TALES OF IAIRIA
ASHES OF ASCENSION

by

Tyler Tullis

authorHOUSE®

AuthorHouse™
1663 Liberty Drive
Bloomington, IN 47403
www.authorhouse.com
Phone: 1-800-839-8640

First published by AuthorHouse 8/7/2009

ISBN: 978-1-4490-1183-3 (e)
ISBN: 978-1-4490-1182-6 (sc)

Library of Congress Control Number: 2009907794

Printed in the United States of America
Bloomington, Indiana

This book is printed on acid-free paper.

For the girls,

Jenna, Amanda and Macey

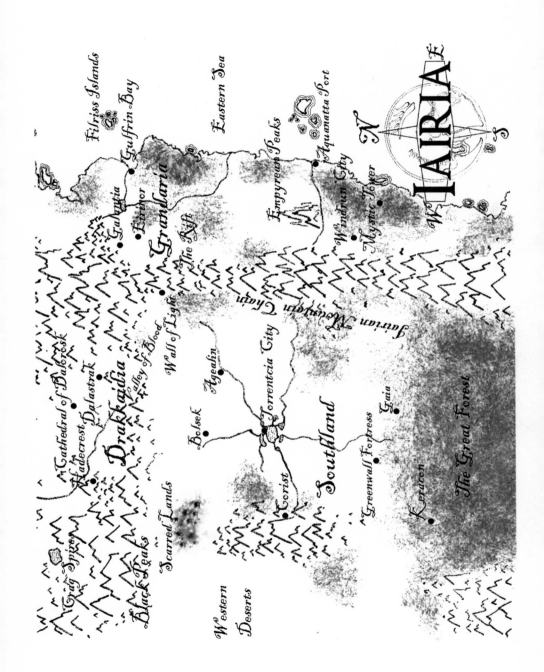

Prologue

<u>Elemental Disorder</u>

A new era had been ushered in for the two nations in the northern lands of Iairia, Grandaria and Drakkaidia. The most bitter of enemies for over a thousand years, the events surrounding the Days of Destiny and the Third Holy War had forced the two great powers to look past their hatred for each other and see a distant but possible road to peace. But while the political situation to the north shone brighter than ever before, turmoil and disarray had slowly been engulfing the sprawling nation of the Southland. Thanks to the expansion and internal growth of the traditionally independent regions of the four lands within the Southland's borders, a national identity had begun to develop forcing the weak central governing body in Torrentcia City to evolve at a pace faster than it could handle.

The growing populace did not require a strong central government or all-prevailing religion to live by like those maintained by their neighbors to the north, but the need for a unifying law code to structure the provisional local governing bodies was becoming painfully necessary. Not equipped to deal with the growing demands of the people for protection of their lands and citizens against internal threats ranging from the lawlessness of bandits and Mavens to organized marauders such as the Purging Flame, the Southland Legion and its commanding Sarton had grown increasingly overwhelmed with keeping order. The Legion had been created in the Second Holy War as a broad shield to protect the northern and western borders of the nation from invading armies, not to put down local uprisings and bands of marauders taking advantage of the limitless freedom the Southland was founded upon.

The far more dangerous and immediately threatening problem forcing Southlanders to call for aid was the rising number of elemental disturbances flaring up across the four lands. While Grandaria and Drakkaidia had sitting Elemental Warriors to establish elemental order when out of check, the last of the Southland's warriors had just died. With no Mystic Sages left alive to anoint new Elemental Warriors, the disturbances had grown progressively worse. Golthrout attacks in the Great Forests were being reported in the calm years when they were supposed to be in hiding underground; wyverns in the Empyrean Peaks had begun preying on passing humans for the first time in history; the Jagged Pike in the Eastern Sea were tearing apart any ship that sailed beyond the horizon of the shore, leaving the island colonies stranded; and Lavlas Boars in the west were lighting more countryside ablaze by the day.

Though the Sarton had assembled the Southland Legion and dispatched small units of it across the lands in an attempt to restrain the disturbances, in small numbers Legionnaires were militia at best. Most had no idea how to grapple with magical elemental disorders. Growing desperate, the Sarton called a meeting of representatives from the key locations across the Southland like Windrun City, Greenwall Fortress, Corist Village and Torrentcia itself. Though none of them could discern what more they could do without Elemental Warriors to aid them, a Windrun Warrior informed the Sarton of reported activity within the Mystic Tower in the Sage's Valley near his post. Having heard the rumors that a surviving Mystic Sage was traveling abroad in Iairia, the desperate Sarton quickly dispatched several riders across the lands to search for the whereabouts of this last hope to gain control of the elemental disorder before it consumed all of the Southland.

Part One
Ancient Vendetta

Chapter 1

<u>Frozen Summit</u>

The sky was quiet over the Border Mountains northwest of Grandaria. Snow had fallen the previous night, but the overcast clouds had parted that morning to reveal tight bursts of sunlight shining down on the rugged mountain peaks and the enormous stone platform that rested over their highest summit.

The portal to the void.

Snowfields and glaciers surrounded the massive edifice, yet even in the midst of the fiercest winter blizzard, somehow not so much as single snowflake ever fell upon its intricate surface. The portal was engraved with beautiful, sweeping designs of angelic wings and curving feathers all converging toward the elaborately detailed center where the Sword of Granis stood erect in all its glory. The sword, the Grandarians' most sacred and revered talisman of power, had been locked into the center of the mammoth portal for nearly sixty years. It was first planted inside by Arilia Embrin during the Days of Destiny, only to be reinforced by her daughter Kaylan Tieloc and the new Granic Crystal she fixed to the blade twenty years later. Ever since, the golden glow from the small crystal had cast a sheen of brilliant light across the engravings on the portal—the only defense against the evil locked beneath the its surface.

As the ashen clouds began to release a faint flurry of snowflakes lofting down through the frigid atmosphere, a bank of snow on the glacier leading up to the summit slowly began to shift, parting down the middle as if making way for the robed figure stepping through it with a hand outstretched before him. When the figure eased his spread fingers and pulled them back into the gray cloak around his body, the snow bank ceased moving and he continued trudging forward over the white field toward the colossal edifice sprawling out hundreds of feet before him. Arriving at the stone platform several minutes later, the figure stepped on. His frame eased and momentarily halted as a wave of warmth surged through him as it did to any who touched the immaculate surface. Deeply exhaling with relief, he let the faint, semitransparent layer of energy dissipate around him that had warded off the biting cold on his path to the summit.

While the frigid mountain atmosphere would have ensnared anyone else on the arduous journey without the magical protection of a warming Lavlas Rock, the figure had felt no more than a fleeting shiver on the way up. Still wrapped tight in the flowing cloak draped around his body, he raised a hand to his neck to grasp a circular silver pennant bearing an uncommon emblem and loosened its hold over his robes. He wore simple dark blue garb beneath his cloak with sturdy black boots and a thick leather belt the only other attire present. With his full mobility restored, the figure pulled the concealing hood further down his face and started forward again, vigorously striding across the enormous portal toward the shining golden talisman at its center.

As the long minutes passed by with the Sword of Granis growing closer, the man's frame grew taut until his heart began to beat so fast and hard he had to seal his blue eyes and take a deep breath to calm himself. At last he slowed to a halt when only a few feet away from the legendary talisman, gulping and letting out an audible breath of anxiety. The light from the brilliant Granic Crystal remained steadily shining from its place on the magnificent hilt of the weapon where it met the golden blade infused with the power of Granis himself. Motionlessly staring down at the shining gem for several long moments, he finally raised his gloved hands to gingerly pull back his hood and reveal the face that rested inside.

The moment the hood fell to the back of his neck, the light from the Granic Crystal flashed with life anew and focused to shine out to him as if recognizing the familiar face that had first collected it years ago. Seeing the crystal and the spirit within react to him, the man let a weak smile spread across his bearded face, a faint layer of liquid forming around his eyes. He gulped hard again and knelt before the talisman. Pulling off the dark blue glove on his right hand to reach out with bare skin, he ran his fingers along the edges of the gem. There was a friendly warmth emanating from its surface, forcing the man's smile to broaden.

The face of the boy named Revond had aged and matured over the forty years since the conscious Granic Crystal last shone its light upon him, having acquired a short black beard and numerous lines in his face to mask the youth once found there. The robust visage now belonged to the Master Sage of the eighth generation of the Order of Alberic. Since giving up his nomadic life as a Maven after his quest to restore the seal to the portal he now stood on, Revond had traveled back to the Mystic Tower in the eastern Southland to begin his training as the Scion of the Order of Alberic—the group commonly known as the Mystic Sages. The magical group of men responsible for the record of all knowledge across the world was Iairia's longest standing institution but had been all but exterminated by the demonic forces of the Drakkaidian tyrant Valif Montrox in the Days of Destiny. In their absence the sentient power of the Sage's Draught, the liquid life-force that stored the order's ancient power, had imbued its raw strength into Revond at birth, thus selecting him to be the next scion to regenerate their ranks and commence the new age.

It was a fate Revond had run from through all of his younger years. With no sages left alive to teach him how to tame and use the raw strength bestowed upon him by the consciousness of their draught, it manifested itself through Revond's emotions in dangerous eruptions of power. Unsure of where the destructive power had come from or why it was his burden to bear, the boy abandoned his identify as Revond and became a nomadic mercenary; a Blue Maven named Edge. The catalyst that drove him to his reclusive lifestyle was a dream that had triggered his power to flare awake one night and level his entire village in the eastland, killing everyone in it except him. Overwrought with grief and self-loathing, Revond tried to end his own life several times but was always resurrected by his mysterious power, keeping him alive whether he liked it or not. Unable to rid himself from the world, he learned to suppress his power by hiding his emotions and adopted a strict policy of avoiding contact with everyone he could.

Though believing his soul to be cursed by Granis, fate finally caught up to him in the form of the spirit of the legendary Mystic Sage Zeroan. Appearing before him one night, the sage revealed Revond's lineage and charged him to protect a daughter of the Tieloc House, Kaylan, on a journey to restore the seal to the portal to the void before the evil power of Drakkan could escape it and destroy the world. At first Revond remained vehemently opposed to the idea of his responsibility to an ancient order he knew nothing about, as well as accepting that the unbridled power inside him that had caused so much pain and death could be used for good. It took the love of Kaylan Tieloc to show him his life indeed had a purpose to be fulfilled as hers did. The young Tieloc had sacrificed her existence in the mortal plane to activate the Granic Crystal that would restore the portal to the void. Finally understanding his destiny through hers, Revond embarked to the Mystic Tower after his quest with Kaylan to be trained by not only the spirit of Zeroan, but by Mystic Sages past who now dwelled within the draught itself, comprising its life-force.

Forever inspired by Kaylan's selflessness and sacrifice for him, Revond committed himself early on to becoming the strongest, wisest sage he could be. Zeroan in particular proved invaluable to his training, quickly becoming the father figure the boy never had and guiding him every step of the way through his first attempts to control his potent power. Though Revond regarded Zeroan as one of the greatest members in the order's history because of his great power and wisdom that had protected the world on multiple occasions, the renowned sage was also the last person Revond wanted to end up like. Zeroan had made more of a difference in the history of Iairia than arguably anyone, but the sage's untrustworthy and manipulative manner to achieve his goals with cold ruthlessness was something Revond constantly feared developing as a consequence of the vast knowledge he would acquire. Zeroan's seemingly dark, callous side reminded him too much of the brooding Maven he had left behind.

This distant fear proved to be the least of Revond's worries as he trained. The long and arduous process to master the sages' seemingly infinite knowledge as well as the complex power of their draught proved to be as great a challenge for him as first accepting his volatile power in his quest with Kaylan Tieloc. Over the long years of his studies, Revond found himself lost in them. Despite his many achievements there was always more to learn and master.

Training in the tower and at times the chasm within that contained the very draught with the spirits of the sages to guide him, Revond learned to control his amazing power not through his emotions as he once had but through his very will.

Far more complex and difficult to grasp than any other power ever known to the world, the scion spent entire years experimenting with fusing his mind to the core elemental matter around him to manipulate and create it for himself in amazing displays of white light he found himself able to birth out of nothing at all. While developing his power, he perused thousands of pages of text in the great libraries of the tower, delving into the collective knowledge and wisdom complied by millennia of human existence until it saturated his mind. As the years turned into decades, he could feel all the information besieging him to the point that migraine headaches became the norm. While so much time in the tower would have worn a normal man to madness over the years, by this point Revond had begun sipping the Sage's Draught to prolong his life and give him a unique sense of clarity as was custom for the members of the order.

The more he learned, the farther it seemed he was from answering all the questions that continued to appear. At one point he realized the sages' spirits had ceased communicating with him altogether, but remembering what Zeroan had once told him in his first years there, he knew he would not have their blessing as the Master Sage until he himself knew he was ready. As the decades rolled by his senses became so attuned to all matter around him that he could sense a single leaf falling from a tree in the middle of the forest surrounding the tower, yet still he didn't feel his mastery complete. The years went on like this long after Zeroan and the others faded for good, keeping Revond cut off from the world inside the libraries of the tower until one day he happened upon a unique book he had never thought to open before.

Discovering the Iairian Almanac of History, he noticed the enchanted book was recording history for the eighth generation of the Order of Alberic on its own. Remembering that this phenomenon commenced only with a new generation contingent on the arrival of the new Master Sage, Revond realized that despite all he had yet to know he had learned enough to assume his responsibly and become what he was born to be. Perhaps his greatest lesson was that he could not absorb the complete history and the full extent of mystic power he was capable of wielding in the tower merely by reading or private meditation alone. He was left with experiencing the world for himself and learning the rest along the way.

Donning the silver emblem bearing the ancient insignia of the Order of Alberic on his cloak, Revond stepped out of the Mystic Tower as the new Master Sage for the first time to embark into Iairia. Though men had been pounding on the tower's door for years crying out for anyone inside to help them deal with the elemental crises that had been plaguing the lands of late, the sage had a final task to see to before he was ready to begin the long list of chores and duties waiting for him. Though he appreciated the desperate need for him to sort out the array of troubles waiting for his hand to mend since the end of the last generation of sages, he knew he could not truly begin his work as the Master Sage until he first paid homage to the girl who had given him the chance to do so. Besides, after all they had battled through to ensure the portal to the void remained intact, he wanted to see for himself that the power of the Sword of Granis was still fully active. Leaving the Mystic Tower behind to take a deep breath of crisp air wafting through the Sage's Valley, Revond looked out on the massive world to realize he was alone. He was the only sage at the beginning of his undertaking for Iairia without any friends or allies.

He still had his partner from his adolescence, Zephyr, but the purple Sky Sprite had been living back and forth between his home in the Empyrean Peaks and the Mystic Tower. While Zephyr was his best friend, the single Sky Sprite was far from informed on the current affairs of the wide world. Mentally delving through the vast sea of knowledge within his mind, he quickly remembered the sages always had a few old friends left from the time of the gods and the natural races so long ago. Calling into the wild of the eastern forests with the silent beckoning of his mystic power, the last member of the race of Morlans appeared in its usual form of the horse-like creature known to the sages as Nighcress. Almost sheepishly greeting the enchanted steed for the first time as he trotted out of the woods to his right moments later, Revond smiled and gently swept his hand along the creature's face. Silently communicating with each other without the use of words, the sage lifted himself upon the creature's back and asked for him to take him to the northern snow.

Though Nighcress was capable of ferrying him to the Border Mountains within hours at the supernatural pace he could run, the sage was in no particular rush and wanted to take in the world he had not seen for decades as they traveled. Though it looked as if not much had changed when he started out, he was eager to learn of what had transpired since the Third Holy War and conversed with villagers and rangers moving across the plains when encountering them. Learning as much as he could over the current political status between the nations and the fate of those who had once led them during his time as a boy, the Master Sage stopped frequently and did not arrive at the base of the Border Mountains for a month. Leaving Nighcress at the snowcapped mountain foot to wait for him while he hiked up the glacier roads to one of the summits, he arrived within a day using a spell from his sway over the element of fire to keep him warm.

A wave of memories of the beautiful blond haired Grandarian girl he had once loved flushing through him as he released his hand from the surface of the Granic Crystal her soul now resided in, Revond continued to kneel over the portal and reminisced his short but blessed time with her. It was Kaylan that had made him come to terms with the once volatile and precarious power that flowed within him, giving him new purpose and reason to live after all the despair and emptiness that had filled him before. If not for her he would have been consumed by his power and left dead as he had wished himself to be before meeting her. Though devastated to have lost her, the memory of the love they once shared was still powerful enough to propel him forward on the new path fate had laid out for him. There was no record in the Mystic Tower of what existence was like as the soul of the Granic Crystal but the sage knew some part of her was still alive within its brilliant glass shell and smiled once more as the light from its beautiful little edges shone out to warm his face. He knew she would be proud of him. He had become the person she wanted him to be—the person she had made him want to be.

The Master Sage blissfully stared at the Granic Crystal for several long minutes, aware he was happier in this moment than he could remember being for years. All that he had worked to achieve and all the knowledge he had mastered over the years was justified as Kaylan's spirit shined out to him as if to congratulate him and wish him luck on the stage of his life still to come. Sensing the presence of something swooping down from the sky behind him amid the falling snowflakes, the sage unhurriedly swept a hand through his shoulder length black hair to reach behind him and pull up his gray hood.

Standing and pulling his right glove tightly back against his hand, he looked down at the shimmering Granic Crystal once more to faintly bow his head. Rotating his body, he began marching back across the portal with his gray robes whipping up behind him. Scanning his sharp vision to the edge of the intricate stone portal hundreds of feet ahead, he spotted a familiar winged figure standing with taloned feet secure to the border. Watching the Master Sage approach him over the next few minutes, the finely feathered body of the Sky Sprite named Zephyr lifted off the portal in a semitransparent sphere of Lift Power, running his miniature hands over the long tail feathers.

"I don't need looking after like Edge did, Zeph," the Master Sage spoke from behind his hood, his voice deep and calm. "You were supposed to remain at the Mystic Tower to keep watch until my return. This isn't going to work anymore if you don't do what I ask, partner." The small purple Sky Sprite merely shook his head and opened his yellow beak to speak, his rich purple eyes wide with concern.

"I'm sorry, Master Sage," he replied quickly, "but I thought you should know something right away. Another band of men just arrived from Torrentcia the other day desperate for help. There's an elemental disturbance in the west." Revond exhaled sharply and nodded.

"There's an elemental disturbance everywhere these days, it sounds like," he replied solemnly as a wisp of frigid wind rustled his hood. "What is this one about?"

"As per your orders I didn't ask them myself but it sounds like something's happening at Mt. Corist. It's been rumbling for weeks and villages around the mountain have been evacuated. The fires are getting out of control over there."

"Lavlas Boars can't affect the volcano," Revond said mostly to himself, breaking eye contact with the little sprite. "If that's true there must be another cause..." Letting the sage think for a moment, Zephyr watched as he turned to glance back at the shining Sword of Granis on the portal again. There was a long silence, but eventually Zephyr felt the need to say something.

"I really am sorry to interrupt, Master Sage," the sprite repeated again, aware of how long the man had been looking forward to this day and what it meant for him to be there again. Revond quickly spun around and shook his head.

"You did the right thing, Zephyr," he replied softly. "And for the hundredth time, you are the last person in this world who ever needs to stand on ceremony for me. I told you forty years ago before we left Eirinor, you can call me Revond." Zephyr's wide beak grinned as his small shoulders merely shrugged.

"I knew it then and I know it now, but you've earned that much respect at least, Master Sage. You better get used to hearing it wherever you go."

"No one even knows I exist yet, Zeph," Revond returned, shifting in his robes.

"Well that's about to change, isn't it?" the merry sprite returned, his optimism infectious as always. "Nighcress is still at the mountain foot. Care for a ride down?" Revond fixed his blue eyes on his best friend, unable to hide his beaming smile.

"Even after all these years, what would I do without you, partner?" the sage spoke as the little sprite extended his open hands to wrap him in a similar sphere of Lift Power and lift him off the stone platform.

"Granis only knows," the sprite whispered to himself as he lifted the Master Sage off the portal to the void to soar over the snowfield and back down the mountain glacier, leaving the white summit peacefully quiet once more.

Chapter 2

<u>The Content Son</u>

Trumpets sounded through the humid summer air around Galantia as baskets full of blue and gold confetti lofted down over the walls of the Golden Castle into the assembly courtyard below. Hundreds of Grandarians stood wildly cheering as the regal form of Supreme Granisian Borlain Gilentium appeared on the massive stage assembled near the Grand Vestibule leading into the interior of the massive castle. The long sleeves of his royal white and golden robes fell back as he raised his hands to wave to the energetic crowds of his people, motioning with his head for the two elite guards adorned with ornate silver armor flanking him to hold at the entrance of the stage for his return. As the sovereign of Grandaria slowly marched closer to his elaborate throne in the center of a platform on the stage, several of the applauding citizens grouped together at the gateway to the massive courtyard were caught off balance as a strong figure impatiently jostled through, struggling to hurriedly squeeze his way through the crowds.

"Hey, watch where you're going, kid!" an older man who had been pushed churlishly barked, catching his balance. The young man still maneuvering forward through the crowd spun his head around with an apologetic smile on his sweating face.

"Sorry!" he called, pushing through another group of cheering Grandarians. "My girlfriend's singing in the Diapason!" Seeing the man frowning as he lost sight of the hustling boy in the crowds, the woman at his side smiled at him and told him to relax, remembering young love herself. Continuing to penetrate through the rows of clapping and sometimes jumping Grandarians in the massive courtyard of the Golden Castle, Aeric Tieloc nervously shot a glance to the stage to find a series of white robed figures marching

12

out from either side of the stage toward a series of stairs behind the Supreme Granisian's throne. Aeric gulped, aware he had to get to the front of the crowd within the next minute to make it on time. Pushing on through the masses with apology after apology as they began to fall silent, the boy watched as Supreme Granisian Gilentium stood before his throne while the last of the white robed figures behind him filed into place on the stairs.

"Grandarians one and all," Gilentium called out, raising his hands with a broad smile, "welcome to the Festival of Radia!" His voice was robust and prevailing over the hushed whispers of the crowd, garnering their immediate attention only to be followed by another explosion of cheers. The current Supreme Granisian had been on the throne for nearly two decades, assuming power after the early passing of Maréttiny Kolior. Being the last of her house, Kolior had selected the young and passionate Minor Granisian Borlain Gilentium to succeed her on her deathbed, hoping his boisterous personality and devout faith to Granis would allow him to rule the nation successfully and far longer than she. He had fulfilled her wish so far, leading efforts along with a united Galantian Council to initiate peace dialogues with representatives from Drakkaidia, something unimaginable at the beginning of Kolior's rule.

Thanks to the efforts of the legendary Warrior of Light Tavinious Tieloc and the Supreme Granisians over the years, the golden land of Grandaria that had been on the brink of destruction only forty years prior in the Third Holy War had entered a new era of peace and prosperity unlike anything it had experienced in its long history. The revelation from Granis the God of Light himself that their once mortal foes the Drakkaidians were not born from the black hand of Drakkan the God of Darkness had been a difficult story for any proud Grandarian to swallow, traditionally taught to hate the dark nation to the west. Over the years this enlightening news had finally begun to alter the national conscience of the Grandarians. Slowly, they were realizing Granis did not desire further war with their forgotten brothers but fellowship among all the children of the human race that he created.

Even the vengeful Drakkaidians had begun to slowly embrace a similar appreciation for their original motherland. At last under the leadership of a king and a High Priest without ambitions for world domination that they had been oppressed by since the Montroxs came to power in the First Holy War, a call for peace for the first time in the dark nation's history was issued. Though Drakkaidian hordes under the leadership of Verix Montrox had been in the position to destroy the Grandarian capital city of Galantia itself at the conclusion of the Third Holy War forty years ago, the Drakkaidian Prince had realized the erroneous cause to the conflict and negotiated a fragile but long-lasting peace. It had truly been darkest before the dawn.

Since then the two nations had begun slowly rebuilding within their damaged borders, Grandaria scarred from the Third Holy War and Drakkaidia still in disrepair from the Days of Destiny and the virtual civil war that ensued. While Grandarians had been infuriated to see Drakkaidian troops marching across their lands after destroying the Wall of Light in the war zone, Montrox's fallback when he could have easily razed Galantia to the ground did much to build a foundation of trust never before harbored for the dark nation and its leaders. After passing rule of Grandaria back to Maréttiny Kolior after the war, Tavin Tieloc lay down his sword for good and began to organize the first ever peace talks in neutral grounds like the Border Mountains and the remains of the Wall of Light, once the first defense to keep Drakkaidians out of Grandarian territory.

In Drakkaidia, Verix Montrox was quickly crowned king upon his return from the short lived war. His first act was to disband the two factions vying for control of the nation, the Loyalists to the Throne and the New Fellowship of Drakkan, and centralize the nation back around Dalastrak. Aware of how dangerous and corrupt the Black Church of Drakkan responsible for the fission had become, the ruler called for a radical restructuring of the church. The primary reform was to finally cease worship of Drakkan. While the church's original purpose was merely to pay homage to Drakkan as the deity who kept watch over the land Drakkaidia had been founded on, over the years the nation had come to worship him as their master and a guiding force responsible for their victories.

Montrox knew better than any the true evil nature of the dark god and forbid such veneration. Though it had created large waves of dissension among the traditionalists of the nation, Verix preached pride in their nation as the true Drakkaidian strength and condemned Drakkan as a false god to whom they owed nothing. Under the leadership of advocates for harmony like the Tielocs and Montroxs, the once unimaginable idea of peace had surfaced from the ashes of their thousand year state of war. Soon representatives from Grandaria and Drakkaidia began meeting for the first time in history to discuss their past, present, and future together.

When the Grandarian spectators in the courtyard of the Golden Castle had quieted once more, Supreme Granisian Gilentium continued.

"As you know, we celebrate this longest day of the year by raising our voices in thanks to Lord Granis for his glorious light that continues to guide our golden land toward growth and prosperity. It is therefore my honor to commence this festival by introducing the Diapason Choir, made up of the finest voices across our nation that can be found. I give you the Diapason!"

After another brief round of cheers from the crowd, Gilentium took a seat on his throne and waited for the choir's Lead Voice to step forward to conduct the rest of the group. With an overly elaborate gesture of his entire body to commence singing, the group of over fifty white robed men and women began signing in a low hum. Just as he heard the first voices sounding out, Aeric finally squeezed his way in between the tightly fit front row of the crowd, barred from moving any further to the stage by the row of elite royal guards and the massive lances they held in crosses to block the masses. Panting and out of breath, Aeric pulled up the sleeves of his frayed old tunic and swept a hand through his short black hair he had inherited from his father. Anxiously sweeping his deep blue eyes through the ranks of white robed figures, a broad smile at last spread across his lips as sight of his longtime girlfriend Mina Garrinal came into view, her curly chestnut hair giving her away at once. A crisp breeze jetted down from the clear blue sky above them, caressing the girl's hair against her smooth freckled face. Though still beaming, Aeric's conscious mind slowly began to drift as he stared at her singing figure, still captivated by her beautiful appearance even after all their years together.

Aeric and Mina had been childhood friends since birth as had been generations of Tieloc and Garrinal offspring in the small Eirinor Village in the center of the hills of Grandaria further south. Their early childhood was full of adventure and wonderful memories together, but this changed when

Aeric's grandfather Tavinious Tieloc, the renowned Warrior of Light who had saved all of Iairia from Drakkan himself and valiantly led Grandaria in the Third Holy War, passed away near Aeric's tenth birthday. Charged with assuming his inherited title as the Grandarian Warrior of Light and the seat that came with it on the Supreme Granisian's Senior Council, Aeric's father Darien Tieloc II moved his son and wife to Galantia to better serve his new role. Though Aeric enjoyed his time living in the Grandarian capital city and built a steady group of new friends throughout his adolescent years there, upon turning 19 years old he was sent to the Gulfrin Academy to study as had his father.

While there, he crossed paths with his old childhood friend Mina Garrinal again, this time as the energetic young woman she had become. Mina was the first generation in her family to attend the academy. Her grandfather Jaren Garrinal had been slated to study there but at the beginning of his adventure with his best friend Tavin Tieloc in the Days of Destiny their plans were cut short. Mina's father Roan and her uncle Jak had never been interested in school, making a good living in the small logging business they had inherited from Jaren in his later years. Though Aeric had fallen out of touch with Mina and didn't even know she would be a student there, the two quickly gravitated toward each other as had generations of Tielocs and Garrinals that came before them. Rekindling their friendship at school and back home in Eirinor where the two returned to live in the winter months they had off together, their parents were not surprised to one day find the two had become inseparable and had fallen for each other.

Happier with Mina than he had ever felt in his life, Aeric became accustomed to the small village of Eirinor once more and decided the small community lifestyle he had forgotten was what he wanted after all. Though it had become an unspoken truth between the two and common knowledge to anyone who saw them together, Aeric and Mina silently knew they were going to spend the rest of their lives with each other but wanted to finish school before they made anything official. Both adults in the eyes of Grandarian law at the age of 22, the two found themselves almost finished with their final year at the academy and preparing for life afterward.

Both Aeric and Mina were virtual copies of their parents and grandparents at heart but had grown into their own persons since their coming of age, in large part because of their relationship. Like his father and grandfather before him, Aeric was a steadfast thinker determined to achieve whatever he set out to do. Wherever he saw an opportunity to help in any way he was able, he did. It was that simple— Tieloc instinct, his mother called it. Mina had become the rambunctious and impulsive girl her grandfather Jaren had been in his time and her father still was, but despite the fact she always had so much fun with Aeric, her relationship with him had seemed to mellow her and cultivate her into the compassionate lady she had blossomed into. Aeric's evolution seemed to come from the fact that having found his love and a place in the world, he was already satisfied with life. While Tavin or Darien would have still been craving adventure and excitement at his age, Aeric was content to enjoy what he had and what was to come on its own. Though anyone who knew anything of his family could still see the Tieloc heart alight inside him, his contentedness had developed a passive nature about him that kept his day to day concerns on Mina and his future with her.

Summoned out of the daydreaming of his love by the sudden crescendo of voices ringing through the clear air into the blue skies above the capital city, Aeric watched with his smile broadening once more as Mina belted out her powerful voice to match the others' in the epic traditional song always sung to honor Lord Granis at the beginning of a ceremony. Though everyone who knew Mina knew the captivating and beautiful voice she harbored, Aeric had always melted hearing her sing. She was by far the youngest of any man or woman in the Diapason, but Aeric always told her talent knew no age. Mina had grown into a particularly pretty girl despite an almost boyish face thanks to her daring eyes and defined freckled cheeks, but Aeric had long seen her as the most beautiful girl he had ever known.

As the choir hit the final sustained note louder and higher than all the rest in amazing harmony, the Lead Voice guiding them at last brought his lifted hands to his side to cut them off. As the Diapason Choir fell silent the crowd burst with energetic plaudits once more, clapping and cheering the loudest Aeric had heard them all day. Watching Mina take a long bow to the risen Supreme Granisian along with the rest of the choir, Aeric saw her eyes fall upon him in the front row and gave him a knowing smile to which he merely lifted his hands higher to clap vivaciously. As Supreme Granisian Gilentium thanked them and announced the Festival of Radia had officially begun, the Diapason began shuffling off the stage to the two exits that led into the Grand Vestibule of the Golden Castle itself. Seeing Mina exit the stage to the left, Aeric began darting through the crowd once more, eager to get to the corresponding side of the courtyard to meet her when she came out.

With the crowds dissipating to fall back to the lower tiers of the city where the mass festivities were commencing, Aeric had enough space to comfortably lean against a wall of the courtyard by the side entrance to the Grand Vestibule beside a large green fern growing from a clay pot. He folded his arms and took a deep breath of the fresh summer air, blue and gold confetti still falling down to land in his thick black hair. Reaching up to pull the loose paper out of his short locks with his hands encased in his usual brown carpenter's cut-off gauntlets, he cast them to the mess of others strewn across the tiled courtyard floor. It felt nice to stop and breathe for a moment. He had rushed all the way up to the Golden Castle amid the flood of Grandarian citizens swarming the busy streets from the lowest of the city's four tiers, late from visiting his mother he had not seen in months.

She was helping a friend run a booth selling local cooking wares and had to miss Mina sing, but as usual she had stopped him to make him tell her how things were going at the Gulfrin Academy for far longer than he could afford. He had meant to put on some fresh clothes from their journey but didn't have time to swap out his usual outfit: simple brown pants and undershirt with a long sleeved blue tunic wrapped over him. His limbs were covered with sturdy brown boots at his feet and worn leather gauntlets around his hands and wrists. He had yet to even remove his thick carpenters belt that held several small pouches to keep random odds and ends when he traveled. Though he feared he would be late to hear Mina sing with the choir for her first time after he had promised her he would be in the front row to watch, he took another deep breath of relief knowing she had seen him.

No sooner than thoughts of his girlfriend and her stellar performance entered his mind again, a collection of white robes flying at him from his right caught his attention along with the ensuing sensation of arms wrapping around his neck. Though nearly shocked off his feet, the boy caught his balance and staggered back.

"Granis on high, Mina," the stunned Grandarian managed as his smile appeared. He wrapped his arms around the girl fiercely hugging him. "How do you always do that?" The girl softened her grip around his neck and withdrew her curly haired head to reveal her smiling face and bright green eyes.

"What, manage to scare you?" she asked playfully. "I don't know, but you deserve it after showing up late for something again." Aeric felt his heart drop but held his smile with color flushing to his face.

"Uhg... I was hoping you wouldn't notice," he said shaking his head, watching a group of people pass out of the Grand Vestibule. "I saw your entire performance. My mother just kept me too long again. You know her." Mina giggled and nodded.

"Oh, I love Mother Tieloc so much—I'm only kidding," she told him, brushing off her fake admonishment. "Besides, it's only easy to scare you because you're so busy thinking about me you can't keep your mind straight on anything else around you." Her tone was lofty and lighthearted, jokingly full of herself as usual. Aeric narrowed his eyes but pulled her closer playfully, his smile only widening as he spoke in a teasing tone of voice.

"And how do you know I was thinking about *you* just now?" he asked pushing his nose against hers, to which Mina giggled again.

"I know that look, Aeric Tieloc," she returned coyly. "You can't hide it from me. I think you kind of like me..." Listening to her trail off and letting her brush a lock of his black hair off his forehead, he silently chuckled again and picked her off her feet into his arms.

"I think I kind of love you," he returned softer. Mina quickly found the sincerity she had come to know better than anyone present in his blue eyes. "You were amazing up there, Mina. The choir sounded a thousand times better today." Mina merely gave him a look that told him she loved him too and pulled in to slowly kiss him on the lips.

"She sings with the Diapason one time and she's already got somebody sweeping her off her feet like she was royalty!" came the cheery voice from out of the slowly retreating crowd. Both Aeric and Mina spun their heads to find Roan Garrinal striding toward them with a broad smile behind his thick brown beard. Aeric grinned and quickly let Mina down so she could run to her father and leap at him as well. He plucked her off the ground and swung her around once, his deep belly laugh making Aeric grin as it always did. "My daughter's a songstress in the Diapason Choir! And she's amazing!" Mina giggled and shook her head blushing, at last pulling away from the burly man.

"Thanks daddy," she replied graciously. "I'm glad at least you and Aeric could make it to see me."

"You know your mother and brother would have stormed a Drak fortress to see you but someone has to run the shop with the battalion of new soldiers in the Hills of Eirinor marching through town. They arrived with the Drill Master for summer training last week, remember?"

"I know, and tell them not to worry," Mina replied. "They'll get to see me sooner or later." After laughing and leaning in to kiss her on her forehead, Roan turned to Aeric to shake his hand with a smile. He was dressed in a short sleeved brown tunic and thin tan pants, obviously trying to cool himself down in the summer heat.

"And how are you these days, Master Tieloc?" he asked. "How's the final year of school going for the two of you?"

"Couldn't be better," Aeric said releasing his firm grip. "I've got the trade school's final review to take next month and then I'll be done with just about everything."

"Atta boy," the older Garrinal returned, folding his arms. "Well we finished gutting Carfon's old inn last week so it will be ready for you upon your return. You are still planning on setting up shop there, aren't you?"

"Yes sir," he replied with a smile. "I've actually got some new ideas for what I want to do with the—"

"There he is!" came a voice from behind them, cutting the young man short. Spinning around with Mina doing the same, the trio spotted several of the elite armored guards of the Supreme Granisian himself parting at the entrance to the Grand Vestibule to make way for a familiar figure walking toward them after the last group of the crowd on their way out of the courtyard. As they approached, one of the silver plated guards stood at attention and dropped the tip of his lance against the ground. The remaining citizens still in the courtyard turned and began to clap at the presence of their famous countrymen.

"Presenting the Royal Chief Advisor and Warrior of Light," a guard spoke loudly, to which the caped form of Darien Tieloc shook his head with a silent chuckle and motioned for the guard to stand at ease.

"Thank you, lad, but I hardly need to be introduced to my own son," he smiled, turning to face Aeric. The two quickly embraced, Aeric hugging his regally dressed father covered in blue and gold attire with decorative golden armor similar to that worn by the previous Warrior of Light, Tavin Tieloc. "How are you, Aeric? Did you and Mina have smooth ride from Gulfrin?"

"It was a long one," he answered quickly, releasing his father to step back beside Mina and Roan. "We were both so excited for her performance it seemed like we were never going to get here." Darien merely laughed and stepped forward to hug Mina and tell her what an amazing voice she had.

"Yeah, finally we Garrinals have a claim to fame of our own aside from keeping you Tielocs in line," Roan said jokingly, reaching out to shake his oldest friend's hand as he released Mina.

"Well if anyone was going to accomplish that it would be your daughter," Darien replied narrowing his eyes. "*Your* crowning achievement in life is still getting me and Kaylan into trouble as children." When they all laughed, Darien was quick to turn back to the other professionally dressed figure beside him patiently waiting. "My apologies, Talus. Everyone, this is Supreme Granisian Gilentium's new Chief Advisor, Talus Blanch. I was hoping to introduce him to Aeric while he was here but looks like we got half of the extended family as well." The man dressed in silver robes nodded civilly and smiled with wrinkles in his aged but dignified face appearing.

"My lucky day, then," he said, reaching out to shake everyone's hands. "It is not often I get to meet two of the most celebrated Grandarian families in recent history. It is a great honor to meet you all." Darien ran his hand along his recently shaved face and spoke to the younger members of their party.

"I'm sure you two didn't receive word back at the academy but Chief Advisor Blanch was appointed by the Galantian Council last month," Darien informed them. "He served alongside my father for years on the Senior Council as the Envoy of Foreign Affairs. Blanch was one of the first to accompany your grandfather for the original meeting between Grandaria and Drakkaidia in the ruins of the Wall of Light when you were just a baby, Aeric."

"Oh yes, Tavinious was a great mentor of mine," Talus chimed in. "His passing was one of the greatest losses this nation has ever suffered. But it would appear his legacy of serving Grandaria lives on in his family. What are you studying at the Gulfrin Academy, Aeric?" The young Tieloc took a deep breath and rhythmically tapped the toes of his brown boots on the tiled courtyard ground as he carefully worded his answer to avoid the potentially uncomfortable conversation that tended to follow this question.

"I'm in the trade school in the academy," he replied vaguely, to which the Chief Advisor smiled.

"Ah, a practical skill," he returned warmly. "One can always use a useful ability to rely on later in life after the years have rolled on and one settles in with his family." A lingering silence hung over the group when Talus finished his sentence, no one sure what to say at first. Though he could tell Mina was about to respond for him as her headstrong defensiveness of him usually dictated her to, Aeric quickly spoke up to preclude her from saying anything.

"Actually, I'm planning on applying it sooner rather than later," he spoke courteously, still maintaining his smile. "I'm preparing to open a carpenter's shop in Eirinor Village next year. Thanks to help from Roan and the Garrinals I already have the building picked out and I'm halfway ready to open." The uncomfortable silence fell over the group again. The feigned smile on Darien's lips slightly weakened and he glanced down as the Chief Advisor tilted his head in confusion.

"But I thought your father told me you were of legal age this year," he said. "Are you not—"

"No, he isn't going into the army or the Golden Castle," Mina finally cut in with heated tone, unable to contain herself anymore. Both Roan and Aeric let out an impatient huff at her, but Aeric merely nodded and met the Chief Advisor's unguardedly shocked gaze.

"It came as a bit of a surprise to me too when I had to make the decision to follow in the family footsteps or not, but I've decided that life in the city or abroad really isn't for me," he spoke at last, hoping to have avoided this conversation. "Galantia could offer me duties as the Warrior of Light and I do want to see the rest of the world someday, but I love Eirinor and I really feel happy to have a future there waiting for me." The Chief Advisor gave him a quirky look as if unable to comprehend what he was hearing. Aeric's smile finally faded as his eyes passed to his father's. They were aimed down at his boots as he stood with his hands at his sides. Feeling his son's gaze on him Darien forced himself to smile once more and turn back to Talus.

"I was a little stunned after all the years of him wanting to take after his grandfather and me, but... I support my son and I'm glad he's following his heart," he spoke while swallowing hard, making things even more awkward. Aeric let out a breath and stood silent in the same discomfort he was forced to endure anytime one of his father's associates in Grandaria asked about his future. Aeric knew his father's words were true and he had his love and blessing, but at the same time he knew full well every time Darien was forced to explain what his son was doing with his life it was embarrassing for him. By settling down in Eirinor and not joining the ranks of the Grandarian Army he was denying his claim to the title of the Warrior of Light supposed to be passed on to him.

Since Tavin Tieloc's first becoming the Warrior of Light as an adolescent, everyone had always assumed his descendants would continue the proud tradition of serving Grandaria. Because the God of Light had appeared to Tavin through the Sword of Granis and personally granted him godly power, many of Darien's associates in Galantia and beyond saw his son's rejection of his birthright as a blatant betrayal to Grandaria and Lord Granis himself. Though Darien and Aeric were aware of this, they also realized the potential power of Tavin's descendants would remain dormant within them without the Sword of Granis to activate it. Darien reluctantly agreed that the Warrior of Light had become a political position alone and his son was technically free to pass his right to accept it one day. Breaking the silence, Mina stepped forward to take her boyfriend's hand and speak up to the wordless Chief Advisor before them.

"And we're all very proud of him," she informed him sharply. "He'll be graduating with honors from the headmaster at the top of his class. Aeric has an amazing creative gift for building things." Talus forced himself to conquer his shock and smile once more.

"I'm sure he does," he replied nodding. "Well I'm sorry to depart so quickly but we really must be getting up to the conference chamber to make the Senior Council meeting. It was very good to meet all of you. Shall we depart, Darien?" The senior Tieloc took in a deep breath as he glanced at the faces of the three others before quickly nodding.

"Yes, we can't keep Gilentium waiting," he agreed. Telling Roan he would find him later in the day, he bid Aeric and Mina farewell, aware they had to get back to the Gulfrin Academy and would most likely be off before he got the chance to see them again. "I'll see you back home then, you two. Have a safe trip back, son." Though his father was sincere as always, as he turned to walk back into the Grand Vestibule Aeric could tell that Darien was still wounded by the decision he had made years ago. Feeling his father's disappointment tearing at him like nothing else could, Aeric stood motionless for a long moment before Mina stepped in front of him to meet his gaze. She stared into his hurt eyes hard before pulling close to softly kiss him.

"Keep your head up, Aeric Tieloc," she told him sternly. Though he did not speak back, he eventually nodded and turned with her hand in his for Roan behind them, forcing a smile.

"So are you two heading back today?" Mina's father asked them, purposely changing the subject. Mina shook her head and smiled.

"We didn't come all the way to Galantia to be here for the Festival of Radia not to celebrate ourselves!" she chimed merrily, bumping Aeric's hip with hers. "We're staying with Aeric's friends tonight so we can get in on some festivities then leave tomorrow. We have a few days off from class anyway so we might as well stay for a while." Roan nodded and rubbed his stomach facetiously.

"Well good, because I didn't intend on letting you leave until you got some food with your old man," he told her motioning for them for follow him out the gate of the Golden Castle's large courtyard. "The banquets are the whole reason I come to these things!" Mina shot him a playful frown and slapped his arm, sarcastically telling him she knew he didn't care about her voice. All three merely laughed and finally exited the Golden Castle for the lower tiers of Galantia.

Chapter 3

<u>Wildfire</u>

The western lands of the Southland, blessed by the presence of the Source of Fire that rested in the core of its elemental temple, had always been a humid and tropical region fixed in continuous summer. The soil was fertile for farming across the countryside, as proven evident by the bonanza of exotic plant life over it. Large palm trees and thick patches of orange flowers with petals as big as horses blanketed entire fields in some areas. Other regions provided a home to the unique plants known as Emble Lilies that blossomed with a tiny spark of fire at the center of the flowers, perpetually burning even in the rain. Perhaps the most amazing botanical spectacle of all was the mighty Icrene Forests that bordered the volcanic Mt. Corist and the village named after it at the mountain base. Despite the presence of natural gas pockets that spontaneously burst into flame within, the burning Emble Lilies that drifted over dry foliage in the winds and even the occasional Lavlas Boar that wandered into the woods, somehow they never caught fire. Not so much as a single wildfire had ever kicked up in the Icrene Forests.

At least until recently. For some reason, the usually unburnable trees within the southernmost woods closest to Mt. Corist had erupted into flames almost overnight with no cause to be found. Though the provisional governing village of the westland had been emptied of its citizens for their own safety weeks ago when the monstrous volcano above them had begun rumbling with life unseen in centuries, winds from the east were threatening to push the wildfire into Corist Village and consume it within the next day at least. A collection of local leaders and warriors had opted to stay behind to endeavor to devise a plan to save the village, but none were sure what to do without knowledge of the fire's source. Recalling that increasingly dangerous and unprovoked elemental disturbances had been spreading across the Southland, the few men lingering by the towering plumes of smoke drifting toward the helpless village guessed it had to have something to do with the unusual activity of the volcano beside them. Though they had sent riders for help from Torrentcia City in the wetlands that morning, they all knew the fire would consume Corist before any help could arrive, if there was anyone who could assist them at all.

Desperate, the few remaining citizens of the village had begun digging a firebreak ditch in an attempt to divert the fire when it reached Corist. Though they wouldn't have enough time or manpower to finish it before the wildfire arrived most likely that afternoon, they toiled on through the blistering heat of the day nonetheless. Around noon when the blaze was no more than an hour away from the outskirts of the village, one of the muscular men shoveling away at the ditch he stood inside of suddenly stopped, feeling a low rumbling in the earth around him. Looking up at the smoldering form of Mt. Corist where the elemental Temple of Fire rested inside, his eyes narrowed to observe a trail of molten lava slowly seeping down from the north side of the mountain. Having never seen the enormous crater bubbling with the molten rock overflow, he shouted out for the others to look up as well. No sooner than all of their eyes were pointed upward, they were further surprised to be shocked off their feet by a fleeting earthquake that blasted free several boulder sized molten rocks from the crater. Witnessing the flaming projectiles launched so high they remained airborne for several long moments, the men at last shouted out cries of alarm as they found them raining down amid the village creating large blazing craters as they landed.

Watching in horror as one of the molten boulders plummeted directly for the ditch they stood in with no time to escape, the men were even more amazed to find it slowing in midair until it halted a few feet above the trench. Hanging inert in the air, several large drops of oozing lava fell from the hovering boulder to scorch the dirt at the men's feet. Exchanging baffled glances at how they were still alive or how the rock had suddenly defied gravity, their answer came at the grunting sound of another figure behind them on the edge of the ditch. Spinning around, the group found a man hooded and cloaked in thick gray robes, his arms and gloved hands outstretched as if gripping the boulder hanging in the air before him. With another grunt behind his concealing hood, the figure swept his arms to his side, releasing the boulder as it dropped safely away from the men into a patch of dead grass.

Shocked back to their senses by the rumbling thud of the boulder crashing into the ground, several of the men clawed their way out of the ditch while staring up at the figure desperately trying to guess his identity. At last, one of the group's leaders shook his head incredulously and approached the figure pulling his dark blue gloves tight against his hands.

"A sage?" he spoke almost too quietly to be heard. "I thought you had all gone..." The cloaked figure merely turned to face him and slightly bowed.

"We have returned," he spoke in a disarming voice. "I am Master Sage Revond. I came in response to your request for help to deal with the elemental disturbances plaguing your lands. Can I be of aid?" The Southlander was too astounded to speak at first, his jaw hanging open in shock.

"Of course!" he managed to stutter eventually, rapidly spinning around to motion for his men to hurry out of the ditch. "Your timing couldn't have been better, Master Sage. The west is burning to a crisp. Wildfires have been springing up everywhere in the past months but now they have even made their way into Icrene Forests." Revond nodded as he shifted his footing to stare into the burning woods on the horizon.

"Yes, I saw the plumes of smoke on the ride here," he spoke, motioning with his right hand for the black horse standing on the ridge behind him to come. "The Icrene Forests have always been immune to fires. Something must be out of place within. I understand Lavlas Boars have been roaming freely out of the mountains of late. Is this true?" Another of the men gathering behind the leader spoke, quickly nodding his head.

"They've even wandered into the village in weeks past," he confirmed. "But they have dwelled in Icrene long before this and never have they started a blaze of any size!" Revond silently nodded, waiting for the black horse trotting up to him to stand beside him.

"I know," he returned, trying to calm them with the assurance in his voice. "Something else must be at work here. I will enter the forest and put out the blaze. Is there anything else you can think of that could be of use to me? Anything else strange at work that could be responsible for this?" The men shot each other puzzled glances again but the leader at last spoke up once more with a shrug.

"As you can see the mountain has been violent of late," he said. "It's been getting worse for weeks now. With no Warrior of Fire we have not been able to enter and see to the temple. Are you here to anoint a new Elemental Warrior to aid us?" Revond mounted Nighcress, letting the men catch a better view of his bearded face as he shook his head.

"Not today, my friends," he responded quickly. "For now I must see to these crises myself. Now flee to cover away from the mountain should it spit fire again. I will return to you." Spinning his head toward the forests in the distance he mentally directed Nighcress forward, instantly speeding away from the village. His gray robes flying up behind him as the enchanted steed blasted toward the fire, Revond whistled and looked up into the sky to find the miniature purple form of Zephyr swooping down from far above him to dive and gently latch his talons onto his shoulder.

"I don't know about this, Revond!" the sky sprite shouted, pulling back the pair of wings mounted on his back. "This isn't some little bonfire you can manage like you practiced in the Sage's Valley! It stretches back for miles and it's spreading too fast to contain!"

"We aren't going to contain it, we're going to put it out," the sage responded confidently. "Do you still have your Dew Drop petals?" The little sprite raised an eyebrow at first but unfolded his wings to reveal two of the blue petals from the enchanted Dew Drop flowers the Sky Sprites protected in their sanctuary in the east safely nestled under his feathers. A smile spread across his wide beak.

"We?" he asked to which the sage turned his head to return his smile.

"We," Revond repeated. "Make sure you are high enough for this to work." With that, the bird like creature took hold of the two petals in his hands and focused his magical Lift Power around him, propelling him back into the air. Carefully keeping track of his partner in the skies, Revond at last passed through the first row of trees in the Icrene Forest and began charging into the woods toward the blaze within. Though he could still feel the presence of Zephyr leading him toward the epicenter of the inferno, the smoke made it impossible to see where he was going and Revond was forced to completely trust Nighcress. When embers drifting through the air began to speed by him, Revond scanned the woods for any unnatural presence, sensing a foreign power in the distance that could have been the cause of the disaster. Seeing nothing and feeling the heat of the fire growing near, the sage was forced to concentrate to form an invisible protective barrier of energy around himself and Nighcress, keeping them shielded from the intense heat and flames beginning to reach out for them. Their surroundings had transformed into a rampant inferno, consuming the bark and leaves of the trees supposedly immune to flame.

As Nighcress leapt over a burning log into a small vale where Revond sensed Zephyr had stopped in the air above them, the sage silently communicated for his steed to halt as well. Guessing his partner had found the epicenter of the blaze, Revond dismounted Nighcress to stand amid the wildfire. The Master Sage squinted as a jet of flame from a falling branch leapt passed his face, nearly singeing his eyebrows. Even with his mystic spell to protect them from the blaze they would not be able to linger there much longer. Keeping a hand on Nighcress to better protect him, Revond closed his eyes and concentrated to pinpoint where Zephyr hovered above. Opening his free hand before him, he summoned his mystic power to form a brilliant white light in the palm of his hand that slowly began to take shape as the moments drew on. What had once been an orb softened and lost its structure to fall into a mold of liquid sloshing back and forth around his glove. Having created the artificial water, Revond opened his eyes and threw up his hand with a grunt to send the glistening white liquid flying out of his grip into the sky where he sensed Zephyr.

Making good use of the acute vision Sky Sprites were known for, Zephyr quickly spotted the enchanted water careening toward him out of the burning trees. Dropping into a vertical dive from above the thin white cloud layer where he hovered, he reached out for the shining liquid with the two Dew Drop petals protruding from his hands. Watching the petals collide with the water the Sprite veered off course to sweep back toward Corist Village. The moment the enchanted petals touched Revond's water they began to expand and dissipate to form a thick white gas forming over the forest. As the seconds ticked by, the vapor grew into full fledged clouds, turning darker and thicker until they spread to cover the entire sky over the southern forests and Mt. Corist itself. While Dew Drop petals were traditionally used merely to create a concealing layer of cloud cover around the sprites' home in the Empyrean Peaks by adding water that made them expand, Revond's unique liquid did not merely create white billows but rain clouds that began pouring as soon as they grew large enough to sustain precipitation. Waiting in the burning forest vale, the Master Sage at last felt the touch of water to his skin and smiled. Over the next few moments the gentle mist transformed into a torrential downpour soaking the forests and subsiding the fire.

Though maintaining the protective barrier around him and Nighcress in the epicenter of the fire, as he mounted the black Morlan and looked around, Revond found the fire gradually weakening and losing energy. Satisfied that the rain would completely snuff the wildfire out in a matter of hours, the Master Sage turned his attention back to his scorched environment to look for any clue as to how it had started in the first place. He had already penetrated a fair distance in and seen no sign of Lavlas Boars, the ill-tempered beasts that coughed fire to eat the nutritious ashes that were left behind by vegetation they burned. Revond shook his head and frowned. Even in large numbers they could not be responsible for such a disturbance—they had roamed the Icrene Forest for millennia without incident. Probing the deep recesses of his mind for anything he knew of that could burn fierce enough to ignite the woods, Revond was surprised to notice the fire around him suddenly flaring back up as if in defiance of the rain altogether. Narrowing his eyes uncertainly as he raised his protective elemental shield to keep him safe, his attuned senses detected something coming at him fast from behind.

Wheeling around in alarm with his wet cloak whipping up, Revond's blue eyes opened wide to find the massive form of a beast twice the size of Nighcress leaping at him from the edge of the vale they had come from. Bracing himself for impact in a fraction of second, the momentum of the creature leaping through the air drove him off Nighcress to slam him onto his back into a burning bush on the opposite side of the vale. Still shocked from having the wind knocked out of him by the assailant, Revond struggled to maintain his shield and find the strength to rise from under the claw of what looked to be a massive cat-like creature with a smoldering coat of flame burning off its very skin. Instantly the sage knew what he was dealing with and reacted before the creature could cut his career as a sage short. Waiting for the growling cat to snap its jaws down for where his head rested inside his hood, Revond summoned his mystic power to generate another ball of liquid around his hands. Gritting his teeth, the Master Sage threw it into the cat's burning red eyes as its head careened down for him. With the beast stunned, Revond jerked his head to the right and avoided what would have been a fatal attack.

Seizing on the creature's momentary disillusionment, Revond summoned his telekinetic grip and pushed his open hands forward to heave the creature off him. It soared off its feet with a screaming growl and slammed into a burning tree, snapping the weakened trunk with its hulking mass. Rising and balling his fists to ready his power again, the Master Sage watched the powerful cat tear its way back to its feet and roar out once more, turning to Revond to lower into a position to pounce on him. When it did not move, the human before it narrowed his eyes.

"Moltar," he spoke to himself. "I should have known from the beginning." The catlike creature growled from deep in its throat upon hearing its name, rhythmically swaying its long flaming tail behind it. Even in the falling rain, the burning layer of fire comprising the creature's coat continued leaping off its body in small embers that dissipated in the wet air. "It is not your place to grapple with me, fire beast. Return to your home in the volcano and stay there. You were banished long ago." Reminded of a defeat suffered ages past, Moltar growled deeply again and crouched further with its shoulder blades high off its back. Watching the flaming cat tighten its grip into the scorched earth to steady itself when it pounced, Revond flared a new wave of brilliant white light around his fists, ready to fight. As the creature came leaping through the air toward him however, Revond did not move, sensing the arrival of a small creature hiding inside the trees above them. When Moltar was halfway to the sage with its burning claws stretching out for him, the creature let out a painful cry to find itself slamming to an abrupt halt in midair, a faint sphere of semitransparent Lift Power around it. As the creature roared and struggled to be free, Zephyr dropped out of the branches above it with a painful look on his beaked face.

"It's powerful, Revond!" he shouted, moving his small hands as if to better his grip on the object he held in place. "I can't hold this thing for long!" Wordlessly nodding in acknowledgment, the Master Sage stepped forward with the white light in his hands sloshing into water once more. Throwing them out at the creature the blast of liquid soared through Zephyr's Lift Power into the creature's skull. Moltar screamed in anguish as the jet of water put out the flame on its body, weakening its power. Looking around at the forest as he pressed his attack, Revond saw the flames on the trees and flora beginning to dissipate as well, reduced to mere embers leaping off the bark and leaves. Though holding his assault for another long moment, as he sensed Moltar's energy signature begin to fade dangerously low he let the jet of liquid diminish and disperse. The cat's once passionately burning coat of fire had been reduced to a mere glow of faint flame over its black skin and it hung almost limply in the air. Seeing it immobile, Zephyr set the creature on the ground and loudly inhaled a deep breath, setting down on a blackened boulder sunk into the earth to recover his spent energy.

Tired from the expulsion of so much mystic power at once as well, Revond let his arms drop loosely to his sides. He took a long breath, eyeing Moltar from head to tail to make sure it was no longer a threat. Slowly lowering himself to the beast's side, he pulled back his hood to stare into the creature's still passionately burning eyes.

"You are a relic from the time of the ancients, Moltar," the sage spoke in a low whisper. "Your life was spared then and it is spared again today. If the Order of Alberic finds you causing trouble a third time you will be granted no such mercy. Return to the volcano when you can walk again and stay there." With that, the Master Sage began to rise and turned to find his partner heavily breathing on the rock nearby. Shooting him a quick smile, the sage ran his fingers through his dark hair and raised his head to let the rain fall down on his face. As he stood recovering his strength, Revond was surprised to hear the beast beside him growling once more. Looking down with his brow furrowed, he found the cat's eyes narrowed and again burning with crimson light. Then it did something he could have never anticipated.

"You speak boldly, sage, but it is your defeat that is imminent," Moltar spoke from deep in this throat, catching both Revond and Zephyr off guard. "The Ascension draws nigh, and neither you nor Alberic himself will be able to stop us this time!" Before he could so much as raise his guard, Revond was astonished to watch the passionate coat of flame ignite around the cat once more. Leaping to his four feet the cat tore away with agility and speed even the Master Sage could not stop. As the fire beast lunged into the tree line toward the distant Mt. Corist in apparent retreat, Revond was left behind with his fists alight with white energy, unsure of what was happening. Looking around, he found the last of the wildfire dying in the absence of its cause and decided it was over for now. Dropping his fists and letting the mystic power of the Master Sage dissipate once more, Revond narrowed his eyes and stared into space before him. Recovering from his shock of seeing the seemingly defeated creature escape so easily, Zephyr rose from the boulder using his wings to fly him before Revond's face as he had so many times before.

"What was all that about?" he asked quietly, shooting another glace to the tree line where Moltar had fled. "What's the Ascension? And who is 'us?'" Revond continued staring into the empty space before him for a long moment before eventually reaching up to flip his hood back over his face.

"Something is sorely out of place," he spoke more to himself than Zephyr. Wheeling around, he began walking for where Nighcress had fled behind the tree line with his soaked cloak trailing behind him. "We need to get back to the Mystic Tower." Aware when something had his partner truly vexed, Zephyr swallowed hard and flapped his purple wings to fly after the sage through the falling rain.

Chapter 4

The Ascension

The circular chamber in the basement of the massive Cathedral of Dalorosk lay quiet as always, the dead silence broken only by the faint crackling of the few torches lining the rounded brick walls. Though the chamber had once been visited almost daily by Dark Mages in the time of High Priest Zalnaught, since his death and the reorganization of the Black Church by the Montroxs, the chamber had become a forgotten relic disturbed with rarity. Even the rats that burrowed deep in the infrastructure of the cathedral did not dare penetrate into this chamber, somehow sensing the presence of the massive black form resting motionlessly within. Though its purpose had been altered by thousands of years of politics and wars, the enormous Cathedral of Dalorosk had originally been constructed by the first Dark Mages to protect this chamber and the beast that lay trapped within from which the cathedral's name was derived. The behemoth creature known as Dalorosk hung limply in the middle of the cavernous basement as it had for thousands of years, its massive horned skull the only thing visible to anyone who walked in through the double doors facing it. The rest of its body was submerged in an empty cavern beneath the heavy chamber floor where its head lay motionless with its thick eyelids closed.

Dalorosk had once been the great terror of the northern skies: a winged monster that lived in the Black Peaks and fed on the first humans to arrive in Drakkaidia before the country was even founded. After an old Elemental Warrior of Darkness had weakened the beast enough to be captured, he dragged its hulking mass to an underground chasm beneath the Temple of Darkness where a prison was built around Dalorosk. Siphoning elemental power from the behemoth to create the first Dark Mages, the Drakkaidians built their master cathedral to Drakkan over the spot where Dalorosk was imprisoned to stay close to him and continue to absorb his regenerating power over the years. The Dark Mages eventually developed a painful ritual known as the Runes to keep the beast weakened and unable to break free from the massive chains and stone walls around it. Dalorosk had always struggled to be free, thrashing about in his prison, but over the past few centuries it seemed as though he had given up trying and remained inert.

Even though it seemed they had the behemoth whipped, the Dark Mages still continued the practice of executing the Runes to be sure it remained docile and cooperative when they needed it. Though they did not venture down as frequently as they once did in the time of the tyrants like Zalnaught, today was the day the current High Priest had ordered the ritual done. The quiet of the age old chamber was broken by the creaking sound of one of the thick wooden doors lurching open to reveal the robed figure of a Dark Mage slowly stepping through. Though having nothing to fear from the defeated monster in recent years, even the most steadfast and resilient of mages still felt uneasy when facing the mighty giant. This particular mage had executed the Runes on Dalorosk several times before and frequently wondered why the beast had abandoned resisting at all in the past decades. As he closed the door behind him he noticed the dark creature's mammoth head had slightly turned since last seeing him. The mage took a step closer, eying the monster up and down.

Dalorosk was a hulking figure, humanoid in appearance but for the many abnormalities across his black hide. His head was more like a dog's that a human's, sporting rows of long bloodstained teeth jutting from his lips and two horns mounted on the back of his hairy skull, angled downward toward his back. His muscular body was covered in streaks of red, as if violently tattooed by Drakkan himself. A pair of tattered bat like wings hung limply behind him against the constricting wall of the prison, mounted high on his back where the thick hide was rough and cracked. His legs were comparatively smaller, resembling those of a lion with long claws on his feet. Perhaps most disturbing were the huge short swords wrapped in massive chains around his arms. The ancient Drakkaidian myth told that Dalorosk had fashioned himself duel blades out of the only substance strong and large enough for him to wield—his own black bones. He had once kept them stabbed into his sides using his very flesh as their sheaths, but after his defeat the Drakkaidians had wrapped them as well as his entire body in the most massive chains ever forged, holding his mammoth form in place within the prison.

Staring at the age old monster for another lingering moment, the Dark Mage shook off his concern and turned for a table behind him where several iron glyphs rested, waiting to be heated iron hot for the execution of the Runes that expanded them in dark power to sear over his entire form. As the mage began toiling to prepare them and summon the spell for the ritual, he noticed the torchlight around him dimming and the once bright flame fade to mere embers falling to the floor. Unnerved by the abrupt darkness, he stopped to listen to a sudden suction of air behind him, only to feel another jet of foul smelling wind rush to stir his long black robes. His heart suddenly pounding with trepidation and confusion, he wheeled around to find Dalorosk's large cranium gradually drifting to lean on the floor of the chamber to his right. Watching frozen with fear as the creature's long black hair on the back of his head drifted together until motionless again in the long moments that passed, the mage guessed the creature was merely breathing and let out a deep breath of relief of his own.

As he was about to turn back to continue preparing the runes, however, the man was shocked to find Dalorosk's eye lids suddenly lift open, a deep crimson light from within casting the entire chamber in heavy red. With the room saturated by the ominous light from the behemoth's glowing eyes, the mage felt his heart threatening to beat out of its chest at what he witnessed next. Dalorosk's cavernous jaws slowly opened, a deep, rumbling growl echoing from deep in its throat.

"The time is now," came a deep voice from out of the dark creature's gaping mouth, nearly dropping the Dark Mage to the ground in shock. The next moment, he was horrified to see Dalorosk lower his head only to violently throw it back up through the surface of the large chamber floor, smashing the stone up as if it was nothing. Roaring ferociously and blowing the mage's robes back is if caught in hurricane wind, the monstrous creature flexed its muscular body for the first time in centuries and began snapping the massive chains holding him down to the prison beneath the chamber with relative ease. When his flailing arms were free, Dalorosk reached down to pull out the giant metal spikes that held his clawed feet into the rock, dark blood flying up as they came. Pulling in his massive wings to his back to fit into the chamber above him, the creature violently smashed his way through what was left of the floor and propelled himself up toward the domed ceiling. His bleeding feet took hold on the wall on either side of the Dark Mage, still standing immobile before him with his jaw dropped.

Chains were still wrapped around Dalorosk's torso and the large curving swords around his arms, but the crimson streaks across his skin seemed to pulsate red and make them glow as he came to the ceiling. Balling his massive clawed fists, Dalorosk slammed them upward until he penetrated through to the next level of the cathedral above him. Pulling himself upward and crawling through with his bunched legs and long wingtips disappearing after him, the heavy crimson light from his eyes faded out of the room. Somehow still standing over the little segment of the basement floor not obliterated by the behemoth's violent surge upward, the Dark Mage could only watch as large debris of rubble fell from the gaping hole in the dome of the chamber to drop into the now empty prison beneath him and the darkness that lay beyond.

Because it lay on the outskirts of the Great Forests and its natural defensible position in the otherwise flat plains, Greenwall Fortress had always been an important location for the Southland. For centuries it had served as the unofficial capital city of the nation, but after the construction of the relatively new Torrentcia City on the plateau above Lake Torrent and the Elemental Temple of Water, it was transformed into a trade station in the center of the Grailen. In recent decades, however, it had been forced to resume its previous role as an impregnable fortress thanks to the unpredictable Golthrout attacks on the villages in the Great Forests. Though the subterranean rock beasts of the woods usually came out only for a few weeks every ten years to prey on what humans they could ensnare, lately they had been striking on a monthly basis and leveling entire villages anywhere near the forests. There were rumors there had even been Golthrouts coming out of the forests; something unheard of before these troubled times.

Over the past year Greenwall had become so packed full of refugees from the destroyed villages in the Great Forests that veritable cities of tents had been forced to set up around its outer perimeter. The fortress was large but hundreds of stranded villagers fearing the Golthrouts had been arriving lately; there was just not enough space for them all inside the walls. Greenwall was built out of a massive wall of rock rising from a lone ridge in the Grailen Plains, even thicker and stronger than the Grandarian Wall of Light had been in its time. The city gates were on the opposite side of the fortress where the famous green wall covered in flowing vines and other vegetation rose, giving the stronghold its name. It was here that yet another caravan of fleeing villagers from a small forest outpost near the Temple of Earth had recently arrived to shout up to the wall of another Golthrout attack nearby. The guards of the fortress had been skeptical of their story at first, hearing that no actual Golthrout was sighted—only another massive earthquake similar to many of the ones being reported lately.

Though about to shout down from the tall wall for the villagers to set up their tents somewhere close by where there was space left, the Legionnaire guard speaking with them curiously felt the ground beneath his feet beginning to tremble. Hearing the cries of panicking villagers suddenly spreading both inside Greenwall and out, the guard caught sight of the grassy earth only a few hundred yards away suddenly explode up in a shower of rock and soil. His eyes going wide, the guard watched as two massive stone limbs rose out of the ground to latch onto the nearby earth with rock-strewn fingers. Over the next long moments the populace of Greenwall saw the most massive Golthrout any of them could ever dream of pull itself out of the fissure it had torn in the earth to slowly stand erect on its hulking legs, easily as tall as the wall of Greenwall itself. The creature had similar makeup to a typical Golthrout but for two massive horns of stone jutting into the cloudy sky and the bull shaped head they came from. There was also a strange crimson light flowing underneath the layer of rock comprising its exterior shell, particularly exposed on its chest where some of the rocky skin was missing.

Ignoring the swarm of humans frantically rushing to pound on the doors of Greenwall to its left, the enormous Golthrout set its sights to the north and began walking forward, its powerful strides shaking the very foundations of the earth with each step.

Aside from the constant gusts blowing from the Temple of Wind at its pinnacle, there was no more peaceful a view than atop the summit of the Empyrean Peaks. The highest point in the world where the earth reached out to scrape the top of the sky with the Elemental Temple at its rocky peak, endless blue stretched on for as far as the eye could see. The only living creatures with reason to venture so high were the Triune leaders of the Sky Sprites and a party of Windrun Warriors that annually paid a visit to the Temple of Wind to ensure its enormous prison and the sole occupant within remained intact.

The prison that had been violently shaking all morning.

As the hours rolled on, a series of cracks in the walls of the elemental temple had been appearing with alarming frequency, starting at the base of the structure and working their way up to the top of the highest tower that contained the Source of Wind responsible for creating all the air in the atmosphere of the world.

As a series of loud crashes and ear piercing screams from something inside eventually made their way to the top of the tower, the constantly blowing winds blasting out suddenly ceased. The air was not quiet for long, however, as the cracks on the wall near the roof of the tower suddenly gave way, letting a massive winged creature tumblle out in a storm of rubble and debris. Free at last, the massive wyvern the Sky Sprites had once imprisoned savagely beat its feathered wings and screamed out from its two dragon like heads. Though there had once been a third, the last neck had been severed nearly forty years ago—the last time it had been free. Beating its wings to careen forward at full speed, the enormous blue and green monster shot off toward the northern skies and what lay under them.

The waters of the Eastern Sea had been particularly rough all morning near the largest town on the coast of the Southland, Acquanautta Port. Waves had been steadily crashing into the large harbor seemingly out of nowhere for hours into the morning, leading most of the captains of ships in the area to dock and brace themselves for the vicious storm sure to be coming. The last ship to make berth from the horizon before the storm grew too violent to navigate through was a large fishing vessel just returning from a long voyage into deep waters around the colonized islands. The captain of the vessel stood at the helm facing the large wheel, nervously watching the incoming waves seeming to grow larger with each swell. Turning to instruct his helmsman to direct them into a harbor stall, he heard the sudden cry of the lookout from high on the mast pole.

"Captain!" came the man's delirious cry. "Vortex on the horizon!" Hearing this, the entire crew spun around back for the sea locked with fear. They all knew what a vortex in the Eastern Sea signaled. Squinting his panicked eyes to the building waves in the sea beyond, the captain raised his wide brimmed hat and peered out to look for himself. Seeing what looked to be a whirlpool in the waves, he shook his head and shot it back up to the lookout on the mast.

"You must be wrong!" he shouted back. "The beast has never been seen near the shoreline! Are you sure it's a vortex?" Though strenuously nodding at first, the lookout slowly ceased and tilted his head to the left, staring out with his long spyglass once more. The entire crew anxiously waiting for his report, the man at last shook his head and looked back down.

"It looks to be gone, cap'n!" the sailor eventually returned, to which all the men took a deep breath and relaxed. "It disappeared but I swear to the fog I saw it as clear as day..." Hearing him trail off, the captain exhaled sharply and put his hands on his hips.

"You've been staring at the salt for too long, you incompetent rat!" the captain barked. "Get down here and..." He was the one to trail off this time as another of the crewmen spotted a shadow speeding toward their ship beneath the surface of the waves. Hearing sudden screams, the captain helplessly watched as the head of a long body of blue scales came leaping out of the waves with inconceivable speed, its wide jaws agape as it came lunging toward the center of the deck. As the enormous serpent's tail slipped out of the waves, its head descended to slam into the deck and drive through the hull, snapping the ship in two. Violently blasted off course, fragmented segments of the deck and hull went flying into the air along with members of the crew. Having lost none of its momentum, the long serpent dove back into the waves to continue blasting forward through the harbor, enormous waves washing up behind it to slam into the docks. Though hundreds of spectators in the port had seen the attack and expected similar aggression from the creature, they were amazed to find it swim its way into the massive river pouring all the way from Lake Torrent and disappear upstream.

Since Master Sage Revond had hurriedly departed after putting out the wildfire in Icrene Village that morning, the group of leaders in Corist Village had continued digging the firebreak ditch where they started, just in case the blaze somehow started up once more. Though Mt. Corist's intimidating slopes remained rumbling throughout the day and into the evening, the group had not seen any further hostility from the mountain and decided to take a well deserved break around a fire pit behind one of their homes. Feasting on a large native bird they had cooked as the sun began to sink behind the foreboding silhouette of Mt. Corist, they sat around the fire to relax for what seemed like the first time in weeks. It had been hectic evacuating the local villages closer to the wetlands and the Torrentcia territories while remaining behind to ward off Lavlas Boars and more recently the wildfire, but they all agreed they had done good work protecting their home and cracked open a keg of dark ale to celebrate.

As the night drew on, the group sat around the fire laughing and forgetting the worries of the world, reminiscing of simpler times before the wild elemental disturbances had begun. The leader of the group who had bid Revond goodbye earlier in the day smiled as he once again congratulated the men on a job well done, leaning in toward the fire to warm a remaining piece of meat on a long stick. As it hovered over the slowly dancing flames, the Southlander noticed he was continually raising his stick higher as the flames seemed to be slowly growing. Pulling the meat back with a curious look on his face, all of the men noticed the sudden increase in the intensity of the fire and stood uncertainly, taking several steps back to avoid the heat.

When the leader was about to state something was wrong, he was shocked to find another mass of flame bursting out of the darkness from behind a row of shrubs adjacent to the home they stood behind, rushing straight at him. His eyes going wide, it was all the man could do to drop to his knees as a flaming cat roaring with anger leapt over the suddenly raging fire. Feeling the incredible heat from the creature as it passed over him, the awestruck Southlander rolled along the grass until the speedy cat landed behind him and raced north into the darkness, leaving a trail of fiery tracks in its wake.

"What in the name of Drakkan below is that rumbling?" the incensed High Priest of the Black Church shouted in the sanctuary of the Cathedral of Dalorosk, struggling to keep his footing amid the veritable earthquake threatening to bring down the building around them. A Dark Mage assisting him with a ritual near the altar at the head of the sanctuary was about to respond they should get outside as quickly as possible but was knocked to his feet as the shaking grew worse. The few Drakkaidians present in the rows of pews inside the church immediately shot up to race for the central aisle and the double doors to get out of the massive cathedral. Befuddled at what the cause of the unnatural disturbance could be, the dark robed High Priest was suddenly thrown to his feet as well. The center of the sanctuary's stone floor was blasted up as if by an explosion underneath.

Staring into the falling debris in horror, the High Priest watched as the beastly form of Dalorosk violently climbed his way through the opening he had made, roaring with rage that threatened to bow the very walls of the sanctuary as it came. His gleaming crimson eyes filling the chamber with their eerie glow, the behemoth stood full length until his head smashed through the arching ceiling. Kneeling down to spy the trembling High Priest on the altar, Dalorosk shifted his gaze to the platform on the altar that rose to the Temple of Darkness above them. Growling from deep in his throat, the black creature drove upward through the ceiling until he had exposed the entrance to the temple. Throwing a mammoth, balled fist through the doorway, he reached in with his other to the core of the temple to rip open the supposedly unmovable door guarding the Source of Darkness. Observing the sphere of black energy containing the essence of the element of darkness from a shard of the Holy Emerald, the beast reached forward to seize it in his clawed hand and pull it back to stare at it for a long moment.

With a grin on his face Dalorosk squeezed the ball of energy in his palm, instantly forcing it to dissipate and flow into his body. The moment it disappeared a dark light ignited and radiated from a spot on the left side of his chest. With the Source his, the behemoth at last spread his gargantuan wings as wide as he was able in the confining chamber. His hulking form heaved upward through the remaining floors of the cathedral until he at last punched through the sprawling roof. Pulling his way into the open air for the first time in well over a thousand years, he spread his wings wide and lifted his body into the tempestuous Drakkaidian sky, lightning cracking down from the rolling clouds to strike the already scorched earth. Staring down at the building that had served as his prison for so long, the monster's eyes narrowed and he began to shake with loathing hatred searing his veins. Reaching to the chains around either arm to pull forth his curving short swords carved from his own bones, Dalorosk let out a roar of fury that tore through the air around him. Focusing a wave of swelling dark energy around the edges of his blades, the behemoth savagely swung them down through the air to release two arching waves of throbbing black energy flying down for the cathedral. Exploding with devastating force as they tore through the roof, the people in the surrounding city could only watch as one of the greatest edifices ever built crumbled and fell like a pile of blocks a child had set up and knocked down for fun.

His rage still not satisfied, Dalorosk leapt back in the air to dive down with his energy charged blades raised above his horned skull. He smashed them down into what was left of the destroyed cathedral, sending enormous segments of stone flying out to land in the city and crush buildings as if hit by a catapult. Charging through the rubble with his enormous muscular body blasting back into the skies, the screaming giant beat its wings to propel him forward to the east away from the destroyed cathedral with a deafening roar.

Chapter 5

<u>The Alliance</u>

Aeric and Mina woke late in the morning the day after the Festival of Radia, having spent the night in a house full of Aeric's old friends from his days living in Galantia. Though Aeric's mother was skeptical of letting a single girl stay with a group of seven boys she knew to be loud and raucous growing up, she above anyone trusted her son to make sure Mina was as safe and comfortable as she would have been staying in the Golden Castle itself. Besides—even Mina's own parents acknowledged she still behaved more like one of the boys than the compassionate girl she was gradually becoming in her relationship with Aeric. After waking and gathering the few things they had brought with them into the city, the pair drifted downstairs in the house to find Aeric's friends still passed out on the furniture from their heavy drinking the night before. Grinning and shaking his head at their typical behavior, Aeric wrote a short note for them on the table of the kitchen thanking them for the beds and telling them he would try to see them all soon. Setting down the inked quill in his hand and turning to step over one of his friends asleep in a ball on the ground, he silently grinned at Mina struggling to contain her laughter at the door.

Closing the wooden door and stepping out into the sunlight of the glorious Grandarian morning, Mina made a sarcastic joke that her boyfriend had better never end up like his friends someday. Aeric merely shrugged and told her he knew the good life when he saw it, to which she rolled her eyes and laughed. Aeric pulled in to swiftly kiss his love's forehead and take her hand as they embarked into the busy city streets. He was dressed in his customary blue tunic outfit while Mina wore long traveling pants and a white tunic tightly fit against her upper body. Though so simply dressed with her curly chestnut hair collected behind her back in a ponytail,

Aeric could not help but smile to himself at how beautiful she looked and again how lucky he was when his eyes frequently drifted to her. He had never been one to take anything for granted, having learned to appreciate the joys and rewards of life from the stories of trial and tribulation he had heard growing up. If nothing else, tales of his Grandfather Tavin's adventures and struggles had instilled in Aeric gratitude for the life he lived—blessed with everything he craved and free from such worldly responsibilities.

As the young Tieloc set his arm around Mina's waist and they broke eye contact, he swept his gaze up to the tightly fit buildings and rooftops of Galantia. It always filled a Grandarian with the utmost pride and fulfillment to walk through the capital. Though the oldest city in all of Iairia, Galantia was still one of the cleanest and best maintained. Even the most minuscule details of its structure and décor resonated with beauty and pride. From the simplest of blue and white flowers lining cement containers on the streets to the shining gold placards on buildings to communicate a residence number or a business name, the smaller beauties contributed to the splendor of the city as much as the large. Hundreds of hand crafted blue and gold flags boasting the crest of light and other flowing Grandarian designs over their flapping surfaces waved in the wind, proudly announcing to the world their affiliation.

Perhaps most unique to Galantia as compared to any other city in Iairia were its people. Even on cold winter days away from the summer festivals, the populace was always in good spirits. Some argued it was because the municipality was the most prosperous trade center in the world, while others maintained it was simply because it was the most affluent city in Iairia. Grandarians claimed it was came from the confidence of believing Lord Granis' watchful eyes were always fixed on them, keeping them safe from harm. Many of them agreed that because the Source of Light rested within the city, the populace emanated a particularly friendly and harmonious demeanor. All anyone knew for certain was that the city had nearly been destroyed twice by Drakkaidian forces in the Holy Wars, but still it stood unscathed.

Even the simplest of homes in Galantia were substantially more elaborate and accommodating compared to those in other cities. The house Aeric and Mina had stayed in was in the heart of the second tier of the city where the marketplace and plebian citizens generally resided. The smaller tier above them contained homes for the more affluent families of the nation as well as the more prestigious businesses and institutions of the old city. The top tier of the city harbored the Golden Castle itself, the oldest structure in Iairia that was first erected around the Temple of Light the ancient Grandarians had found long ago. All of the six elemental temples across the lands were happened upon in a similar fashion, believed to have been constructed by the ancient humans who first existed after the Battle of the Gods between Granis and Drakkan eons ago in the forgotten world. While not even the Mystic Sages knew the origins of the ancients or what had become of them with any certainty, all the people of Galantia knew was that the golden bricked Temple of Light rising out of the Golden Castle was the most beautiful edifice any of them would ever see. Its highest peak had even later been christened the Tower of Granis, lofting high above any other point in the city.

The final and lowest tier of the shining capital of Galantia was the protective Gate Yard built after the First Holy War almost six centuries ago when Drakkaidian forces had first penetrated into Grandaria to threaten its capital. A massive wall similar to the now destroyed Wall of Light that had once barred invading forces from entering Grandaria through the war zone, it stretched around the front of the capital to where the natural protective ridge behind the city began. Between it and the old gates to the second tier of the city, a military base was installed as the first line of defense should any enemy ever penetrate into Grandaria again. It was this tier of the city that Aeric and Mina were headed for, having left their horses there with a friend of Darien Tieloc who maintained a stable for the army.

Though a treat to make the trip to Galantia and get away from school for a while, the couple only had a few days off from the Gulfrin Academy on the coast of Grandaria and decided they needed to be heading back that morning. Strolling through the bustling streets of the lower city, they casually ambled toward the Gate Yard taking in all of the activities of the festival still drawing large crowds. They stopped at the booth Aeric's mother had helped station the previous day to find her gone, apparently up at the Golden Castle visiting her husband with Roan Garrinal according to another woman. Though wishing they could have seen their parents again before departing, they knew it would take them all day to visit the castle again and say their goodbyes, so the pair continued moving through the crowds toward the city gates. While walking, Aeric pulled out a small satchel of Seir and bought them a meager breakfast of special pastries only baked on such events as these, covered in sugary frosting that Mina gobbled down as they continued down the side of a stone tiled street. Noticing a small glob of icing on the tip of her nose from her voracious consumption of the pastry, Aeric leaned his head in to lick it off with a swift swipe of his tongue, to which Mina giggled and slapped him away.

As they walked several people who saw them would coo and sigh at how adorable they looked together. All their friends back home in Eirinor and at the academy always told them how perfect they were for each other. If there was one thing anyone familiar with Aeric knew about him it was his enduring devotion to Mina. Her happiness and wellbeing were always his first priorities in any circumstance, sometimes to a fault when he tended to neglect other matters of importance aside from her. Though aware of this and admonishing him for it herself, Mina was ultimately always just happy to know she was unconditionally loved more than anything and let things be.

At last exiting the city to move into the Gate Yard, Aeric and Mina made their way to one of the smaller stables along the wall to find the man keeping their horses and graciously thanked him. Bidding him farewell with smiles as he returned to his work shoeing a horse, the two loaded their supplies into the traveling packs in their saddles and began walking the animals out of the colossal city gates. As they made their way out of Galantia and into the busy marketplace for travelers outside of the gates, Aeric wove his way to the opposite side of his horse to stand beside Mina as they marched forward. She smiled as he took her hand again.

"Now that wasn't so bad, was it?" she asked looking back at the shining city. Aeric shot a glace down to the moat they walked over on the large gates and shrugged.

"You know I love visiting the old place, but I'm always happier to leave for somewhere smaller," he returned.

"I know," she replied wiping a curl of her locks out of her eyes and behind her ear. "After a while all the people in there start to make me feel like I'm going to be swallowed by the crowd. But we always have fun, don't we?" Aeric shrugged again and swept his blue eyes back on the city, looking up to the towering Golden Castle high above them.

"Especially when I get to explain my future to another of my father's associates on the Galantian Council," he said, catching her off guard. "I always love that conversation." Mina quickly picked up on the sarcasm dripping from his every word, letting out a huff of irritation in response.

"Aeric, look at me," she told him, placing a hand on her slender waist. The boy did as he was bid with a faint smile appearing, aware he had just earned a lecture. "You are a grown man now. Why in the name of Granis on high do you still let what other people think weigh on you?"

"Come on, Mina," he spoke with a disarming gesture of his arms, trying to appease her. "You know it doesn't bother me, it's just, you know... I hate having to justify myself to the family name to people who aren't even a part of it."

"You don't have to justify anything to anyone, Aeric," the girl returned heatedly, her passionate side erupting out. "You've worked hard for the life you want. You're just the Tieloc your father is or Grandpa Tavin was, Granis embrace him." Aeric chuckled to himself hearing this and looked down to button shut a loose pouch along his leather carpenter's belt.

"Well I don't know if I'd go that far," he returned, remembering all the tales of adventure his grandfather had told him when he was still alive. "Grandpa Tavin did more for Grandaria and the whole world than most people will ever begin to know, no matter how many embellished tales of the Days of Destiny they hear."

"So because your grandfather saved the world he's a better man than you?" Mina asked as if disgusted by what he was implying. Predicting his non-confrontational nature as he was about to respond and lay the discussion to rest, she cut him off by raising her free hand in front of his face, silencing him before he could reply. "Do you remember the winter of our second year at the academy?" Her question catching him off guard, Aeric tilted his head in confusion. "Remember the trip you were going to take with the boys in our quarter from the sailing guild?" Aeric's face lit up with remembrance at this.

"They were taking me and a few others who had never been on the sea out to the Filriss Islands," he recalled. "Never went though. What made you think of that?"

"Because the story doesn't end there, dummy," she recoiled. "On the day you were set to embark, that ancient roof—that we had been complaining about to the headmaster all year— finally caved in over the general room of your quarter building. And while your buddies left the mess, you volunteered to assist Master Cambren and the others with repairing it because they were shorthanded and needed you."

"I don't quite see where this is going, Mina," Aeric interrupted, a frown appearing on his face as he remembered the rest of the event. "They gave me a hard time for bailing out on the trip for the rest of the year. When they were done people thought I was too afraid to leave the docks to even go for a swim."

"And while you let them get in your head all that time, you didn't realize that it was you who repaired that roof in time for the giant snows we got in the blizzard the day before they got back from the islands," Mina continued, ignoring his rebuff. "If you hadn't been there to lead the project when Cambren hurt his back, there would have been two feet of snow in the beds of those jerks when they got back." Aeric was silent, just staring at her in bewilderment as they walked. Though Mina rolled her eyes at his confusion, she let out a little sigh and walked closer by his side. "Because you were there, doing what you love to do even though they made fun of you for it and judged you for not conforming to what they thought you should be doing, you made a difference. You may not have made it saving the world like your grandfather, but you made it with the same spirit that he was renowned for. The world needs its warriors but its needs it carpenters too. Granis works through us all in different ways, Aeric. Grandpa Tavin had the Sword of Granis and you have the tools in your belt, but you have the same passion for what you do that he did. The same passion for what you care about..." Nearing his face, the girl swept in to gently kiss him on his lips and pull away to see him smiling. Seeing him happy again, she smiled and took his hand. "I know you're a good man and so do you, so don't let your father's friends on the council make you think otherwise."

"What would I do without you, Miss Garrinal?" Aeric merely replied after she finished, silently chuckling and staring at her. "I think you—"Aeric was cut short by a man suddenly walking into him, shoving the boy aside with his shoulder as he passed through the couple. With his eyes on Mina, Aeric never saw him coming, but as he looked back to find the figure walking directly past them without so much as turning apologize, a frown appeared on the boy's face. The middle-sized but strong man had short black hair and dark clothing from head to foot, marching forward with purpose. Though Mina could tell her boyfriend would have loved to tell the man to watch where he was going, she took his hand once again with a smile, drawing his attention back to her. Knowing she wanted him to let it pass without incident, Aeric forced himself to shrug the churlish figure off. Exhaling sharply, he set his eyes back in front of them and picked up where he let off.

As the pair and their horses marched out of the marketplace and into the green Valley of Galantia to turn east for the Gulfrin Academy, the figure that had bumped into Aeric unhurriedly came to a halt in the center of the marketplace before the downed drawbridge of the city. He was an adult with an average sized body and a typical face, no distinguishing characteristics to be found. As Aeric had noticed, his attire was all multiple shades of black from the thick boots and pants to his tunic with long sleeves and rectangular designs along its edges. The only unusual item present on his person was a strange medallion fixed to a metal plate on his left tunic with a strange orb of dark light contained behind glass at the center.

As the figure stood with his fists clenched in the busy marketplace, his dark eyes suddenly drifted to the moat on the right side of the gate. Narrowing his eyes, he watched as the surface rippled and the shadow of something underneath appeared. At last, a man gradually lifted himself out to crawl up onto the grassy land. As his fingers gripped wads of the grass to pull himself up, the figure in black saw rows of blue scales over the backs of his hands slowly fading to meld with the tan skin. Though preparing to stride over to the rising man dressed in clothes identical to his except for their blue hue, a pair of men walking toward him from his left entered the corner of his eye and he spun to face them. They too were dressed in attire exactly like his but one was brown and the other bright red. Curious to see them together, the man in black froze and watched them continue striding forward with their eyes fixed on him. Though the crowd did not seem to notice the four men grouping together while they grew more grave by the second, several passing merchants let out a shout of fright as a fifth figure suddenly dropped out of the sky to land in front of the man in black, crouching over the earth with a thud as he landed.

Though many of the confused travelers took a step back at the unusual display, one of them at last pointed out they were all dressed in similar clothing and guessed aloud they were a troupe of performers on their way out of Galantia from the Festival of Radia. The man in black could overhear a passing mother tell her son they had to be brothers because even their faces were identical. As the figure dressed in purple rose from where he had landed a moment before, several feathers fell out of his sleeves, lofting to the ground. When the other two men walking toward them and the figure who had emerged from the water at last arrived around the others, the group of five silently stared each other down for a long moment, their faces tense. At last, the man in blue spoke.

"I see we all had the same idea," he spoke in a low voice.

"The same priority, you mean," the man in black returned, his tone harsher. "This city reeks of his treacherous stench."

"I could say the same thing of your black citadel to the west," the man in purple adjoined with a frown.

"Are we to continue where we left off, then, scum?" the man in red said taking a step forward, the grass at his feet suddenly smoldering with small flames.

"Wait," the man in black said putting his hands between them defensively. "We came here with a common goal—a common enemy. If we fight amongst ourselves we will be in no state to battle him as well." The man in brown slowly nodded.

"I agree," he said. "I did not come here for any of you. I must destroy him first."

"It is not your rocky hide that will be his end, imbecile," the man in red spoke once more. "It is my claw that will deal his death."

"Like it dealt to his descendant yesterday?" the man in blue snapped callously, prompting the man in red to step forward with his fists bursting into flame. Before the two could meet in the middle of the group the man in black thrust his arms out once more, signaling for them to wait.

"Hold, brothers," he urged them once more. "Before we begin our battle anew, think on this. Our war never yielded any result but our downfall. What if the maggot has a new external power like last time? We have been waiting for this weakness in his defense for eons. What if he has lulled us into a false confidence? If we are separated he will be able to take us one by one as he did before."

"Then what would you have us do?" the man in red bit angrily again.

"Form an alliance, my brothers," the man in black spoke passionately. "Together we can destroy him with ease. Then, once we have all the Sources combined, we can rule the six lands together. There would not have to be one superior to the other. We could all share in the one, ultimate power as if the emerald were assembled again."

"Ridiculous," the man in blue barked, shaking his head. "What makes you think I would trust any of you, least of all you, Dalorosk?" The man in black struggled to hide his impatience but exhaled deeply.

"Unless my eyes deceive me, it appears we all have no choice," he said. "You are wounded from recent defeat the same as Moltar, Vorkoise. I sensed the same descendant of our enemy who stopped Moltar yesterday weaken you in the seas years ago. You will need the combined power of the Sources to regenerate completely." The man in blue recoiled swiftly, anger flushing his face red.

"Wounded? Did you not also sense me this morning when I destroyed my Temple of Water to recover what he stole from me after my defeat? We all have our Sources with us, Dalorosk—you included," he said pointing to the various medallions of light over each of their chests. "I have all the strength I need." The man in black extended his hand to the man in blue's neck, pointing to the two large scars there.

"Your scars tell a different tale," he returned calmly. "You were wounded without the Source of Water in your possession. You will need more than its power to restore you completely. What chance do you think you have to defeat him alone without your full power?" The man in blue was quiet at this, his scowl growing. The man in black turned to the others then, eyeing them up and down. "And what of the rest of you? We have all sensed each other's struggles since our imprisonment. All of you—within the past century—have been scarred. Do you think you will fare any better if our enemy is at his full strength?" The others fell quiet at this, shooting each other knowing glances. The man in red could not hide his scars either, most of them spread across his face from his battle the previous day. Giving in, the man in purple reached up to his shoulder to reveal a large scar of his own. Finally, the man in brown pushed his tunic in to his chest, revealing fresh blood soaking through to stain it.

"What in the name of the shards happened to you, Golthrout?" the man in red managed with a look of abhorrence on his face.

"There was a boy," the man in brown responded after a long moment, his teeth clenched. The man in purple nodded, covering his scar again.

"I lost a head to naught but a girl," he growled, clenching his fist and spinning his head around to the man in black before him. "I want it back. I want the power of the combined Sources." The dark figure slowly nodded, eyeing them all again.

"Then we shall have it, my brothers," he said with assurance pouring form his voice. "My feet still bleed from the spikes the pathetic humans drove through them centuries ago. We have all suffered agonizing defeats. Defeats that never would have occurred had we not been betrayed by our brother the traitor. But today we are free. Today he finds himself without his precious staff or his human minions with the power of the crests to hold us back. Today he finds himself facing all five of us at once. Today, we will take our revenge." Seeing the faces of his four brothers incensed and nodding with the lust for destruction he had seen there countless times before, he pumped his fist into the middle of where they stood. Though slow to follow, the others slammed theirs up against his one by one until they stood in alliance.

On a ridge overlooking the Valley of Galantia and the golden city tucked against the mountainous cliffs behind it, Aeric and Mina rode up the last stretch of the dusty road leading away from it toward the famous Path of Coriell that led between the capital city and the Gulfrin Bay to the east. They were talking about the events of the previous night, still laughing over some of the belligerent activities Aeric's intoxicated friends had engaged in both inside the house and out in the festival. As they began verbally planning out their schedules for their final reviews once they returned to the academy, Mina turned around to pull out a paper she had brought with her in her saddle bag. Facing the Valley of Galantia once more, she suddenly caught sight of a strange shape moving through the sky over the city behind them. Halting her horse to get a better look, Aeric noticed she was staring into the distance and confusedly turned his steed around as well.

"Aeric, am I going crazy or is there something over the valley?" she asked with a hint of concern in her voice. Following her eyes and her finger pointing into the sky above Galantia, he too saw what looked to be a giant bird flapping its wings toward the Golden Castle at the top of the city. Rubbing his eyes to make sure they weren't playing ticks on him, the Grandarian boy shook his head incredulously.

"What is that?" he asked more to himself than her. "No bird is that big."

"It doesn't look like any bird I've ever seen," Mina responded with mounting tension audible in her voice. Continuing to watch as the creature in the blue sky moved closer to the top tier of the city, the pair dismounted from their horses and tied their reins to the branch of a large bush beside them. Hurriedly striding to the top of the ridge to get a better view, both Aeric and Mina watched in baffled horror as a mammoth humanoid creature suddenly appeared as if leaping off the bird into the air beneath it. Their eyes wide, the two young Grandarians jumped in shock as the enormous brown creature slammed into a short tower on the Golden Castle, swinging its huge arm through it to severe it from the castle and blast huge segments of stone flying through the air into the city and countryside beyond. Shaking his head in awestruck bewilderment, Aeric felt Mina taking hold of his arm, too shocked to speak or scream. Forcing himself to tear his gaze off the destruction of the courtyard in the Golden Castle toward a movement in the skies that caught his attention, Aeric found a large stone fragment of the tower the mysterious beast had blasted loose falling down through the sky toward them.

Seeing the approaching rubble plummeting toward their position, Aeric's heart leapt back into his chest. Taking hold of Mina as the shadow of the stone spread over them, the two ran to their left near the large bush and leapt as hard and far as they could as the earth shook with shockwaves upon the loud impact of the tower rubble. Landing on his back to protect Mina's screaming form but rolling over her to shield her, the awestruck boy turned his head to find the huge segment of the tower sitting in a crater where they had been standing moments before, a cloud of dirt and debris gently raining down on them. Seeing their terrified horses running away, Aeric forced himself to conquer his shock and rise to desperately call for them to come back. Mina rose slowly on her own, her eyes wide at what lay before her. Similar chunks of the tower were landing in the fields around them, releasing small tremors with each impact. Turning back to face Galantia, she felt tears appearing in her face as she watched the monstrous creature smashing through the entrance to the Golden Castle.

Chapter 6

<u>The Attack</u>

Supreme Granisian Gilentium's throne room fell into madness the moment the apparent attack on the Golden Castle began. Gilentium had just returned from the daily sacred service to Granis in the sanctuary of the beautiful Church of the Granisians in the third tier of the city. He had been taking a seat on his throne to meet with village leaders from the southern tip of the Grandarian border about building a dam in a large river that passed through them. Before Chief Advisor Blanch could so much as introduce them, the first shockwave ripped through the ground. Everyone but the heavily armored elite guards standing by the doors of the illustrious chamber were knocked off their feet. So harsh was the quake that blasted through the castle that the Supreme Granisian was thrown from his ornate throne to roll down the steps leading up to it and forcefully land on his front over the white marble floor.

The room immediately burst alive with the shouts of servants and captains of the royal guard leaping to their feet to rush to the Supreme Granisian's aid and call for emergency protocols to go into effect. Doors from the back of the room and the front burst open to reveal rows of additional silver plated guards running in the room to take a perimeter around Gilentium, still struggling to rise. Seeing the chaos erupt around him the Supreme Granisian raised a hand and shouted for silence.

"What is happening?" he shouted to a Commanding General of the Grandarian Army rushing into the room flanked by elite soldiers. Taking a quick bow the general shook his head.

"We aren't sure, yet, Your Eminence," he replied as another shockwave shook the castle and forced several plaques and decorations off the walls, loudly clamoring as they bounced across the floor or shattered where they landed. "It must be some sort of earthquake..." He stopped short as the group of men from the southern border began shouting and pointing out the window at something flying through the air. Looking out into the lower levels of the city, Gilentium and the general watched as enormous stone segments of what looked to be chunks of the Golden Castle itself went flying through the air to plummet into various buildings, smashing them to rubble. A look of horror spread across his face as he saw plumes of dust and smoke rising from the lower tiers of the city. Another loud crash shook the throne room, this time directly above them on the roof. Chief Advisor Blanch staggered forward catching his balance, staring out at the destruction in the city.

"What in the name of Granis on high..." he spoke behind the Supreme Granisian.

"My lords!" came an exhausted voice from the large double doors of the throne room, struggling to be heard over the clamor of guards taking positions outside. Gilentium, Blanch and the general turned toward the door to find a standard soldier pushing his way toward them, out of breath. "There is... something huge destroying the Grand Vestibule!" Hearing this, the general's brow furrowed but he rushed forward to grip the man's shoulders and pull him up.

"What do you mean 'something huge?'" he repeated disbelievingly. "Is something inside the castle?"

"Darien Tieloc sent me," the messenger managed to say through his sporadic breathing. "He said to get the Supreme Granisian out of here!" Hearing mention of the Warrior of Light, Gilentium pushed his way through his guards toward the solider.

"Where is Tieloc?" he said as another earthquake originating from the west side of the castle tore through the room. The solider shook his head, struggling to keep his balance.

"He and half the royal guard have fallen, Your Eminence," he reported, his voice shaking with fear. Everyone who heard these words momentarily froze, their mouths going wide. Before the general could inquire further as to what was responsible for the assault on the castle, the sound of screams sounded outside the arching hallway leading up to the throne room. Gripped by his uncertainly and dread of whatever could be coming, the general quickly ordered the elite guards inside the throne room to take the Supreme Granisian to the back of the chamber and form a protective barrier between him and the door. Drawing the blade at his side, the general ordered the rest of the silver armored guards to follow him out the double doors and take position along the stairs leading up to the throne room. As they left he ordered the doors sealed shut and not to be opened until it was silent outside.

Standing at the top of the stairs with the most elite soldiers in Grandaria lining each step up to him and the walls of the illustrious hallway below, the group fell quiet as the clashing of steel and the screams of men from beyond the curve in the hallway grew louder. Sweat beading from his face, the general watched as the body of one of the royal guards flew into their hallway to slam against the wall with his own sword jammed through his chest armor and streaks of blood strewn over his lifeless corpse. Though the seasoned guards stood strong in the face of the bloody display, even the general himself flinched and swallowed hard contemplating what the mysterious assailant that drew near could be to deal out such death and destruction.

The answer appeared as a group of four men dressed in identical attire but for their various colors came steadily walking around the corner of the hallway, their expressions unchanging as view of the dozens of soldiers before them stared them down. Though the Grandarian general had expected a demonic beast or some freakish juggernaut of dark power to appear before them, he quickly spied the orbs of light mounted on the men's tunics and knew they were indeed enchanted by some evil power. Screaming for his men to dispatch of them, the rows of silver armored royal guards charged forward with sword and lance points extended for them. Without slowing their march forward, the group of men kept their eyes on the double doors behind the general while the man in red suddenly leapt forward with his body erupting into flames. As he jumped through the air with the fire around him flaring up, the elite troops were shocked to find his body morph shape into a large cat with jaws of long teeth agape for the first of them.

Stunned and staring at disbelief at what they had just seen, the guards were left vulnerable and terrified as the large cat bowled into their ranks, slashing and biting as it came. Moving so fast and setting the hallway ablaze as it plowed through the helpless soldiers before it, the burning creature left a bloody path for the other three men behind it, one dressed in black, the other blue, and the last brown. Their pace still unchanged, they began walking up the cleared stairs leading to the throne room as the fiery cat at last reached the Commanding General of the Grandarian Army. Though shaking with fear, the general grit his teeth at his impending death and valiantly swung his blade down toward the charging beast. Darting to the right the creature avoided the attack and shot its left claw forward to bat the man off the stairs with the flesh on his chest cauterized from the creature's molten claws.

Hearing the carnage and roars of the mysterious creature responsible for it outside the closed doors, the Supreme Granisian and his remaining royal guard inside the throne room froze as the hallway beyond suddenly fell quiet. Staring at the doors in bewilderment, Talus Blanch looked down to the cracks under the door to find fire creeping up on the doors. Though they slightly budged as if someone was trying to find a way to open them outside, the occupants of the throne were horrified to find them suddenly blast open and shatter against the walls in an explosion of fiery debris as the monstrous cat leapt into the room with a menacing roar. Falling back over themselves in fear, the Supreme Granisian's guards watched it stand motionless with a deep groan echoing out of its throat as three men appeared behind it. They entered the chamber slowly, sweeping their eyes around the crowd as if trying to find its leader. As they made their way up to the flaming cat the Grandarians were further shocked to find it rear back on its hind legs to transform into a man identical to the other three beside him.

As the four mysterious figures made their way to the base of the stairs leading to the Supreme Granisian's throne, the room fell completely silent. Still unsure of what he was dealing with, Gilentium could only watch the four men as they stared up into the ranks of his guards and advisors. As the last of the embers lofting off the man in red's body dissipated in the air around him, the figure in blue looked down to his tunic to find a streak of blood left from one of their victims. Reaching down with his index finger he swept it along the wet cloth and put it in his mouth, licking the blood clean. At last the man in black let out a deep breath and folded his arms before his chest as if impatient of something.

"Which of you heads this city, then?" he asked, shifting the weight between his feet. There was no response at first. Gilentium could feel one of his servants pulling back on his sleeve, obviously not wanting him to say anything. Letting out a sharp breath, the man in black slowly blinked and rolled his eyes. "I will ask a second time. There will not be a third. Who leads?" Though the silence lingered on for another long moment, the silver robed figure of Talus Blanch at last rose and raised his hands in a disarming gesture.

"I am the one you seek," he said slowly. "There is no need for further violence. I will cooperate—whatever you ask." The man in black's eyes shifted over the Chief Advisor's figure up and down, studying him. After another long moment he reached down to pick up one of the loose short swords at his feet and tightly gripped it around the leather hilt. Though motionless at first, he abruptly threw back his arm to cast it forward and launch the blade at the silver robed figure, impaling him with such force he flew back over the stairs to tumble backward to his death. Standing to try and rush to his fallen Chief Advisor's side, Gilentium was held back by his elite guards. Seeing the elaborately robed figure rise, the man in black locked his eyes on him.

"No man who leads so many would submit with such haste," he spoke callously. "The man in the golden robes is the one we want. Kill the rest."

"Enough!" the Supreme Granisian shouted, thrusting his arms away from his servants and pushing through the ranks of his guard. "I am the leader here. Spare these men— you have me." Though the man in red was about to transform into the blazing cat once more, the man in black extended an arm before his chest to block him. Keeping his dark eyes fixed on Gilentium, he motioned for him to come down. Gilentium did as he was bid, slowly making his way down the steps to face the four figures. "I am Supreme Granisian Gil—"

"Where do you keep the white Source?" the man in black cut him off. Seeing the Supreme Granisian's confusion the dark figure spoke again to preclude his question. "Your Elemental Temple. Where is it?" Gilentium swallowed hard, unsure of what he should say if the mysterious attackers did not even know of the famous structure's location when it was right in front of them. Guessing he should not try their patience or test their resolve when so many more potential victims lay at their feet, however, the Supreme Granisian decided not to lie to them again.

"Even with the power you obviously possess you could not gain access to the temple," he informed him as civilly as possible. "Only the Warrior of Light can open the door to the Source."

"Let us worry about that," the man in black returned heatedly. "Where is it?" Gilentium gulped hard again, desperately trying to think of a way to avoid divulging the temple's location.

"If you would tell me what you desire than perhaps we can negotiate—"

"Wyrik!" the man in black suddenly cut him off, his face tightening with anger. The next moment Gilentium felt the room shake as something on the roof of the building leapt off and the sound of massive wings beating through the air caught his attention. Before he could ask what was going on the man in black viciously grabbed hold of him and pulled him to a window in the golden chamber in the direction the wing beats were headed. Though the guards came to attention at once Gilentium shouted for them to remain where they were. Shoving the Supreme Granisian against the opening in the castle wall, the man in black grabbed the back of his hair with one hand and pointed out the window with the other.

"Do you see that tower in your precious castle?" he snarled, his face bunched up in fury. Before Gilentium could respond he saw a massive creature soaring down from the sky. It had enormous feathered wings mounted to its back with four powerful legs beneath it and two heads jutting off from long necks. Held firm by the man in black, Gilentium could only watch in horror as the flying monster reached out with his front legs to crash into the tower and demolish it to a pile of falling rubble raining down onto the third tier of the city below. The man in black spun the Supreme Granisian around and grabbed hold of his ornate robes, bunching them in his fists. "Do you hear the screams of you people? Such will be the fate of your entire city if you do not tell me what I want to know!" Though Gilentium held his composure in the face of the shouting assailant holding him under his strong grip, he could not stay silent any longer.

"Please, call your monster back," he begged. "I will tell you where to find the temple."

"Then what are you waiting for!?!" the man in black blasted, throwing him back against the window and towering over him to push half his body out into the open air.

"It is inside this very castle!" Gilentium shouted. "It is just behind us! Please stop this!" The man in black froze at this, his furious expression slowly easing to grow confused. He turned then, looking back to the other three figures standing behind him. Spinning back around, the man in black pulled Gilentium back through the window and set him on his feet.

"Take us there," the man in black commanded. Though hesitant, the Supreme Granisian knew what would happen if he disobeyed and decided in the best interest of his people to save what lives he could. They would find it on their own even without his help now. The man in black shouted out the window for the creature loosed upon the city. Somehow hearing him, the massive winged creature turned from the demolished tower it stood on and spread its wings for the Golden Castle. As it came, the identical men gathered by the window picked Gilentium up by his robes, hoisting him high with unnatural strength. Though shouting for them to let him go, as the massive winged beast slammed into the wall beneath them the men leapt out of the window with Gilentium in tow, sliding down one of the creature's long necks onto his back.

With its passengers on its back, the large creature released its hold on the wall and lunged off, soaring back into the sky to gain altitude. Though the Supreme Granisian's remaining guards rushed after him they were helpless as he flew away from the tower. The man in black stood on the creature's back, instructing the Supreme Granisian to point to the temple, to which Gilentium extended his arm down to the golden structure rising out of the center of the castle. The man in black stared down as if mesmerized. The Golden Castle was literally constructed around the Temple of Light. There was a circular gap between the two structures, connected only by a small bridge that led to the temple's large doors. Noting the single tower and its pointed spire shimmering in the sunlight, the man in black grit his teeth and instructed his compatriots to land on the bridge connecting the two buildings. With that he turned and leapt off the soaring creature to freefall through the air. As he fell the orb of dark light on his chest flashed and his human form began growing and expanding. His skin building into black muscles streaked with glowing crimson scars symmetrically embedded into his hide, his form quickly grew to cast a shadow on the Temple of Light beneath him. As the horns and blades stabbed into his thighs jutted out of his body, the behemoth called Dalorosk spread his massive bat like wings and slowed his rapid decent to aim his towering body at the tower beneath him.

Slamming into the spire with his clawed feet, Dalorosk slid down its long surface until half way between the tip and the base. Taking hold of the tower with one hand and casting back the other, he balled his fist and powerfully slammed it into the golden stone to smash through it and send half of the Tower of Granis toppling over to slam into the castle. Raising its massive form to gaze inside the tower, Dalorosk's crimson eyes searched for the Source of Light but could not find it. Growling, he continued smashing the temple bit by bit until he had made his way all the way down to the base. At last he came to a door that burned his dark hand when he touched it. Narrowing his beastly eyes, the behemoth took hold of one of his black blades and formed a layer of dark energy along its edge to slam down into the exposed chamber and pry the door off. Staring inside, Dalorosk found a pedestal similar to the one he had taken the Source of Darkness from, but no Source of Light on it. It was already gone.

Slowly quaking with untold rage, the monster thrust his head up to release a howl of fury into the air audible to the entire Valley of Galantia. Spinning around for Wyrik and the Supreme Granisian on his back, Dalorosk reached out to pluck him off his brother and bring his terrified body before his face.

"The Source is gone!" he blasted with such volume the man in his grip had to shield his ears. Consumed by his anger, Dalorosk threw his arm out to cast the sovereign of Grandaria flailing away to fall to the city and his death. Spinning his head back to the others next to Wyrik, Dalorosk sheathed his blade back into his leg with dark blood spraying out and pointed a finger into their ranks. "The treacherous worm must have sensed us coming and stole it before we arrived. He can't be far and he can't transform for he knows we will sense his location. Tear this city and the countryside apart until you find him! I want his bones ground to *dust!*" Hearing this, the other men quickly transformed from the appearance of humans into the monstrous creatures they truly were. Leaping down from the Golden Castle, they began slamming into the city to tear it to pieces. Still standing on what was left of the Temple of Light, Dalorosk looked down at the surrounding green countryside for any sign of movement. He could smell the same stench of his eternal enemy as he had upon first finding the city. He was out there somewhere. Bellowing with rage once more, the black behemoth spread his wings and leapt into the skies to begin searching with the others.

Chapter 7

<u>A Precious Gift</u>

Mina sat on her knees over the grassy ridge overlooking the smoking city of Galantia, a horror stricken expression on her tearstained face. While Aeric had temporarily left her to retrieve their fled horses, Mina had been unable to tear her gaze off the once unassailable capital of Grandaria crumbling to rubble before her eyes because of the monstrous creatures crashing through it. While she had been shocked enough by the appearance of the rock monster that smashed apart the courtyard of the Golden Castle, the strength in Mina's legs gave out as she saw another black beast appear out of the skies to smash the Tower of Granis on the Temple of Light in two, sending the renowned spire crashing into the city shrouded in a plume of rising dust. As she sat limply over the long grass, her heart fell to mesh with her guts. It couldn't be real. The city that had stood firm for over a thousand years was being blown apart; the pride and soul of Grandaria was being ripped to shreds before her. Forcing herself to break eye contact from the besieged city, new tears that had been welling in her eyes dropped to slide down her freckled cheeks as her head fell.

After a long minute of sitting by herself struggling to make sense of the gruesome display, she heard the fast approaching footsteps of someone behind her and forced herself to spin around, her bouncing chestnut hair flying up with her in its ponytail. It was Aeric, rushing to her side out of breath. His brown boots and pants were dusty from running back to her through a patch of loose soil.

"The horses are long gone," he managed, leaning down to prop himself up by putting his weight on his thighs. Too choked up by her emotions to say anything back, Mina merely shifted her gaze back at Galantia, observing a portion of the third tier of the city catching fire.

"Granis..." she murmured at last, shaking her head in disbelief. Noting the girl's shaking voice, Aeric brought his gaze back up to the city as well. It looked like Galantia was in the grip of every apocalypse ever imagined all at the same time. The Temple of Light had been leveled, most of Golden Castle was falling around it thanks to an enormous black beast smashing it to pieces, a massive fire was spreading over the third tier down to the second, and a segment of the wall in the Gate Yard had been penetrated by a jet of water exploding from the inside as if flooded.

"This can't be happening..." he trailed off quietly. "What in the name of Granis on high is going on down there?"

"What are those things, Aeric?" Mina asked him, spinning back around. "What are those things destroying Galantia?" Aeric kept his eyes on the mammoth black creature soaring over the city as if looking for its next target, roaring so loudly it rumbled through their hearts even on the ridge. He could not find the words as he finally looked down to Mina, but she spoke what was on his mind for him. "They're demons, aren't they? Like the ones your grandfather fought in the Days of Destiny." Aeric stared at her uncertainly for a long moment, trying to sort out everything that was happening to determine the best course of action. At last he reached down to take hold of Mina's waist and pull her back to her feet.

"We are not going to stick around here to find out," he replied at last, looking back into the fields behind them for any sign of more of the terrifying creatures. Mina froze stiff at this, shooting him a staggered glance.

"What do you mean?" she returned questioningly. "What are we—"

"We're getting out of here, now," he cut her off, wheeling around to face her. "We'll make for Eirinor. Hopefully we'll find the horses before we get to the hills or someone who can help us—"

"Help us?" Mina repeated, interrupting him. "Aeric, all our help is down in that city! We have to go back!" Aeric eyed her skeptically, his brow furrowing.

"Are you crazy, Mina?" he asked her quickly. "Can you not see what's happening down there? Galantia is already destroyed! Half the city is on fire or in rubble! If we go back our fate will be the same as anyone inside the walls and I won't let that happen."

"So you want us to retreat to Eirinor and hide there?" she asked him incredulously, balling her fists and going rigid. "Who will help us stop those creatures there? The army and the Temple of Light are here! Our family is here! Are you going to leave your own mother and father like this?"

"Well what do you want me to do, Mina?" Aeric grilled her, awestruck at what he was hearing. "If we go back in there what could we do to help? We'd be as powerless as the army or the Granisians in the temple clearly are, because in case you haven't noticed, the Gate Yard and the temple aren't there anymore! You think I want to leave our parents to die at the hands of those monsters? If there was some practical way we could help I would but sometimes you don't have a choice, Mina."

"But we have a choice, Aeric!" she nearly shouted at him. "I know you want to protect me but there's more at stake here than us! You have to look past me for once! If we lose Galantia what do we have left? If we give up on it what will there be left to stop these things?"

"I'm not letting you run into your death, Mina," Aeric told her sternly, stepping closer to take hold of her shoulders. "I know we're Grandarians and Galantia is our heritage but that's not the issue here. It's not that this isn't our fight, it's that this fight is already over. Galantia is gone. The only thing we can do now is take care of ourselves, and I intend to. We have to get out of here and warn everyone else." Though she stared at him hard for the next long moment, obviously torn between her Grandarian pride and Aeric's logic, she at last gave in and nodded, lowering her head with fresh tears appearing. Seeing her upset and knowing his words had just condemned their parents to death, Aeric swallowed hard and wrapped his arms around her. As he stood holding the besieged girl, his eyes drifted up to the smoldering city in the background. The fire had spread to engulf every tier of the city and the demonic beasts ravaging it had leveled nearly everything. There was no sign of life from either the Gate Yard or the Golden Castle. It was practically over already.

Though about to release Mina and take her hand to begin leading her away from the Valley of Galantia as fast as they could move, the sound of hoof beats from his right suddenly caught his attention amid the roars from the creatures in the city and he spun around to find their source. Though wary it could be another of the dark beasts, both Aeric and Mina caught sight of a single rider dressed in white on a brown horse appearing over the ridge, wilding scanning around him as if looking for the creatures as well. Though Aeric was about to flag him down for help, the rider spotted the pair on his own and kicked his steed forward with renewed vitality, driving it up the ridge for them. Though oddly dressed in all white from his tunic to his boots, the man looked Grandarian enough and seemed as frightened as they were. The figure pulled back on the reins of his horse to come sliding to a halt beside Aeric and Mina, leaping off the horse before it was even completely stopped. Seeing him up close, Aeric noticed how exhausted the man was and offered a hand to help him stand.

"Are you alright, sir?" Aeric asked quickly, to which the man merely shook his head and began reaching up to grasp his chest. "Did you manage to escape the city before—"

"We have no time, young Tieloc," the man interrupted him, surprising both Aeric and Mina when he spoke the boy's name.

"I'm sorry, have we met before?" Aeric returned confused, watching the man grip a strange glowing medallion on his right chest. The man in white quickly rotated it to the right, unlocking it from the small metal plate in his tunic to pull the medallion out.

"I am in no condition to ride after eons in this form," the man spoke out of breath, shoving the medallion into Aeric's hands. "You must take this medallion and this horse and ride to the Mystic Tower to the south with all speed." Squinting his eyes with confusion to Mina, Aeric shook his head and fumbled for the words to respond.

"Sir, please wait," he begged shaking his head. "What are you talking about?"

"I told you there is no time to waste, young Tieloc!" the man in white shouted, motioning for them to mount his horse. "They will be scouring the fields for me in moments if they are not already! I will remain here to throw them off your trail. You must ride!" Though the man was trying to help Mina mount the horse, Aeric grabbed his forearm and stood between them.

"Sir, I don't know who you are or how you know my name but—"

"I have been looking for one of you since the Ascension began, child of the Tieloc house," the man in white told him quickly. "By right you are the one who must bear my burden to the descendant of my order. This is the Source of Light. You must get it to the new Master Sage in the Mystic Tower. Give him this as well." Reaching into a pocket in his white tunic, the man pulled out a small note of paper and put it into one of the leather satchels on the carpenter's belt around Aeric's waist. "I am sorry to heap this charge on you but fate has already chosen you by sparing you from my brothers' wrath today. You must continue on for the sake of not just your own people but every race and creature in all of Iairia." Though Aeric merely stared at the man in white uncertainly, he shook his head again and raised the medallion in his hands to glance at it skeptically.

"This is the Source of Light?" he repeated disbelievingly. "Um, I don't know why you would think this but the Source is in the Temple of Light..." The boy trailed off, seeing the figure suddenly spin around toward the Valley of Galantia, his eyes wide with alarm. Following the man in white's eyes, Aeric and Mina observed a strange beast that looked to be covered in flames sporadically running across the fields as if searching for something. The man in white spun around again and spoke in a hushed voice.

"Both of you hide!" he whispered harshly, pointing to the large bush they had tied up their horses by when first arriving on the ridge. "It will be over if they see you so stay put until they are gone. I will try to lead them the wrong way so you will have your chance. Remember—get the Source of Light and that note to the Master Sage in the Mystic Tower. Time is of the essence, my young friends. I'm sorry I could not be of more help to you. Now hide!" Pushing the two youths toward the large bush on the ridge, the man in white began running back toward the right side of the ridge where he had come from. Seeing the fiery beast in the fields growing closer and wary that more may be approaching as the figure warned, Aeric decided to believe him and followed Mina into the undergrowth of the bushes to hide and wait to see if anything happened.

Though they continued watching the man in white run down the ridge for the next several seconds with nothing happening, they were surprised to find him suddenly halt where he stood. Curiously staring, Aeric and Mina saw him ball his fists and look into the sky as the form of a massive shadow appeared over him. Before they could so much as lift their heads to observe the source of the shade, the colossal form of the bird like creature they had seen before the attack on Galantia began came crashing out of the skies at frightening speed to slam into the ridge and pin the man in white's body to the ground. Both Aeric and Mina flinched where they lay, terrified at the fearsome creature's sudden landing and what it meant for the man in white. No one could have survived a blow under the weight of such a creature. The beast looked like a massive wyvern that lived in the Empyrean Peaks in the Southland but for its long reptilian tail and dragon-like heads jutting from its upper body. While Aeric's jaw dropped open and Mina put a hand to her mouth in horror, the winged creature thrust its two long necks into the air to shriek out so loud both Aeric and Mina screamed and were forced to press their hands against their ears.

Though the pair could feel their ears ringing after the sheiks ended, both of them could feel the rumbling in the ground of something else drawing near. Hearing the sound of the earth tearing open from below the ridge and shaken by the ensuing earthquakes, Aeric and Mina gulped hard to find the colossal minotaur of rock appear to snarl from deep in its scarlet throat as view of the man in white came into view. Though the couple was surprised to find a man similarly dressed to the man in white but for his blue clothes suddenly morphing into a massive snakelike creature from the rock monster's back, Mina let out another gasp upon seeing the man in white still intact and breathing underneath the wyvern's clawed foot. Pointing at him for Aeric to see, he too noticed the man was somehow still alive. Hearing a wild roar from down the ridge, they next found the flaming cat they had seen earlier leaping over the hill to land beside the blue snake.

Aeric and Mina were most terrified at the coming of the final creature, the massive black behemoth that leveled the Tower of Granis. Staring up through the branches of the concealing bush as his powerful black form dropped out of the sky, he roared for the others to make way. Standing over the wyvern and looking down at the man in white staring back up at its crimson glowing eyes for the next long moments, the behemoth at last shocked Aeric and Mina by speaking.

"Hello, brother," the enormous black creature articulated with what looked to be a smile appearing over the shining teeth in its mouth. "It has been too long."

"Or not long enough, Dalorosk," the man in white managed to speak, his voice calm and strong compared to what the two humans listening to him thought he should. "You were all banished. And now you have destroyed more innocent life because of your pointless battling."

"Oh, but as you can see, brother, our war is no longer with each other—only you," the figure in black growled, his voice angry and low upon the last words. "I promised you there would be an Ascension. I warned you to be prepared for this day when you betrayed our birthright with your scheming. It took us eons but now we are back to reclaim what is ours."

"All that you have left is your prison, Dalorosk," the man in white returned. "Before this is over you will be returned there or destroyed, but this will be set right as it was before. The world does not belong to us, but to man."

"It should have belonged to us!" the behemoth blasted in a shout, swatting the wyvern away to lower his beastly skull down to the man in white's. "It would have been ours if not for your treachery! Now your staff is gone and the last of your pathetic humans with the power of your crests along with it. There is nothing to stop us this time."

"There is still me," the man in white stated undeterred, inches away from the behemoth's gaping jaws. The creature called Dalorosk was quiet at first hearing this. At last, his twisted smile returned and he lifted his head back into the air with what sounded to Aeric and Mina like laughter.

"You?" the monster repeated, looking to the other creatures around him. "Then why don't you transform and do so, brother? Strike us down as you did before! Why have you not done so already? Oh, yes, I forgot. You have become so infatuated with the idea of the humans' rule that you have tried to become one yourself, living within their cities as one of them. You have forsaken your birthright of mastering them, and after so long living in that pathetic shell devoid of power you cannot even summon the might to return to your true form. Is this not so?" The man in white remained quiet at this, merely staring up at the beastly form of Dalorosk.

The silence was at last broken by the flaming cat, suddenly leaping forward to stare at the man in white then back up to Dalorosk.

"The Source is gone!" the creature growled, causing all of them to look down at the man in white's chest with their massive frames going tense. Dalorosk's face instantly lost its smile, thrusting his head back down to observe the man in white's tunic. His glowing eyes narrowing, he barked at the other again.

"Where have you taken it, Alberic?" the behemoth quietly grilled. The man in white remained silent, still just holding the beast's gaze. His fury mounting again, Dalorosk lifted one of his fists to slam it back down into the earth next to Alberic's side. "Where is the Source of Light!" Aeric and Mina felt their hearts raise in their chests at this, remembering the object the man in white had given them before the creatures arrived. They both looked down to the medallion resting in Aeric's grip, worriedly exchanging glances.

"It is hidden somewhere you will never find it, my brother," the man in white returned slowly. "Somewhere none of you will ever find it." All of the creatures around him were furious at this, growling and screaming down at him. The massive rock creature even lifted his brown fist to throw it downward at him in rage. Blocking the attack with his own forearm, Dalorosk spun around to face the minotaur.

"We may need him if we cannot find it ourselves," the behemoth spoke angrily to them all. Slowly turning his gaze back down to the man in white beneath him, Dalorosk shook his head. "But it will do us no good to torture you, will it? You will not break so easily. Fine then. If you will not give us what we want we will find it ourselves, and you will watch as we do." Raising his monstrous body full length, Dalorosk violently swiped the man in white from the ground into his right fist. "He could only have sensed us coming yesterday and he could not transform to carry it far so the Source must be nearby. He probably entrusted it to another of his wretched humans. Look for villages. Start with the city, then tear every inch of the countryside apart until you find it. Kill everything." With that, the various beasts around Dalorosk roared in anger and split up to take off in different directions to look for the missing Source of Light. At last the monstrous frame of Dalorosk spread his gargantuan wings and savagely beat them to lift him off the ground and back toward Galantia, rustling the branches of the bush Aeric and Mina hid in.

When they were at last alone once more on the battered ridge, the Grandarian pair could feel their hearts pounding at all they had just learned and all that had unfolded before them. Wordlessly turning their shaking eyes to each other, they both eventually looked down to the shining medallion in Aeric's hand the five monsters were tearing Grandaria apart to find.

Chapter 8

<u>Hunted</u>

As soon as they were confident none of the monsters attacking Grandaria remained in the proximity of the ridge, Aeric and Mina crawled from the bush they had been hiding under and began silently dashing to the south as fast as their feet would carry them. The horse the man in white had given them had disappeared, probably scared off by the creatures as their own horses had been. Not willing to wait a moment to postpone their retreat however, Aeric seized Mina's hand and began rushing her down the ridge toward the Hills of Eirinor in the distance. As they began running as quickly as they could from cover to cover in the open green fields, both were too shaken by the unimaginable encounter between the man in white and the demonic beasts who had taken him to speak. Their imaginations had gripped Aeric and Mina's thoughts, conjuring up images of who the mysterious man in white could be to have been holding the Source of Light and what the creatures would do if they found it in their keeping before they could get to an adequate place to hide.

Forcing their minds to concentrate on the dire predicament at hand, the pair at last began to talk as they made it safely away from the Valley of Galantia with no sign of any of the five beasts on their trail. Though in agreement that their next move and sole priority should be finding well hidden shelter before the night arrived, a heated debate ensued when talk of their larger plan came back into the discussion. Though the violent dialogue the monstrous creatures had with the man in white had convinced Mina they were in possession of the Source of Light, Aeric remained skeptical even after the unbelievable display and was trying to slow her down from talk of traveling to the Mystic Tower. They were frequently close to screaming at each other over the dispute thanks to the unthinkable events of the late morning still

74

tearing at their stressed minds, but at last the pair agreed to wait to decide what they would do with the medallion until they found shelter and a place to rest for the night.

Though both of them had heard the story of their grandfathers Tavin Tieloc and Jaren Garrinal running through the Hills of Eirinor through the night to avoid the demonic minions of Valif Montrox during the Days of Destiny when they were fleeing to Galantia for help, despite being in particularly good physical shape, Aeric and Mina were far too exhausted from the traumatic day to continue on through the night and desperately began searching for any kind of refuge as the sun began to sink behind the towering Iairian Mountain Chain in the west. They had been hiking through grass up to their knees for half an hour, gently swaying in the night breeze until smashed down under the weight of their thick boots ferrying them forward. Though cover was rare in the rolling green Hills of Eirinor they had worked their way into by dusk, fortune finally dealt them a kind gesture as they happened upon a small indentation of rock sunken into a hillside ahead of them.

Climbing inside the hidden enclave as the last remnant of sunlight faded into the darkening sky, the pair found a fixed boulder sitting inside and took a seat. Groaning as she finally lifted the weight of her exhausted body off her sore legs, Mina rubbed the muscles along her limbs attempting to coax away the ache. Though eager to sit as well, Aeric's primary concern was still keeping them hidden from any of the wandering creatures looking for them. Noticing the long grass hanging down over the entrance to the small indentation of rock, Aeric reached down to his carpenter's belt to pull forth a short dagger. Quickly cutting away a collection of soft grass from the earth above them and outside on the hill, he brought armfuls in to pad the hard rock for them. Satisfied they would be safe and as comfortable as possible for the night in the enclave, Aeric at last allowed himself a deep breath and sat beside Mina, wiping away the sweat on his forehead with the leather gauntlet on his arm. Reaching down to sheath his small blade, the boy took hold of the small flask at his side and took a quick gulp of water they had found in a small creek behind their shelter a few minutes ago. Offering some to Mina, she fumbled for it through the darkness and took a hearty drink herself, emptying half of it. Though it was a fairly warm summer night as usual for this time of year, he could hear Mina shuffling to cross her arms and bringing her knees up to her body as if to warm herself.

Setting the flask back along his waist, Aeric scuffled closer to her in the dark and gently took hold of her bare arms to rub them for heat where her white tunic sleeves ended. Though he could barely see anything in the dark notch in the hill with only the slim crescent of moonlight above them, he could feel Mina pulling away to set her back against the rock.

"I'm not cold," she whispered, her voice cracking. Letting her go and just listening to her quickening breaths over the next long moments, Aeric could hear her sniffling, trying to hold in the emotion building up in her throat. She was struggling not to cry. Though his girlfriend rarely shed tears over anything with such a bubbly and audacious persona, Aeric remembered all they had been through today and wasn't surprised at her emotions. Though he had been determined to keep his mind on the present and getting them to safety, now that they had finally stopped to rest he could no longer keep the images of the destruction they had witnessed from his own mind. Guessing thoughts of the destroyed capital and of her father they had left behind as it collapsed had entered Mina's mind as well, Aeric let out another heavy breath and slowly leaned closer to her to lean his shoulder against hers, just to let her know he was there.

Feeling the warmth from his body, Mina at last swallowed hard and began audibly weeping, reaching out to take hold of the boy's arm and hold it in hers. Aeric let her cry for several long minutes before reaching around her to pull her closer to him, her head falling against his chest to send locks of her curly hair across his tunic. They had fallen out of her ponytail hours earlier, now messily draped around her dirty tunic and face. There was no point in telling her he was sorry or that everything was going to be all right. After all they had just lost, neither one of them was sure it would be. All he could do for her was stay beside her and continue protecting what he had left.

After Mina's tears subsided to mere sniffles once more, she finally spoke, her voice cracking with emotion.

"Do you think there's a chance any of them are still alive?" she whispered, clutching Aeric's free hand tighter in her lap. Aeric slowly exhaled at her question, struggling for what to say. Though he thought about telling her Tielocs and Garrinals had made it out of worse situations than this before, he knew he couldn't compare the Days of Destiny to that morning. His grandfather Tavin Tieloc had been armed with the legendary Sword of Granis to ward off demons in his day—his father and the Granisians didn't have any magic left to wield in its absence and that of the Source of Light, if it truly rested with them now.

"There is always hope, Mina," he told her at last, remembering his grandfather's favorite line. She had heard it before and taken confidence from Tavin Tieloc, but with him gone and the city he defended in ruins, the words seemed hollow and devoid of the meaning they once resonated. Galantia was the backbone and soul of all Grandaria—with it gone nothing felt safe. All she had left that made her feel secure was the boy holding her. Swallowing hard once again, the girl slowly rotated her head over his chest until her forehead bumped into something underneath his old blue tunic. Raising her eyes to it, the girl found a faint white light shining from underneath the faded cloth. Slowly bringing her hand up to his chest, the girl pushed the object up until it came out of his tunic to faintly illuminate the entire enclave in its light. Feeling Mina push the medallion out of his shirt, the boy looked down to study it for the first time. It was crafted in a white metal he had never seen before, nearly an inch thick with octagonal sides. In its center rested an orb of shining light incased by a glass cover on its front side. As Mina slid her fingertips over the surface of the glass she shook her head, mesmerized.

"It's warm," she spoke more to herself than Aeric. The boy stared down to her illuminated face, letting out a dissatisfied huff. Knowing what he was thinking, the girl raised herself off his chest to look him in his blue eyes. "I'm telling you Aeric, this has got to be the Source."

"How do you know that, Mina?" he returned with a gentle but questioning tone in his voice. "What makes you think this tiny little glow is the one, legendary Source of Light? It doesn't make any sense. The Source can't be moved from the Temple of Light. The Granisians can't do it and the Warrior of Light can't do it. It's never been moved in the history of Grandaria."

"Just because something's never been done doesn't mean it can't be, Aeric," Mina replied. "Remember what the creatures said today? They said they had the other Sources. If the other elemental Sources can be taken from their temples why can't the Source of Light?"

"We don't know if those things really have the other Sources," Aeric pointed out. "And what do we know about this man in white? The things that destroyed Galantia knew him. What if he's one of them? What if he was trying to trick us?"

"What possible reason would he have to do that?" Mina answered with mounting irritation in her voice. "He knew your name, Aeric! He said he was looking for you. Don't you think that means something? He saved us for Granis' sake! If he hadn't told us to hide when he did those creatures would have found us." Aeric was speechless at this. If the man in white had lied to them about anything and meant them harm why would he have saved them the next moment? Seeing him pondering, Mina continued to press her argument. "I know it seems unbelievable, Aeric, but after what I saw today there is nothing I wouldn't believe anymore."

"Even if this is what he said it is, what do you want us to do about it?" the boy returned eventually, throwing a hand up. "You want me to take this medallion all the way to the Mystic Tower? What would that achieve? The sages have been dead since the Days of Destiny. No one could help us there any more than anyone in Eirinor."

"What about the rumors, Aeric?" Mina suddenly exclaimed. "We've heard them even as far north as Gulfrin. They've been saying for years there's been activity in the Sage's Valley. What if it's the sages? What if they aren't all dead? If anyone could help us it's them!"

"And what if they are just rumors?" he rejoined. "Grandpa Tavin told us the stories of the Days of Destiny as children. Zeroan's spirit himself told him the sages were gone. How could they have just come back?"

"We just agreed there is no reason the man in white would have lied to us and he charged us to take the medallion to the sages. If you want to talk about your grandfather then let's talk about what he would do if he were here. Remember his charge from Zeroan? Did Tavin and my grandfather Jaren have anything more to believe Zeroan's words when he told them they had a shard of the Holy Emerald to protect? They had no more reason to trust him than we have to trust this man, but they did and thanks to them the world was saved.

You were born with the same blood as your grandfather, Aeric. This is our responsibility now."

"If anyone was going to lecture me about my responsibility to Grandaria I though you would be the last person, Mina," Aeric shot back. "I am not my grandfather— I'm no warrior. My responsibility is for you." Upset with her boyfriend's negative responses, Mina tightened and yelled at him.

"All I know is that if there is even the slightest chance of saving the rest of Grandaria or stopping these creatures we owe it to your parents and my father to at least try!" she practically shouted, surprising him. "I know you love me and this isn't what you wanted, but it's just been thrust into you hands whether you like it or not. You think I wanted any of this to happen any more than you did?" Though about to respond that he was just trying to sort through all this realistically to make sense of the insane situation they found themselves in, he was cut short by the sudden howling roar from far outside the entrance to the enclave. Both of them falling silent with dread, Aeric pulled Mina to the ground where they huddled with eyes wide and hearts racing at what might have found them. Afraid her outburst could have given away their position, Mina trembled and silently whispered she was sorry over and over. Placing a finger before his lips to signal for her to remain quiet, Aeric gulped hard and quickly concealed the luminous medallion back into the confines of his tunic. Dark and silent once more, Aeric at last tugged on Mina's hand to pull her towards the entrance to their shelter to peer out onto the dark fields for any of the terrifying beasts looking for them.

Their eyes gazing out onto the fields, the pair saw nothing but the dark curves of the rolling hills and the swaying grass upon them. Letting out a long huff of relief, Mina turned her gaze to Aeric with her eyes still quivering. Gulping hard himself, Aeric turned to her. Before he could say anything however, a sudden light out in the hills caught his attention and he spun back around with Mina doing the same. Looking far ahead to the next hilltop to the south, the couple saw a collection of flames suddenly appear over it to illuminate the night with their burning fervency. Their eyes going wide, Aeric and Mina identified the burning figure as the flaming cat they had seen earlier in the day. Though it stood still for a lingering moment, sweeping its fiery eyes across the hills before it, it leapt down with incredible speed and agility toward something that caught its eye below it. Following the creature's movements down to another larger enclave of rock in the hillside across from them, Mina gasped as it tore inside and stiffened its muscular frame to send a jets flame leaping off its fiery coat to ignite the entire enclave in a moment. It emerged quickly after, continuing to scan the hills around it for movement or more concealing areas. As it found another to its left and ran off, Aeric felt his heart threatening to pound out of his chest and wheeled back to Mina.

"It's going to find us if we stay here," he told her in a whisper.

"What are we going to do?" she returned, peering down at the cat running to the next notch in the hills. "If it's already gotten ahead of us it could have already been to Eirinor. Where are we supposed to go now?"

"We take it one step at a time for now," the boy eventually returned trying to calm her down, prying his eyes off the flaming cat. "We can't outrun it or hide from it on open ground if it's burning all our cover. We need a way to get away from it..."

"What if we use the Source of Light?" Mina asked fumbling for an idea. Sensing her desperation, Aeric shook his head.

"No, we don't know what this creature is," he returned. "If it isn't empowered by dark elemental energy the Source would do us no good. Besides, I'm not exactly sure how we'd 'use' it anyway." He trailed off again, looking down to his focus his thoughts. Spying the flask of water at his waist, the boy was hit with an idea. "But I bet this thing is connected to the element of fire. If we can get back to that creek we saw earlier we might be able to hold it back."

"What?" Mina returned in disbelief. "You want us to *fight* it?"

"Not fight it," Aeric corrected, "just run from it. Light probably won't hurt this thing but I'm betting water will. It's basic elemental principals. The monster might not be able to get to us if we're surrounded by water, and if we can get into the creek we can follow it all the way back to the border and one of the villages there."

"You really think that little creek is going to hold back something that destroyed Galantia?" she spoke uncertainly.

"I don't think we can afford to stay here and take our chances," he returned. "If we're lucky we can slip back to the creek without the creature ever knowing. If we stay here, we're dead for certain." Though Mina was hesitant, she stared back onto the fields as the blazing cat ignited its fur into another enclave and at last nodded in agreement. Telling her to stay close to him and be ready to run, Aeric took her hand tightly in his and helped her to her feet. Waiting until the monster of fire turned and begin sweeping the opposite hillside for more hiding places, they silently crept out of the entrance to their enclave and began scuttling down the hillside toward the sound of the creek. Though the two slipped through the silence in the long grass for several long minutes with confidence they had vanished from the beast's view, as they ran in a hunch Aeric was suddenly terrified to find the medallion in his tunic fall out to shine its brilliant white light out into the open fields. Though fumbling to tuck it back into this shirt as fast as he could, the silence was immediately broken by the sound of a furious roar blasting into the night air behind them.

Wheeling around in terror, Aeric and Mina found the flaming cat leaping from the top of the hill where they had been, lunging after them and leaving a trail of flames igniting the grass in its wake. Screaming for Mina to run, Aeric spun back around and began running as fast as his legs would move for the creek basin at the bottom of the hill. Now their only chance was that the humble stream could hold the fearsome creature at bay, provided they could reach it before it ensnared them in its molten claws. Sprinting down the slope at full speed in the dark while keeping their footing proved to be a daunting challenge, and it was not long before Aeric heard the sound of the girl beside him tripping and falling into a tumble. Wheeling around to race back and pull her back to her feet, they both looked up to find the flaming cat had quickly closed the gap between them and would be at their heals in a matter of moments. Yanking her after him, Aeric audibly pleaded to Granis for speed and continued racing forward as fast as possible. The creek was now in sight but it ran dangerously shallow at this point and they would have to get to the center quickly for any kind of protection from the beast.

Running along the rocks at the basin the two could feel the heat on their backs from the monster roaring. They stumbled into the modest creek to painfully land on their sides after tripping over unseen pitfalls under the flowing water. Though Aeric pushed himself up and thought it was over for certain, as he wiped away the water from his eyes no killing blow came. Staring to the water's edge in disbelief, the pair found their gambit had worked as the flaming cat had stopped short, roaring out at them in fury. Though the creature attempted to dab its paw in the water, a sharp hissing of steam echoed through the night air and the beast pulled back in apparent pain. Rising with their wet clothes sticking to their skin, Mina clutched onto Aeric in fright and hurriedly asked him what they should do. Though they appeared to be beyond the creature's reach for the moment, Aeric recalled there were still four more of the beasts looking for them and seized Mina's hand to begin pulling her downstream toward the south.

The flaming cat growled from deep in its throat and followed them from the shore as they ran, careful to keep its claws away from the water's edge. Though it followed its prey for several long minutes, at last Aeric heard its flaming body halt. Looking back in surprise to find it staring at them and pulling back its head in a crouch, Aeric guessed it was going to leap over the creek and claw at them as it came. Dropping to his front to shield his body from the coming attack with Mina doing the same, they were both surprised to find it merely let out a terrible roar that forced them both to cover their ears with their hands. It lasted for several long moments, tearing through the very air with deafening volume. When it finally stopped, Aeric and Mina turned back to it to find it merely sitting, its burning eyes staring them down. Though daring to hope the creature had given up, as Aeric sat up with the water up to his waist he heard another sound in the distance that made him realize what the flaming cat was doing.

It was calling for help.

Turning his eyes to the northern skies, the Grandarian boy swallowed hard as the sound of wing beats echoed their way into his ears followed by another massive roar twice as deep and powerful as the flaming beast's. Shouting for Mina to rise and start running again, the pair continued down the creek with the wing beats growing closer by the minute. Before they could even get around the bend in the river past the next hill, Aeric felt his heart drop when he saw the massive black silhouette of another creature dropping out of the sky to slam its clawed feet on either side of the creek with such force it nearly knocked him and Mina to their feet. Standing in front of the girl protectively, Aeric watched as the massive form of the behemoth called Dalorosk lowered its frightening head to roar down at them. As its bleeding red eyes fell upon Aeric's shaking frame, the beast spoke as it had to the man in white.

"I will never find it indeed, Alberic," he spoke as if to himself, leaning his beastly head in front of the two shivering Grandarians. "I can taste your fear, humans." Surprised the creature would toy with them after witnessing his maddening impatience and rage earlier, Aeric attempted to collect himself and think of any way they could survive. "Give me the Source and you may be the first to become our pets." Aeric froze at this, unable to remove his eyes from the glowing red pair burning into him. His mind racing, he decided to take his one chance to save his and Mina's lives. Opening his mouth to take a deep breath, the boy saw the creature growling and raising its arm to smash him. Throwing up an arm defensively, Aeric reached into his tunic with the other to pull out the medallion. The behemoth flinched upon seeing it but quickly smiled as it came into view. Mina's eyes burst open with dread.

"What are you doing!?!" she whispered, beside herself. Holding firm, Aeric remained quiet as Dalorosk reached down for the medallion. When his black fingers were nearly to it, both he and Mina were surprised to see Aeric suddenly reaching up with his free hand to pull the glass window holding the Source within free. The next moment light flooded the Hills of Eirinor, covering every blade of grass in brilliant white radiance. Though Aeric stood with his eyes closed to shield him from the light, he heard the behemoth above him scream out in pain and tumbled back over the earth in searing pain. When the massive creature fell over onto its back shrieking out, the shockwaves knocked Aeric and Mina to the ground with the Source of Light falling out of his grip into the river. The light remained shining out nonetheless and Aeric was forced to continue shielding his eyes as he groped under the water for it.

Splashing through the water as they rose back to their feet, both the Grandarians heard several more of the monstrous roars erupting to life around them and guessed all five of the creatures had converged on their location.

The water and the Source of Light would have no effect on them. It was over. As Aeric desperately searched for the white medallion lost in the creek, he heard the sound of splashing to his right and prepared for a killing blow to come. As he held Mina, however, he was surprised to be picked up out of the water and placed on the back of what felt like a horse with Mina sitting behind him.

"Hold on to me!" were the words from the figure sitting in front of them. Though more confused than he had ever been, Aeric did as he was bid and felt Mina latching onto his waist. Feeling the horse gallop forward, the glow from the Source of Light at last vanished as quickly as it had come and the dark of the night was restored. Though expecting to see the five beastly creatures that had destroyed Galantia drawing near, all Aeric or Mina could see was impossibly fast moving scenery around them blurring into a mess of dark colors in the night.

Chapter 9

<u>The Tower</u>

Aeric and Mina desperately held onto the large man sitting in front of them for the next several minutes, the world around them a blur of shadowy hues speeding by faster than they could see. Though he still felt his heart beating and the sensation of wind jetting across his tightened face, Aeric could not help but wonder if his spirit had passed on to the next world as the amazing display of magical light continued to rush by around them. The last thing he remembered seeing before the blinding luminosity of the Source of Light engulfed the Hills of Eirinor was the massive form of the behemoth Dalorosk bearing down on them along with the four other creatures looking for them. Had they dispatched of him and Mina after all or did the mysterious figure sitting before them on the large horse somehow save them?

It wasn't until he could at last feel the galloping steed they rode beginning to slow and the captivating display of slurring colors fading into coherent physical images that the young Tieloc's bemused mind began to regain its senses. He could still feel Mina fiercely gripping him and the damp clothes on his frame stick to his skin, sensations suggesting his continued presence in the mortal realm. The blurring darkness slowing to reveal concrete images of grass and trees around him, Aeric blinked in amazement as he found himself on a thin dirt road in the heart of a forest.

Spinning around with fret, he found Mina still clutching onto him, her head pressed against his shoulder, trembling. As the girl's nervous green eyes flickered open, she too found the magical display of racing light replaced by a milieu of the moonlit forest and the valley ridges surrounding it. Slowly lifting her cheek off of Aeric's frame to stare up at the treetops in bewilderment, their eyes at last met, reflecting each other's confusion at what had just happened to them.

Though too mystified to speak, Aeric quickly looked her up and down to make sure she was safe and unharmed. Her tight white tunic had been ripped and mud stained from the creek, but she looked otherwise alright. As the galloping horse slowed to a trot, the two confused Grandarians slowly fixed their gazes to the grey cloaked figure before them. As if sensing the two shifting, the figure at last turned his head around to stare at them, his face concealed by a hood and the darkness.

"Are you both alright?" he asked in a deep but disarming voice. Aeric and Mina remained speechless at first, but at last both nodded.

"I think..." Mina returned before Aeric could find his own words. "What just happened to us? Are we...?" The figured kept his gaze on them but let out a dry huff of laughter from behind his hood.

"Dead?" he finished for her as if amused. "Thanks to Nighcress here, not today, young lady." Mina raised an eyebrow at this, swallowing hard and brushing a lock of damp hair sticking to her forehead behind her ear. "The display of light you just saw was hardly passage to the next world, merely to the south. The horse you ride on is no horse at all, but an enchanted Morlan from the time of the gods capable of running at speeds beyond anything the world has ever seen. Nighcress is the last of his race and an ally of mine."

"And who are you?" Aeric asked, searching for a face in the man's concealing hood.

"A friend," the robed figure spoke with a disarming gesture of his right arm. Though he was about to elaborate further, the figure suddenly shot his gaze skyward and paused. Wary at what had his attention, Aeric and Mina looked upward to find a small winged creature deciding from over the treetops to hover before the figure in a sphere of semitransparent light. Having encountered enough deadly beasts over the past day to make him wary of any foreign looking creature, Aeric instantly recoiled and raised his body to cover Mina. "Easy, young man. Zephyr here is another friend of mine. He will do you no harm." Having heard of Sky Sprites before, Aeric and Mina relaxed some but still stared with incredulity at the levitating creature eyeing them up.

"You found them," the sprite spoke, trying to smile at the other two humans behind the man in gray.

"Only just barely," the man returned. "What news from Haven?"

"I never made it," the purple sprite returned. "There was fire and death from Windrun all the way to the Empyrean Peaks—I helped as many as I could but Wyrik has definitely escaped. There was talk of the beast in every village."

"Yes, I saw him in the north with the others," the robed man confirmed. "It is as I feared." Baffled at what the two were talking about, Aeric forced himself to find his voice.

"Excuse me, but what's going on here? Who are you two?" the boy pressed, prompting the man and the sprite to turn back for him.

"We have much to discuss, my young friend, but it is conversation better saved for the safety of indoors," he answered quickly, turning back to the sprite. "Zephyr, something far more terrible than we can imagine is at work this night. Return to the outpost on the ridge of the valley and keep watch to the north for anything out of the ordinary. If you see Wyrik or anything else approaching fall back to the tower at once." The Sky Sprite gave a single nod and shot skyward once more, moving so fast Aeric and Mina barely saw him disappear back over the trees around them.

Though about to protest once more that they needed to know who their mysterious savior was, both of them fell silent as they came around a turn in the dirt road parting the trees to observe a lofty structure rising from the ground before them. It was a long tower that rose high into the night sky, polished dark stone and gaping windows comprising its thick exterior. The many levels of the edifice seemed to grow smaller as it rose into the air—wide and spacious on the first floors but compact and confined toward the pointed spire at the top. The tower stood on a flawlessly flat but unnatural looking plateau rising from the forest floor, perfectly rounded on all sides except for a narrow pathway leading up to the base that the steed called Nighcress began to stride up.

As they arrived through the pathway and onto the plateau before the tower, Aeric and Mina exchanged glances, silently guessing what the amazing structure must have been. At last stopping before a large staircase leading up to the double door entrance of the gargantuan tower, Nighcress halted and the robed figure asked the couple to dismount behind him. They did quickly, Mina sliding down first, followed by Aeric and then the man in grey himself.

"Aeric, you're bleeding!" Mina suddenly exclaimed, surprising both the boy and the other figure. The girl wiped a lock of her chestnut hair behind her ear and gently took hold of his right arm, to which the boy looked down to find a deep cut in his thick carpenter's gauntlet and a dark bloodstain at its edge where it met his blue tunic. Unable to remember sustaining the wound, the young Tieloc raised it to better examine it in the weak light. Before he could tell Mina it was nothing the robed man spoke.

"It looks as though Moltar nicked you before I arrived," he said. The Grandarians turned to him curiously.

"Moltar?" Mina repeated uncertainly.

"I notice his glove is charred above the cut," the man observed. "The flaming cat's claws are molten hot and most likely responsible for the wound. It looks to be minor but we'll see to it inside." As he finished, Aeric and Mina were silent, surprised at how large the man was standing at full length. He wore dark blue attire underneath his flowing gray cloak and hood and the thin moonlight revealed a short beard on his sharply angled face. Most curious of all was the silver medal fixing his robes together and the emblem upon it. It was the same emblem engraved on the twin pillars on either side of the staircase beside them.

"You're a Mystic Sage, aren't you?" Aeric suddenly spoke, forgetting his arm and breaking the silence between them. The figure shifted his gaze down to the boy and tilted his head beneath his hood.

"What would lead you to such a conclusion?" the man asked dispassionately.

"This building," Aeric began shifting his view up to the pointing spire lofting far above them, "looks like something my grandfather told me stories about as a child. The Mystic Tower, where the sages gather. That emblem on your robes is the same as the one on the tower. Your attire even reminds me of the way grandfather spoke of Zeroan himself." The figure tilted his head at this, curiously staring down at the boy.

"Zeroan has been gone for nearly sixty years now and few of his limited friends ever saw this tower," he mused more to himself than to the Grandarians. "Who was your grandfather, I wonder, to have such uncommon knowledge?"

"Tavinious Tieloc of Grandaria," the boy answered with understandable pride. The robed figure froze at this before taking a step closer, to which Mina grasped Aeric's hand tighter.

"...You are children of the Tieloc house?" the figure asked as if shocked beyond all belief.

"Aeric is Tavin's grandson," Mina returned for him, intrigued at the man's shock. "I'm his girlfriend, Mina Garrinal." The figure shifted his gaze to the girl as she spoke then slowly stared into space to his left for a short moment.

"That might help explain why they attacked you then, Aeric Tieloc," the sage at last stated more to himself than then either of them. He withdrew his hood at last, revealing his dark haired head and the robust face staring at them. "Before we continue this any further allow me to introduce myself. You are of course correct about who I am and where you are. My name is Revond, and I am the Master Sage of my order."

"I thought you were a sage, but I also thought all the sages died after the Days of Destiny," Aeric replied.

"They did indeed," the sage confirmed, shuffling in his robes. "I have just recently restored our ranks by beginning a new generation of sages. It is too complicated a story to explain now but I will enlighten you in the future. For now, I need to know what is going on, young Tieloc. You must tell me how you came to possess the Source of Light and why five of the ancient elemental beasts are on the hunt for you." Upon hearing of the Source of Light, Aeric instantly remembered losing it in the creek in the Hills of Eirinor and wildly spun around to Mina to ask if she had it. Before she could respond, Revond spoke again. "Fear not, young one. I have what you seek." Turning back to the Master Sage, Aeric and Mina observed him pull a familiar white medallion out of his robes to hold in the palm of his right hand. "I took it from the creek bed before we fled from Grandaria." Aeric stared at it for a quick moment but decided it best the sage hold onto it.

"Speaking of which, how did you know to come for us, Master Sage?" Mina spoke up from beside Aeric, trying to remain as respectful as possible despite her confusion. "The man in white told us to bring the Source to you here at the Mystic Tower. We weren't expecting you to find us." Revond perked up at this, his brow furrowing.

"What man in white?" he pressed, lowering the glowing medallion back into his robes.

"We met him this morning," Aeric answered, retelling their story. "Mina and I had just made our way out of Galantia when those creatures started their attack on it. We were watching and a man in all white clothing appeared on a horse. He gave us that medallion and told us to bring it to you at all costs. We didn't know what he was talking about but before we could ask or object the creatures found him and attacked. Mina and I hid under a bush but we heard them demand the Source of Light from him. After that the black monster picked him up and ordered the others to destroy Grandaria until they found it. They found us in the Hills of Eirinor and you know the rest." Revond stared at them both hard for a moment, trying to sift through their strange story to decipher what was really going on.

"And this man in white did not tell you how he came to have the Source? He did not even tell you his name?"

"He never told us *his* name but somehow he knew mine," Aeric informed him. "He said he had been looking for me since something called the Ascension started." Revond froze again at this, his eyes growing wide as he remembered what Moltar had told him at the end of their struggle the day before.

"Did this man give you any other clue that could help me reveal his identity?" the sage asked quickly. "Anything he said or did that could give me greater insight?"

"We thought you would know who he was," Aeric confessed. "We even thought he was a Mystic Sage himself at first, but after he called the beasts his brothers we weren't sure what he was..." He trailed off for a moment, remembering something else. "One of the creatures called him Alberic, if that means anything to you."

"What?" Revond interjected. "Alberic was the first sage who lived eons ago. He has been dead for thousands of years."

"Well there is another one now because I remember the beast calling him that too," Mina affirmed. Aeric was about to elaborate when he saw Mina jumping to face him from the corner of his eye and reaching down to open one of the pouches on his belt.

"I almost forgot," she began pulling free a rolled piece of paper, "the man in white gave us this note for you as well." Revond swept forward to snatch the paper from her as quickly as possible hearing this, rolling it open to read whatever the message was. As his focused eyes raced across the paper, Aeric and Mina could only wait for him to react. Though Revond's face grew confused as he reread whatever words were on the small paper, he at last lowered it and stared into space again, obviously collecting his thoughts.

"Did the man in white tell you anything more about this note?" he asked them quickly.

"We never even looked to know what it says," Aeric told him, rubbing away the dampness in his short black hair with his left hand. "He just told us to deliver it to you." Revond kept his gaze on them for an uncomfortably long moment but eventually rolled the paper into his robes. He looked around for anything else in the Sage's Valley, narrowing his eyes as he peered into the quiet trees. Seeing nothing, he flipped his gray hood back over his face and motioned for the two Grandarians to make their way up the staircase toward the doors of the tower.

"Hurry inside then, and we'll see if this man in white is who he says he is," Revond whispered, gently nudging them forward to emphasize the need for speed. Guessing the note had revealed the man in white's identity, Aeric and Mina did as they were told and practically sprinted up the stairs toward the doors of the Mystic Tower with Master Sage Revond driving them from behind. As they drew near the entrance, the sage extended one of his gloved hands toward the door, opening his fist to spread his fingers wide. The Grandarians were amazed to find the massive wooden doors hurriedly open by themselves, the lurching of the old hinges moaning into the night air. Stepping through them and into the expansive foyer of the tower, they looked back to find the Master Sage turning in his robes to close his hand into a fist once more. The next instant the doors slammed shut, even locking on their own. Guessing they were under the influence of the sage's telekinetic grip that they had heard about from stories of Zeroan, Aeric and Mina exchanged glances that confirmed this man really was a Mystic Sage.

Still pressing forward, Revond took the lead and quietly beckoned them to follow him through the foyer. Though forced to take powerful strides to keep up with the swift sage, Aeric and Mina took the time to sweep their gazes around the massive room that few had ever seen. The central chamber of the Mystic Tower was three stories tall with arching staircases on either side of the room leading up to the next levels, all complete with smooth railed balconies along the walls. From what they could see, the sage's tower was simple and only barely decorated compared to the ornate hallways of the Golden Castle in Galantia. There were a few hanging tapestries with cloaked figures and ancient emblems similar to the one Revond wore on his cloak over the sparse walls, but aside from the numerous torches lighting the expansive circular chamber it was barren. Mina shuddered with a chill running up her spine as she walked through the eerie silence broken only by the crackling fires, stricken with a nameless fear knowing they were the only ones in the empty tower. Shifting her gaze to Aeric still staring at the upper levels in wonder, she gently grasped his hand in hers and hastened her steps behind the sage.

As the trio continued toward the far side of the foyer and the many arching passages lining its curving wall, Revond turned back to the Grandarians, sensing their discomfort of both him and their surroundings. Speaking low, he began to talk again.

"But I have still not answered your question, Mina Garrinal," he started suddenly, getting their attention. "You have trusted me with your story so perhaps I should now trust you with mine. As I told you before, I have just recently assumed my role as the new Master Sage of the Order of Alberic. Over the years I have sensed the various elemental disturbances across Iairia that you have undoubtedly been hearing about. One of my roles is to anoint the Elemental Warriors of the Southland to deal with these disturbances and maintain order, but I fear my return to the world was too late. Early this morning before the attack on Galantia began, I sensed the various Sources in the elemental temples across the lands disappear, including the Source of Light now in our possession. I am still unsure how this could have happened but it obviously has something to do with the elemental beasts of the ancient world that you encountered in Grandaria."

"Wait, elemental beasts?" Aeric repeated. "We thought those creatures were demons."

"Though the beasts you saw destroy Galantia may resemble those you have heard stories about from your grandfather in the Days of Destiny, young Tieloc, those are no demonic creatures. They are five of the remaining elemental beasts that have survived since the ancient world after the Battle of the Gods. I have studied them all over my years in the Mystic Tower but they have never interacted or come out of hiding on so grand and destructive a scale before. I am not sure what they are up to but we are going to find out."

As he trailed off, Aeric and Mina kept their gazes on the back of his hood, waiting for more to this story. Eventually he asked them to describe the man in white as best they could, leaving out no detail of his appearance or mannerisms. Aeric and Mina weren't sure what more to say at first, merely stating he was an average looking middle-aged man dressed in white from head to toe. Thinking more carefully however, Mina remembered that he was originally carrying the medallion he gave them on the left side of his tunic in some sort of a lock. Though this obviously intrigued the Master Sage, he said nothing and led them through the central passage into a short hallway.

"And there was nothing else distinguishing about his appearance," Revond pressed, looking back at them as he continued marching down the torch-lit hallway.

"Not that I can think to remember," Aeric returned hopelessly. "I would never have guessed he was anything more than an average man if I didn't know any better. He had the face of any Grandarian you would just bump into on the..." The boy trailed off for a moment then, his pace suddenly slowly. Feeling her boyfriend lagging, Mina spun around to see the astonished look on his face.

"What is it?" she asked worriedly. Hearing this, Revond stopped and looked back to them as well. His eyes going wide, Aeric shot them up to Mina's.

"That man who bumped into us as we were leaving Galantia," he said abruptly.

"That rude man in black?" Mina remembered if vaguely. "What about him?"

"I didn't get a good look at him, but now that I think about it he looked exactly like the man in white," Aeric said shifting his gaze to Revond. "There was another man that looked just like the man in white at the gates of Galantia when we were leaving. He was even wearing the same tunic and outfit as the man in white, but all in black." Revond raised an eyebrow at this, unable to make any connection.

"You think these two men are somehow related?" the sage asked questioningly.

"I... I don't know," Aeric confessed, suddenly unsure where his observation was going. "All I know is they looked like twins. It must have something to do with this." Revond held the boy's gaze for a long moment before deeply exhaling and shaking his head, seemingly upset.

"This grows more confounding by the minute," he mumbled to himself. "Hurry. We may have little time. The light from the Source blinded the beasts and coupled with Nighcress' lightning speeds they will not have seen in which direction we escaped, but if our horrid luck holds this will be the first place they look for you."

"Can they sense the Source of Light here?" Mina asked worriedly.

"No, only active power can be sensed by those with the capacity to feel it across the lands. Like all talismans of magic the Source is passive unless in use. But the creature Wyrik knows the location of this tower and might lead the others here. We must be quick." Spinning around with his robes flying up behind him, Aeric and Mina continued following him down the hallway until they arrived in a smaller circular room with a stone platform in the center. Looking up, the Grandarians were amazed to find no ceiling but for the tallest point in the tower dozens of levels up. "Step onto the platform, my young friends."

"What is this place?" Mina asked in wonder as she eyed the stone platform she was stepping onto beside the others.

"The fastest mode of transportation in the Mystic Tower," Revond answered, waiting for the two to stand beside him in the center of the platform. "The center of the tower is hollowed to allow we sages access to any of the thirty-four floors without having to climb endless stairs."

"How does that work?" Aeric asked doubtfully.

"Like so," the sage responded, extending his hands toward two opposite sides of the circular platform. Clenching his grip into the air as if grabbing hold of something, he slowly raised his hands with the platform rising with them. Finding herself moving through the air past the various levels of the tower, Mina gulped and stood closer to Aeric once more, tightening her grip on his hand.

"Amazing," she whispered, feeling the platform slightly accelerate. Thinking the same thing himself, Aeric shifted his gaze back to the Master Sage beside them, effortlessly raising the massive platform into the air. As the seconds ticked by and the three climbed higher into the halls of the Mystic Tower, Revond eyed the young Tieloc tapping the toes of his thick brown boots on the platform and refastening his loose carpenter's belt while the girl checked him over for any further cuts they had not noticed in the darkness. Though wrapping his mind around other matters pertaining to recent events, the sage could not help but notice the familiar blue eyes he had seen in the face of another Tieloc years ago. His curiosity getting the best of him, he spoke.

"You are the son of Kaylan Tieloc, Aeric?" the sage quietly asked, to which both Aeric and Mina stopped what they were doing stared at him peculiarly.

"Kaylan is my aunt," Aeric responded after a lingering moment, his brow furrowing. "My father is Darien Tieloc, her brother." Revond gave him a single nod in response, forcing himself to look away from the two. Aeric and Mina shot each other disturbed glances, curious at his question. After a long moment with no follow up question from the sage, Aeric asked one of his own. "Master Sage, how do you know of my aunt? I thought you didn't even know who I was until now." Revond merely raised his head upward to see the final level of the tower approaching and began to slow the platform with his mystical grip.

"That is another story for another day, my young Tieloc," he returned mysteriously. "When this crisis has abated, ask me again and I will tell you another story of your family that you have not heard." Aeric raised an eyebrow skeptically at this, wondering how even the Master Sage could know something about his family that he didn't. Feeling Revond was holding back more than he was telling them, Aeric could no longer contain the question burning within him since they had first been saved by the sage in the Hills of Eirinor.

"Revond, do you know what is happening?" he asked, his eyes hard as if prodding the sage for the truth. Revond was quiet at first but as the platform came to a halt hundreds of feet in the air near the highest ceiling of the Mystic Tower he met the boy's gaze.

"I have a... theory, but one that would turn the basis of history upside-down if proven true," he spoke quietly. "Step off the platform into the passage." Though hesitant at first, Mina pulled Aeric after him into the passage where Revond followed after beginning to lower the platform back down to the base of the tower with his mystic power. Turning around to face them, he began walking up the stairwell toward a strange wall bearing the emblem Aeric and Mina had seen countless times in the tower. Slowing before it, Revond spoke once more but kept his gaze on the wall. "I have been training to become the Master Sage within these walls for nearly forty years now. I have explored every room, hidden passageway, nook and mouse hole in this tower. I am intimate with every inch of it." He paused for a moment, reaching into his robes to pull out the note the man in white had written for him. "Except for those that lie behind this wall."

He turned back for the Grandarians then, stepping aside to let them better view the wall.

"This is the highest level of the tower. There is nothing here except for one room behind this wall, but not even I have the power to budge it. Only Alberic, the founder of our order, has ever set foot beyond here. These were his private quarters—his watchtower over the land that lies beneath our stronghold—sealed shut after his departure. No one knows what lies within. It had been passed down through the years that this wall will only move with the correctly spoken password, but Alberic did not leave it with any of his disciples. None of us have ever been able to guess it. I searched for any clue of it in the libraries for years but I assumed it was lost with him. Now, it might be that it was recovered after all." Though confused, Aeric and Mina were surprised to find Revond lift the note before them for them to read. Squinting to make out the black ink on the page, they found the words "the password is Ascension" quickly written out.

"So you think the man in white somehow knew of Alberic's password?" Mina asked. "How would he know if he isn't connected to the Mystic Sages?"

"I wouldn't have known what this meant at first," Revond admitted, "but there is an amazing—if farfetched— possibility of this man's identity revealed to us by what you heard earlier today. You said the behemoth called the man in white Alberic. Though I'm of his connection to the elemental beasts, perhaps this man is indeed a direct ancestor of the first Alberic who lived millennia past. Whether he is or not, we will know in a moment." With that, Revond turned back for the wall blocking their way and took a deep breath before speaking a single word. "Ascension." No sooner than the last syllable escaped his lips, the trio was surprised to hear a sudden grinding of stone on stone from behind the wall. Staring, they were shocked to find it suddenly rising into a slot in the ceiling to reveal the dark room that lay behind it. His eyes going wide and his heart pounding, the Master Sage Revond flipped down his hood and turned back to stare at the two Grandarians who had brought him the key to the mystery that had so long eluded him.

Chapter 10

<u>The Cebrach Book</u>

Revond inched into the darkened chamber with caution, his guard up for any enchanted defense in the once permanently sealed room. With a sweeping gaze over what lay before him unveiled to human eyes for the first time in millennia, he stepped fully inside. Aeric and Mina stood uncertainly waiting behind him in the narrow stairwell, watching the Master Sage amble forward until his robes were merely a silhouette in the darkness. At last he came to a halt and raised a hand out of his robes to motion for them to follow after him with the flick of his fingers. Curiosity and wonder at what so secret and small a room could hold to baffle even the Mystic Sages for so many years, the couple took each others hands and ambled after him through the raised wall into the chamber. Though dark at first compared to the torch lit corridors of the lower tower, Aeric and Mina quickly noticed moon and star light pouring in from arching windows all around the circular walls of the room. They could see the entire Sage's Valley below stretching out to the hills around it.

Caught up with the sprawling view beneath them, the two were surprised to hear a heavy snap from Revond's gloved hand, followed by several torches around the perimeter of the chamber leaping to life with white flame. Staring at his exposed face, Aeric and Mina found he was as mesmerized by the chamber as they. At last they found his eyes lock onto something and followed them to the object they had noticed resting in the center of the otherwise barren chamber. A cylindrical stone pedestal rose out of the floor holding a large leather-bound book propped up on a slanted wooden brace. Surprised that the great mystery of the tower's sole hidden chamber was only an old book, the Grandarians watched in silence as Revond slowly approached it, his head shaking with wonder.

"It can't be..." he murmured to himself, coming to a halt when towering over the pedestal and book. The Master Sage pulled off the gloves on his hands and tucked them inside his robes before cautiously leaning down to blow the heavy layer of dust free from the hard cover. His eyes widening, the sage ran one hand over his gruff black beard and the other slowly along the book's edge to gingerly open its cover. "It's been right here, under our noses for millennia..." Unable to contain his curiosity as he peered around the sage to eye the large book, Aeric mustered the courage to speak.

"What has?" he asked breaking the silence between them. The sage kept his focused eyes on the book as he fully opened it for the first time in untold years, not wishing to reply until he could validate his hopes with proof. Finding it on the title page of the book, he let a faint smile spread from the corner of his lips and softly spoke back to the bewildered Grandarians.

"This is the lost volume of the Cebrach books..." he trailed off, his eyes wildly racing up and down the ancient paper beneath him.

"Is this all Alberic was keeping in here?" Mina asked, still unconvinced a mere book could be the first sage's great secret. His smile dissipating as the girl's question registered in his mind, Revond carefully rotated the top of the swiveling pedestal holding the book around, walking after it so he could face the young Grandarians.

"This is one of our greatest treasures, thought to be lost to time or bandits in the first years of the order," he returned, finally shifting his gaze back to them. "There are twelve books kept in the libraries below us called Cebrach books. They contain the sages' greatest mysteries and exploits over the long years of our existence, written and stored in chronological order. They are named after one of the original sages who developed the enchanted ink they are written in, allowing the words and images being described to come to life before the reader when read aloud. Every sage including myself has read every book but one: the very first volume that went missing even before the library was fully built. We have been searching for it with no avail since its disappearance. And now, here it lies..." Aeric and Mina exchanged confused glances at this.

"Why would Alberic hide it in here then?" was Aeric's question. "I thought he was known for sharing his great discoveries about the world. Why would the original sage of your order hide the very first of your recorded history from you?"

"Your guess is as good as mine, Aeric," was Revond's befuddled response looking back at the book, "but there is only one way to find out." Dragging his fingers along the title of the first page, he looked back up at the boy. "As you pointed out, the contents of this book appear to be about one of the last voids in our records of history that even we sages are uncertain of." The sage took a pause before opening his mouth to read the words on the page, aware of the reaction that would come. "The title reads, 'The Ancients and the Forming of the Six Lands.'" No sooner that the last word escaped his mouth, Aeric and Mina were surprised to see the page he read from flash blue and illuminate the entire chamber, startling them nearly to the point of falling backward. Slowly, the pulsating particles of light hovering over the book began to swirl together and spread out in the room, covering the area around the pedestal. Their hearts racing and their curiosity stirred to no end, the Grandarians slowly began to approach the glowing book. Revond held up and hand for them to halt. "You will have a better view if you stay where you are, young ones."

"What's going to happen if you read more, Master Sage?" Mina asked, a hint of trepidation in her voice.

"Nothing that can cause you any harm, I assure you, Mina," he told her. "What you are about to see are merely shadows from the past playing out as the writer remembered them, who in this case is most likely Alberic himself. We'll know for sure in a moment. I'm only going to skim through anything that may give us a clue as to who this mysterious man in white is or what is at work here. Listen and watch carefully, for you may discover a clue that could prove useful." Clearing his throat, Revond flipped the page and set his eyes upon the first block of text under the first chapter of the book, squinting uncertainly at the different structure of this book from the other volumes he had read. There was no outline of information; no table of contents or other introduction to the book, merely text without a heading of any kind. Without any direction, the sage merely took a deep breath and began reading from the beginning.

"'My fellow sage,'" it opened, light slowly rising out of the book with each word uttered. "'I am not sure who you are or when you are, so I must word what follows carefully from the rest of the Cebrach books that have been compiled at the beginning of this order. While the pages in other volumes after this one have been written from the perspective of history and to tell of our ventures across this world, I am compelled to write not for the sake of lasting education but of dire warning of the events in your present about to occur or that are already occurring. Besides my own, your eyes are the first to read this text." As Revond continued to read, Aeric and Mina could detect another voice articulating the same words as the Master Sage, emanating from the random, twisting displays of light before them. "Judging from the fact that you are reading this now, I can only assume the worst has happened and the Ascension has come. While I was confident the threat this day has brought could be avoided by the measures I took in my time to be detailed in the pages that follow, it would seem my best efforts at precluding this doom have failed. I am of course Alberic, the first of this order that came to be named after me which safeguards the knowledge of the world.'"

Though the Master Sage was going to continue the paragraph and go on to the next page, he was interrupted by the sudden gasp of both Aeric and Mina from in front of him. Looking up in alarm, he found the two staring with mouths agape at the image of light collecting before them in the air. Staring at the image's back from his position behind the pedestal, Revond could only make out an average looking man with brown hair and gray robes draping along his back, obviously depicting Alberic in his younger years.

"Are you surprised by his appearance?" the Master Sage asked them. Awestruck, the two Grandarians merely shook their heads, unable to tear their gazes off of the image in front of them.

"This is *the* Alberic?" Aeric managed to ask, taking a step closer to the image's motionless face, made still from Revond's pause in reading. Revond tilted his head in curiosity at this, taking a step away from the book and towards them.

"I am reading from Alberic's words, so you are seeing him, yes," he answered curiously. Aeric gulped at this, letting his arms down in disbelief.

"You need to see this, Master Sage" was all he could say, shaking his head incredulously. His brow furrowing at what could have the two Grandarians so shocked, Revond quickly strode around the pulsating images of light until facing the front of the man depicted.

"What is wrong?" he asked, eyeing the figure up and down without noticing anything peculiar. Aeric and Mina slowly exchanged glances with each other before looking at Revond, their eyes sparkling.

"Look at what he's wearing," Aeric told him. Growing frustrated, Revond turned to observe the sage's gray robes once more. Looking more carefully however, he saw the garb underneath was solid white from his boots to his tunic neck lining. The moment he guessed what had the two so unnerved, Mina spoke out.

"This is the man in white we saw this morning!" she exclaimed, throwing her arm out as if to offer up the man's appearance to the sage. It took a moment for the outrageous statement to sink into Revond's ears before slowly rotating back to her with a disbelieving look on his face.

"That cannot be, my young Grandarian," he returned with a disarming gesture of his hands. "Again, the original Alberic has been dead for thousands of years and he is the man the book is depicting for us. This cannot be that man you encountered earlier." The looks on Aeric and Mina's face remained steadfast.

"All I know is this is the man we saw today," the girl returned, growing flustered. She gently pushed Aeric and locked onto his eyes. "Tell him Aeric!" The Tieloc boy let out a sharp breath but nodded his head as he turned it back towards Revond.

"She's right, Master Sage," he affirmed. "This is too close to be even a distant ancestor. This is the exact face and clothing of the man in white, minus the cloak. This is him!" Though letting out an irritated huff at first, Revond forced himself to forestall his judgment on the two as he looked into their sincere eyes. He could tell they honestly believed the two men were the same whether it was true or not.

"I appreciate your earnestness, my friends, but how could you have seen someone who has been recorded dead for millennia?" he asked, imparting the logic of his argument. "Even with the power of the life elongating Sage's Draught, no man could live that long. Alberic is gone." Though stopping to ponder this fact for a lingering moment, when he looked back up at the inert face alight before him, Aeric shook his head again.

"This is him," he answered quietly with confidence. "I'll prove it to you. Let me see the Source of Light." Both Revond and Mina stared at him uncertainly at this, but with reluctance the Master Sage reached into the confines of his robes and pulled forth the white medallion they had obtained. Taking hold of it in his right hand, Aeric slowly turned for the image of Alberic and approached, the motionless light parting like a thick haze as he reached through it. Extending his arm out through the light toward Alberic's chest, Aeric held the medallion up to the empty metal lock on his right chest. Slowly turning back to Revond and Mina, he pushed it forward until its edges fit perfectly into the mold. "This is where the medallion was when he first met us. He twisted it off and gave it to us. You can even see where the grooves link into the lock on his chest."

Revond remained still at first, slowly tilting his head and taking a step forward to better examine the medallion somehow carrying the Source of Light.

"How can this be...?" he murmured, his heart racing at what he was seeing. It was an exact match. "You are both sure of this beyond any doubt?"

"It's him, Revond," Aeric confirmed, his eyes confident. Revond merely felt a pang of uncertainty in his heart that he had not felt since before stepping out into the world as the Master Sage. Revond slowly let his gaze stare off into space. Desperate for answers to the riddle they had uncovered, Mina slowly gripped the sage's arm underneath his gray robe to get his attention back.

"I think we need to read more out of the book," she told him, looking into his blue eyes. Coming back to his senses, the Master Sage gave her a slow nod and turned back for the pedestal in the center of the chamber.

"I think you're right," he returned just loud enough to be heard. Seeing the sage was convinced of the man in white's identity, Aeric lowered his arm and the medallion back to his side. He slowly stepped out of the misting light back beside Mina, staring at him with wonder mirrored in her frightened eyes. They both watched and waited as the sage moved over the Cebrach book, preparing to read again. As soon as he found his place and inhaled to speak the light began moving once more, Alberic's voice speaking in unison with Revond's.

"I am of course Alberic, the first of this order that came to be named after me which safeguards the knowledge of the world. I am ashamed to report to you however, that there is knowledge from the beginning of our world that I chose to withhold from this order and the world at large. I made this decision not because I deemed anyone unworthy of the truth, but rather because of a mistake I made within this book. Contained in the pages of this Cebrach book are more than the events in the ancient world which is why you read this now, but record of other places beyond the six lands and powers that I found there. In my excitement to record my adventures and discoveries in these pages, I wrote down details I later realized I could not leave with the first members of the Order of Alberic, as some of my early brothers could not be trusted with knowledge of such power. This enchanted ink cannot be erased, however, and so I had no choice but to hide this book away until now when the true history is needed to prevent disaster. Now that this book is in your possession you can judge for yourself if my decision was prudent or foolish, but the accounts that follow are true either way.

"I supposed I should begin at the beginning. As you already know courtesy of Grandarian record, our world was created by the life giving Holy Emerald that once contained the six elemental energies that create all matter in the universe. The emerald was shattered in the Battle of the Gods by Granis and the Drakkan, sending its six shards flying across the world to rest in six different locations.'" As the story began to unfold, Aeric and Mina were amazed to see the light from Alberic disperse to recreate an image of Granis and Drakkan racing toward a glowing emerald, only to have it shatter into the six shards when they both touched its gleaming surface. In another flash of brilliant light, they watched the shards race towards different corners of the chamber to disappear, one of them passing in between their heads only to dissipate into thousands of miniscule particles beyond. Captivated, the two Grandarians couldn't help but glance at each other with wonder and stare on as the spectacle continued. "At this point, Drakkan was sealed into his Netherworld along with his evil race of demons, while Granis disappeared leaving behind his race of humans. While the Grandarian's history turns to legend and myth here, my story now begins, as the tale of the shards' effect on the world is only just beginning. This is the account of the old world and the Ancients, as I have come to call them, who came into existence there.

"'Like all talismans of power, when the six shards of the Holy Emerald were separated from each other and fell across Iairia, their power faded into passivity. Because the emerald was broken, however, the elemental energies within did not merely fall into a dormant sleep as they would in an intact talisman of power. They began to seep out onto the lands they fell to, being slowly absorbed into the earth and sky around them. Over time, the regions where the shards fell took on the characteristics of the elemental energy that shard had once stored, giving birth to the terrain and life present there today. Once the six lands where the shards fell became saturated with the elemental energies of the emerald, creatures of great power came into existence comprised of elemental energy. The strongest of these creatures eventually came to rule over their respective lands, protecting and fostering life on their own. These creatures were the Ancients. Their sway over the elements was so great that one day they began mustering the energies that had seeped out of the emerald shards to them. They focused all of the energy that had been absorbed into the land, the atmospheres, and themselves, into one, concentrated sphere of raw elemental power that they could tangibly possess and control. The creatures came to call these spheres of power the Sources of elemental energy.

"'For a time, it was good, and there was peace across the six lands. The problem came when Granis' race of light, the humans, began gradually expanding and multiplying outside the northeast lands they had been born in, upsetting the delicate elemental order the creatures had established. Angry at their coming, the Ancients began attacking and destroying humans until all but those in the northeast lands where they had come from perished. It was in these attacks that the creatures encountered one another for the first time. Already incensed by what they viewed as trespassing by the humans and arrogant by unchallenged rule in their lands for so long, the Ancients went to war with each other to exterminate any element but their own. The war went on for many long years, causing destruction not seen since the Battle of the Gods and shaping the world to look the way it does today.'" As the shimmering light from the Cebrach book swirled into images of the elemental creatures lunging at each other with voracious rage, Mina couldn't help but gulp and tighten her grip on Aeric, admittedly a little afraid at how realistic the display of slashing, biting and tearing appeared.

"'By now, though, you must be wondering how it is I have knowledge of this when neither the ancient Grandarians nor anyone else in the order does,'" Alberic suddenly wrote, freezing and slowly dissipating the images of the elemental war. Caught off guard, Revond, Aeric, and Mina looked into the light to see Alberic appearing again. "The reason I have memory of these events to record them here in this Cebrach book is because I was there, fighting to protect the northeast lands and the remaining humans who lived there. Though I was always assumed to be human, I am in fact one of the six elemental creatures. I am the Ancient of Light, Alberic—created not from Granis or Drakkan but from the raw power of the shard of the Holy Emerald that carried the energy of light. As you can see, I am capable of altering my true appearance to one more suitable for speaking with you, as can my brothers, which is how I was able to live among humanity. I have been alive for a great longevity—depending on the time you live in—and still am, provided one of my five brothers has not killed me. Only they have the power to do so, as I am, like them, comprised of pure elemental energy. There is, at least at this point in history, no other force besides the Holy Emerald that can hold such energy at bay.'"

Revond paused at this, raising his hand to run his fingers through his hair and take a breath to ease his disbelief at what he was hearing. The history of his order was not only being rewritten with every word he read, but that of the entire world. Aeric and Mina shifted their gazes to him again, waiting for him to continue the narrative. Though the sage could barely bring himself to carry on, he conquered his doubts and forced himself to turn the page.

"'Getting back to the story, our war grew to consume every inch of our six lands,'" the two voices slowly began again. "'My brothers and I were once majestic and beautiful creatures, but as we went to war our appearances grew monstrous and we became beasts. In the beginning we merely did battle with one another, but as the years wore on we used our Sources to create armies in our images to expand the scope of our war. Golthrout, the Ancient of Earth from the forests to the south, created his race of smaller Golthrouts that he named after himself. Wyrik, the Ancient of Wind from the eastern peaks, gave birth to Wyverns, steeds of the skies. Vorkoise, the Ancient of Water that took refuge in the wetlands, created the Jagged Pike, his ravenous watery predators. Moltar, the Ancient of Fire, breathed life into packs of Lavlas Boars whose constant flame burned everything they came in contact with.'"

As Revond eyed the images of the Ancients racing back and forth before the Grandarian couple, a deep rooted frown swept over his face, remembering his less than favorable encounters with several of the beasts listed from the distant and recent travels of his life.

"'Then there is my opposite and the most wicked of my brothers—Dalorosk. A behemoth of dark power, he created the teeming, poisonous Siarchs. He altered them purposefully to pose greater threat to my regal Fethiotts, enormous birds of white. Our war was the birth of the elemental races across the lands. The other races—Sky Sprites, Morlans, Cronoms, and the Celestrians now all but vanished—were the natural races present even before Granis and Drakkan created the humans and demons. Though they once thrived all over the world even through the Battle of the Gods, our armies nearly wiped them all out to extinction.'" Aeric couldn't help but smile as he witnessed several of the gnome like race of Cronoms bounce playfully in the enchanted light, remembering stories of them from his grandfather during the Days of Destiny.

"'And so the story ends unhappily, as war inevitably does,'" Alberic continued in his writing. "'Because we all possessed an equal Source of elemental energy, we were all squarely pitted against one another and none of us could defeat another. Our battles remained deadlocked for years. Eventually I foresaw the complete destruction of the world if things continued, so I left Iairia in search of another power that could stop the constant warfare my brothers and I had plunged the six lands into. In my travels I indeed found a new power apart from our elemental energies that I could use to stop the conflict, the circumstances of which are detailed in later pages within this book. It came in the form of a staff I fashioned that could absorb any magical power it encountered. Bearing this staff I returned to Iairia and used my brothers' powers against them, taking their Sources and banishing them underground as Granis had done to Drakkan.

"'With the war at last over and my brothers contained, I charged myself with making sure they remained banished and restoring the war torn lands they had once protected. I began by using the staff I had obtained to erect the Elemental Temples across the lands that would safeguard the Sources we had created and rejuvenate the lands with their slowly radiating power.'" A tear gently caressed Mina's cheek as an image of the once towering Temple of Light and the Tower of Granis in all its glory shimmered before her, now lying in rubble after the events of the morning. "'I wandered the lands in my human form, ensuring that my brothers remained within the small regions I allowed them to roam. As the years rolled into centuries and I existed apart from my Source of Light, I lost the ability to transform back into my true form. Though I could still stave off my brothers if they tried to emerge again with my staff, I knew that cut off from my power I was weakened and would not be able to manage them anymore. So as humanity began to grow and evolve into the beginnings of Grandaria, I delegated my task to others.

"'Using my staff and the remaining elemental power it still contained from holding the Sources, I bestowed six humans with the means to give them sway over the elements and in turn the beasts and their races. If any of my brothers attempted to escape their prisons these Elemental Warriors would be there to stop them. Seeing the humans take to the task with such verve, I decided to establish a wise group of them to continually anoint new Elemental Warriors when the others perished or grew unable to continue their duties. This is the true origin of the Order of Alberic. Though it grew into the Mystic Sages whose task was to record and preserve all knowledge in Iairia, this was its original and primary purpose. After establishing the first age of our order, I entrusted my staff to them and departed back to the northeast land that I had been born in to live in peace the rest of my days with the Grandarians.

"'There is one final element to the story which is the reason you are reading this now. There was a final battle between my brothers and me in our elemental war when I banished them away to their underground caverns and distant mountaintops. In his vengeance, my brother Dalorosk promised me that he would return one day to finish what he started and conquer the other elements. He promised that there would be an Ascension—a day when he and the others would rise up and destroy me. While it was a threat I worried about at length in my time overseeing their banishment on my own, I am now confident as I write this that the system I have set in place is infallible. The Elemental Warriors are in place to keep the Ancients banished and their races in check, and the order is here to ensure the warriors always remain. And even if something were to happen to them and the chain broken, there is the Staff of the Ancients that I have entombed in the lowest chamber of this tower that any of my disciples are capable of wielding to defeat my brothers again. There should be no way elemental order can falter now.'"

Revond stopped once again, his heart suddenly racing as he remembered the most recent story surrounding the Staff of the Ancients. In his anger over the loss of Kaylan Tieloc, he himself had destroyed Alberic's staff years ago after it was stolen by the Drakkaidian High Priest Zalnaught. Revond let out a long breath of dissatisfaction with himself before forcing himself to continue the end of the page.

"'But of course, if you are reading this, the system I am so proud of and put so much faith in has obviously failed after all. The Ancients would not have risked emerging with the warriors present to stop them or the staff intact; they will remember how easily they fell to me before. But they will be able to sense if the warriors or the staff are no more, and if these checks are not in place Dalorosk and the others will surely rise up to continue their campaign of devastation. I on the other hand, separated from my Source of Light, have lost this ability to sense the fate of these safeguards, and because I am not explaining all this to you myself, it means I have either been captured or killed by my brothers during their Ascension. It falls to you then, my brother or sister, to find a way to stop the Ancients from fulfilling their pledge to destroy Iairia. If you are reading this it means you have the power to anoint new Elemental Warriors, but you must do so quickly. If my brothers find you first or take their Sources back before you can anoint warriors there may be no hope of stopping them.'"

Revond stopped reading there, the light from the image of Alberic waning as he did. Aeric and Mina shifted their awestruck gazes to the Master Sage in the silence, not knowing what to make of any of this. It was Revond who finally broke the silence, raising his head to fix his suddenly desperate eyes on the two Grandarians.

"Aeric," he began softly, "do you know if the elemental beasts had the Sources with them this morning?" The young Tieloc let the question digest before slowly turning to Mina, already staring at him with a look of horror in her trembling eyes. Seeing the way they looked at each other, Revond knew the answer to his question before they even told him. Letting out a deep breath and slouching to lean over the pedestal with his heart sinking in his chest, he silently reread the last sentence from Alberic's book. If the Ancients claimed the Sources before he could use them to anoint a new batch of Elemental Warriors, there may be no hope of stopping them.

Chapter 11

<u>Besieged</u>

As the light in the small chamber on the highest floor of the Mystic Tower began to slowly dissipate from Revond's extended pause, Aeric saw that the sage already knew the answer to the question he had asked. Swallowing hard and holding the Master Sage's intense gaze, he opened his mouth to speak anyway.

"The Ancients told Alberic that they had already taken their Sources," he answered softly. "They were practically mocking him for not having his..." Revond let the words digest before slowly nodding and closing his eyes. He remained still for a lingering moment but eventually swept his fingers under the cover of the Cebrach book to lift it and flip it shut. The remaining light in the room vanished as if pushed away from a wisp of wind as soon as its cover fell closed, shocking both the Grandarians who were waiting for more from its texts. "Is that it?" Aeric asked almost angry.

"That was the end of the chapter," Revond returned, barely audible. Mina's brow furrowed in disbelief hearing this, her passion flaring up.

"That was how he ended it?" she asked critically. "He didn't even tell us what we're supposed to do now!" Revond placed his hands on the edges of the rotating pedestal holding the Cebrach book, leaning his weight down upon it before he responded.

"I fear there may be nothing we can do, my dear," he said, a hint of anger underneath his words. Mina let Aeric's hand go and took a step toward the sage at this, her face tightening with incredulity.

"What do you mean there's nothing we can do?" she bit at him, shocked at his answer. "Those creatures are out there destroying the world looking for us, killing entire cities of innocent people as they go!" Aware her grief from the day's events was fueling her words and she was becoming upset, Aeric gingerly grasped her forearm.

"Mina, try to stay calm," he tried to tell her before she spun back at him and pulled away, looking back and forth between the two as she continued.

"No! This isn't a time to be calm! He's the Master Sage! Alberic himself told us to come find you so you could help! How can you say there is nothing we can do?" Though Aeric was about to grab her again and pull her back from Revond, remembering he was in fact the Master Sage, the cloaked man shook his head and raised himself up from the pedestal, slowly ambling around it until facing them.

"She has every right to be angry, young Tieloc," he told him, looking at Mina. "There is fault here on my part. If I had taken the steps to anoint new Elemental Warriors earlier when the warning signs of this day began years ago, it might not have come to this. Now it is too late, for even if I had capable men and women to anoint Elemental Warriors, they can only be given their power by being immersed in the Sources with my hand present to imbue them with the power. With the Sources in the clutches of the Ancients this cannot occur. My delay to this responsibility with the knowledge I was the last of the order may have cost the world more than I can repay." The Grandarians were quiet at this. Aeric wasn't sure what to say, lost in all that he had just learned that felt leagues above his head. He could only stand firm as Mina turned for him with tears welling. Her anger had been flushed out of her system only to be replaced by the mounting grief that had been building all day. As she pressed her head against his in uncharacteristic sorrow and the Master Sage lowered his in what looked to be defeat, the boy refused to believe it could be over just like that.

"Well there must be something else that can be done, Master Sage," he fumbled. "What about this staff that Alberic defeated the Ancients with in the first place? He said you had the power to use it." Revond was silent for a moment at this, seemingly searching for the words to respond. Staring into space before him, he finally did.

"The Staff of the Ancients will do us no good, Aeric," he answered. "It was destroyed nearly forty years ago by a foolish and impulsive Maven who lacked the foresight to see its importance. It was broken in two and its fragments discarded in the fields outside of Galantia. The staff has been lost to time." Though cringing at the hidden truth of the entire story behind the destruction of the staff, the sage forced his mind back to the matter at hand and looked back at the boy. "Both of Alberic's safeguards to prevent the Ascension are gone."

"Well if there was no hope from the beginning why did Alberic give me the Source of Light in the first place?" Aeric grilled. "Why would he bother to warn us if we were already doomed?"

"I'm not sure how Alberic knew of you or why he was looking for you specifically, Aeric," Revond started, "but as he told us in his writings, he could not have know the Staff of the Ancients was destroyed or the last of the Elemental Warriors was dead. I'm sure he merely wanted someone he could trust to get the Source of Light out of the reach of the Ancients, maybe even for me to anoint you as a Warrior of Light like those in the beginning of the order. Whatever his purpose was, it will not come to fruition with his safeguards already vanished."

"Wait," was the teary voice of Mina, suddenly pulling her head off of Aeric's shoulder to turn it to Revond. "What about all this power that Alberic was talking about in other lands? What if we could find more of that power like he did? What if we made a new Staff of the Ancients? We only read the first chapter of his book—maybe there is more information that could help us." Revond exhaled slowly at this, again choosing his words carefully.

"I fear that now, with this doom already upon us, it is too late to travel to uncharted lands far beyond our shores in search of otherworldly power as Alberic did," he told her softly. Seeing the tears well in her eyes once more and realizing it was the only hope they had left, however, he nodded. "But it is worth looking, isn't it? Perhaps there is more that could be of aid to us." The Master Sage turned slowly, letting his eyes meet with Aeric's as he did. Though only looking into them for a moment, the young Tieloc could see the truth mirrored there that hit him like a hammer as it sank in. It was already over. No matter what they found in the book it would not stop the Ancients from tearing apart the world looking for them.

Attempting to gulp down this truth and stand strong for Mina, the young Tieloc felt himself trembling the same as she, torn between his grief for all he had lost earlier in the day and his disbelief that any of this was happening. There was no opportunity for a quest or the means to avert this doom as his grandfather had in the Days of Destiny—it was just over. Gripped by his fear of this penetrating fact, Aeric felt the threat of what he always worried to be true about him being the weak link in the chain of his courageous family weighing down on his mind. Unlike his courageous grandfather had been when facing the doom of his time, he was powerless—unable to do anything but hide and wait for the fires of apocalypse to claim him. Instead of generating daring ideas or endless determination like his grandfather, all he felt was fear.

Walking back toward the pedestal and the Cebrach book, the Master Sage Revond slowed, his keen senses catching a faraway sound in the night that no other could have detected. Peering out through a window of the small chamber into the calm night sky over the Sage's Valley to listen more carefully, he identified the sound as a familiar whistling of alarm he had heard countless times as a boy. His muscles going tense, the sage rushed to the window to hear the shrill cries of his Sky Sprite partner far over the trees but growing louder by the second. With his adept hearing focused on the small purple dot jetting through the night toward the tower, Revond could make out a few words amid the frantic cries.

"...to the woods! It's on the watchtower! Get out of the tower, Revond!" were the distant but audible screams of the little sprite. Processing them carefully, Revond peered past him toward the old watchtower on the northern edge of the valley. Though nearly invisible against the black night sky, the sage observed a mammoth silhouette standing motionless high above the tree tops—waiting. By now both of the Grandarians had noticed the sage's apparent alarm and were moving around the pedestal to see what had caught his attention.

"What is it, Master Sage?" Mina asked quietly, her heart racing. Shifting his gaze back to Zephyr racing toward their position as fast as his Lift Power would let him soar, the sage merely swallowed hard and spoke calmly.

"We must abandon the tower now," he told them quickly. "They are—" The sage was interrupted by a loud screech from outside in the valley shattering the night silence, immediately followed by the colossal frame of a birdlike creature swooping down out of the sky directly behind Zephyr. Revond's eyes shot open as he recognized the beast as Wyrik, carrying four smaller figures on his back as its duel heads shot forward with clamping jaws for the comparatively minuscule body of Zephyr desperately soaring to get away. Acting before he knew what he was thinking, the Master Sage threw up his hand from inside his robes and willed an intense white light around it. Both Aeric and Mina jumped back in surprise. Waiting a short moment for the white energy to collect into a shining ball underneath his open palm, the sage closed his fingers around it forcing the mystic power to yield from its previous shape into a long shaft of light jutting from either side of his hand. Lifting the rod of light over his shoulder and locking his face with determination, the sage cast his arm forward and heaved the spear out the window at impossible speeds that further shocked the Grandarians, still without a clue of what was happening.

Slicing through the night air, the missile hurtled hundreds of feet in mere seconds toward the rapidly approaching Sky Sprite and Ancients on his tail. Seeing it coming in a split second, Zephyr veered off course from the tower toward the tree tops below, leaving the spear to pierce the space where he had been seconds before and slam into the right skull of Wyrik. Though not stabbing all the way through, the saber of white light remained protruding from the creature's head that screamed in painful unison with the other. It turned on its side in agony, throwing the other Ancients on his back down toward the earth far below. Though the winged beast flailed wildly, Revond knew it would still slam into the tower in mere moments at the rate it was careening forward and wheeled around with his gray robes flying up around him. Yelling at the top of his lungs for Aeric and Mina to run for the door, he extended his open right hand for the Cebrach book on the pedestal, instantly responding by soaring into his hand. Tucking it under his shoulder, Revond pushed the Grandarians forward so all of them stumbled for the doorway to the chamber and the narrow hallway beyond. With his free left hand Revond began lowering the platform hovering in the center of the tower with his telekinetic grip.

"*Jump!*" he bellowed to the two Grandarians in front of him.

"Are you crazy?" Aeric yelled, observing the platform already descending at an alarming rate. He wouldn't have time to argue as the Master Sage pushed them forward again, the momentum forcing the two over the edge toward the falling platform. The moment their feet left the floor of the hallway the three could hear Wyrik's screaming heads smashing through the wall of the tower behind them, obliterating the entire top level of the tower and sending stone rubble hurtling after them. Though most of it slammed across the open expanse of air between the top hallway and the wall across from it, several large chucks of the falling roof and ceiling came down after them as they painfully landed on the stone platform sinking into the lower levels of the tower. Though Revond managed to extend his hands upward upon landing to catch several of the falling debris with his power that would have otherwise crushed them, a few chunks managed to slam through the platform's opposite side, tearing large holes and cutting it almost in half.

Though it took all the concentration the Master Sage could muster to hold off the falling rubble and keep the platform steady at the same time, he knew Wyrik was still smashing its way down the tower and would be within range to clamp its jaws around them in mere moments. Aeric rolled to his side after landing on his chest, desperately scanning for Mina who had landed beside him near the collapsing side of the platform. Though barely able to hear anything in the chaos, her abrupt screams of pain immediately caught his completely attention. Her left leg was pinned under one of the large stones that had not punctured through the platform. Yelling for her to hold on, the boy rose to his feet as quickly as possible and began heaving away the heavy rubble to free her. Though trying to help them as well, the besieged Master Sage could not balance the platform and fend off Wyrik at the same time and was left with no choice but to turn his attention to the beast clawing its way down the shaft, its muscular taloned legs reaching at them.

Wiping away the last of the major rubble from the air above them, the sage dropped his hands to his sides and began casting another spell of mystic energy around them. Though having never had to cast such powerful or destructive spells before, he grit his teeth with resolve, knowing only the most potent of his attacks would have an effect on the mighty beast. When both of his open hands were alight with power,

Revond threw his arms up until slamming into each other along with the passionate energy detonating into a flurry of sharp spears of light. Soaring upward in a storm of white needles, the spears slammed into Wyrik's heads and necks, painfully piercing him over and over.

Screaming out in anguish once again, the Ancient of Wind decided to pull back before the sage could inflict any more pain on his body. It crashed back up the tower to spread its massive wings and lift off into the night air again. With the beast stunned for the moment, Revond let his arms down and spun to Aeric, finally pushing the rubble off of Mina's screaming frame to plummet over the side of the broken platform. He rushed to her side to lift her head and upper body off the stone surface, raising her arm and pulling it behind his back so he could attempt to lift her.

"Is she alright?" the sage asked quickly, panting heavily. Aeric shook his head as a bead of sweat fell from his dirtied face. When he tried to lift her by her back and legs she screamed again, pleading to be put down. Gently but swiftly racing his fingers down her tight brown traveling pants he could feel a bone out of place.

"I think her leg is broken!" the boy returned, spinning around to face the sage, unsure of how he could move her without causing her pain. Desperation on his terrified face, Aeric looked up to see the ceiling of the tower gone, replaced by the starry night sky. He could hear the cries and powerful wing beats of Wyrik circling above. "What are we going to do?" Revond was obviously flustered himself but quickly collected his thoughts and continued pushing the platform down with his mystic grip.

"They are all here but we may have a chance to escape if we can get to the basement," he spoke so quickly his words ran together. "There is a network of hidden passages that run under the tower. If we can reach the forest floor undetected we can call for Nighcress and escape. You'll have to carry her—" The sage was again interrupted as another quake ripped through the tower, this time from beneath them. Dashing to the edge of the broken platform, Revond looked down to find the lowest level cracking and bending upward. Before he could tell the Grandarians to hold on, the entire surface smashed upward, revealing the scaly skull of Vorkoise slowly rising up through the ground with water spilling out on all sides, flooding the first floor.

With a constricting motion of his fingers, Revond halted the descent of the platform, aware they had been cut off. His mind reeling for another idea, he was left with no time when the serpent's jaws spread agape and began overflowing with water. Remembering the last time he had faced Vorkoise as a young man and what this action signaled, he yelled for Aeric to grab Mina and get her off the platform into the hallway across from them. Though imploring that he couldn't move her, the sage barked he must do it if he wanted any of them to live and raised the platform back to the next level above them.

Telling her he was sorry for hurting her as he gathered her in his arms, Aeric took hold of Mina through her screams of pain and turned to carry her off the platform into a torch lit room with rich red carpet and elaborate glass windows. Turning back for the Cebrach book lying on the edge of the levitating platform, Revond again called it to him with his telekinetic grip. Waiting for Aeric and Mina to be safely in the next room before releasing his grip on the platform, he saw the attack from below coming and wheeled around to join them. Leaping off the platform to land in a roll behind the Grandarians, a speeding jet of water came rocketing up through the shaft of the tower, smashing what was left of the platform and heaving it into the night air.

Turning to observe the wall of rising water mere feet behind him, the sage rose again and yelled for Aeric to keep going into the room down the hallway to his right. Aeric did as he was bid but found it difficult to hold Mina amid the constant earthquakes. Racing past a stained glassed window he had fallen out of nearly forty years ago with Kaylan Tieloc, Revond swallowed hard at the gambit he was about to risk. The Sage's Chasm, the well that contained the enchanted draught of the order, lay in the stone chamber at the end of this hallway. It was a potentially suicidal risk, but it was their only hope.

Though screaming for Aeric to run faster, his words were lost in the crash of the window behind them, shards of stained glass flying around them as they ran. Spinning around with his robes flying up to contend with whatever was responsible, Revond found an enormous brown hand composed of rock racing in after them. Though summoning his mystic power to drive it away, it flew past him with surprising speed to take hold of Aeric and Mina and pull them back toward the window. Hearing the two scream under the pressure of the rock fingers, Revond dropped the Cebrach book and charged a massive wave of power around his right hand to form another white saber, this time slamming it down into the wrist of the rock strewn arm. The fist holding Aeric and Mina opened to drop them at once, flying out of the hallway in apparent pain and further smashing the walls as it fled. Knowing Golthrout would not give up so easy, the sage raced to the window with his arms extended outward. The massive stone giant hung from the side of the tower, its horned head and scarlet eyes fixed on the man who had wounded it. Finding the ledges the rocky minotaur held with its hands and feet to keep it suspended in the air, the Master Sage made grandiose sweeping gestures with his arms and upper body, closing his fingers as if grasping something that wasn't there and heaving it away. In response to his mystic grip, entire ledges and balconies that held the minotaur began to crumble and break off the tower itself, weakening the beast's hold.

While Revond dismantled half the side of the Mystic Tower to send Golthrout plummeting for the plateau below, Aeric managed to roll back to his feet again with his head ringing and spinning from the crashing noise of the attack. Forcing himself to focus, he witnessed half of the hallway split down the middle, sloping down toward the open window. Among the rubble sliding toward the opening stories above the ground was Mina, desperately trying to claw her way back to him. Though ready to run to her aid, he was cut short by a sudden roar from behind him. Spinning around, he observed a deep orange glow building in the stairwell just ahead of the stone chamber beyond. Surprised at how fast the creature within could move, Aeric ducked as the flaming form of Moltar came bursting out of the large stairway, smashing the sides of the doorway as it came. Lunging so hard that it leapt over him completely, Aeric thanked Granis he had ducked and shouted to Revond in warning. Though not finished with Golthrout, the sage wheeled around upon hearing the boy's cry. With just enough time to roll to his side and avoid being pounced upon, he jumped up to his feet at the creature's side, summoning a sloshing white liquid around his hands.

Recognizing the sage's attack from the last time they had clashed, Moltar roared and leapt to his side with a burning paw slashing up for his adversary. Though able to block the brunt of the cat's molten claws with his mystic energy, the sage was struck with force enough to send him flying back across the hallway to land on Aeric, still rushing forward amid the battle to try and get to Mina. With the sage and boy scrambling to get back on their feet and on the opposite side of the hallway, Moltar turned its attention to the girl lying mere feet beside it and sliding toward the window. Looking past Revond's robes as he struggled to rise, Aeric saw the Ancient of Fire descending over her helpless form, raising his claws for her. Though the boy screamed out as loud as he could and fought his way to his feet amid the tremors, she would have been dead if not for the purple bullet smashing through what was left of the window. Wrapping Moltar in a sphere of semitransparent Lift Power as he had before in the Icrene Forest, the miniature form of Zephyr spun around with his feathered hands outstretched to heave the heavy creature out the window, screaming as it fell.

Though relieved for the moment, Aeric was again horrified to see the ground under his love's body crumbling for good and her helpless form sliding toward the puncture in the tower wall.

"Grab her, Zephyr!" was the powerful order from Revond as he spun Aeric around and pushed him toward the chamber at the end of the hallway once more.

"What are you doing?" Aeric shouted, fighting to push against the sage and rush back to Mina. Grabbing him and heaving him back down the hallway with all his strength, the sage fiercely shouted in his face with blood leaking from his mouth.

"Saving your life!" he bellowed back. "Zephyr has her, now move!" Though unable to run anywhere but further down the hallway with Revond pushing him along, Aeric kept his gaze on Mina's dirtied form and the small creature holding her life in his hands. Zephyr quickly wheeled back after casting Moltar from the tower and focused his Lift Power onto the Grandarian girl, lifting her immobile body from the ground and ferrying her down the collapsing hallway after the two men. Keeping his gaze behind him as he stumbled into the Sage's Chasm, Aeric watched the selfless little sprite dart and dodge her around segments of the falling ceiling.

"Hold on, Mina!" Aeric shouted as Revond pushed him into the chamber toward a large hole in the ground behind them. The girl screamed something back to him but through the chaos of the moment her words were lost. Though they made it almost all the way down the hallway after Revond and Aeric, the two men were dismayed to observe the rocky body of Golthrout reaffirming his grip on the tower outside and spreading its jaws to furiously roar into the hallway. Maneuvering through the falling hallway as fast as he was able, Zephyr still wasn't fast enough to outrun the mighty brown hand crashing down the hallway after them. "Revond, do something!" Aeric yelled with his voice going hoarse.

Though the sage pulled Aeric behind him with one hand while he charged another with an electrified burst of white energy, they were both surprised to hear the wall behind them suddenly break free with rubble falling into the room around them. Entire segments of the wall fell into the Sage's Chasm itself, vaporized the moment they touched the shimmering but volatile white liquid. Forced to use his power to hold the onslaught of falling stones from crushing Aeric and himself, the Grandarian boy watched in agony as Golthrout's thick hand snatched both Zephyr and Mina, trapping them inside as it quickly withdrew. Besieged from all angles with Golthrout behind them and Wyrik blasting through the wall in front, Revond grit his teeth and turned his head to watch his partner and the girl disappear into the night.

The sage's chaotic environment seemed to slow and dim to slurring colors and faint noise for a moment as he realized the world was caving in around them and there was nothing more he could do to stave off disaster. Revond set his eyes on the boy reaching out down the hallway, the veins in his neck tense from his screaming. In his moment of pause, the Master Sage knew the two of them were the last chance for the world and their last chance to survive was that moment. The chasm full of the white draught beside them was their last hope. As a stinging bead of sweat dropped into his eye from his tense brow, Revond felt time accelerate to full speed again and acted as fast as he could.

Seeing Aeric about to charge back down the crumbling hallway after Mina, the sage summoned every pocket of strength he had left and threw the rubble he held back flying into Wyrik's body as it emerged through the wall, pelting him with blow after blow of the heavy rocks. With the Ancient of Wind stunned for precious seconds, Revond wheeled around to grab Aeric and hoist him off his feet into his arms. Though the boy cried to be released while tears streamed down his cheeks, the sage merely wrapped his robes around him and leapt off the floor of the room into the open Sage's Chasm for the brilliantly shimmering liquid contained within. A barely visible layer of mystic energy surrounding them both as they fell, the two plunged into the liquid with a mighty splash that sent the draught flying up around the stone walls of the chasm. As the two disappeared beneath the surface, it slowly fell silent again while half of the tower around them came crashing down in the night.

Part Two
Apocalypse

Chapter 12

<u>Emergence</u>

What remained of the chamber containing the Sage's Chasm was dead quiet as it had been for centuries under the careful watch of the Mystic Sages. Only they and a rare handful of their allies had ever seen or heard of the enchanted draught entombed within the tower, as its mysterious power aside from that of the six elemental energies of the world was too potent for any others to behold. It was said the sages had derived the essence of their mystic strength from the well of the draught and had transfused its harvested energy into their beings such that their souls could communicate with other sages through the draught even after their deaths. A mere glance at the shimmering white liquid from a mortal being could sap days off of its life; touching it would incinerate anything not protected by a variant of its power. This famed myth commonly whispered by the people of Windrun that lived around the Sage's Valley had been proven true during the attack on the Mystic Tower by the Ancients, as massive segments of rubble from the tower walls had been blown free to plummet into the draught and vanish to oblivion upon splashing into the white surface of the liquid. The draught was perhaps the most volatile and dangerous substance ever discovered anywhere in the world, though even the sages were unsure of its origins.

It was this shining white liquid, usually lying perfectly still and undisturbed within the protection of the massive tower, that suddenly rippled and gave way to a single hand rising out of it to latch on to one of the stones along the circular wall of the chasm. Though concealed underneath a dark blue glove as it fiercely gripped for a hold above the surface of the rippling liquid, the muscles inside flexed as they struggled to hoist up the heavy mass they were attached to. After splashing more of the white draught up while the hand reached higher to grasp another stone, a forearm emerged from under the surface as well. It was faintly covered in a semitransparent veil of energy that the Sage's Draught quickly slid off without touching the vulnerable matter underneath. With moments ticking by and the nearly invisible layer of energy slowly dissipating, the fingers of the gloved hand suddenly tightened to the point of digging into the dark obsidian stone making up the walls of the chasm. Immediately after the forearm flexed with all its might, it heaved two figures up through the splashing draught to sail dozens of feet upward to the rim of the chasm.

Latching onto it with his free right hand, the greyly cloaked Master Sage Revond gasped for breath from exerting so much mystic energy to leap the incredible distance while holding on to the young man in his other arm. Grunting and gritting his teeth, Revond lifted the coughing form of Aeric Tieloc up from beside him to gently toss him above his head and over the side of the chasm onto the floor beyond. With both arms free, the sage gripped the rim of the chasm with either hand and crouched on the vertical wall he hung from. Mustering the remaining strength in his legs he kicked off the obsidian wall with such strength that he flipped over the ledge. Spinning full circle as he flung himself out of the Sage's Chasm, Revond landed on his feet and hands in a crouch over the fragmented stone ground beside Aeric. Both still breathed heavily from the exhaustion of the battle they had just escaped and the effects of the incredible risk the sage had taken to allow them to do so.

As the moments slowly passed, Revond at last forced himself to control his fatigue and racing heart to quiet his mind and mentally will away the fading semitransparent energy around both of their bodies. With his mystic power sealed away once more, the sage quickly turned to the coughing and shuddering boy beside him, his body in apparent shock. Flipping back the concealing gray hood that hid his face, Revond hurriedly propped the boy up by his back and told him to breath. Though Aeric couldn't feel his own body for several long moments, at last the sensation slowly returned and his fierce coughing began to subside. Revond watched as his eyes slowly opened to reveal bloodshot red streaks as if they had been burned. Giving the boy another moment to recuperate from what he had just put him through and the severe effects it had taken on his body, the Master Sage pulled him toward a large chuck of debris that had been blown off the wall of the chamber to rest against. Watching the Grandarian shudder and look around as if lost, Revond set a hand over the boy's shoulder.

"Aeric, listen to me," he cooed gently. "You must try to breathe easy and relax your body. If you don't settle down and rest you could fall into a seizure or sleep from which you may never wake. You must calm down." Though the Grandarian's eyes sporadically shot back and forth as if lost in a frightening disorientation, he could see Aeric taking in his words and slowly relaxing. Eventually, the boy swallowed the excess saliva drooling from his mouth but violently shuddered as if a painful jolt of cold had rushed up his back.

"Mina..." he spoke, looking around again. Seeing the young Tieloc still not aware of where he was or what had happened, Revond leaned directly in front of his face and fixed his eyes on the other's.

"Aeric, you are in the Mystic Tower," he said sternly. "You are safe with me for now but your body is struggling to cope with your time in the draught. Do you remember?" Hearing this, Aeric finally ceased his shuddering and forced himself to try and summon his most recent memories. When his eyes passed the rubble strewn across what was left of the floor he lay on, his searching eyes at last went placid, fixed on something behind the sage. Observing him staring at something with his mouth slipping open, Revond slowly turned to find what had occupied his attention. Seeing it himself, the sage's brow furrowed and he slowly rose from beside Aeric to stand full length and survey more of the horrible view behind them.

Though having barely noticed his surroundings after emerging from the Sage's Draught and seeing to Aeric, Revond was awestruck to find the rest of the tower that had once stood around and above them completely vanished. All that was left of the smashed chamber that held the chasm was the little floor they stood on strewn with debris and dust. Beyond where the hallway and stairwell had once been was only open air, revealing a far more terrible sight beyond the decimated tower. Unable to believe what he was seeing, the Master Sage slowly walked through the rubble to the edge of the floor and the dark atmosphere that lay beyond. Revond's eyes widened as he swept his gaze from left to right, scanning far into the horizon to the edge of the valley around them.

It had been laid to waste.

The entire Sage's Valley was utterly devastated. The once thick forest at the base of the plateau the tower stood on was all but gone, replaced by a few sparse tree trunks jutting up from the scorched black earth. The ground and the hills in the distance were still smoldering from recently burning fires with smoke still rising from beyond the valley's borders. The atmosphere was just as dark. Though it looked to be day, thick rolling clouds hung over the otherwise stagnant sky painting the world in the shadows of night. There was no sound; no sign of life anywhere. Casting his gaze down over the side of the edge of the crumbling stone at his feet, Revond saw the plateau beneath them covered in huge piles of stone rubble, furniture, and ripped pages from the books of the libraries scattered across the ground in a heap of destruction. Most of the Mystic Tower lay beneath his feet in ruins.

So caught up in the carnage before him, Revond never heard Aeric rise from the rubble to weakly stand, sweeping his horrified gaze around the valley to find it devoid of life as far as he could see. With his breathing quickening again and sweat rolling down his forehead, the boy shook his head in disbelief any of this could be real. His fears coming full circle to one thing, the boy forced himself to find his voice and speak at the robed figured motionless in front of him.

"Where's Mina?" he managed to utter, bringing Revond out of his trancelike state. The sage swallowed hard but kept his gaze out on the desolated world around him.

"Have I already failed so quickly?" he whispered to himself. "All in one flash of hatred... everything is undone..."

"Where is Mina?" Aeric asked again, finding his voice and its volume. Hearing the boy trying to take a step forward, the sage forced himself to turn and face him. He could see the emotion ready to burst from the Grandarian's face and knew he remembered what had happened.

"We were... lucky to escape with our own lives, Aeric," the sage returned softly. Aeric was still at this for a long moment, letting the dead silence over the entire valley hang as if he couldn't comprehend the words. Shaking his head, he felt a tear stream down his face.

"Where is she, Revond?" the boy pressed, ignoring the vague answer in hopes a clearer one would yield a more favorable answer. Revond merely exhaled sharply and shook his head.

"Mina is gone, young Tieloc," he responded blankly. "You saw as well as I what happened to her and Zephyr. I am very sorry." Aeric's face was flush with color by now and he was already shaking his head in rejection of the sage's words before he was finished with them.

"You don't know that," he said angrily. "She could still be... somewhere... Where are the Ancients? They had her— maybe they took her with them like they took Alberic!"

"Aeric, I told you that you must remain calm until you can get some rest or your body may react to the draught in an ill fashion," Revond told him, trying to veer him away from thoughts of Mina. The Grandarian completely ignored him.

"We have to go after her," Aeric pressed at once. "We were only gone for a few minutes. They can't have gotten far." Revond let out a sharp breath and stepped forward to stare the boy down.

"Aeric, you saw the Ancients destroy Galantia yourself," he reminded him. "You know those creatures leave none alive, and we may have been gone far longer than a few moments. My intent here is not to be cruel, my young friend, but I guarantee Mina is dead. If Zephyr had managed to save her and himself I would sense my friend nearby on his way to us by now. They are both gone." Aeric eyes acquired a fresh layer of salty water over them as he swept his gaze around the charred Sage's Valley, desperately trying to come up with a way she could still be alive that the sage had not thought of. Though about to suggest they couldn't know for sure, the Grandarian remembered the guarantee of her death came from the Master Sage himself. Tightly sealing his eyes and fighting back the sorrow threatening to overflow out of his sinking heart, the boy suddenly grit his teeth and locked his irate eyes on Revond.

"This is your fault!" he exclaimed, channeling his grief into rage to avoid feeling the true emotion in his heart. He took a step toward the sage with an accusing finger pointed at his face. "I was trying to reach her down the hallway but you pulled me back! I could have saved her! *You* could have saved her!"

"If I had let you go you would have met the same fate," Revond responded, growing frustrated himself. "We were besieged from all angles and if we didn't retreat when we did we would both be dead now—"

"I never asked for your help, sage!" the boy screamed, to which Revond started striding toward him. "She needed me! She was innocent in all this! She had nothing to do with your damn Order of Alberic or your war with these Ancients! This isn't our fight—" The boy was stopped by Revond shooting his hand up to the boy's neck to tightly grab hold and drop him to his knees, forcing him to stop shouting.

"I'll spell it out for you, Aeric. Calm down or you could die from shock," he stated harshly. Aeric reached up to try and pry Revond's fingers away from his neck but even at his strongest he could never have loosened the powerful sage's grip. Seeing the boy struggle, Revond softened and said something else. "Do not make the mistake of thinking you are the only one between us who just lost the most important person in his life." Aeric gradually stopped struggling at this, his tear-filled blue eyes meeting with Revond's which he noticed for the first time were also moist. Losing himself in his emotions, the Grandarian let his arms limply drop to his sides and he began to cry. Seeing Aeric calm down, Revond gently released him and let him fall to rest on his knees through his sobbing tears. The two remained on the tower for several long minutes while Aeric cried, cursing himself for not being there for his love when she needed him most. Though consumed by his sorrow, after turning to see the powerful Master Sage wiping away a tear of his own, Aeric forced himself to hold back his emotions and make sense of the incessant madness that had befallen them since the attack on the Mystic Tower. Managing to curtail his crying to soft weeping and wiping his tearstained cheeks with the sleeves of his ripped and dirtied blue tunic, he took a deep breath and summoned his voice once more.

"What happened?" was all he could think to ask. "How did we survive?" Choking down his own grief, Revond shifted in his robes and resisted the urge to collapse on a chunk of rubble, standing tall.

"I'm sure you've heard stories from your grandfather about Zeroan and the enchanted draught that kept him alive for over five centuries," he started, catching Aeric off guard. "That draught is the source to the power of the Order of Alberic. It was passed down that Alberic himself discovered it and filled a chasm in the Mystic Tower with it before the founding of the order. Though dangerous and unstable beyond measure in its raw state, he developed a means to harvest the energy it radiates for our use, perhaps with the Staff of the Ancients. In light of recent revelations from Alberic himself I can't attest to the validity of this story now, but the draught has remained in the Sage's Chasm for millennia. In its raw liquid state it is so potent that normal matter would be incinerated with a mere touch, but as my power stems from the draught itself I was able to wrap us in a cocoon of protective energy that shielded us, or rather, you, from its energy. The Ancients obviously knew what it was as they did not dare to follow us in or attempt to destroy the chasm to force us out, for even they would have been seared by the draught. It was a great risk for me to do what I did because only Master Sages have ever been submerged in the liquid, but we were left with no other alternative." Aeric held the sage's gaze for a long moment, soaking in the story. At last he spoke again through his tears.

"What was the risk?" he asked confused. "And what did you mean I could die if I don't calm down?" Revond peered over at the glowing walls of the chasm behind Aeric before responding.

"As I said, there has never been one besides a Master Sage to be submerged in our draught," he repeated. "To be honest I wasn't sure what would happen to you. Though confident I could shield you from being destroyed with my power, as it seems I managed to do, I was not sure if you would come out alive or what effect the emanating strength of the draught would have on your body. Seeing as you would have been killed anyway if we didn't jump in, I decided it was a risk worth taking. You appear to be fine, but you will feel ill until your body rests and flushes the radiation out of your system. I am sorry, but I imagine this experience probably cut several years off the end of your life. The emanating effect of the draught is extreme. I wish there had been another way that we all could have escaped unscathed, but under the circumstances it is truly a miracle the two of us survived at all."

Aeric kept his eyes locked on the Master Sage for another long moment in the silence but eventually stared into the space between them. He couldn't believe any of this. First Galantia had been destroyed in front of him with his parents inside, now his one true love—the joy of his life and meaning to it—was gone. With this truth pounding through him threatening to rip his soul in half inside him, he wished Revond hadn't saved him. He had no desire to live anymore. Not without Mina.

Amazed at the destructive power of a group of only five creatures most believed existed only in myth, it was all the beleaguered Grandarian could do to stare out at the smoldering fields of the Sage's Valley wondering how it was possible for his life to fall apart in front of him like this.

"So why aren't they here to kill us now?" the boy asked sullenly. "Where are they?" Revond took another deep breath before squinting his eyes out onto the horizon, taking a moment to confirm what he guessed would be the answer to his question.

"More time may have elapsed for the Ancients to achieve this destruction than you know, Aeric," the sage responded at last. "There is another element to our escape into the Sage's Draught that I counted on to ensure our survival. Time is a fluctuating force within the draught. As you already know, one of its functions is to delay the passing of time on a body that wields its power when it is consumed slowly. I have spent time beneath the surface of this chasm before for what felt like years to me when only minutes transpired on the mortal plane. It's too complicated to explain this with any detail, but by using my power within the liquid to protect you, we may have altered this effect and experienced time slower than the rest of the world outside. I'm not sure if this is the case or not because this was only a theory of sages long since passed, but looking around the valley I'd say it is possible we have been gone longer than the few minutes we perceived to pass in the draught."

"How long could we have been away?" Aeric asked, to which Revond blew a breath through his shut lips and shrugged.

"Days; possibly even weeks," he guessed out loud. "I can't say for certain as this has never happened before. Obviously enough time passed that the Ancients grew tired of waiting for us to reemerge." Aeric looked back at the glowing chasm behind him at this, wonder and perplexity tearing through his thoughts at what the incredible Sage's Draught truly was or how it could do something as amazing as slow the passing of time. Deciding more pressing matters warranted his attention as the warm sensation of fresh blood spreading down the skin on his right arm brought him to his senses, the overwhelmed boy turned back to face the Master Sage staring at him.

"Then what do we do now?" he asked hopelessly. Though uncertain of that answer himself with the desperate circumstances before them, the sage focused and objectified the situation as he would any.

"Despite our extreme losses, we take measure of what we have left," he answered as confidently as he was able. "Aeric, if you look under your tunic on your chest, you will see we still have something of great value that we should thank Granis did not fall into the possession of the Ancients." Looking down through his tears to his chest to see what Revond was talking about, he noticed a faintly glowing light underneath his tunic. Reaching to the chain around his neck, he pulled it up to reveal the white medallion that contained the ever shining Source of Light within. "If the Ancients had taken that from you the situation we now face would be all the graver. As we learned from Alberic's writings before the Ancients found us, if they were to assemble all six of the Sources they could create power that rivals that of the Holy Emerald itself. Our first priority now must be to keep that medallion out of their grasp."

"What about the rest of Grandaria, Revond?" Aeric questioned. "What about the rest of Iairia for that matter? Those things are still out there looking for this. What are you going to do to stop them?" This was a question the Master Sage had no clue how to answer, and Aeric could see it on his face as the moments passed in silence.

"Considering all that has befallen us in the past few days, I think for now it is all we can do to concentrate on our own survival, young Tieloc," Revond responded at last. "I can sense the Ancients abroad using their power so we will have warning should they approach, but for now it appears we are safe. If they return, though, I do not wish be caught on this decimated tower with you virtually poisoned by the Sage's Draught and my strength nearly exhausted. For now, let's make our way to the valley floor. I need to salvage what I can from the ruins of the Mystic Tower. After that we have a journey ahead of us to see what fate has befallen Windrun and the rest of the world. From there we can make further plans." Though this answer sounded to Aeric like Revond's way of giving him false hope that there was in fact something they could do to stop the onslaught of the Ancients when in reality they were powerless, the Grandarian boy had no reason not to trust the sage. There was no one else he had left to trust. Though continuing on seemed pointless to him now, Aeric slowly nodded and rose to his feet, suppressing his tears. If there was any hope Mina was somehow still alive, that was all the reason he needed to stand and follow Revond off the tower, he thought. If they were doomed to die along with the rest of Iairia then at least he would find Mina in the next world and be free the misery this one had heaped upon him.

Helping the ailing Grandarian boy to his feet and directing him to the edge of the stone floor on the annihilated Mystic Tower, Revond cast his gloved hand down to the overhang they stood on and spread his fingers to seize it in his mystic grip. Clenching his fingers together as if grasping a ball in his palm, the Master Sage broke the overhang from the rest of the floor and levitated it away from the tower to slowly descend through the stagnant air to the plateau beneath them. The farther away from the remains of the Mystic Tower they floated, the more the two cringed at how it had been torn to pieces. Half of the tower lay in rubble around its base and the other half that still stood had been slashed and blasted apart nearly to the point of toppling over. On the way down Aeric felt his stomach twist and he leaned over the side of the levitating stone to vomit into the air, obviously caught in the sickness Revond had warned him about from exposure to the Sage's Draught. It felt like his insides had been shaken apart and every inch of his body was bruised to the bones.

Though struggling to keep hold of both Aeric and the platform, Revond at last brought them safely to the scorched forest floor around the outskirts of the largest debris from the tower. The stone they stood on landed diagonally over the ground nearly causing Aeric to lose his balance but the sage kept him standing and slowly lowered him to the steady earth. Telling the young man to remain there and lie down to get some sleep, he temporarily left to wade back into the rubble of the tower and search for anything they could use. Most importantly, Revond told him he had lost hold of the Cebrach book during the attack on the tower and had to try and find it. Though he feared it destroyed, he remembered there might be more information within its pages that could help them face the Ancients and deemed it too important not to at least check. Telling him he would not be far off, the Master Sage navigated the rubble back toward the plateau of the tower and began sifting through the crumbled stone with his mystic power, carefully checking as much as he could for supplies that could be of use to them.

Though Aeric sat with his back against a boulder in the earth for several long minutes while the sage began his search, the boy knew he would not be able to fall asleep. He felt nauseous and beaten, not to mention that he was still bleeding from dozens of cuts across his body despite the cloth pressed against them he and Revond had applied a few minutes before. His black hair was a tangled mess, dirtied like his attire. Between the bloodstains, rips, and frayed ends of his tunic and brown traveling pants, it looked like he had just been trampled by a stampede. As soon as he was alone with his thoughts, he couldn't help but start crying again. Memories of Mina and the horrible end she must have faced would not leave his mind. He was too afraid to fall asleep knowing the nightmares about her death that he might conjure up. He couldn't bear the thought of her suffering or her absence from his life. It was as if the best part of his soul had been ripped from him and he was forced to continue on in an empty shell of his former self. He felt as devoid of life as the world around him.

Struggling to deal with the reality that he was alone in a doomed world with only the faint hope the Mystic Sage behind him could find a clue to their salvation buried underneath hundreds of tons of stone debris, Aeric tried to numb his tormented mind by staring out at the burned ground ahead of him. Sweeping his gaze past a row of scalded and heaved up trees to his left, the young man's eyes fixed on something he hadn't noticed before. He could barely make out a small fire burning behind a felled tree trunk closer to the plateau and the tower. Slowly sitting up to peer at it further, he wondered how it could still be ablaze when the rest of the Sage's Valley was as dead and burnt as it was. Rising, Aeric slowly fumbled down what was once a path through the trees of the forest closer to the fire not twenty yards away. Getting closer, he tilted his head in confusion. The fire was lit over a collection of organized dry logs and twigs, obviously not burning from the fires of the Ancients. Wary, the boy turned back to the tower to raise his voice to Revond as the sage cast aside the remains of a wooden bookcase with the flick of his wrist.

"Revond, I think someone was just here!" he shouted, catching the sage's attention. Revond turned from the rubble at the base of the plateau and found Aeric standing thirty feet behind him.

"What did you see?" he returned, stiffening with suspicion.

"There's a fire here still burning," he returned. "It's manmade." Revond narrowed his eyes at this, sweeping his gaze around the surrounding ground the boy stood over to spot the fire for himself. Silently agreeing that it must have been built by someone not long ago to still be cracking with embers, the sage failed to notice the swift movement from behind a massive section of a wall next to Aeric until it was too late. Before he knew what it was, Aeric felt the sharp tip of steel suddenly press against his neck and an arm take hold of him from behind. Though still hard pressed to stand, he went stiff and looked down to find a chipped dagger against his vulnerable skin.

"What have we here?" was the rhetorical question from a voice directly behind him, speaking just below a steady shout. "A robed figure and what looks to be a bloodied Grandarian lad digging for buried treasure in what's left of the sages' tower. Sounds like converts up to no good to me."

"Wait!" Revond shouted as he slowly raised his hands disarmingly. "Do not hurt the boy. We don't want any trouble."

"Well that's precisely what you're looking for when you venture out of your little shrine to do your masters' bidding and cross paths with a free man, convert," he snapped sharply. "What errand have they sent you on this time? Pilfer what power you can from the Mystic Tower for your masters to absorb? You know, I never get tired of cutting you sycophantic slavers down but you take the fun out of it when you show up half dead already." Revond was confused at his words, having never heard of this "convert" term with which they were being labeled. Observing the long blue scarf around the man's neck the sage could surmise what he was.

"Listen to me, Maven—you have mistaken us with another party," he said, slowly working his way down through the rubble closer to Aeric and the attacker. "I am Master Sage Revond of the Order of Alberic and that young man is a mere Grandarian lad." The dark expression on the Maven's face was suddenly swept away with melodramatic surprise.

136

"Oh, you're a Mystic Sage now!" he returned in a mocking tone. "And here I thought you had all been dead for near sixty years!" The Maven's face tightened again and he drew his dagger tighter against Aeric's neck. "It amazes me how dull you converts are after just a few months of becoming their lapdog pets. The sages have been gone since well before the Ascension and as you can see, their tower was the first thing to be destroyed in the fires. If you want to fool someone make sure they're a fool before you try. And if you take one more step closer I'll open your Grandarian's throat." Revond halted immediately, again raising his hands defensively.

"I tell you, man," he began locking his eyes onto the Maven's now only several yards away, "I am who I say I am. If you would but lower your knife I can give you proof—"

"Sorry, but you know as well as I the time for trusting other people went out the door a long time ago in this world," the Maven interrupted. "When you sell your soul to Dalorosk it might as well be to Drakkan. Give him my regards when you show up in the Netherworld, scum." Sensing the Maven about to pull his blade along Aeric's neck, Revond's already raised hand clutched its fingers into the air, taking hold of the dagger and yanking it out of the Maven's hand with his mystic grip. Before the Maven could so much as raise his eyebrows in bewilderment, the sage's other hand shot forward with fingers pointing at his head to send him flying away from Aeric and onto his back over the black earth. Free at last, Aeric took a deep breath of relief and fell to his knees with his balance still wavering. With Aeric's assailant held down under his power, Revond motioned with the sweep of his fingers for the levitating blade to float to the Maven's throat where it had been on Aeric's. Baffled at what was happening, the Maven's incredulous eyes swept up to Revond's now standing directly over him.

"Do you require further proof, Maven?" was the sage's caustic question. Though the Maven's eyes remained wide and stunned for a lingering moment, at last he tried a quirky smile and swallowed hard.

"I think we started our relationship on the wrong foot," he spoke with his suddenly friendly voice cracking nervously. "Maybe we could start over. My name's Erland. Lucan Hauk Erland. A sage wouldn't have any need for a Blue Maven, would you?" Through Revond eyed the man distrustfully, he slowly willed the dagger pressed against the Maven's throat into the air until its hilt landed in his hand for his fingers to wrap around.

"Fortunately for you, my cynical friend," the sage started coldly, "the code of my order does not harbor your doubts of humanity's inherent goodness. Rise." Though staring at the robed figure for a lingering moment, the man gradually turned over on the charred ground to push himself upright and stand, dusting himself off and flinging the long scarf back over his shoulder. Once on his feet, Revond tossed his dagger back at his chest. The flustered Maven caught it with a fumble and tucked it back into a sheath on his brown belt. Seeing the sage return his attacker's weapon, Aeric found his voice again.

"Are you really going to trust someone who was about to try to kill us, Revond?" was his skeptical question. The Maven narrowed his eyes and let out a dry huff.

"Give me a break, kid," he said throwing his hands up. "I've run into my fair share of converts since they started rummaging through the world looking for their prize and that has never ended well for me, so you'll have to pardon my paranoia. I think I'm entitled to some being one of the last free men in Iairia."

"I'm not a kid, and if it's killing you're after I think you're wearing the wrong colored scarf, Maven," Aeric returned harshly, rubbing his neck where the blade had been pressed moments before. Before Erland could respond with a sneer, Revond stepped between them.

"What do you mean you are one of the last free men in Iairia?" the sage queried, his brow raised in confusion. The Maven matched his puzzled expression at this question, unsure of how he could have misunderstood.

"Well I'm certainly not a convert, if that's what you're getting at," he returned defensively. "And I'm a little far south to be part of the resistance, don't you think?" When the sage and the Grandarian merely stared at him clueless, Erland slowly tilted his head to stare at him skeptically. "You have no idea what I'm talking about, do you? Maybe I'm the one who should be asking you who you are and where you've been until recently. I mean, I thought the Mystic Sages have all been dead since the Days of Destiny. Who are you really?" Revond let out a disgruntled breath, seeing the man was growing wary and defensive again.

"It is a long story, Lucan Hauk Erland, but my friend and I may have been gone for longer than we know," he answered vaguely in keeping with the most famous sages that came before him. "How do you know of the Ascension?" Lucan's eyes shot open at this and a quick laugh escaped his mouth before he realized the sage wasn't joking. His face awestruck, the Maven narrowed his eyes.

"You're serious," he stated as if to confirm it for himself. "Who's fool enough... I mean, doesn't know of the Ascension? It's consumed everything. The Ancients left nothing intact or alive from the old world. They've killed or enslaved nearly every person on the continent in their search for the last Source. How could you not know? Where have you been for the last year?" Both Revond and Aeric's eyes burst open at this, staring at the Maven incredulously.

"We've been gone for a year?" Aeric asked to no one in particular, shocked.

"Erland, when did Galantia fall to the Ancients?" Revond asked quickly. The Maven froze for a moment but looked around into the sky as if calculating the answer.

"Well if my memory is right, the sun tables paint the longest day of the year tomorrow, and the Ascension began right after the Festival of Radia in Grandaria, so... almost a year to the day," he answered, still stunned that neither of them knew what he was talking about. Revond froze at this, turning to stare into the charred earth at his feet. They had spent an entire year in the Sage's Draught; it was already over.

The world had already been destroyed.

In a year, creatures as powerful as the Ancients would have time to level and burn Iairia ten times over. The scorched Sage's Valley could only be a preview of what lay beyond.

"Erland," Revond spoke in a whisper, "have you seen the lands beyond here? Is the rest of the world in this condition?" The Maven kept his stare on the sage but sullenly nodded.

"I haven't seen all of it myself since it began," he started, "but trust me when I tell you, sage: everything is destroyed. I haven't even seen the sun in months. The Southland looks more like Drakkaidia these days, and Grandaria..." Aeric shot his head up to the Maven at this.

"Is what?" he pressed, his voice taut.

"Well, Grandaria looks like something else entirely," he answered as if not wanting to impart any more to the obviously distraught young man. Hearing this, Aeric felt a rush of sickness and nausea sweeping up his throat from his stomach again. Losing his balance even on his knees, the boy fell down to bolster his body up by his arms and he threw up again. Seeing his sickness resurface, Revond knew he would be in danger if he didn't get sleep fast. Telling the Maven to wait a moment, the Master Sage picked the boy up and carried him to the softest patch of loose earth he could find beside a row of felled trees and laid him down. Reaching up to the boy's eyes, he spread his fingers and slowly pulled his hand down, sealing them shut as it moved.

"Sleep now, Aeric," the sage told him. "Wake when you are recovered. Try to dream of hope and not of sorrow, my friend." With that, the sage's already soft and echoing words faded and the already dark world fell into complete blackness.

Chapter 13

<u>Dead World</u>

Unfortunately for Aeric, his dreams strayed to what Revond had bid him to avoid. Though he slept for several long hours through the day, he was frequently in a sweat from nightmares about the beastly Ancients engulfing the world in flames along with everything that mattered to him. Gradually worsening and growing more realistic as they drew on, Aeric eventually dreamt he was running down a long tunnel dragging Mina behind him. Though there was a faint light ahead of them, the black form of the behemoth called Dalorosk looming behind in the darkness grew closer by the second. Feeling Mina ripped from his grasp and forced to watch her disappear into the void behind him with only her screams ripping through his mind, he at last came awake. His eyes shot open and he flung his upper body off the ground where he laid, desperately panting for breath. Looking around in terror as if to find Mina before she disappeared in the Ancient's clutches, the young man realized it was only a dream and remembered where he was. The burnt Sage's Valley around him was even darker than the last time he had seen it hours previous, obviously under the veil of night, but was illuminated by a small fire crackling beside him. He was still in his worn clothes but a frayed brown blanket was draped over him to keep him warm in the chilled night.

"They say you can overcome your nightmares with your dreams," came a voice from beside him that prompted Aeric to spin his head around to find a figure sitting on a log to his left, staring back at him with a smile. "I say whoever said that didn't live in a world where the worst nightmare is waking up from one back into reality. Feeling better?" Aeric focused his blurry gaze on the man speaking to recognize him as the Blue Maven he had encountered the last time he was awake. He sat with his back lazily draped over a tree

141

trunk and his legs asymmetrically folded over each other, shaving the stubble on his face with a small dagger. His messy shoulder length brown hair was collected into a bunch behind him so as not to stick to his wet cheeks while he worked. As before, he was dressed in a thick black tunic and gray traveling pants sewn with extra large stitching up the sides. Though not wearing it, there was a thick belt beside him with leather pouches for assorted tools meant to be slung over his shoulder beside his blue scarf.

Grinning as he found Aeric staring at him uncertainly, the man cleared his throat and sat up straight to dip the blade in his hand into a can of water and flick it off before setting it down. Running his fingers along his face to make sure it was evenly smooth with one hand he outstretched the other to the Grandarian beside him. "Lucan Hauk Erland. We met before, remember? In a fashion, at least. Sorry about the whole almost-killing-you greeting, again. I guess you don't really understand where I'm coming from being gone as long as you have, but the world isn't exactly the delightful place you remember." Though still a little confused and taken aback at the man's sarcastic manner, Aeric slowly pulled his arm free from under the blanket on top of him and reached out to shake the Maven's hand.

"I'm Aeric," he replied softly but still breathing hard, obviously still shaken up from his nightmare.

"Glad to know you, Aeric," Lucan replied, releasing his hand. "The sage is out in the darkness somewhere going through the ruins of the Mystic Tower. Left me to watch you until you woke. Here." The Maven thrust a thick leather flask of water at the boy. Aeric took it slowly, unsure if he could trust the man. Seeing him hesitate, Lucan grinned again and leaned back against the trunk behind him while raising his legs to fold them up and set them on a rock, assuring him it was only water. With his mouth as dry as it was, the boy decided to believe him and take a long swig. After pulling it away from his lips and setting it back where the Maven had picked it up, Aeric found the man staring at him as if waiting for something.

"You said Revond is nearby?" the Grandarian asked, breaking the uneasy silence.

"Right over yonder about," he said pointing with one of his hands out into the darkness before setting it behind his head along with the other one. "He's your friend, is he?"

Aeric continued to stare the man down uncomfortably at this, unsure of what he should say, if anything. Seeing the distrustful look in the young man's eyes, Lucan spoke again. "You know, while you were asleep the sage and I worked out an agreement to see if we can't help each other. I'm supposed to be keeping an eye on you and filling in the blanks for you two since you both seem to be oblivious."

"And how are we supposed to help you, since you clearly seem to know more about what's going on than we do?" Aeric returned guardedly, lowering the blanket over his body so he could prepare to rise if he needed to.

"I'm always looking for an opportunity," the Maven responded with a shrug. "They don't come about very often these days. But when someone hears a Mystic Sage has returned after sixty years of extinction anybody's interest would be piqued. A man in my position has a lot to gain from throwing in with someone like the Master Sage himself."

"And what position are you in, exactly?" Aeric grilled. The Maven raised an eyebrow and leaned forward to speak in his physically bombastic manner.

"You know for someone who's living at the hospitality of another at the moment, you aren't the most gracious guy," Lucan recoiled, growing impatient with his skepticism. "Not that I'm the most optimistic and unquestioning person I know, but seeing as I have personally cleaned and wrapped all your cuts, fed and watered you while you thrashed around in your sickness this afternoon, *and* given you my favorite blanket to sleep with tonight, I think you can afford to trust me a little. You could be infected, hungry and cold—not to mention dead. Things could be worse, you know." Though Lucan's words attested to his trustworthiness, the final statement left Aeric cold.

"Things could be worse?" he repeated with quiet ire. "I don't know who you are, Lucan Hauk Erland, but you have no idea what I've been through the past few days. You have no idea what I've lost." The Maven softened at this and slowly brought his hands down to fold over his lap.

"I heard about that, actually," he returned quietly, what sounded like empathy in his voice. He unfastened his brown hair behind his neck from the twine that held it in a bunch and looked around the darkness, searching for the words to elaborate. "The sage told me what happened to you two inside the tower and how you ended up skipping through time to end up here. I'm sorry about your girl." Aeric went silent again at this, his blue eyes drifting down to the fire as another image of his lost love flashed before him. Feeling his sorrow rising up at the mere thought of her, he forced himself to keep talking and push the grief inside.

"You never answered my question," he stated, ignoring the Maven's attempt at sympathy. "Who are you, Lucan? What is a Maven doing in a world as devoid of life as you say it is?" Lucan cocked his head and let out a deep breath.

"The same thing as anyone else I guess," he responded vaguely. "Just trying to stay alive as long as I can. Before I tell you anything about myself you should probably hear... what happened. I already told most of this to Master Sage Revond but I'll give you the padded down story if you want. You know how it starts because apparently you were there to see it. The Ancients, as they call themselves, appeared outside the Elemental Temples across Iairia and destroyed them, stealing the Sources inside. Soon after they joined together to destroy the Temple of Light in Grandaria and take the last Source inside. When it wasn't there they went on rampage and started destroying everything in their path, starting with Galantia. In a matter of days it seemed like the entire world was on fire or crumbling. Most died in the first few weeks..." The Maven stopped there, his words growing distant after he paused as if to decide whether or not to say what was clearly on his mind.

"That's when Terrea and Lauress died. My wife and little girl. I was a Windrun Warrior for years near a village outside of the Empyrean Peaks. Seems like just yesterday Lauress was born there. I remember picking her up for the first time and taking her to the window to hold her in the sunlight. I told her the world would be hers to do anything she wanted." Lucan paused and faintly smiled at the precious memory he rarely had time or occasion to let surface. "She was nearly walking when I was called away from the village after reports came in that Wyrik had escaped from the Empyrean Peaks and was on its way to Windrun City. By the time my regional unit got there Windrun was already in ruins and the warriors dead or scattered to the winds. Like most of us I broke ranks to get back to Terrea and Lauress but... it was too late."

Aeric watched as the usually animated and witty Maven reached up to preclude a tear from falling onto his cleanly shaven cheek, shaking his head and staring into the fire as if he were fine.

"Afterwards, we tried to reorganize and call for the Legion to be assembled but rumors were already coming in that Torrentcia City had been leveled and the wetlands were destroyed. By this time there wasn't much left of anything. We learned that four other beasts similar to Wyrik had emerged and laid waste to everything. Mainland Grandaria had been turned into a crater and they were in no condition to fight back either. The story goes that during the weeks after the Ascension, what was left of the Grandarian army traveled to Drakkaidia led by the Warrior of Light to try and build an army together that could stand up to the Ancients." Aeric froze at this, having believed his father was killed in the first attack on Galantia.

"The Warrior of Light? What happened to him?" the boy pressed quickly. "Is he still alive?"

"Well, Valguard Montrox, the King of Drakkaidia, had survived the attack on Dalastrak and was already on the warpath. He was all too happy to take even the Grandarians in but before they had time to get far they were discovered by the Ancients looking for them in the Valley of Blood. Tieloc and half the Grandarians were already wounded from the attack on Grandaria but did what I never would've thought possible and joined with Drakkaidians in battle. Montrox led the charge and supposedly managed to wound Dalorosk with his supernatural power, but in the end he was crushed along with the entire army. None survived." Aeric felt his heart sink once more, again having to feel the loss of his father after momentary hope of his survival had been restored. Lucan let his body sulk and his tone dampen further as he continued.

"After that there was no power or courage left to stand up to the beasts. Everything was in ruins and most of humanity wiped out, but the Ancients were as furious as ever. After Valguard Montrox's death they spoke to the few left in Grandaria and said they were looking for the Source of Light. Dalorosk and the others had been building some sort of castle atop the ruins of Galantia for a while at that point, and announced it would be the new Holy Shrine where they would keep their Sources. We guessed they were growing desperate after tearing the world apart and still not finding the Source of Light, because Dalorosk himself promised that all who swore allegiance to the Ancients and vowed to help them search for the Source would be allowed to live under their rule." Aeric gulped at this, guessing that Revond had not told the Maven that the Source he kept talking about was right before him in his possession.

"So these are the converts you kept talking about earlier," Aeric remembered, wanting more of the story.

"One and the same," Lucan breathed with disgust. "All the cowards in the world charged out from Grandaria in search of the Source. Along the way they found any refugees of the old world who just wanted to escape Iairia and brought them back to the Holy Shrine to be enslaved. If they refused they would be killed on the spot. It's gruesome…"

"You've seen it?" Aeric asked uncertainly. The Maven gave a single nod, rolling up a sleeve on his shirt. Aeric winced as a he found a strange circular emblem with five dots burned into his skin.

"They brand their new converts. I was one of the lot the first crusade of the slavers found," he answered. "I was scavenging outside of the Windrun outposts further south when hundreds of them descended on us. Most of us died fighting but I was knocked unconscious and the next thing I knew I was being chained up and walking north. I was taken inside the fortress of the shrine and lined up with the rest of the captured. We had to swear allegiance to the Ancients and dedicate our lives to finding the Source of Light or be killed. The first few of us tried to fight free or tell Dalorosk to shove his horned head up his backside, but all of them were hacked to pieces by the converts. When it was time for me to swear or die, I decided living would be in my best interests so I lied through my teeth and swore allegiance. They pair the new converts with masters to test their loyalty when they go out in search of the Source or survivors they can enslave, but neither of them were seasoned warriors and I killed them both once we were out of Grandaria. I ran as fast and hard as I could to be away. That's why I thought you and Revond looked suspicious when I found you. You looked like master and slave. Most of the converts in their little hierarchy were homeless or downtrodden a year ago. It's sick but most of them seem to see their enslavement as a position of power in the 'new world order,' as they like to call it.

"Ever since I've been alone," he continued, his voice reverting back to its impassive and comfortable tone. "I earned my freedom and decided to use it while I have it. I found a weapons cache after I made my way back down to the Empyrean Peaks and became a Maven. I've been scavenging the ruins of the Southland for months now, trying to find other free men still stranded out in this godforsaken world. I help those I can and relay messages back and forth between my few contacts to keep hope alive. I run into a few new faces on occasion but, like me, people are hesitant to dole out trust these days. Keep in mind that most of the people wandering the world in the wide open are disguised converts trying to lure the free into traps." Aeric shook his head as the Maven prodded the fire with a stick to mix the logs and kick up the flames. The Grandarian couldn't believe anyone, especially his proud countrymen, would sell their souls to the evil ambitions of the Ancients just to survive.

"Is the entire world like this?" Aeric asked in disbelief.

"Essentially," he replied. "I've heard rumors of safe houses and underground villages from credible friends here and there but civilization as you knew it is gone. Wanderers like me don't know the locations of the underground communities because if one nosey convert stumbles onto them the Ancients would be there in search of the Source of Light in a second. The most tantalizing rumor is there is a resistance movement in the mountains west of Drakkaidia. It's said that an Elemental Warrior of Darkness, the son of Valguard Montrox, leads them, but even if there is a resistance it isn't like they're in a position to do anything when Valguard Montrox himself fell with a full army behind him. The hope this will ever come to an end is something no one dares to believe, least of all me." He paused again, a seriousness in his eyes not commonly found there. "I thought about giving up after I lost Terrea and Lauress, especially when I had the chance to die in the Holy Shrine, but Terrea was always proud of me for helping people and giving them hope. I may have abandoned it myself, but for her, I keep going. When I find converts I kill them and leave them on display to inspire others to fight. Guess I'd rather see people die standing than live kneeling."

He trailed off then, taking in a deep breath before dropping his smoldering stick into the fire and shrugging, pulling back to set his folded hands behind his head once more and lean on them.

"Anyway that's what the world's come to and who I am," he responded as if to conclude. "At the end of the day I'm just another free man trying to stay alive and do right by my own council for as long as I can. I figure that includes helping you and your friend, especially since that friend is someone as promising as a Mystic Sage. I had about as hard a time swallowing his story as I'm sure you did swallowing mine, but if anyone would know how to help the world, I'd bet my Seir on him."

"Your confidence is appreciated, Lucan, but I suggest saving your currency for more probable and tangible ends," came the low but gentle voice from beyond them in the darkness. While Aeric spun around to where it had come from with fright, Lucan merely shifted his to the approaching silhouette in the darkness and grinned.

"Ah who am I kidding? I don't think anybody has much use for Seir anymore," he joked as the large form of Master Sage Revond appeared to stride around another felled tree on the opposite side of the fire. Upon reaching them he flipped down his gray hood and set his eyes down on the young man lying by the fire, staring up.

"Is your strength somewhat recovered, Aeric?" was his concerned question. Aeric slowly nodded before looking over to Lucan sprawled out on the log he sat on.

"Thanks in large part to you and Lucan, I suppose," he returned, to which the Maven gave him a modest gesture of his hand reaching down from behind his head.

"I already told you, I'm just trying to be a helpful fellow," he responded with a smile, if a bit sarcastically. Revond looked the Grandarian over for a moment before nodding and taking a seat as well on the log behind him. He reached up from inside his flowing robes to pull off his gloves and bring his chilled hands beside the fire.

"Your body looks to have purged the radiation of the Sage's Draught," he observed. "And despite his reserve, our new friend did indeed help expedite the process. We are indebted to you, Lucan Hauk Erland."

"I offered you my services, didn't I?" he said, making light of his contribution. "I'm more concerned to see you come back empty handed." Aeric's eyes drifted back to the sage at this, seeing him take a long breath and slowly nod.

"I'm afraid there was little left intact in the ruins of the tower," he replied at last, obviously disappointed. "While you slept, Aeric, I have been looking under the tons of rubble for any remain of Alberic's Cebrach book that we had been reading before the attack on the tower, apparently an entire year ago. While it may yet be buried somewhere underneath the enormous pile of debris and wreckage, I fear I will never be able to locate it if I have not yet. I unearthed countless stones, shattered pieces of furniture, and sorted through hundreds of torn pages from the books of our libraries, but I recovered no trace of the missing Cebrach book. I fear it may have been destroyed along with most of the tower's artifacts after I relinquished it that night." Aeric felt his heart sink again at this. The book and the remaining knowledge within may have been their only chance to stop the Ancients. With it gone, he knew the powerful but admittedly inexperienced Master Sage had no clue what to do.

"It wouldn't have mattered anyway," the dejected Grandarian spoke, to which the sage eyed him with his brow furrowing. "It's already too late. The world is destroyed. It's already over."

"Perhaps not," Revond replied, causing both men before him to stir with new energy. Seeing he had their attention, he continued slowly. "After my search through the rubble I took a moment to reflect on the top of the tower—to take measure of what we have left." The sage looked at Aeric, reminding him of what he had said earlier in an effort to instill hope through his abundant despair. "After hours of delving through all the knowledge I have absorbed in the long years of my training to become the Master Sage, searching for any possible means by which we could retaliate against this onslaught, I arrived at the only conclusion I could think of. It is true, Aeric, that much has been lost. And while there is no known power left that can be wielded against the Ancients and the bulk of civilization has fallen before their attack, the world still exists along with great power. There may yet be another way that we can stop this fire from consuming all life across the world and eventually undo the damage that has been done."

"Do you know a way to defeat the Ancients?" Lucan asked for both Aeric and himself, impatiently waiting for him to elaborate.

"I do not," he admitted, "but there is one who might."

"Who?" Aeric pressed. Revond took a deep breath and readied himself for the long conversation to ensue after his answer.

"Alberic," the sage responded plainly. Aeric froze at this, his face cringing with skepticism.

"Alberic?" he repeated, discouraged. "Surely he must be dead by now, Revond." The sage shook his head.

"The Ancient of Light and founder of my order still lives," he responded confidently. "The other Ancients are still looking for the Source of Light to fuse it with the others. We can surmise at least this much from the construction of this new Holy Shrine of theirs, modeled after the one that existed in the time of the complete Holy Emerald itself. They will need Alberic alive to bolster the full strength of the Source of Light should they find it. They would not kill him and risk weakening the full extent of the power they seek to control."

"It's true," Lucan concurred. "Dalorosk publicly decreed that someone named Alberic was the first prisoner put into the vast dungeons the converts use under the Holy Shrine."

"While the Elemental Warriors and the Staff of the Ancients may be gone," Revond continued, "if anyone would know a way to restore them or find another way to overcome the Ancients it would be him. He was the one who authored the lost Cebrach book and therefore is aware of its complete contents. He may know another weakness of his brothers' that we could exploit. For the sake of the world, we must find out for certain."

"Umm..." Lucan began, sitting forward with a raised hand, "how are we going to do that when he's under lock and key of Dalorosk himself?"

"We will journey to the Holy Shrine and release him," Revond answered, flooring both the men sitting before him. Lucan remained silent for a long moment but at last faintly smiled and laughed in spite of himself.

"I think you've been stuck in this draught of yours for a little too long, Master Sage," he said glancing at Aeric to see what he made of all this. The Grandarian boy let out a disappointed huff and sulked back against the log before looking up to Revond.

"That's your idea, Revond?" he asked with a touch of frustration in his voice. "Haven't we already lost enough without marching headlong at the Ancients to be killed ourselves?"

"This will not be an end, but a beginning for a world lost in darkness," Revond responded, keeping his calm and composure. "You forget, my young friend, that we still have something of great value hanging around your neck even now that could turn the tide in this struggle." Looking down, Aeric saw the lump in his tunic where the medallion around his neck hung. Slowly grasping the thin chain that held it there, he pulled upward until the white medallion was free to shine its constant light out into the night air. Lucan raised an eyebrow at the glowing object in the young man's hands.

"What is that?" he questioned doubtfully.

"That is the reason Aeric and I were attacked in the Mystic Tower and forced to flee through time in the first place, Lucan," Revond answered. "That is the Source of Light that the Ancients are after." The Maven's already incredulous eyes narrowed at this revelation. He swept his gaze back to the Mystic Sage, finding his momentarily lost voice.

"That little pendant is *the* Source of Light?" he asked suspiciously.

"In a disguised state transformed by Alberic himself before the Ascension began," the sage replied. "The only reason the Ancients could not find the Source of Light since the Ascension is because Aeric has had it with him, given to him by Alberic during the destruction of Galantia. I thought they would realize that Aeric had it with him and would wait for us to reemerge from the Sage's Draught, but apparently they believed we had somehow disappeared and transported elsewhere out of their grasp. This is the only explanation for how they continued searching for the Source across Iairia."

"How will the Source do us any good, Revond?" Aeric asked. "If they find us with it they'll take it and become all-powerful."

"But if we can get to Alberic, we can use its power to rejuvenate him," the sage replied. "And if we have a Source, I can also use it to anoint an Elemental Warrior of Light as was originally intended. You, Aeric, could assume this role. With an Elemental Warrior, Alberic and myself we may be able to change the fate of this world." The Grandarian froze at this, disbelief in his eyes.

"Revond, I'm the last person you want to help you do that," he replied lamely.

"There is already dormant power within your blood, Aeric," Revond reminded him. "If anyone were to take up the title of the Warrior of Light it would be you."

"I'm telling you I can't do it!" the boy suddenly snapped, his anger surprising both Revond and Lucan. Seeing the shock on the sage's face as he stared at him uncertainly, Aeric slouched again. "...I was going to be a carpenter before all this started, Revond. Now... now I'm nothing. I'm not the man my father or grandfather was. I barely even know how to use a sword..." Revond was quiet for a moment, staring at the boy confused. He was surprised to hear such a negative and pitiable response from the offspring of Tavinious Tieloc himself. He knew firsthand the courage of the Tieloc family from his adventure with Kaylan and this was hardly the strength and bravery they were renowned for. Remembering the simple life he led compared to his grandfather before him and the pain he had been subjected to after the loss of everything that mattered in his life, however, the sage was quick to be empathetic and forgive.

"I know you are beleaguered by doubt and torn by your grief, Aeric, but you must remember Alberic gave you that Source for a reason," he told him smoothly. "No one expects you to live up to the legacy of your grandfather, but you have been chosen by fate the same as he was. You know better than I he was reluctant to accept his charge when Zeroan appeared to warm him of the danger of Drakkaidia but he took it up in the end as you must now. You asked me what we can do earlier. This is it. Our only chance to make a difference."

"What difference can we make, Revond?" Aeric returned, tears welling in his eyes again. "Everything's already destroyed. My grandfather had something to fight for. I don't..."

"You are wrong, Aeric," the sage recoiled quickly, struggling to contain his frustration for the boy's pessimistic attitude. "Look to your left. There is free man sitting there still alive and a part of this world. And though their cities may be destroyed and their lives shattered, countless more are alive as well. Do not be so quick to write off the world as doomed. As long as we hold that Source hope is not lost. We are still in a realm full of suffering people who need help. It may be a slim chance but if there is hope we are obligated to try." Aeric sulked all the lower at this. He knew the sage was right and that there was still a world of people desperate for help no matter how broken that world was. It just felt like his was already broken beyond repair. Without Mina all of his convictions and beliefs instilled in him by his family of treading the high path for others seemed meaningless and empty. As his thoughts drifted to his lost love, he cringed again knowing what she would think of him if she were still there. She would be ashamed that he was using her as an excuse not to do what he knew he had to. Keeping his gaze on the dark earth below him, Aeric spoke in a whisper.

"You must think I'm a coward, don't you, Revond?" he asked passively. The sage exhaled and shook his head.

"I think you are a simple man who has suffered much more than you ever should have," he answered. "But whether you were a warrior or carpenter before all this, you know what must be done now and all you need for it is courage. I think you have it buried beneath all your sorrow, and if you look for it you will find it." Aeric brought his tearstained eyes up to the sage and swallowed hard. He knew what he had to do; what Mina would have wanted him to do. Though deciding, there was no fierce determination in his eyes that would have been in his grandfather's, only ambivalence.

"Then I'll go with you to rescue Alberic, Revond," he said slowly. "Whatever I can do to help save what's left of the world, I'll at least try." Revond gave him a single nod before raising a hand to his face to run his fingers down his black beard with a breath of relief.

"That is all anyone can ask of you, Aeric," he returned gratefully. With that, the Master Sage turned to the Blue Maven sitting with eyes wide at the conversation that had unfolded between the two, completely confused at what they were talking about. "Lucan, you offered your services to me when we first met, and Aeric and I are in need of a guide. We are going to the Holy Shrine." The Maven was still for a long moment, staring Revond down with an unfriendly look on his face.

"Good luck," he said unsympathetically, raising a hand to point north. "It's that way." Revond frowned and eyed him judgingly.

"What happened to the fellow just trying to be helpful?" the sage asked, repeating the Maven's own words back to him. "We'll need someone with knowledge of the interior of the Holy Shrine. This is your chance to help." Lucan made an amazed expression on his face and leaned forward to quickly smack his lips and summon the words behind them.

"No, this is a chance to commit suicide," he returned. "What you *need*, among many things, is a miracle. You should be talking to Granis, not a Maven."

"Who was it who said he'd rather die standing than live kneeling?" the sage asked, once again throwing his words back in his face.

"Rushing into certain death is not the solution I had in mind!" the Maven recoiled, already standing to collect his things and be off, having heard all he wanted to from the obviously insane Mystic Sage. "Fighting against the converts when I have the chance is one thing, but the Ancients themselves? Not all of us have supernatural powers, Master Sage."

"You told me you were looking for an opportunity before, Lucan," Revond said, still sitting over the log. "One has found you. You could help us find a way to save this world."

"Well I could do a lot of things," Lucan agreed, grabbing his belt on the ground and hoisting it over his shoulder. "I *could*, climb up what's left of your tower and jump off. I *could* throw myself into a river and drown myself. I *could* stab myself with my own dagger. Hell, I could even make love to the ugliest woman—if you could even call her that—I've ever seen down south traveling with this pack of rangers who... Well, you don't need the details, but the point is just because I *can* do something doesn't mean I want to." Exasperated at the mere notion of what the sage was asking, Lucan dropped the supplies he had gathered and turned to lock his incredulous gaze on him. "I mean, do you realize what the converts would do to me if they found me back in the shrine? I've already been branded—that means they would know I'm a run-away. They'd chop me to bait for Jagged Pike the second they saw me."

"Do you think Aeric risks less by carrying the Source of Light into the heart of our enemies' territory?" the sage questioned calmly.

"Which is why he should be heading the opposite direction of the Holy Shrine too," he explained with his face turning red from frustration. "Look, I vowed I would never set foot in Grandaria again. I didn't escape just so I could walk back in and be butchered by mindless slaves of the Ancients. And think about what you're doing, for Granis' sake! Do you know what will happen if they discover you and the Source? The world really will be over!"

"Do you know what we risk if we don't act to save Alberic?" the sage answered by posing another question. He didn't give Lucan the time to answer. "Nothing. The world will continue on like this under the rule of the Ancients anyway until they destroy it all on their own, which they will. We'd just be letting it die slower." Lucan bit his tongue at this, silently agreeing with the sage on that note. Still convinced what Revond was proposing was suicide, the Maven let out a long breath and put his hands on his sides, shaking his head.

"Well what do you plan to do?" he pressed incredulously. "Barge in to the shrine and demand to be taken to Alberic? Even if we get inside, what chance do you think even you have against all five of those things and the army of converts they have under their feet? Even a Mystic Sage—the Master Sage—isn't enough." Letting the silence hang between them for a moment Revond slowly raised his hand to run his fingers through the dense black beard on his face and slowly turn his eyes to Aeric.

"Aeric, would you please inform our Maven friend of your name," he asked, catching them both off guard. Aeric shot him an uncertain glace before realizing what he was asking. The young man turned his eyes to Lucan, staring at him curiously.

"It's Tieloc," he said, fulfilling the sage's request. "I'm Aeric Tieloc of Eirinor." Lucan raised an eyebrow at this, shooting his eyes back and forth between the Grandarian and the Master Sage.

"...You mean, as in... *the* Tieloc?" he asked puzzled. "The Warrior of Light, Days of Destiny, Tieloc?" Aeric gently nodded his head yes.

"Tavinious Tieloc was my grandfather," he confirmed. Lucan's eyes widened even further and he tilted his head, sweeping his gaze up and down the young man.

"This is the son of Darien Tieloc; the grandson of *the* Tavinious Tieloc?" he asked as if awestruck.

"He is," Revond answered for him. "There is destiny and power in his veins the same as the generations of his family that came before him. He did not obtain the Source of Light by chance. He may not know it himself yet, but this lad has the power to change the world for the better as did his grandfather before him." Lucan Hauk Erland held the sage's gaze for a long moment and then slowly shifted it to Aeric's, searching his eyes as if to confirm the truth for himself. Slowly sitting back down on the scorched tree trunk and nodding, he spoke.

"*The* Tieloc, huh..." he murmured, trailing off as he slowly folded his arms and leaned back. He lowered his head back behind his back and softly groaned into the night air. Flipping it erect once more, he rolled his eyes and blew a blast of air out of the corner of his mouth. Shifting his gaze to Revond and rhythmically patting his knees, he shrugged and spoke. "I'll do it."

Chapter 14

<u>Trio</u>

The unlikely group of three took the rest of the night to rest beside the wreckage of the Mystic Tower, primarily to allow Aeric more time to rest his body and let it recover from the adverse effects of the radiation from the Sage's Draught. By the next morning he felt like himself again and rose to stand full length over the earth where he had slept to stretch his dirtied body, stains of crusted blood breaking apart on his faded blue tunic. Lucan Hauk Erland was again there to greet him when he woke, preparing a meager breakfast over the small fire from the store of supplies he had just scavenged from a nearby destroyed outpost of Windrun City. Aeric was quick to inquire as to the missing Master Sage's whereabouts, to which Lucan replied he was taking a final glance through the rubble of the tower before they left the valley.

Before the Maven would give Aeric any food he had him remove his bloodstained tunic and dressed all his wounds again. Taking off his clothing and bandages from his waist up, the Grandarian observed most of his cuts had begun to heal. The deep one on his arm where Moltar had clawed him had even been stitched closed. Guessing Lucan had mended him while he was out cold the day before, he turned to the Maven to find him throwing a new tunic at him that landed over his head. It was pale blue with a gray layer of heavy cloth over the shoulders and thick stitching similar to Lucan's attire up the sides and sleeves. Before pulling the thick cloth down over his head Aeric dabbed his exposed skin with water and the leaves of a common fern that travelers used to keep their bodies clean and smelling refreshed. With the tunic on he strapped his worn carpenters belt and brown leather gauntlets over his hands, leaving only his fingers exposed from out of the cutoff gloves.

Aeric and Lucan ate breakfast and split the supplies the Maven had gathered on his latest excursion in separate packs to be worn over their backs while they traveled. Though Aeric loaded the pouches on his belt with assortments of the Maven's gear, he was surprised to find Lucan pulling a dagger off the belt on his chest to shove it behind the Grandarian's belt, telling him to keep it close. By the time Aeric had finished cramming his backpack full of rations and the warm blanket Lucan had entrusted him with, the towering silhouette of Revond came lumbering back into their camp, his gray hood down to conceal the bulk of his face as usual. Apparently he had come across no better luck searching for anything of value in the remains of the tower than the day before. Seeing Aeric in good condition once more, he informed them they would be off at once for the north. Though Lucan retained the humor and usual sarcasm that the two had come to identify as normal for the Maven throughout the morning, they could easily see the ambivalence and disbelief of the journey he was about to embark upon through his jumpiness and curtness when he spoke.

Detecting the anxiousness and stress of both of his companions as they smothered the fire and strapped on the packs over their backs, Revond looked into the cloudy morning sky and took a long breath. Both Aeric and Lucan gradually froze and stared at him, seeing him slowly shut his eyes and loosening as if lost in deep thought. Waiting for him to return to his senses, they were surprised to find him remain in his trancelike state and slowly open his mouth to speak.

"I give you no illusions, my friends," he said slowly, "we have lost much. You both know this better than I, having lost your loved ones and entire ways of life. The evil we face is all consuming and perilous beyond belief, as will be our quest to extinguish it. Unlike the heroes who have ventured to save the world before, we enter a plane already ravaged by darkness. There is... an emptiness about the world I have never felt." He paused there, opening his eyes to see the faces of Aeric and Lucan staring at him uncertainly. "But while there is barrenness, I also sense life. I sense it abroad and I see it before me, even in this otherwise devoid valley. Though we have lost much, the three of us have endured, men, and so has Iairia. For the sake of that, I will not give up hope our world may be restored. I've seen willpower overcome impossible odds before. It will be so again. We *can* do this."

Though Aeric still harbored his doubts that they could even get to Grandaria, much less rescue Alberic and find a way to reverse the destruction of Iairia, the young man knew Revond's plan was all he had left and gave a single nod, holding the sage's powerful gaze. Returning the Grandarian's gesture, Revond shifted his eyes to find Lucan staring at him with an eyebrow angled skeptically. Though both he and Aeric waited for the doubtful Maven to respond, he merely gave them both a look that told them his faith in their hopes of success wasn't as steadfast. Eventually though, he smacked his lips and let out a short huff of breath, grinning.

"You had me at death and destruction, Master Sage," he said sarcastically, repositioning his backpack and motioning with his head for them to follow him. "It's a long way to Grandaria. Let's get moving." Swiping a lock of brown hair out of his face, the Maven started forward to the opening at the west end of the valley. Still more than a little unsure of their guide, Aeric shot a quick glace at Revond. Though the sage gave the Grandarian a knowing look, he faintly smiled and nudged the young man forward after him.

Less than an hour after the trio embarked on their rescue mission for Alberic they emerged from the scorched Sage's Valley for the world beyond. Upon seeing more of the ruined landscape Aeric and Revond were sickened at the devastation. Though there had once been thick trees on the road between the Mystic Tower and Windrun territories, all they could see was scorched earth with sparse trunks occasional jutting up from it. The terrain was smoldering in every direction with no sign of life anywhere. The stagnant morning was eerie without the sounds of birds chirping and leaves swaying in the wind the area had once been famous for, being near the Elemental Temple of Wind atop the Empyrean Peaks on the horizon. It truly felt dead.

Darting through the open terrain toward what cover he could find, the Blue Maven leading the group reminded them of the peril lurking in the seemingly lifeless world. Though aware the Master Sage knew more about the Ancients they were aligned against than himself, he was quick to remind the two on their way out of the Sage's Valley to keep their guard up for the converts. Many of the wayward men and women wandering the lands as he did were converts in disguise and they could afford to trust no one. Instructing them to trust his judgment when it came to taking routes to keep them out of harm's way, he informed them he knew of several hidden spots that he found in his flight from Grandaria where they could rest and take refuge.

Once they arrived in the northeast nation, Lucan was less confident he could ensure their safety. He told them the night before that he knew a little of the interior of the shrine being a prisoner inside once, but he had no idea how they would penetrate that far into the fortress. Despite his doubts, Revond assured them both he had a plan for getting into the Holy Shrine that he would reveal once he could survey the structure and acquire more details about the organization of the converted populace inside.

As the group quickly made their way north across the Windrun territories without encountering a sole, they remained quiet throughout the day and stopped to rest only once darkness had set in around the overcast sky. Though Revond had tried to call Nighcress to him the day before to hasten the journey, he did not respond, leading him to believe the Morlan had been killed in the attack on the Mystic Tower. That night Revond left his companions around their small fire to reconnoiter their immediate surroundings. Remembering the stories his grandfather had told him about the enigmatic Zeroan, Aeric guessed he was secretly leaving them like the legendary sage had with his Grandfather Tavin. Zeroan had used the night hours to energize himself with the vial of Sage's Draught that perpetuated his life when consumed in extreme moderation. By themselves, Lucan and Aeric were left to their awkard conversation until they went to bed early. The two trusted each other and got along without crossing, but both were still unsure of the other having just met and been thrown into their journey together.

Lucan put great stock in the Grandarian's potential given his identity but was doubtful how a descendant of Tavinious Tieloc himself could be so unconfident and seemingly fragile even in the face of his recent losses. Aeric was still bemused by the fact that knowledge of his identity alone could persuade the Maven to join them when before he had been so adamant about leaving Revond and himself to their perilous quest on their own. Though Revond had reminded him earlier in the day just how renowned his grandfather's adventures and legacy had become to those even far beyond the borders of his home country, Aeric couldn't see how the mere mention of his famous name could have such influence to one who had never even met anyone by it.

Deciding it was just a testament to how amazing a man his grandfather was, Aeric let it go and focused on his own venture now laid out before him. Though he still felt eclipsed by the shadow of his family's legacy and that he had no business being here, he remembered Mina's words to him in the Hills of Eirinor during their flight from Grandaria. She hadn't wanted this anymore than he did but it had been thrust into his hands whether he liked it or not. If there was any chance of saving Grandaria or their families he owed it to them all to at least try.

Over the next two weeks the party of three silently darted up the desolated lands of the eastern Southland in a similar fashion. While Aeric and Lucan remained uneasy in their travels, nervous of each other and what waited ahead around every turn, Revond was the most disturbed and strained by the situation he found himself in despite his outwardly calm and amiable appearance when around his younger companions. While away from them every night investigating the ravaged new world and consuming the drops of his enchanted Sage's Draught, the sage let the frustration and disbelief he fought to suppress rise out. He saw the state of the world as his personal failure. It was his lack of foresight and clairvoyance to see what was really at work behind the elemental disturbances occurring during the long years of his training that allowed the Ascension to occur unchecked. He was the one who had failed to maintain the Mystic Sage's longest tradition of anointing Elemental Warriors; he was the one who had destroyed the Staff of the Ancients back in his adolescence as the Maven named Edge.

When Revond told Aeric of his vague plan to rescue Alberic in the northern Southland, the Grandarian mentioned that it sounded like he was keeping secrets as Zeroan had from Tavin Tieloc back in the Days of Destiny. Though the Master Sage was quick to retort he was not Zeroan and he had no interest in keeping them out of the loop, he wondered if his failure was because of his differing methods from the legendary sage that preceded him. Long had Revond resented Zeroan and his breed of sage for their concealing ways, having been victim to them himself when Zeroan chose not to reveal the fate awaiting Kaylan Tieloc until after she had met it.

161

Now he couldn't help but think that if Zeroan had been in his place, the legendary sage's wisdom could have somehow averted this dark fate. Zeroan had always been the master tactician that never left any detail to chance no matter how small. Revond, on the other hand, retained his experience from his days as a Maven that ultimately any situation came down to spontaneity and instinct. Trusting himself and his vast skills to come through for him as they always had, he had never been one to plan as far ahead as Zeroan. Zephyr once guessed his days of being so reactive as a Maven had left this imprint on his methods.

Revond knew that if the spirit of Zeroan was still speaking to him he would say that this wasn't of his doing and he could never have seen this hidden doom approaching thanks to Alberic keeping it hidden over the years, but the Master Sage still ultimately faulted himself. Regardless of the differences between the two sages, his inexperience had cost the world and Aeric Tieloc nearly everything. Even with his greater power as the Master Sage he failed to save Mina Garrinal and his own best friend Zephyr when they needed him most. He had been charged by generations of past sages to safeguard the lands against evil, the likes of which that had consumed the world during his watch. Remembering his own words, however, he knew he was still alive and able to fight so it was now up to him to use the little experience he had to try and reclaim the lands for humanity. He hadn't watched Kaylan Tieloc sacrifice herself into the Granic Crystal only to have all she fought for lost.

As they traveled north, Revond noticed another odd trend of his companions: misjudging his powers and assuming he was capable of preposterous feats of magic. Staggered with Lucan's blind faith in the Master Sage simply because he harbored a power he couldn't explain and Aeric's continuous comparisons of him to Zeroan, Revond took the time to impart the nature of the power employed by the Order of Alberic and the Master Sage in particular to help them grasp the reality of his abilities. While Lucan had always thought the sages capable of seeing into the future and projecting their will into others with mere thoughts, Revond explained his skills and knowledge fell somewhere in between the ridiculous notions of power Lucan subscribed to and the constraints of a standard Mystic Sage like Zeroan.

Over the course of a few days he explained how the Sage's Draught worked to give the sages the power to manipulate the universal field of latent elemental energy present in all matter and the sage's supernatural connection to it even in death. Remembering the sage's displays of uncanny power during his struggle with the Ancients in the tower, Aeric was quick to inquire why he had never heard of Zeroan possessing such power. Reminding him that he was the stronger Master Sage chosen before birth by the will of the draught and the past sages comprising its consciousness, he told of the additional power he possessed in the form of the potent energy he could summon and craft called Hallador Might.

Though this combat art that had been long developed by the Master Sages was extremely powerful when mastered, he confessed it was far too weak for combating beasts as powerful as the Ancients when they possessed their Sources to empower them. Explaining that the bulk of the mystic power he possessed was rooted in memorized spells designed to perform a specific action when cast, he told them most were too complicated for those outside of the order to comprehend without years of training and study. Deciding as his grandfather had that the true nature of the Order of Alberic's power was beyond him, Aeric let the subject go and just accepted Revond was an amazing sorcerer beyond even Zeroan.

With all three of the trio driven by their desperation to affect whatever change they could, they continued on to the north until at last coming to the provisional border of Grandaria. Upon reaching this checkpoint Lucan Hauk Erland grew even more nervous about the risk of detection from the hidden danger across the land and took greater measures to lead them to cover and be particularly vigilant when passing across open distances. Unfortunately there were many, as the majority of the surface of the once green fields of Grandaria had been reduced to craters after the Ascension. Aeric in particular was sickened at what had become of his golden land, scorched and blown apart everywhere his grief-stricken eyes strayed. Between the desolation of the terrain and the constantly black skies above, even Revond agreed even Drakkaidia was most likely in better condition.

The group found dried up rivers, entire mountains on the horizon smashed and any remains of towns or villages blown to splinters around the craters where they had once rested. Even Eirinor Village that once lay quietly in its hamlet in the hills was completely vanished as if it had never been. Lucan led them past it toward a small burrow in the ground where his former convert master had led him to rest for a night. Though Aeric wanted to run into the sunken earth where the village once rested to see if anything was left at all, Lucan assured him there wasn't and venturing outside this close to the Holy Shrine was madness. Though he had led them clear of any converts roaming the hills, he implored that there were patrols constantly moving around the proximity of the shrine and they were about to start running into them within the next day. Though their guide was sure they would be caught if they moved any closer to the destroyed Valley of Galantia, Revond remained confident and bade him to lead on when the morning came.

The next morning they embarked into the hills in a soft rain falling from the rolling black billows above them. Aeric was feeling particularly dreary after stepping into a charred patch of earth that morning that gave way and twisted his foot. Though able to walk, it had been an annoyance all day and with the rain beginning to come down in the unseasonably cold atmosphere, it was a miserable trek through the hills. They proceeded on for several hours until Lucan's fears came true and they saw a group of men appear from a ridge in front of them near the end of the Hills of Eirinor. Caught in the wide open with no time to hide, the Maven froze and looked back to the Master Sage still walking forward past him.

"What in the name of Granis are you doing?" he asked in a whisper though still far out of range for the men nearing them to hear. "Where there is a group of converts there are always more nearby." Revond merely kept walking undaunted with Aeric behind him.

"Keep walking behind Aeric. You said yourself we look like master and slave, did you not?" he asked, catching both Lucan and Aeric off guard. "We'll walk right through them." The Maven grimaced and widened his eyes incredulously, his moist scarf flying back in a breeze to stick against his face.

"That's your plan!?!" he returned, filing in behind Aeric and furiously pulling the blue cloth out of his face. "In the circumstances before at the valley I was wary of you but this close to the Holy Shrine you'll never pass for one of them!

You don't know their customs! *This* is how you're going to get us past a city of converts and out again!?!"

"This looks like a suitable opportunity to see if that strategy would be viable," he replied coolly, eyeing up the four figures now pointing at the sage from the ridge as they grew closer. "Let me handle this and we'll be fine." Aeric looked back to shoot Lucan a nervous glace to which the Maven merely bit his tongue and silently cursed under his breath. As Revond led his party up the ridge he found the group ahead of him drawing short swords as they made their way down to meet them. The man in front was draped in a tattered red cloak while the three behind him were strapped in ragged tunics and leather armor. One of them was even chained by the hands. Inhaling a long breath and drumming his fingers along his palms inside his gray robes, Revond narrowed his eyes and readied himself.

"Don't remember ever laying eyes on this mug," the man in red said with his voice soaring through the falling rain. "Where are you coming from with these two maggots?" Revond remained silent until he was only a few yards away and sneered.

"Maggots indeed," he repeated. "I'm not the one abroad with one of mine still bound. Looks to me like that one has treachery in his eyes." The man in red stopped where he was walking, scowled at Revond and shrugged, stabbing his blade into the earth at his feat where he stood to lean on it.

"Don't put any ideas in his head," the convert responded. "That one's still fresh, is all. Took a while to break him—had to take him down into the dungeons to get the job done. But I'd worry about your own fortunes. I'm not the one coming back what looks like empty handed. You know the Black Ancient has ordered the dungeon guard to kill returning soldiers who don't bring back new recruits or the Source."

"Which is why I would not return without something to show for my efforts," Revond responded, not missing a beat. Without turning his gaze from the convert he reached back for Aeric to grip his tunic and violently pull him forward. Shocked, Aeric felt the sage push him away between him and the convert. The man in red raised his eyebrow.

"Why didn't you take him to a stockade post? What, this one surrendered willingly?" he asked doubtfully.

"When faced with the prospect of death you know as well as I how quickly some fold without a fight," the sage continued darkly, amazing both Aeric and Lucan at how convincing his act was. "I hardly require the stockades when—"

"Sir! That one has a remnant!" the unchained man beside the convert in red suddenly shouted, pointing behind Revond to Lucan, who froze where he stood. The master of the converts spun his head around and picked up his sword, scowling as he approached Lucan.

"Well what's this?" he asked to all of them, raising his blade up to the blue scarf around Lucan's neck. "A remnant insignia? What, do you think you're a Maven or something with this scarf?" Thinking quick to contain the situation, Revond made a disarming gesture with his right arm.

"He's a spoiled whelp. I just let him wear it to keep his neck warm—"

"You know the law!" the convert yelled, to which Lucan froze even stiffer. "All remnant signs and emblems from the old world are to be destroyed and the penalty for carrying one is death! For someone I've never seen with a new convert who isn't bound and a slave carrying remnant you're starting to look suspicious, man." By now the slave of the man in red who first noticed the scarf was drawing a short sword along with one of the other two behind him. "I should have all of you killed for allowing this violation to the Ancients' will. Now kill your man for his violation or be counted as a traitor to the new world order yourself." Revond let out a sharp breath before giving the man a single nod. His face going serious like Aeric had seen it before during their escape through the Mystic Tower, he watched as Revond raised his gloved hand to quickly seize the short sword in the convert master's hands, pulling it away from Lucan's neck with the flick of his wrist.

Awestruck, the man watched the blade flip around and jut into his belly under the control of Revond's power. Witnessing the magic display and their master run through by his own blade, the two converts behind Aeric raised their swords and charged for them. Hearing them coming the Master Sage spun around with his hand still outstretched in front of him to pull the sword out of the man in red's gut and send it flying into one of the charging converts. Though seeing his fellow convert knocked off his feat from the force of the blow the other kept charging at the sage, incensed. Keeping his eyes on Revond, he failed to notice Lucan pull a dagger from the belt along his chest to throw it by the blade at him. Spinning through the air and rain it pounded home in his chest. Still falling forward with his blade outstretched, he watched Revond grip onto his tunic and pull him up by it. Throwing his arm to his left, the sage cast the man flying away down the hillside to land with fatal impact over a collection of rocks.

Still standing in place with an incredulous look on his face, Aeric turned around at the sound of the shaking chained convert behind him falling backward on the wet ground. Noticing the final member of the enemy party as well, Lucan leapt toward him, reaching down to pluck his dagger off the ground from where it had fallen when Revond threw the body it slammed into.

"Lucan, wait," was the fast but controlled command from the Master Sage. The Maven stopped short in front of the trembling man as Revond strode up to him to look down on his pitiable form. "You just recently converted to the rule of the Ancients, did you not?" The man didn't respond, not sure what he should say to the man who just killed his master. Seeing his fear, the sage reached down with a fist to spread it open, forcing the cuffs on the man's hand to break open around his wrists. "Take heed, man. You will be spared but flee now and never return to these lands." Motionless for a moment as he gazed up at the robed figure through the rain, the freed man at last nodded and rose, running past the trio and down the ridge into the hills. Watching him flee, Lucan let out a huff of disbelief and shook his head.

"He won't make it far in that state before he's found again," the Maven spoke coldly, shoving his dagger back into a sheath on the belt at his waist.

"The farther away from here he is the better chance he has," Revond replied, looking to Aeric and Lucan. "Are you both alright?" Before Aeric could respond he was fine Lucan was throwing his hands in the air and cursing out loud.

"Alright!?!" he repeated amazed. "Did you think that was going to end any other way? You walked us right into that mess!" Revond shuffled in his robes and remained calm as he responded.

"And yet we would have walked out without incident were it not for your scarf," he answered. "You'll need to hide or discard it for the next time we run into them."

"There's not going to be a next time, you insane sage!" Lucan recoiled, backing away. "This is your plan for rescuing Alberic? Pretending we're converts? We'd never pass ourselves off. Neither of you know the way they are or what to expect, as you clearly demonstrated here."

"While careful planning and perfected contingencies are preferable in normal circumstances, a little improvisation and quick thinking can be equally effective, Lucan Hauk Erland," Revond returned. "My years as a Maven taught me that. If we can fool one we can fool them all, especially in a city teaming with converts. The last place they would expect to find free men is walking through the streets of the Holy Shrine in their midst. We can use this to our advantage to gain entrance and penetrate to Alberic." The sage reached down to point at the shackles he had pried off of the convert from before and lifted them with his mystic grip to Aeric. "Our story is I am the master returning with Lucan, my servant, and Aeric will be the new recruit we found further south. We just learned from the convert master that sometimes it is necessary to break captured men in the dungeons we are trying to get to, so I'll 'insist' Aeric needs to be taken to the prison thanks to his unruly nature and love of freedom."

"And what happens if they refuse your insistent attempts to get us all into the dungeon?" Lucan pressed, worrying the sage's persistence could not overcome the laws inside the Holy Shrine he knew nothing about. "Do you really think your little improvisations can get us past their entire system of converting new captives? What happens if they take Aeric to be converted at the Bloody Square like I was? You have no idea what will happen if we just barge in there."

"Between my persuasion and your knowledge of the inner workings of the fortress I am confident we can get inside and navigate the dungeons," Revond said. Lucan's jaw fell open as he searched for the words to reply. Exasperated again, he looked at Aeric equally disturbed by what Revond was proposing.

"*This* is the best a *Master Sage* can come up with?" he asked to either of them aghast, pointing with his entire hand at Revond. "That's not even a plan, it's throwing us into the fire and seeing how bad we get burned!"

"You have already witnessed us effortlessly fool the converts, Lucan," Revond reminded him. "Acting is reacting. Unless we run into one of the Ancients themselves we can fool any hostile authority in the fortress. You have already been branded if anyone wishes to see, and with his hands bound between us Aeric will look like a captive. I tell you, this will work. I have more than a few tricks up my sleeves that they won't expect. Believe it or not, I've penetrated into an unfriendly city through hundreds of hostile occupants to rescue someone before and emerged successful. Sometimes desperation calls for one to have faith in his instincts. All I'm asking from you is to continue having faith in me."

"Reason has a funny way of getting in the way of faith, Master Sage," Lucan returned, folding his arms over his chest. "As does common sense. This is absolutely insane." He turned to look at Aeric. "What do you think of all this?" Aeric swallowed hard at this, sensing Revond's eyes pass to him as well. He raised one of his hands to run his fingers through his black hair and search his thoughts. Lucan was right that there was no plan, just Revond's confidence he could somehow fool an entire city of hostile servants to the murderous Ancients. Staring at the sage's gray robes, he remembered the stories of Zeroan his grandfather had told him and the incredible odds the sage helped him overcome. The Master Sage had already saved his life several times over the course of their weeks together and was supposedly more powerful than Zeroan ever was, despite his inexperience. Though the doubt around this plan was so thick it threatened to suffocate him, Aeric looked into the sage's hood through the rain and held his gaze.

"Let's do it," he stated simply, to which Lucan slouched and rolled his eyes. With both of their eyes and the pressure on him again, the Maven slowly reached up to start unfastening the scarf around his neck.

Chapter 15

<u>Rescuers</u>

After Revond quickly scattered and hid the remains of the felled converts with his mystic power so as not to raise an alarm among other passing converts back to their city, he and his two slaves pressed on through the afternoon and the Hills of Eirinor toward the ravaged Valley of Galantia. They arrived on its outskirts as evening fell and the soft rain from the clouds abated, swallowed by the rolling black masses growing darker the closer they traveled to the new Holy Shrine. They found the valley utterly destroyed as view of the once green and sprawling milieu appeared on the horizon, looking more like the glassed over bottom of a dead sea. Other parties of converted slaves to the Ancients began constantly appearing around them, making their way to or from the Holy Shrine nestled against the mountains in the distance where Galantia once stood. Though the trio was nervous as they found themselves entering a valley jostling with the converts, most of all Lucan who was still convinced they were walking toward their demise, Revond powerfully strode forward exuding his usual air of confidence and control.

Aeric and Lucan didn't see how his resourcefulness alone had any chance of fooling an entire city of the converts, but they saw for themselves it was working so far. By the time they entered the former Valley of Galantia they had passed several groups of converts, some comprised of over two dozen men, none of whom had recognized them as free men or what they referred to as stranded. A few masters like the red cloaked man Revond had killed earlier occasional barked at them asking what they were doing, but the sage returned their hostility by telling them to mind their tongues and their own business. Though Lucan felt his heart sink with every word Revond spoke, waiting for one of the converts to call his bluff and expose them, none did and they passed through several more large groups unchallenged.

Though instructed to keep his head down and look as pitiable as possible while they traveled to maintain the illusion of their act, Aeric couldn't help but raise his eyes to the devastation around him to take it all in. Grandaria, the proudest and longest standing nation in Iairia that had endured since the dawn of humanity eons previous, had been subjugated and essentially erased in less than a year. Seeing everything he had ever known gone reminded him of the day he had seen Galantia fall. The pain of losing his parents and Mina seared at his heart as it had the first moments he lost them. He was perhaps the last vestige of the proud people he had known. Though this fact ate at the already weak motivation and resolve keeping him walking forward, the young man found a nameless strength in the knowledge he was the last remnant of Grandarian society, as if compelling him to embody it properly. If he was to meet his end, he would have it be one befitting the courageous tradition of his family and people. He owed his grandfather's legacy and the memory of all that was lost this much at least.

Beginning to meld with the various parties of converts converging toward a beaten path leading to the huge structure ahead of them, Revond and Aeric saw for themselves why Lucan had swore an oath to never return here again. Standing over the ruins and lingering rubble of the once greatest and oldest city on the face of Iairia was a series of messily erected wooden towers and ramparts. They lead toward the enormous Holy Shrine high above them where the Golden Castle had once rested. The first and second tiers of the city where the Grandarian army's Gate Yard and the lower city had been were obliterated, now only a collection of rubble and wreckage where the rectangular wooden towers rose to survey the rest of the valley and activity in it. Passing over a ditch in the road where the moat surrounding the wall of the Gate Yard had been, Aeric's face contorted with disgust as an atrocious stench found its way into his nostrils. Looking around for the source of the horrid odor, his eyes widened and he found himself slowing as he looked to his right near a larger ditch around the debris of a stone tower where converts were throwing dead bodies into a messy pile. Aeric swallowed hard as he observed several corpses rotting with bones protruding from the flesh in decay. Even the Master

Sage narrowed his eyes and swept his fuming face over to the site of the barbaric display.

The three were quickly forced to focus back on the Holy Shrine and the city ahead of them as the groups of converts began crowding together into a mass. While streaming in and out of the city, many revealed their ill tempers as they jostled into each other and shouted curses. Through trying to keep his head down and attract as little attention as possible, Aeric found masters of the converts approaching as they walked by to grab and inspect him, asking Revond where he found him. The sage lied he had been wandering a road near the Empyrean Peaks and pulled Aeric back after him, continuing on toward the gates of the broken city and the guards standing there with rusty lances perpendicular to the ground. They were covered in dirtied Grandarian armor, looking over the converts entering and exiting the city, obviously for anything unusual. Though Lucan was certain they would never make it past them with Aeric outside of a stockade without being interrogated, Revond pressed forward at his steady pace without being stopped. Just as they were nearly clear, one of the guards called out to a man in gray, obviously Revond.

"Found a stray, did we?" he asked once Revond had turned to look at the guard walking toward them. Though Revond was about to respond the guard interrupted him. "Let's see your branding." Thinking fast, the sage called back to Lucan.

"Be quick about it, slave," he snapped. Taking a deep breath, Lucan raised up the sleeve on his left arm to show the scarring of the convert brand, to which the guard nodded. Seeing his approval, Revond spoke again, turning to continue on into the city. "Now hurry—the two of you have delayed me enough already on this trip."

"Then you're a poor leader but you still know the drill," the guard shouted. "No one enters the city outside a stockade group without showing your mark. I'll be seeing yours as well." Lucan and Aeric exchanged glances at each other frantically at this, though Revond merely rolled his eyes and let out an impatient huff.

"My sleeves are tucked into my gloves and I haven't the time to—"

"Hey!" the guard shouted, raising his voice and walking to Revond to stare up into his hood. "I don't care how much of a rush you're in, show me your damn brand, scum!" Seeing onlookers stare suspiciously, Lucan and Aeric knew they were dead. Though the Maven was ready to reach for his knives and prepare for his last stand, he was astounded to find Revond rolling up his left sleeve while cursing under his breath. Both the Maven and Grandarian were shocked to find a scar high on his arm, exactly matching the brand on Lucan's.

"Now hurry up, you two," the sage yelled back to his stupefied companions frozen behind him. Shaking off their shock they both sprinted behind him past the guard motioning them to be on their way with a frown. Quickening his pace to stride on the sage's left side, Lucan was about to ask how he could possibly have been branded and why he didn't tell them before. Summoning his voice, he stopped short when observing the mark slowly disappearing from his clean skin as Revond rolled his dark blue sleeve down again. Though baffled and waiting for an explanation from the sage, he merely continued marching into the city around the Holy Shrine with his gaze fixed ahead. Lucan looked back to Aeric who returned his bemused glance.

Letting the matter pass, the trio continued on into the dirty streets of the makeshift city. It was a horrible and disgusting sight. Not even Dalastrak or its surrounding villages during the Black Winter of Drakkaidia were so downtrodden and impoverished. Everywhere the group looked they saw people lying on the streets begging for food or fighting over shelter. Most of the city was comprised of the ruins of Galantia. A few building walls from the old city still stood amid the rubble with tents and shabby wagons where merchants were trading with the converts. There was violence all around them, growing progressively worse until the group came to a winding path up a hillside that led to an open courtyard outside of the Holy Shrine itself. It made Aeric sick to see the violent and savage world that had replaced all he had known before. It was as if humanity itself had regressed back to primal ages of legend.

Walking up a dirt path past a felled white pillar that held up an archway leading into the old Golden Castle, the trio walked into a wide expanse that had once been the assembly courtyard. There was a large mob of fighting and cheering converts gathered in a circle around a wooden stage where several men in chains were being tied up or beaten.

Observing a man in a red cloak reaching out with a short whip to crack it over one of the tied men's backs, Revond could guess where they were.

"This is the Bloody Square, then?" he asked to Lucan just loud enough to be heard over the cries of the mob.

"The one and only," he returned eyeing the stage where he had once stood, a rush of painful memories flushing into him. "Those men must be prisoners from the dungeon they are trying to break. Once they agree to convert, they'll be branded there like I was. Any who refuse will be tossed into the crowd to be hacked apart."

"The dungeon is directly ahead inside the fortress of the shrine then?" Revond pressed.

"The fortress *is* the dungeon," Lucan replied. "All that's in there besides the top level where the Ancients keep the Sources are cell blocks and torture chambers. There are a few entrances around it leading into the lower cell blocks. One is behind the Bloody Square at the top of that staircase." Looking past the rows of screaming converts watching the bloodshed on the stage, Revond peered to the plain stone wall of the Holy Shrine and the opening above a staircase. The shrine was a large and forbidding but simple structure, built with six long stone walls stretching hundreds of feet in each direction. It was only three or four stories high but there was another wide tower that stood higher off the center. Lucan had told them the rumor was that the Ancients had built it in less than a day with their elemental powers and incredible strength to aid them. Guessing that was where the Ancients were storing the Sources, Revond narrowed his eyes with resolve.

"Once we get inside be prepared to act fast and react quickly to whatever I do," the sage stated.

"Look, I don't know how you managed that little trick with the guards at the city entrance but these won't be fooled so easily," Lucan said quickly. Heeding the Maven's words, Revond looked back to guards standing attentively at the gates then back up at the tower of the shrine. He knew this situation called for a diversion but he couldn't do anything too grandiose as one or more of the Ancients could have been in their false Holy Shrine. Though the beasts couldn't sense his mystic power like normal elemental magic, they would surely notice too bizarre a spectacle if they were nearby. Groping for an idea as he continued forward, the sage cast his eyes back on the noisy Blood Square to their right. Deciding on his course of action, Revond lifted his hand outside of his robes and spread his fingers toward the mob. Having seen the Master Sage summon his power like this before Aeric guessed something was about to happen and looked into the square.

Suddenly, he heard a loud cracking noise as if wood was being split. Watching as the men atop the stage fumbled and the crowd quieted in confusion, Aeric saw Revond tightening his fingers as if grasping onto something and breaking it in his hands. Observing the commotion for himself, Lucan watched with his eyes widening as the several legs of the stage that kept it elevated above the ground began shattering and breaking apart one by one, toppling the stage to the ground and sending everyone on it on a collision course for the mob. As the tied up captives found their way to their feet, they were amazed to find the bonds around their hands and feet breaking apart and flying off of them into the crowd. Free, they lunged away through an opening in the mob one of the falling planks of wood had made. The incensed converts around them immediately came to their senses and began charging after them, screaming and waving swords as they ran. Lowering his gloved hand back into his robes, Revond shifted his gaze back to the opening in the wall of the fortress to see the guards coming alert and running into the Bloody Square to see what was happening.

Stepping to their right to avoid the rush of guards charging past them, Lucan and Aeric found the entrance to the dungeons free and clear. Once again shooting each other amazed glances, they merely quickened their pace to keep up with the Master Sage now jetting across the barren earth for the Holy Shrine. Quickly ascending the stairs past rows of torches, Aeric looked back into the crowd to see the incensed converts breaking into a full riot in the chaos of the moment. Eager to be out of their range of sight before someone could spot them and figure out what was happening, the Grandarian spun back to pass through the dark gate leading into the Holy Shrine.

Revond slowed his pace once they were inside a torch lit hall, as plain and simply constructed as the fortress' exterior. Though they were alone in the wide hallway for a moment, at last they heard a rush of footsteps from a hallway beyond and observed a group of guards striding toward them demanding to know what was going on. They came stumbling around a corner in torn and filthy clothes, stains of blood and some sort of black substance like ash smeared across them all. One of them was missing an eye and the other was so overweight he was sweating profusely and could barely keep up with the others.

"What's all this ruckus then?" one of the converts asked as he peered behind Revond's hooded form for the opening into the Bloody Square outside.

"Some of the prisoners escaped," Revond returned, turning to grab hold of Aeric and pull him forward again as the boy was becoming used to. "This is one of them. I was ordered to have him locked up. They need more men outside to quell the riot."

"Riot?" one of the other guards repeated. "What in the hell is going on out there?" The man reached to his belt and pulled free a ring of keys, throwing it to one of the guards at the back of their number. "You take this one to the bulk cell. If we aren't back in a few minutes send out the rest of the jailers on the main level. I don't want the Black Ancient coming outside to see we've lost control of his shrine." With that, the jailers rushed to the door grabbing weapons off of the wooden armory stand there. The lone jailer fumbling through his keys and grumbling something to himself reached out to grab Aeric by his bonds and pull him after him as they began walking down the hallway.

"Get back outside and help them, man," the jailer yelled back through the hall at Revond. Though Lucan was about to lean in and tell the sage they couldn't leave Aeric or they'd never see him again, Revond was already walking after them taking care to keep his footsteps as quiet as possible. Lucan followed with his back pressed against the wall on his tiptoes as they walked behind Aeric and the jailer down the hallway until coming to a turn that led down to a stairwell. Hearing the distant screams and moans from the bottom, they watched as the jailer shoved Aeric forward so hard he fell over, landing with a painful thud on his front. As the jailer heaved him to his feet by his tunic, he cursed the boy and slammed him up against the bars of an empty cell. There were several cells in the room, including a larger one where several men and women sat cowering in the corners, obviously the bulk cell one of the guards had spoken of before. Further down the hallway were more cells containing bloodstained tables where prisoners were tortured and broken until they succumbed to the converts' rule. In one room Aeric saw a man lying dead on a table.

As Aeric tried to pry his eyes off of the gory sight, the jailer had reached up to pry his keys into the door of a chamber next to the bulk cell and open the door. Turning when he heard the massive sound of the metal bars opening, Aeric's eyes narrowed as view of a large silhouette appeared behind the jailer. Seeing the shadow cast on him, the jailer turned to find Revond and Lucan walking toward him, looking around to make sure none of the prisoners were watching.

"What do you two think you're doing down here?" he barked turning to face them. "I told you to—" He would never have the chance to finish. Revond quickly fired his right hand forward through a bundle of gray robes to latch onto his neck. Struggling for breath, the jailer reached up to pry away the sage's powerful hand with no avail, finding himself being raised off his feet. Moving swiftly with an expression that looked more like vengeance than determination to Aeric as he watched from the bars, Revond heaved open the door and viciously flung the jailer inside against a stone wall. Tasting blood in his mouth as he fell to the floor, the jailer was stunned to find Revond following him in and grabbing hold of him again, lifting him against the wall.

"Where do the Ancients keep the one called Alberic?" he grilled in a hushed growl.

"You're mad," the jailer returned, shaking his head with a scowl. "This is the new world order! You'll be dead before you can get out of this cell block!"

"And you'll be dead before you can get out of this cell if you don't tell me what I want to know," Revond pressed, pushing him harder against the wall. "Where is Alberic held?"

"Prisoners escaping!" the jailer yelled to which Aeric and Lucan cringed, aware there would be more of the converts nearby. Though he was about to yell something else, Revond's face tightened with rage and he lifted the man off the wall only to slam him into it again. Turning back into the cell to find a table and several sharp tools lying over it obviously intended for torture, Revond threw the jailer down onto the table with bone breaking force. Reaching down to grab one of the hooked knives beside the convert's legs, Revond raised it to his chest to rip away the man's shirt and press the tip against his exposed hairy chest.

"If you want to scream for help I'm going to give you reason to," Revond breathed with acid dripping from his words. "But I promise you," the sage said slightly shoving the tip of the hook into the convert's skin, "one way or another you are going to tell me what I want to know. This can be quick and painless or excruciating in ways you can't comprehend, but you will tell me where Alberic is." As the hook descended further into the man's chest, he screamed out in agony and began to babble he would tell him whatever he wanted to know.

"The Ancients keep him above the dungeon in their quarters!" he yelled struggling against the sage so hard even Revond could barely hold him down. "There's a staircase leading up at the end of the cell block! Follow it up to the highest level! Please, I just work for them!"

"How many men guard him?" Revond pressed, still holding down the hook.

"None! The Ancients are the only ones in the top level of the shrine!"

"How many of the Ancients are up there?"

"I don't know!" he said to which Revond lowered the hook lower into the man. Though he screamed he insisted he didn't know and began crying hysterically, soiling himself. Satisfied the jailer had given them all he was going to, Revond jerked up the guard's head. Slamming it back down on the table with nearly lethal force, he ensured the convert would remain silent until they were long gong. Surprised at his violent ruthlessness, Aeric and Lucan waited for him to emerge with the jailer's keys and shut the door to the cell. Revond could see the shocked expression on his companions' faces at what he had done.

"There is no room for mercy today," he said, pretending to fumble with his keys and tuck them into his robes. Aeric and Lucan held his gaze uncertainly, not having believed the usually calm and collected Master Sage capable of such brutal aggression. "How many guards can we expect between here and the top levels of the fortress, Lucan?" The Maven swept his gaze around the cell block as if gathering his memories from the last time he was there.

"I only remember a few jailers managing my cell block last time and I think the rest of the men assigned to this one ran outside," he said. "But I don't know what lies beyond this hallway. Could be more—or worse, torturers." Revond gave him a single nod and whispered for them to keep following his lead.

Starting forward again with Aeric in tow, the trio was spotted by several of the prisoners who called out to them, having heard the screams of the jailer moments before. Though Aeric was about to suggest they let them free since they had the keys to their cells, Revond twisted his head toward them and barked out for them to be silent or he would have them thrown into the Bloody Square. Again surprised at the sage's behavior, Aeric guessed letting them go or even letting them think the three of them were anyone but convert master and slaves could arouse suspicion and blow their already shaky cover before they could even get to Alberic. Staying silent and continuing to trust the unwavering Master Sage, they made their way to the end of the wide hallway to another chamber with a few cells and three staircases leading in different directions. Guessing the one that spiraled would lead the highest, Revond turned and led them toward it past a collection of bones lying to their right on the floor.

Stepping through the entrance, the trio ascended the spiraling stairwell up several floors past more cell blocks defiled with blood on the floors and screams echoing through to them. Seeing greater light coming from the end of the stairs up ahead, they stopped short before they could exit onto the next floor. Though subtle at first, all of them could feel a slight tremor shake the stone beneath their feet and they paused. Remaining motionless in the silence, they felt the tremors grow into large quakes until all at once they disappeared. While Revond listened carefully with his acute hearing, Lucan and Aeric glanced at each other both silently guessing an Ancient was nearby. At last the silence was broken by a large door slamming open from above them inside whatever chamber lay beyond the exit of the stairwell. Hearing a lone set of footsteps ambling through the chamber then fading into silence, Revond narrowed his eyes and slowly crept against the wall up the stairs until he could peer out of his hood into the chamber beyond.

There was a massive but barren circular room before them with a few doors lining the chamber like the exit to the stairwell they stood in and a stone staircase leading up to another level in the center. Though he had just heard someone walking about there was no movement anywhere but for the dancing torches along the walls and in several metal baskets on the rising staircase. Taking the setting in for a long moment, he eventually turned back to Lucan and Aeric waiting for his report behind them. Before they could ask what he saw, the sage reached up with his left hand to grip Aeric's shackles with his power and drop them from his wrists at last.

"If the jailer told us the truth about the converts not being allowed past the dungeons, that means the footsteps I just heard belonged to an Ancient," Revond told them. "There is a chamber that lies before us, empty but for a staircase leading up to another floor. I don't know what we'll find but we have to keep going. I would have you two wait here but if an Ancient passed by in the meantime you would not be the better for it. Aeric, keep the Source of Light close." Remembering they would need it to revive Alberic when they found him, Aeric recalled its effectiveness against the mammoth beast called Dalorosk as well and gripped the medallion underneath his blue tunic.

Turning to take a final look into the still chamber, Revond motioned with two fingers for them to follow him into it. They trio emerged quickly, darting across the open expanse of the torch lit room toward the staircase in the middle. When they reached it, Revond scanned the other doorways around the room to see if any of them led to another room that could contain what they were looking for. Concluding that they were all stairwells, the sage turned his attention back to the level above them and began leaping up the stairs with his gray robes trailing behind him along with Lucan and Aeric, excitement and fear gripping them at the prospect of what they might find at the top level of the Ancients' Holy Shrine.

Chapter 16

<u>The Ancient of Light</u>

Revond was the one to emerge in the open air atop the fortress of the shrine first, coming up the final stairs through the ceiling of the chamber beneath them. Feeling rain drops coming down on their bodies, Lucan and Aeric realized they were going outside as well and looked up to find rolling black clouds above them as they ascended the top steps. Though Revond thoroughly checked over the side of the opening in the floor of the top level for any hostile presence, he found his worries quickly replaced by his amazement of the other objects at rest around him. Seeing the Master Sage's mouth slip open in what looked to be astonishment, Lucan and Aeric were quick to join him atop the roof to observe what had captured his attention. The surface of the large top level of the Holy Shrine was flat, stretching over a hundred feet from side to side, but for six pedestals around the perimeter and one large one in the center beside them. Levitating over the six pedestals was a sight that all three of them couldn't help but stare at through the falling rain with wonder.

Lighting the atmosphere and their bodies with various hues of glowing energy were the other five elemental Sources once stored in the Elemental Temples. They looked just like what Aeric's grandfather had told him—massive perfect spheres of light reflecting the color of their element, taller and wider than any man. All of them hovered a few inches over the stone pedestals where they had been placed, seemingly inert but shining with power and strength that Aeric swore he could feel radiating into the back of his mind. Sweeping their gazes around at the floating orbs from which all elemental power in the world stemmed, Aeric was surprised to hear a sudden gasp behind him. Wheeling around to find Revond fixed on one of the platforms, Aeric's eyes drifted to it to notice there was no Source levitating there. Guessing it had been crafted for the still missing Source of Light now merely fifty feet away around his neck, Aeric noticed there was something else lying atop the surface of the pedestal. Narrowing his eyes in disbelief, Aeric found the broken and dirtied figure of the man in white who had given him the medallion he clutched over his chest lying there chained to the stone floor.

It was Alberic.

Coming to the same conclusion based on the image he had seen in the Cebrach book over a year previous, Revond tightened his body with purpose and leapt from the middle of the floor to rush over to the platform holding the weak figure with Aeric and Lucan behind him. Seeing the feeble man in white stir at the sound of his footsteps, Revond slowed at the side of the pedestal and slowly raised his hands to lower the gray hood behind his back. The Master Sage's eyes were sparkling with wonder, overwhelmed at the thought of standing beside the being who helped shape the face of the world and established the order to which he had dedicated his life. Despite the incredible longevity of his life and his broken state, the man looked younger than he. Alberic's white attire was ripped and soiled to match his bruised and swollen face, but there was no blood anywhere on him including from the numerous cuts across his skin. He lay slouched over on his knees, chained by the wrists and ankles that allowed him enough room only to shift position or lie down on the small pedestal.

The man in white slowly lifted his head to open his dim eyes and observe the three men standing before him, blinking and remaining still as if studying them. When Revond at last overcame his amazement and forced himself to step onto the pedestal and lean down to the beaten man, Alberic's eyes shifted to the silver crest holding his cloak over his chest. He faintly smiled as he raised his eyes to Revond's.

"The young Tieloc found you, then," he spoke almost inaudibly. "Hello Master Sage." Revond couldn't help but smile back upon hearing the man speak and gave him a single nod.

"He did indeed, Master Sage Alberic," he returned slightly bowing his head. "We have come to liberate you from the Ancients." The smile on Alberic's face dissipated as he slowly shook his head.

"You risk too much by coming for me," Alberic stated, his eyes shifting back to Aeric. "Your resourcefulness is proven evident by your getting this far, but I will be too great a burden for you to escape with me through the ruins of Galantia."

"You will not be a burden for long, Alberic," Revond returned, turning his head to his companions and motioning for Aeric to approach. The Grandarian did as he was bid, stepping onto the pedestal and leaning down to the man in white he had last seen over a year ago. "We have brought something to rejuvenate you." Hearing this, Aeric reached inside his tunic to slowly pull forth the white medallion hanging at his neck, glowing from the shining orb in its center as always. Seeing the Source of Light, Alberic winced as if in pain.

"You brought the final element to the very place my brothers seek to use its power for their evil ambitions?" he asked as if shocked. Revond was silent for a moment, realizing for the first time just how much he had risked in his plan when the criticism came from the greatest of his order.

"I didn't know what else to do, Alberic," the Master Sage confessed. "Your Cebrach book was lost in their attack on the tower and the checks you set in place to prevent the Ascension are gone. I knew of no other power to seek that could prevent the destruction of the Ancients from spreading." Alberic took a long breath and stared at the Source of Light, obviously thinking. Before Revond could continue, Lucan's voice sounded from behind them.

"Uhh, I don't mean to interrupt," he whispered, "but could we please hurry this up? If you recall we are in the heart of enemy territory and will be ripped to shreds if someone sees us."

"My friend is right, Alberic," Revond began again. "You must take the Source and use its power before we are detected."

"I cannot," he replied, to which all three of the humans before him froze and stared at him incredulously. "Dalorosk is here in this very fortress. If we use the Source he will sense it here and destroy us. I cannot yet fight him in my weakened state even with the power of the Source of Light." Revond let out a quick huff of dissatisfaction, having hoped the Ancient of Light would be strong enough to provide the means to their escape once reunited with the Source.

"Very well then," Revond replied, thinking quickly. "We will just have to make our escape the way we came. Hold still while I sever your bonds—"

"Wait!" Alberic cut him off, suddenly gripped with shock and terror. Freezing as well, Revond and Aeric heard the cause of his distress. The sound of footsteps from beneath them echoing out of the hole in the ceiling where the staircase ended caught their attention, warning them someone was coming. Guessing it was an Ancient, Revond wheeled around to look to Alberic. "Hide behind a Source! Quickly!" Deciding they had no hope of winning a fight with an Ancient with Alberic chained and weakened, Revond nodded his head and hoisted Aeric off his feet to silently dash toward the nearest Source on their right. Lucan followed as quickly as he could, tiptoeing with every step as the sound of someone ascending the staircase echoed into his ears.

Leaping behind the pedestal where Revond and Aeric lay in a crouch with a massive red orb of floating energy above them, the three fixed their gazes on the center of the floor where the staircase ended. Waiting with their hearts pounding for several long moments, they watched as a figure dressed in all black at last emerged from the stairs into the rainy atmosphere. Remembering the man in black who had bumped into him over a year ago the day he and Mina were leaving Galantia, Aeric gulped and shoved the Source of Light back into this tunic with his hand over it to ensure no light escaped.

The figure in black dragged a quivering man by his leg with one hand, leaving a bloodstain on the floor to be slowly washed away by the rain. Moving toward the pedestal that held Alberic, the trio watched as the man in black released the shaking prisoner he held and slowly sat on the pedestal beside Alberic, his face emotionless and controlled. He flexed his fingers in and out of a fist as he opened his mouth to speak, staring out into the rain before him with Alberic to his back.

"Gloomy day, isn't it, brother," he said impassively.

"As they have all been since your return, Dalorosk," the man in white returned weakly, staring down at the man quivering below the pedestal. "You don't have to do this."

"I know I don't," Dalorosk returned, lowering his hand to rest upon his knee. "I wouldn't if you would tell me what I want to know. Is today my lucky day?"

"This and every other since you have been free have been your lucky days, brother," Alberic spoke, a drop of rainwater dripping from his chin. "Soon your luck will change." Dalorosk frowned at this, turning around to stare at the man in chains with a peculiar look on his face.

"A little spirit seems to have gripped you today, brother," he observed keenly. "You haven't been in the mood for such banter in months. What provokes this sudden challenge, I wonder?" Alberic was quiet at this, looking down to the man still cowering beneath Dalorosk's feet, then closed his eyes.

"It is out of your reach now, Dalorosk," he said, knowing what was coming. Dalorosk stared at him for a lingering moment before shrugging and turning around again.

"Your time is over, Alberic," Dalorosk said as he reached down to grab hold of his prisoner's leg again. "Mine is the face of the future." Latching onto the man's leg he flung him up into the air with what looked to be no effort at all. Once the crying man was over Dalorosk's head the Ancient of Darkness let him go to send him flying over the walls of the tower and plummeting to his death far below. Listening to the man's scream until it was gone, Aeric felt his jaw slip open in shock. "We'll try again tomorrow then." Dalorosk rose and started back across the floor without looking back. "You realize someday we're going to run out of people for our little game. What will you hold out for then, Alberic?" With that, the man in black stepped onto the first step leading back down into the Holy Shrine.

As he disappeared, Aeric and Lucan let out long breaths of relief and let their bodies unwind. The Master Sage was already back on his feet, however, silently dashing back to Alberic. Struggling to catch up with him, the two younger men crept across the floor, keeping their eyes on the staircase to make sure Dalorosk was indeed gone. Arriving back beside Alberic, Revond lowered his hands to seize the chains around his wrists and take hold of them with his powerful mystic grip. Pulling his fists apart as if snapping a thin twine, the chains quietly shattered and fell to the pedestal.

"Lucan, help me carry him," he whispered, to which the Maven stepped onto the pedestal to swallow hard and grab the Ancient of Light's left arm. He gently wrapped it around his neck while Revond bolstered up his right side.

"Can you walk at all, Alberic?" The age Ancient grimaced as they lifted him to his feet and shook his head.

"I haven't stood for months," he said replied.

"Do you know a safe way out of the Holy Shrine?" he pressed, lowering him off the pedestal. Alberic shook his head and told them he knew as little about the interior of the fortress as they did. "Where has Dalorosk gone? Will he be in the shrine or leaving?" Again Alberic replied he didn't know. Revond let out a huff of dissatisfaction but knew every moment they wasted was one more they could be found by someone. Instructing Aeric to keep ahead of them and check around any corners they came to, the group made their way to the stairwell and began descending it for the empty chamber below them. Though Aeric silently peered down to scan the room for movement, remembering Dalorosk had been here no more than a minute ago, he gave the all clear and the three behind him slowly began to creep down the stairs, Alberic's feet dragging on the stone steps as they moved.

At last reaching the bottom with all eyes scanning the doors for any movement, they remained alone and began creeping toward the doorway to the spiral staircase of the cell block they had come from. Too wide with all three to fit through the entrance, Lucan and Revond rotated into a line to fit through. As Aeric started down the steps he stopped short, hearing the sound of voices echoing up from further down the stairwell. Guessing the jailers they fooled into going outside had quelled the riot and returned, Aeric spun around and silently motioned for them to retreat back into the chamber to preclude them from walking into a room full of armed converts.

Pulling Alberic out immediately, Aeric told them they would have to try another way less risky. Dashing to the nearest opening to peer into the next room and see what was there, the boy was shocked to run into something as soon as he turned the corner. Shocked, he fell backward onto his backside with an audible thud that caused Revond and the others to spin around with their hearts leaping into their chests. Staring into the doorway, the group found Dalorosk standing there with a shocked expression on his face, staring at the boy that had ran into him as if wondering how it was possible for him to be there.

Revond and Lucan felt Alberic's weak frame tighten. Turning to observe the other three standing to his right, a look of furious disbelief found its way into Dalorosk's shaking eyes. Aware their only chance to survive was immediate action, Revond extended his free hand to the ground beneath Dalorosk's feat and clenched his open fingers together. The next moment the thick stone floor beneath him split and gave way, sending chucks of rubble and the Ancient of Darkness standing over them through the floor. So shocked at what he found in the chamber, Dalorosk didn't have time to react and he disappeared into the hole.

"Aeric!" Revond bellowed the next moment. "Give Alberic the Source!" Still shocked himself, the young man only stared at the gaping hole in the floor in front of him.

"*Come on, kid!*" Lucan screamed, hearing a massive yell of fury sound beneath their feet. Aware he had to act, Aeric leapt to his feet and pulled out the Source of Light to bring it to Alberic.

"Lock it back onto my chest," the Ancient of Light spoke weakly. Remembering the image of Alberic he had seen from the power of the Cebrach book and how the medallion once fit in the mold on his chest, Aeric raised it to place it into the mold as he had on the image of light. Twisting its edges in the locking the grooves inside the mold, Alberic grunted and jerked back as if the boy had taken a hold of his heart. Releasing the medallion and taking a step back, Aeric watched as it began to glow and cover Alberic's body in a thin veil of brilliant light. Still looking besieged, Alberic spoke.

"Take me back to the roof, quickly," he whispered to Revond. Though Revond was about to tell Lucan to make for the stairs with all speed, the ground beneath them began to shake as if caught in the grip of a massive earthquake. "Dalorosk will not risk damage to the Sources by transforming in the Holy Shrine but he will be on the roof after us within moments. Hurry!" Hearing this the Master Sage instantly whirled around to push Lucan away and grab onto the shimmering Ancient of Light on his own, setting him over his shoulder and leaping to the staircase in the middle of the chamber with speed that shocked Aeric and Lucan, starting off behind him amid the tremors shaking the fortress. As the two sped behind Revond, they could see the thin layer of light around Alberic widening and intensifying by the second, spreading to engulf the Master Sage's hands. Racing up the stairs back to the top level containing the Sources, Revond found the light pounding against his body with unexpected force, straining his grip on the man.

When they at last came up to the roof, the light around Alberic's body had completely hidden him inside and was growing by the minute into a solid sphere. Forced to drop him onto the surface because he couldn't maintain his grip, Revond watched with Lucan and Aeric as the light transformed into an orb as big and luminous as any of the other five surrounding them. Though amazed at the at the spectacle before them, the trio of humans heard a massive crash from behind them and wheeled around to find the gargantuan head of the behemoth Dalorosk rising from behind the black Source of Darkness on the opposite end of the tower. The beast spread its enormous jaws and roared out so loudly Lucan fell to his knees with his hands pressed against his ears. Leaping in front of Lucan and Aeric, Revond stood full length and clenched his fists with the unique white energy of Hallador Might flaring around them. Though Dalorosk was about to reach over to the sage with his hulking arm to slam his fist onto him, they were all surprised to find a blinding golden light abruptly flare up from behind them that forced the Ancient of Darkness back to spread his bat like wings and flee into the open sky.

Turning around as the flash faded, Revond, Aeric and Lucan found the Source of Light shrinking into the body of an oversized white horse rearing back on its hind legs. It had hooves of shimmering gold light that left a trail of golden contrails wherever they moved and a long flowing mane of similar golden hair. Perhaps the most amazing were the two angelic wings attached to the horse's sides. Though tucked into it, the creature still stood high over them, easily double the size of any normal steed.

"On my back quickly!" came a loud and robust voice from the horse's mouth as it turned its head to face them. Though the three were shocked to hear it speak, they quickly realized this was the true form of the Ancient of Light and darted from where they stood to lift themselves up and straddle the beautiful creature. As soon as Revond and Lucan helped Aeric's struggling form up to take a seat, they were forced to hold on for their lives as Alberic abruptly galloped forward with his golden tail waving up after the rest of his body. Running toward the edge of the tower, the three humans' eyes widened to find the creature they rode leaping over the ramparts into the open air. Though feeling gravity take hold of them as they descended past the tower's pinnacle, they watched in awe as the wings once tucked tightly against Alberic's sides spread wide, lifting them back into the sky as they beat the air with power.

Wondering why Alberic had waited so long to lift them away from the tower, Aeric was shocked to find a massive black sword sweep down into the space where they might have been moments before. Turning with his eyes wide and heart pounding, the Grandarian observed the colossal figure of Dalorosk beating his enormous wings behind them, roaring out with untold fury as he kicked off from the tower of his fortress and soared after them over the skies above the Holy Shrine. Observing the threat as well, Revond summoned his mystic power again and crafted a long staff of white light in his right hand. Raising it up behind him, the sage cast it away from them to soar back toward the ancient behind them. As it began to fall, the staff shrank into a small sphere of light that detonated once the behemoth flew beneath it, showering him with raining bolts of stabbing energy.

Though Dalorosk screamed out, Revond could tell he was more annoyed than in pain and the Ancient only charged forward harder. Sensing his dark kin drawing nearer as well as he swept them up past a dark cloud with contrails of shining gold appearing from his hooves, Alberic focused a burst of light in his mouth. Sensing the power being charged, Revond turned to find the Ancient spit back something from his mouth. Reaching to his right to catch it in his gloved hand, the Master Sage observed it was the Source of Light in its medallion form again. Turning back, he handed the Source to Aeric.

"Use it!" he yelled over the wind rushing past them. Though Aeric was unsure why he had to be the one to use the power of the Source, he remembered what he had done to stun Dalorosk before in the Hills of Eirinor and turned back to face the rapidly gaining behemoth. Staring the creature down, the Grandarian raised the glowing white medallion above his head and reached up to open its glass cover and reveal the power within. Aware of what the boy was about to do, Dalorosk grit his teeth and swept one of the two massive blades he carried in an arch toward them, sending an electrified wave of energy racing toward them. Sensing it coming, Alberic was forced to violently sweep downward to avoid it, causing Aeric to lose his grip on the talisman and send it falling through the air. Not willing to let it go as it fell beside him in their dive, the young man summoned his courage and pushed himself out from the Alberic's back to reach out and take hold of it with the tips of his fingers. Reaching back with his other arm, the boy fiercely grabbed onto the Ancient's golden tail. When Alberic came out of the dive to maintain their altitude in the sky hundreds of feet above the scorched Valley of Galantia, Aeric hung loosely from the backside of the steed desperately calling out for help. It came as Lucan Hauk Erland lunged over the creature's back to take hold of his arm with both hands and heave him up with all his strength.

Hearing Dalorosk so close he could hear his wing beats louder than Alberic's as Lucan tried to tighten his grip over the gauntlet on his hand, Aeric turned to find the behemoth within striking distance behind them. Just as Dalorosk was about to attack again, Aeric reached with his index finger around the medallion to the glass cover and pried it open, instantly sending brilliant rays of white light shining out in all directions. Just like the last time the burning light fell upon his dark flesh in the hills, Dalorosk screamed out in pain and dropped back, the strength in his wings deserting him. Keeping the Source of Light open for several long moments, Aeric waited until he heard the distant sound of Dalorosk's hulking mass impact the earth below them before sealing the medallion closed again and cutting off the shining light.

With the skies clear behind them, Lucan took a breath of relief and lifted Aeric all the way back up to sit on Alberic's back. Still breathing harder than he had in his entire life, Aeric could only turn to meet the Maven who saved him and the Master Sage staring at them both. When no one said anything, they all looked down to the dark earth below them to find the giant form of Dalorosk sprawled out in a crater, struggling to rise. As Alberic beat his wings harder to lift them into the dark clouds, they lost sight of the Ancient of Darkness and what remained of Grandaria, disappearing into the evening sky.

Chapter 17

<u>Wasteland</u>

Tightly clutching both the Source of Light and the back of the winged horse he sat on, Aeric flew through the dark night sky with Revond and Lucan for several hours after their slim escape from the Holy Shrine. Though they were far from Grandaria by the middle of the night, Aeric could still feel his heart pounding from all that had transpired inside and out of the Holy Shrine, particularly his near death experience at the claws of the most fearsome Ancient of them all. Still amazed he drew breath after penetrating into the Holy Shrine's city and fortress, rescuing Alberic and eluding Dalorosk, the young man could only sit quietly reflecting over the incredible odds they had overcome that evening. In sharp contrast, Lucan had expressed his shock at all that had befallen them at the fortress in his usual bombastic and animated manner, not sure whether or not he should laugh or cry after they were finally clear of immediate danger. Easily the most uncomfortable of the three on the Ancient of Light's back as he flew, the Maven wasn't about to ask one of the oldest and most legendary creatures in Iairia to touch down and let him off.

As the group conquered their disbelief soaring through the night sky, Lucan was quick to break the momentary silence and raise the question of what they were supposed to do now. Though Revond told him their first priority was retreating far from the Ancients with Alberic and the Source of Light back in Aeric's hands, Alberic was quick to interrupt as he turned his beautiful white head back to them. Though still amazed at the Ancient's incredible appearance in his true form, the Master Sage could somehow detect the fatigue and weakness in the creature's gilded eyes. Even after using the Source of Light to rejuvenate him, he hadn't transformed from his human appearance in so long he was still weak and exhausted. Though the Ancient of Light told them he would take them anywhere they wanted to go, he informed them he couldn't continue on for much longer without rest.

His mind reeling for what their next move should be and a safe location to hide in the meantime, Revond searched his mind in silence for a long moment before turning back to Lucan. Asking him about the rumors of the resistance in Drakkaidia he had mentioned before, Lucan confirmed that there was supposedly a movement of free Drakkaidians and other men from across the lands that were gathering against the eastern edge of the Black Peaks. Though he wasn't sure how large it was or exactly where they were in hiding, Revond decided if there were any sympathetic to their cause with resources to aid them, that would be their best bet. They had no where else to go. Turning back to Alberic, Revond asked them to continue west into Drakkaidia to ferry them to the Black Peaks. After the hours they had been flying they had already soared over the Border Mountains between Grandaria and Drakkaidia and the former Wall of Light. Making a turn to the north for Drakkaidia, Alberic continued beating his massive feathered wings with what strength he had left.

They continued on for nearly another hour before the Ancient of Light's final reserves of energy were depleted. Though they had penetrated into central Drakkaidia, Alberic turned to Revond to tell him he could go no farther in his state. Observing the white horse's already weak wings faltering in the sky and letting them glide down toward the black earth far below, Revond nodded his head and shouted back to him.

"I fear we have asked and expected too much of you in your weakened condition, Alberic," Revond told him shaking his head and looking down to the terrain below in the bright light of the full moon, trying to locate a good spot to land. "If you are able, try to veer us toward those plains." Hearing this, Lucan's eyes went wide and he leaned forward with alarm.

"He can't get us to the peaks?" he asked loudly through the wind passing around them. When Revond shook his head no and told him they had to rest for the night, the expression on the Maven's face was grave. "Revond, we can't just land in the middle of Drakkaidia. There's something else I haven't told you." Both Revond and Aeric's ears pricking up at this, they leaned in closer to stare at him with worry, waiting for him to elaborate.

"What is it?" Revond asked annoyed, as if they didn't already have enough arrayed against them.

"Well, I'm not sure," Lucan replied vaguely. "But there have been rumors spreading of a nameless danger in the land that was Drakkaidia since the Ascension. No one knows what it is but the converts say that it wasn't the Ancients that laid waste to Drakkaidia: it was something else. Supposedly even the Ancients themselves haven't set claw or scale in the northwest lands for months." Revond was silent at this for a moment but eventually narrowed his eyes and brushed his concern off.

"There is nothing left to challenge the Ancients, Lucan," he returned. "I wouldn't put too much stock in the rumors of the converts."

"All I know is every convert that's ever set out to search for the Source of Light in Drakkaidia has never come back," he returned. "If the Ancients and their lapdogs don't want to be here that I certainly don't think we should either. Can't Aeric give Alberic back the Source to give him some more vigor to reach the Black Peaks at least?"

"The Black Peaks are still Drakkaidia, the same as here, Lucan," Revond replied as they began to quickly lose altitude while Alberic glided down toward the plains below them. "We cannot use the Source or the Ancients will sense it and be on us even if there is something they fear in Drakkaidia. I'm sure it's just the Siarchs or some other elemental disturbance the converts are being ensnared by." Though not so sure based on the disturbing stories he had heard, Lucan gulped and realized they had no choice but to risk staying in Drakkaidia. Flying down through the otherwise still night air, the large winged horse touched down on the rocky ground with his hooves of golden light casting shimmering energy around the earth. Immediately Alberic let his wings droop to touch the ground and collapsed where he stood, sending the three humans on his back falling over to land on the hard ground on their sides.

"I am sorry, friends," Alberic spoke through his exhaustion. His once bright shining mane and tail were faded and dim, along with his weakly glowing hooves. "I must revert to my disguised form to rest."

"Apologize for nothing, Alberic," Revond replied as he rose from the ground brushing off his long gray cloak. "You are free now. Get your rest." Seeing the white horse nod, all three of the rising humans watched as a faint layer of light shone off his body and suddenly flashed for a moment, illuminating the dark Drakkaidian night if but for a moment. Lucan swallowed hard at this, realizing if there was anything lurking in the darkness it surely would have seen it. Looking back where Alberic's once enormous form had rested, they found it replaced with the body of the man in white Aeric had first seen on the day the Ascension began. He looked restored and healthy again; all his attire was repaired as good as new and the bruises and cuts on his body had vanished. Alberic slowly blinked his tired eyes and rose to his feet, brushing his white clothes off.

"Shall we make camp?" he asked wearily to which Revond couldn't help but smile, seeing the man who he had studied and revered for most of his life standing before him as if he had never been gone.

"Indeed," Revond concurred, raising his gray hood back over his head as usual. Telling his companions to get to work clearing out a space for them to sleep and eat something while he took a quick look around, Lucan and Aeric began unpacking some of their rations and helping Alberic sit while Revond turned to hike up a small ridge beside them. Aeric unrolled the blanket in his backpack to give to the Ancient of Light like Lucan had given him that night in the Sage's Valley. Though Alberic accepted the blanket, he graciously declined the food, telling them he didn't need to eat and they should save it for themselves.

Though surprised at this revelation at first, Aeric shrugged it off realizing he was one of the six creatures to spawn from the elemental energies of the Holy Emerald itself, and it was no wonder he didn't need such simple means for energy as food and drink like a mere human. Cleaning up a place to sleep, Aeric and Lucan couldn't tear their eyes off Alberic, amazed at how natural and human he appeared despite the fact he was one of the oldest and most powerful beings in existence, having seen and done more than either of them could ever imagine. Despite living on a plane neither of them could understand, he spoke to them casually as if he were one of them and was as vulnerable as any of them.

Listening through the night, the three heard Revond approaching from the ridge in the darkness and turned to face him as he strode back into their dark camp.

"Look past that ridge," he told them all calmly, surprising even Alberic. Worried he had seen a threat, they worriedly spun around to look past the ridge into the dark night. "Squint hard and you'll see it." Doing as he was told, Aeric continued to peer through the darkness until he caught view of the silhouette of a massive image lying in the shadows. His eyes going wide, he spoke to no one in particular.

"It's a tower," he said.

"It's Dalastrak," Revond clarified. All three of his companions shot him a glance of wonder before locking their eyes back onto the image in the distance. "Or what's left of it. You can't see much from here but atop that ridge the entire former capital of Drakkaidia can be seen. It has been torn to pieces the same as any city but the towering castle of the royal family is still more or less intact up there." Aeric stared intently at the castle he had heard stories about from his grandparents. It had been destroyed before in the Days of Destiny thanks to Valif Montrox unleashing Drakkan and the demons of the Netherworld onto the city, but it was restored by the Holy Emerald. Now, it was in shambles again.

As stories of the Days of Destiny bounced across his mind and Aeric slowly scanned the darkness behind the ridge, his searching eyes caught sight of another image superimposed into the black sky. Squinting even harder, he could make out of the form of something moving, its round body standing on a cliffside nearer to them. Though keeping his gaze on it to be sure his eyes weren't just playing tricks on him, the boy was stunned to observe a quick flash of crimson light blink across the top of the moving image then disappear, almost looking like eyes.

"There's something out there," Aeric breathed in fright suddenly, catching the rest of his group's attention at once. "I saw something move."

"Where?" Revond pressed, gazing out into the darkness around Dalastrak. Though Aeric pointed out to the cliffside he had seen the light appear, his brow furrowed again to find the entire image had vanished in the blink of an eye.

"There was something out on that cliff but... it's gone now," he replied softly. Though guessing the boy's imagination was acting up after hearing Lucan's story about there being something in Drakkaidia, Revond was not going to take chances and continued sweeping his focused eyes out into the night. After several long moments of silence, he at last widened his eyes, seeing something as well. Raising up his hand into the air to the east, he gripped his fingers and took hold of something with his mystic grip. Hearing a small shriek in the darkness, Aeric, Lucan and Alberic all spun around to find a small winged creature racing toward them through the air.

"Do not be alarmed," Revond spoke quietly, seeing Aeric and Lucan ready to jump out of their skin. "This little creature can do us no harm." As it slowed and moved over Aeric and Lucan's heads, a small black creature resembling a common bat fell into Revond's right gloved hand, going limp. It had two wings stretching only a little over a foot in total length, small claws at the ends of each wingtip. Though small, its body was furry and muscular with a miniature head sporting two white eyes and a row of baby teeth from its mouth. Revond turned the creature around and presented its opposite side to Aeric and Lucan, staring uncertainly.

"It's just a lone Siarch," he told them.

"The creation of Dalorosk," Alberic chimed in, his tone clearly discontented.

"I had never seen one alive but I have studied these creatures at length in the Mystic Tower," Revond continued. "They are packs of winged animals that live in the deep caves of the northwest. Alone it is harmless, but in great swarms, these little beasts have a powerful weapon." He drug a finger over the small sets of claws at the base of the Siarch's body to provoke a gooey substance out of their tips. "The Siarchs numb their prey with scratches from these talons that secrete a temporary poison that renders it paralyzed. With no Drakkaidians left to frighten them off from cities, they have roam of the countryside. This is most likely the 'beast' that has been ensnaring the converts, Lucan, and this is what you saw, Aeric." Aeric was silent for a moment, unsure. Whatever he had just seen far in the distance looked far bigger than this small creature and emitted a light the little Siarch couldn't have.

Though he was about to express his worries to the sage that it was not what he had seen, they were all surprised to hear a sound approaching from the direction Revond had ensnared the Siarch. Hearing a faint but shrill mess of shrieks like the one the Siarch had made a minute prior, Alberic suddenly stood, his eyes wide with alarm.

"We must get to cover!" he shouted, shocking the others. Suddenly aware of the source of the sound growing louder by the second as well, Revond dropped the Siarch in his hands and wheeled around with his robes flying up behind him.

"Aeric! Lucan! Run!" he bellowed through the night air. Though the two of them had no idea what was going on as they took off after the two Master Sages running toward the ridge Revond had climbed, they looked back with in astonishment to find what looked to be a razor sharp cloud of black ripping through the air above them in swirling jets of fury. Hearing hundreds of miniscule shrieks like the one the Siarch they had captured before, both of them quickly realized what was after them. There were hundreds of Siarchs jetting through the air in a frenzy, abruptly sweeping down in an arch toward the retreating humans below them. Running as fast as their legs would carry them, the party of four ran ahead toward the ridge and the declining slope to its side that Revond shouted for them to make for. Racing toward it they all saw several large holes in the rock they could jump into for shelter. Though not sure if it would be enough to dissuade the apparently ravenous predators behind them from continuing the chase, Aeric knew it was the best chance they had and pressed forward with all his strength.

Though the group was only a few feet away from the depression in the ridge and the shelter inside, an arching wave of the shrieking Siarchs suddenly burst up from behind the ridge to come sailing over it and the holes they had planning on jumping into. Planting his feet to halt himself and grab Alberic before he could jump, Revond spun his head around and shouted for Aeric and Lucan to keep running up the ridge. Moving past them in their steady climb, Aeric observed a small indentation in the rock near the top of the ridge that they would just barely be able to crawl through. Careening forward almost out of control as they heard a column of the Siarchs descending for their position from the sky directly above them, the four leapt over a gap in the earth and landed in front of the indentation in the rock. Dropping to their hands and knees they started worming their way inside. Lucan pulled through first and slammed his back against the rock inside to turn and pull Aeric through as hard as he could, ripping the boy's tunic and bruising his abdomen.

When almost all the way inside, the Grandarian felt a sharp sting on his right leg and heard the Siarchs swarming around the earth behind him. Though Lucan heaved him through just in time, the two could only watch as Revond and Alberic were consumed in the storm of Siarchs ripping past them with unbelievable speed. Though they could see Revond summoning the white energy of Hallador Might around his fists as he forced back a wave of the churning Siarchs with his power, too many of them penetrated his defenses and scratched his back and arms with their scraping clawed feet. Though Aeric tried to reach outside the opening of the hole in the rock to grab hold of the Master Sage's foot, the white light of his power slowly faded and he was picked up off his feet along with Alberic, already motionless beside him, to be lifted into the air. Though Aeric shouted the Master Sage's name, he found the storm of ravenous Siarchs outside the hole begin to blur and their once strident shrieks fading. Feeling his outstretched hand going numb, the last thing he remembered was being held back against a rock wall and the feeling of his wet saliva dripping across his skin from the corner of his mouth.

Chapter 18

<u>Natives</u>

Aeric came awake slowly to the faint light of the dark sky above him, once again overcast with rolling black billows even in what looked to be daylight. Rapidly blinking his eyes to focus his gaze, the Grandarian found a strange tingling sensation running along his right leg as if being tickled from the inside. Struggling to lift his upper body with a grunt, he looked down his body to find Lucan Hauk Erland pulling a dampened wad of green mush out from a cut in his exposed leg. Seeing the young man rise, Lucan shifted his irritated eyes to him while casting the green substance in his hands over his shoulder and wiping the residue off along his gray pants.

"One of these days I'm not going to be here to patch you up while you're unconscious," he remarked rolling down the boy's pant leg over the cut and turning to grab his boot and throw it at Aeric. "That's two you owe me now, Tieloc." Lifting his body upright and reaching down to massage his tingling leg, Aeric raised his eyes curiously to the Maven.

"What happened?" he asked, looking around to observe them lying outside of the indentation in the rocky ridge where he and Lucan had taken refuge during the Siarch attack. "Where are—"

"Let me save you the trouble," Lucan interrupted, sitting on his backside to tuck a cloth back into a satchel on his belt along with a sharp metal tool of some kind. "Those Siarch-bat-things took Revond and Alberic and I have no idea where they are; it's close to noon the next day; and you were cut and poisoned by the numbing agent in the talons of the little beasts. It wasn't enough to paralyze you but it conked you out for nearly twelve hours. I worked it out of you so you should be fine. Oh, and I'm fine too, by the way. Thanks for asking." By the end of the Maven's sarcastic rant

Aeric was shaking his head with frustration, wanting him to slow down.

"Will you hold on for a minute?" he asked irritated. "What do you mean I was poisoned? And how did you cure it?" Lucan sighed and reached into another satchel along his belt to pull out a light green leaf similar to the travelers fern they used to keep themselves refreshed.

"You and I escaped the Siarchs in the little hole behind me, but they nicked your leg with their poisonous claws in a couple places," Lucan began. "Like I said, it wasn't enough to paralyze you like Revond told us about but you fell unconscious and starting drooling all over yourself last night. Thankfully, being the prepared and knowledgeable Maven I am, I had a chopped branch of a Messlean shrub. Windrun Warriors use it to coax out poison from spore traps in the forests of the east. I thought it might do the job on the Siarch poison so I filled the wound and sure enough it absorbed just about everything. So once again thanks to me, it looks like you'll be fine." Aeric looked back down to his leg, running his fingers over his pants where the last tingling sensation rippled down his skin near the cut from the Siarch talons. Grabbing his boot to pull it back over his foot, he looked back up to Lucan.

"I guess thanks are in order then," he said flatly, guessing Lucan saw him as more of a chore than anything else. "But we're pretty far from fine, Lucan. What are we supposed to do now?" The Maven was still and silent for a moment before grabbing his blue scarf and hoisting it over his back again.

"I've been puzzling over that since the Siarchs disappeared with our powerhouse friends," he returned in a quiet tone, folding his hands together over his legs. "Revond was always the one with all the answers. I'm still just trying to figure out why I'm still here." Aeric frowned at that, finishing securing his boot on his foot and tucking the ends of his pants into it.

"What do you mean?" he returned worriedly. "Do you think we should start after them?"

"No, I mean I'm wondering why I'm not running out of Drakkaidia as fast as my legs can take me," Lucan said, rising to his feet. He leaned over and picked up the backpack on the blackened earth to sling it over his back. "My part in this is— was—done a long time ago. If I had my way I would've had

Alberic drop me down in the Southland and let me hike back to the eastland from there. Now I'm stuck in the last place anyone in the world wants to be with the Ancients looking for me, these Siarchs things around every corner, and Granis knows what else lurking out there. No offense, but despite the fact you are your grandfather's grandson, I think you're bad luck, kid." Seeing him turning to make his way down the ridge, Aeric leapt to his feet with worry in his blue eyes.

"Lucan, wait!" he pleaded, grabbing the pack beside him and strapping it on his back. "How can you even think about leaving? Revond and Alberic are still out there! They need us!"

"What they need, Aeric, is a miracle, and after that stunt we just pulled at the Holy Shrine I'm fresh out," Lucan returned gesturing with a sweep of his arm that he was finished. "We have no idea where they are or if they're even still alive."

"So you want to leave the best chance the world has to survive out there to be eaten by Siarchs?" he asked in disbelief.

"Hey I wouldn't even be in this mess if it weren't for those two," Lucan replied, turning to face the boy. Aeric remained adamant as he drew closer to the Maven's face with his own fortified with determination.

"You were the one who volunteered to help," the Grandarian returned heatedly, "because you knew then like you still know now that those two are the only chance we have to save what's left of this world. Are you really going to let all we went through to rescue Alberic be for nothing by abandoning him now before he's even had a chance to help us? Are you really that much of a coward?" Surprised at the young man's unusual display of spirit and resolve, Lucan was taken aback and chose not to recoil.

"This is big talk coming from someone who wanted as little to do with this quest as I did the night Revond told us about it," he said softly, hitting Aeric harder than he could have by shouting. Though faltering for a moment, the Grandarian remembered Mina and what she would want him to do if she were there. Trusting that, he knew why he had to press on.

"I still don't know if Alberic will be able to help or not, but whether he can help us save Iairia or not, all that matters to me right now is my only friend left in the world who's saved me time and again needs me to save him, and I intend to," he said with confidence that surprised even himself. Lucan raised an eyebrow at the boy, soaking in his words filled with the determination and power that the Tieloc name was famous for and had made him trust the young man and Revond in the first place. Taking a deep breath, Lucan let out a little groan and swept his eyes across the dark clouds in the sky above Dalastrak.

"Do you still have the Source of Light?" he asked abruptly, catching Aeric off guard. Looking down to his tunic, he saw a lump over his chest where the white medallion lay hidden. When he replied yes, Lucan let out another melodramatic huff and repositioned the pack on his back. "While I was holding you in the ridge last night I saw the Siarchs head west. Let's head that way." Earning a broad smile from Aeric, he nodded and the two turned to begin hiking down the rest of the ridge and start off over the barren earth for the west.

The pair set out at an enterprising pace, jogging over the flat earth when they could and hurriedly climbing over or around rocks in their way as fast as they were able. Aeric remembered Lucan's fears that they could already be too late to save their friends from the Siarchs but pulled his companion along without rest for hours. He knew if they were still alive, every moment that passed was another they could use to find them before it was too late. Though Lucan had no idea how to track flying creatures he had never even heard of prior to the previous night, he recalled from Revond's explanation that they lived in caves and told Aeric they would have to check any cavern or hole in the rocks they passed by. Aeric agreed it was the only course of action they could take but worried that even if they found the cave containing the immense swarm of miniature predators they would not be able to penetrate their vast numbers and escape with Revond and Alberic, most likely unconscious and paralyzed. The two proceeded forward fully aware that hope was slim, but no slimmer than it had been so far in their quest.

Lucan and Aeric ran on through the blackened plains in central Drakkaidia for another hour until the last remnant of Dalastrak disappeared from view behind them and they stood in an open wasteland of rock. Though they had seen a few small openings to caves along the way, none of them were big enough to house the swarm of Siarchs and they continued on. Eventually the two stopped for a break to rest their legs and have a bite of what rations they had left. By then the last tingling sensation in Aeric's leg had disappeared and though tired from the events of the past day, insisted they keep going shortly after taking a gulp of water from a flask.

Starting off again, the two found themselves coming up upon a series of sloping cliffs on the horizon. Guessing they would be a prime area for caverns large enough for the Siarchs to congregate, they pressed on through the afternoon until working their way into a tight basin of dark rocks with large boulders veering up around them. Weaving their way into the basin that lowered into a small canyon at its lowest point, the two slowed their pace so as not to carelessly trip and fall down a slope of rock that could prove fatal.

As the duo at last reached the bottom of the basin and the narrow path that wove through it leading to the opposite side, Aeric heard the faint sound of rocks tumbling down one of the sloping canyon walls to his left. Slowing his pace and gazing up to the top of the wall he found a few loose rocks tumbling down ahead of them. Since the wind had been blowing most of the afternoon and knocking loose small stones and dead branches of plants across the plains, Aeric was content to ignore it and move on but Lucan had come to a halt in front of him with a hand on the hilt of one of his daggers. Aeric stopped as well before almost running into him, raising an eyebrow and whispering.

"Siarchs?" he asked, looking back up to the top of the canyon wall.

"We'd hear them if there were Siarchs around," the Maven replied.

"Well do you think there's something up there?" the Grandarian pressed, waiting. Lucan narrowed his eyes but gradually let his hand off of his dagger.

"It's probably just the wind but keep your head up and eyes alert," he warned. "It'd be real easy for someone or something to get the drop on us in here." No sooner had he finished his sentence and began cautiously walking forward again, a sword point thrust out from behind a boulder in the canyon floor they were walking past, extended at Lucan's neck. The Maven and Aeric froze instantly while two men appeared on the top of the wall where the stones had come from with bows strung tight and arrows pointing down for them.

"Easier than you think, Maven," came a scratchy voice from ahead of them behind the turn in the road. Lucan and Aeric stood motionless and watched as a large figure adorned with black armor over his body and a long red cape appeared from beyond the turn, walking toward them. He was big man, almost a foot taller than either Lucan or Aeric with a muscular frame underneath the angular armor on his chest, shoulders and appendages. He had short black hair but a face covered with stubble, suggesting he had been out in the wild for several days at least. His flowing red cape was tattered and dilapidated at its ends but kept tight against his body even in the wind thanks to a huge double sided axe hanging over his back. The expression on his visage was cold and focused and left both Lucan and Aeric fearful of what he was capable of as he lumbered forward, sweeping his eyes up and down their figures.

Still shocked they had run into other humans in the desolate plains Aeric failed to notice the sharp Drakkaidian emblems on the black chest plate of his armor until he was mere feet away, stopping before them with his dangerous frown spreading.

"My friend and I aren't looking for trouble," Lucan spoke to the large Drakkaidian, breaking the silence.

"And neither am I," he returned coolly. "Which is why there won't be any so long as you cooperate and answer the question I'm about to ask you honestly."

"All right," Lucan replied, a touch of aggravation in his voice. The Drakkaidian folded his arms in front of his armored chest and locked his hostile eyes on Lucan.

"Who are you and what are doing in Drakkaidia?" he asked quickly. Lucan took a deep breath before responding.

"We're Mavens from the eastern Southland looking for two of our friends," he answered slowly, to which Aeric shot him a quick glance wondering why he withheld Aeric being from Grandaria. "They were taken by Siarchs late last night."

"And what business would two Mavens or their friends have in Drakkaidia in the first place?" the Drakkaidian pressed.

"We're trying to get to the resistance we heard about in the Black Peaks," Lucan returned composedly. "Are you with them?"

"I'll be the only one asking questions, Maven," the Drakkaidian snapped. "I'm sure you are indeed trying to find the resistance to have penetrated this far into Drakkaidia, but you still have not told me your reasons for doing so. Perhaps you are free men in search of sanctuary, but perhaps you are converts trying to locate the base who would bring the Ancients to destroy it."

"We are no converts," Lucan stated with verve. The Drakkaidian gave him a slow nod and unfolded his arms, walking toward him again. When he was walking directly past Lucan he shot his arm up to the Maven's shoulder to rip his sleeve and expose his arm. Lucan felt his heart sink, aware his convert branding was exposed for them to see. As soon as the Drakkaidian laid eyes on his he reached up to cock his elbow in front of him them slam it into Lucan's back, dropping him to his knees.

"Not converts indeed," the Drakkaidian snapped with his calm tone burned away by words drenched in acid. Stepping past the downed Maven he turned to the other Drakkaidian holding the sword. "Bind their hands." Though Aeric tried to tell them they could explain Lucan's brand and show them he had no mark on his arm, the Drakkaidian struck him as well and told them to be quiet or he would filet them on the spot. As the other two archers from the top of the canyon came sliding down to the floor to help tie their captives' hands behind their backs, the man in charge strode back down the path Aeric and Lucan had come from toward the slope that led back to the plains behind them, letting a loud whistle fly into the air. Sitting on his knees as his hands were bound, Aeric heard the sound of hoof beats above the canyon wall and a rider dismount. Listening carefully, he heard the Drakkaidian in charge yell out for him to ride to the primary party for Dalastrak and tell them to swing back to the cliffs to meet them. With that, he turned back to the men around his new captives and ordered them to bring them back up to the top of the basin after him. Heaved to his feet and shoved forward, Aeric knew their already dim hope of saving Revond and Alberic had all but disappeared.

Chapter 19

<u>Leader</u>

The party of Drakkaidians led their two captives back up the canyon road they came from until reaching the edge of the rocky basin where it began. Though Aeric in particular had pled for their captors to hear them out and that they were not converts, none of them, particularly the ill-tempered Drakkaidian in charge, were interested in listening and fiercely barked for him to shut his mouth if he valued his ability to speak. Trying to ask Lucan what they should do, the two Drakkaidians behind them hit him over the back of his head with the shafts of their bows and shoved him forward when he tried to talk. Though nervous of what was in store for them when they reached wherever they were going, Aeric was most concerned that the longer they remained in the Drakkaidians' custody the more their chances of rescuing Revond and Alberic would dissipate. The soldiers had taken their few weapons, including Lucan's belt now slung over the light chest armor of one of the archers behind them. Aeric was in no position to try and escape with his hands bound and his captors heavily armed but kept mentally groping for an idea.

As the Drakkaidians marched them down from the mess of boulders leading to the canyon, Aeric and Lucan found themselves back in the dark plains with evening approaching. Silently guessing they were going to be taken back to the ruins of Dalastrak or some other outpost where more of the Drakkaidians were hiding, Aeric swept his eyes ahead to find the leader of the group jumping up onto a large rock along the path and unfastening his oversized axe from behind his back. As he lifted it into the air and began swinging it back and forth, Aeric watched puzzled at what he was doing. With the moments slipping by both he and Lucan discovered the reason for his waving, as the sound of distant hoof beats galloping across the plains became audible. Shooting each other nervous glances before looking back out into the fields, they spotted a rising wave of dust approaching them with several horses kicking it up as they ran.

Seeing the coming riders as well, one of the Drakkaidian archers behind them moved ahead of the captives to get a better look and count off the number of horses in his head.

"How many are left?" the Drakkaidian behind Lucan asked.

"Looks like they're missing at least two," the other returned with an outstretched finger pointing to count each of them. "Do you think they encountered any?"

"If they did they wouldn't be riding toward us right now," the first of the two replied.

"I don't know about that. The Warrior of Darkness is still at the head, after all." Aeric froze hearing this. According to their captors, the rumors Lucan had told him and Revond about an Elemental Warrior in Drakkaidia were true. This meant that these Drakkaidians could be members of the resistance after all. As Aeric thought about what he would say to the son of Valgard Montrox when he arrived to convince him they were allies, Lucan seized on their captors' lack of attentiveness and cleared his throat loud enough to get Aeric's attention. The Grandarian shifted his eyes to him where he stood, observing the Maven's mouth slowly moving. Reading his lips, Aeric found him wording his name and the words "get ready." Though not sure what the Maven had in mind with both of them bound and their captors mere feet away, he tightened his body and gave him a quick nod, his heart rate beginning to rapidly increase. Keeping his eyes on Lucan waiting for him to make a move, he saw the Maven's face suddenly cringe with what looked to be extreme pain. Remaining silent but for taking a deep breath, Lucan grit his teeth and suddenly wheeled around to the guard behind him. Rearing back his head, the Maven sent it flying forward to slam his forehead into the Drakkaidian's exposed face, toppling him over as he cried out in surprise.

Before Aeric could turn around to wrangle with the other Drakkaidian coming alert behind him, he was amazed to find Lucan bring his arms back in front of him, somehow free of his bonds around his right hand. Reaching down to pluck one of his daggers out from the belt around the felled Drakkaidian's torso, he shot back up in one fluid motion and threw the dagger as hard as he could. Racing past Aeric's face so close it might have shaved him if he had more than the stubble on his cheeks, the blade slammed into the other Drakkaidian in the joint of his armor where the chest met the shoulder plate before he could loose an arrow at them. Watching him drop his bow and stagger backward in pain, Aeric rushed ahead and kicked him in the gut of his armor as hard as he could, sending him falling over as well. By now the other two Drakkaidians ahead of them had turned around to observe their party members fall and were already rushing back for them.

Reaching down as he yelled for Aeric to follow him, Lucan yanked his belt off the Drakkaidian lying at his feet, bleeding from his broken nose. Pulling off another dagger, he reached back to quickly heave it up through Aeric's bonds to free him as well. While Lucan's hands rushed past his, Aeric winced in shock as he saw how the Maven had freed himself from his bonds. His right thumb had been dislocated to allow him more room to fit his hand through the bonds, obviously the source of his grimace of pain before he head butted the first Drakkaidian. Lucan quickly pulled it back into place as they ran, yelping in pain.

Running as fast as they could, the two rushed back toward the series of boulders leading into the canyon with the hope that they could lose the two Drakkaidians chasing them and evade the horsemen all together if they could weave their way back inside. Though the armored Drakkaidians behind them weren't more than ten feet away, Aeric and Lucan quickly pulled ahead without the burden of armor and weapons to weigh them down. Looking back as he ran over the blackened earth to the sound of shouting and hoof beats right behind them, Aeric saw the Drakkaidian's party on horseback had arrived past the boulder the man with the large axe had been standing on and were charging after them as well.

Knowing they wouldn't last out in the open, the Grandarian scanned ahead for a quicker means to escape them. The sloping canyon wall that led to the base was only twenty feet away but another steeper incline beside a massive boulder was just feet to their right. Yelling for Lucan to leap toward it, the Maven veered off course and prepared to jump into the canyon for the uncomfortable ride down. Just as they were about to lunge as hard as they could for the steep rock slope, Aeric heard the discharge of an unusual sound behind him. Before he could look back to see what had happened, a ball of electrified crimson energy flew past his head to slam into the boulder on their right, blasting it apart in a fearsome explosion of energy and dust. Shielding their faces through the falling fragments of the devastated boulder and shocked beyond belief, both of the retreating men came to a skidding halt, temporarily blinded by the display.

Coughing through the dust and waving it away from their faces, Aeric and Lucan lowered their arms to get their bearings. Before they could jump for the canyon slope, the two noticed several sword points reaching out for their necks. They froze again, realizing the horsemen had cornered them. Though several of the armored Drakkaidians prepared to swing down and finish them, a barking voice ordered them not to be touched. As the dust settled, Aeric and Lucan remained still and swept their eyes over the several horses and their riders surrounding them. Though Aeric knew the Warrior of Darkness must be among them as proven evident by the powerful display of dark energy a moment ago, he didn't have much time to guess which of them it was. Two of the horses were pushed apart by the man with the double bladed axe who had first discovered them. A look of boiling hatred adorned his rough face and he gripped the long handle of his weapon as he jostled his way through to them, batting away swords and lances in his way.

"No one will harm them," he spoke with quiet rage in his voice. "This convert scum is mine." Seeing him about to raise his weapon, Aeric frantically raised his hands in a defensive gesture.

"I'm telling you, we are not converts!" he shouted desperately. "We are free men looking for the resistance you are all obviously a part of!"

"Asinine," the large Drakkaidian snapped. "If you claim friendly to that cause and identify us as part of it, I find it strange you would attack us and try to escape!"

"Only because we don't have time for any of this!" Aeric continued heatedly, to which Lucan eyed him nervously praying his words would appease the Drakkaidian. "Our friends have been taken by Siarchs and we have to get to them before it's too late! One of them is a Mystic Sage! He's here to help you!" The Drakkaidian let out a loud grunt of disgust and shook his head.

"I've had enough of your pitiful lies, cowards!" he shouted, raising his axe.

"Hold, Captain Asthatch," came the voice of burly man wrapped in black armor from head to toe. Aeric and Lucan both shifted their gazes to the man as he looked them up and down. He was middle aged man, looking to be a veteran warrior from the scars on his rough face and over his shaven head. "I am the Warrior of Darkness, leader of the resistance. Do you have any proof of your claim?" Aeric held the Drakkaidian's gaze for a moment, in disbelief he was in the presence of a Montrox, the most infamous family in Iairia. Shooting a quick glance at Lucan to see if he could think of anything to prove the truth of their story, he found only a bemused look in his dreadful eyes. Turning back to the Warrior of Darkness uncertainly, he was struck by a sudden thought that forced him to tilt his head with sudden skepticism in his eyes. Mustering his courage to say what he had to, Aeric opened his mouth to slowly articulate his words.

"I can tell you that you are not the Warrior of Darkness, sir," he spoke quietly but as respectfully as possible. All the Drakkaidians were silent at this so Aeric continued. "Valgard Montrox was a young king, only in his late twenties when he ascended to the throne. With all due respect, judging by your age you look as old as he would be if he were still with us." Though the man in black before them was about to say something further, another voice from behind him started first.

"You seem to know much about Drakkaidia and its royal family for being from outside its borders," came the surprisingly high and feminine voice. Raising an eyebrow in surprise, Aeric watched as one of the riders behind the row surrounding them dismounted. Though the Drakkaidian wielding the axe spun around and told the rider to let him handle this, he was pushed aside to reveal a young woman emerging past the horses to meet Aeric's gaze with hard but curious eyes. Aeric was speechless at her appearance, not having noticed a girl with the Drakkaidians before. She was almost exactly as tall as he was and her slender body was encased in tight black garb from the neck down.

Though Aeric would have immediately gone as far as to label her figure striking to the eye, her feminine curves were masked by a gray shawl draped around her shoulders that stretched down over her front and back almost to her waist line where the ends came together at a triangular point. Jagged black glyphs were embroidered into the front of the gray material similar to the emblems found on the Drakkaidians' armor around her. She had a unique set of dark red armor over her forearms and legs, smooth and pressed tight around her limbs but for the thin silver edges around each piece.

The shawl and her short red hair that barely touched her shoulders gently waved in the breeze rustling past them. She put her hands on her hips as she narrowed her unusual but striking red eyes on Aeric as if to search for the truth of his story. At last she took a step closer and wrapped her fingers around the hilt of a short sword at her side attached to a thick brown belt with a fearsome buckle shaped like a cracking lightning bolt at its front.

"I am Valeri Montrox, daughter of my late father the King of Drakkaidia," she announced suddenly, still keeping her distrustful but intrigued eyes on the young man's. Taken aback by this revelation and momentarily disbelieving her, Aeric found that as he let the words digest and he stared at her hard face she was telling the truth. She looked just like how his grandfather described his grandmother Arilia Tieloc, once Arilia Montrox, back in the Days of Destiny. The girl's red hair and eyes were the same as hers and she even dressed similarly to what both his grandparents told him they had seen Verix Montrox look like as a youth.

Waiting for her to say something further, Aeric realized she had yet to take her gaze off him even to so much as glance at Lucan. Feeling uncomfortable, he prepared to say something but was cut off when the girl saw him open his mouth.

"In times like these it's necessary to hide my identity when dealing with possible converts. But we aren't the ones answering questions here, and you still haven't answered the one that decides whether we consider your story or kill you where you stand. The only proof I can see is the kind not good for you, since your friend has a convert brand on his arm." The Grandarian summoned his courage to respond to the authoritative girl.

"It's true," Aeric returned carefully, "my friend was branded as a convert. But he escaped his master after they left the shrine of the Ancients and he's been a free Maven ever since, fighting against converts." Aeric slowly reached to his right arm to pull up his sleeve tucked underneath his leather gauntlet and reveal his skin. "If we were convert spies trying to find the location of the resistance I'd be branded too."

"Not necessarily," the girl replied warily, shaking her head. "If the converts were smart they'd disguise you by keeping your arm clean."

"If you've ever encountered a convert you'd know they aren't that smart," Lucan spoke. Valeri Montrox's face abruptly tightened as she spun to face the Maven with a finger pointed up at him.

"I don't remember asking you a damn thing!" she shouted surprising both him and Aeric with the commanding power of her voice, to which the Drakkaidians extended their sword points closer to his neck. Her eyes calming, she turned back to Aeric obviously determined to work him down alone to test his authenticity. "What's all this about a Mystic Sage? And if you aren't a convert who are you? How do you know anything about my family?" Aeric mulled her question over in his mind, realizing something for the first time at the mention of her family in such general context.

"Well," he began timidly, awestruck at what he was about to say, "I actually am part of your family." She raised an eyebrow at this, a look of disgusted confusion ripping across her face.

"What are you talking about?" she bit at him.

"My name is Aeric Tieloc of Grandaria," the young man said slowly. "My grandfather, Tavinious Tieloc, took your great aunt, Arilia Embrin—or Montrox—for his wife. We have the same great-grandfather in Valif Montrox." A hush befell the entire group. The Drakkaidians' faces slowly loosened and shifted to one another, not sure what to think of such a claim. Lucan let his mouth drop and his incredulous eyes drift to his companion, just as blown away by the revelation as any. Valeri softened at this and stared at Aeric uncertainly, her grilling tempo and steadfast expression thrown off by the explanation she never could have seen coming. Seeing her falter, the brutish form of Captain Asthatch shook his head with a distrustful look and lowered his axe to the boy's neck.

"You claim to be the son of Darien Tieloc?" he grilled. "I was the commander of the guard at Dalastrak and met him with Valgard Montrox before the final stand against the

Ancients. He told Montrox his son was dead when he and the Grandarians joined with us. You look healthy for a dead man, convert." Though Aeric momentarily softened at the news his father believed him dead after the Ascension began and the pain it must have caused him, the Grandarian tightened with anger in the face of the accusation and he reached up to shove the flat of the axe beside his neck up and away from him.

"My father thought me to be dead because I was and have been with the Master Sage of the Order of Alberic since the Ascension began, who has been trying to get here to help you!" he shouted at Asthatch, his courage fueled by his anger. "And that sage, your resistance's best chance to survive the Ancients and come up with a plan to stop them, could be dying in a cavern of Siarchs right now because you won't let us go to help him!" At the end of the young man's passionate outburst, even Captain Asthatch was quiet, suddenly not so sure of his accusations. Seeing all eyes on him, Aeric set his own back onto Valeri Montrox's, still staring at him and struggling to penetrate to the truth of his words. "How the Master Sage and my party came to be here is a long and hard to believe story to be sure, but you have to trust me or it will be too late to save him and our other friend. If you won't help us at least let us go so we can try." Valeri remained silent at this, running her thoughts back and forth through her head. Seeing the dilemma about her unusually vulnerable eyes, Asthatch stepped forward into her view.

"Your Highness, please," he said. "Use your reason— the sages have been gone for over half a century and he has no proof of anything he is saying. I heard Darien Tieloc tell your father his son was dead myself." Though taking in his words, Valeri motioned for him to stand back with a sweeping gesture of her head. With her path clear, she continued stepping toward Aeric until only a few inches away from his face, her eyes determined and piercing again. She tilted her head as the breeze rustled a lock of her crimson hair over her face and the front tip of her shawl out to touch Aeric's tunic.

"You look like him," she said quietly at last, surprising them all. "I've seen your eyes before..." Hardening, she took a step back and put her hands back on her hips. "Are you telling me the truth?" Aeric nodded and told her he was, to which Asthatch let out a sharp huff and prepared to say something. Predicting his words, Valeri spun around to hold a hand before her to signal for quiet. "I know what you would say, Asthatch, but his eyes have convinced me of the truth. And the Maven is right—the converts aren't smart enough to come up with a ruse like this. They would never make it this far into Drakkaidia with the Siarchs and our mystery beasts roaming the flatlands. They are who they say they are, and I'm going with them to find this Mystic Sage who's looking for us." The Drakkaidians on horseback gradually lowered their weapons at this, obviously surprised at her decision by the way they looked back and forth at each other. Asthatch's eyes widened with disbelief.

"You'd trust them just like that?" he asked skeptically. "Put us all in harm's way based off an unsubstantiated story? Your father would never—" He stopped short when the girl before him tightened and a wave of crimson electricity jolted up from her clenched fist to shoot up her arm.

"I am not my father, captain," the girl told him coldly, narrowing her red eyes at him. "I am Princess of Drakkaidia and will do what I judge best. Two of our men were taken by Siarchs when they were scouting last night in the hills north of Dalastrak so I've abandoned the mission and have been tracking their swarm all day. I'll take these two with me into the Siarch cavern to rescue our men, and if there is indeed a Mystic Sage then we'll know they are telling the truth. If not, then you'll have your corpses." Aeric gulped at this, having never seen a lady exude such authority or ruthlessness.

"Surely you don't intend to go by yourself, Highness," another of the Drakkaidians behind her said dreadfully.

"I will move faster and more safely without the patrol," she returned. "I can control the Siarchs but the more of you there are for them to prey on, the more I have to concentrate on to keep you safe. Besides, I can sense the colony in the cliffs above this canyon and your horses will not be able to follow. I will take only the Grandarian and the Maven."

"Your Highness, this is madness—you can't trust them!" Asthatch practically shouted. The Warrior of Darkness merely frowned and locked her eyes on him.

"If anyone left alive is equipped to deal with the dangers of this world, it is me," she replied frigidly. "I want you to take the horses around the canyon to the far side of the cliffside where it slopes back down into the fields and wait for us to return. Should one of the beasts find you without me you won't survive so you are to find the best cover you can and stay silent. Those are my orders and they are not open for debate or interpretation. Now get going. I want to be on our way back to Hadecrest by nightfall." Though obviously wanting to challenge her, Asthatch knew he was in no position to do so and bit his tongue. With reluctance, the Drakkaidian captain slung his oversized axe behind his back and turned to mount one of the horses with his red cape swaying behind him.

"We'll be in position, Your Highness," he spoke with an overtly frustrated grunt, kicking his steed forward and calling for the rest of them to follow him. With all of the Drakkaidians on horses, they backed away from Aeric and Lucan and proceeded to gallop after Asthatch in the lead. As they sped up to ride around a series of boulders and disappear from view in a cloud of dust their steeds quickened into a run. Aeric and Lucan turned to glance at each other before fixing their eyes on the Drakkaidian princess standing before them, staring back. Standing in the silence with the girl looking at him the way she had before as if still searching for the truth about his identity, Aeric spoke.

"Do you really believe me?" he asked, amazed she had so suddenly reversed her stance to help them. She continued staring at him for a lingering moment before shrugging.

"It doesn't really matter what I believe," she said walking toward him. "I think you are who you say, but if you aren't and there is no Mystic Sage, you'll both be dead and I'll be no worse off, so I have nothing to lose." She walked in between the two, staring forward toward the sloping canyon wall leading toward the bottom of the basin and the cliffs ahead of them. "Keep up with me." With that, she leapt down over the slope to slide down and disappear from their view. Though shooting each other uncertain glances again, Aeric and Lucan hurried behind her to continue on for Revond and Alberic.

Chapter 20

Siarchs

With Valeri Montrox leading them, Aeric and Lucan quickly sprinted through the canyon basin where Captain Asthatch had discovered them shortly before. They made their way deeper in until approaching the first of the rising slopes leading up to the cliffs where the Warrior of Darkness guessed the Siarch colony to be. The two men she led remained quiet as she pressed them forward at a surprisingly strenuous pace, merely observing the Drakkaidian princess. She kept her gaze fixed toward her objective most of the time, but every few minutes she would occasionally glance back at Aeric to sweep her eyes over him when he wasn't looking, sizing him up as well. Observing her taking in the Grandarian between her dexterous movements across the treacherous terrain, Lucan felt a pang of distrust of the commanding princess ripple through his mind. He was both disheartened and skeptical that a mere girl led the fabled resistance to the Ascension he had heard stories about since it began.

Though Aeric was the most insecure in the trio and was hesitant to say anything, when they came to a narrow crevice leading out of the canyon toward a cliff wall above them he broke the uncomfortable silence hanging between them all by asking her how she knew the Siarchs would be in those cliffs for certain. The princess turned back for him as she leapt across a gap in the rocks and began crawling her way up the steep incline, taking another look at him before replying that she could feel them nearby. Though seemingly impatient that he didn't already grasp her abilities as an Elemental Warrior, she explained she could sense where Siarchs gathered as well as command them with her power the same as generations of her family had been able to do before. It was the same with other Elemental Warriors able to influence races comprised of their elements. Though

216

mockingly asking him how he didn't know this when he came from a line of Elemental Warriors himself, the boy merely ignored her and asked what she and her men were doing so far from the Black Peaks the resistance was rumored to operate from.

Fixing her eyes on him as if gauging what or what not to tell him as they came to the top of the crevice and the flat plateau looking over the canyon behind them, she cleared her throat and began to speak to address them both for the first time.

"The men with me are some of my best. I was leading them to the ruins of Dalastrak to investigate something," she answered vaguely. When she left it at that, Aeric searched his thoughts to guess what the something might be.

"It must be something pretty important to your resistance to risk bringing its leader out into the world with all the danger abroad," Lucan told her, pressing his luck to extract more out of her. The girl slowly rotated her head back around to face him at this, narrowing her cold eyes. Remembering how incensed she had become when her own captain had doubted her ability to keep herself safe, the Maven sank back and closed his mouth.

"You aren't worried about the Ancients, Your Highness?" Aeric asked for the silenced Southlander, taking care to address her in a proper fashion. "Even though you're an Elemental Warrior, there is still great risk." The girl shifted her gaze to him before sweeping it back to the dark earth before her.

"You should know better than any the kind of power I bear," she replied curtly. "Like you have the potential to become a Warrior of Light with power hindered only by your will to use it if you took up your Sword of Granis, my family's strength stretches beyond the normal boundaries of conventional elemental power as well. We're infused with strength originally taken from Dalorosk himself, developed by generations of Dark Mages and Montroxs to grant us power limited only by our spirit and determination—something you'll find Drakkaidians keep in hearty supply. My power flows from means other than the Source of Darkness, but I'm stronger, faster and more powerful than any other Elemental Warrior regardless. The only power ever to challenge ours was your family's and your Sword of Granis." Valeri paused then, realizing she had worked herself up and let out a breath

217

to calm down. "Besides, the Ancients haven't set foot or claw in Drakkaidian since Dalorosk first escaped the Cathedral. They aren't why we're here."

"Then what were the beasts you and your men were talking about, princess?" Aeric asked, remembering the Drakkaidians' multiple references to beasts they were fearful of encountering. The princess took in a long breath before looking up to the side of a cliff they had worked their way beside and coming to a halt. Narrowing her eyes and peering up its sides to observe a series of caves halfway up the jagged wall, she turned her body back to the men behind her.

"Dalorosk and his accursed brethren, though the primary enemies of the free peoples of Iairia, are not the most immediate threat upon us and our resistance movement against them," Valeri informed them, resting one of her hands on the hilt of her silver sword hilt along her waist. "There is something else moving across Drakkaidia; something else that leveled half of the countryside and maimed our people while the Ancients were to the south combing the lands for the final Source. We've seen movements of creatures in the night and heard strange reports of gruesome deaths near our base in the mountains, but no one at Hadecrest knows what they are. I came to Dalastrak to investigate a theory, but thanks to the Siarchs preying on what's left of Drakkaidia and abducting my men we didn't have time to stay."

The girl stopped there and pointed up to the multiple caverns in the cliff above them.

"I can sense a colony of Siarchs in there," she said, quickly changing subjects. "Like I said, I can protect you from them but only if you stay close and do exactly as I command once we're inside. If your friends are still alive, they'll be in a coagulation net—where the Siarchs slowly bleed their prey and feed on them. Siarchs always feed on the oldest prey they have first, so depending on if they captured my men or your friends first, they may already be dead. Whoever we find, we'll make our way to the coagulation net and release them."

"Well that's all fine and good, Your Highness, but how do you plan on getting all the way up there?" Lucan asked skeptically, looking up to the cavern openings several dozens of feet above them.

"Just follow me, Maven," the Drakkaidian girl retorted, spinning around for the cliff wall again. Doing as he was bid with Aeric beside him, the two men followed her over the rugged terrain until they worked their way around the cliff wall to another slope on the opposite side of the plateau they hadn't seen before that lead up to one of the lower cavern entrances. When Lucan asked her how she knew the concealed path was there, she informed him she had been in these caverns before as a child with her father when she was just learning to come to grips with her power. Remembering they were only a few hours away from Dalastrak, Aeric continued to trust the Drakkaidian princess and followed her up the narrow slope.

After several long minutes of nervously scaling the cliff side with the ground below stretching farther and farther away, the trio at last came within a few feet of the lowest opening in the wall several feet above them. Though Aeric thought it was still too far out of range, he was shocked to see Valeri Montrox leap up with surprising height and latch onto the vertical cliff wall with her bare hands. Kicking her feet into footholds, she looked down to the men below her and asked them what they were waiting for. Uneasy, both of them slowly took hold of the rocky cliff and began slowly climbing it after her. Within moments Valeri was hoisting herself up into the maw of the lowest cave entrance, turning back to help pull Aeric and Lucan inside after her. Though Aeric lost his footing and might have fallen as he took the girl's hand, she held him firm and lifted him up beside her with impossible strength for a girl her size. She frowned as she lay him down beside Lucan.

"There won't be any room for slip ups or mistakes in here, Master Tieloc," she told him frustrated, using his name for the first time. "It will be night soon and they'll be waking up in a hurry so we have to be quick about this. Be careful and do as I say or the Siarchs will be all over you despite my power to ward them off." Before she could say anything else, they heard the sound of a small shriek from behind them in the darkness of the cavern. Spinning around, Valeri observed a speeding image bolting for her out of the darkness.

Reaching up her left hand, she opened her palm and let it hang in the air for a moment while a lone Siarch sailing toward them veered up to bat its wings around the air above them, making Lucan and Aeric nervous. Eventually, it calmed and landed to lock its miniature talons around one of Valeri's fingers. Though they worried it would poison her the same as it had Aeric the night before, the small creature merely wrapped its wings around its petite body and lowered its head, slowly spinning it back and forth as if soothed. Bringing up her other hand to gently stroke the small space between the Siarch's ears, the girl raised an eyebrow at the two men slowly rising beside her.

"They really aren't that imposing when tame. They've worked themselves into a frenzy with free reign over the lands but no prey in them. Before the Ascension they would never had fed on humans but they're left with little choice. This one's just a baby." To Aeric and Lucan's shock, Valeri raised the little creature to her face and gently kissed it on its furry forehead with a lock of her short red hair falling over her face. As she raised her arm to command it to be on its way, they found her faintly smiling for the first time they had seen. The contented expression quickly dispersed as she rose and told them the adults would not be so friendly if they caught them feeding and told them to stay close to her as they moved into the larger cavern beyond.

Carefully ambling into the darkness, the trio continued along a flat surface of the cave until coming to a narrow opening above them where they could hear hundreds more shrieks gently echoing through the cavern. There was a wall in front of them and another on the sides of the opening of the lowest cave mouth they had come from, creating a natural fissure. Making her way to the side of the wall in front of them, Valeri took hold of a ledge then flipped around to shove her feet against both of the rock walls between them. Motioning for her companions to follow, she began climbing the gap to the cavern above her. Though having greater difficulty than the nimble and supernaturally powerful Drakkaidian princess, both Aeric and Lucan found a larger ledge in the wall to stand on as they rose through the fissure beside Valeri to peer out into the cavern above them.

The largest cave in the cliff stretched for nearly a hundred feet in front of them with almost fifty feet between the ground and ceiling, covered with stalactites and hundreds of sleeping Siarchs hanging from them. Aeric's felt his mouth slip open as he let their incredible numbers wash over him. It was as if the entire ceiling was moving. There were more inside the massive fissures similar to the one they stood in littering the ground and several of the little creatures were coming awake, flying up from the ground around a column of rock toward the back of the cave. Before Aeric could get a good look at it, he heard Valeri quietly curse and looked at her curiously.

"We don't have much time," she told them in a whisper. "See the coagulation net?" Aeric and Lucan peered to the end of the cavern, only illuminated by the several openings in the wall behind them where light from the failing afternoon sky was seeping in. Hanging above the column of rock Aeric had noticed before was a slimy green net oozing a mucus-like substance onto the cavern floor. There were several Siarchs climbing along the uneven net like insects, apparently strengthening its weak spots. Peering at the bottom of the net where the weight hung was a sight that made Aeric's heart jump high into his chest. Laying immobile in the center of the dripping coagulation net were two decaying corpses and the slimy bodies of Revond and Alberic, their limbs jutting out of the openings in the net.

"Revond," the Grandarian whispered out loud, to which Valeri narrowed her eyes at the figures in the net. Telling them to hurry but move conservatively, she gradually lifted herself out of the fissure to stand full height in the cavern of Siarchs. As the men rose beside her, Valeri lifted her arms and took a deep breath, causing several of the Siarchs jetting toward them to slow and merely fly in circles above them in the soggy cave air. Keeping her arms aloft as if offering a disarming gesture to the creatures of darkness, she began to walk forward over the treacherous cavern ground. Aeric and Lucan kept pace behind her but nervously prayed the floor would not give way from their weight with the loose rocks and fissures everywhere. Lightly hopping to stout ledges, the two anxiously kept their eyes on the Siarchs swooping around them.

After a few minutes of navigating the perilous floor of the cave, the trio at last came to the oozing green net hanging from a stalactite at its rear. While Aeric leaned in to observe Revond and Alberic's condition, Lucan immediately pulled a dagger from the belt on his chest and set to work sawing the surprisingly tough net even at its weak points. Valeri stood beside Aeric, peering in and exhaling a discouraged breath to see two sets of Drakkaidian armor covering rotting skeletons, obviously already consumed by the Siarchs. Though disheartened at the loss of her men she eyed the others with wonder, observing the gray cloak on one of them like the one she had heard stories of about the Mystic Sage Zeroan.

Shifting her gaze to the young man standing beside her, the Drakkaidian princess was uncertain again, clinging to the possibility the Grandarian was telling the truth and was indeed there to help her. Staring at him while Lucan continued to cut away at the net mumbling to himself how disgusting it felt, Valeri forced herself to come back to her senses and reach up for several of the Siarchs moving across the net above them. Motioning for them to come down and land on Revond and Alberic, they obeyed and began sinking their talons into their flesh again. Though Aeric was quick to spin to her and ask what she was doing, the girl brought a finger before her lips to signal the need for silence.

"The Siarchs like to feed on live, moving prey," she told him in a whisper, leaning into speak in his ear. "They carry an anti-venom to undo the effects of the paralyzing chemical they use to catch their prey. I'm coaxing them to use it on your friends. They should return to us fairly quickly as long as they are otherwise unspoiled." Turning back to watch the Siarchs inject his friends with the chemicals from their talons, Aeric observed Lucan finally cut through enough of the netting to allow Alberic to slide through. Catching him before he fell, the Maven hoisted his slimy body to Aeric while he continued working Revond out. Aeric gathered Alberic in his arms and wiped away the slime over his face, barely able to believe the mighty Ancient of Light could fall victim to the dangers of the world like any of them.

As Lucan was pulling Revond free and preparing to sling his heavy form over his back to carry him out, a deep tremor in the ground caught the attention of the entire group and they froze. Dozens of the Siarchs along the ceiling felt it as well and came awake, unfolding their wings to take to the air in the cavern. Raising her hand to them to soothe and ward them off, Valeri told them it was time they took their leave. Before they could so much as turn around, however, they felt another tremor in the ground and were shocked to see scores of the Siarchs suddenly tearing through the air out of a fissure in the ground beside them on the right side of the cave. Though Valeri tried to control them and direct them back to the ceiling, she was surprised to find them in such a frenzy she could barely ensnare even a few of them under her control. Most of them were making for the opening of the cave into the open air.

Baffled at what could have provoked them into such a frightened state, the Warrior of Darkness turned back for the deep fissure they had emerged from as another tremor shook the cavern, this time much stronger. Turning to observe the origin point of the shaking for themselves, Aeric and Lucan watched as a faint red light began to line the fissure walls, steadily rising to shine out into the cave. Feeling their hearts beating wildly, the trio watched as the tips of two massive wings similar to the Siarchs pointed out of the hole, followed by a set of claws tearing into the ground with a loud crash that woke the remaining Siarchs from their slumber.

Though Valeri continued to shield them from the winged creatures, she stood as alarmed as her companions as the shape of a large oval body with a sunken head rose from the fissure. A pair of glowing red eyes bulged from its head and radiated into the cave, locking onto the three humans before it. The creature had a smooth black body but its arms and legs were covered in a mess of veins and arteries reaching all the way to its clawed hands and feet. Its limbs and joints were like hydraulics that pumped in and out to produce its strength, thin and disproportionate to its round body. Taking the fearsome creature in, both Aeric and Valeri remembered stories of a creature similar to its appearance from their grandfathers and felt their jaws drop open in dread.

It looked like a demon of the Netherworld.

A Valcanor.

It was one of the many creatures that plagued the lands of Iairia during the Days of Destiny, summoned from the underworld pit by Valif Montrox to do his bidding. Though not sure how one of the dark creatures could be standing before them when the seal to the Netherworld was firmly in place, both Aeric and Valeri knew what the creature was and what it was capable of. It took a lumbering step toward them, growling from behind its non-existent mouth in its sunken head. Not willing to wait for the creature to act first, Valeri Montrox tightened her face with determination and extended one of her raised hands toward it with her fingers spreading wide and a charge of flickering crimson light appearing around them. Before Aeric or Lucan could look back to investigate its source, they were astounded to find a flash of light and an electrified burst of dark energy flying from the girl's fingertips to slam into the large creature, batting it back to send it falling off balance to land on its back over the fissure it had crawled out of.

"Run!" she screamed as loud as she could to the men beside her, spinning around to leap back over the unsteady terrain of the cave toward the openings far ahead. Not needing to hear anymore to know they were in serious trouble, Aeric and Lucan started after her as fast as they were able amid the storm of Siarchs that had erupted above them and the quaking ground thanks to the thrashing of the demonic beast behind them. Keeping pace with Valeri this time proved to be an impossible task, as they were both burdened with men heavier than they on their shoulders and easily lost their balance on the treacherous ground riddled with fissures and pitfalls. Valeri quickly realized they couldn't match her speed and turned to shout for them to hurry. Between keeping the Siarchs under control and watching the furious form of the Valcanor rise back to its feet, she was in no position to help them, having her own hands full.

As the two men rushed past her for the largest entrance of the cavern, Valeri stood her ground and mentally ordered a slicing storm of the Siarchs she had mustered to rush at the demon already stomping after them. The storm of the small creatures shot past her, sending her silky red hair and shawl up as they flew. Colliding into the massive creature, the Siarchs scratched with their razor sharp talons to inflict as much damage as possible. Though they clearly had it annoyed and were slicing some of the veins along its limbs, with a few massive swipes of its mangled arms the Siarchs were beat away and began flying around crazily again, somehow out of Valeri's control. Seeing the creature start after them again, Valeri heard Aeric desperately calling for her to leave it and hurry after them.

Wheeling around to see the men halfway across the cavern, the girl grit her teeth and ran to catch up, leaping over rocks and the few safe surfaces with amazing agility. Quickly arriving beside Aeric and Lucan carrying Alberic and Revond, she knew she wouldn't be able to control the Siarchs and fight the demonic creature chasing them at the same time. Compromising as best she could once they were nearing the fissure where they had emerged minutes before, she screamed that they wouldn't have time to climb down and ordered them to run for the largest opening in front of them. Though Lucan was quick to remind her there was no ground beneath them there, she bellowed for him to do it.

Turning to glance at the Drakkaidian princess as he ran, Aeric saw her lifting both fists above her toward the center of the cavern's ceiling while a pulsating charge of energy began to grow around them. When it had illuminated the entire cave with volatile power, the girl let out a sharp scream and let a beam of passionate red energy explode from her fists toward the jagged ceiling, careening into it with such force Aeric and Lucan nearly fell over even as they came to the flat surface of the cave's mouth. Seeing the Siarchs desperately dash for the exit around them as Valeri let her dark power fade and the beam disperse, Aeric watched as she wheeled around to avoid the collapsing ceiling beginning to rain down around her. Though feeling his heart beat so fast it threatened to leap out of his chest as she barely dodged falling stalactites, Aeric saw her summon the fleeing Siarchs around her as she dashed toward them.

"Jump!" she yelled as the entire cave began collapsing around them. Though Lucan shot her a look of confused disgust, having seen nothing below them for dozens of feet but clear air, he was left with little choice when the bodies of Siarchs began pushing him onward. "Hold onto your friends!" Valeri yelled as she arrived by their side, looking back a final time to see the Valcanor being pummeled and buried by falling rock. Her view obscured by the Siarchs around her, she looked back to jump out of the cave entrance with Aeric, Lucan, Revond and Alberic around them just as the mouth itself collapsed and fell to crush the remaining Siarchs lingering there. The rest of the winged creatures remained below the party's feet, desperately struggling to rise. It was then that Aeric realized what they were doing. Though they would have fallen to their deaths on the cliff by jumping without them, the Siarchs were slowing their fall.

As they descended through the storm of Siarchs cluttering beneath them, the group at last fell on the hard rock at the base of the cliff wall with a painful but non-lethal drop. Scattering and dispersing into the air as soon as the humans were safely on the ground, the Siarchs shot back into the sky to form into their concentrated storm and fly off to the north at once. Watching as they departed into the dark sky, Aeric could only turn in amazement to the Warrior of Darkness who had saved them with her incredible power and quick thinking. Though ready to say something, the Grandarian was cut off by the feeling of Alberic stirring beneath him.

"Alberic is coming to," Aeric told Lucan at once, to which the Maven nodded and rose from his back on the ground.

"Revond too," he replied.

"Their ability to move will be restored soon," Valeri informed them, jumping to her feet and pulling them up by their tunics. "Now hurry! That thing might still be alive in there and I don't want to be here if—" The girl was cut off by the sound of several strident shrieks echoing from the southern sky. Wheeling around, all three of them saw particularly foreboding storm clouds building in the sky. Remembering what rolling storms signaled, Valeri swallowed hard and helped lift Alberic. "Those are no Siarch cries. We have to get to my men at the base of the cliffside, now!" Her words were desperate and fearful for the first time Aeric and Lucan had heard and they shot each other dreadful glances as she helped Aeric lift Alberic and move him along the cliff wall. Taking hold of Revond with what strength he had left, Lucan followed them terrified of what may have been racing toward them in the storm.

Chapter 21

<u>Valcanor</u>

The trio scurried around the cliff walls and down the western slope where Valeri Montrox had ordered her men to be waiting as fast as their feet would carry them. Though tired from the frightening encounter with the demonic Valcanor in the Siarch colony and burden of carrying Alberic and Revond's slimy bodies, the three pressed on as the distant shrieks in the sky sounded through the windy air. Running toward the end of the plateau beneath the cliff, Aeric continued to feel Alberic stirring with life. Though he tried to coax him awake, Valeri was quick to tell him not to waste his time as the Siarch venom was too strong for anyone to recover so quickly.

Coming around to the west side of the cliff, the group found a long slope leading down to the plains below them riddled with boulders and uneven rocks jutting up. Though it made for a treacherous path down to the horsemen they could see assembled a few hundred feet away, the frequent obstacles proved to be a blessing in disguise. On so steep a slope even Aeric and Valeri together might have gained too much momentum and lost their balance with Alberic on their shoulders. Thankfully the footholds and boulders to lean against on the way down ensured they never moved too fast with their precious cargo.

By the time the group neared the base of the western slope of the cliffs the large caped Drakkaidian named Asthatch was already shouting out to Valeri asking if she was alright. Though she could hear her captain's voice, his words were lost to the increasingly savage winds ripping down from the ominous black clouds rolling above them. When the Warrior of Darkness and her companions emerged from the last of the rocks, Asthatch and two of the men behind him dismounted and rushed to help lift the immobile men they carried. When Asthatch single handedly took Alberic from Aeric and Valeri he felt the ooze over the man's body and shook his head with disgust.

"Blasted Siarchs," he cursed to himself before fixing his gaze on Aeric uncertainly. "Is this...?"

"The other looks to be the sage, captain," Valeri answered for the Grandarian. "They're both still out from Siarch venom but it looks like our new allies were telling the truth." Asthatch was silent for a moment at this, sweeping his distrustful eyes over Aeric before turning to order his men to help the incapacitated man in his arms up to a horse.

"What of our men?" Asthatch asked, turning back to the Drakkaidian princess.

"We were too late," she replied with a hint of sorrow intertwined in her voice. She pointed to the two empty horses riding with the group and motioned for Aeric and Lucan to mount them. They did, sitting behind Alberic and Revond limply mounted in front of them. "Asthatch, one of the beasts was hiding inside the Siarch colony. It attacked us and I think there are more on the way here now coming with the storm." The Drakkaidian was still at this, her words slowly sinking in.

"You believe it is as we feared then?" he asked, aware of what the coming of storm clouds meant. She nodded and took hold of the saddle of the black horse beside her, mounting it and taking hold of the reins.

"I never got a good look at the portal in Dalastrak but there's a dead Valcanor buried in the caves of the cliff. Obviously the seal is somehow broken. We'll never make it to Hadecrest if we're being followed and I can't fight more than one so we have to get to cover outside of the plains," she stated with authority. Asthatch's face buckled with fortitude and he gave her a single nod, climbing up to sit on his horse. Before he could say anything he was cut short by Lucan, turning to shout to Aeric with energy coursing through him.

"Revond is trying to speak!" he exclaimed. "I think he's coming to. We should wait and see if he wakes up. He'll know what to do." Though Aeric was hopeful hearing this, Valeri was quick to interject.

"Mystic Sage or not, he won't be of any help to us in the state he's in," she said, rejecting his idea. "His only chance, as is ours, is to get away from here as quickly as we can."

"We ride west with all speed!" Asthatch shouted to other Drakkaidians around him. "Fly as if the spirit of

Drakkan was behind you!" Kicking his steed forward, the Drakkaidian captain led the party of horses away from the slopes of the cliff behind them and started back into the flat plains as fast as they could run. Asthatch and Valeri took the lead with Aeric and Lucan behind them and the rest of the Drakkaidian soldiers making up the rear, all of them constantly looking back to scan the dark skies. The once distant and blurred shrieks were right behind them and loud enough to cause the riders to cringe when they ripped through the air. Though the wind blew at their backs from the black billows seemingly chasing them, the group could only move so fast with Aeric and Lucan holding onto the reins and the motionless men sitting before them as well as the two wounded archers at the rear still bleeding from the Maven's wounds inflicted earlier.

Though they rode on for several minutes into the dark plains, when the sun at last disappeared behind the thick clouds obscuring it and evening fell, Aeric saw Valeri spin her head around and look into the clouds above them as if sensing imminent danger. Following her eyes into the sky, the Grandarian was horrified to see three mammoth creatures suddenly drop out of the clouds screeching as they came. All three had eerily glowing eyes like the demon they had seen in the cave but their bat like wings were spread wide to allow them to swiftly glide down in a steep dive for the party of horses running beneath them. Valeri was the first to draw her sword, the look on her face fearful but resolute.

Tightly clenching the hilt of her weapon as she rode, a faint layer of red energy began to pulsate up and down the blade. Shooting the weapon skyward, she released a thin beam of crimson energy crackling through the air toward the Valcanor. Seeing it coming, the three rolled to their right with surprising maneuverability for creatures so large. Only the demon on the far right was caught in the wing by Valeri's attack, slicing down its middle. Unable to maintain its altitude or balance in the tempestuous air, the shrieking demon slowly drifted to the south until slamming into the earth, grounded.

Though improving their odds, Valeri still knew they she could not contend with two of the savage demons at once and attempted to send another slash of energy flinging from her blade to stop them. While Aeric watched the demons evade it entirely and continue after them, he heard Alberic mumbling something and turned back to check on him. When his eyes were turned back, they shot open with terror to observe another Valcanor diving down from the clouds ahead of them. Though he shouted Valeri's name as loud as he could and pointed forward as the creature rushed to meet them head on, she noticed it too late.

Only a dozen feet above from the ground, the winged demon slashed its massive arm down as it passed over the riders. Slamming its claws into their horses, Valeri, Aeric and Alberic were sent flying from the head of the column. It narrowly missed Asthatch, slashing out for the creature with his oversized axe. Though Aeric and Alberic landed in a patch of loose soil when flung from their horse, Valeri landed on her back over gravelly terrain and rolled to a painful halt on a sunken boulder in the earth.

Hearing her cries of pain, Asthatch immediately turned his horse back for her only to find the other two Valcanor originally trailing them sweeping through the rear of his men taking hold of a few of them and their horses with their clawed hands. The demons savagely threw them into the air to fall to their deaths far beyond. As they rushed by him Asthatch let out a barbaric scream and slashed his mighty axe into the creature's middle. Only scratching the surface of its thick hide, the Valcanor was affected little and Asthatch was thrown off his horse with his axe flying out of his grip from the force of the collision.

Lifting back up into the sky, the three remaining Valcanor joined together and set their piercing gazes on the red-haired girl struggling to rise on the boulder, identifying her as the only real threat to their defenses. Swooping down and crashing around her with their clawed feet fragmenting the earth from the force of their landings, Valeri was knocked back to her side. Seeing herself surrounded and the creatures reaching for her, she rolled as hard as she could to avoid being grasped by their clawed hands, flipping back up to her feet and lifting her sword.

Before the Warrior of Darkness could muster her dark power to defend herself she was finally plucked off the ground into one of the demon's clutches with dizzying force. Watching her being seized, Aeric felt his already rapidly beating heart raise high into his chest with dread. He shouted for Asthatch or any of the remaining Drakkaidians to help her, but none were nearby and he was unarmed. Holding the powerful girl in its bleeding hand, the Valcanor began to squeeze with crushing force to which the Drakkaidian princess screamed out in anguish. In his desperation to help her, Aeric remembered the Source of Light hanging around his neck and its effectiveness in dispelling creatures of darkness. Though aware he would be announcing their location to Dalorosk and the Ancients by using it, he knew he had no choice if he wanted to save Valeri. Leaving Alberic and rushing toward the demons while reaching inside his tunic, the boy slowed when he patted down his shirt but felt nothing inside.

His eyes going wide with horror, he realized it was gone. He spun around to look for the white medallion somewhere on the earth, guessing it had been lost when he was knocked over by the Valcanor. Though scanning the ground for the powerful talisman in a panic, he heard Valeri screaming even louder and knew he had no time. By now the first Valcanor Valeri had dropped had marched up to her as well, its wing bleeding as it came. Though defenseless, the boy charged forward for the princess to do anything he could to help her. He could see her attempting to use her dark power to blow the creature that held her back and force it to release her but she could barely find the strength to breathe in its grasp much less muster her elemental power.

Just as all hope looked like it had faded and Valeri could feel the crushing darkness enveloping her, she and Aeric were both amazed to find a shaft of shining white light suddenly protruding through the Valcanor's prodigious round gut. Noticing this for itself, the demonic beast looked down through its pain to find itself speared through the middle by the white light. Before it could paw at it or attempt to pry it out, Valeri and Aeric were amazed to see it suddenly spread vertically up and down the creature to cut it into two halves that slowly fell to separate on the dark earth. There was no blood, as if it had been cauterized down the middle, and as it dropped dead the large fingers around Valeri at last loosened and she pried her way free. Painfully crawling away, she spun her head around to see where the attack had come from.

Looking past the defeated hulk of the winged demon to the last standing horse in the distance, Valeri, Aeric, and the other three Valcanor observed the figure wrapped in his slimy gray cloak sitting upright with one of his gloved hands shining with white energy. Though in disbelief at how it was possible, Aeric grinned when he saw the Master Sage Revond gritting his teeth and raising his hand to lift the halves of the sliced Valcanor and heave them at the three demons staring at him uncertainly. The attack sent the creatures staggering back, trying to swat the corpse of their kin away. Though the winged monsters were about to lift off and fly over to attack this newest threat, Aeric was surprised to see them all suddenly turn toward him. Though baffled at why they were staring in his direction, his doubts were answered when a white mass of something huge flew over his head and slammed into the Valcanor, leaving a trail of golden contrails behind in the air above the Grandarian.

Staring in wonder, Aeric saw Alberic landing in front of Valeri in his true form and standing up on his hind legs with his angelic wings spread wide. Though the Valcanor were frightened by the golden light the strange creature exuded, they lunged at it with their gnarled limbs slashing out. Alberic struck first, slamming his already raised front legs into one of them and knocking it to the ground. Stomping it with his hooves, intense light flared up to incinerate the top half of the demon's body while he beat his wings to escape into the sky before the other two Valcanor could reach him. Watching as if in a trance as the demons lifted off after the white horse to battle it in the sky above her, Valeri Montrox shook her head wondering what the creature that saved her was or where it had come from.

Though Alberic made quick work of one of the demons by slamming its hind legs into its head and burning holes through it with his golden hooves, the creature's lifeless form dropped where it died and began plummeting like a rock through the sky. Realizing it was coming straight for her, Valeri returned to her senses and tried to lift herself but found her body too sore and bruised to even rise to her feet. Staring up at the enormous dead corpse falling for her that would certainly crush her to death while the white horse did battle with the other demon, Valeri was surprised to feel someone behind her dragging her by her arms and lifting her into his. Looking up she found Aeric Tieloc holding her and running as fast as he could away from the falling Valcanor just before it slammed into the earth where she had been moments before.

Knocked off his feet by the force of impact, Aeric fell on his back but held Valeri in front of him to protect her from the brunt of the fall. Though she let out a sharp yelp of pain when landing, she looked back to the dead Valcanor a few feet behind them where she would have been crushed if not for the young man. She looked back at him with an incredulous look on her face and in her wide eyes, seeing him panting hard and already staring at her. When neither one of them said anything, they heard the remaining Valcanor screech as Alberic kicked it down to the earth to destroy it as well. Landing on the plains over its vanquished foe, the white horse looked up to survey his friends around him, spotting Aeric and Valeri first. Trotting over to them, Aeric felt Valeri clutch onto him tighter in fear of what the creature would do. When it stopped above them and lowered its head to reveal its shining gold eyes to them, Valeri was amazed to hear it speak.

"Are you alright, Aeric?" Alberic asked in his majestic voice, to which Valeri's eyes widened even further. Aeric let out a deep breath of relief that the mystical being was restored.

"I'll live thanks to you," the Grandarian returned. "How did...?"

"I recover so quickly?" the Ancient of Light finished for him. "I've been conscious since you rescued me, young man. I have been poisoned by Siarchs many times before, and as our new friend knows, it is possible to build up a natural resistance to Siarch venom the more one is exposed to it. Besides, I took this from you to provide a quick boost of strength—just enough so my brothers would not be able to sense it." A faint light flashed in Alberic's mouth then quickly faded as he opened it to drop something at the boy's feet. Looking down, both Aeric and Valeri saw a white medallion lying there. Relief washing through him again, Aeric gently leaned to his side with the Drakkaidian princess in his arms to pick it up and tell the white horse he thought it had been lost.

"And as for me," came another voice from behind Alberic's large form, "the Sage's Draught in me helps to purge poison or sickness with relative speed. Quickly enough for me to muster a little power to aid you, it would seem." Aeric, Valeri and Alberic all turned to find a horse carrying Lucan Hauk Erland and the Master Sage Revond appearing from behind the Ancient of Light. Though Revond looked exhausted, he was sitting upright with a faint smile as he looked down to the two youths on the ground. He raised his hand to wipe a lingering batch of slime off his black beard as he opened his mouth to speak again. "But Alberic and I owe you three our lives for saving us first. I am Master Sage Revond of the Order of Alberic. We are in your debt, Princess Montrox." Valeri tilted her head and stared at the man in gray before glancing back at Aeric, to which he nodded at her in confirmation he was who he said he was.

"Is this... creature of your creation, Mystic Sage?" the girl asked, looking at the white steed once again while it pulled in its feathered wings. Though the sage tried to respond, he turned his head to cough and fell victim to his fatigue.

"That's the long part of the story I mentioned before, Your Highness," Aeric answered for him. The girl looked back at him to peer into his eyes at this, to which Aeric realized he was still holding her over him and blushed red. "Umm, can you stand, Your Highness?" Shaking off her own discomfiture, the Drakkaidian girl told him she was sore from falling off her horse and being squeezed by the Valcanor but that she would recover quickly. Seeing Aeric in need of help, Lucan dismounted and slowly helped her up while the young Tieloc stood full height again. Before she could ask any more of her many questions to the Mystic Sage sitting before her, the group heard the calls of Asthatch racing toward the princess with his red cape flying up behind him and his oversized axe in his hands. Seeing him ready to defend her, Valeri lifted one of her sore arms for him to stand down. As he raced toward her and saw her signal for him to hold, the ill-tempered captain slowed to a jog but nervously gripped his weapon tighter when looking over the large white horse that had defeated the Valcanor.

"What manner of beast is this?" he asked to no one in particular, sweeping his eyes over Alberic.

"I'm not sure, but as it just saved my life, I think you can assume it is of no threat to us, captain," Valeri told him weakly, clutching her side. Seeing her in pain, the captain shoved Aeric and Lucan aside and braced her himself, asking her for orders. Turning to observe the rest of her group, she saw all of her men other than Asthatch dead across the plain and their only horse carrying the exhausted Master Sage. "We have to get back to Hadecrest as quickly as possible. We'll need to find transportation somehow. We're in no condition to travel by foot."

"I may be able to assist you with that, Your Highness," Alberic spoke to her, nearly shocking Asthatch out of his skin. "I have just enough room on my back to ferry the five of you anywhere you'd like to go."

"Do you have enough energy to fly, Alberic?" Lucan asked, remembering he had still not gotten the rest he needed from the last time they touched down.

"As long as our destination is not too far off I can manage it," the Ancient replied. Though Aeric could see the hesitancy in Valeri's eyes at riding on the strange creature, he stepped into her view and told her she could trust him. Keeping her eyes on the Grandarian for a lingering moment, the Drakkaidian princess nodded and raised her right hand to brush a lock of her short red hair behind her ear.

"To Hadecrest then," she said. "We'll sort everything out once we've all recovered." Nodding in agreement, the group waited for Alberic to lean down and allow them to slowly climb over his back, taking great care to be gentle with Valeri and Revond particularly. When they had all mounted the white horse's back, Alberic began to trot forward until in a gallop. Stretching his feathered wings away from his body, Valeri and Asthatch were amazed to find them lifting off the ground into the night with lines of golden light streaking behind them. Seeing the Drakkaidians' amazed faces, Aeric looked back to Lucan and took a deep breath. The Maven returned his exhausted but relieved expression, praying they would finally be safe for the moment.

The Bloody Square outside the southern wall of the fortress of the Holy Shrine was a mess. After the wooden stage where new converts were beaten and branded had mysteriously collapsed and splintered into the mob around it the night before, the ensuing riot generated by the escape of the prisoners had spread to engulf the entire area and even the top half of the makeshift city where the third tier of Galantia once stood. Though the guards and jailers in the dungeons of the Holy Shrine had attempted to subdue the violent unrest for nearly an hour, it was finally quelled by the reappearance of the Ancient of Darkness lumbering back through the city on foot, smashing anything in his path as he weakly stumbled through entire stone buildings and tall watchtowers the converts had constructed. Seeing the fearsome behemoth crashing through the city in a fit of rage, the converts immediately fell quiet and retreated to the outskirts to avoid his vehemence.

When Dalorosk arrived at the base of the Holy Shrine he slowly climbed up its exterior to the top level where he and the other Ancients stored their Sources, driving his horned feet into the walls as if the rungs of a ladder. Observing the destruction of the Bloody Square below him as he climbed, he grit his massive bloodstained teeth in his colossal jaws and guessed the intruders had caused this as well. Reaching the top, he slowly transformed into his smaller human form to crawl onto one of the six pedestals and into the dark orb of light levitating above it. The Ancient of Darkness lingered inside the black sphere of energy for several long minutes before stepping out, his dirtied and torn attire refreshed and his face composed once more. Taking a deep breath, he opened his dark eyes and walked across the floor to the staircase leading to the shrine.

The Ancient of Darkness waited inside a chamber of the fortress for nearly a full day before the first of his brothers arrived. It was of course Wyrik, landing on the top of the tower beside his Source of Wind as always. Next came Golthrout, blasting out of one of his fissures in the earth adjacent to the city to transform into his human form and walk into the shrine through the dungeons. He found Vorkoise waiting for him at the entrance, having just burrowed in from the Eastern Sea through a muddy riverbed. By the time they ascended the multiple levels of the tower discussing what they had sensed the day before that caused them to return to the shrine prematurely, they heard a loud roar from outside in the city. Continuing up the stairwell from a cell block on the first floor, they emerged in the central chamber of the shrine beneath the roof where the Sources rested to find the gaping hole in the floor that Revond had made the previous day. As they stood puzzling over why half of their Holy Shrine was in disrepair, they turned to find flames escaping from one of the nearby staircases followed by Moltar leaping out of it the next moment. Transforming into his human form as he landed in front of them, he found the other figures staring at him.

"I suppose being as small and pathetic as you has its advantages at times, Moltar," Vorkoise said with a mocking grin on his face. The figure in red sneered and continued walking past them toward an arching doorway along the wall.

"As I recall, I managed to slip past your scouts onto your lands on my own more times than any of you ever breached mine in the old war," he recoiled abrasively. "And I suppose being an overgrown sea-worm has its disadvantages when traversing those lands, doesn't it, Vorkoise?" Though the Ancient of Water was ready to leap at him, Golthrout raised a hand to his chest to signal him to stand down and silently followed Moltar into the doorway. When the three were inside, they found Wyrik in his human form standing with his arms crossed beside a table, picking feathers out of his sleeves. The chamber was bare except for the table and single chair at its end and the few torches on the walls to illuminate it. He was speaking to a figure in black sitting at the table with his back to the entrance and the other Ancients.

"All I'm saying, brother, is the humans have their uses," Wyrik continued, turning to observing the coming of his kin. "And besides, we're all here so we should decide this together—like everything else. How many times must you be reminded that we act as one, Dalorosk?"

"What are you demanding now, Dalorosk?" Vorkoise asked, walking beside Golthrout and Moltar as they approached the long table scattered with oddly cut pieces of dark stone and long scrolls messily draped over its edges.

"He wants to wipe out the humans just because they let one slip past them," Wyrik informed him disbelievingly.

"It isn't just because of the disciple!" Dalorosk abruptly shouted, slamming a fist against the table. "We can't trust any of them! We never should have used them in the first place—they're just sacks of meat that conspire to survive like a disease spreading wherever it can. What have we got in return for allowing them to live? More humans? The entire reason behind their existence now is to find us the Source. Every one of them let it slip by yesterday!"

"Hold on, what's this about a disciple? What in the name of the shards happened yesterday? I sensed the traitor empowered," Golthrout said, stopping behind Dalorosk's chair with the others. The Ancient of Darkness turned his attention back to the stones he was fitting together in his hands, fusing them with the dark energy radiating from his fingertips.

237

"One of the treacherous dog's disciples—probably the one you let disappear inside the tower the day we first attacked—survived the Ascension and penetrated into the shrine. He carried the Source of Light and used it to free Alberic." The three Ancients who just arrived froze at this, their faces shocked.

"The Source was here?" Moltar repeated aghast. "Under your very nose? And you let it go?"

"Perhaps if one of you idiots had been closer by we could have tracked Alberic or cut him off!" Dalorosk barked with such rage that spit flew from his lips. "There was also a boy with the disciple who could wield the power of light. He used the Source of Light against me."

"You sensed the Source of Light but didn't have the foresight to take the Source of Darkness from the shrine to counter it? What did you expect would happen, Dalorosk?" Vorkoise grilled. Dalorosk slowly rotated his head to lock his irate eyes on the figure in blue.

"If the Sources are not in place at the shrine we cannot communicate over long distances, brother," he spoke with quiet malice dripping from his every word. "I had to leave it to call for help, but here you are arriving an entire day later! Once again your bumbling idiocy fails me!"

"So they have disappeared?" Golthrout inquired.

"They were heading west," Dalorosk responded, spinning around to continue working. "The disciple is surely using his power to veil Alberic from us even when transformed."

"They probably headed for the old Drakkaidia," Wyrik said. "My humans—in their limited but existing usefulness—inform me a resistance against us builds there. The disciple probably knows this as well."

"There is nothing left of Drakkaidia except my Siarchs and the minions of Drakkan," Dalorosk said, quietly fuming. "His demons leave none alive, and they can prove a match even for us, which is why we agreed to leave the northwest to its fate. Alberic had to have headed back to the south. He always tries to trick us... to play his little games..." Hearing the Ancient of Darkness trail off, Moltar spoke.

"So what will we do?" he asked for all of them.

"We find him before he can concoct another cowardly plan to defeat us," Vorkoise said clenching his fist.

"There is no power left with which he can wield against us," Golthrout responded.

"That was what we thought last time when he disappeared for all those years, but he returned with power none of us could repel," Dalorosk reminded them quickly. "With the help of his disciple and this boy he might find another way to stop us. I... we can't take that chance. Find him."

"What of Drakkaidia?" Moltar asked. "It should be searched—"

"I will sweep my lands when I am ready!" Dalorosk barked, keeping his attention on what he was working on. "If you want to charge in to face the demons so badly, be my guest. We already know there are no humans left in the northwest, so scour your own lands and destroy any of the miserable creatures you find."

"I tell you, Dalorosk, the humans can still be of use to us," Wyrik told him heatedly. The Ancient of Darkness let out a long breath and sat back in his seat, trying to maintain his calm.

"If Alberic is free, he will seek a new way to use the humans against us as he did last time with his little Elemental Warriors," Dalorosk told them. "The risk the humans present with him on the loose if far greater than the measly benefits they present on rare occasion. Just kill them. Kill them all." Though the other Ancients glanced to each other as if to decide whether or not they agreed, Moltar finally broke the silence.

"He's right, the humans are worthless," he replied. "If they were capable of finding us the Source they would have done so by now. We planned to exterminate them once we found it anyway." Wyrik rolled his eyes and let out a long disgruntled huff.

"Fine," he agreed at last, letting apathy take hold.

"Start with the city below us," Dalorosk said, motioning with a gesture of his right hand for them to leave him. "I grow tired of their stench." Black sparks flew from his fingertips again as he pieced together another of the carved stones on the table.

"Why do you waste so much time toiling on that, brother?" Golthrout asked, observing the light. "You may be vulnerable to the Source of Light but the rest of us are capable of retrieving it once it is found."

"I am working to make sure days like yesterday don't happen," he snarled back. "It's my own business, now get out of my sight."

"Just get on the way to the northwest soon, Dalorosk," Wyrik returned for them, turning to walk out of the torch lit room back down into the larger chamber beyond. Once they were gone, Dalorosk set his full attention back on the circular stone object he was assembling in his hands, ignoring the screams of dying humans suddenly echoing through the chamber from the dungeon beneath him.

Chapter 22

<u>Mountain Stronghold</u>

Nearly two hours later Alberic broke through the cloud line along the eastern end of the Black Peaks of Drakkaidia, the golden contrails from his shining hooves slowly dissipating behind him as he began gliding down through the night sky. Though the Ancient of Light was weary again and in desperate need of rest that had been denied to him since breaking free of his chains atop the Holy Shrine, the white horse continued gently flapping his enormous wings as Captain Asthatch pointed down to a wedge in the mountains where several rising cliffs bowed in to come to a point along a jagged peak. Though the Drakkaidian warrior was still nervous of the flying creature he found himself riding and not sure how to speak to it, he tried to yell above the wind to descend toward the wedge and make for the top of the cliffs.

Alerted by the Drakkaidian's voice, Aeric and the others on Alberic's back all looked ahead to peer through the dark night to where he was pointing. Though the moon was full, only a few rays of its white luminosity managed to penetrate through the thick clouds to illuminate the mountains rising before them. The group could only barely make out the unnatural edifice rising from the top of the cliffs in the wedge. Buried into the peak was a gap in the rocks where a single tower rose from what looked to be a fortress lower in the mountainside.

When the group lifted off from the plains of central Drakkaidia hours before, Valeri told her new companions of their stronghold in the Black Peaks where the resistance gathered. Apparently Hadecrest had long been a secret Drakkaidian fortification in the peaks that Veriod Montrox, the first of the infamous royal family to live during the First Holy War, had discovered in ancient times. He ordered it to be rebuilt in the event his lands ever fell under threat of invasion.

One of the best protected strongholds in all of Iairia thanks to the natural wedge in the edge of the Black Peaks that would bottleneck armies trying to penetrate to the fortress high in the cliffs overlooking the land below, Veriod Montrox had been confident no force would ever manage to breach it if it was ever needed.

Valgard Montrox could only pray Hadecrest's fabled invulnerability was true after hearing of even the mighty Galantia's fall before the onslaught of the Ancients. Before he marched the Drakkaidian armies to meet with Darien Tieloc and what was left of Grandaria in his doomed battle against the beasts, he ordered his daughter be taken to Hadecrest. Should the battle go ill and the rest of Drakkaidia fall defenseless, she was to take the throne in the secrecy of the Black Peaks where she would stand a better chance defending her nation than at the more exposed citadel in Dalastrak.

Though the Drakkaidian princess revealed the story to Aeric and the others behind him, usually kept secret to ensure no convert ever discovered its existence, she could not continue talking for long as her exhausted body was in a great deal of pain from her struggle with the Valcanor. Despite being the powerful Warrior of Darkness and as fierce a warrior as any, the girl's energy was dangerously depleted and her entire form was bruised from being squeezed by one of the Valcanor and the rough fall from her horse. Though Asthatch tended to her as they flew, Aeric was the one sitting behind her. After seeing her struggle to keep her balance on Alberic's back, he offered to let her lean against him so she could rest. She ignored him at first, only looking back at him with her tired red eyes probing his again. Eventually she turned forward and continued hunching over on her own. Though Aeric guessed the proud Drakkaidian princess didn't care for his charity, he noticed her gradually pulling back and leaning into the folds of his chest and arms as the minutes ticked by. Before long she completely loosened and let the Grandarian hold her, giving into her fatigue and abandoning her pride.

They flew on like this for another hour until Alberic dropped out of the clouds to start his descent for the stronghold of Hadecrest. Though Valeri had fallen in and out of sleep on the way, she leaned upright and cleared her throat as they soared into the wedge toward the top of the cliffs ahead of them. Asthatch directed the Ancient of Light to a wide wall stretching out from the cliffs that looked down over the wedge and beyond. Though there were no torches along the wall, obviously to keep the wedge hidden in the night to any passing outside, Aeric could see movement along the fort at their coming and the shouts of men along with the drawing of swords ringing through the night. Beating his wings to keep them aloft as they dropped out of the air and onto the stone wall top, Alberic lowered his body to allow his passengers to dismount. Before any of them could drop they were surrounded by dozens of Drakkaidian soldiers pointing swords and lances out for the winged horse, illuminated by his glowing hooves.

Though shocked at the bizarre creature's appearance and arrival, the men were even more stunned to find Captain Asthatch lunging off the horse and batting away their weapons with his forearm, ordering them to stand down for the princess. Hearing this, the Drakkaidians all shot their gazes back to the horse to find Valeri Montrox slowly dismounting with Asthatch helping her down and immediately sheathed their weapons. When several of them asked for orders the young Montrox attempted to straighten herself as best she could and speak with authority. Telling them she had found allies on her venture into the central lands, she ordered Aeric and his friends be extended the full hospitality of Hadecrest and that they be tended to immediately having just come from battle.

After Aeric, Lucan and Revond lowered themselves from Alberic's back, the entire group and all the soldiers were surprised to find the winged steed suddenly pulsate with a faint golden aura then begin shrinking and morphing into a smaller humanoid form. Though the Drakkaidians were awestruck and frightened at what they witnessed, Revond was quick to order Aeric and Lucan to help Alberic up once he had transformed back into his human figure. Alberic weakly smiled as they bolstered him up by his shoulders, telling them he needed rest.

With several servants rushing out onto the wall after being summoned by one of the soldiers, Valeri was quick to order them to direct Alberic and the others to the infirmary. She was cut off by Asthatch commanding the servants surrounding the princess to take her to her quarters immediately. Watching the red haired girl be whisked away by servants and soldiers alike before he could say a single word, Aeric found Asthatch slowly turn toward them and approach. Informing them he would have a light banquet of food and drink set up for them in a gathering hall that would be ready once they were out of the infirmary, he told the servants to take good care of them. Before he turned to be on his way after Valeri, the gruff Drakkaidian captain surprised Aeric by bowing before him and thanking him for saving her. Though speechless when before the captain had not trusted him at all, the Grandarian managed to bow back and tell him he barely did anything.

When Asthatch left, the servants around Aeric and the other three in his party were quickly led off the wall into a passage in the cliff wall that led into a torch lit hallway. Guessing that Hadecrest was built into the mountainside as well as the castle above them, they pressed on until weaving their way into a large chamber decorated with several Drakkaidian flags draping from the ceiling and dark tapestries on the walls. It was a tall rectangular chamber with three floors, looking to be a central hub that linked the fortress, or at least this lower segment apart from the castle. Entering another hallway the servants led the four into the infirmary where they were separated to be tended to by the few healers that had been awakened. Though seeing to their various cuts and wounds from the Siarchs, all of them insisted they were otherwise fine and just needed to rest. Alberic fell asleep the moment his head fell upon a pillow, to which Revond took a deep sigh of relief and sat down on a chair beside his bed, removing his crusted gray cloak still covered in dry Siarch mucus from the coagulation net.

Though Revond told the healers he needed no attention other than a bath and a new set of clothes, they insisted on looking him over. Deciding it prudent not to offend their hosts when taking sanctuary there, the sage bit his tongue and let them examine him. By this time Aeric and Lucan had their few scrapes cleaned and patched and were ready for sleep. Aware the sage needed none with the vial of Sage's Draught in his robes and that he would want to stay at Alberic's side through the night, Aeric told Revond they were going to get a bite to eat and some rest.

Before the servants could surround the Master Sage he strode beside his two companions and leaned down to them to avoid being heard. Whispering, he told them to take advantage of the hospitality of the Drakkaidians but not to say anything more about their quest or of Alberic than necessary. Assuming Revond would want to explain everything to them formally when the time came, the two nodded in agreement. The sage weakly nodded and told him they would talk in the morning.

Once again led by a few servants, Aeric and Lucan left the infirmary to walk back through the hallways and into the central chamber. Aeric in particular felt more than a little uneasy in the stronghold, surrounded by Drakkaidian culture everywhere he looked. Though grateful to be there and trusting Valeri in particular, he knew any Grandarian would be unsettled walking in the heart of Drakkaidian society even after the talks of peace began prior to the Ascension. He couldn't explain why but it just felt like he wasn't compatible with the environment and he shouldn't have been there.

Lucan was in sheer disbelief at his surroundings, still amazed at the situation he found himself in. A few weeks ago he had been planning on traveling south past the borders of Windrun into the hot blue coastal regions to look for survivors and maybe find a more permanent residence with them, and now he had been thrust back into the struggle against the Ancients with the Drakkaidian resistance itself. Though confident the Ancient of Light and the Master Sage Revond would be able to figure out a way to undo the damage caused by the beasts and keep him safe in the process, the Maven couldn't help but feel like all of this was beyond him.

Their misgivings were alleviated as the servants led them to the top level of the chamber only to find another spiraling staircase leading up. Passing up it in silence, Aeric and Lucan found themselves emerging in a similar room but more decorated and polished. Asking where they were, the servants replied it was the castle of Hadecrest at the top of the cliffs where the princess and the Drakkaidians stayed. Apparently the bulk of the resistance members living at Hadecrest lived further down the cliffs or around the exterior of the castle in makeshift camps, while the leaders under Valeri operated within the small castle.

The servants led Aeric and Lucan down a hallway on the right side of the dark foyer until they reached a set of double doors opened to reveal a room with long tables and a few men sitting around one them. They were eating from several plates of old bread and dried meat strips, softly talking amongst themselves. Aeric and Lucan immediately noticed Asthatch sitting at the end closest to the door ripping at a dried strip of meat in his hands, rising as he noticed them coming. He had removed his long cape and the armor from the waist up, obviously just taking a moment to rest as well. Throwing the meat to a plate before him he bid a few of the other men around him to rise. One of them was an older blonde man dressed in a light brown tunic elaborately stitched around the collar, unusual for a Drakkaidian.

"Master Tieloc," Asthatch greeted. "Do you and your friend find Hadecrest hospitable?" Aeric summoned his voice and volume as he nervously replied they had been very well taken care of. When he finished Asthatch looked back to the door as if waiting for someone else to emerge. When no one else came he turned his questioning eyes back to Aeric. "Where is the sage, then?"

"Well, um..." the Grandarian trailed off, not sure what he should say for Revond, "He is seeing to our friend Alberic."

"Are our healers and medics not adequate?" Asthatch asked, raising an eyebrow. Though Aeric wanted to tell him Alberic wasn't just any wounded man, he remembered Revond's warning to keep the truth of their situation mum and fumbled for something else to say. Seeing his dilemma, Lucan cleared his throat and spoke.

"You saw for yourself that Alberic isn't quiet normal," the Maven said folding his arms with a forced smile. "I'm sure you understand that the Master Sage is in a unique position to see to his health." Though cringing at Lucan's initial sarcasm to the usually ill-tempered captain, Aeric shrugged it off and focused back on the Drakkaidians before him.

"They should both be fully recovered tomorrow," he offered. "I'm sure that Master Sage Revond will want to explain everything to you himself then."

"Of course," Asthatch nodded, lingering distrust present in his eyes as they swept over Aeric. "In the meantime perhaps you could enlighten us with a general story of what you have been doing with a Mystic Sage since the Ascension. These men," Asthatch said, turning and raising a hand toward the few men eagerly staring at the young man and Maven, "are the representatives of the old world that guide the resistance." Before he could introduce any of them they began stepping forward to do so on their own, ushering in a look of mild irritation on the captain's face.

"Asthatch tells us you are the son of Darien Tieloc, young Grandarian," the blonde haired man began. "It is good to see the face of a fellow Grandarian after so long among the people of our neighbor to the west. My name is Alam Tielance of Grandaria. I knew your father—I was once a scout under his command. I am the sole voice of the golden land that remains here." At the mention of his father, Aeric softened again but gradually took the man's hand and shook it by the wrist, greeting him heartily. The next man was bulkier and hidden by a thick brown beard stretching down from his face. He approached Lucan and reached out for his hand.

"And I am Comdon Broll, once a man of the deep Southland," he told the Maven. "I represent her as best I can. I'm afraid I didn't get your entire name from the captain here." Lucan gave it to him and released his hand only to be greeted by the last of the three with dark attire and leather armor over his chest.

"Welcome to Hadecrest, Master Erland," he greeted in a deep voice. "I am Markus Desrum, caretaker of this stronghold since the rule of Verix Montrox. It isn't a city citadel but I trust you'll be comfortable here." As soon as he released Lucan all three of them began yammering over each other, all trying to ask how they came to be there or what power they brought with them in the form of the winged horse they had heard of. Seeing Aeric and Lucan besieged, Asthatch loudly grunted and stepped in between the representatives grilling them.

"I'm sure our guests are tired and hungry," he said loudly, raising a hand for them to make their way to the opposite side of the table and sit. "As you can see, the men of our council here were most enthusiastic to hear of a Mystic Sage looking for us. Perhaps too enthusiastic." The three went quiet at this, shooting Asthatch unappreciative but submissive looks.

"Your propensity to distrust leaves you cold to optimism as usual, Captain Asthatch," the Grandarian named Alam Tielance spoke, taking a seat opposite Aeric. The Drakkaidian captain merely reached for the strip of dried meat he had been eating and ripped at it with his powerful jaws, fixing his eyes into space before him as he responded.

"My propensity to distrust is why most of you are still alive and stay that way, Tielance," he returned coldly. "I have little cause for optimism these days."

"And yet you tell us Princess Montrox's first order upon her return was to spread word of a closed meeting of our council tomorrow so our new guests can explain why they have come," Tielance said looking down the table to him. "Thankfully not all Drakkaidians have abandoned the hope that our resistance may yet fulfill the purpose it was charged." Seeing the irritable captain about to respond with anger in his eyes, Lucan spoke to cut him short and see if he could get them back on topic.

"Perhaps you could more clearly lay out that purpose for Aeric and me, sir," the Maven spoke, reaching for a slice of bread in front of him. "In my travels since the Ascension I have heard many rumors of this movement but never more than a whisper of its aim or structure."

"Surely, Master Erland," Markus Desrum returned, taking a sip of water from a light goblet he held. "The princess was moved here at the order of our late king Valgard Montrox should he fall in his battle against the Ancients. After his death and the ensuing destruction of most of Iairia, Her Highness found herself ruling only a few patrols of the Drakkaidian army previously under my command, a few survivors who managed to escape the Ancients after the battle in the Valley of Blood like the good Captain Asthatch here, and whatever stragglers who managed to trickle up through the peaks from the rest of the lands. Though we kept Hadecrest a secret to ensure our princess' safety, in the first few months a handful of travelers who heard of a Drakkaidian refuge arrived at the wedge seeking sanctuary. But as time rolled by we saw less and less. You and your friends are the first to enter Hadecrest since the Ancients erected their shrine and began their bloody new world order.

"There are a few other men not of Drakkaidia here like Tielance and Broll, but including the men who were stationed here there are only over five hundred people at Hadecrest. The wisest and strongest of the refuges were identified by the princess and her men from Dalastrak like Asthatch and a council was assembled. In the beginning our objective was merely to ensure the secrecy and survival of Hadecrest and those living here, but as per Princess Montrox's charge to us months ago, we have tasked ourselves with retaliating against the Ancients any way we can. Though we have no force or power with which to repel them, we offer sanctuary to all those free men still lingering across the six lands and beyond. In the meantime we have been devising anything we can do to stand up to the Ancients, but..."

"All anyone can think of is to try to locate the remaining Source of Light before they or their converts can," Broll finished for him, making Aeric swallow hard and take note of the white medallion still hanging around his neck. "Valeri insists she will one day use her elemental power to try and destroy Dalorosk at least, but—"

"If her father could not break the dark beast with the full army behind him do you think she will fare any better, Broll?" Asthatch interjected, looking down at his plate as he bit into a meager piece of moldy bread.

"The princess herself admits she is the last pocket of strength left in the free world, Asthatch," Desrum said.

"It is that kind of talk that encourages her willfulness, Commander Desrum," Asthatch snapped, spinning to face him with a flash of resentment in his eyes. "She may be our princess but she is still young and impetuous to say such things. I was charged by her father to keep her alive. I will not let her go to her death."

"Perhaps she will not need to after the events of this day, captain," Alam Tielance said from the opposite end of the table. "Now that she has found a Mystic Sage who claims to bring good tidings perhaps we will be presented with another alternative to curb the Ancients' insatiable appetite for destruction." Seeing Tielance's eyes drifting toward him as if preparing to ask him what Revond was going to tell them, Aeric quickly turned to Asthatch to ask a question of his own.

"How is the princess, Captain Asthatch?" he asked, veering away from the subject the conversation was leading to. "Will she be alright?" Asthatch let himself cool and took a deep breath, dropping his bread and peering up to the Grandarian.

"Despite her appearance and gender, Princess Montrox lives up to the name of her house laid down by the generations that preceded her, Master Tieloc," he informed him proudly. "As I'm sure you've gathered from your brief time with Her Highness, she is very... strong willed. Though she is getting her rest now I'm sure she will be up and about well before she should. Her power grants her strength beyond that of a normal woman—or man for that matter—and she has inherited her family's unmatched fortitude. Sometimes to a fault, but it serves us well. She will be fine." The Drakkaidian captain sat forward and pushed his plate away, sweeping his eyes over everyone at the table. "Which brings me to her orders. I was bid to tell you all she will hold council in the war room tomorrow at midday. I trust your friends Alberic and the Master Sage will be recuperated by then so they may enlighten us with whatever it is they have searched us out to say, and how in the name of Drakkan below that winged horse saved us today." Aeric froze at this, still unsure of what to make of Asthatch. Though he seemed to have their interests and those of Valeri in particular at heart, his abrasive and distrustful manner made it difficult to warm to him.

Guessing the conversation would lead to a discussion Revond had warned them to avoid if he lingered any further, the Grandarian rose from his seat along the table, taking a final gulp of water from his cup.

"I look forward to tomorrow then," he told them, looking over the faces of all the men at the table. "I'm afraid I've had a long day...days... and I really need my rest."

"You and me both, my friend," Lucan seconded as he rose beside him, tossing his frayed blue scarf over his shoulder. Asthatch stood at this and clapped his hands twice, signaling two servants waiting outside the doors of the chamber to swiftly enter.

"Take our guests to their rooms that we arranged," he ordered, turning back to face the men across the table. "They'll wait to wake you until late into the morning and have bathes prepared for you. I'll look forward to hearing from you again at the council. Sleep well." Noting Asthatch's suspicious tone, the two bowed to the Drakkaidian and the other three standing as they turned to depart. Before leaving Lucan snapped his fingers and jumped back to grab several slices of bread off the table to take with him to his room. Grinning as Asthatch watched him with a blank face, the Maven hurried next to Aeric's side and they took their leave from the chamber after the two servants guiding them back into the foyer of the small castle of Hadecrest. Weaving into another of the torch lit hallways branching off on the right side, the servants led Aeric and Lucan up a staircase and a barren stone hallway with several wooden doors along its sides.

"These are the rooms where the masters of the stronghold once held quarter in," one of the servants said. "They currently belong to the council members and our military leaders. The princess' room is just down the hall up another staircase. Hadecrest was not built to hold many and certainly not royalty, but you should find it comfortable, I hope." The servant who spoke stopped before one of the doors on his left and bid Lucan to enter while the other led Aeric down to another room on the right a little further down the hallway. Receiving a gracious dismissal from Aeric and Lucan, the servants bowed and made their way back down the hallway to disappear down the stairs. Alone at last, Lucan turned back to Aeric while shoving a slice of bread into his mouth, chewing and looking down the empty hall.

"Can you believe any of this, kid?" he asked suddenly, still chewing with his mouth open. Though Aeric frowned at the kid reference yet again, he took in a deep breath and gingerly shook his head no.

"I still can't believe a lot of things," he replied softly, lowering his eyes to the ground. "I don't know how we keep cheating death in a world consumed by it."

"You'd make for a pretty depressing philosopher," the Maven bantered, leaning his shoulder against the stone frame of his doorway. "For having such a bleak outlook and such little faith in our mission at the beginning of this thing, you've represented your last name pretty well, you know." Aeric's eyes narrowed and he looked up to the Maven uncertainly.

"What do you mean?" he asked guardedly. Lucan shrugged and took another bite of bread.

"Well, considering how shaken up you were by everything that happened before we met, as you were well justified to be, of course, you've turned out to be a regular beacon of courage through all this darkness. You held it together in the Holy Shrine on the very gravesite of the world you once knew when Revond was dangling you like bait on a hook; you looked death in the face—or more like spat on it—when you used the Source of Light to stave off Dalorosk in our escape; you convinced me to stay the course after we lost Revond and Alberic when things looked bleaker than ever; you talked down a Drakkaidian princess and her elite guards, getting them to help us no less; saved her from being crushed—yeah I saw that, it was smooth—and last but not least, you just held your ground in the face of all these big mouthed, makeshift politicians trying to twist you around their fingers. I didn't see you coming, Aeric."

"See me coming?" Aeric repeated, confused.

"I'm just saying, give yourself some credit," Lucan told him simply. "At the beginning of this thing you were sulking so low I didn't even imagine you'd make it to Grandaria, but here you are delivering the long lost Alberic and the Master Sage to the only people who might be able to help us, and doing so looking like you know exactly what you're doing. For someone who claimed he was nobody with nothing to fight for, you're getting dangerously close to living up to that legendary family name of yours." Aeric was quiet at the end of Lucan's speech, letting his words digest. Though things had been so desperate and moved so fast since he set out with Lucan and Revond in the first place and he had never stopped to think about all that they had made it through, now that he heard it dictated to him he found himself surprised. Despite the grief still tearing at him from all he had lost and Mina still haunting his thoughts whenever he had a free moment to think, he had indeed endured more than he thought he possibly could when he first set out.

Allowing himself to faintly smile from the corners of his lips as the Maven grinned at him, still chewing away at his bread, the Grandarian slowly nodded and turned to open his door.

"Thanks, Lucan," he said quietly.

"Get some rest, kid," the Maven returned, opening his own door and stepping through it. "You've earned it." With that, he stepped inside his room and tightly shut the door behind him, leaving Aeric alone in the hallway. Silently chuckling to himself, the young man opened his door wide and entered his own room. Securely shutting the door behind him and leaning against it as he took a deep breath to think over all the Maven had said, he swept his tired eyes around the small room. It was faintly lit by a few candles near an old wooden bed frame on the left side of the room. As his eyes casually peered into the darker side of the room and a cabinet along the wall, they shot open and his heart leapt up into his chest at what he saw sitting on it. Nervously standing erect but still, he watched as the dark frame of Valeri Montrox shifted where she sat then tilted her head, her eyes staring hard as they had earlier in the day.

"Your Highness...?" he said uncertainly, trailing off. Valeri remained sitting on the top of the cabinet but crossed her legs and placed her hands in her lap, still staring. She was dressed in a long black tunic much too big for her that draped over one of her shoulders leaving it exposed. Its frayed ends reached down to cover her white legs to her knees. Her bare feet hung limply in the air right above the ground. There were a few white bandages along her arms where she had been cut by the Valcanor, and her short hair was still frazzled from the flight on Alberic but patted down nonetheless.

"I heard everything the Maven said," she told him, finally breaking the silence. "It sounds like you are indeed your grandfather's—my great uncle's—kin." Aeric was silent at this, incredibly thrown off by her presence and desperately groping for something to say. Seeing him searching for words, she continued. "Have my servants taken care of you?" Aeric swallowed hard as he mustered the courage to respond, slowly nodding.

"They have," he said, so quiet he was embarrassed. "I just need some rest and I should be fine by tomorrow..." Trailing off, he was once again mortified by his words, sounding as if he was trying to shoo her out like a common servant.

"From all you've been through in the past few days I can only imagine," she returned, finally hopping down from the cabinet to walk toward him, making Aeric even more uncomfortable. He could see the girl wincing with every step as if in pain. Remembering the ordeal she had just been through with the Valcanor hours before he was surprised she could even stand. Though she was obviously still sore and weak, Aeric couldn't help but notice the girl's slender figure as she approached, even more striking than he had originally observed with no armor and shawl covering her skin. Feeling like he was staring, he swallowed hard and glanced down. "I apologize for startling you. I just wanted to talk before tomorrow. Asthatch told you of the council I ordered, I trust."

"He did, Your Highness," the Grandarian returned. Valeri let out a slight smile and swept a lock of her crimson hair behind her ear.

"Please, Aeric," she told him. "I didn't sneak into your bedroom in the middle of the night with Asthatch's guard watching my front door to talk to you formally." Aeric was suddenly terrified of what she would say next, desperately wanting to take a step back but standing frozen. Keeping his gaze locked on the Drakkaidian princess, he watched as she looked away from him and took a seat on a chair beside his bed. She folded the creases of her long black tunic between her legs and set her strange but striking crimson eyes back on him. "I just wanted to talk to you before tomorrow so I have an idea what's coming before it hits me in the face out of nowhere. And maybe to gauge what kind of man my second cousin is a little better." Though Aeric allowed himself to take a deep breath of relief at this, he remained on edge by the door. Seeing his obvious discomfort, Valeri smiled again and shook her head. "You can sit down, you know. I just want to talk to you person to person, as I'm sure you can tell by my extremely informal attire." Seeing her lighten and make a mild joke, the Grandarian loosened some and blushed red, giving her a single nod and walking to the edge of his bed to sit.

"All right," he said at last, swallowing hard again. "I have to tell you though, the Master Sage Revond wanted me to wait to tell anyone about the circumstances leading up to our coming here. Like I told you before, it's a long story. Too long and complicated for a casual chat, I'd say, and to be honest I'm still not sure of half of what I've been through recently." Valeri went blank at this, her eyes flickering back and forth across his face as if accepting his explanation.

"Very well," she said. "Maybe you could just tell me about you then."

"Me?" he asked. "What about me?"

"I mean who you were before all this," she said plainly. "Before the Ascension. The Maven said you had reason to be 'shaken up by everything.' What was that everything, I wonder?" Aeric looked down into the space between them at her question, surprised at her forthright questions but pulled back into his empty sorrow at the mention of his losses.

"I'm sure my story isn't all that different from yours, Your... Valeri," he said quietly. "I just lost everything."

"A woman, then?" she asked, catching him off guard. He brought his eyes back up to hers, wondering if he was so transparent or if her searching eyes did their work surprisingly

254

well. When he nodded and told her yes, she pressed on. "Were you married?"

"...No," Aeric responded, looking down into space again, "but we would have been." He paused, his memories of the life he knew before all this somehow drawn out by her gentle words. "I knew her since I was a baby. We grew up together; went to school together. Our families had been best friends since the time of my grandparents. But she loved me for who I was and not for the person everyone wanted me to be. She made me realize who I wanted to be. But when I had to be something I *needed* to be, I wasn't there for her. I let her go." Valeri was quiet when he finished, observing her questions had provoked tears falling down his cheeks.

"I'm sorry, Aeric," she said almost inaudibly. The princess tilted her head and lowered it to force him to look into her red eyes. "But though you may be no warrior, you honor her memory by being that person you need to be now. True strength is keeping everything together when everyone expects you to fall apart, and here you still are in one piece." Aeric's watery eyes shifted back onto hers and squinted uncertainly.

"You don't know me at all, Valeri," he told her blankly. "How can you say that?" The redheaded girl sat back in her chair but kept her gaze sternly on him, confident.

"I may have only met you today, Aeric, but I can surmise all that I need to know about you already," she told him. "You're an honest man; honest men are easy to decipher. You are clearly no warrior as you displayed today with your recklessness and indecisiveness in battle, yet you stand by your allies in their moment of need regardless. There has been desperation and insecurity in your voice when dealing with me from the moment we met, yet you stand your ground with passion when you need to. You obviously had a different life planned aside from the one your family's legacy is known for thanks to the girl, but I'm sure the rest of Grandaria saw that choice as a betrayal and never let you forget it right up until the end.

"Now you hate yourself for not choosing that life because you think if you had and gained the skills and poise in conflict like your father and grandfather had, you might have been able to save her, and the last thing you can see in yourself is the courage that comes with your family name because of that failure. But though you may not see it, it's there. You are a Tieloc; your grandfather's blood. I can see it. I could see it from the first moment your eyes looked into mine with courage in the face of what I might have done to you. It's a different kind of courage—desperate and unconfident—but it drives you on the same as it did to Tavinious Tieloc. It's what made me trust you in the first place. It's why I trust you now."

Valeri stopped there, her eyes fixed on his intently staring back at her. Though she looked empathetic as she sat looking at him, she maintained her air of confidence of all she had said as if she had just read all this from a book in black and white pages. Astonished at how she could surmise so much about him from the little time they had known each other or how she could be so wise to know the intricacies of his heart merely by the little clues she had gathered, he slowly shook his head in amazement.

"There's clearly more to you than anyone around here lets on," he said, to which the princess smiled faintly.

"That may be true," she said coyly, "but reading people isn't hard: I just pay attention. The question is, do you?"

"If there's more to you than what's on the surface, I might need more than my attentiveness to read a person like you, Valeri," he returned, faintly smiling himself. The girl tilted her head and curiously let her smile widen as if tickled.

"Try," she said. Aeric felt uncomfortable at the notion of dismantling his host and exposing her as best he could when he barely knew her, but seeing her eyes on him he suddenly felt compelled and narrowed his eyes.

"All right," he said slowly, locking onto her. "While their may be more to you than you let on or that people in this stronghold want to see, for one reason or another they don't see it. Asthatch's loyalty is without question, but his care for you obviously extends beyond a mere captain to his princess. They way he talks about you and rushes to your side when anything is wrong or he feels you in danger, it's as if he's trying to be the father you lost, especially since it was your father who ordered him to look after you in the first place. You must care about him a great deal as well, but I think you're upset by the fact that his dedication to your safety holds you back. He doesn't think you're ready to make hard decisions on your own, even though you can clearly take care of yourself.

"It's made you all the more headstrong, though, and unlike me trying to escape my family's shadow, you're trying to cast your own longer and wider. It's why you snapped at Asthatch when he compared you to your father today and it's why you told him and his men to wait for you while you charged into the Siarch colony with only two strangers to back you up. It's why you were bold enough to be waiting in here for me despite how it would look to anyone who found out and why you're direct enough to ask me about my personal life so quickly without batting an eye. And while you depend on Asthatch because you know he's the most loyal and capable you have, his leash on you only enflames your independence, maybe to a fault if what I heard about you wanting to take the fight to Dalorosk yourself is true. Either way, you remind anyone who thinks you incapable because of your age, gender, or inexperience that you are the boss around here whenever they second guess your orders."

Aeric stopped there, seeing the surprise on the girl's face from having him break her down in detail she hadn't expected. Taking in her fiery hair and eyes, he was reminded of something else and continued softer.

"You're the person my grandmother Arilia might have been had she not been taken from Drakkaidia as a child," he said. "She had your independence and drive, just not the hard Drakkaidian side that makes you..." He stopped there, realizing he had said too much.

"What?" Valeri asked him, narrowing her eyes curiously. When he didn't respond she answered for him. "Outspoken? Discourteous? Cold?"

"...Mature," he said at last, nervous but undeterred. Valeri went blank again at this, waiting for him to elaborate. "It's not like I find you disagreeable, just unusually worldly for your years, as I'm sure being your father's daughter and a princess have made you. And I wouldn't go so far as to say all this is posturing, but I can tell by your smile there's another person behind all that." The Drakkaidian princess remained still and emotionless in the long moments that followed, making Aeric nervous again as he thought over all he had said. He was put at ease when she finally let a coy grin overtake her face and stood up, the long ends of her dark tunic waving around her knees.

"Maybe there's more to you that *you* let on, Aeric," she said looking down at him.

"I guess we're just running in circles then," he returned with a faint smile of his own. The girl's grin broadened and she raised a hand to sweep it through the Grandarian's messy dark hair.

"I guess so," she replied. "I haven't talked to someone like this in a long time. Thank you." With that she turned for the right side of the room, silently stepping over the stone floor with her bare feet sticking as they touched down. As she ambled across the floor, she spoke back to him. "I'll hear the details from the Master Sage tomorrow then. Get some rest. You *have* earned it." Watching her, Aeric observed her slowly opening the old wooden shutters on the window in his wall and tilted his head with curiosity.

"What are you doing?" he asked. The girl jumped up to the stone hole and smiled back at him, leaning out into the night air.

"I told you," she said. "Asthatch's guards are watching the front door to my bedroom." Smiling at him one last time, the Drakkaidian princess leaned out of the window and took hold of some sort of cloth hanging outside. Grabbing on tightly, she pulled herself up until out of view. His eyes wide, Aeric rushed to the window to gaze out into the night. There was a vertical wall outside that led down two stories to the rocky basin around the castle where the makeshift camps of refugees lay quietly. Looking up, the Grandarian found the tails of the cloth disappearing into the window above him and heard the sound of wooden shutters closing.

Though shocked at what she had just done and the uncomfortable conversation that had just taken place, Aeric couldn't help but smile as he pulled his head back into his own room and closed the shutters sealing out the night. Sitting back down on his bed, he realized it was the first time he had truly smiled because he was genuinely happy since the Ascension over a year ago. Though not sure what that meant and still stricken with grief as his thoughts drifted to Mina once again, he crawled into the sheets of his bed feeling better than he had felt for the first time in as long as he could remember.

Chapter 23

<u>Breakfast</u>

A light tapping against his bedroom chamber door in the castle of Hadecrest was what woke the sleepy Grandarian the following morning, rustling him out of his dreams as the noise grew steadily louder. Lifting his heavy head off a thin pillow and rubbing his blue eyes with the butts of his hands, he blinked rapidly and set his gaze on the door.

"Yes?" he asked with a groggy voice, propping his upper body up with his elbow.

"I'm afraid we must wake you, Master Tieloc," came a voice from the hallway, blurred by the wooden barrier between them. His senses sharpening, Aeric tossed sheets and blankets over him and swung his legs out from the bed. He set his feet down on the cold stone floor, sending a chill through his entire body. Rising full length and trudging toward the door, he opened it and peered out to observe three servants standing in the hallway, one carrying a set of clothing and two more behind him struggling to lift a steaming tub of water. The man in front had a curious expression on his face as he scanned the younger man up and down.

"The princess and the council expect you in the throne room in a little over an hour, sir," he said. "We have brought you a bath and fresh attire for the day. Step aside." Before Aeric could open the door wider to let them in, the Drakkaidian in front pushed it open himself and brusquely barged in, ordering the other servants to drop the tub on the spot on the ground where the light from the window was coming in. Before Aeric could express his thanks the leader threw the clothing over Aeric's bed and jostled the others back into the hallway, taking hold of the door to leave after them. Before closing it shut he told Aeric to hurry and that breakfast had been prepared in the kitchen he had been in the night before. With that he practically slammed the door and disappeared down the hallway with his powerful footsteps fading.

Though raising an eyebrow at the servant's churlishness, Aeric remembered that Drakkaidians were not known for their manners or patience. Living in a place constantly under siege from enemies, beasts and weather at every corner of their territories coupled with the dark influence of Drakkan seeping out from the land itself from the eons of his reign over it before the Battle of the Gods, the Drakkaidians had always been a hard people that spared no time for kindness or warmth.

Aeric quickly let their behavior slide, as the only warmth he cared to receive was from the steaming tub on the floor beside him. Reaching over his shirt to pull out the white medallion around his neck he had slept with, far too cautious to let it out of his grasp unless absolutely necessary, he set it on a small table beside his bed. Slipping off the undershirt and pants he had also slept in, the young man slowly dunked himself into the small tub and its torrid, bubbling water. He hadn't felt the relaxing sensation in weeks, or far longer depending on how he perceived his awkward passing through time since the Ascension. Dunking his head beneath the water and rubbing the soap into his scalp, he emerged several moments later with his black hair sticking to his forehead. It had grown longer than he liked it, almost to his eyes.

Though content to linger in the soothing water until all the heat escaped, the young man remembered he was pressed for time with the council ahead of him and wanted to meet with Revond and the others beforehand. Finishing scrubbing his body, the Grandarian rose from the tub and quickly dried himself in the chilly air of his bedroom with a long blanket lying beside the tub. Shaking off the beads of water from his dripping dark hair, Aeric hastily dressed himself in the light garb the Drakkaidians had brought for him including a simple white shirt cut at the neck and brown pants similar to his own. Pulling a fresh pair of socks over his feet followed by his boots, Aeric stood while breathing deeply and ferociously rubbing his hair to dry it as quickly as possible. As he turned to grasp the Source of Light on the table beside his bed, he heard his door opening and spun around to find a familiar face revealed as it swung open all the way to the wall. Lucan Hauk Erland stood there, wearing a simple black tunic and what looked to be a new blue scarf tied around his neck to signify his Mavenhood.

"That was the first time I've slept in a bed in months," he said, scratching his head through the tangle of damp brown hair. "Or taken a full bath."

"Both were much needed I'm sure," Aeric said with a faint smile, placing the Source of Light back over his chest thanks to its thin chain.

"Well aren't you chipper when you get to sleep in?" the Maven asked sarcastically. "But what would any morning be without breakfast? Hurry it up, Grandarian." Lucan turned and motioned for him to follow him out the door with a sweeping gesture of both arms, to which Aeric smiled and darted after him as he disappeared around the doorway. Closing the door to his room and tucking the Source of Light into his shirt to keep it hidden, Aeric strode beside his companion and walked with him to the end of the hallway where it opened to a staircase leading down the first level of the castle. As they moved they heard voices from below them and wondered out loud where Revond or Alberic were. Though Aeric could guess the Master Sage would be waiting for them already completely rejuvenated and ready to face Valeri and her council, neither of them was as sure if the Ancient of Light would be at full strength yet. Though they had traveled with him across half of central Iairia in the past few days, they still knew little of the famous creature or his abilities beyond what they had gleaned from Revond talking about him with almost youthful reverence.

Their answers came when they made their way into the foyer of the castle amid its few lightly armored guards and other Drakkaidians making their way to and fro. Standing under a large red and black tapestry looking out of an arching window into the Black Peaks was a figure concealed in a black robe with a hood over his head. Though guessing the man to be a Drakkaidian as they passed by him, Aeric was surprised to hear him speak with his words coming in a familiar deep voice.

"Good morning, my friends," it came. The hood turned to reveal the robust bearded face of Revond looking at them, rotating his body and grabbing the end of one of his black gloves to tighten it against his hand. Where he had once been encased in dark blue garb he now wore faded gray, but his silver broach bearing the seal of the Mystic Sages was still upon his left shoulder holding his cloak in place. Though not expecting the figure to be the wise Master Sage, Aeric quickly smiled up to him and opened his mouth to speak.

"Good morning, Revond," he said, admittedly relieved to find the powerful sorcerer returned to them in good health. "How are you feeling?"

"As you both appear, refreshed," Revond returned, taking a deep breath. "Thanks to the hospitality of Hadecrest we all look to be on the mend." At the mention of all of their party, Aeric was quick to remember Alberic. Before he could inquire to his whereabouts Revond beat him to the punch. "To save you both the trouble of asking, Master Alberic is finally rested and recuperated himself. While, like myself, he doesn't need to eat, he is currently doing so in the kitchen adjacent to this chamber. I'm sure he would enjoy seeing you both." Lucan agreed and quickly ran past a passing servant toward the kitchen on the right side of the foyer. While anxious to see the Ancient of Light as well, Aeric lingered as he saw Revond turn to peer back out the window.

"What are you looking at, Revond?" the young man asked. Revond shrugged but stepped to his right allow Aeric room to see out the window as well.

"See for yourself, young Tieloc," he replied, motioning with his eyes for him to look out. He did, setting his hands on the stone windowsill and peering out, a small breeze rustling his black hair. Though the jagged dark mountains of the Black Peaks under the perpetually overcast sky were the first thing to catch the Grandarian's attention, the noise from beneath him signaled him to look down and find something that took his breath away. Though they were on the first level of the castle, below the window was a sharp drop on the jagged pinnacle of the mountain wedge that opened into a cavern beneath them where the rest of the stronghold was located. Around it and on either side of the window were camps of makeshift tents and loose wood huts. Small campfires burned throughout with hundreds of rundown men, women and children slowly moving around them.

"This is the resistance?" Aeric asked more to himself than Revond.

"The refugees that the resistance looks after, but yes," Revond responded softly. Aeric was horrified at the meager and miserable conditions the people lived in, revealed to be nothing more than a slum. Most of the camps looked to have little to no food over their fires and the majority of the noise coming from the crowds were groans or the banging on steel and wood. Though keeping his thoughts to himself, Aeric couldn't help but think the resistance didn't look to be in a condition to resist anything. Aeric was once again disheartened at the state of the world after the Ascension, especially since this rundown refugee camp could have been the last free city of humanity in Iairia.

"Not what you were expecting," Revond said looking back out on the rows of tents and huts as well. "Nor I. And yet it is the card fate has dealt us so we should be thankful these people are here at all. Quickly now. We have much to discuss." Rotating his body and striding away from the window with his black robes wafting around him, Aeric took a last glance at the people outside and turned to walk after him into the kitchen. The smile on Aeric's face was swiftly restored upon seeing Lucan sitting across from a familiar man in white attire from his neck to the soles of his boots. He was nibbling on a wide but thin slice of soft bread that a cook had toasted for him along with several links of dried meat.

"So if you don't need to eat, why bother?" Lucan asked the Ancient of Light with his brow furrowing as Aeric and Revond approached. A beaming smile overtook Alberic's relatively youthful face as he took another bite of the bread and began chewing.

"Well there's a long and complex explanation to that question that involves the millennia I have been living as a human and my body's mutation when I became the first Master Sage, but primarily," he said with his mouth full, "because it tastes good." Lucan froze at that, raising an eyebrow high as his eyes flickered with surprise at the simple answer. His face overtaken with a grin, the Maven turned to see his other companions arrive beside the table, both staring at the Ancient of Light looking up at them from behind a cup of water. When he set it down and gulped down the liquid in his mouth, he smacked his lips and sighed, contented.

"Hello again, Aeric," Alberic said smiling. "Care for some breakfast? There's plenty." Aeric couldn't hide his smile at the mighty Ancient's strangely genial and human behavior anymore than Lucan could and nodded, taking a seat next to the Maven.

"My family always told me the one thing I definitely inherited from my grandfather is his appetite," the young man returned merrily. "How are you, Master Alberic?"

"Full," the Ancient replied, leaning back in the chair he sat on and holding his stomach. "And you are not of my order, Aeric—there is no need to stand on ceremony for me. I feel rested for what feels like the first time in forever thanks to our hosts and the medallion still safely around your neck." Aeric looked down to the Source of Light gently glowing through his shirt, almost brighter now that it was so close to the being that shaped it. "After two short but potent charges within the white sphere after millennia apart from it, and of course a good night's rest, my former strength is restored. After all the study and experimentation with the order... I had almost forgotten the feel of my own natural power..." He trailed off for a moment, his blue eyes glimmering as they looked up and down his immaculately clean attire, so light it seemed to brighten the very room. Aeric's smile grew, observing the once broken and drained Ancient of Light they had first found atop the Holy Shrine truly happy in what he guessed to be the first time since the Ascension. "And it's the three of you I owe. You saved my life."

"You have already returned the favor in spades, Master Alberic," Revond said shifting his robes where he stood. "And your voice at the coming council will put us farther in your debt than you could ever be in ours." Aeric and Lucan eagerly glanced at each other at this, remembering the reason they had rescued him in the first place.

"Do you know of a way to stop the other Ancients, Alberic?" Aeric asked almost desperately, looking back at him. The smile on Alberic's face gradually dissipated as he set down the cup in his hands and fixed his gaze on the boy's eyes.

"I think it best if you wait to hear what I have to say until the time comes, young Grandarian," the Ancient of Light responded, confusing both Aeric and Lucan. "There is no clear answer to that question, for as you know as well as any, much has been lost. Some that we may never get back." Seeing the deep regret and pain surfacing on both of the faces sitting across the table from him, Alberic tried his best to smile. "But it is not too late to abandon all hope, my friends. I bid you to stay strong. And as long as we continue to hold onto that Source, we can stave off my brothers from destroying what's left of Iairia."

"Why did you give me the Source in the first place, Alberic?" Aeric asked. "How did you even know of me to begin with?" The Ancient of Light smiled at this and picked up a strip of meat from his plate to begin chewing on.

"The answer to that is far simpler," he said. "I have been living amongst humanity for a very long time now. I hear the same rumors and stories as any, including the exploits of your family. I've been watching the Tielocs since Taurin Tieloc took up the Sword of Granis in the First Holy War. My power allows me to sense other light based energy around me active or passive, including the energy signature in your veins. When the Ascension began and I sensed my brothers coming for the Source of Light, I took it from the elemental temple in the Golden Castle. It had to be hidden for I knew Dalorosk would find it with me sooner or later. I was originally going to give it to your father but by the time I had it he was already in battle with the other Ancients and you were my last hope. I knew I could trust you to keep it safe and use it should you need it. With the power of light already in your veins you may prove to be an amazing Warrior of Light." Aeric was quiet when Alberic finished, glancing at Revond who had already deduced most of his explanation. Seeing the boy's eyes on him, Revond took a seat beside Alberic.

"I trust our friend will make the rest clear when he is ready," he said. "We agreed earlier that I would introduce him to the council and outline the Ascension from our unique point of view including the ensuing quest for the Holy Shrine. If you are asked to speak do so truthfully but with caution. Drakkaidians tend to upset easily, and while I am grateful to this young Montrox for taking us in, I am cautioned by the fact she is in fact a Montrox. If whatever Master Alberic has to tell her does not yield the answers she was hoping for when she found us, she may seek to use what power we have for a plan of her own." Aeric's brow furrowed at this.

"You think Valeri will try to take the Source of Light from us?" he asked as if offended.

"As I said, I think she is a Montrox, and a desperate Montrox to boot," he returned dryly. "I am merely concerned she may try to pressgang our party into direct battle against the Ancients if no other plan is arrived at, which would obviously not end well for us. Keep in mind the Drakkaidians are a fierce and militant people who loathe the thought of being subjugated or forced to hide from their enemies." Though Aeric didn't buy into the idea that Valeri was only helping them to use them as a means to an end, he remembered that the caution came from the Master Sage himself and kept silent, knowing his suspicions were warranted. Though Aeric and Lucan in particular remained bent on discovering what Alberic had to tell them as they sat and tried to talk of smaller affairs for the next half an hour, at last Captain Asthatch appeared at the door to the kitchen dressed in black leather armor over his chest with his long red cape and oversized axe on his back once again. Taking powerful strides as he lumbered forward, Aeric caught sight of him first and looked up to the gruff face of the man even taller than Revond.

"Good morning," he greeted powerfully to them all. "If you are ready the princess' council is gathering above us." Though Lucan was still gulping down a mug of water and waiting for another plate of fruits to be brought from the kitchen, Revond rose from his chair and swept his gaze over them all, silently beckoning them to follow his lead. Though letting out a deep breath of remorse at missing more of the food the kitchen had been lavishing on him, the Maven rose alongside Aeric to see to the reason he was there. Having not yet met Revond or Alberic formally, the Drakkaidian captain bowed as they arrived before him and introduced himself.

The two Master Sages did the same, once again thanking him for caring for their party so well. Seeing Aeric and Lucan refreshed with eager expressions on their faces as well, Asthatch bade them all to follow him for Valeri's provisional throne room higher in the castle. Passing into the foyer once again, the group made their way to a central staircase in the chamber with torches and long but narrow red flags hanging over the stone railing. While they began ascending the stairs, the few guards and servants passing through the foyer and leaning out of doorways watched them go by, whispering amongst themselves of the rumors they had been hearing about a Mystic Sage present among them.

When Asthatch came to the top of the staircase on the second level he led the group down a narrow but tall hallway leading to large double doors at its end. Throwing his arms forward with the weight of his large body behind them, the Drakkaidian pushed open the doors with a lurching creak of the hinges along the walls bouncing into the chamber beyond. Peering past Asthatch, Aeric saw a large chamber with no windows along the walls. Seeing daylight pouring in from above, he looked up to find a slanted glass window giving view to the stagnant clouds choking the sky. In the center of the chamber was a large wooden table where several figures sat, swinging their gazes around toward the doorway and the party standing in it. Before Aeric could step into the chamber he found Revond and the others halting in front of him while Asthatch stood at attention.

"Princess Montrox and the Council of Hadecrest," he announced powerfully, "I present Aeric Tieloc of Grandaria and his party." Though surprised to hear the captain name him at the head of the group of four, Aeric saw Revond turning to stare at him from behind his black hood and gesture for the young man to step ahead of him. Doing so with his heart beating rowdily, Aeric found Asthatch standing aside to make way. Scanning the table the Grandarian found several faces all staring at him curiously. Closest to him were three of the council members he had met the night before including Alam Tielance of Grandaria, Comdon Broll of the Southland and Markus Desrum, the former commander of Hadecrest.

Beside them were two additional faces Aeric had never seen. At the far end sat Valeri Montrox, her hard and authoritative demeanor returned. She was dressed in similar attire to the first time they had met but her light crimson armor was not present and the sleeves of the tight black garb across her upper body only stretched down to her elbows. After Asthatch had stepped aside, Valeri raised a hand from the table and gestured toward the empty chairs at the opposite end of the table.

"Welcome Master Tieloc and friends," she greeted in her feminine but commanding voice. "We have been eagerly awaiting your arrival. Please sit." Gently nodding his head in response, Aeric forced himself to calm his nerves and walked to the closest chair at the end of the table. His companions followed, bowing to Valeri and taking their seats beside Aeric. When Asthatch took a seat on Valeri's left, the entire table was full and the princess leaned in with her hands folding over the top. "Will my council all please introduce themselves?" She looked to Asthatch first, who frowned, aware they all already knew him, but did as he was bid and introduced himself again. This time he reminded them he had once been captain of the royal guard in Dalastrak to Valgard

Montrox and was currently Valeri's first captain and head of her security. To his left was one of the men Aeric had not recognized; a shorter old man with white stubble across his weary face. He informed them he had once been an advisor to the Montrox family from the Cathedral of Dalorosk and was one of the few to escape it when it was destroyed at the start of the Ascension.

To his left were Tielance and Broll who informed Valeri they had met Aeric and Lucan last night, but then introduced themselves to Revond and Alberic. Desrum went next on the opposite side of the table, then the younger man sitting beside him who revealed himself to be a former lieutenant of the Drakkaidian army. When he finished they all looked back to Valeri, thanking them with a nod.

"These men are the Council of Hadecrest and leaders of the resistance against the Ancients," she said sweeping her gaze over the newcomers to her table. "They are the strongest and brightest from those who managed to make it to our mountain refuge after the Ascension. We hold meetings with the people outside the castle walls on a weekly basis for them to hear our thoughts and decisions, but this group meets every day. While it was once our mission to merely survive the Ascension and protect the people gathered here, we have decided we cannot outlast the Ancients cut off from the rest of the world and have pledged to find a way to stop them. Unfortunately we are left with little power to attempt such a feat, so we are all very hopeful at the presence of a Mystic Sage here today. Please say whatever you have searched us out to tell us." With this, Aeric, Lucan and Alberic all turned to Revond sitting at the opposite end of the table from Valeri, motionless in the confines of his dark robes. Taking a deep breath, the sage nodded and raised his gloved hands up to lower his hood and reveal his face to them all, his focused blue eyes confident as he opened his mouth to speak.

Chapter 24

<u>Lost Details</u>

"My name is Revond, and I am the current Master Sage of the eighth generation of the Order of Alberic," the sage began, his powerful voice resonating through the stone throne room of Hadecrest. "I must again thank you for helping my party, including Aeric Tieloc son of Darien Tieloc the Second, the Blue Maven Lucan Hauk Erland of the east, and our ally Alberic." Repositioning himself in his wooden chair as he prepared for the long story to come from Revond, Aeric silently wondered why the sage chose to conceal Alberic's true identity in his initial remarks. "We are in your debt for the rescue and taking care of us here. As you are all aware, we have searched you out to bring you a new perspective on the events surrounding the Ascension so we might come up with a way to stop the fires of apocalypse from spreading any further.

"To begin with, you should all know exactly what we and this resistance are arrayed against in this struggle. The Ancients that have united against us are five mythical beasts that have lain hidden underground since after the Battle of the Gods eons ago. They are the creatures spawned from the raw elemental power of the shards of the Holy Emerald that fell across Iairia to shape the lands with their influence. It was these mighty creatures who first created the elemental Sources to use for their own ends. Eventually the beasts went to war with each other for control of all Iairia, but a sixth Ancient that you have not heard of defeated them all and developed a system to keep them subdued over the years. It was this Ancient of Light who created the first set of Elemental Warriors and a talisman that he first used to end their war called the Staff of the Ancients. Before the five warring Ancients were imprisoned across the lands they issued a threat that they would return; that they would overcome the safeguards set in place to keep them banished.

"This is where our story becomes more recent. While the Ascension itself did not occur until that fateful summer day last year, the events that triggered the rise of the Ancients surround me and my origin. As you know, the seventh generation of Mystic Sages was completely wiped out during the Days of Destiny by the minions of Valif Montrox. Whenever the Master Sage of a generation of sages falls, the collective spirits of sages past select a new soul to be endowed with the power of our order. It occurs randomly; the first human to be born closest to our Mystic Tower and the Sage's Draught within receives this gift. I was this child, but in my case the power I was born with was more of a curse. With no other sages left to claim me and train me to control my power, it was left raw and dangerous. Eventually the spirit of the fabled Guardian Sage, Zeroan, came to me and summoned me to the Mystic Tower. Inside the tower walls and the hills of the Sage's Valley, I trained for over forty years to master my power and the collective knowledge of all sages that came before me. It was not until a few days before the Ascension took place that I emerged into the world as the new Master Sage to commence the eighth generation of the order.

"In the long years of my seclusion, however, the last of the Elemental Warriors that we sages have anointed since the time of the Ancient of Light died. The Staff of the Ancients that was used to control them had also been destroyed. Few know that the true cause of the Third Holy War between Grandaria and Drakkaidia was because the former High Priest Zalnaught and his Dark Mages infiltrated the Mystic Tower shortly after the Days of Destiny and stole the Staff of the Ancients. I was the one who took it from him and destroyed it as a boy so its power would never again fall into the wrong hands. Unfortunately, time has proven my rash action unwise as I did not yet know of its true purpose and importance. With the staff destroyed and the last Elemental Warrior dead, the Ancients sensed the safeguards set in place to control them gone. They were at last free to reemerge unchecked and unchallenged to take their vengeance on the Ancient of Light who imprisoned them in the first place." Revond paused for a moment, shifting his gaze from Valeri and her council to the man in white beside him.

"The man sitting beside me named Alberic is the Ancient of Light," he said suddenly, to which Drakkaidians and others on the council shot forward uncertainly. "As I'm sure you have noticed, his name is the same as my order of Mystic Sages. It was Alberic, the Ancient of Light, who created the Mystic Sages and Elemental Warriors as the first line of defense in keeping the other Ancients in check. He is the one who built the elemental temples across the lands to house the Sources that he and his brothers created. Though even his disciples in the order named after him to have always assumed him to be human, Princess Montrox and Captain Asthatch witnessed his true form yesterday in the plains of central Drakkaidia. He is an immortal creature spawned from the energy of a shard of the Holy Emerald and has fought for the survival of mankind as our unsung champion for eons. Once he set the tradition of sages and Elemental Warriors in place, Alberic left us to live as a human in his native land that would become Grandaria.

"Unfortunately, the events of the Days of Destiny and the Third Holy War exposed a rare flaw in his otherwise self-sustaining system to control the other Ancients that left us vulnerable. Sensing Dalorosk, Moltar, Golthrout, Vorkoise and Wyrik suddenly emerge from their prisons across the lands and steal back their Sources, Alberic took his own Source out of the Temple of Light in Galantia to hide in the hands of Aeric Tieloc before he could be discovered by his brethren seeking revenge against him. They found him shortly after the destruction of Galantia and imprisoned him atop their false Holy Shrine. Thankfully I was able to sense the rise of the Ancients as well and managed to locate Aeric before the Ancients could kill him. I took him to the Mystic Tower but it proved to be of little sanctuary as they tracked us to it in short order and trapped us inside. With the beasts closing in, I was left with no choice but to throw Aeric and myself inside the chasm where our enchanted draught is kept. Within the draught we experienced time slower than the rest of the world and emerged to find Iairia devastated by the fires of the Ancients an entire year later.

"We met Lucan Hauk Erland in the Sage's Valley after our emergence, who informed us what had transpired in our absence. Finding ourselves out of options, he guided us to the Holy Shrine in hopes we could rescue Alberic. It was not an easy task, but thanks to Aeric using the Source of

Light to counter Dalorosk, we escaped into Drakkaidia with hopes of finding this resistance we had heard of. From there I assume you all know the rest. In our fatigue Alberic and I were overwhelmed by a passing storm of Siarchs and while Aeric and Lucan tried to rescue us they encountered Princess Montrox and her party, leading us here." Revond paused to take a long breath again, examining the faces of Valeri and her men struggling to take in the incredible story he had only barely skimmed the surface of. Between the tale of the Staff of the Ancients in the Third Holy War surprising even Alberic and the notion of Revond and Aeric skipping through time, the entire table was in shock. Glancing at Alberic again, the Master Sage knew the time had come to switch voices.

"This is where we stand," he said powerfully. "Though we still have the Source of Light in our possession here at this very table, it is only a matter of time before the Ancients eventually come after us and find even the remote stronghold of Hadecrest. Though I myself am at wit's end and know of no other means to fight the Ancients, I would like to present to you a being far wiser and more knowledgeable than myself who knows the Ancients better than anyone, being one himself. I am not sure what ideas if any Alberic has to offer this council as the entire system he put in place to ensure this fate would never come to pass has failed thanks to me, but I bid you to hear him out nonetheless in the hope that between all of us we may come up with a way to at least prepare ourselves for the coming storm." There was an uncomfortable silence at the end of Revond's speech when he turned to look at the Ancient of Light almost helplessly. Aeric had never seen him so dejected and ashamed, obviously truly believing this was his personal failing. Shooting a glance down the table to Valeri and her advisors, the young Grandarian saw them staring captivated at the man in white, whatever questions they surely had overridden by their desperate curiosity to hear whatever he would say.

Still staring at Revond with a faint smile on his clean cut face, Alberic gently lifted one of his hands to pat the Master Sage's forearm caringly.

"This was not of your doing, Revond," he said gently with his eyes still on Revond's. "If anything, fault for the Ascension lies with me." He released Revond and turned to face the rest of the council, his smile dissipating. "I had several chances to ensure this day would never come, yet I ignored

Dalorosk's blatant warning that he would be back one day and left the world vulnerable. At the end of our war with each other, I could have destroyed my brothers with the power of my staff yet I let them live in hiding. My hubris in the system of Elemental Warriors I created proved to be my undoing and cost the entire world. I thought that between the warriors, the constant order of sages to anoint them and the staff that I left in their care, there would always be adequate safeguards to preclude this doom. Yet now my brothers' patience has paid off and the Elemental Warriors are gone along with the staff. The Sources are back in the hands of the Ancients, so we cannot anoint new warriors even if anyone was left to be anointed. All the defenses I set up have failed."

Alberic was silent for a moment, breaking eye contact from the men and girl to set his eyes into space before him, contemplating what he would say next.

"But while we have lost much and hope is now very dim," he began slowly, his eyes still distant, "there may yet be a way to not only stop the other Ancients, but completely reverse all of the damage they have caused and the death they have spread." Aeric was the first to shoot forward with eyes wide, his heart leaping up in his chest, beating wildly. "It is a long shot to be sure, but there is a way to restore the land and banish my brothers forever." Seeing the shock on the faces of all those around him, Alberic turned to his right to look at Aeric. "I was there in the crowd of Galantia the day your grandfather announced he had fulfilled the prophesy of the Three Fates, Aeric. He didn't say it in so many words but I knew the Holy Emerald had been absorbed back into the world along with its universal power. But though the emerald is gone, its power still remains in our plane atop the imposter shrine my brothers built over the ruins of the golden city.

"The six Sources were formed from the concentrated energy of the shards of the Holy Emerald themselves. The reason Dalorosk and the others have been so vigorously seeking the Source of Light is so they can fuse them all together into one. A Source of All. With this one Source combining all the elemental power of the world together, it would bestow them with power rivaling the Holy Emerald itself. If we could take the Sources back and fuse them ourselves, we could use that limitless power to undo everything the others have done and restore the lands exactly the way they were before the Ascension. Virtually as if it had never happened." Aeric froze at this, the very blood pumping through his veins momentarily motionless. He couldn't believe it—there may yet be a way for him to save Mina and get back the life he had lost. Hope brimming in his blue eyes, he found tears welling in them and reached up to wipe them away before they could stream down his cheeks.

"So you're telling us if we storm the Holy Shrine and take back the elemental Sources we could restore all of Iairia and bring back everything that has died in the Ascension?" Valeri asked incredulously at the opposite end of the table.

"The Source of All would have the power to return life to the world," Alberic confirmed, "but let me be clear: I am not advocating storming the shrine and fighting the other Ancients. You must remember Princess Montrox, that even with your power, Master Sage Revond, myself and the Source of Light to aid us, my brothers have their Sources to wield against us. A direct attack would leave us all dead and the last Source in their possession." Valeri looked frustrated at this, the fierce stubbornness and battle-hardiness that Revond had warned them of appearing on her face.

"Then what are you proposing, Alberic?" she asked heatedly. "How else will we obtain the Sources? Are we to sneak into the shrine as Aeric and the others did?" Alberic shook his head, sinking lower in his chair as a new frown built on his face.

"That will not be an option either," he returned quietly. "I'm afraid I have recently sensed my brothers using their power for destruction once again. My guess is they are unnerved by the resourcefulness of the humans thanks to my escape and are killing them all to be sure their shrine is not penetrated again. We will not be able to get anywhere near Grandaria now. The only people who could get by the Ancients and join the Sources should we acquire them are Elemental Warriors."

"But you have said yourself that they are all dead, with the exception of the princess of course," Alam Tielance said. Alberic nodded but leaned forward in his chair over the table, preparing to say something slowly.

"Though the sages have always anointed Elemental Warriors by means of the Sources," he began, "there is another way." The table went dead silent at this, anxiously staring at the man in white. Revond was the most engrossed by this revelation, a glimmer of hope flashing across his eyes that had not been seen in a long time. Alberic leaned back and looked up into the space before him as if reminiscing. "After I ordained the first group of Mystic Sages, I sent them out in search of men and women who could bare the burden of becoming an Elemental Warrior. While they searched, I remained in the tower we were constructing to craft the power these warriors would wield to control the six elements. The original warriors were not immersed in the energy of the Sources as has become custom over the years since: they were given an external talisman of my creation. I fashioned six different metal crests bearing the insignia of each element over their surface and submerged each of them within their respective Sources. Using the unique power of the Staff of the Ancients, I transferred, or rather copied, the power of the Sources into the crests. When my disciples returned with brave men and women to be anointed, I gave them each one of the six crests that would give them the power of an element to manipulate. This was how the original Elemental Warriors were anointed.

"While everything went according to plan for several years, eventually I realized the crests could prove to be dangerous. One day the Warrior of Fire was traveling near Mt. Corist when a bandit stole his crest from him. Using it for his own designs to cause chaos, it took three other Elemental Warriors and myself to subdue him and recover the crest of fire. My sages and I knew that we had to constrain the power of the Elemental Warriors better in the future to ensure this could not happen again. From then on we began immersing the warriors themselves directly into the Sources to instill their power into their very bodies. This way no other could misuse the power. Ever since it has become tradition for sages to inscribe the image of the crests on the back of the hands of Elemental Warriors. With the crests no longer necessary, we tried to destroy them so they would never fall into the wrong hands. Unfortunately, their power was directly linked to the Sources and as long as they remained radiating their energies, so too would the crests. Unable to rid ourselves of them, we hid them by burying them with the bodies of the original Elemental Warriors when they died.

"I buried them myself in a graveyard at the south end of the Sage's Valley where they would never be disturbed. There they rested and were watched over until I took my leave from the order of sages and left a new Master Sage in charge.

I forbade my fellow sages to record existence of the crests so they would be forgotten and to remove temptation of any who would seek to use them for dark purposes in the future. Over the centuries they passed out of knowledge to everyone except me, explaining why Revond has never heard of this. But because the Sources are still present, the power of the crests remains; power enough for us to anoint a new batch of Elemental Warriors to fight the Ancients and fuse the Sources." While even Revond was speechless at everything he had just heard, it was Lucan who finally broke the silence.

"So we have to get back to the Sage's Valley and get these crests," he announced, following Alberic's plan to its inevitable conclusion. The Ancient of Light exhaled at this and shook his head, surprising the Maven and everyone else.

"I'm afraid that will do us no good, Lucan," he said dejected. "If the crests were still beside the Mystic Tower I would have flown their after our escape from the Holy Shrine."

"I thought you said that you buried them with the original Elemental Warriors, Alberic," Aeric said confused. "Why wouldn't they be there?"

"After I renounced my position as the Master Sage of the order," Alberic began again, "I traveled back to the Sage's Valley on occasion to secretly observe the tower and pay my respects to the graves of the warriors and others who were buried beside them. However, on my last trip to visit them almost five centuries past, I found something most disturbing in the graveyard. The coffins holding the original Elemental Warriors' bodies had been dug up and were missing. I searched the tower for them in case the sages had dug them up for some reason and then looked for years in the east for any sign of them, but I never found so much as a trace. Though they are active talismans of power that I would normally be able to sense, I sealed them in the coffins with a spell that hid their presence. Eventually I assumed they had been stolen by grave robbers years before my discovering them gone and abandoned the search. Though nervous of what could have become of the crests, I took solace in the fact that if anyone ever used them for evil I would be able to sense it and stop them. To this day I have not sensed so much as the slightest display of power from the lost crests. I have no idea what has become of them—only that they are lost."

The entire table sulked back in their chairs at this, most of the faces of the council members either dejected or angered to have hope restored only to be ripped away again.

"So we're back where we started," Valeri said blankly.

"Not necessarily," Revond said sitting up straight in his chair across from her, to which they all perked up again.

"Do you know what happened to the crests, Revond?" Aeric asked hopefully.

"No, I do not," the sage responded shaking his head, though his eyes were sparkling with hope. "But there is... a story. A myth, as it is more aptly described. There are fragments of writings from sages over the years that tell of something commonly referred to as the Scavenger—a creature with delicate senses that wanders the six lands searching for talismans of power. The first of the twelve Cebrach books I ever read in my training at the Mystic Tower was the most recent to be written—by the hand of Zeroan himself. One of his earliest entries in the book tells of the desecration of the grounds in the southern side of the Sage's Valley. Though Zeroan had never known of a graveyard in the valley, one night he discovered a recently dug fissure with several ancient coffins strewn about inside.

"Observing tracks of several heavy objects being dragged through the earth to the north, Zeroan guessed that some of the coffins had been stolen. He tracked whoever was responsible for weeks all the way into Drakkaidia until he at last lost the trail. Zeroan wrote that he searched for any sign of the thief for weeks but eventually gave up. Because he knew he was trailing several of the heavy objects he guessed to be coffins but never found evidence of more than one person dragging them across the lands at impossible speeds, Zeroan guessed the thief to be the mysterious Scavenger. Never sensing any strange power or anything out of place, however, he relinquished the coffins to whoever took them and forgot the incident."

Revond paused and swept his eyes to Alberic, already staring at him intently.

"So the coffins and the crests within could be somewhere in Drakkaidia..." Alberic trailed off softly. Revond nodded, his movements animated and excited again.

"The stories seem to fit," he concurred, looking back to Valeri. "Your Highness, have you ever heard stories of such a person or creature in Drakkaidia?" Though caught up in the

277

excitement of this newest development as well and quickly scanning her mind for any story or legend of a Scavenger, she eventually frowned and shook her head. Before she could tell them no, however, another voice sounded through the throne room.

"Wait a moment," Markus Desrum interjected, leaning forward with eyes wide. He spun around to Asthatch at the far end of the table. "What about the man in the Crag Spires?" Though Revond and the rest of them were confused, they eagerly awaited for the captain's response.

"The recluse?" Asthatch returned raising an eyebrow. "He's an old man who can barely get about. How could he be this Scavenger?"

"No, of course not," Desrum said quickly waiving his hand as if to strike Asthatch's words from the record. "But what if he knows something about this Scavenger?"

"Hold on, what are you two talking about?" Valeri interrupted, her frustration evident.

"There is a reclusive man who lives in the Crag Spires to the northwest—the lowlands of the Black Peaks, Your Highness," Desrum informed her quickly. "Before I took command of Hadecrest I was a captain leading a scouting party through those peaks. One of my men was captured by Siarchs in the Crag Spires but an old man saved him and returned him to us. Asthatch knows the story as well." Valeri turned to her most trusted captain, shooting him a look asking for confirmation.

"It's true, Your Highness," he told her quietly. "There are stories of a veteran soldier or something of the sort who knows all of Drakkaidia like the back of his hand living in the Black Peaks. Desrum is the only man I've ever known to claim to have met him, but if the tales are true, he might know of this creature or whatever it is." Valeri frowned again at this but curiously looked back to Desrum.

"Why would anyone choose to live by himself in an area as treacherous as the Crag Spires?" she asked doubtfully.

"He is a recluse from the rest of Drakkaidia, princess," Desrum responded. "Supposedly he was a soldier seeking peace from the battlefield after his long years spilling blood. All I know is he rescued one of my men and led us down a safe path through some of the most dangerous terrain in Drakkaidia. He would know where to find something."

"You say this recluse is an old man, Desrum," Valeri pressed. "What use to you think he would be to us in such a condition? How do I know he is even still alive?"

"That I can't answer, Your Highness," Desrum admitted. "But if there is indeed a Scavenger lurking about Drakkaidia, this is the man who would know where it is." Seeing Valeri chewing over his words, Alberic spoke up again.

"It seems to me this is our best lead to finding the crests and in turn stopping the Ancients before it is too late," he said while the redheaded princess met his gentle gaze. Taking in the Ancient of Light's words, Valeri slowly nodded, her resolute expression returned.

"Then it seems as though we have a recluse to track down," she said with authority. "Who is coming with me?" Asthatch rolled his eyes and deeply exhaled at the princess' fortitude, aware once she made up her mind there was no changing it.

"I will be happy to take you anywhere you need to go, Your Highness," Alberic told her with a smile. Though Valeri nodded in response at this, Revond leaned forward shaking his head.

"Wait a moment, Master Alberic," the sage said holding out one of his gloved hands. "If it is indeed the will of this council that we assemble a party to go in search of this recluse and the crests, we must also consider another element to our plan. As all the great quests have been over the years, time is arrayed against us and we must act to conserve as much as possible before it is too late. The Ancients are sure to be incensed at the loss of Alberic and the Source of Light and will be all the more aggressive in trying to track us down even in Drakkaidia. We are going to have to separate our forces if we are going to anoint a new group of Elemental Warriors before they find Hadecrest and the Source of Light."

"What else needs to be done that would require us to divide our forces, Master Sage?" Valeri asked raising an eyebrow.

"Even if we locate the crests, Your Highness," Alberic answered for him, "we will still need men and women to anoint as Elemental Warriors. We must also be searching for them across Iairia at the same time."

"There is no need," Valeri said quickly, dismissing their worries. "Even in days as dark as these I assure you there is no shortage of warriors in Drakkaidia. I can provide double the capable men we need to fulfill this charge."

"I'm afraid we can't cut corners, Princess Montrox," Revond said shaking his head. "Not just any capable soldier can be anointed an Elemental Warrior. It is no mere tradition that we match warriors with the element of the land they hail from. A man from Drakkaidia, the land soaked with the element of darkness, would not correspond with the Source of Earth, or at least not as effectively as one from the Grailen or great forests where that element holds sway. While I understand it would be more expedient to simply anoint a handful of your greatest warriors here at Hadecrest, to maximize the power of these Elemental Warriors we must recruit them from the respective lands of the Sources. We will need every bit of strength we can muster to make a stand against the Ancients." Though clearly frustrated at the Master Sage's report, Valeri at last nodded.

"I agree," she told him at last. "What do you propose then?" Revond swept his gaze over the faces of his companions as if deciding the best course of action and where they would do the most good.

"Though severely outmatched against the Ancients as we stand now, we nevertheless have several powers at this very table to defend ourselves," he stated. "We should delegate them to where they will do the most good. First, I will have to be present on the quest for new Elemental Warriors as I am the current Master Sage and therefore the only one who can anoint them. It must be my judgment in their selection. Master Alberic will also need to come with me to be my transportation as we have far greater distance to cover in the Southland than here in Drakkaidia. Between my power and his we will be able to take care of ourselves should we run into trouble."

"So you would leave Princess Montrox to fend for herself in the Black Peaks?" Asthatch asked irately. "Against the demons? Against whatever this Scavenger might be?"

"Valeri Montrox will not be alone either," Revond returned calmly. "I do not know what this Scavenger might be and I am still not entirely sure how Drakkan's evil race of demons have managed to slip onto our plane, but she will have the means to repel them. This separation would leave the princess and Aeric to go out in search of the recluse and the crests. With her power as the Drakkaidian Warrior of

Darkness that she inherited from her family activated by the Black Church, she will be able to hold off Siarchs and even a few of the demons should you encounter any. If you are overwhelmed by them or Dalorosk should find you, you will have Aeric with you holding the Source of Light to repel them. This would of course be the last defense as your location would be sensed by the other Ancients, but Alberic and I would also sense it and could come to aid you. I know there is great danger in separating our forces, but it is a necessary risk to take before the Ancients can find us. Time is short and we have no alternative."

"This entire plan rests on chance, sage," Asthatch stated coldly. "We don't even know if this recluse is still alive, much less if he knows anything about the Scavenger or the crests. For the wrath of Drakkan, you can't even tell me for certain that it was this Scavenger that took them or if it even exists!" Though Revond was about to respond, Valeri spun around to face him with her crimson eyes narrowed.

"Desperate times call for desperate action, Asthatch," she told him coldly. "We could not be any more desperate. Though far from safe this is the best idea we've had since the forming of this resistance and we're going to act on it. If you want to stay behind, no one is stopping you." Through clearly frustrated, Asthatch swallowed his pride and bowed his head.

"You know my first and only concern is for your safety, Highness," he told her in a humble tone. "I will follow you to whatever end to ensure it." Silently giving him a single nod, Valeri turned across the table for Markus Desrum.

"Do you still remember the way to this recluse in the Crag Spires, Desrum?" she asked.

"I do, Your Highness," he responded. "It will be my honor to guide you there." Seeing Valeri look back to him, Revond continued.

"And I will need a guide as well," he spoke, shifting his gaze to the Maven fidgeting with the tails of his blue scarf in his hands. "Someone who has seen the world before and after the Ascension and who knows where to look for what warriors remain across the lands." Lucan's eyes widened hearing this, realizing the sage was talking about him.

"You're kidding," he stated dropping his scarf. Revond shook his head.

"You have been with me this far, Lucan, and you have not led me astray," he said. "This is still your opportunity to help; to undo the destruction you have witnessed and the loss you have felt. If we succeed you could bring back your family. Do it for them." Though staring at the sage unconfidently for a lingering moment, the Maven glanced down the table to see all eyes on him. Gulping, he forced a grin and opened his mouth to speak.

"You had me at death and destruction again, Revond," he said, to which the Master Sage couldn't help but smile. Turning to the young Grandarian sitting beside him, Revond noted the doubt and insecurity lingering in his eyes.

"Are you satisfied with this plan, Aeric?" he asked. Aeric knew the sage could see his nervousness and doubt in himself at the responsibility that had just been heaped on him. It was the responsibility he had never wanted—the duty that came with his family name he had renounced long ago. Though remembering Lucan and Valeri's words to him the night before that told him they saw his family's famed courage alive in him through his actions and words so far, he still feared he was only a carpenter. Even with the Source of Light all he would do is slow Valeri and her men down. Letting his thoughts drift to Mina, he also knew this was the only way he could ever have her back. He had already let her down once—he wasn't going to do it again. Swallowing his fears, the sweating Grandarian fixed his eyes back on Revond's.

"I am satisfied, Revond," he said simply, surprising the Master Sage. Though Revond had expected him to ultimately agree this was his charge now whether he wanted it or not, he predicted the young man would need to be told so for him to accept it. Guessing Aeric had finally found the bravery in his heart and that his love for Mina easily pushed aside his self doubt, Revond nodded and set his gaze back on Valeri across the table.

"It appears we have a plan then, Your Highness," he said confidently with a faint smile on the corner of his lips. Valeri took a deep breath before responding, looking over the faces of her council all nodding in agreement of their decisions.

"Very well," she confirmed. "We will set out first thing tomorrow, then, fully recuperated and ready for whatever lies in store for us. I leave the details of my party for Desrum and

Asthatch to arrange, and I will have servants prepare us all the supplies and rations we will need. While much remains uncertain of what lies ahead, I am certain that if there is a way to heal this world and bring justice to our enemies, this is the group that will accomplish it. For Drakkaidia, and Iairia." Valeri rose then, immediately followed by her council and then the companions at the far end of the table. Informing them to spend the rest of the day making themselves ready for their departure the next morning, she adjourned the council. As the members began filtering out the doors of the throne room to see to the details of the coming day, Valeri approached Aeric, Revond, Alberic and Lucan with her face alight as not even Aeric had seen the previous night. "Thank you for bringing us hope, Master Sage. It's been long since we've... since *I've* had any." Revond bowed his head in response and set his eyes on her.

"You owe Alberic and these young men as much gratitude as me, Your Highness," he responded, flipping his hood back up to cover his head.

"Of course," Valeri confirmed, turning to slightly bow her head to Alberic in particular. "It's an honor to meet the fabled Alberic. I can barely believe it. But now isn't the time to be grilling you with questions. You'll all need more time to rest before we embark tomorrow. I'm sure Asthatch and my council will keep me occupied for several hours to come but let's reconvene for dinner downstairs later." The princess paused then, glancing over her shoulder to observe Asthatch talking with Markus Desrum and Alam Tielance too far behind her to hear. Turning back to sweep her gaze between Revond and Alberic, she took a step forward and spoke in a quiet voice. "Do you really think we have any chance, you two? Is there any hope for this plan?" Revond was the one to respond, quickly shooting a glance at the Ancient of Light.

"There is more hope than we had this morning, Valeri," the Master Sage replied in an equally hushed tone, addressing her informally. Though she was not filled with any more confidence by his answer, she knew he was being completely honest with her and took what comfort she could from it.

"Yes," she said nodding to herself. "I'll see you all soon then." With that the Drakkaidian princess bowed to them all, stepping back and turning to make her way for the doorway where Asthatch stood waiting for her. Before she walked out the girl turned her fiery colored head back to let her eyes meet with Aeric's already staring at her as she walked away. Slowing her pace so she could hold his gaze a moment longer than she should have, she at last turned away toward her men who immediately descended on her with questions and issues requiring her attention. Watching as the Drakkaidians disappeared and they remained alone in the throne room, Aeric turned back to find Lucan nervously rolling back and forth on his toes to his heels.

"So we're really going to do this, huh?" he asked to no one in particular. Revond responded by shifting in his robes and taking a deep breath.

"We are really going to do this, Lucan," he answered. "If I were you I'd start brainstorming some candidates for Elemental Warriors."

"That's a little easier said than done," he replied dryly. "Please remember that most of humanity is dead and gone. I don't know who you expect to find out there. Besides, I'm more worried about sending the kid off with a party of Drakkaidians after some creature we know nothing about in demon infested mountains." Aeric gulped nervously at this, not appreciating the Maven's cynical assessment of the situation he found himself in.

"Aeric is no mere kid," Revond replied, shifting his gaze onto the Grandarian. "He is a Tieloc; a new breed, at that. And just what this journey calls for. His caution and pragmatism will be a good compliment to Valeri's brash willfulness. They'll make a good team." Though Aeric silently worried they may be more like oil and water mixed together in a pail, he remembered how easy it had been to speak to her informally and hoped they would be compatible after all. He trusted her—admired her strength—and he could tell she trusted him as well. Keeping silent, Aeric followed Revond and Alberic out of the throne room beside Lucan, walking back into Hadecrest for the last night before their departure.

Part Three
Recruitment

Chapter 25

Departure

The Ancient of Light stood alone in his human form the next morning in a small archer's balcony, gazing out at the activity of Drakkaidian soldiers over the wall top in the mountainside of Hadecrest and the overcast skies to the east. He had slept peacefully the night before, his full strength and elemental power of light completely restored for the first time in eons—since the last time he transformed into his true form after banishing Dalorosk into the mountains he now stood in. After defeating his brothers with the absorbent power of the Staff of the Ancients, he had cast their weak bodies into various natural prisons across their lands. Golthrout had been thrown deep underground under the Great Forests, Vorkoise out into the Eastern Sea, Wyrik atop the highest of the Empyrean Peaks, Moltar in the core of Mt. Corist, and Dalorosk in a large cavern in the Black Peaks.

Though each of them had grown bold enough to venture out and cause trouble over the long years of their imprisonment, they had all been pushed back into their lairs by Elemental Warriors or other champions bearing great power. Alberic frowned as he looked onto on several of the jagged peaks of the mountains around him, reminding him of Dalorosk. The Ancient of Darkness had been the most ferocious and troublesome of the group, constantly flying out from his caves to challenge the Warrior of Darkness in the early years. Eventually the Drakkaidians of the Black Church captured him and used his power to fuel the order of Dark Mages, but even bound in chains under the cathedral they built around him Alberic could always sense his brother's rage teaming to be unleashed.

As the man in white reflected over the banishment of his powerful kin he heard footsteps behind him from a stairway inside the mountain stronghold. He let his eyes drift back onto the soldiers below him, waiting as a figure in gray garb with a flowing black cloak arrived to stand over the rock balcony beside him and join him in staring.

"Good morning, Master Alberic," Revond said from inside his concealing hood. Alberic smiled and turned to face him, gently setting his hands on the rock beneath him.

"I am not the Master Sage anymore, my friend," he said easily. "You are welcome to call me by my name alone."

"You are the founder of our order and always will be," Revond replied, still keeping his gaze down on the wall top. "If anyone has earned the title of Master Sage it is you."

"And yet first and foremost I am the Ancient of Light, Revond," Alberic reminded him. "My title is merely my name. It makes me remember purer times when I hear it. Simpler times, before the war of my brothers and complexity that I began with the sages." Revond turned for him, raising an eyebrow from inside his hood.

"You make the nature of the order sound like an evil, Alberic," he observed curiously.

"You know as well as I that good and evil are perspectives held by imperfect creatures such as ourselves," Alberic replied. "The order I began has accomplished what we perceive to be good and served its purpose well until recently, but I always lamented introducing the foreign and manipulative power the sages came to use into Iairia. This was the one unpolluted place in our world where life was primed to thrive only from the simple, raw elements."

"Is that why the origins of the draught and the staff were never recorded, Alberic?" Revond asked through the warm morning air as a breeze rustled past his hood. "Because you found them off the shores of Iairia and saw them as a disruption to the natural order of our lands?" Alberic was silent at this, holding Revond's searching gaze for a long moment before looking out at the dark sky on the horizon.

"Everything is recorded somewhere, Revond," he said at last. "I see you didn't read much more than the beginning of my Cebrach book."

"There wasn't exactly time to read hundreds of pages the day the Ascension began," the Master Sage returned. "If you'll permit me to ask, Alberic, why did you conceal so much from the order? The Ancients and the forming of the Sources; your true identity; where you retrieved the staff; even the origin of the draught that gives us our power. For all the extensive knowledge we have compiled, these questions from our beginnings remain mysteries."

"You question my keeping such things secret," Alberic stated quietly, looking down as if defeated. "As well you should, for time has proven many of my decisions during my years as the Master Sage imprudent." Seeing the Ancient of Light's dejected expression, Revond lowered his black hood behind his back and fixed his eyes on the other's.

"Do not mistake my intent, Alberic; I am the last person to criticize after the disaster that occurred on my watch," he said humbly. "I am just curious why you left us—the sages—in the first place with so much left unsaid." Alberic let out a deep breath before shaking his head and looking upon the Master Sage's bearded face.

"First of all, you may be the Master Sage now, Revond, but this disaster is of my doing, as you pointed out, by keeping so much truth in shadow," he stated. "As I told you yesterday my hubris is the reason we now face this doom. At the end of my short centuries as the Master Sage things looked different than they do today or even a few hundred years ago at the start of this age—brighter; clearer. There were no nations or strange powers rampant across the lands. Iairia was still completely unspoiled and just beginning to grow. The gods had long been away and we knew nothing of the Holy Emerald yet; mankind was still just a small pocket of life in the northeast lands surviving off the remnant power of Granis; my brothers and their troublesome races were contained; and the natural races like the Sky Sprites and Cronoms were coming back. Even the few remaining Morlans and Celestrians took confidence in traveling in the open freely. I believed my task as the world's protector to be done. I left because I didn't want to influence the world or disrupt the destiny of mankind anymore than I already had. It was their world now. My brothers and I were merely the byproducts of chance that didn't fit into the destiny Granis had in mind for the humans.

"You were a part of the world nonetheless, Alberic," Revond reminded him. "If you subscribe to that line of thought you must believe you were meant to be here as well."

"Perhaps," Revond agreed, gently nodding. "But I preferred the human existence to the one I had been given. Life was so much more beautiful for them. They could build and create all manner of things beyond what I could ever imagine. They appreciated life so much more because it was not infinite for them. I supposed I respected that about them; envied it even. It's why I have defended them over the years. But in my relative youth and experience with humanity only in its infancy in those days, I assumed things would carry on this way forever."

Alberic slouched where he stood again and faintly shook his head.

"I was wrong," he almost whispered. "I forgot that Granis did not create the humans in his gentle image but as creatures with a propensity to fall victim to their desires. I witnessed the volatile and violent side of humanity split and fracture itself over and over again. First there was the split in Grandaria when Godsmark uprooted itself into the skies to disappear forever. Then came the political unrest that drove half of Grandaria away into Drakkan's lands to be slowly subverted by the dark energy that shaped them into the fierce people they are today. Later I saw the expansionists almost go to war with the rest of Grandaria but instead break away into the land that would become the Southland. Then the wars started between Grandaria and Drakkaidia. Terrible years of death that stretched on for a millennia until cumulating in the Holy Wars. I could barely understand their lust for blood and conquest. The tear in religion; the confident ideologies that defied the very principals Granis had first instilled in them; the doctrines of law created to knowingly enflame conflict; all of them were followed without question, driving man to take life for his misguided ambitions when the world had been peaceful and just to begin with. It never made any sense to me..." Hearing the Ancient of Light trail off, Revond searched his thoughts for the right thing to say.

"Few of us are able to grasp the entire historical narrative as you, Alberic," he said. "Such is the nature of humanity. It's why we can't see definitive good or evil, as you reminded me. When we completely devote ourselves to belief in one of those religions, ideologies, doctrines, or even primal desires—whatever it may be—we cannot see past them to some universal code of ethics, if one even exists to be comprehended by creatures as shortsighted as we. True belief in something requires us to become consumed by that belief. Depending on the nature of that belief or conviction, it can lead us to peace and prosperity or war and destruction. Tavin Tieloc had the same belief in his mission during the

Days of Destiny as Valif Montrox had in his. Good and evil don't even enter into it. They just knew what they had to do. But while this consuming belief can prove dangerous, consider that without it—without a purpose or ideal to devote our lives to—what meaning would life retain?" Revond paused there, seeing Alberic struggling to sort through all he was saying. "This is why you kept so much hidden, isn't it? You feared knowledge of power beyond our world would fall into our hands and contribute to this destructive side of humanity."

"I simply wished to protect humanity from itself," Alberic returned. "I hadn't yet witnessed man's capacity for destruction, but I feared what might happen should I tempt them. In my desperation to stop the endless cycle of ruin from my brothers in their war, I left these shores to search for power elsewhere. Well I found it, Revond, on lands far from these where elemental power is merely a backdrop to a world of magic and energy I could barely comprehend. I brought back but a fragment of that power to contain my brothers and form our order. In my self-righteous judgment I deemed it too great a risk for humanity to uncover. I wanted mankind to discover it on their own when they were ready so I sealed my Cebrach book and all of its contents from even my most trusted disciples. I now see the cost of my lapse in judgment. I could not see that I am the same imperfect being consumed by his beliefs as well." When Alberic fell quiet Revond let the silence hang for a moment, casting his gaze back onto the wall top to observe Aeric Tieloc and Lucan Hauk Erland appearing from the right side slowly walking down while munching on something in their hands.

"Time may have proven you right, Alberic," Revond said, watching the two young men stroll and talk. "I do not doubt humanity's inherent goodness or I would not have dedicated my life to this order, but sometimes I wonder if we will ever overcome our shortsightedness. Perhaps we would have destroyed ourselves long before the Ancients ever got the chance had we acquired such power before we were ready. And we aren't yet. For all my studies of the Sage's Draught and its power I still know so little of its true nature. Some things may be beyond us."

"But that was not for me to decide," Alberic returned, also catching sight of Aeric and Lucan. "If I had put that Cebrach book on a shelf of the tower that day I left, this entire doom may have been avoided. Instead I hid it all from you and gave up my duty to monitor my brothers. In doing so I invited apocalypse." Hearing this, Revond was unsure of what more he could say to alleviate Alberic's guilt. Parting through all the philosophy and ideals they had delved through in the past few minutes, the Master Sage forced himself to think back to the earliest days of his training and remember something he had heard on his first day in the Mystic Tower.

"A hardnosed realist once told me it is easy to see the difference between right and wrong," Revond said. "He said that is the role of wisdom. What's hard is choosing the wrong that's more right. You did what you thought best, Alberic." Revond put a hand on the Ancient's shoulder. "That was your only duty, and it was fulfilled. You still fulfill it now." Feeling the hand on him, Alberic turned to meet Revond's gaze with a raised eyebrow.

"Who was this realist?" he asked, to which Revond faintly smiled.

"Who else?" he asked withdrawing his hand back into the folds of his cloak. "Zeroan." Alberic silently chuckled at this, leaning his weight onto the rocky edge of the balcony.

"I wish I had known that one," he said with a fleeting smile. "I think I would have liked him." Looking back down at Aeric as he laughed at something Lucan had said, Alberic's face went blank again. "This is our mess to clean up, Revond. Is it fair of us to bring Aeric into it? To ask him to risk his life venturing into the most dangerous terrain in Iairia with only a party of Drakkaidians after a creature we know nothing about other than its desire to hoard power?"

"It is no less fair than when Zeroan came to Aeric's grandfather sixty years ago," Revond answered. "But it is just as necessary. The princess will need him. Though it is battered with grief and self doubt, his heart is strong. That and the Source of Light will protect him." Alberic smiled as he rotated his gaze to Revond.

"You have great faith in the Tielocs, don't you?" he asked. Revond slowly nodded, glimmers of a time long past flashing across his mind.

"I knew one well myself," he replied softly. "She was the bravest person I ever knew..." Alberic's smile widened at this, watching Revond's eyes drift into space. Lifting himself upright, the Ancient of Light's white attire began to softly glow.

"Then it looks like we have all the hope we need," he said, his voice growing deeper. "Shall we?" With that, the sheen of white over Alberic's clothing stretched to cover his entire body. Jumping up to land on the balcony with both feet, he leapt forward into the open air to morph before Revond's eyes into his amazing true form, his angelic feathered wings spreading wide as the light faded to reveal the white horse softly touching down on the wall top with his golden hooves shimmering upon impact. Contented to see he had lifted the Ancient of Light's spirits, Revond smiled again and reached up to pull his hood back over his head. With a mighty leap of his own Revond jumped up to the balcony to heave himself into the air. Flipping down to his feet, the sage landed far beneath on the wall top in a powerful but graceful crouch, his black cloak gently falling around him. Raising himself up full height, he found the Drakkaidians and his companions staring in amazement at both Alberic and himself. While Aeric rushed to Alberic's side to greet him, Lucan strolled up to Revond with his hands behind his head.

"You always make an entrance," he said with a grin, to which Revond replied he was merely following Alberic's lead. Ambling up to Aeric, Revond saw that he and Lucan were dressed in the clothes they had arrived in, washed and reinforced with patches and stitching where needed. They had fresh packs of supplies on their backs, obviously ready to depart early as Valeri Montrox had instructed. Seeing Revond appear around one of Alberic's pulled in wings, Aeric smiled and repositioned the pack on his back.

"Hello Revond," he said merrily, his dark hair blowing in the passing breeze. "Looks like you three are ready to go."

"We are indeed," he stated, glancing at Alberic's golden eyes. "Where is Valeri? I thought she was coming to see us off."

"She told me she'd be down in a moment," Aeric informed him. "She had some last minute business to see to after breakfast I suppose." Revond nodded, looking to the opposite side of the wall and the opening into the stronghold to see it clear of the Drakkaidian princess or any of her men. Taking a step closer to Aeric, the sage spoke to him in a hushed tone of voice.

"Then before she arrives and you depart listen close," he said. "I know this isn't the path you were expecting or wanting for your life, Aeric, but it is laid before your feet nonetheless. I am proud of you for finding the strength to do this. But be warned: you must be cautious on this next stage of your quest. You must think for yourself now. Trust Valeri and her men but use your own judgment—be a voice for prudence and reason as you travel. While you will be protected by her power and the Source of Light, you march onto unknown ground after this mysterious Scavenger. Only use the Source if absolutely necessary but keep it close and ready should the need arise. Be diligent for the demons. Neither Alberic nor I can account for their presence, but something is obviously amiss across Drakkaidia for them to have escaped the Netherworld." Though Revond could see the boy nervous again at his cautions, Aeric swallowed his fears and nodded.

"This is my only chance to save Mina. I won't let you down, Revond," he avowed. "We'll find the crests." Revond couldn't help but smile at this, noticing Valeri and several of her men strapped in dark armor appearing from the opening in the cliffside to the wall top.

"If anyone can, it will be you, Aeric," he returned. Knowing the sage meant it by his friendly and sincere eyes, Aeric smiled again before turning to face Valeri Montrox, Asthatch and Markus Desrum flanked by guards on either side. Seeing his companions staring at something behind him, Alberic turned his large body to see the Drakkaidians as well and dipped his head at the princess' coming, the shimmering golden hair of his mane spilling down over his head. Her eyes as full with wonder as they had been the first time she looked upon the Ancient of Light's true form, Valeri struggled to maintain her serious royal composure as she arrived before them and motioned for them to rise.

"You're ready to embark, then?" she asked looking over the trio standing beside Aeric.

"Yes, Your Highness," Revond told her. "We will be off immediately. Though I can guarantee you no certainties, I am optimistic that we can find the four we need with relative quickness. If half of the rumors Lucan has heard are true, there are still ample pockets of underground civilization that endure, so I have hope we can find our Elemental Warriors as soon as possible."

"Then I can only hope to match your speed, Master Sage," Valeri replied bowing her head. "We will be off as soon as we have seen you away. I wish you a safe journey."

"And to you, Princess Montrox," he replied with a bow of his own. With that Revond turned to pull himself onto Alberic's back, motioning for Lucan to follow him. Taking a deep breath, the Maven first turned back to Aeric with a strange expression on his face. Though Aeric was about to ask him what was wrong, the Grandarian was surprised to find him rushing to tightly hug him where he stood, telling him to be careful out there. Chuckling in response and embracing the Maven as well, Aeric told him he would and for them to do the same. Pulling away as he mumbled he would see him soon, Lucan tossed his blue scarf over his shoulder and reached up for Revond's hand to help him onto Alberic's back.

Once the two were secure behind him, Alberic bid the group around him to stand back while he stretched his wings. Flapping them hard where he stood and telling Revond and Lucan to hold on, the white horse slowly lifted into the air until he rose higher than the ramparts. Moving over the wall top, Alberic suddenly plummeted past it, disappearing. Rushing to the side to see where he had gone, Aeric, Valeri and the rest were surprised to see him shoot back into the sky with the momentum and speed he had built and soared off out of the mountain wedge.

Laughing out loud at the thought of Lucan losing his breakfast from the sharp takeoff, Aeric turned to find Asthatch and his men not finding anything so amusing. Seeing the Grandarian's smile dissipating, Valeri let one spread across her own lips and told him it was their turn to set out. Silently nodding, Aeric walked beside her as they turned for the exit to the wall top back into the mountain stronghold.

Nearly an hour later Aeric took hold of the rough side of a boulder beside him to bolster himself up on the steep path he was walking up, pausing to turn around and observe the distance he had traversed since departing Hadecrest. Looking through the breezy air that blew his blue tunic and black hair back and forth where he stood, the boy took a moment to pause and take a last look at the only trace of civilization he might see for a very long while. The castle of the mountain stronghold was barely visible through the rocks of the tips of the peaks surrounding it, and he was about to make his way down a ridge that would obscure his view of the edifice completely. He, Valeri, Asthatch, Desrum and three other elite Drakkaidian soldiers handpicked from the resistance army by Asthatch had set out from the castle in the distance the moment Alberic and the others had lifted off, covering considerable ground to the north of Hadecrest for an hour.

There was a large plateau around them but now they were beginning to descend a mountain slope that led into the most jagged and rough terrain Aeric had ever seen. Turning away from Hadecrest to look back out into the seemingly endless Black Peaks ahead of him, the Grandarian took a deep breath, still in disbelief he was setting out into them. Though energized after his rest at Hadecrest the thought of hiking and climbing over the vast mountains before him filled his mind with fatigue. He wasn't sure what he found more daunting: embarking out into the unknown or doing it without the power and wisdom of Revond to guide him. The sage had been there for him since the beginning to protect him and determine the best course of action in any situation. Now all he could rely on was the judgment of a few Drakkaidians he had only met a few days before.

As thoughts of his current party members echoed back into his mind, Aeric was brought back to his senses by the sound of a thick boot kicking against a foothold in the slope to propel a large body up behind Aeric. Looking back again, the Grandarian observed Captain Asthatch heaving himself up to the top of the ridge as well, raising his cold eyes to the young man's.

"Keep pace, Master Tieloc," he said, striding past him and repositioning the oversized axe on his back to untangle his flowing red cape around its handle. "We move in this formation for your protection. Our scout and guide at the front and myself and the soldiers in the back to keep you and Her Highness protected at either end. Guard column formation, it's called." Taking a final glance at Hadecrest before turning to rush down the ridge after the Drakkaidian captain, Aeric swept a hand through his hair and tried a smile as he walked beside him.

"But what will you do if we're attacked from the side, Asthatch?" he said lightheartedly. The large Drakkaidian merely shot him a blank glance and let out a short huff before telling him to hurry back into formation, obviously not seeing the humor. His smile dissipating, Aeric felt embarrassed and quickened his pace as they passed down a narrow road leading down the ridge. Though the rest of his party was well spaced out with Markus Desrum and a scout far ahead looking down a crevice in the rocks, he was surprised to find Valeri standing still with her body half rotated back for him as if waiting.

She was dressed in the same attire and curving crimson armor he had seen her in the day they met. Her short red hair and the tips of her gray shawl swayed in the gust blowing past her, forcing her to sweep a lock of hair blown into her face back behind her ear. She stood leaning on one foot with her hands resting on the hilt of the short sword at her waist, hung on the belt with the metal lightning bolt buckle. Waiting for the young man to arrive beside her she began walking again, silently chuckling. When she saw Aeric's eyes on her, curious at her behavior, she merely shook her head and rolled her eyes.

"You'll have to forgive the captain," she said almost playfully. "His sense of humor is non-existent. Sarcasm is a different story, but he doesn't have much of a taste for comedy."

"I noticed," he replied, shooting a glance back at the gruff captain walking several yards behind them. "Sure to make for a long journey."

"It won't be that long, hopefully," Valeri responded. "If we march fast and hard, which we will, the Crag Spires are only a few days northwest. Then we'll have to take our time."

"What is it that makes this place so dangerous, Valeri?" Aeric asked.

"The Crag Spires?" she asked as if surprised he had never heard of it. "It's possibly the most hazardous spot in any mountainous region in Iairia. It's said Drakkan and Granis did combat there once during the Battle of the Gods, blowing away half the mountains around them. The Crag Spires are a region of near vertical cliffs and towers of rock stretching high into the sky; columns of stone that spiral and twirl around each other. There are few tales of anyone venturing into the spires and coming out. Desrum and my grandfather are the only ones I know of who successfully navigated them."

"Your grandfather?" Aeric asked, curious. "You mean Verix Montrox?"

"That's right," she confirmed, glancing at the Grandarian. "You're curious about him?" Aeric shrugged.

"My Grandfather Tavin would tell more stories about your grandfather—my great uncle—than anyone else," he confessed. "He respected him more than anyone he knew. I guess I'm just wondering what happened to him. My grandfather said the last time he saw Verix Montrox was at the first peace council between Grandaria and Drakkaidia in the ruins of the Wall of Light and after that no one from Grandaria ever saw him again."

"Nor Drakkaidia," she replied setting her gaze back in front of her. "He left Dalastrak when I was still a toddler. I never knew him. They say that after the Third Holy War and the reunification of Drakkaidia under my grandfather, his exploits over the years finally became widespread knowledge and seemingly overnight he became the most celebrated king in the history of our house. Though many were hesitant about his reform of the Black Church and his talk of peace with Grandaria, the people loved him for helping them rebuild and revive the sense of glory from the old days. In the face of near destruction at the hands of our great grandfather Valif Montrox and the threat of civil war in the years to follow, my grandfather restored Drakkaidia to its former power in just a few short decades. Everyone loved him.

"Too much, perhaps. Though no one but my father really knows why he did it, my grandfather left the capital without a word over fifteen years ago. He was due to lead a battalion of troops against the barbarians from the north encroaching on our borders but he departed the night before, naming my father the new king in a written decree. My father told me that grandfather felt he had been in power too long and seen too much. He was still a strong man, but he said his body had grown weary of the stresses of being king despite his love for his country and decided it was my father's time to rule. Apparently the Black Church and the nobles didn't feel the same. They told Verix he was loved by his people too much to give up his crown to his young son before his death. They feared it could undo all the gains he had made as king.

"So grandfather left them no choice. His final order as king was leaving instruction for Valgard to be crowned, explaining he had other loose ends to tie up before he could rest. My father led the army to a tremendous victory against the barbarians so the people rallied around him and the church anointed him the new Warrior of Darkness, but no one ever saw my grandfather again. All I have of him is this." She swept her right hand down the curves of her chest over the gray shawl she wore. "It was made from the coat he wore when he was my age. Probably the one he wore when traveling with your grandfather during the Days of Destiny." Though Aeric was amazed by this and wanted to look over the cloth closer, he found himself staring at the girl's chest and forced himself to look away before he started blushing.

"I had no idea of all that," Aeric said mostly to himself, surprised the legendary King of Drakkaidia who had battled with and alongside Tavin Tieloc over the years had so suddenly vanished. Shifting his gaze back to the girl walking beside him watching him blush, Aeric changed the subject. "When did you become the Warrior of Darkness, Valeri?" he asked. The girl opened her mouth to say something but she cut her self off, rephrasing whatever she planned to say.

"Well technically, I'm not the Warrior of Darkness," she admitted, surprising him. "The power was brought out in me by the Dark Mages when I was a child as my father's and grandfather's had been so I could train and develop it over the years, but I was never formally ordained. Verix Montrox wasn't either, despite his legendary power. You see, my mother died of sickness during the Black Winter shortly after grandfather left. Without a son, my father was left only with me as his heir. It was another radical change of the Montroxs—there has never been a ruling princess or queen on the highest throne of Drakkaidia. Had the Ascension never happened and my father lived, he would have faced an even more difficult dilemma seeing his child crowned that his father before him did. He trained me the same as he would have a son, though, showing me no less mercy than his father had shown him growing up. My grandmother insisted I have a bower of women and girls my age to groom me into a lady as well, but my father always told me I should have been born a man." She looked to Aeric who was staring at her uncertainly at this, to which she smiled. "In Drakkaidia that's a rare compliment, Aeric. I'm not the warrior my father was but he always said I would outgrow him someday. Sometimes I wonder if the Ascension will give me that opportunity or take it away."

The princess trailed off at that, her eyes momentarily distant before she shook off her deep thoughts and lit up with remembrance.

"Which reminds me," she said suddenly. She spun around to one of her soldiers covered in light black armor with a sharp red insignia painted over the torso plate, calling him out while she walked backwards beside Aeric. Sprinting from where he had been walking, the soldier raced past Asthatch until within a few feet of the princess so he could bow. "One of your swords, please," she asked opening her hand. Quickly reaching to his side, the Drakkaidian pulled off one of the swords sheathed at his waist to present it to her. She thanked him and turned back around, to which the man ambled back into his place at the rear of their formation. Watching the girl spin back around, Aeric was surprised to feel her shove the weapon up against his chest. "We can't have you unarmed where we're going," she told him. Though Aeric raised his gauntlet covered forearms to take hold of the blade, he let out a soft breath of dissatisfaction and looked at her.

"You should save this for your men, Valeri," he told her. "I'm not much good with this sort of thing." The girl raised an eyebrow incredulously at this.

"The son of Darien Tieloc never learned how to use a blade?" she asked sounding almost aghast. Aeric frowned and lowered the weapon to his side.

"I never said that," he returned affronted. "This just isn't my sort of tool. I was going to be a carpenter before all this, not a soldier. You said yourself I'm no warrior. I wouldn't have much use for this." Valeri frowned as she placed her hard gaze on the boy.

"Well I'd wager my grandfather's shawl you're going to get use out of it before this is over whether you trained for it or not," she returned abrasively. "And we don't have much use for a carpenter out here. I suggest you reprioritize the skills you should be familiar with from here on out." Aeric's irritated expression escalated to a full frontal glare hearing this and he allowed himself to forget he was addressing a princess.

"Well pardon me for not having been drilled with combat my entire life," he snapped. "Don't belittle my life just because you never had a choice to pick yours." Valeri's eyes flared at this, spinning on the Grandarian beside her with a flash of anger suddenly in her crimson eyes.

"I am what I need to be," she blasted back. "That's why I'm ready for anything and everything that comes my way whenever and wherever it comes, which is more than I can say for you, Grandarian. Keep your softness and frailty and see how far that gets you. You're in Drakkaidian now, Aeric." Though Aeric thought about responding, he was cut short by the girl spinning her head away and leaping off to the side of the ridge beside them to slide down a gravely slope down to the winding trail beneath them where Markus Desrum walked looking out at the road ahead of them.

Watching as she disappeared amid the dust and rolling gravel, Aeric bit his tongue and took a deep breath, trying to settle down. Sweeping his eyes down to the sword, he felt a wave of remorse and shame washing over him, aware he had just pushed away his only friend on his new journey. Though wanting to scream at himself that he was an idiot for getting flustered by nothing and offending her, the Grandarian merely shoved the sheath of the sword into the carpenter's belt at his side and continued walking. Remembering Asthatch trailing not far behind, Aeric glanced back to find the captain's eyes on him, narrowed and clearly unhappy. Gulping, Aeric whispered a prayer to Granis to be with him as he traveled with the cold Drakkaidians.

They continued marching on down the ridge for another hour before coming to another cut through the mountains leading back up to a higher road. Hiking on up and down through the peaks for the rest of the day with virtually no break to speak of, the party at last came to a halt for the night beside a series of jagged boulders. Though Desrum was confident they could reach a marker on the road to the Crag Spires if they pressed on for just a short while longer, Asthatch refused to travel in the darkness with the threat of the demons abroad in the Black Peaks and insisted they camp immediately. Agreeing with him, Valeri ordered a small fire be made and her scouts to search the immediate perimeter for anything out of the ordinary.

The group around the fire ate a meager meal in silence only occasionally broken by Asthatch telling Valeri and his men of dangers in the terrain they would need to be wary of and avoid. It had been awkward ever since Aeric and Valeri's confrontation early in the day, neither of the two speaking to each other even though Aeric knew he had to make peace early or risk leaving her permanently upset. Though he wanted to say something to the girl when Asthatch rose from the fire to see to the sentry keeping watch at their rear leaving them alone, the princess quickly rose and wandered back beside one of the large boulders away from the fire.

Pretending to pick at something on his tunic behind him so he could turn around to glance at her, he saw the princess was looking at him as well but hurriedly shot her gaze elsewhere and pressed back against the rock where she sat on her still folded bedding. Alone for what might have been the only time the rest of the night, Aeric let out a long breath and summoned his courage, knowing he had to talk to her before her anger could settle and keep things uncomfortable in the long run. Rising from the small blanket he sat on sweating with nervousness and with no clue what he was about to say, he turned to slowly amble toward the boulders. Though he saw Valeri pretend not to notice, he stopped alongside one of the giant rocks beside her and leaned against it so she would not be able to miss him. When her eyes drifted up to him they were not angry or frustrated, just blank as if expecting something. Aware of what he had to do, the young man just spoke the first words to come to mind, unfiltered and raw.

"I'm sorry for earlier," he said softly, just loud enough to be heard. "I overreacted for some reason. I just... I didn't plan for that quip about you not having a choice to be what you are to come out mean." Valeri's expression remained unchanged but she raised her legs to her chest and wrapped her arms around them as if pressing her own body heat into her. "If anything I'm probably just a little insecure that the girl I'm traveling with is a powerhouse who knows more about combat and worldly pursuits than a simple carpenter like me ever will. I'm... sorry, Valeri." He stopped there, not sure what else he could say without stammering over himself and appearing desperate. He fixed his gaze down on the girl waiting for a reaction. Eventually she tilted her head and leaned it against the boulder she sat against, a faint smile appearing on the corners of her lips.

"Come down here, Aeric," she told him cavalierly. Aeric remained still at first, feeling oddly uncomfortable at such a request. Not wanting to upset her again, he lowered himself to sit against the rock across from her so they were facing one another. Valeri let a sharp stream of breath escape from her lips as she looked up into the dark sky. "If anything you were right. I've never regretted my life but it's true that I've never had much of a choice in it. I shouldn't have gone off about those old Grandarian pigeonholes. Maybe I'm just jealous that you were in a position to choose your own destiny. I'm sorry if I belittled that." She brought her gaze back down to meet the young man's, her eyes gentle and casual as they had been the night they talked in his room at Hadecrest. "But you are the last person who should be intimidated by me—you're the first person I've ever known who I'm envious of." Aeric raised an eyebrow uncertainly at this.

"Envious of me?" he repeated in disbelief. "You're a princess, Valeri. What possible reason would you have to be envious of someone like me?" The girl shrugged at first, her eyes slowly passing up and down his figure.

"You have something I never will," she returned distantly. "Don't get me wrong, I meant what I said about never regretting who I am. I've never wanted for anything. But I have... wondered what life outside of castle walls and royal bowers is like. Life without the responsibility. Without the duty on my shoulders. I'd bet it feels liberating." Seeing Aeric speechless, Valeri smiled again and tilted her head further on the rock. "And you were right. Just about every man I know besides Asthatch and my father has been insecure with me since I came of age. Few like the idea of an attractive girl with power far beyond them, both politically and physically. It's scared off any would-be suitors over the years. I've never known what it's like to be in love... like you are." She paused for a moment, her searching eyes probing into his again. "What's her name?" Aeric remained quiet for a moment, once again surprised by her question. Delving into his memories to conjure up the beautiful form of his long time love smiling at him in his thoughts, he took a long breath and spoke.

"Mina," he said, forcing a smile at Valeri as he battled to suppress his rising emotions at the thought of his girlfriend. "She's my Mina." Valeri returned his smile, still peering unblinking into his eyes.

"Mina," she repeated, testing out the sound of the name from her own voice. "Maybe it's her I envy." Aeric shot her an uncertain look hearing this, staring back into her gaze.

"There's never been a man willing to speak to me as you do. Honestly. As a peer and a friend and not a subject. My father had guards that would talk to him as an equal in private at least. I only have... well, Asthatch, and he might as well be my second father. I guess I'm just jealous of that part of your life at least." Aeric didn't know what to say after she finished, still just gently staring at him. Though he considered saying something trite like how he could easily see a desirable girl within despite her strength, he was precluded by a deep voice calling from the fire beyond.

"Your Highness," it said powerfully, causing both Aeric and Valeri to spin around to find Asthatch standing in front of the fire looking at them with a cold expression on his hard face. Valeri did not respond but to turn back to Aeric and lean off the boulder behind her, pulling her legs back in that she had let slip beside Aeric's. Not having noticed before, Aeric quickly leapt back to his feet to brush himself off in the uncomfortable silence. Valeri took her time, grabbing her blanket she had been sitting on. Yawning, the princess told him they should get some sleep and wandered past him back to the fire where Asthatch continued staring, unmoving.

Aeric wasn't sure whether he was more uncomfortable by the Drakkaidian girl's words to him in the minutes before or the large captain continuing to stare him down until Valeri wordlessly tapped the armor over his middle and he slowly turned to unfold his own bedding. Sensing that Asthatch didn't appreciate his presence as Valeri seemed to, Aeric wandered to the other side of the fire and tried to fall asleep, aware he would need all his strength and more for the rest of this journey with them.

Chapter 26

<u>The West</u>

A lone sparrow slowly let its wings relax beside a wisp of cloud above Mt. Corist. Though the skies over the Southland had been devoid of nearly all life after the Ascension, a few remaining birds had survived, particularly in the traditionally fertile lands of the west where pockets of plant and animal life refused to perish. The small bird hovering in a rising thermal from the heat of the volcano had been scavenging alone for months now, surviving off insects and seeds from the vegetation that had cropped back up amid the burnt soil and ashes of the Ascension.

It was sight of the little sparrow lofting in the thermal that drew a smile to Lucan Hauk Erland's face as he dropped out of the clouds beside it on Alberic's back. Spying the winged creature as they soared by, Lucan let a small but relieving wave of hope fill him up. Though he had been doubtful that anyone or anything could have survived the Ascension when telling Revond and Alberic of their first stop to find a contender he knew of for the Elemental Warrior of Fire, the Master Sage urged him not to underestimate life's resourcefulness to endure even the destruction done by the Ancients.

"Life is a remarkable occurrence, young Maven," he had said while they flew south from Drakkaidia. "It's always finding ways to carry on. No matter how hard death besieges it, as long as matter exists you never know where it may turn up next." Lucan remained skeptical, only aware of rumors of lost pockets of civilization hiding across Iairia. He informed them that the first person they should seek out was to the west beyond Mt. Corist. He had heard that a nomadic group of survivors led by a Red Maven scavenged the remains of the once lush and fruitful land. Though Lucan wasn't sure if the rumor was true or if this leader was even the Maven he had in mind, he was the only person he could think to vouch for rumored to still be drawing breath.

"They used to call him the Stain," Lucan began when telling his companions of the rumor. "Short for Bloodstain. Before the Ascension he was an infamous Red Maven that specialized in assassination jobs, human and beast alike. He was a hunter, proficient beyond anyone I've ever seen with the bow. When I was a Windrun Warrior my patrol was on our way to Haven in the Empyrean Peaks when we encountered him trying to kill a wyvern on the slopes. Apparently he had been hired by a noble in Windrun who just wanted a head he could mount on his wall. It's against local law to kill them, but with the help of a partner he actually brought it down. We caught them both and were bringing them in but he escaped and after he sprung his partner that night we never heard from him again. Neither he nor the woman he was working with were exactly the most cordial of Mavens I've ever known but they were good. And lethal. I don't know if that's a prime candidate for a public position of power but that's about the best I can give you if you're asking for someone in particular. I don't know how the Stain ended up in the west looking after a rabble of villagers but that's the rumor. Maybe he had a change of heart."

Though Revond was less than impressed by the apparent character of the morally ambiguous Maven, he bore in mind that he would be presented with few options for alternates and had to make the best of what they had. Agreeing that they should at least try to search him out as the Maven could have a group of others with him who might also offer potential for recruitment, Revond asked Alberic to hurry them to the western territories of the former Southland. As they traveled through the constantly clouded skies, Revond and Lucan quickly noticed the Ancient of Light taking bizarre turns whenever they dropped out of the clouds to rest, heading all four directions. When they asked him what he was doing, Alberic replied that even with Revond's mystic power to veil his presence from the other Ancients, it was necessary to mask the direction they were heading visually as well. He reminded them that the other Ancients would be out looking for them now and if one spotted them and the direction they were heading he could have the other Ancients converge on them.

Though Revond was confused at how an Ancient could relay such a message to the others when they were separated over the six lands, Alberic informed him that his brothers had discovered a way to communicate with each other over long distances so long as their Sources remained together atop their false Holy Shrine. Because his Source was not a part of their collection Alberic could not hear their conversation, but the others could now speak to each other over any distance so long as their Sources remained together. Though nervous at this revelation, the trio pressed on for the south taking care to watch the skies and land below for any sign the Ancients. They arrived in the western mountains after a day of erratic flight to throw off any trackers, beginning to sweep the lands for any sign of a group of wandering humans. Revond had the Ancient of Light pass over the remains of villages first, occasionally touching down to look for any sign of recent activity. Though all three of them were skilled trackers and knew what to look for, none of them could find any evidence anywhere that anyone had passed by recently.

Continuing the search through the morning and afternoon on the day they arrived, Revond began to grow frustrated and asked Alberic to touch down over a ridge on the mountains they flew over. Mt. Corist was just a few miles to their right from the spot the white horse touched down on, his golden hooves illuminating the ash covered rock with shimmering light as they did. Coming to a standstill, the Ancient turned his head back to view a glimpse of his riders. Revond was staring out at the fields to the west of the mountains before shaking his head and exhaling a sharp breath.

"This is getting us nowhere," he said frustrated. "Searching aimlessly from the sky isn't going to yield any results when this wandering group, if it exists at all, is sure to be in hiding most of the time either underground or in the mountains. We need a better tactic." The Master Sage turned back to Lucan readjusting the scarf around his neck. "Do you know of any natural hideaways or specific areas where this Maven and his band are rumored to be?" Though Lucan wished he could provide the sage with additional detail he shrugged and shook his head.

"I already told you everything I heard," he returned, "and that I wasn't even sure this rumor was true. Keep in mind that I'm from the east—I haven't a clue about the geography out here."

"And though I have traveled out here before, Revond," Alberic chimed in, "the land has changed much since my time as the Master Sage. I wouldn't know where to begin."

"So we have to comb every inch of the Southland," Revond finished for them, his voice unguardedly aggravated. "The odds are not in our favor at finding a small group of humans trying to hide from anything resembling the Ancients. This may take longer than I thought if our luck doesn't improve." Watching as the sage withdrew back into his thoughts to silently brainstorm a new strategy for searching out the nomadic group, Lucan noticed something on the horizon and leaned to his right to gaze past Revond's black hood. Narrowing his eyes as if to assure himself his observation was what he thought it was, he pointed up to the horizon.

"Maybe our luck just flamed back up," he said catching their attention. "There's a column of smoke rising from out in the fields on the horizon." Hearing this, Revond and Alberic spun their heads around to gaze out at the charred fields and observe the plume of smoke for themselves. It was far away and small but spreading with each passing moment, obviously revealing a fresh fire. Though it might have been natural, Revond told Alberic to take them skyward again so they could investigate for themselves. Nodding and spreading his wings out, the Ancient of light galloped off the rock and shot back into the air with newfound energy and speed for whatever lay beyond. They blasted through the breezy air with ferocious speed the likes of which they had only witnessed in their escape from the Holy Shrine. Though Revond peered ahead to keep his view on the nearing tower of smoke, he grew increasingly frustrated with Lucan desperately prying his arms around him to ensure he wouldn't fall off the soaring steed.

After several minutes quickly passed with Alberic and his riders blasting through the sky they at last reached the base of the plume of smoke and the its source. As they came over a hillside in the once green plains several leagues away from the basin of Mt. Corist, the trio observed a voracious wildfire spreading across the plain. Though confused at how such a fearsome blaze could have started when the land was already scorched and there was barely anything left to burn, Lucan's eyes spread wide as he saw the base of the fire itself was moving and only leaving sparse embers in its wake. Before he could alert Revond or Alberic to the bizarre phenomenon, he was surprised to feel Revond jolt forward to yell something ahead to Alberic. Looking down to where Revond was pointing as he shouted to be heard above the passing wind, Lucan was further amazed to find several dozen people ahead of the blaze running for their lives. Many were women and children, moving too slowly to keep ahead of the fires for long. Their road through the open fields was also narrowing as they ran toward a rocky ridge that would force them to turn either north or south.

"We have to stop them from advancing!" Alberic yelled, his majestic voice ringing out. Lucan reeled back in confusion at this.

"What are you talking about?" he yelled back distraught. "We have to get them out of there!" Revond spun around shaking his head at the Maven's response.

"Not the people," he corrected, pointing down to the front of the fire, "them!" Narrowing his gaze uncertainly, Lucan stared down to the fire to see several jostling figures racing along the ground. They were portly creatures running on four stubby legs, jets of fire racing along their charred, arched backs. Heated red tusks jutted from under the mouths, all frothing with hunger for the humans they chased.

"What are they?" Lucan asked aghast.

"Lavlas Boars," Revond answered as Alberic swept to his right to swing down to the earth in a dive for the fire. "When they gather in great numbers the fires from their backs combine and spread over each other to create wildfires. If we can make them disperse and separate the blaze will fail. We must contain them quickly!" Revond's voice was stout with determination. Alberic quickly raced ahead at full speed, beating his massive feathered wings hard against the hot air growing warmer by the second. Soaring in front of the wildfire and reaching the stragglers in the party of humans only a few yards behind it, Alberic dropped to the ground with incredible force and wheeled around to face down the approaching blaze.

Keeping his large wings spread, the Ancient of Light began fiercely batting them forward to send waves of powerful wind rushing into the charging Lavlas Boars. Though the powerful jets of wind managed to bat down the flames of several of the fiery boars racing toward them, the creatures on their far right and left would still penetrate. Seeing this himself, Revond reached out for the ground on either side of him and clenched his hands into fists. Closing his eyes and focusing hard, the Master Sage slowly lifted his arms. The moment they began to rise Lucan was shocked to feel the ground beneath him begin to rumble. Looking to his left and right, the Maven observed columns of soil rising from the earth to block as much of the plain as possible to the coming boars.

Gritting his teeth and letting out a loud yell, Revond cast his arms forward and in turn the walls of soil, falling into the front line of the Lavlas Boars. Though they scattered uncertainly and hesitated for a lingering moment, the blazing beasts continued forward through the soil. As Lucan was certain he was about to be consumed by the wildfire, he was surprised to see all the boars halting once they reached the empty ground where Revond had pulled up the loose earth. With them temporarily immobile, Alberic continued hammering gusts of wind into them powerful enough to extinguish the rising flames from their backs. As the boars separated to make their way around the holes in the earth, the wild inferno began dying down to just the individual flames rising off of their arched backs. With the wildfire dying, Revond raised a leg over Alberic's back and jumped over the side.

"Hold them here while I lead the people out of harm's way, Alberic!" he yelled. "Lucan! Come with me!" Though hesitant to leave the safety of the mighty Ancient of Light, the Maven did as he was told and jumped off Alberic's back to follow the Master Sage already dashing toward the retreating people. Alberic shot back into the sky almost immediately, using his powerful wings to blow away the fire and further segment the Lavlas Boars, pushing them back to the east. Catching up with Revond, Lucan listened as the Master Sage yelled that they were there to help and commanded them to follow him as fast as they were able. Though several of the dirtied Southlanders stared at his cloaked form uncertainly, Revond halted where he stood when he found one of them standing in front of him with an arrow strung in a taut bow aiming into his hood.

"That's far enough," the young woman barked. "Get some swords on these two!" Before Revond or Lucan could say anything they found several of the armed men around them racing to extend rusty sword points out for their necks. Twisting his head around to look at the woman, Lucan's eyes opened wide and he froze, staring at her. Observing the Maven's reaction, Revond slowly raised his arms as if to surrender and met the gaze of the woman pointing the arrow at him. She wore dark brown garb from her neck to her feet, complimented by her long brown hair wrapped into a loose ponytail behind her back. "You converts grow bolder each time I run into you. Showing up with an Ancient itself? You must be getting pretty desperate for free people to brainwash." The woman turned and shouted for the rest of the people to keep running until the Ancient was gone.

"To the contrary, we are here to help you, young lady," Revond told her quickly. "I am Revond, Master Sage of the Order of Alberic." The woman let out a dry laugh before drawing her bow string tighter.

"You're a Mystic Sage?" she repeated mockingly. "Converts are getting dumber by the day. If you're going to lie to us at least try to make it believable." Though Revond was about to respond more adamantly, he was precluded by a sudden scream of a woman behind the one holding the bow.

"Maglin! My baby is still out there!" came the woman's cry. Spinning around to look at the crying woman as she began bawling hysterically and rushing forward, the woman holding the bow spun back around to look past Revond's hood with her brown eyes going wide. Wheeling around themselves, Revond and Lucan saw a crying child sitting in the dust with one of his legs singed and two of the Lavlas Boars that had worked their way around Revond's gap in the earth approaching it. Tightening her face with resolve, the woman swiftly redirected her arrow away from Revond and toward one of the boars as it swung its head back in preparation to spit fire at its prey. Closing one of her eyes to take better aim, the woman let her missile fly. Though Revond was about to knock the swords around his neck away and rush out to the boy to help him, he was surprised to see the woman previously threatening his life rushing past him before her arrow had even found its mark.

Watching as the projectile slammed into the Lavlas Boar's throat to release molten blood and drop it instantly, Revond held his ground as he curiously observed the young woman blast ahead while stringing up another arrow. This time she fired it into the remaining creature's back, bouncing off its thick hide but diverting its attention from the child now directly in front of it. As the woman raced to the boy's side she pulled a third arrow from the quiver on her back and lifted a flask of water from her side, turning it upside down and slashing it open with the arrowhead just before sprinting full speed at the boar. At top speed, the woman leapt over the Lavlas Boar and threw the ripped flask down on its head as it opened its mouth for her, searing over its heated face.

Landing on the ground beside it in a dexterous roll, she instantly leapt back to her feet and strung the third arrow into her bow, waiting for the creature to turn away from the boy and toward her. In its rage and pain from the touch of the water it turned toward her instantly, rearing back its head to breath fire at its foe. With its throat vulnerable as its kin had been, the woman released the arrow down into it to tear open its flesh and send a stream of liquid fire streaming out of the wound. With both of the Lavlas Boars dead she spun around to observe the rest of the pack that had been chasing them dispersing thanks to the strange white horse flying above them. She pulled the bow in her hands over her head and down her chest, running up to the crying boy and back to the people rushing to meet her. The boy's sobbing mother was the first there, gently taking him out of the woman's hands and thanking her through her tears. Eyeing the woman up and down and noticing the red scarf around her neck, Revond discreetly turned his gaze to Lucan to speak to him in a whisper.

"Is this the Maven we are here to find?" he asked quietly. Lucan turned his head and looked at him uncertainly.

"Not the one I was thinking of, but this might work out even better," he said hopefully. "This vixen and I go way back. Just let me handle this and she'll be eating out of our hands." Seeing her two captives silently talking, the woman in the scarf pulled off her bow once more and drew her last arrow toward Revond again.

"Everyone run!" she ordered. "For some reason the Ancient is attacking the Lavlas Boars. I'll take care of the converts." Seeing her prepare to let her arrow fly at Revond, Lucan stepped forward and tried his best to smile and make a disarming gesture with his arms.

"Maglin Byre," he said, surprising both her and the men around her at how he knew her name. She pointed her arrow at him. Seeing he had her attention, Lucan swallowed his fears and forced himself to continue. "You don't want to kill an old friend, do you?" He trailed off then, seeing her eyes widening and her face lighting up with remembrance.

"Lucan Hauk Erland," she stated dryly, anger building in his face. "What a truly pleasant surprise. I think this will be twice as satisfying." Her face tightening with rage, the woman let her arrow fly mere feet away from Lucan's face. Though the Maven saw his life flash before his eyes as she let the wooden shaft slip from her fingers toward him, Lucan was amazed to find it suddenly stop mere inches in front of his nose, floating harmlessly. While he let out a deep breath of relief, the woman in the scarf and the men around Revond froze and locked their gazes on the sage, watching as he lowered his outstretched hand and dropped the arrow with his mystic grip. Though Revond shot Lucan a glare, he lowered his hood and lowered his blue eyes to the young woman standing awestruck before him. "How did that happen? What... did you do?"

"As I already told you, young lady," Revond said gently, "I am an ally. I am Master Sage Revond and I am here to help you." The woman named Maglin Byre held the sage's gaze for a long moment, letting his unbelievable but proven words sink in. Before she could say anything, the woman was shocked to see a large shadow sweep over her immediately followed by the winged horse she had seen before landing beside the man in the black cloak, its shining hooves and mane more beautiful than anything she had ever seen. Soaking in the horse's regal appearance, she at last let her incredulous eyes sweep back to Lucan nervously staring at her with his quirky smile returned.

"How do I know this isn't some trick of the Ancients?" she asked slowly.

"Maglin," Lucan began raising a hand defensively, "though you appear to still be a little sore at me for last time, I think you know you can trust me on this. We just saved your peoples' lives. And honestly—me a convert? So what do you say we call a truce until you have a chance to hear what Master Sage Revond has to say?" Maglin Byre's uncertain gaze slowly shifted back into a hard stare burning into Lucan, but eventually she lowered her bow and took a step closer to him, narrowing her eyes.

"Fine," she replied at last. "Follow me. But this story had better be one for the ages. About the sage, and last time." With that, Maglin walked past him pushing his shoulder away with hers as she passed. While she walked after the bulk of her people, Lucan turned back to Revond, staring at him with a deep rooted frown on his face that conveyed everything he might have said. Lucan merely shrugged and grinned his quirky grin.

"Women," he stated. "They never let anything go..." Revond merely frowned again and brought his hood back up to cover his face, asking Alberic to transform and follow them on foot.

Catching back up with the majority of her fleeing people to organize and calm them down, Maglin Byre led all of them west across the dark plains beside Mt. Corist into a small valley where several scorched tree trunks rose around an empty riverbed. Though a few of the scattered Lavlas Boars had continued chasing them, they were quickly driven away by Revond and his Hallador Might. Though the Red Maven leading them remained unnerved at the presence of a Mystic Sage and the power he possessed, she breathed easy as he drove away the last of their beastly assailants and decided to trust him at least for the moment. She had little time to speak with either him or Lucan as they swiftly marched into the valley over the next hour, preoccupied with managing the fatigued and upset people around her. There were nearly forty of them from what Revond counted, all dirtied and downtrodden as if they had been wandering the barren land for longer than a year. Most of them were injured or malnourished to the point of looking gaunt.

Only Maglin and a handful of stout men could move with any speed and looked to be in a healthy condition. The Maven herself was no larger than an average woman her age, which Revond guessed to be her late twenties like Lucan, but she moved with rare energy and dexterity that she had flaunted in her rescue of the child back in the plains. There were streaks of dark dirt across the cheeks on her face and her forehead but she was unusually eye-catching for a female Maven by trade. Her straight brown hair was thin but stretched down almost to her waist in the loose ponytail she kept it, mingling with her red scarf hanging over her back as she ran to and fro seeing to the distressed people she led.

As they all began trickling into one of the dried up riverbeds of the valley, Revond and his companions were surprised to see the people filtering underneath a small overhang of earth held in place by thick roots of a felled tree interweaving through it. Under the overhang was a collection of debris and salvaged goods from villages in the area including wooden planks, blankets, candlesticks, tunics, and a few boxes of rations. While watching the people creep into the protection of the overhang to sit and relax their aching feet from the long run, Revond heard a voice from beside him and turned to find Maglin Byre coiling a length of rope around her forearm and looking at the people sitting down to rest.

"This is one of the few places we found for any kind of shelter," she said, obviously taking to the sage. "Hidden from anything looking for us and spacious enough to store emergency supplies for days like this."

"You look after this group then, Maglin Byre?" Revond asked, looking down at her. The woman cleared her throat and turned her head to spit before nodding and motioning for them to follow her down to the end of the overhang where a few large boulders once submerged beneath the river lay exposed and cracking.

"You could say that. I lead them back and forth scavenging for what food we can find around Mt. Corist. The Ancients burned everything but the soil is still fertile here so we can find a few fruit bearing plants here and there. We've even tried planting seeds in a few hidden plots of soil in the plains. That's where we were today when the pack of Lavlas Boars stumbled onto us. We had been growing that garden for months—they burned it all. My people were tired after the journey down from what's left of the Icrene Forest. Would have been easy meat if not for..." The Maven trailed off at this and set her gaze on the man in white garb she had seen morph from the enormous winged horse that had saved them. Shifting her mystified gaze back to the other Maven standing before her, she hardened her expression and balled her fists. "Which brings me back to you. After the Ascension, my one relief was knowing that at least *Lucan Hauk Erland* would be dead. You've got more nerve than I would have guessed to come looking for me after the last time." Lucan cocked his head as if unsure what she meant.

"First of all," he began, tossing his blue scarf over his shoulder, "wishing an old friend dead is not nice at all. Second, I didn't bring Revond and Alberic here looking for you. You were the last person I was expecting to find out here."

"Well I wasn't too eager to stay in the east after becoming Windrun's most wanted criminal overnight, thanks to someone," she snapped, the anger blaring from her eyes.

"Pardon me for interrupting," Revond said raising a hand, "but perhaps one of you could see fit to explain the nature of your association in the first place. It was my understanding you two were friends, but judging by Maglin's reaction to your presence, Lucan, that doesn't seem to be the case."

"Friend?" Maglin repeated incredulously. "Try backstabber." Though shooting the woman a frown, Lucan turned back to look at Revond and Alberic staring at him doubtfully.

"In the years before the Ascension the Southland was having a mounting problem with Mavens, Reds in particular, roaming across the land unchecked doing anything they wanted whether for jobs or not. It became the Windrun Warriors' top priority to deal with them by whatever means necessary. Even if it meant hiring Mavens ourselves to track down and eliminate the more notorious ones that routinely slipped past our nets. Maglin here was one of the Mavens we hired to help us contain the flow of Reds in the east. We didn't want it getting out that we were employing the very people we were trying to get rid of though, so we kept it very quiet. I was her only contact to the Windrun for years."

"Until the day when you decided everything I had done for you—all the blood I spilled cleaning up the messes your little boy scout patrol didn't have the stomach for—didn't matter and you burned me," Maglin interrupted. Lucan cringed once again but fought the urge to turn around and defend himself to her.

"Remember that story about that Maven called the Stain I told you before?" he asked Revond, to which the sage nodded. "Well the Stain was the single most wanted man anywhere in the Windrun territories for months. Then one day as a patrol of my men were coming down the Empyrean

Peaks we found him and his partner poaching wyverns. One guess who his partner was."

"So after all the work I had done for him over the years, Lucan here had me captured and arrested, scheduled to be hanged in Aggiest Village the day after he locked me in a jail half full of people I put there," she finished for him.

"What did you expect me to do, Maglin?" Lucan exclaimed, finally spinning around to face her. "You knew full well how much we wanted Stain when you partnered with him. What were you thinking? I had to take you in!"

"I didn't work exclusively for you, Erland!" the Red Maven shot back. "Even amongst Mavens we have something called loyalty, a virtue you obviously have never heard of."

"I was going to get you out that night," he returned, throwing his hands up in the air.

"With all of your little bosses that you were so intent on impressing watching? I'm sure," Maglin replied sarcastically. "But we'll never know because Stain came back for me after he escaped from your idiot guards to spring me on his own. So thanks to Lucan, I was right behind Stain himself on the most wanted list of criminals in the east."

"Do you really think I wanted that to happen, Maglin?" Lucan said taking a step closer. "You were the reason half of the worst Reds got swept out my territory or finished off. Keeping you around was the reason I was promoted as fast as I was. You knew how much I owed you."

"Which makes what you did all the more disgusting," she replied, folding her arms in front of her chest and sneering at him. Taking a deep breath, Lucan let his frustration fade and put a hand on her shoulder.

"No, that's the reason you know that I would have freed you before that morning came no matter what it looked like to my superiors," he said earnestly. "Come on, Mag. As far apart as we operated all those years you have to admit we were friends once. I never stopped thinking of you that way even after you disappeared." Though the woman kept her hard gaze on him, her biting eyes softened as they stared into his, remembering the sincere face of one of her few friends. She broke her gaze off from him and looked into space, backing away out of the reach of his arm.

"So how did you end up with a Mystic Sage?" she asked looking over Revond and Alberic again. "I thought all of the sages were dead decades before the Ascension."

"They were," Lucan responded. "But this is a new sage starting a new order. He found me in the east about a month ago outside the Mystic Tower itself. We're looking for... people who can stand up to the Ancients."

"So you came out here looking for Stain?" Maglin asked. "Well sorry but he's been dead for almost a month now. Pretty inglorious death. He was scouting the mountains and fell into a crevice leading into a fissure of molten rock. Even the safest places are treacherous out here these days. After he and I escaped from Windrun we came out here with a plan to start over. I knew the land because I was born here. Unfortunately our plans changed when the Ancients started ripping the world apart. We managed to gather about fifty survivors together last winter and we've been moving them from place to place trying to keep them alive ever since. I thought about going out looking for help but around spring we started running into these converts out looking for the Source of Light. It's not even safe to wander past Corist these days."

"Well at least your problems with the converts are gone," Lucan told her, to which she tilted her head in confusion. "Thanks to us the Ancients are just killing every human they find again like when it started."

"What do you mean, 'thanks to you?'" she asked skeptically. Turning back to Revond, Lucan let the Master Sage step forward and continue, not sure what he would want to tell her himself in explaining their situation. Bidding her to sit, Revond took her through a simplified version of their story so far and explained to her who Alberic was. After he told her what they were trying to do to stop the Ancients once and for all, Maglin slowly stood again with disbelief in her eyes.

"You're telling me we could kill the Ancients and undo all the damage they've done just with a new group of Elemental Warriors?" she asked incredulously.

"If I can anoint a new team of Elemental Warriors we will be able to defeat the Ancients and unite the six Sources to reverse the destruction of the world, yes," he replied keeping his calm and composure as always. "That is why I have come to the west, young Maven. I am looking for a capable person of character and skill as a combatant to become the Warrior of Fire. Is there anyone you would recommend for such a responsibility?" Maglin held Revond's gaze for a lingering moment at his question but slowly shook her head.

"I wouldn't go so far as to call any of the men with me skilled combatants, sage," she answered. "And all of them have families they wouldn't want to leave so they can go risk their lives against the Ancients themselves. I think you're barking up the wrong tree."

"Though I came looking for a man at Lucan's suggestion, I didn't specify that this warrior must be a male, Maglin," Revond returned. Both Lucan and Maglin were silent and still at this, staring at the Master Sage as if unable to believe what he seemed to be hinting at.

"...Me?" Maglin asked, pointing to her dirtied face. "You want me—a Red Maven and wanted criminal—to be an Elemental Warrior?"

"Uhh... Revond?" Lucan almost whispered, eager to voice his concerns to this idea as well.

"The only person who wants you now is me," Revond told her, cementing his implications in black and white. "We came looking for a Red Maven that Lucan vouched for in the first place, and we found one that he depended on for years. He obviously trusted you, and I trust Lucan. I will trust you." Maglin shot Lucan an awestruck glance before fixing her gaze back on Revond, shaking her head.

"You don't even know me!" she explained. "How can you trust me? I would have killed Lucan earlier just because I was angry with him over something that happened years ago! Is that the type of character you want in an Elemental Warrior?"

"I have seen both your true character and your skill with the bow, Maglin," Revond informed her. "You displayed them both in taking great risk to dispatch of those Lavlas Boars before they could harm the boy."

"Who wouldn't stand up for a child, sage?" the woman replied, letting out an impatient huff. "Look, ask Lucan. We may have been friends but he knows they don't call me Maglin the Terrible because I *don't* do terrible things. As eager as I am to see the Ancients fall, I'm not the girl you want for this." By now, several of the men further down the overhang in the riverbed had heard the conversation going on between Maglin and the mysterious sage and were gathering amid the rocks to watch and listen.

"To have earned your reputation you obviously possess great skill as a combatant and are determined to accomplish your goals. You may have previously walked a dark and even bloody path as a Red Maven, but I know better than you realize how a cold soul can warm. I was a Maven myself years ago and was in a far darker place than you, but years later I sit before you as the Master Sage of an order dedicated to protecting the greater good of the world. You have a good heart—I can see that. It's why you defend this lot of frail refugees when you would be better off on your own. And you were born here in the west so you can wield the element of fire stronger than another from across the Southland. It was not mere chance that I stumbled upon you here, and a sage does not offer this title and responsibility lightly. But I offer it to you." At the end of his speech, Maglin was flabbergasted, staring at him and groping for words. Though Lucan had shared her hesitancy at first, Revond's words of redemption quickly convinced him. He had known the Red Maven for years and though she appeared callous and cold-blooded at first glace, he knew perhaps better than any the true soul of the good person shining out of her.

"Come on, Mag," Lucan said, catching her attention. "Do one last job for me."

"I... I have responsibilities here now," she said. "What about these people?"

"We will carry on without you if we must, Maglin," one of the men from behind the rocks said, catching the entire group by surprise. Maglin turned to see them walking around the rocks into plain view. "You would aid our interests best by stopping the Ancients and restoring our lost world. We will protect our families here." She stared at the man who spoke for a moment before setting her gaze down into the space between her and Revond. Slowly nodding, a smile crept across the corner of her lips.

"The Warrior of Fire, huh?" she said as if to test out the title. She placed her gaze back on Revond, readjusting the red scarf hanging on her back and around her neck. "I guess that would be the suitable element for me. Let's turn the fire against the Ancients, then." Lucan smiled at this, meeting her gaze. Revond rose, nodding his head and pulling his hood back over it.

"Very well," he said, his voice pleased and almost excited. "One down and three to go then. Thank you, Maglin Byre."

"If anything I should be thanking you, Master Sage," the woman replied. "But I warn you—I know absolutely nothing about this Elemental Warrior business beyond what you just told me. I don't know the first thing about what I'm supposed to do."

"That will come with time, my friend," Revond replied. "For now I think we should all take some time to rest. I'm sure Alberic needs to recuperate his strength from our long flight and the battle with the Lavlas Boars, and since night is coming we will depart in the morning." Agreeing she would like some time to prepare as well, Maglin told them she would have dinner prepared for them and bedding put down. When some of her men bid Revond and Alberic to follow them down into the overhang, Maglin turned to look at Lucan unable to hide her smile.

"Just like old times, I guess," she said, to which Lucan nodded.

"Hopefully this time we can part on better terms," he said with his quirky smile taking hold. "I'm sorry for that business in Aggiest, Maglin." She took a deep breath but shrugged, leaning down to pick up the rope she had been coiling several minutes before.

"I guess I should have trusted that you wouldn't let me stretch," she admitted. "But you still owe me for arresting me in the first place. If anything your men should have given me a fat mug of ale for that shot to the wyvern from the slopes. You saw it. In that wind no man alive could have made that shot."

"Glad we've got the woman, then," Lucan said, chuckling to himself. As they began to walk after Revond and Alberic, Maglin looked down to Lucan's neck and curiously raised up the blue scarf around his neck, to which Lucan told her it was a long story.

Chapter 27

<u>The Crag Spires</u>

Valeri Montrox stood over a high ridge in the Black Peaks with one leg straight to the ground and another propped up in front of her, leaning on a split boulder protruding from the rock as she gazed out at one of the most amazing natural wonders she had ever seen. After marching four days northwest of Hadecrest over leagues of dangerous mountain paths, she and her party had at last reached the infamous Crag Spires. A series of razor sharp columns of winding stone with gaping fissures and expanses of deep canyons lay before her, stretching on as far as she could see into the cloudy horizon. Most of the spires were isolated and inaccessible, shooting out of the low canyons far away from each other into the sky. While few ever had reason to venture past the Crag Spires further north into the Black Peaks beyond even Drakkaidia, it was said there were enough spires close to each other to yield a route across them. From where she stood Valeri could make out several plateaus and ledges jutting out from various columns as if reaching out for each other, while some were actually connected by narrow bridges of crumbling stone.

As the princess stood staring into the cliffs and canyons attempting to chart the fabled path through the spires, a gust of wind blew down from the rolling clouds behind her that whipped her short crimson hair and the front tip of her gray shawl. Watching the gust jet into a nearby spire she had been looking at for its narrow stone bough connecting it to another rising column, her eyes widened in surprise as the evidently weak bridge began to crumble and collapse in the grip of the gust. The girl gulped, momentarily nervous at their chances of making it through the dangerous road. Though she had prepared for the coming hazards with her usually indomitable confidence on the journey there, a nameless worry had been occupying her recent thoughts. It was said only two men had ever made it into the Crag Spires and emerged with their lives—three, if the recluse supposedly living atop one of the spires was actually there. Thankfully Valeri had one of these men with her, scouting ahead with one of her soldiers down the steep road to one of the smaller spires. Markus Desrum had ventured into the spire before and knew the safe road to take, if it still existed.

Though Valeri was uneasy to navigate the Crag Spires, it was another unknown danger lurking in the shadows that had her worried. She couldn't sense any active power other than the distant Ancients ravaging Iairia, but she had felt a presence behind her for days now as if something was watching her—waiting for the opportune moment to reveal itself. Just as a shiver of cold ran down her spine from such thoughts, the Drakkaidian princess was surprised to hear a loud snapping of rock directly behind her.

Spinning around with her hand flying to the hilt of the sword at her waist, Valeri swept her gaze down to the small cliffside she had just scaled, ready to face whatever threat presented itself. Staring down to the edge of the cliff, her face taut with anxiousness, she was relieved to find the source of the noise only Aeric Tieloc. He was still struggling to grab onto a hold in the ground where she stood and climb free of the cliffside. Letting out a deep but silent breath, Valeri released her white-knuckle grip over her weapon and let a faint smile appear on the corner of her lips.

Though fiercely concentrating on what he was doing to make sure he didn't lose his grip and fall back down the cliff, Aeric noticed the girl's edgy reaction and raised his eyes to her uncertainly. She met his gaze with an amused smirk and leaned over to offer her hand to the tense Grandarian, forcing her paranoia of whatever else could be out there from her mind. Pulling him up beside her while he strenuously fought to keep his grip on the rocks, Aeric let go of her hand and leaned over to prop his arms on his knees. His face flushed red and his heart remained racing from climbing the steep cliff. Valeri smiled seeing him so worked up, trying to hold in her laughter at his earnestness in trying to keep up with her and her men.

"Are you holding up all right?" she asked. Though Aeric struggled to catch his breath before replying, he tried to stand up straight and nod, wiping away a streak of sweat on his forehead with one of his blue sleeves. No sooner than he opened his mouth to reply, he was surprised to feel the rock around his right boot break and fall down the cliff, nearly sending him over the side with it. Reaching out with both hands to take hold of his tunic and pull him forward, Valeri threw off his balance further and he fell into her almost taking her down as well. Holding him steady until he found his footing again, Valeri giggled at his voracious breathing in spite of nearly losing him. Her arms were pressed together in front of his chest with her fingers spread over his tunic, gently pushing him back. Though scared out of his mind at the fate that had almost befallen him several times so far on their journey, Aeric quickly realized his face was within an inch of the girl's and he stepped back. Controlling his breathing, he finally responded to her question.

"About as well as the mountain around me," he said to which Valeri giggled again, surprising him. Though she was about to say something else, the two heard a groan from below them on the cliff and looked down to find Asthatch rising behind Aeric, heaving himself to his feet and glaring at the Grandarian as he rose.

"In the future please try not to kick rocks loose down a cliffside while someone's still climbing it, Tieloc," he snapped sarcastically.

"Oh poor Asthatch," Valeri said putting her hands on her hips and returning his sarcasm. "Savor these easy cliffs while you can. We're about to start the hard part." Aeric's eyes widened with dread at this, noticing for the first time the full view of the Crag Spires behind her. He slowly leaned to his right to gaze past her, his jaw slipping open with dismay.

"...We're going through that?" he asked slowly.

"More like over it than through, Master Tieloc," said another voice from across the ridge they stood on. All three of them turned to see Markus Desrum walking toward them, refastening a loose plate of light armor on his shoulder.

"Have you navigated the path we're going to take, Desrum?" Valeri asked, regaining her serious tone. Desrum nodded and stopped when standing before the others.

"As best I can for now, Your Highness," he replied. "The other men are down the ridge testing the integrity of the ledge leading to the first spire. I remember the road I took into the spires on my own and the one that the recluse showed us out on, but they only ever got me halfway. I can guarantee you a relatively safe route until that point, but afterwards I'm not sure how we're going to find wherever the recluse is. The Crag Spires are a very big place if you count the canyons below us and he could be anywhere."

"Then we'll just have to make our way to the highest point we can and survey as much of the spires as can be seen," Valeri informed him. "If this recluse found you last time perhaps he will find us."

"If he is still even alive," Asthatch mumbled to himself just loud enough to be heard. Though Valeri frowned at her captain she shook off his doubts and ordered for Desrum to lead them to the ledge he told them of. The group hurried over the cliff top toward another slope leading down to a long ledge that hung over the side of it toward a flat on the closest spire rising out of the canyon far below. Aeric gulped as he witnessed one of the Drakkaidian soldiers leaping off the side of the ledge onto the spire, sliding over the loose rocks on its surface as he landed. As they walked out to the ledge Desrum began speaking once again.

"As you all know the Crag Spires are one of the most dangerous and unforgiving places in all Iairia," he began. "Much of the ground between the spires and paths protruding from them is slanted, narrow, thin, crumbling, eroding, or disintegrating in general. Every step you take on the spires is one that could send you tumbling down into the dark canyon below no matter how safe it may look, so take your time and concentrate on one step at a time. The only way from spire to spire is to jump from ledges like these, the small cliffs on their sides, or the occasional rock bridge connecting them. I've seen how treacherous these paths are before, so trust my judgment if I say a road is too dangerous. Stay close to each other to help someone if they slip, but never hold onto them while you walk because if one of you takes a tumble off a cliff the other is sure to go as well. Remember—the first moment you aren't giving these spires your full concentration they will betray you, so keep your minds alert on what you're doing out there. It's easy to be enamored with the canyon but be careful. There's an ancient Drakkaidian saying—the abyss gazes also."

With these ominous words Desrum motioned for his companions to wait while he edged out to the end of the ledge, calling out to the other Drakkaidians already on the spire to be ready for the princess. Walking back to them, he instructed her to run off the ledge with some momentum and the soldiers would brace her when she landed on the spire. Nodding confidently, she glanced at Aeric to see him gulping and staring at the gap at least several feet long. Gently taking hold of the young man's forearm, she smiled and told him it was just a hop. Trying his best to smile back and relax his irregular breathing, he watched as Valeri turned to sprint to the end of the ledge and clear the gap with ease, landing in a crouch amid her men on the base of the spire. Conquering his fear, Aeric jumped after her followed by Desrum and Asthatch. Once they were all across and onto the first spire, Aeric couldn't help but gaze down at the seemingly endless canyon and the dark abyss it sheltered. As the group started to walk around the edge of the spire, Asthatch gently nudged him forward, warning him to keep his mind on the road and nowhere else.

Traversing the ledge around the spire, the party began its expedition into the Crag Spires. For the next hour they slowly and cautiously made their way around the cliffs of the rising rock columns, jumping from other ledges, climbing short rock faces, and traversing narrow bridges rising from the canyon. No one spoke above a whisper for the duration, following Desrum and Asthatch's advice to keep their minds on their footing. Though they came to several twists in the path on which Desrum debated the road to take with Asthatch and Valeri, he continually chose safe roads that barely cracked and crumbled at their passing. He would frequently call for them to hold behind him while he cast a stone onto the ground ahead, testing weight on the thin paths. Though Aeric was sure the ground beneath him was going to buckle and give way as he passed with his back against the walls of the spires on the narrower roads, he remained safe and suspended on the tops of the spires every time.

Eventually they came to a hangover of loose rocks between them and the next ledge leading up to a higher spire that forced them to halt and examine every step they would have to take. Though Valeri suggested jumping, Desrum and Asthatch both agreed that she would be the only one who could ever clear such a distance and the rest of them would still need to plot footholds to get across. Deciding to press their backs against the wall and creep along the sturdiest rocks they could find, Desrum went first, taking care to press as little weight as possible on each wobbly stone beneath him. Though their hearts all jumped when a few of the loose rocks gave free under his boot, the commander of Hadecrest made it safely across and beckoned for the others to follow. Though Valeri planned to jump as she suggested, as she was leaning down to charge the strength in her legs, Aeric heard a faint cracking noise in the ground she stood on and rushed to grab her shoulders.

Though she fell back onto him with a fright, nothing happened and she slowly asked what was wrong. Before he could reply a much louder crack sounded through the air under his own feet and both Aeric and the soldier behind him felt the ground under their feet give way. Though Asthatch didn't have time to grab at his fellow Drakkaidian as he tumbled down the side of the spire, Valeri was already clutching onto Aeric and held him firm as he slipped through the ground. Twisting her body around to lay flat on the ground, she yelled for the other soldier at her side to help her lift him. Though they pulled him back without any harm done to him, Aeric felt his heart racing faster than he had ever felt and looked back into the darkness gaping back up at him from the hole he had made. Listening to the faint screaming of the lost Drakkaidian as he plummeted down, Asthatch grit his teeth and barked that Aeric had just cost the man his life with his rash action. Though not sure what to say, Valeri was quick to control her strenuous breathing and tell him the Grandarian was only trying to protect her. Ordering them all to calm down and continue, the group made their way over the gaps in the road on to the next spire.

After almost another two hours of carefully weaving their way around the spires deeper into the treacherous canyon they rose from, the party came to the longest stone bridge they had yet to see stretching hundreds of feet to a row of compact spires nestled against each other. Though it was a foot wider than most of the narrow bridges they had traversed so far, this one did not rise from the canyon surface but hung between the spires with only the abyss below. There was a gaping ravine between them and the next spires along their road. Desrum halted upon reaching the ledge leading out onto the bridge, looking around as if he had lost his bearings.

At last he spotted something far to their right and kicked a stone at his feet in frustration, to which Asthatch asked him what was wrong. Desrum pointed over to another spire several hundred feet to their right and the thicker, safer looking bridge leading to the same collection of spires on the other side of the ravine. Explaining that he must have chosen the wrong path along a spire behind them and that he had been trying to get to the opposite bridge, the group's guide informed them this bridge wasn't safe enough and they had to go back.

Though no happier than any of them at this news, Aeric was surprised to observe Valeri not paying attention and staring with intense eyes behind them as if searching for something. When Desrum again told her they had to start backtracking she raised a hand for silence, making them all nervous. Aeric had noticed she had been unusually focused and alert since she had saved him nearly an hour ago, constantly looking back as if expecting something. Turning his head around to gaze back into the towering spires they had traversed as well, Aeric scanned for anything out of the ordinary that could have been the cause of her apparent concern. Though the entire group remained silent as they all stared back into the Crag Spires waiting for Valeri to say something, the stillness was broken by the sudden shifting of rocks far behind them. None of them could see any movement but the sound of tumbling rocks echoed through the expansive canyon for several long moments.

Just as Valeri was opening her mouth to say something, her red eyes shot open wide as she observed a swift movement behind one of the spires. The others noticed it soon after, tightening in fear and dread as they watched three sleek and muscular creatures on all fours blasting down a path twisting around a spire and leaping off of a ledge onto another one, dexterously sprinting over terrain that had taken them hours to safely navigate. Turning their heads to observe the party of humans standing in shock far ahead on another spire, all three of the strange creatures sent a loud howl into the air and charged forward with renewed purpose driving them on. Hearing the frighteningly loud howls, Valeri at last conquered her shock and wheeled around to shout to her companions.

"Demons!" she yelled, drawing her sword. "Run!"

"Your Highness, this bridge may not hold!" Desrum fumbled immediately, to which Valeri merely shoved him forward with the utmost resolve on her face.

"She is right!" Asthatch responded for her. "Even Valeri cannot hold three demons on terrain as treacherous as this.

We must cut them off! Valeri can destroy the bridge once we're all across." Though Desrum tried to reply that Valeri probably wouldn't need to destroy the bridge if they all tried to cross it at once, he was cut off by Asthatch angrily pushing him forward along with the other two Drakkaidians. Aeric and Valeri followed after them, nervously looking back and forth between each other and the demons lunging between the wall of a spire onto a nearby cliff after them. Though none of them were confident enough to run on the thin bridge hanging over the darkness of the canyon around them they pressed on as fast as they could hearing the impossibly fast creatures growing closer by the second.

As he dashed ahead Aeric shot glances back past Valeri to better observe the nimble creatures perusing them. They were built like prowling wild cats but were more compact and infinitely more agile, able to run faster, jump higher and perform feats along the spires the Grandarian could barely believe. They had no hair or scales, covered only in pale white hide with large splotches of diseased blue skin from their round heads to short tails as if they were infected with some plague. The rows of teeth and banks of claws at their feet were all dark yellow and stained as if by blood. Remembering stories of the Days of Destiny and his grandfather's encounters with the demons of the Netherworld, Aeric guessed they were the sleek hunters called Arnosmn.

Though eager to keep watch on the rapidly advancing demons to determine if they had any chance to outrun them, Aeric nearly stumbled along the narrow path at his feet and forced himself to keep his gaze locked on what he was doing. By the time they were halfway across the bridge over the expansive ravine he could hear the stone underneath them cracking and fragmenting with every step, obviously straining to hold the weight of several running humans. Though Aeric concentrated with every ounce of energy he had to keep focused on the ground and nothing else, as he approached the end of the bridge he couldn't help but notice the footsteps behind him had stopped. Wheeling around he found Valeri standing in place looking back at the opposite end of the bridge with the wind blowing her hair back. Looking past her Aeric saw that the three Arnosmn had reached the bridge and were catapulting after them.

Knowing she had to stop them before they got any closer, Valeri tightened her muscles and gritted her teeth, summoning a wave of crimson energy swirling to life around her. As red and black electricity danced across the curves of her body, Aeric saw the force of her power further fragmenting the ground she stood on.

"Valeri!" he called, desperately running back to reach her. "You'll bring down the entire bridge! Just come on!" The girl didn't respond other than to flare her aura of power greater and grip the hilt of her sword tighter, its blade beginning to pulsate with a glowing layer of power. With her attack charged, the Drakkaidian princess raised her sword over her head and slashed down in a horizontal sweep, sending a thin but powerful arc of crimson energy leaping from the blade to slash into the center of the bridge.

As soon as her weapon was at her waist again she flipped the hilt around in her hand and swung it back up, unleashing a second arc of energy cutting the bridge a second time just in front of the sprinting Arnosmn. Though the rock only budged at first, as the seconds slipped by, the chunk of the bridge in between Valeri's slashes began to give way and fall into the darkness of the ravine below. Though two of the sleek demons immediately locked their feet against the ground and came to a sliding halt before running onto the falling segment of the bridge, the one in the lead shot forward with unbelievable vitality and lunged off the falling rock even as it began its freefall.

Soaring through the air propelled by enormous momentum and howling as it came with its front claws reaching out, Aeric and Valeri were amazed to find the creature clear the entire fallen segment and slam into them. Though the princess raised her blade when she saw it coming and managed to pierce it through its underbelly as it landed on top of her, she was pinned down and stunned by the force of impact. Aeric had drawn his sword as well but was knocked off balance as the girl fell into him, sliding off the side of the bridge. His weapon fell onto the stone path before he ever had a chance to use it and his heart leap higher in his chest at the feeling of nothing beneath his feet. Fiercely gripping at the stone bridge to keep from falling to his death, the young Tieloc grabbed hold of the opposite side and kept his upper body on the bridge with his legs dangling into the canyon. Though he could see Asthatch and the others scrambling to run back for them they had only just noticed what was happening and Aeric knew they wouldn't reach them in time to help.

Turning the other way he found Valeri pinned underneath the bleeding demon with her aura of dark power fading from being stunned by the creature's attack. She had been forced to release her sword to hold back the demon's head, fiercely struggling to reach her with its snapping jaws drooling saliva around her. Aware she wouldn't be able to hold it long with the creature only reveling in its own pain, Aeric screamed and affirmed his grip on the rock. Knowing he didn't have time to try and climb up, he let go of the rocks with his right hand and gripped the hilt of his sword lying in front of him.

Gritting his teeth, the boy slashed at the creature's head, cutting a deep laceration into its skull and making the demon flinch as dark blood dripped into one of its eyes. Seeing the attack Valeri realized Aeric was still beside her and found her strength again. Seizing on the Arnosmn's cringing recoil she lowered one of her hands from its neck and balled it into a fist burning with crimson energy. Screaming with all her might she slammed her empowered fist across the side of the demon's head, forcing it off its balance and falling over the side of the bridge toward Aeric.

The demon desperately fought to grip something as it fell but its clawed feet remained around Valeri's legs. Unable to grab onto anything with the Arnosmn clawing at her, Valeri's heart rocketed into her chest as she realized she was going to fall. Slipping over the side of the ground with fragmenting pieces of rock around her, she watched the demon fall first, dropping past Aeric and plummeting down with a final howl. As she helplessly dropped past the Grandarian with her life flashing before her eyes, the Drakkaidian princess was shocked to suddenly be jerked up, suspended in the air by the straps of her backpack under her arms. Flipping her head up, the girl saw Aeric still dangling from the side of the bridge holding it with one arm and her backpack with the other. His face was bright red and taut with strain, calling on strength he didn't have. Though unable to turn in the position she hung in to grab onto him, Valeri watched the boy hold firm as he grunted and fought to keep his failing grip on both the rock and the leather strap of her backpack.

Just when they both thought his strength to keep them suspended in the air above the endless darkness was about to fail, Valeri heard voices telling them to hold on and feet sliding above them. Looking up again, she saw Asthatch reaching down for her while Desrum and one of his men held onto Aeric, swiftly pulling him up while the captain grabbed Valeri's forearm and heaved her back to the bridge. Laying both of the young companions down and giving them a moment to breath, Asthatch scanned them both over for wounds. Finding none, he propped Valeri's upper body up against his and gently patted her on the back. Though still panting heavily, the princess immediately let her awestruck eyes pass to the Grandarian struggling to breathe in front of her, sweat dripping from his flushed face.

"He'll be fine," Desrum told Asthatch and Valeri, patting the young Tieloc's chest and giving him a drink of water from a flask. "His arms probably feel like they've been stretched on a torture table but he'll live." Taking a long gulp of water and spitting up some of it on his blue tunic, Aeric met Valeri's amazed gaze. Though he could tell she wanted to say something she remained quiet, staring at him as if awestruck.

"We're even," he managed to utter through his heavy breathing, giving the flask back to Desrum. Remembering the previous hour when he she kept him from falling off the spire she faintly smiled in spite of the situation and prepared to respond. Before she could, Asthatch was heaving her back to her feat and pointing off to their right.

"We're not out of this yet," he said with his arm outstretched to the opposite bridge Desrum had meant to lead them to in the first place. Spinning their heads toward it, the party saw the remaining two Arnosmn racing along it toward the collection of spires in front of them. Realizing it was too late to blast the bridge and stop them, Valeri forced herself to focus and rise tall again. Ordering them up at once, she told them to run for the tall spires before them and prepare for battle. Though exhausted after his ordeal on the bridge, Aeric rose beside her and shot forward again, readjusting the pack on his back and running off the bridge. As they stepped off, he and Valeri exchanged glances again, a million thoughts racing through their minds that they forced away, aware there were far more pressing matters at hand to worry about. Heading up a steep slope for the tallest spire they could see, the party pressed on with the howls of the two demons behind them echoing through the Crag Spires.

Chapter 28

<u>The Spire Top</u>

Dashing over a series of ridges wedged between the close collection of spires rising from the dark canyon below them, the party from Hadecrest ran ahead with all speed to find a way to cut themselves off from their pursuers or an open expanse to make a stand. They found neither as they struggled to jump over the jagged terrain, narrowly confined to the loose ground jutting off of the spires. Hearing the howls of the two Arnosmn on their heels growing nearer by the second, Aeric brought up a hand to clutch the object inside his blue tunic in case he had to use it. Though remembering Revond's warning not to use the Source of Light unless absolutely necessary for fear it would attract the Ancients, the Grandarian guessed it might be their only chance if they could not outrun the demons or if Valeri could not hold them back. Looking at the Drakkaidian princess running alongside him at the rear of the group, he watched her rip a fresh sword away from her belt and glance back to make sure the Arnosmn had not caught up with them yet.

Running with a southern wind beginning to pick up at their backs, the group at last came to a rising slope branching off of a large spire toward a wider cliff jutting out of the canyon. Though revealing access to several spires in spiraling paths that wove around their circular walls, the largest path led to what looked to be a cliff top with open ground. Deciding that was their best chance to defend themselves, Markus Desrum bolted up the slope past the group of spires shouting for everyone to hurry and stay close. Observing that the outskirts of the slope looked unsteady and were most likely fragmented, he kept to the center of the path and carefully planned each step as best he could. Obviously not heeding Desrum's warning to stay close to him, the soldier that ran ahead of Valeri drifted to the right side of the wide slope to give Captain Asthatch more room. Oblivious to the fragments of loose rock chipping away on the edges with his every step, the Drakkaidian was surprised to find his boot cleave clear through the stone beneath him in a thin spot, instantly splitting the rock around him and tearing the path down the middle. Before he could so much as fill his lungs with the air to scream he slipped through the fissure he created and was gone from sight.

Though Desrum and the last of the Drakkaidian soldiers had cleared the breaking path before the fissure spread to cut it in half, the three behind them were left running forward as the ground around them began to cave in. With less than a second to react, Asthatch instinctively lunged forward before the ground gave way and flew to land on the edge of the broken slope. Caving in under his weight, the edges broke free and the large captain fell through them. Though Valeri charged ahead confident she could make the jump over the gap and Asthatch, Aeric knew the ground was fragmenting at both edges of the gap and she would never make it. Reaching out to grab hold of the princess' left arm and lock his feet to a halt on the ground, he pulled her back just as she was about to lunge forward. With the edges giving way beneath her weight as Aeric predicted, one of her legs fell over the side and she quickly kicked back to stumble into the young man.

Clawing at the jagged path as his waist slipped past it, Asthatch caught hold of a rock with his right hand and jolted to a painful halt, grunting and swinging his other arm over for something else to grab. By this time Desrum and the last Drakkaidian soldier had heard the commotion behind them and spun around to help Asthatch back up to the top half of the remaining slope. Rising to his feet, the captain spun his eyes around for Valeri, nowhere to be found. Jerking his head back, he found the princess and the young Grandarian standing on the other side of the gap now over ten feet wide and still crumbling. Though he was about to leap back for her, Desrum took hold of his waist and pulled him back, screaming he would never make it with the path still disintegrating. On the other side of the path Valeri shot her irate eyes to Aeric while she backed away from the edge.

"What did you do that for?" she bellowed, breathing hard. Aeric leaned down to prop his upper body up with his hands on his knees, fighting for breath.

"The ground would have buckled under you even if you could have made that jump," he managed to say. "And I never could have..." Though obviously frustrated at being hampered, Valeri quickly loosened and realized he was right and had probably just saved her again. Seeing him bleeding from where he had been cut on a sharp rock while reaching for her, she told him to hold it tight and wait. Spinning around she saw Desrum and the others on the other side of the slope.

"Valeri!" Desrum yelled with a hand beside his mouth. "Make for one of the passes up the spires we saw! Try to find a ledge close to the cliff top and we'll meet you—" The commander of Hadecrest was cut off by the echoing howls of the demons right behind the spires. Their hearts racing, Valeri and Aeric spun around with their swords raised waiting for them to charge around the side of a spire. Though nothing came, Valeri could hear the sound of falling rocks at the other end of the spires and guessed they had less than a minute.

Grabbing Aeric and heaving him after her, she shouted for him to hurry and raced back down the slopes to get to the spiraling paths leading up around the spire closest to them. Peering around to be sure the coast was clear, she bolted to the path with Aeric struggling to keep up behind her. Running as fast as they could up the spire, they at last reached the relatively flat summit high over even the cliff the rest of the party was scrambling to reach. Looking around nervously, Valeri and Aeric observed several more flat tops to the spires above and below them, some even connected to theirs, but no ledge leading across the gap between them and the cliff top.

Hearing the sound of the Arnosmn clawing up the same path they had just ascended, Valeri furiously grit her teeth and strapped an expression of determined rage on her face. Pushing Aeric behind her, she assumed her battle stance on the top of the spire with the wind blowing down to caress her red hair against her face. Though Aeric told her he wouldn't let her face them alone and tried to move around her, she blocked him off with the tip of the sword she held and told him he admitted himself he was no warrior. Aware she was right and he would probably just get in her way, destroying any chance they had of staving off the demons, he reached into his tunic and pulled up the white medallion around his neck, laying it down across the blue fabric rustling in the wind. As his fingers slid to its surface in the silence Valeri began charging her dark power around her until a faint aura of erratically pulsating crimson energy beat against her frame and swept up and down her blade.

Though the next moments seemed like an eternity for the two while waiting for the Arnosmn to lunge forth from the spiraling path around the spire ripping and clawing, consumed by their bloodlust, they were surprised to find the first of the pale creatures slowly rise into view, its black eyes staring at them as it revealed its entire body. Gradually the second demon emerged behind it, making its way alongside the first until they came to a halt evenly before their prey. With his hands latched onto the Source of Light, Aeric felt his heart beating wildly at the sight of the two pale monsters before them, just as his grandfather Tieloc had described. Their rows of bloodstained teeth oozed saliva slowly dripping from their open mouths onto the ground and their long claws. Though doubting even the Warrior of Darkness could match their great speed, he had to give her a chance before he opened the Source and betrayed their position. With her expression indomitable and her crimson irises glowing with power, Valeri stood at the ready, staring the two creatures down.

Denying the speedy Arnosmn the first move, Valeri slashed her glowing sword down at them both, unleashing an electrified arc of energy similar to the two she had used to destroy the bridge and drive them away several minutes ago. Reacting even quicker than she expected, the two Arnosmn leapt off the ground as Valeri's attack shaved away a corner of the spire and sent it sliding down tumbling off the side and into the canyon. Counting on the demons to leap above her attack, Valeri flipped herself forward to roll over the ground and raise her blade with a sharp yell as the demon on the right shot back down for her.

Catching it in the middle of its underbelly as it landed where she had been, the Warrior of Darkness raised a hand just as it turned back for her with a roar, charging a blast of energy in the palm of her hand. Shoving it forward just as the demon's jaws opened wide for her, she screamed and fired a blast of heavy crimson energy into its skull, shearing away the layer of pale white and blue skin that had been there before. Shoving it back several feet across the top of the spire, the Arnosmn nearly slammed into its kin.

With its lightning fast reflexes the unscathed demon leapt over the first, slashing its claws out for Valeri before she even knew it was airborne. Observing the attack a split second too late, the princess was unable to evade or block with her blade and felt the demon's razor sharp claws tearing into her side and right arm, forcing her to drop her blade as feeling rushed away from her hand. By the time she could scream out in pain the Arnosmn had landed on her, shoving her down with her red haired head dangling over the side of the spire top.

Though Aeric had raised his own blade to deliver a killing stroke to the first demon shrieking out from the damage done to its head and belly, the Grandarian shouted the princess' name as loud as he could upon seeing her fall with blood from her grievous wound streaking a line along the ground. Pulling the tip of his blade out of the first Arnosmn's head, Aeric rushed behind the other and thrust it down into its back. Though heaving it down with all his strength, the young Tieloc could barely penetrate its thick hide much less stab all the way through.

Reeling in pain from the blow, the demon lifted off Valeri and spun around with speed and force great enough to wrench the sword out of both its back and Aeric's hands. With his weapon flying through the air to land on the top of another spire several yards away and knocked off his feet by the enraged Arnosmn's backward charge, Aeric found himself helpless once again. Though the Arnosmn barked at him while black blood poured down its back where he had stabbed it, the creature immediately turned back for its first wounded prey. Feeling the demon pressing one of its clawed feet down on her chest just below her neck, Valeri squirmed to be free but found her strength rapidly deserting her as she felt the warm sensation of blood flowing across her skin. The aura of crimson energy around her quickly faded as the seconds passed by, completely gone by the time Aeric had fallen back.

Seeing the Arnosmn descending on Valeri again, Aeric knew he had no choice but to use the Source of Light and fumbled to reach for it on his chest, desperate to save her. Just as he was about to flip its glass door open and as the demon spread its jaws preparing to close down on the girl, Aeric was shocked to see his sword coming flying back through the air directly into the demon's open mouth with fearsome force, lodging itself deep in its throat and dropping the Arnosmn lifeless where it stood. Falling to Valeri's right, the demons slid onto the shaved corner of the spire she had cut and plummeted off into the darkness of the canyon below. Unable to believe what he had just seen, both Aeric and Valeri looked up and back from where the sword had come to observe a figure standing on a nearby spire top with its long black robe flying in the wind.

The figure was motionless for a moment, standing in a hunch with an arm cast forward as if it had just thrown something. Slowly rising full length, Aeric and Valeri watched as the figure took hold of a long wooden stick leaning against his right shoulder and began walking toward them. He moved slowly and hobbled on his right foot as he came but looked anything but frail as he stared the two down. His face was wrinkled but robust and covered in a short gray beard with the shoulder length hair on his head the same hue. Underneath his black robe was simple gray garb and a hefty leather belt lined with a few satchels much like Aeric's. Though much of his face was hidden behind his beard they could both see an intolerant and hostile look about it, primarily from his narrowed eyes. Once he ambled onto the spire top adjacent to them he set his walking stick down and leaned it back against his shoulder, sweeping his eyes over both of them.

"What possible business do two children have in the Crag Spires?" the old man asked, his voice scratchy but surprisingly powerful. Neither of them said anything at first, still amazed at what they had just seen.

"...How did you do that?" Aeric asked almost too quiet to be heard over the wind. "We could barely cut through its hide." The old man sniffed in hard through his nose and raised his head, looking down on the young Grandarian.

"Even demons have their weaknesses," he returned gruffly. "All that is necessary to exploit them is to know of them, as I do. Now answer my question." Though Aeric wasn't sure he trusted this mysterious man, his appearance and words so far led him to only one conclusion.

"We're looking for someone," he said. "A recluse that lives in the Crag Spires. Are you him?"

"If I were a recluse that by nature seeks isolation and seclusion, why would I appear before two wandering children and a pair of demons?" he asked, leaving Aeric a loss.

"Then who are you?" Aeric asked, slowly rising back on his feet. The old man kept his gaze on them for a lingering moment before taking hold of his staff and turning his back on them, walking away.

"I can tell you what I'm not," he replied. "A babysitter for a Grandarian and a princess wandering one of the most dangerous roads in Iairia—even more dangerous in the wake of the Ascension. Go back to Hadecrest or wherever you came from. There are greater perils than Arnosmn or Ancients wandering the Black Peaks of late." Though Aeric was about to ask him how he knew who they were, when the Grandarian looked down to see to Valeri and noticed the pool of blood beneath her, his heart began to race again and he rushed to her side. Gently lifting her wounded arm he saw why she had been silent in the moments before. She had already lost a huge amount of blood and was turning pale. Her usually intense red eyes were dimming. Jerking his head back up to the old man walking away he shouted out for him to wait.

"Please stop!" he yelled as loudly as he could. "The princess is badly wounded! I need help!" Hearing this, the man came to a stop and quickly turned around, looking down to see the revealed pool of blood gathering beneath her from the wound. Gritting his teeth and picking up his walking stick, the old man shot back across the spire he stood on and jumped down to the one below him with speed and strength that surprised both Aeric and Valeri. Leaning down on the other side of the girl, the old man inspected her wounds and shook his head, silently cursing in an old Drakkaidian dialect Aeric couldn't understand. Reaching down to his belt, the mysterious man pulled off a flask of water and a large sash that had previously hung from his right side.

"Press this against her side and wrap it around her arm," he ordered quickly, tearing the sash in two. "The wound is deep—she's bleeding out. We'll need to take her to my hut. I can't treat her here." As Aeric wrapped the sash around her wounds as best he could, the old man lowered the flask of water to her lips and told her to drink. Though she spit up most of it and tried to say something, the princess' eyes began to flutter. Seeing her eyelids growing heavy the old man sprinkled some water across her face and gently patted her cheek. "You've got to keep her awake. Her chances will be better. Lift her gently and follow me." With that the old man rose and quickly leapt back up to the higher spire top. Though Aeric gathered Valeri's cold body in his arms as tenderly as he could, he looked back over to the cliff top.

"We've got friends on that cliff who can—"

"They can't help her," the old man said, turning back to him impatiently. "I can. This is going to be close. Hurry now!" Though hesitating to trust the mysterious old man, as he looked down to Valeri's placid face and unusually vulnerable eyes staring up at him, he knew it was her only chance and he had to risk it. Though exhausted from their confrontation with the Arnosmn, Aeric pulled the princess tight against him and lifted them up onto the adjacent spire after the mysterious old man.

The once green and vivid Valley of Galantia brimming with activity at the gates of the golden capital of Grandaria was dead quiet, motionless but for a few still burning fires across the rubble of the city. It was the first time the valley had been devoid of human life since the creation of humanity eons previous. The ground was soaked with the blood from all the converts that had been butchered several days before, seeping into the earth to stain the once golden land red. The only movement besides for the few rising embers over the city was the massive silhouette of the Ancient of Darkness standing on a peak on the mountains behind the ruins of the city, his massive clawed feet digging into the rock to keep him upright. The behemoth was still and silent, staring through the dark afternoon sky at the five shining orbs of light on the top of the stone fortress lying far beneath him. With them all collected together, they enabled their creators to communicate with each other over whatever distance with no more than a mere thought. Though unable to see through his brothers' eyes, Dalorosk had been quietly waiting atop the small mountains for word from any of his kin, due to report their findings sometime in the day.

Dalorosk sniffed a massive swell of air into the enormous nostrils on his dog-like face, shifting his black body into a new stance on the rocks and resting his clawed hands around the hilts of his swords stabbed into his thighs. He grunted and twitched his head as one of the long pointed horns protruding from the back of his head toward his back stabbed into him, sharp enough to penetrate even his thick hide. He hated waiting. He had done nothing but wait for eons—for longer than he could remember. But as then, he now had nothing else to do with his time. He could have been helping his brothers scour their lands for Alberic and the missing Source, but though he was evenly allied with the other Ancients he hated the thought of working at their sides; of sinking to their level. He hated having anything to do with them. He hated them almost as much as he hated Alberic. They were all his enemies; all beneath him. It was almost more than he could bear not to attack them all as soon as he saw them the day of the Ascension, but he knew then as he knew now that he needed them. At least for the moment.

The behemoth shook his head and tried to drive such thoughts from his mind. He had to be careful not to dwell on his thoughts too hard or the others would be able to hear them through their mental link. He already knew they didn't trust him and were suspicious of his every word but couldn't completely give himself away until the time was right. For just a while longer, the beast had to bide his time. Besides, he didn't have any desire to speed into Drakkaidia to look for the Source because of what he could sense lurking there. Being born from the element of darkness he could sense more clearly what his brothers could not—the presence of demons across the northwest that rivaled his own power and that together could weaken him. Without his Source it was too great a risk. He had to wait. As Dalorosk tried to place his thoughts on Alberic and his hatred for his treacherous brother, the faint echo of a sound bounced through his thoughts as a thrown stone would ripple through still water. As the seconds passed by, Dalorosk listened to the ripple morph into a voice inside his head.

Hear Golthrout, brother, the voice spoke in a menacing rumble. *I have still found nothing in the south. The forests are empty of everything. My minions have not even found a Cronom tunnel of late.*

And Vorkoise has seen no sign of the Source of Light in the riverbeds from the great lake to the sea, another voice said, having heard the last. *I have even begun walking across the isles in my human form but I still find nothing.* The Ancient of Darkness let out a loud huff of air and a slow growl at the news from both of his brothers, aware his waiting would have to continue.

Stay out there until you find him, he barked inside his mind. *He can only hide for so long and—*

I have seen him, Dalorosk, came a third voice, excited as it raced through all three of their minds. Dalorosk tightened his enormous frame at this, his wings lifting up erect along his back.

Do you have his location, Moltar? the black Ancient grilled.

He is hiding above the clouds as he travels, brother, the Ancient of Fire responded. *I just saw him moments ago in the midlands through a part in the sky. I lost him but he was headed east. Converge on my position so we can find and destroy him!*

Wait, Dalorosk said, hearing Vorkoise and Golthrout drooling at the chance to attack as well. *We hold for now. Do not reveal yourself.*

What? Moltar yelled through his mind. *Why would we hold?*

I told you before, Dalorosk returned, speaking to them all. *Alberic is probably up to his tricks again trying find some new means to defeat us. We should follow him and see where he goes—find out what his latest treacherous scheme is.*

Nonsense, Vorkoise recoiled quickly. *The best way to stop Alberic from gathering some new power against us is to destroy him as quickly as possible so he doesn't have the chance!*

And what if his disciple or the boy with the power of light are not with him? Dalorosk asked impatiently. *What if the missing Source is not with him? If we attack and defeat him we will be back where we started when the Ascension began and his little humans will still be out there preparing his schemes. But if we follow him he may lead us to the Source or his humans so we can know for sure.*

Every moment we don't attack is another he slips farther out of range, Dalorosk, Moltar reminded him heatedly. Dalorosk violently roared into the air and slammed his foot down on the rocks, fragmenting a large segment of the peak he stood on.

We must not allow any threat to our rule! he shouted into the clouded sky. *Do as I say!* There was silence across the mental link for a short moment but at last Golthrout spoke.

Be mindful of yourself, Dalorosk, he said in his deep rumble. *You will not scare us into submitting to your temper. We make the decisions as one.* The link was silent again. *But I believe Dalorosk is right in this matter. We should wait to attack until we know where the Source is for certain. Vorkoise and I will meet Moltar in the midlands and find the traitor again. Dalorosk and Wyrik will scan the skies above us to make sure he doesn't escape. Are we in agreement?*

I am, Vorkoise replied.

Fine, Moltar said.

Then hurry into position, Dalorosk told them. *I will pass word to Wyrik.* With that, the echoing voices in the behemoth's mind began to steadily fade and the rippling water went still again. Alone with his thoughts to himself once more, Dalorosk balled his hands into fists and spread his wings, beating them hard against the air to lift him off the peak and into the air high above the Valley of Galantia. The black Ancient grit his rows of sharp teeth as he shot forward with fury driving every beat of his wings. He was growing tired of this game he was forced to play with his brothers. He hated holding in his fury. He hated waiting.

Chapter 29

<u>Ceruleana</u>

Maglin Byre stood with her dripping wet face mesmerized, staring at the stretched out form of the white horse named Alberic peacefully sleeping underneath a small alcove of rock with his sweeping wings tucked close to his sides. Drying her skin with the ends of her red scarf and rubbing her eyes to work the sleep away from her short nap in the previous two hours, she carefully took a step toward the sleeping Ancient taking care to tiptoe so as not to wake him prematurely. Alberic was the most majestic thing the Maven had ever seen, his every hair and feather shining white while his mane and tail shimmered gold. When they were open his eyes were solid gold as well, just like the glowing hooves made up of slowly swirling light. Unable to contain her curiosity and wonder, Maglin slowly reached down with her hands tightly wrapped in black bandages for gripping her weapons and ran the tips of her fingers over his hooves. They slid across it like over melting ice, though instead of a frigid touch a wave of warmth spread down her arm. Seeing the golden light emanating from her hand she pulled it back to stare in awe as thousands of miniscule particles danced off her fingertips, dissipating into the air.

Slowly turning her head as the light around her hand faded, Maglin locked her astonished gaze on Lucan Hauk Erland sitting a dozen feet away by a small cracking fire. Slowly rising and grinning uncontrollably, the Red Maven ambled over and took a seat on a brown leather pack sitting on the ground across from him.

"He's like something out of a dream," she said quietly, reaching back to flip some of her long brown hair over her shoulder. "I still can't believe he's real." Lucan smiled back, having never seen the woman beam with pure, simple joy like this before.

344

"He's been getting that reaction from a lot of people lately," the Blue Maven told her, raising a long stick with a piece of meat from Hadecrest on the end over the flames. "But there he is. The lost Ancient of Light and original Master Sage himself."

"Do you really think it's a good idea for him to be lying... like that, out in the open while the other Ancients are looking for him?" Maglin asked, turning to gander back at the winged steed. Lucan raised an eyebrow as he slowly rotated the stick over the fire.

"Lying against the walls of the Cataract River basin is hardly 'out in the open,' I'd say," Lucan stated. "He gets better rest in his true form than his human disguise and he certainly needs his rest after flying us all the way from behind Mt. Corist to the Torrentcia Territories, so there's not much we can do about it. Besides, Revond said it was safe, and that's good enough for me."

"The sage's word is infallible, is that it?" Maglin asked, cocking her head sarcastically.

"In time you will learn, Maglin," Lucan replied, pulling the meat back from the flames to quickly touch with his fingertips, "that when this Master Sage character says something, you can pretty much bet your life on it. I would." Though Maglin frowned and remained skeptical of this man Lucan seemed to put such great stock in, she remembered he was in fact a Mystic Sage. So far everything she had heard about him from both Lucan and his own lips seemed to suggest he knew more about the world and everything in it—at least what was left of it—than anyone she had ever known. It made her feel all the more excited and honored to know he was following her lead and advice to locate the next Elemental Warrior he was looking for.

After taking the night to rest among Maglin's people, the Red Maven gathered up her things and prepared to depart the day after they rescued her people from the Lavlas Boars. While she was nervously climbing up onto Alberic's back for the first time, she heard Lucan and Revond talking about where they were headed next to find another Elemental Warrior. Lucan, apparently the sage's guide, had heard a rumor of a hidden underground city somewhere in the central lands of Iairia that the people of Torrentcia had fled too after the destruction of the silver city beside Lake Torrent. Though Lucan didn't know much more than that, it was enough to spur a memory in Maglin's head and she quickly stopped him, laughing out loud in Revond's direction at the lackluster guide he had found.

When Lucan wheeled around to scathingly ask her what more about it she knew, the woman turned for the overhang of soil and yelled out the name of one of her men standing and waiting for Alberic to lift off. As he came forward Maglin told her new companions that this man had been a Legionnaire who once protected the Sarton himself during a raid of the infamous marauders of the Purging Flame in the upper Grailen Plains. Turning back to the man, she asked him to tell Revond what he had told her about the emergency hideaway of the Sarton.

The man explained that though he had never seen it himself, there had long been a secret city underneath the Cataract River stretching from Lake Torrent to the Great Forests. A Legion patrol discovered it occupied by marauders and bandits almost two hundred years ago and cleared them out, yielding a secret emergency fortress for the Sarton should the Southland ever fall under invasion again. Though he confessed it was only a rumor and he wasn't sure it even existed, he told them the entrance was supposed to be behind one of the falls in the northern Cataract River. Curious that the wandering sages like Zeroan had never found such a place, Revond was skeptical the underground city would be anything more than a bunker if it existed at all but thanked the man for his tale and told Alberic this would be their best bet to find a candidate for the Warrior of Water.

With a destination set, Alberic shot forward and bounded into the skies leaving the west behind. Traveling for several days they at last reached the once blue and watery middle of the Southland. The group began flying up and down the empty channel where the Cataract River once flowed, trying to gauge which of its many falls could be the entrance to the underground city. While Revond quickly searched several dried cliffs on foot looking for any kind of entrance or cavern, he had found nothing after days and grew frustrated they could be on a wild goose chase. Setting Alberic down alongside the last major cataract in the northern half of the river on their third day of searching for the city, Revond told his companions to get some rest while he went out looking one last time before they abandoned the idea in favor of another of Lucan's rumors. Lying down underneath an alcove once overlooking the massive falls in the river, Alberic quickly went to sleep while Lucan and Maglin took shifts doing the same and keeping watch for any sign of the other Ancients.

Finally both awake and eating a late lunch while they waited for Revond to return from his typically long searches, the pair was surprised to see the black cloaked figure of the Master Sage appear from the shadows above the alcove where the Ancient of Light slumbered to drop down beside them, back unusually quickly. He raised full length and shifted in his robes, reaching up to pull back his hood and reveal his bearded face. Meeting their gazes but remaining silent, the sage turned and walked beside Alberic, gently placing one of his gloved hands on his neck and shaking him awake.

"It's time to wake, my friend," Revond told him tenderly. "Rise." Feeling the man's touch and hearing his voice, the white steed's eyelids slowly slipped open to reveal his gilded eyes. Taking a step back as the Ancient of Light woke and began to lift his head from the ground, Maglin and Lucan watched in amazement as a thin aura of light enveloped Alberic's body and he began to quickly morph into his comparatively small human form, sitting on his backside in his usual white garb as the light faded. Shaking his head and blinking his eyes rapidly, Alberic smiled and stood beside Revond with a smile appearing. Lucan couldn't help but grin at the irony of his appearance in his human form. Here he was, the first Master Sage and one of the oldest and most powerful beings alive, and he stood almost a foot shorter than Revond and maintained an almost boyish youth on his clean face. Lucan never understood why one as strong and wise as Alberic appeared to them so young and simple.

Walking beside Revond as he dusted himself off, Alberic's smile widened when he saw the two other humans around the fire.

"Good morning, Mavens," he said energetically for having just awakened.

"Almost," Lucan replied with a grin. "It's been afternoon for a few hours now if you recall." Alberic laughed at himself and shook his head again, taking a seat beside Maglin and reaching for some of the rations in another pack at his feet.

"Ah, of course," he replied. "But I think I've worked up an appetite for breakfast nonetheless." Lucan laughed again and squinted his eyes as if trying to piece together the puzzle of why the Ancient acted this way.

"But you don't have to eat, Alberic," he said. "Can you really have an appetite? How did you develop all these peculiar human traits when you're so much more?" Alberic merely shrugged and smiled, shooting a knowing glance up to Revond.

"Perhaps I just find the human way of life appealing," he returned, taking a bite of bread. "I've been living it with relative success for several hundred years now, anyway. Perhaps that's why I can forget the time of day on occasion." Maglin beamed at him at this, just as curious as Lucan at how the powerful Ancient could appear as such a relaxed and easygoing man no different than they despite all the knowledge and experience he harbored. While Revond smiled as well as he watched Alberic eat, his expression turned serious quickly after and he moved around the fire to be better seen by all of them.

"I'm afraid we won't have time for a full meal here and now, Alberic," he began. "We need to pack up and start out on foot. I may have found what we're looking for." All three of them livened at this, leaning up and setting down whatever was in their hands.

"You actually found this underground gathering?" Lucan asked in disbelief.

"Something, perhaps," he returned vaguely. "There is a small entrance to a cavern behind one of the cataracts where the waterfall would have been, as Maglin's man informed us. There was torch light coming from within. I didn't venture too far in but it may be what we're looking for, and even if it isn't there must be someone in there for a torch to be burning. In any case I want all of you with me when we make contact with whoever is in there. Time is short so let's pack up and get moving." Hopefully exchanging glances with each other, Lucan, Maglin and Alberic all shot up and began gathering their things back into their packs. Dousing the fire and hiding any sign they had been there, the group assembled behind Revond and began trailing after him through the basin beside the huge riverbed.

The Cataract River had been the biggest in Iairia, rivaled only by the east flowing river that ran into a natural underground aqueduct under the Iairia Mountain Chain then into the Eastern Sea at Acquanautta Port on the coast. The mighty river got its name from the several waterfalls along its route through the wetlands and the Grailen Plains before segmenting into the Great Forests. Along the many cataracts were green basins and cliffs that overlooked the wide river, some hundreds of feet high. Since the Ascension, the river and its source, Lake Torrent, had all but dried up and much of the life around it had died. Thankfully for Master Sage Revond, the dry conditions had made his task in finding the secret entrance to the rumored underground city that much easier.

Leading his band up the basin at an enterprising pace, they quickly arrived in front of the cataract they had seen from the air earlier in the day. There was a smooth cliffside before them stretching up over a hundred feet but the walls of the basin were much wider on either side. While the waterfall would have obscured a series of narrow ledges along the cliff, with it gone Revond led them up the one on the western side of the basin, telling them to watch their step as it was a long way down to the riverbed. Pressing along behind him in single file, the group navigated over the pebbly ledge until halfway across the cliff where Revond stopped and peered up to a fissure in the rock a few feet above his head. Though narrow along its sides it was tall, stretching almost to the top of the cliff. If the waterfall were still there it would have been impossible to detect and very dangerous to reach with the rock wet and slippery.

Ordering the others to group around him, Revond reached down with both hands and made a quick sweeping movement with each of them, slicing the stone at their feet into a circular platform. Clenching his fingers as if taking hold of something in the palm of his hand, the sage lifted the stone slab and everyone standing on it into the air. Though Lucan was always more than a little unsettled when the sage used his amazing power on him without informing him first, he was surprised to find even Maglin taking a step closer to him and gulping uncertainly at whatever was happening. Before she could express her discomfort of levitating above the ground high over a tall cliff, she found herself even with the entrance to the fissure and Revond instructed her to slowly step into it. Mustering her courage, the Red Maven gingerly entered the split in the rock, followed by Lucan and Alberic. Revond entered last, turning his head to look back at the rock and gently drop it back down to the spot he had lifted it from so nothing looked out of place.

When they were all inside the narrow fissure Revond stepped back into the lead, weaving his way around the others in the tight surroundings. Bidding them to follow him quietly, they were surprised to find the narrow passage expanding and widening as they began to walk down a slope leading toward what appeared to be torchlight on the walls. While Lucan and Maglin shot each other mystified glances, Revond abruptly halted in front of them and held up a hand for them to do the same. Peering down into a flat segment of the cavern where the torch light seemed to originate for a long moment, he spun around and turned back for them, flipping down his concealing hood.

"It seems we have indeed found someone—there are two Bullocts sitting inside the cavern ahead," he said in a whisper. "They look to be guarding a carved staircase at the end of the tunnel." Lucan frowned at this, having never liked the large breed of dog known for its ferocity.

"So let's send Alberic in and have him transform in front of them," he suggested. "The only thing that will scare a Bulloct is something bigger and meaner. I bet a glowing horse could do the trick."

"I'm afraid that may not be prudent, Lucan," Alberic answered from behind. "Revealing the true form of an Ancient for any human that may be around a corner to see might generate a panic. Revond can handle this."

"Agreed," the Master Sage confirmed. "Just be ready for anything. We don't know who might be occupying this cavern." Seeing the two Mavens nodding in compliance, Revond turned and continued down the end of the slope until his entire body was revealed in the flat part of the cavern. There were a few torches hanging from either side of the cavern walls, illuminating the muscular and fearsome gray build of the Bullocts. Equipped with hulking jaws and muscular black bodies, they were known for their difficulty to train but famed uses as guards.

Walking quietly so he wouldn't disturb the two Bullocts resting alongside the staircase in the wall at the end of the passage, the sage knelt on the rock and let a soft whistle escape from his lips. The two dogs' pointed ears pricked up immediately and shot their heads up, scanning ahead to find the man in the black cloak kneeling down and motioning for them to come with his hands. Leaping and lunging forward barking at the stranger, Lucan and Maglin gulped as they charged at him ready to use their massive jaws that could easily snap a bone in two. Before they could reach him, Revond turned his hands upside down and slowly lifted them higher, raising the Bullocts off the ground and replacing their barking with whining and whimpering at the sudden lack of the sensation of gravity.

With the dogs suspended into the air before him, Revond slowly rose and reached up to touch each of the ferocious animals on their heads between their eyes. Though Lucan was sure the sage was going to lose his fingers by doing something so foolish, he was surprised to find the dogs suddenly passive and quiet at his touch. When they dropped their ears and ceased their whining, Revond lowered them back to their feet and knelt beside them, reaching up to each of their heads to stroke them and quietly word something none of his companions could make out. Amazed to see the Bullocts panting serenely and even trying to lick Revond's gloves, Lucan stepped forward with disbelief in his blue eyes.

"How in the name of Granis...?" he trailed off, walking beside the Master Sage with his hands on his hips.

"Merely a spell to soothe the angry mind," Revond spoke as he scratched one of the Bullocts' over his chest. "It won't work on a creature with a sentient mind like a human but on a Bulloct here it is an effective tool to calm their natural propensity for violence."

"Huh," Lucan uttered, nodding his head. "For some reason I had the idea you could only manipulate elements and not things that are actually alive."

"Everything is made up by the elements to some degree or another, Lucan," Revond responded. "The power of my order cannot infringe on human free will and we generally have a rule not to take physical hold of living creatures with that power, but as you just witnessed it is possible." Though slightly confused, Lucan nodded and let the matter pass. Seeing the Bullocts so docile, the Maven reached down to pat one on the head but recoiled when it began growling and lifting its pointed ears as if preparing to snap out at him. Taking a large step back, Maglin laughed at him and told him the Bullocts were a good judge of character.

Rising, Revond told them both the spell only truly worked for the wielder and they should still keep their distance. Before they could say anything else, the group was surprised to hear several footsteps from the staircase sounding into the cavern. Wheeling around to face whoever was coming, Revond and the others found several men wearing brown leather armor marked with an old emblem of the Southland Legion emerging from the stairs, brandishing swords at the sight of the strangers. Guessing they had heard the Bullocts barking, Revond raised his hands above his head as if to surrender while they came forward.

Though surprised to see their Bullocts calm and motionless before the figure in the black cloak, the armed men remained hard and pointed their blades out for him.

"Alert the captain that a few unlucky converts have wandered into the cave," one of them at the front said, shouting back into the staircase. Hearing this Revond spoke up with his commanding voice soaring through the cavern.

"To save you the trouble we are not converts," Revond said, growing experienced with facing such accusations. "My friends and I are allies to the free people of the Southland and are looking for shelter. I am Master Sage Revond of the Mystic Sages. I'm here to talk with your leader." The men around the staircase went quiet and still at this, looking at each other and mouthing the part about the Mystic Sages back and forth. At last the man who first spoke shook his head and ordered a few of his men up to detain them.

"The Mystic Sages have been gone for years," he replied cynically. "I don't know how you found this place, convert, but it's already time for you to leave. Throw them out of the fissure and be sure they are dead. Keep one of them for questioning—there might be more out there." Hearing this and seeing several men approaching her with rope to bind her, the Red Maven spun around one of them and drew a knife from her thigh to press against his neck.

"You should listen to the Master Sage," she said with quiet malice in her voice. "Tell your men to back up and drop their weapons."

"That won't be necessary, Maglin," Revond said, extending an open hand in her direction. Tightening his fingers he grabbed the knife from her with his telekinetic grip and floated it through the air into his opposite hand. The men around them made aghast noises of disbelief at what they saw, whispering to each other again. "I think these men have ample proof of who I say I am." No sooner that he finished his sentence, even his own companions were surprised to see his body slowly disappearing into thin air, leaving only Maglin's knife levitating in the air. Watching in amazement as it began moving across the distance between where he had been standing and the apparent commander of the men, they were shocked to find the sage reappear in front of them in the blink of an eye, lowering the knife to his side. "My party and I are here to help you, my friends. Please trust us. We need to see your leader." The man in charge remained frozen in shock at first but slowly nodded, coming back to his senses. Obviously convinced, he spun his head around to one of his subordinates.

"Send word to the Sarton personally," he said. "Inform him a... Mystic Sage is awaiting him at the city gate. Make haste." Nodding, the man sheathed his weapon and turned to sprint into the stairs leading further down underground. Hearing the order, Revond narrowed his eyes uncertainly.

"The Sarton of the Legion is here?" he asked incredulously, to which the man nodded.

"This is his city," he replied. "Have you not come for him?" Revond replied yes but that he didn't know the Sarton himself would be here. Lucan and Maglin exchanged hopeful glances at this new revelation, letting themselves believe the underground city might exist after all. Though they waited for several minutes while Revond answered a few of the questions the Legionnaires had for him about where he and the Mystic Sages had been for so long, a clamor from the stairway echoed up to them and the men parted to make way for an additional unit of armed men arriving in front of Revond.

At the center was a man dressed in white and blue, pushing his way through the Legionnaires and scanning the cavern for the man in the black cloak he had been told of. He was a medium sized man with silver gauntlets over his arms and dark hair that stretched down over his ears, complimented by facial hair around his mouth and chin. Though wearing a thick belt he had a silver sash over his left side down to his knees, a sign of nobility among the citizens of Torrentcia City.

Spying the towering form of Revond at once, the man let a slow smile spread over his face as his eyes drifted to the silver emblem on the sage's cloak. Seeing his eyes on it, Revond spoke.

"You are familiar with the insignia of the Order of Alberic, then," he stated. The man kept his eyes on it for a lingering moment while he nodded yes, his mouth slipping open.

"I have not seen it except in the pages of a book, but yes," he replied, shifting his gaze to Revond's eyes and beginning to smile. "My men tell me you claim to be a Mystic Sage. Can you offer any proof?"

"I suggest you ask your men, sir," Revond answered.

"I'd like to see something for myself, if you don't mind," the man replied. Though Revond knew it was forbidden to use his power so lightly and felt especially uncomfortable doing so with the founder of his order standing behind him, he let out a sharp breath and opened the palm of his hand, summoning a white light over it that grew to illuminate the entire cavern as the seconds passed. Closing his fingers around it, the light shot through them in rays of waning particles before fading altogether.

"I can perform cheap parlor tricks all day, sir, but the real proof I offer is in the council and tidings I bring in this dark hour," Revond said, lowering his hand back into his cloak. "I am Master Sage Revond and I have come to speak with the Sarton." The man in front of him let the sage's words digest and his faint smile grew into a grin.

"I am the Sarton," he said, extending his hand out for Revond. "By the name of Jax Morrol."

"Morrol?" Revond repeated surprised. "There has been a Sarton by that name before."

"Correct," the Sarton affirmed. "I am his son, once a lieutenant in the Legion and then elected to its head several years ago the same as my father. And I have been waiting for this day nearly every day since." Revond reached up took hold of the man's forearm, shaking it.

"What day is that, Sarton Morrol?" Revond asked.

"I have been looking for you since before the Ascension even began, Master Sage," he informed him. "There were rumors that a lone Mystic Sage had emerged from your tower in the east and was traveling Iairia. I dispatched dozens of riders to search for your whereabouts so you might help us deal with the growing elemental disorder ravaging the Southland, but alas, we were too late. But now, here you are after all. How did you survive the Ascension?" Revond released the Sarton's hand and gave him a knowing look.

"I'm afraid it's a very long story that brings me here, Sarton," Revond replied. "It would be best if we could sit and speak privately. And my friends could use a meal." Jax Morrol nodded and ordered his men to make way, yelling that they had guests.

"Please follow me, Master Sage," he said, looking past him to the others standing at the opposite end of the cavern. "You all as well! The hospitality of Ceruleana is yours." Though confused at the strange name none of them had ever heard, the group quickly made their way up to the Sarton to shake his hand and introduce themselves as well. After the introductions the group began following him down the carved out staircase leading deeper underground.

"Pardon me, Sarton Morrol, but what is Ceruleana?" Revond asked for them all as they walked with the Legionnaires filing in to follow them down. Morrol looked back up through the torchlight of the stairs with a smile.

"A secret even from the vast knowledge of the Mystic Sages, it would appear," he replied merrily. "Ceruleana is an underground oasis discovered during the days of the first Sarton, taken from the clutches of the Purging Flame marauders. It is a hidden city left only for emergencies of the Southland and for the Sarton to evacuate to if Greenwall Fortress, or later, Torrentcia City, ever fell. Since the Ascension we've put it to good use." He paused for a moment as the light began to transition from the red of the flames to a strange blue glow coming from further down at the end of the staircase. "But please. You'll want to see for yourselves." He turned back then, hurrying down the stairs to part the crowd of people that had gathered there, looking up the staircase to see who was coming. Surprised to see so many people in what looked to be good health and clean cosmopolitan attire, Revond and the others emerged from the staircase to be stared at by dozens surrounding them and whispering to each other.

Behind them was another sight that stole the breath away from even the Master Sage and the Ancient of Light. They stood over a wide ledge looking down on something none of them could have predicted. Laying out below them was a massive cave with a waterfall coming out of the opposite side. It fell into a small lake at the bottom of the cave surrounded by amazingly detailed buildings around its perimeter, all of them carved and assembled from cerulean stone that encompassed the walls of the cave and collections of enormous shells as if from the bottom of the Eastern Sea. The ledge they stood on stretched down into the collection of buildings then back up again to a single bigger one built on the left side of the cave overlooking everything. Above them over the staircase was a wide shell jutting out from the rock as if to shade them with a plaque on the end that had the word Ceruleana etched over it.

Though the cave was well lit with torches around the walls and the buildings, perhaps the most amazing aspect of the cave was the blue glow emanating from the waters of the lake. There were hundreds of miniature lights swimming back and forth under the surface as if generating the light that filled the cave. Unable to believe what he was seeing, Revond turned to Sarton Morrol standing with a smile amid his people and Legionnaires, his hands at his sides.

"Welcome to Ceruleana, Master Sage," he said.

"How is such a place possible?" Revond returned almost in a whisper.

"By keeping it a secret," Morrol answered, folding his arms. "Come. Allow me to give you a tour of the city." Motioning for them to follow him again, the Sarton began ambling down the ledge that led to the houses of blue rock and shells. Following him but staring captivated at the cave around them, the group listened as their host began to tell them about Ceruleana. While they walked, the crowd slowly followed them, keeping several feet back but listening intently. "Though we call it a city this cave can only hold about a hundred occupants comfortably. We have nearly two hundred crammed inside. After the Ascension and the destruction of Torrentcia City I evacuated to the south. We were originally headed for Greenwall Fortress but when we learned it had fallen under attack by Golthrouts and was destroyed we came here. I led as many survivors across the lands inside as I could, but few to none in the wetlands survived and we didn't have time to go into the Grailen when we heard of what was happening.

"We've been here ever since. Though Lake Torrent has drained after the Ancients stole the Source of Water, it will be several years at least before the underground reservoirs of water dry up. That's where the small waterfall you see is coming from. With fresh water and the supplies already prepared here in case of an emergency, we can last in the city for another year or two before we have to start venturing out looking for food elsewhere. We even have some livestock and gardens growing over in the left corner of the cave." Alberic looked down into the city to see streets and lampposts alight with fire beside most of the major buildings.

"Who helped you build these structures?" the Ancient asked. "This kind of construction seems impossible."

"Almost," Morrol replied, looking back to the man in white. "The city was constructed almost two hundred years ago after we found the cave, but the Sarton enlisted the help of the Warriors of Water and Earth to help shape and erect the unique houses that make up the city. Most just have a few rooms with a little furniture brought down here long ago, but the Sarton's Watch where I stay is considerably larger with several rooms where I conduct Legion business on behalf of what people we have left." Morrol pointed up to the other ledge leading up to the far left side of the cave where a much larger and more elaborate house stood. It was a larger house built into the cave wall with a balcony that looked out over all of Ceruleana.

Lucan could barely believe all that he saw as he scanned the amazing blue cave. In a world that had been nothing but barren and destroyed for longer than he wished to remember, he was nothing short of awestruck at the luscious and beautiful scene before him. He had forgotten such a place could exist. "From there my men and I plan excursions out into the world to gather information and continue looking for any survivors. These days we've had to be more cautious and guard the entrance better because of the converts. But we have remained safe here without detection of any kind since we arrived."

"Sarton Morrol," called Lucan as he found his voice. "One thing has still got me—where is that blue light that illuminates the entire cave coming from? It looks like..." Trailing off for fear of sounding like a fool for even thinking what he was, he was surprised to hear Morrol finished his statement and confirm his guess.

"Fish," he said, to which the others raised their eyes incredulously. It was Alberic who broke the silence, nodding in understanding.

"Ah, I should have known," he started. "I've seen glow fish in caverns similar to this before. Their very scales shine to illuminate the water around them so they can see in the darkness of underground places like this."

"Exactly," the Sarton confirmed. "Though we're deep underground, between our torches and the glowing Trouck Fish, as they're called, Ceruleana remains constantly alight. Our haven is a truly remarkable place." Having reached the bottom of the ledge leading down from the entrance to the city the Sarton stopped and faced the main street leading into it. "But please, I'm sure you're weary from your travels and require food and water. Our biggest storehouse is the gathering hall in the center of the city against the back wall. My men will escort you there. When you've had a chance to rest we can continue our discussion, Master Sage. Agreed?" Though aware his party had just rest before coming to the city, Revond didn't want to offend the Sarton or his people's hospitality and accepted.

"Very well, Sarton," he said. "Thank you for taking us in." Morrol merely swept a hand through his hair and bowed before his guests.

"No, thank you, Master Revond," he returned with a smile. Ordering a few of his men to lead them to the gathering hall down the street, the Sarton watched as Revond and the others turned to make their way into the amazing miniature city.

Chapter 30

<u>Recluse</u>

Aeric let out a huff of worry and irritation upon seeing Valeri starting to bleed again, a warm drop of red liquid staining the cloth tightly wrapped around the wound on her right side. Dragging the wooden chair he sat on closer to her bed, he raised her bandaged right arm dangling by the wound over her chest so he would have a clear path to her side. Pulling off his leather gauntlets for greater mobility of his hands and fingers while he worked, he carefully reached out to lift the girl's black shirt a little higher up. Revealing the whole of the bandaged area, he began to swap out the dressings for new ones again. The princess had been in and out of sleep since she arrived in Aeric's arms at the small house on the cliffs looking over the Crag Spires. It was barely more than a small and rickety shack built into a depression in the rocks and from some kind of black wood Aeric had never seen. The old man who had come to their rescue in the Crag Spires assured him they would be safe there while he tended to Valeri. Setting her down on a bed, the mysterious owner of the house ordered Aeric to stand back but be ready to help him when he called for assistance.

Valeri had lost a dangerous amount of blood from the deep slashes on her waist and arm and she was numb around both areas from what the old man guessed to be a strange poison on the claws of the Arnosmn that had wounded her. Removing his black robe, the old man quickly hobbled into a nearby room to pull a red cloth off a shelf, along with a needle and a handful of bandages. Telling Aeric one always needed to be prepared for disaster in a place like the Crag Spires, he set everything down on the end of Valeri's bed and began pouring an old jar of liquid over the red cloth. Ordering Aeric to hold Valeri down with all his strength, he cast the cloth against her wound to which she screamed out and violently

359

struggled to rise, tears of pain welling in her eyes. Struggling to hold the supernaturally powerful princess down even in her weakened state, Aeric demanded to know what he was doing to her. The old man told him to trust him, continuing to clean the wound and sew it up as best he could.

Over the next hour he had stopped the hemorrhaging and ensured the wounds wouldn't become infected, then finally backed away from the Drakkaidian princess saying he had done all he could. Aeric was amazed at how well he had repaired the girl using strange liquids and herbs but did not bother asking what any of them were, preoccupied with keeping a constant vigil on Valeri. Though he knew Asthatch and the others were still somewhere out on the cliffs of the Crag Spires and he had to go after them, the old man told him he would never make it back if he ventured out the door alone. Ordering the Grandarian to watch Valeri and make sure she didn't lose any more blood, the man put on his robe again and gathered his walking stick. Telling him he would find the others and bring them back, he promised to return soon. Though Aeric was no healer and didn't feel comfortable being left with Valeri in her unstable state by himself, he knew it had to be done and agreed, thanking him for his generosity. The old man merely let out a dry huff and slammed the door to his simple house, disappearing into the dark afternoon.

It had been almost an hour since the old man had left them alone and evening was beginning to darken the sky. As Aeric worked to pry off Valeri's bandages and wrap her in new ones, he reached over to a nearby table to grab a candle and bring it closer to better illuminate his surroundings. Dripping sweat as he nervously peeled off the last of her bandages, he found the princess stirring once again, her eyes slipping open and drifting over to him. Looking down to see him touching her bare stomach stained with blood, she cringed and tightened. Seeing her muscles tense, Aeric raised a hand to her head to sweep his fingers over her hair and gently tell her to calm down.

"Valeri, just relax," he coaxed her as tenderly as he could. "If you tighten up you'll start bleeding again and you can't afford to lose any more blood. Just calm down."

"Where am I?" the girl asked, wincing in pain. "I... It hurts bad..." Aeric brought his hand back down to her wound to begin dabbing her skin with a wet cloth and wipe away blood before bandaging her again.

"I know Valeri, I'm sorry," he told her sincerely. "The old man that killed the Arnosmn brought us to his house in the cliffs next to the Crag Spires. You're going to be in a lot of pain for a while but you're safe here."

"Where is he?" she asked, looking around the room with sweat beading on her face.

"He went to go find Asthatch and the others," the Grandarian answered. "He should be back soon. He promised." Aeric stopped what he was doing as he accidentally pulled a bandage too hard and caused the princess to yelp out in sharp pain, her face grimacing. "I'm sorry, Valeri. The old man used some chemical I've never seen before to stop your bleeding. He said it was the only way to stop you from losing too much. It's working—even closing your wound somehow—but he said it will burn pretty bad until it wears off and your body takes its course. You were cut pretty deep." Though gritting her teeth and breathing hard, the girl forced herself to relax as best she could and shift her tearing eyes back to the boy slowly wrapping her again.

"How long have you been tending to me?" she asked softly. Aeric glanced at her staring at him again and shrugged.

"Since he left," he replied simply. When he finished wrapping her he gently took her arm again and lay it to rest beside her, taking a deep breath and wiping the sweat off his brow with his sleeve. Meeting her gaze, the young Tieloc leaned closer and dabbed a wet cloth against her forehead. "You're going to be alright, Valeri, I promise. You're one of the toughest people I've ever known. If anyone can pull through this it's you." The princess stared into his eyes for a long moment after he finished, her breathing finally relaxing back to a minimal pace.

"You think this man is the recluse?" she asked quietly.

"He fits the description," Aeric returned. "An old man living alone in the Crag Spires. And he saved us just like he saved Desrum before. He knew who we were and how to treat demonic wounds. And while he isn't exactly the warmest or most civil individual, he definitely saved your life."

"With your help," Valeri added softly. There was a long silence that hung between them after, both of them just staring at each other while Aeric dabbed the sweat from her head. The silence was broken by the sound of footsteps echoing

361

into the room from outside the house. Standing up to look out the glass window above Valeri's bed, Aeric saw the old man leading Asthatch, Desrum, and the last Drakkaidian soldier down into the depression the house sat in. Telling Valeri he would be right back and to call out if she needed him, Aeric rose full height from his chair and strode out of the room for the main chamber. The rickety structure was dreadfully old, simply decorated with splintering wooden furniture and a tattered Drakkaidian flag on one of the walls. Apart from the bedroom and another storage room where the old man kept supplies, he had seen nothing more of the house except the small, dusty depression it sat in that the man called his yard. Opening the front door and stepping outside into the evening air, Aeric waited for the others to march up to him. Seeing Asthatch peering through the darkness to make out the boy's identity, Aeric opened his mouth to speak.

"Are you alright, captain?" he asked as they arrived before him.

"Where is the princess?" was Asthatch's response, urgency tearing through his voice. Aeric frowned at his manners but remembered how much the princess meant to him and raised an arm to point back into the house.

"She's recovering on a bed inside," he replied. Walking past Markus Desrum, the Drakkaidian captain told Aeric to stand aside as he reached for the door. Before he could they were all surprised to find the old man lift his staff and shove it against the door, blocking him off. Asthatch wheeled around toward the old man with a scowl on his face.

"What do you think you're doing?" he barked. The old man kept the dark but determined expression on his bearded face.

"The girl needs to rest and does not need anyone else swarming around her for now," he said flatly. "You may go to the back end of the house and into my storage room for the night." The large captain flared up at this and stood before the old man, only slightly taller.

"Princess Montrox is my responsibility and I am going inside," he stated with equal resolve.

"No," the old man returned, to which Asthatch cursed him and reached for the door again. The old man immediately flipped his staff around his arm with surprising dexterity and flung an end down into the captain's hand. When Asthatch wheeled back to reach for his oversized axe, the old man shot the end of his staff out again, this time slamming into the large man's temple and dropping him to the ground. Though Desrum and the soldier reached for their weapons Aeric raised his hands defensively and told them to wait. Standing over Asthatch, the old man flipped his staff around to the opposite end to press the sharper side down against the captain's neck.

"Youth is a gift of nature but age is a work of art. Don't let my wrinkled skin fool you, captain—I'm still a masterpiece of war. I am the one who just found and saved you and your princess. You are alive because of me, taking advantage of my hospitality in an otherwise most inhospitable place. While you are doing so, you will do what I tell you, when I tell you to do it, and that will be the end of it. Or it will be the end of you." Holding his staff against Asthatch's neck for a long moment while his words sank in, he told Desrum to help him up and take him around back and that they would be allowed into the house in the morning after Valeri had more time to rest. Helping Desrum lift their dizzy companion, Aeric felt the commander tap on his shoulder and lean in to whisper something in his ear.

"This is the man we're looking for," he said, pulling back to look into Aeric's eyes. Giving him a single nod in acknowledgement, he let the Drakkaidian soldier help lift Asthatch and they retreated to the back of the old man's house, disappearing around a corner.

"How is the girl?" the old man asked, opening his door and looking at Aeric. Turning to face him, he shrugged and followed him inside the house.

"Her bleeding is almost completely stopped but I had to change her bandages again just now," he said. "Whatever you rubbed on her to stop the bleeding has her in a great deal of pain." The old man nodded as he closed the door behind them and securely locked it, shaking his head and pulling off his black robe to throw it over a chair beside a large table in the center of the central room of the house.

"It acts to essentially cauterize the wound and completely disinfect it at the same time," he explained. "It's an ancient and very painful remedy but the most effective I've ever come across. She'll make a full recovery much sooner than with traditional healing methods. As for the pain, if she's truly a Montrox it should be of little consequence." Aeric frowned at this, never happy to hear assumptions made about someone because of one's name alone. Knowing Valeri was indeed stronger than most men he had ever known and the old man was probably right, he let it slide and walked into the bedroom containing the princess.

Valeri looked up at them both as they entered, wincing while struggling to bury her cold feet under some blankets at the end of the bed. Though feeling uncomfortable as he did it, Aeric had taken off most of the princess' clothing after he lay her down on the bed, leaving only her tight black shirt and undergarments. She had been feverishly hot when entering the house, but judging from the way she shivered now she looked to be freezing. Aeric quickly shot to the end of the bed to raise a blanket over her.

Before the Grandarian pulled it up to her chest, the old man looked to her side to observe her freshly bandaged wounds, slowly nodding and scratching his gray beard.

"It will be a long night, Highness," he said, shifting his gaze to her face, "but you will make a full recovery. It was a close call to be sure and you have lost much of your blood, but you will live."

"I don't have time to recover," she said with powerful tone but weak volume. "How long before I can get up and walk?" The old man took a seat in the chair Aeric had been sitting in with a long breath escaping as he lay his back against it, loosening his obviously fatigued body from such a tiresome day.

"You will be able to walk tomorrow if you are half as strong as your family is given credit for, but not much else beyond that," he answered brusquely. "You need rest whether you have time for it or not. You are in no condition to be ambling out into the Crag Spires or anywhere else for that matter." He paused for a moment, reaching to the door to pick up his walking stick lying against the frame and lean it into his shoulder. "Which begs the question of what a princess of Drakkaidia is doing this far north away from civilization in the first place." The girl was quiet for a moment, trying to say something but wincing and gritting her teeth. Seeing her in pain, Aeric told her to save her energy and let him talk to the old man. Turning to stand and face him, Aeric answered his question.

"I already told you," he said. "We came here looking for you." The old man frowned and folded his hands on his lap.

"You don't know me," he said quietly. "How do you know I am the one you seek? And why would a princess and her elite guard be searching for an old hermit living in the Black Peaks?"

"One of the men in the back is the former commander of Hadecrest," Aeric replied. "His name is Markus Desrum. You saved him and his men from Siarchs and led them out of the Crag Spires years ago. He recognized you. He told us you would be the one to help us." The old man was silent for a moment before raising his head.

"And what does the princess need my help with?" he asked. Aeric swallowed his doubts and tried to formulate his answer as best he could.

"We understand you know everything there is to know about Drakkaidia," he said. "We were hoping you know of someone or something called the Scavenger. We're trying to find it." The wrinkles in the old man's face bunched together as he deepened his frown.

"Everything there is to know about Drakkaidia," the recluse repeated in a disgusted mumble more to himself than Aeric, looking down at the floor and sitting up straighter in his chair. He rolled his eyes but eventually placed them back on Aeric. "Well it seems you found me at least, boy. But I'm sure you and the princess are not searching out a creature that few have ever even heard rumors of simply for the pleasure of the hunt. The only logical reason you would be after the Scavenger is because you are looking to reclaim something it scavenged, am I right? So to be looking for the Scavenger is to be looking for means to do what?" Sensing the skepticism and doubtfulness in the old man's voice, Aeric knew he had his task cut out for him in explaining their story.

"Are you familiar with the Mystic Sages?" Aeric asked, catching the recluse off guard.

"I am," he replied, leaning forward with his curiosity piqued.

"Well a new Master Sage has returned to Iairia and has devised a plan to stop the Ancients that have destroyed it," Aeric continued. "Though they have the elemental Sources, there is another way for the Master Sage to anoint a new group of Elemental Warriors to take them back and banish the Ancients forever. The original Elemental Warriors who lived eons ago were buried with copies of the Sources' power in a graveyard beside the Mystic Tower of the sages. These copies of the Sources are called crests. Unfortunately, we think this Scavenger creature stole the coffins with the crests that were sealed inside and dragged them north into Drakkaidia."

"So you're looking for the Scavenger in hopes of finding your missing crests," the old man finished, piecing together the story. Aeric nodded and replied yes, shooting a glance down at Valeri staring up at him. The recluse was still and silent for a moment, slowly shifting his gaze around the room until he at last frowned and shook his head. "This sage has sent you on a fool's errand," he said gruffly, surprising both Aeric and Valeri. He rose then, heaving himself up by his staff and turned to make his way for the door. "I cannot help you. My house is yours until the princess recovers, then you will make your way to Hadecrest." Seeing him hobble toward the door, Valeri's face tightened angrily.

"Wait right there!" she shouted through her pain. "Did you not hear him? We have a way to save our world from the Ancients. We have come all the way here for your help. You will provide it." The old man spun around hearing this, his face suddenly taut with anger as well.

"I will do what my own mind decides, little princess," he snapped back. "The only thing that lies north of here is death. This sage obviously has no idea what he's sent you to do—what he's sent you after. I will not help you commit suicide by continuing on into these mountains."

"I am your princess!" Valeri shouted louder than before. "I am ordering you to—"

"Save your decrees for your brainless servants outside, Highness," the old man cut her off. "I have served Drakkaidia my entire life; given her everything I had and more. And while I am retired from my previous duty I serve her still by judging that it is not in her best interest to send the only remaining heir to her throne to the single most dangerous place on the face of the continent to die. The road you seek is one more perilous than you can imagine, and even if you weren't nearly crippled; even if you had this Master Sage of yours with you; even if you had in your hands the Source of Light itself to dispel the evils of these mountains, you would not have a chance to survive." At the end of the old man's rant, Aeric reached down into his tunic to pull up the white medallion hanging there and lift it in his right hand for him to see.

"You mean this Source of Light?" he asked, to which the old man froze and went blank, staring at the shining object in his grasp. Tilting his head and studying it for a long moment, he looked back at Aeric with probing eyes.

"Why would a boy carry the Source of Light with him?" he asked quietly. "Who are you?"

"My name is Aeric Tieloc of Grandaria, son of Darien Tieloc," the young man said with perhaps more pride than ever. "The Source was given to me by Alberic, the Ancient of Light himself. I carry it for our protection against these evils you worry about here in the peaks." Though Aeric expected the recluse to be surprised at this revelation, it was the first thing he said that brought a bedazzled expression over his bearded face.

"Tieloc?" he repeated almost inaudibly. He took a step closer to Aeric and looked hard into his eyes, probing like Valeri had the first time she met him. "You are... the grandson of Tavinious Tieloc?" Aeric nodded and replied yes, guessing tales of the Days of Destiny had reached even the ears of the old hermit living isolated from the world. The old man stared at him for another long moment before shifting his gaze into the space between them and slowly sitting back down in the chair.

"Perhaps it is not my place to deny the destiny of a Tieloc," he said at last, slowly looking back up to the young man. Both Aeric and Valeri were shocked at his abrupt turnaround and stared at him uncertainly. Valeri glanced up to Aeric with a doubtful expression at the man's strange behavior, surprised the revelation of his name alone could so suddenly persuade him when the Source or the story about Alberic had slipped past him without notice. Nodding, the recluse reached up to scratch his beard as he let out a long breath. "I suppose you two will be heading north after the Scavenger whether I aid you or not, won't you?" Both Aeric and Valeri replied yes at the same time. The old man rolled his eyes and leaned his staff against his shoulder once more. "I thought as much. It appears as though I am left with no choice but to assist you as best I can then, for the princess' sake at least. But I warn you both, there is danger beyond these cliffs greater than anything either of you can fathom. The odds either of you will return alive are virtually nonexistent. Do you understand this?" Undaunted, Valeri told him she feared nothing before wincing at her pain. The recluse let a silent chuckle escape from his throat at her response.

Leaning forward in his chair, he swept his eyes back and forth between the two young people and spoke in the gravest tone they had yet to hear from him.

"Then listen well, for you must appreciate the peril that lies in wait for you if you are truly serious about continuing," he started. "The creature you are seeking is not a creature at all—it is a woman. A witch, called Sakkdra. A terrible, soulless witch corrupted by the taint of Drakkan himself. Many centuries ago there was a servant to the High Priest of the Black Church who wanted to become a Dark Mage. But the servant was a woman, and appointing female Dark Mages is strictly forbidden so she was ignored. Eventually she was thrown out of the Cathedral of Dalorosk altogether after her relentless petitioning for an exception in the tradition finally left the High Priest exasperated.

"Alone and consumed by her desire for power equal to that of the men, she traveled to Dalastrak and broke into the royal citadel. Penetrating all the way into the chamber containing the Netherworld Portal itself, she descended inside to offer her soul to Drakkan in exchange for power and duty as great as any man's in the church. The legend goes that Drakkan granted her wish, making her soul immortal and granting her a duty as important as any. Unfortunately for the woman, the price of her gains was greater than she had bargained for and her change was not what she had in mind. Though her soul was immortal and still in her possession, she was tasked with keeping eternal watch over the Lake of the Undead by herself, far away from the rest of Drakkaidia."

"Wait," Valeri interrupted, skepticism in her face. "The Lake of the Undead? You're telling me that old children's ghost tale is real?" The recluse narrowed his eyes and locked his gaze onto the girl's.

"I have seen it," he told her, replacing her doubt with shock. "The lake is as real as Lake Torrent. It lies many leagues north of here in a valley hidden within the Black Peaks. It is a cursed body of water created by the ancient church where damned souls are sent to be punished for all eternity. Only the worst offenders and enemies of Drakkaidia are sent there to be stuck in limbo between life and death; hovering over the placid waters of the lake. Besides the Netherworld Portal itself, it is the most unholy ground on this plane of existence, and Sakkdra the Witch is its keeper."

"So how does this witch fit into the tale of the Scavenger?" Aeric asked, still confused. "If she is bound to this lake how can she be the one who stole the coffins containing the crests?"

"Over the years Sakkdra found loopholes in her service to Drakkan," the old man continued. "She has grown bolder over the years with the expansion of humanity over the lands and the magics of old slowly fading from the world. Feeling safer in venturing away from her charge for longer periods of time, she began searching for talismans of power across the lands in an effort to appease the God of Darkness and gain her freedom. Hoping to bribe him with new power she could offer at the Netherworld Portal as she once offered her soul, she began hoarding all manner of powers and talismans that she could find. Somehow she could sense magics even in a passive state when no others could, and her collection began to grow. She is a shape shifter—a wraith that moves across the lands in shadows and disguises, searching high and low for energy she can offer Drakkan. She collects the spoils of her efforts on a small island in the center of the Lake of the Undead, putting them out of the reach of any who would seek to take back what she rightfully stole. She has been at this for several hundred years now, coming and going as she pleases without fear of Drakkan, especially when news of his imprisonment in the void world reached her ears."

The recluse stopped for a moment, looking hard into Aeric's eyes.

"As I said, this is a fool's errand," he told the young man harshly. "If Sakkdra has indeed stolen these crests as the sage fears, they are beyond your reach. None but she can cross the Lake of the Undead to the island where she hoards her stolen treasures."

"Well we have to keep going so there must be a way," Aeric avowed, brushing off the man's doubts. "And how do you know all this? Who are you exactly?"

"I know about the witch because she has told me her tale herself, many long years ago," the old man said, looking down in space as if reminiscing. "Sakkdra is a treacherous foe—a demon in her own right. There is no confronting her; no getting around her. She is the keeper of the lake and the only way across it."

"How do we know she'll even be there?" Aeric asked. "If she is out looking for power all the time what makes you think she'd even be there to stop us?"

"Oh she is most definitely there now," the recluse said with certainty. "With Drakkan's minions loose across the lands she will be frightened at the possibility of his reemergence and will not risk being found away from her station. And even if she were gone, she is still the only one who can cross the lake. If a mortal soul were to pass over those unholy waters, the damned spirits trapped there would rip it from the body, pulling it under into eternal torture with them. There is nothing we can do." Letting the silence hang with Aeric's and Valeri's eyes still on him, the recluse let out a long huff of air and repositioned his stiff body in his chair. "And yet this is our road. If we cannot find a way to reclaim these crests of yours this world will remain in ashes forever. Perhaps we could..." Aeric perked up at this, his eyes widening with hope.

"What is it?" he pressed quickly. The recluse was silent for a moment, twisting his hands along his wooden staff.

"Sakkdra is a complicated antagonist," he returned secretively. "Her mind is consumed by the darkness of the Netherworld and she does not think rationally, but she is still sharp and cunning when it comes to her ambitions. In this regard she still retains some traces of her humanity which we may be able to exploit. We may be able to... barter with her."

"How?" Valeri asked from the bed.

"I once had something she wanted," the old man stated mysteriously. "I doubt her desire for it would remain in the condition it's in now, but it may be worth a try to offer it to her in exchange for these crests."

"What is it?" Aeric questioned, his eyes sparkling with curiosity. The old man drew out of his mysterious state of mind at this and hardened again.

"That is my concern, not yours," he responded abrasively. "But it may be our only chance, and as long as we have some hope, no matter how slim, I suppose it's worth trying." He narrowed his eyes again and shot a forbidding glace at both Aeric and Valeri as he leaned forward on his staff again. "But I warn you again, this journey will be fraught with danger. There is terrain far more treacherous than the Crag Spires on the road to the lake that I barely managed to navigate in my prime. Even with your power, princess, in your current state you will be vulnerable the entire way through. And you,

Grandarian, cannot use that Source because it would betray our position to Dalorosk and his brethren.

"Once we reach the lake and Sakkdra there is no guarantee she will be in a bartering mood, much less that we can even get to her door. And most dangerous of all are the demons crawling out of the Netherworld Portal. After the Ascension, all the mass destruction and blood that was spilled weakened the veil between our worlds and drew the demons out of their accursed pit. Now they roam the world looking to kill what life remains. The ones you have encountered are nothing compared to some of the enemies I know of. There is evil abroad on wing and claw even at this very moment powerful enough to challenge even the Source of Light. Our chances of success are slim to none."

"You plan to come with us, old one?" Valeri asked incredulously. He sneered at her and rose from the chair, looking down into her crimson eyes.

"Even at my considerable age, I am the best defense you have and the only one who can guide you on the safest route through the Black Peaks, Highness," he told her coldly. "It seems we are both left with no choice." He turned again then, making his way back to the door. "But we may have little time. Though you are wounded, princess, we will have to set out as soon as possible. Tomorrow, even." Though Aeric was about to protest that there was no way he could expect her to travel in her condition so soon, he felt the girl grab his arm and tug him back. Looking down, he saw her silently telling him to agree. Though angry, he kept silent, aware they had to make it back to Hadecrest with all speed.

"Very well," Valeri said. "Thank you for helping us. But wait—you still haven't even given us your name." Aeric froze at this, realizing he still didn't know anything about the recluse other than the fact he knew a great deal about Drakkaidia for being a hermit. The old man stopped in front of the door as he reached down to grab its knob and push it open. Turning his head back he spoke deep and quiet.

"Drakkaidian," he told them. "My name is Drakkaidian." With that, he told them to get their rest and sleep well through the night and if they needed him he would be in another room to their right. Disappearing into his house and blowing out candles as he went, Aeric and Valeri were left alone in the bedroom staring at each other in wonder over who the strange recluse was.

Chapter 31

<u>Random Chance</u>

Lucan Hauk Erland sat at a circular table beside the corner of a house in the center of the subterranean city of Ceruleana, stuffing his mouth with a freshly cooked meal of potatoes and freshly grown vegetables from a garden behind the house on the other side of the cavern. Around the table was his old friend Maglin Byre as well as an elderly couple that invited them in for supper. They and three boys who had apparently lost their parents in the destruction of Torrentcia City lived in the small house. It was a beautiful little home with its cerulean rock walls that shimmered from the reflections of the lake in the center of the cave, even modestly decorated with a few trinkets the couple had managed to save and bring with them in their exodus from Torrentcia. Though dazzling, it was far too small to hold all of them comfortably. The boys slept on the floor each night while the couple took the small bed, all of them sharing only two blankets. As the two Mavens had been led through the small city they saw just about each house suffered from the same lack of space and supplies, crammed full of refugees while some even slept outside.

Though the people of Ceruleana were congested and weary of living in such conditions, Lucan and Maglin were surprised to find them all in good spirits and extending their party every courtesy. The elderly couple, seemingly privileged to be feeding and hosting the outsiders, revealed during the meal that most of the people that made it inside the city were justifiably terrified at what was going on outside the cavern walls and what would become of them in the distant future, but they were first and foremost thankful to still be alive when thousands of others hadn't been so lucky on the first few days of the Ascension. On the streets of the little city the two Mavens were even more captivated at its rare and exotic beauty, unlike anything they had ever seen despite having both spent considerable time in the central regions of the Southland.

The architecture of the miniature houses was a feat unlike anything Lucan or his friends had seen, completely comprised of slabs of the cerulean rock and massive shells a Warrior of Water had apparently found in the lake when he first entered the cave almost two hundred years ago. The rest of the city was equally beautiful with white fences and chains roping off the few patches of earth and soil where they grew vegetation. Beside the gardens was a grassy yard where livestock was being raised. A central storehouse contained all the supplies and beside it was a larger house where a few healers looked after the health of the refugees. There were even lampposts lining the streets that further illuminated the cave primarily lit by the swath of glowing Trouck Fish in the lake, jetting to and fro under the surface with their blue scales. On the banks of the diminutive lake the many children of Ceruleana would stand and watch the fish dart back and forth, some even climbing the tall rocks beside the thin waterfall constantly dumping in and providing its gentle sound echoing through the cave.

Though it was easy to loose track of the time with the unchanging lighting in the cave cut off from the sun, by the time Lucan and Maglin sat down to begin their meal it was apparently evening and a few rations were being passed around the refugees for the night. They ate little to conserve what food they had but extra portions were handed out in celebration of the first new arrivals they had seen in months. While they ate, several groups of the refugees passed by the house where the Mavens sat, looking in and whispering amongst themselves at who they could be and if they might be servants to the Mystic Sage or sages themselves. Periodically looking out the window at the city in amazement as he ate, Lucan finally caught sight of a familiar cloaked figure walking along the smooth rock road past them heading toward the ridge leading up to the Sarton's Watch and the entrance to the city. Rising and excusing himself for a moment, the Maven tossed his scarf over his back and ran from the table outside to catch up with Master Sage Revond, striding forward at his usual brisk pace. He and Alberic had opted to make their way away from the crowds of refugees and stand in solitude by the lake after their arrival, wishing to reflect by themselves for a while before Revond went to inform Sarton Morrol why they had come.

Arriving beside the Master Sage, Lucan lifted up his belt and the front of his pants by his buckle and smiled into the sage's concealing black hood. Before he could say something to get his attention Revond spoke.

"This is quite the hidden bunker after all," the sage told him, keeping his gaze ahead of him. Lucan wasn't surprised the sage didn't have to look to know he was there.

"I still can't believe there's an underground town hidden in the middle of the Torrentcia Territories," Lucan said, looking around the expansive cave again. "How the converts never learned of this place in all the chaos and confusion after the Ascension I'll never know."

"Knowledge of this haven was concealed even from the sages," Revond returned. "The Sarton and his men probably didn't try to send word for refugees outside of Torrentcia to evacuate here for fear of its location being compromised to the Ancients—a policy that has probably kept them alive since. Morrol seems to be a wise leader as his father was back in the Days of Destiny."

"You're going to talk to him then?" the Maven asked, to which Revond replied yes.

"I anticipate his cooperation," Revond said hopefully. "If we can recruit a Warrior of Water here our recruitment will be going ahead of schedule. We have been lucky so far."

"Let's hope it holds," Lucan said, stopping in the road to let the sage continue without him. Before turning to be on his way back to Maglin and his meal, he shouted out one last question to the sage. "Where is Alberic?"

"He is... pondering, by the lake," Revond shouted back. "Leave him be for a while. Enjoy the satisfaction of a warm meal while you can." With that, he turned back and began walking out of the houses up onto the rising ledge leading up to the Sarton's Watch. Shifting his gaze to look out into Ceruleana as he began ascending the trail to the top of the cave, Revond watched Lucan disappear back into a house to rejoin the soon be anointed Warrior of Fire within. Quickly running over his recent conversation with Alberic by the lake regarding the Blue Maven, he took in a deep breath and nodded to himself to affirm the decision they had made was the right one. Reaching the top of the ledge looking over the entire cave and the front steps of the largest house within sitting there against the wall, Revond prepared his thoughts for the coming conversation with Morrol. Seeing two armed Legionnaires at the open archway leading into the cerulean structure parting and standing perpendicular to it, Revond gently bowed his head to both of them and stepped up into a beautiful chamber.

There was a large table in the center surrounded by chairs and a few burning candles in the center. On the walls were a few older maps of the Southland and a mounted sword over another doorway leading into at least one other room. Though glancing into it when hearing voices inside, the sage guessed the Sarton was finishing with business and turned to his right to find one of the walls of the room missing. It was replaced by a balcony that looked over the city below. Stepping up to the white arching railing Revond looked down, taking in Ceruleana from the high vantage point. With its unique stone makeup and lofty heights it reminded him of the Sky Sprite sanctuary of Haven that he had visited before as a boy.

The sage frowned at himself for letting his mind drift again. Even with the gravest of circumstance to occupy his thoughts as of late, he found his thoughts still frequently drifted to his years as the Maven called Edge. The adventure he had lived out the first time he was charged with saving the world was still the great lesson of his life he looked to for guidance when faced with dilemmas as the Master Sage. Everything reminded him of his journey with Kaylan Tieloc and her dark half, the vessel of Drakkan who called herself Kaotica.

The two girls and his time with them had shaped him into the man he would become more than any of his training or studies in the Mystic Tower over the years. It was Kaylan and her love that showed him it was alright to live—that no matter how dark his life had been before there would always be light ahead waiting for him if he chose to walk toward it. He had fallen in love with her—fallen in love with them both. For all her dark power and the destruction it brought because of her naivety and raw desire, Kaotica had taught him there was more to darkness than the opposite of light. Though she had been born from the gloom and shadows of Kaylan's soul and been destined only to destroy, she sacrificed everything for her opposite half to live.

As his thoughts drifted over the images of the two girls he had lost in his quest over forty years ago, the sage was brought back to his senses by the footsteps of someone entering the chamber behind him. Turning around with his black robe twisting about his frame, the sage found Jax Morrol entering the room and walking around the table to extend his hand out in greeting. Lifting back his hood to reveal his face, Revond took his hand and shook it.

"Hello again, Master Sage," Morrol greeted with a smile. "I'm sorry to keep you waiting—I wasn't expecting you so quickly."

"My apologies, Sarton," Revond said. "Your guard and the refugees were most hospitable in providing us with food and drink to keep us occupied, but as I'm sure you can guess I have little time and must be quick about all my business." Morrol released his hand and gestured for the sage to sit at the table along the side near the balcony.

"Of course," he stated understandingly. "Apologize for nothing, my friend. Can I get you a drink? I'm afraid all we have is water." Revond thankfully declined, to which the Sarton took a seat across from him, folding his hands together on the table. "So what is this business of yours, Master Revond? And how did you know of our city?"

"I didn't actually," Revond returned. "I was brought here by my guide, Lucan Hauk Erland. He is a wandering Maven who up until recently has been fighting converts in the east and helping what free people he could. He and the other Maven named Maglin Byre had collectively heard of this hidden shelter. None of us had any idea it would turn out to be such an elaborate refuge."

"Yes, Ceruleana is responsible for the lives of all the refugees present here," Morrol confirmed, nodding his head. "If not for this shelter I don't know what we would have done. And yet, I fear we cannot outlast the Ancients here forever. I haven't the heart to lay such concerns on the already frightened people down there, but my few men and I know it is only a matter of time before the destruction of the world above us eventually reaches our doors."

"Your worries are well founded, Sarton," Revond told him calmly but with a grave tone. "Which is why I am happy to bring you hope that we may yet be able to stop the rampage the Ancients wreaked during their Ascension." Morrol sat forward in his seat at this, his hands gradually pulling apart and his eyes spreading wide.

"What?" he asked as if awestruck.

"It is true," Revond responded with confident eyes. "Though the elemental Sources are lost to us—held captive by the Ancients for their dark designs—I have found other means to anoint a new group of Elemental Warriors and am searching for men and women across the Southland to recruit for this charge. With new Elemental Warriors we can challenge the Ancients and take the Sources back to restore life to Iairia. I am here looking for a candidate to become the Warrior of Water and I am hoping you can suggest a man or woman you would feel capable to bear the responsibility." Morrol was speechless at this, barely able to believe what he heard. Raising a hand to gently pass over his beard as his eyes shifted up and down the table, he at last met the Revond's gaze again.

"Elemental Warriors," he repeated as if an almost forgotten myth from a lost past.

"Indeed," Revond confirmed. "I am in need of someone with skill as a combatant, able to think quickly and rationally in the face of conflict and danger. A natural leader. He or she must be courageous and stout hearted, for the trial that lies in wait for this person will be perilous to say the least." Morrol was quiet again at this, his smile fading.

"Well, I can't begin to express my happiness of this news, Master Sage, but I..." he trailed off there, prompting a confused and surprised look on Revond's face. "You may have come to the wrong place looking for such a warrior, Master Revond. The few men I have here are a collection of random patrols of the Legion that fled their posts after the attack on Torrentcia began—it's the only reason they are still alive. My elite guard are all dead. And with more and more of the men I send out on patrols or reconnaissance missions not returning, I'm afraid I'm terribly shorthanded as it is. I can't afford to spare any of them." Revond was silent at this, half disturbed and half awestruck. Forcing himself to keep his cool, the sage took in a deep breath and shifted in his seat.

"Well what of the refugees?" he asked, glancing down at the city behind him off of the balcony. "Surely there is at least one among them strong and experienced enough to take up the mantle of the Warrior of Water." Morrol's expression remained skeptical and he shook his head.

"In the long months we have been crammed into this cave I have met and gotten to know each and every one of the men, women and children living down there," he stated. "Most of them are commoners from the capital city or bordering villages, but none of them are any kind of warriors. There are a few strong and determined men among them who might agree to step up to what you are asking under different circumstances, but all of them have families to be responsible for. I fear you would have no better luck with them." Revond felt his temper slipping a little at this and let out a sharp huff of dissatisfaction at the Sarton's unexpectedly negative responses.

"With all due respect, Sarton," the sage began, "we are in the most desperate of situations and I need a Warrior of Water born and raised in the wetlands. You have said yourself these people are all that remain of that group. Under the circumstances I am prepared to be lax with my judgment on traditional standards required for this title—courage will suffice. Perhaps if you would but let me ask one of them they could answer for themselves."

"To be honest, Master Sage," Morrol said, leaning forward again, "I'm trying to keep these people safe, not put them in harm's way. It isn't that I don't trust you or your plan, but I have seen first hand the indiscriminate power of the Ancients and I am doubtful even Elemental Warriors can hope to stand up to them without the Sources in our possession. Even with courage what chance do you think any of them would have facing the fury of one of those beasts roaring out in front of them? I am the only man in the cavern with any real combat experience."

"Then why not you, Sarton?" Revond asked quickly. Morrol paused for a moment but quickly rejected the idea, shaking his head and groping for the words to respond while maintaining his civility.

"Out of the question," he returned at last. "I can say with no ego I am the only chance these people have to survive the coming winter. If this sanctuary should be compromised they will need my leadership to get them out and away safely."

"You know as well as I that should this cavern be found by Ancients with these people inside, not one of them would escape alive, Morrol," Revond returned sharply. "Your only act on their behalf would be to courageously die by an

Ancient's tooth or claw. But if you come with me and become the Warrior of Water you will have an opportunity to stand against the beasts and deal a fatal blow to their evil once and for all. With that power you can bring your people out of this dank cave and back into the sunlight where they belong. You would serve them best by leaving with me."

"I'm afraid I can't take that chance, Master Sage," Morrol replied, shaking his head. "I wish you luck on your recruiting but you won't find any people here up to the challenge. I've got a cave full of them I'm trying to keep alive." Revond narrowed his eyes in antagonism at this, leaning in over the table.

"You're only letting them die slower, Morrol," he said in a nearly menacing tone. "You said yourself you won't last in here forever. What will you do when the Ancients track you here? If you don't take a stand now all of these people will die. They can continue on without you if they have to for the immediate future, but eventually this sanctuary will fall. That isn't a responsibility you want on your head." Morrol rose from the table, keeping his eyes on the sage.

"I'm afraid I will say no more on the matter, Master Sage," he stated simply. Revond found himself glaring at the Sarton at this, pushing back his chair and rising as well. Staring him down for a long moment in the silence broken only by the waterfall and the faint embers crackling off torches on the walls, Revond at last flipped his hood up over his head and spun around, making his way for the door of the chamber. When he reached it he turned his head back to address the Sarton a final time.

"I appreciate your concern for your people, Sarton," he began, "but your lack of action on this matter condemns them to death. You can dig your own grave if that is your wish, but I cannot let you stand in the way of this effort. Whether you like it or not, I am going to ask your people for a volunteer. If there is one among them with the courage to do what you will not, that person will be welcome to join me." Morrol was still but narrowed his heated eyes at the sage.

"I forbid it," he said in a low rumble.

"Again, with all due respect, Sarton," Revond replied, "try to stop me." With that, he turned back to begin walking down the steps and out of the Sarton's Watch back into the open cave. Leaving the Sarton standing alone in the silence behind him, Revond felt more frustrated than he had been since the Ascension began, amazed at the lack of foresight and wisdom from the man he hoped would possess both. Clenching his fists within his cloak as he began his descent down the ledge leading back to the city, the sage gradually slowed his pace, feeling something strange tingling in the back of his mind. Realizing it was actually a small sensation from the ground racing up his body, Revond identified it as faint tremors shaking the cave around him. Coming to a halt and turning down into the city to look for what could have been amiss, he was surprised to hear the distant but incredibly loud voice of Alberic sounding out above the noise of the waterfall all the way from the side of the lake.

"*Revond!*" he shouted as loud as his voice would carry. "*They are coming!*" His eyes shooting open with alarm hearing this, Revond felt his heart rising in his chest as he felt the vibrations steadily growing to shake the entire cave. Hearing a loud grinding noise from his left, the sage spun around to the waterfall to find the rocks around its mouth shuddering and giving way as a blue scaled skull slammed through it. Watching in horror as the long snakelike body of Vorkoise dropped out of the hole in the cliff wall and plunged down into the lake with water exploding up around him, Revond shouted as loud as he could for the people watching the beast arrive to run. Frightened deeper into the lake by the presence of the beastly Ancient of Water, the Trouck Fish scattered and the light from their scales disappeared leaving the cavern darkened and the entire populace beginning to panic and run out of their houses screaming.

The cave was quickly illuminated once more by the white light of Alberic transforming into his true form and galloping off the ground into the air of the cave. Looking down to the bottom of the ledge Revond saw Lucan and Maglin were already there leading people up the other path leading to the entrance of the city. While they stood herding the rush of Southlander's along, Vorkoise at last reared its snakelike head out of the water with the oversized gills and fins around it fanning out.

Spreading its jaws wide before Alberic could gain too much altitude, the serpent threw its head forward to unleash a torrent of water blasting from its mouth down into the city, consuming anything in its path. Watching in fury as the Ancient blasted away half of the houses and people running out of them for their lives, Alberic thrust himself forward over the lake to charge his watery brother head on. Soaring around the incoming beam of water spraying from its wide jaws, Alberic flew over its head to pound his golden hooves into it and force Vorkoise to relinquish its attack, shrieking out in pain as Alberic lifted higher into the cave.

Back on the top of the ledge beside the Sarton's Watch, Morrol had ran out of his structure to observe the Ancient inside Ceruleana. Crying out for his few men, he drew his sword and ordered them down into the city. Though Revond shouted out for him to wait as Morrol and his men ran past him down the ledge for their people, the sage knew he must first contain Vorkoise and set his open hands together to begin summoning a white ball of energy between them. Before he could launch an attack of Hallador Might down on the serpent, however, he was surprised to feel another massive quake ripping through the cavern that disrupted his concentration and almost dropped him to his feet. Hearing a near deafening crash of rock from above him, the sage looked up to find the hulking form of Golthrout dropping down out of the smashed ceiling of the cave to slam down into the city with a crash that shook the very foundations of the earth.

Landing amid the pile of blasted houses while crushing several more beneath his rocky feet, the Ancient of Earth began smashing its arms down after the retreating humans. Watching as the minotaur's fists slammed down onto several refugees, Revond cursed out and rose full length to muster his mystic power again. This time in the form of a raging ball of white electricity between his hands, Revond threw them down toward Golthrout with his fingers spread to send several cracking bolts of lightning flying into his gravely exterior and blasting free small segments of stone where they landed. Tripping back in shock and pain, the Ancient fell onto its backside, struggling to rise.

Watching as Revond and Alberic contended with the two Ancients, Lucan and Maglin continued leading what refugees had survived the initial attack up the ledge toward the exit of the cave. Lining up on either side of the cave door, they directed the slow and frightened people out first, telling them to run south when they came to the exit of the cave. The two held their ground until every last man, woman and child had escaped the cavern and was safely ascending the staircase leading out. When Maglin asked above the chaos erupting if they should stay with Revond and Alberic or flee with the others, Lucan wasn't sure what to tell her and shifted his gaze back to Alberic. The Ancient of Light was diving down to slam into Vorkoise again as the serpent attempted to clamp its beastly jaws down while he passed. Though not wanting to leave his or the Master Sage's side, Lucan knew that Revond would tell him his first responsibility was to ensure the safety of the otherwise defenseless people.

Spinning around to tell Maglin they had to follow the refugees out and lead them to safety, he noticed a strange light in the corner of his eye and looked into the staircase to observe a heavy red glow appearing on the walls. Horrified to hear the sudden sound of screams echoing down the staircase, Lucan felt an uncomfortable warmth radiating within. Dreading another Ancient had found them, his fears were confirmed when a jet of fire raced out of the exit of the cave passing directly between him and Maglin. Falling over onto their backsides in surprise, the two Mavens watched as a final bloodstain was sprayed against the stairs and the beastly form of Moltar came slamming its way down the stairs toward them, furiously roaring as it came. Though the two struggled to rise Lucan knew they wouldn't be able to outrun it and even it they could they were trapped in the cave. Moltar had killed every one of the refugees that passed up the stairs and now it was coming for them.

Preparing for the flaming cat to squirm through the tight passage and lunge out at them, Lucan was surprised to find a mighty jet of wind slam past them into the staircase causing the Ancient of Fire to scream out when its fiery skin was temporarily blown out. Looking behind him, Lucan saw the white horse dropping onto the ledge beside them, ordering them to mount him at once. Doing as they were told, the two Mavens scrambled to jump onto his back as he began galloping into the air spreading his feathered wings wide again. Bellowing for the humans to hold on, Alberic swung to his left to avoid a coming rush of water from Vorkoise still blasting out at him from the lake. Swooping down and back up past Golthrout to the opposite ridge where a lone figure stood raining white fire and lightning down on the two monsters, Alberic shouted out and landed beside him.

"We are overwhelmed!" he shouted with his usually majestic voice shaking. "They share a telepathic link; Dalorosk and Wyrik are surely on their way here as we speak if they have not already arrived! If they do we will never escape! We must be away!" Though shouting out in rage as he unleashed another flurry of lightning down onto Vorkoise that spiraled and constricted his long body, Revond at last wheeled around and leapt up onto the Ancient of Light's back behind Lucan and Valeri.

"Down to those men at the base of the ledge first!" Revond shouted, pointing to Morrol and his last surviving guard as they struggled to drive into the city shouting for survivors. Running down the path with incredible speed as his golden hooves left behind surges of light with every step, Alberic quickly reached the base where the Sarton and his man turned to face them. Reaching down as they ran by to seize both Morrol and the Legionnaire with his mystic grip, he lifted them onto Alberic's back as the horse spread his wings and beat them hard to lift above a slab of cerulean stone thrown at them by Golthrout. Though they soared just above it and Alberic managed to kick off it as it passed under his hooves, in the turbulence Revond lost his grip on the Legionnaire and the man was caught by a fragment of falling rock to be pulled back to the ground to his doom.

Lifting up into the cave as hard and fast as he could, Alberic narrowly dodged as many of the attacks as he could. As they passed above the ledges again, he was forced to bank to his right as Moltar's entire body came leaping out for them, grazing Alberic's tail but otherwise missing them. Seeing the horse struggling to regain its altitude and balance in the barrage, Vorkoise spread its jaws to unleash a final beam of speeding water up for them. Seeing the attack coming, the Master Sage Revond brought up his free right and focused hard to halt the attack with his mind, holding it back as if with a massive invisible shield as he had done once before many years ago. Struggling to hold onto Morrol's struggling form while he held back the wall of water, Revond shouted for Alberic to hurry for the hole Golthrout had punctured in the ceiling. Rising through it and passing through a dangerously narrow tunnel of sharp splintered stone on their way to the surface of earth, Alberic at last lifted clear of the cave and emerged back into the open air to land on the ground.

Pulling in his wings to rest them for a moment, the Ancient of Light began running hard and looking around for any sign of either of the two winged Ancients waiting for them. Not seeing any sign of them yet, Alberic turned his head back to yell at Revond.

"We were lucky," he shouted as he ran. "They must have been looking for us in the area but stumbled upon the cave by pure chance."

"Then Dalorosk and Wyrik are probably coming from the north and east," Revond shouted back. "Head southwest as quickly as you can." Nodding his head and spreading his wings again, Alberic lifted them off the ground and into the sky with his momentum to hasten their ascent. Lifting up into the night sky past the clouds, the group disappeared from view below with only Sarton Morrol's cries of pain and lament filling the air.

Chapter 32

<u>Drakkaidian</u>

Aeric slept in the wooden chair beside Valeri's bed during their night in the recluse's house beside the Crag Spires. Though the man who called himself only Drakkaidian told him of another room he could use which Valeri implored him to take advantage of, the Grandarian wanted to stay beside her through the night to keep a constant vigil on her wounds and tend to her if she needed him. Neither of them got much sleep as a result: Valeri in constant pain through the night and Aeric forcing himself to stay awake to monitor her.

Though her bleeding had completely stopped and her wounds were as clean as could be, the side effects of the strange liquids and herbs Drakkaidian had used to mend her and supposedly restore her strength gripped the princess in agony through the night, burning pain searing across her right side and arm. As the hours rolled by Aeric fetched her water and wiped the beading sweat from her face as she cringed in anguish. He even let the powerful Warrior of Darkness grip his hand when she tensed up to let her know he was there, though it felt like she was breaking his bones with her vice-like grip.

By the time morning came Valeri had finally gotten a few hours of sleep, falling into her dreams while clutching her caregiver's hand. Aeric woke a few hours after dawn to the sound of someone shuffling about in the central room of the house beyond their closed door. His tired blue eyes slowly opened to gaze around the room, at first not remembering where he was. Feeling the Drakkaidian princess' hand in his, he looked down to observe her sleeping peacefully on the bed beside him and remembered all that had transpired the previous day from entering the Crag Spires to being rescued by the mysterious recluse who agreed to aid them in their search for the Scavenger, revealed to be a witch named Sakkdra.

Leaning forward in his chair to sweep his gaze up and down Valeri's frame and see how she looked after a night's rest, he observed her skin had regained much of its color and her bandages were still clean with no trace of any blood. She had kicked off the blanket over her in the night, bunched in a wad around her feet leaving her bare legs exposed. In the night Aeric stripped off the last of her ripped and dirtied clothing, leaving her only in undergarments and the simple white tunic he had slipped over her upper body to cover her revealed frame. Apparently it was a dangerous risk to leave the scent of blood even indoors for long in the Crag Spires. Drakkaidian quickly took her stained garb outside to bury it, leaving only her gray shawl and crimson gauntlets and grieves.

Though not seriously wounded himself, Aeric had been more stressed and mentally spent in the past night than since first arriving in the apocalyptic world from the Sage's Draught. With the powerful princess lying incapacitated and the next part of the daunting journey still lying before him, the Grandarian felt hopelessness taking hold of his heart again. Even though they had found the mysterious recluse and they still had their trump card in the Source of Light, with Valeri so severely injured and the road ahead anything but certain except for the ever present peril, it seemed like Aeric's chances of saving Mina and restoring their world before the Ascension were dissipating with every failing breath the princess exhaled. Though Drakkaidian had promised she would make a full recovery once her bleeding had abated, Aeric retained his doubts that so serious a wound could be healed so quickly if at all.

The Grandarian let his eyes gravitate toward her sleeping face. He wasn't used to seeing her usually commanding and indomitable visage so gentle and serene. Though belied by the immense power she wielded in battle and on her throne, when her guard was down she was beautiful like a fragile flower alone in an otherwise barren field. She had the look of an uncomplicated and innocent girl out of place amid such dangerous affairs. Remembering the few casual talks they had shared when she chose to willingly reveal herself this way to him, Aeric knew his concern was not about losing the strongest warrior in his party that would help him find the crests, but the only friend he had among them.

Letting his eyes slip up and down the curves of the sleeping princess' body, he jolted up in his seat when he heard a quick knock at his door followed by a raspy voice telling him to wake and prepare Valeri for the day. Recognizing the voice as the old man's but hearing him walk away, Aeric gradually relaxed and felt his face flush with color, turning his gaze away from Valeri's revealed form. Surprised at his constant fixation on the princess when before it was all he could do to think of anything but Mina, Aeric suddenly felt uncomfortable with where his thoughts were leading him. Taking a deep breath and remembering the necessary gap he had to maintain between them, he forced himself to refocus his association with the princess.

As he was about to gently tug on her hand and try to wake her, however, he was surprised to feel her fingers tighten around his. Shifting his gaze to her face, he saw the girl stirring and her eyes unhurriedly slipping open. Looking around as if to get her bearings, she spied Aeric sitting beside her, freezing as their eyes met. Though still heavy from sleeping, Aeric could see the girl's crimson irises alive with color again. He guessed Drakkaidian's care coupled with the little rest her body allowed her had done its work well and she was going to pull through. Remembering the long night behind her and how Aeric had tended to her every need and wince of pain throughout it all, the princess could only faintly smile and keep her hand in his.

"Thank you, Aeric," she uttered almost inaudibly as she searched for her voice. Aeric shook his head modestly and swallowed to clear his throat.

"How do you feel?" he asked, glancing down her side again. Valeri's smile faded and she looked down to her wounds as well.

"I'm not sure," she replied with palpable nervousness in her voice. "The burning pain is gone but there's this heavy ache across my entire body—almost numbing. But I feel like I have my energy back." Though Aeric was about to tell her to stay in bed until he could gather her some food and water, she released his hand and slowly lifted herself upright in the bed, swinging her bare legs out over the side to gently place her feet on the cold wooden floor. Though her breathing was tense as she struggled to move on her own for the first time since the Arnosmn slashed her, her disciplined strength won out over her fatigue and soreness and she slowly rose to stand beside the bed. Though she looked a little unsteady as Aeric rose from his chair to offer his support, she brushed him away and took a deep breath. The young Tieloc was amazed that she could find her energy so quickly after being so gravely wounded the day before.

Telling her that Drakkaidian ordered them to get up and prepare, the two wiped away their sleep and groomed themselves as best they could with the last clean bucket of soap and water on the floor. Once they had refreshed themselves Aeric turned while Valeri pulled off the white tunic she wore and attempted to dress. Reaching for the stack of clothes Drakkaidian had left them the previous night, she pulled on a loose black tunic and traveling pants obviously intended for a medium sized man. She could only pull the tunic around her neck and the pants to her ankles, quickly discovering that she couldn't lean or stretch too far or the wound on her side would throb with her stitches pulling tight.

Though uncomfortable and humiliated, the proud Drakkaidian princess asked Aeric to help her dress. Trying to keep his eyes off her half revealed body as he finished pulling down her tunic and lifting her pants up her smooth legs, Aeric finished by draping her gray shawl over her head and strapping her light armor over her forearms and legs. He took particular care not to pull the leather straps holding the armor on too tight on her right arm, remembering the wound on its underside, and tucked her feet into thick socks and old boots. The whole while Valeri stood quietly, staring at him tenderly securing her attire as best he could while taking care not to rush and hurt her.

When they were both dressed again, Aeric picked up their traveling packs with one hand and helped bolster Valeri with his other. Insisting on her leaning against him with her left arm over his shoulders until she was walking on her own again, the two unhurriedly made their way to the door and opened it, revealing them to the occupants of the central room. Rising from their chairs around a wide table were Asthatch, Markus Desrum and the last soldier, all tightening with worry at the sight of their princess weakly standing with an arm draped over the young man beside her. Observing her men standing at attention, Valeri attempted to straighten herself up as best she could and restore her usual strong expression to her visage. Though gently pushing Aeric back and trying to stand by herself, the princess lost her balance for a moment and cringed, forcing Aeric to swing in and lift her back up. Seeing the young Montrox so weak, Asthatch crashed forward knocking over a chair to rush to her side with worried eyes.

"Your Highness," he started looking her over, "please let me assist you." Though ready to shove Aeric out of the way and support her by himself, Valeri shook her head and pulled closer to Aeric.

"I'm fine, captain," she said with her voice strong and resolute in spite of the aching pain from her side. "Master Tieloc has proven himself more than capable of tending to me. Just give me some room, please." Though a look of confusion and conflict spread over Asthatch's face, he let down his arms primed to lift her up and took a hesitant step back.

"How bad is it really, Valeri?" he asked solemnly, breaking his usually sharp discipline to address her by her first name.

"Thanks to our host and Aeric," she said, repositioning herself against Aeric to eventually lift free of him and stand on her own, "I'll live. Whatever this Drakkaidian did to treat my wounds, his methods were effective. I'm still fairly sore and my mobility is severely lessened but I will be able to press on." Aeric shot her a perturbed glance, knowing full well she was putting her condition lightly. Though Asthatch was about to tell her to slow down and tell him everything that the recluse had done to her over the past night, another voice entered the chamber from another room on the back side of the house.

"Montroxs have a renowned aversion to death," it said followed by a few coughs from the old man who spoke. Turning their heads, the group found the one who called himself Drakkaidian walking into the room with his walking stick helping to prop him up. Though scanning the faces of all before him, he quickly placed his prickly gaze on Valeri, dressed and standing on her own. "Feeling better, Highness?" Valeri's face remained impassive but she gave him a single nod and replied yes.

"As I said," she spoke in her noble tone, "well enough to press on. Does your offer to help us still stand?" Drakkaidian continued walking up to her until stopping to lean his weight against his staff with both of his wrinkled hands over it.

"I am a man of my word," he answered with a single nod. "Including when I told you we must be away quickly if you are serious about this journey. I've already fed your men. Take a moment to eat with the boy then we must be off."

"Hold your tongue there, old one," Asthatch interjected quickly. "I don't know what kind of deal you arranged with the princess last night but she is obviously in no condition to travel in her state. We will leave when she is ready."

"And I will be the judge of that, captain," Valeri answered for him. Asthatch and the others turned to face her as she continued. "This man is indeed the recluse we came to find and he has agreed to lead us to the Scavenger that lies further north in the Black Peaks. As you know we have little time to find the crests for Master Sage Revond before he returns to Hadecrest with the Ancients surely not far behind. We set off again today." Though Asthatch was about to speak with his face tightening with anger at her order, Markus Desrum stepped forward to preclude him from erupting.

"Your Highness, look at yourself," he said with a gesture of his hand out to her middle. "You are critically wounded and lucky to be alive. Even you with all your power are in no condition to travel further into the most dangerous mountains in Iairia. You must give yourself time to heal."

"Every minute we lose standing here is one more our enemies have to search us out and destroy us before we are ready to face them," Valeri shot back, her voice determined and powerful. "Even now I can sense dark power exploding across Drakkaidia coming from Dalorosk. He is closing in on us. We must find those crests now." Seeing both Desrum and Asthatch about to object further, Valeri's face locked up with anger and she raised a hand for silence, gritting her teeth. "My orders stand. We go north with Drakkaidian to guide us."

"He is coming with us?" Asthatch asked incredulously. "He can barely walk!"

"Just like your princess, captain," Drakkaidian chimed in with a dark smile on his bearded face. Asthatch glared at him and raised a finger to his face.

"Do not push me, old man," he growled. "I still know nothing of you and don't trust you at all."

"Trust this," the recluse said raising his eyebrows at Asthatch. "I saved the life of everyone in this room; fed and watered you all; used my best Lacerative Liquids on Princess

Montrox; and have agreed to risk my life leading you to the most dangerous place in Iairia. If I wished any of you harm I would have left you in the Crag Spires to die. But seeing as the girl is my princess as well and the boy is a Tieloc, I am compelled to offer what aid I can. And all that I ask in return is your cooperation and compliance as I lead you to your destination. If I don't get it, well, you can find your own way to where you're going." Asthatch was silent at that, distrustfully staring the old man down. At last Valeri spoke again.

"You have our cooperation, Drakkaidian," she confirmed. Nodding, the old man told Valeri and Aeric to sit while he gathered them some food from his storage room. While they sat waiting for him to return, Valeri and Aeric explained all they had learned from Drakkaidian the previous night about the identity of the Scavenger and where their journey was about to lead them. Though the others were skeptical at best that the recluse knew what he was talking about or that he could successfully get them to the mythical Lake of the Undead, they realized it was their only option and time was running out.

After they ate breakfast and refreshed their supplies, Drakkaidian put on his black robe and walked out the front door of his house with the remaining party from Hadecrest behind him. Locking his house and dousing the lamp beside the front door, he turned and began walking out of the small depression where the house sat to the north end and a slope leading back to the cliffs beside the Crag Spires. Though the ground around them still hung over the deep canyon that lay beneath most of the spires, Drakkaidian informed them as they were leaving that they had made it through the worst of the Crag Spires and would be far beyond it by the end of the day.

Though all of them felt better at this revelation, their spirits were further lowered when Drakkaidian informed them there was far more dangerous ground lying in wait for them on the road to the Lake of the Undead. Warning them that they would have to pass over high mountain ridges possibly snowcapped even in the summer and then the infamous Electric Flats that led into the valley where the lake rested, the old man informed them plainly that most of them probably wouldn't make it to their destination, himself included. Though taking solace in the fact that he had traveled this route before and knew of the safest road to take through the mountains, the entire group saw Drakkaidian constantly looking around in the skies and the horizon for any sign of what they guessed to be more demons. The group traveled on for several hours at a much slower pace than they had originally maintained upon leaving Hadecrest, thanks to Drakkaidian's age and Valeri's wounds keeping her ambling forward at a sluggish pace.

Though she required help from Aeric and Asthatch as they marched to get over hazardous terrain and climb slopes, they were all shocked to see the old recluse leaping across gaps in the rocks and climbing up steep roads with impossible speed and strength for a man his age. Watching him use his staff to push a heavy rock down a slope to gauge its durability, Aeric turned to Valeri to ask her if she had any clue to who this man could have been in his younger years to be capable of such feats and have knowledge of so much. Though she remained silent and merely shrugged, Aeric could see her thinking and eyeing the old man the way she had eyed him when they first met, obviously having at least a suspicion.

The Grandarian kept pace alongside Valeri for the entire morning and most of the afternoon after departing from Drakkaidian's house and the end of the Crag Spires, helping her along rough spots in their road and making sure she was as comfortable as possible. When they set out Aeric had guessed that Valeri would try to keep him at arm's length in their travels, wanting to prove she could get by on her own. She had always been the one helping him along prior to being wounded and with their roles reversed he assumed her fierce pride would keep her from asking for as much help as possible.

As the hours rolled by, however, Aeric was surprised to find the princess allowing him to stay at her side and help her whenever he deemed necessary. Though he rightly predicted she would virtually never ask for his help, she wordlessly accepted it whenever he offered, allowing him to lift her over obstacles, lean against him when she grew tired, and give her water whenever he thought she looked thirsty. Though she ordered Asthatch and Desrum back into formation behind her when they tried to assist Aeric, Valeri let the Grandarian stay by her side the entire day. Aside from pondering over the true identify of Drakkaidian on occasion, they conversed little, both content in their silent presence. Though Aeric frequently wondered why she had suddenly opened up to him even if only by letting her physical guard down to him exclusively, he guessed it was for the same unknown reason he felt better beside her as well. It was as if just walking beside her and helping the princess move gave him a new purpose and sense of responsibility he could assume on their quest.

As the afternoon began to transform into early evening and the daylight began to fade behind the thick rolling billows above them in the sky, Aeric finally left Valeri's side when she asked him for a moment to consult with Asthatch about their new guide. The two could frequently hear the captain grumbling about the situation to Desrum as they walked and Valeri wanted to assure him she knew what she was doing. Agreeing to give her a moment Aeric walked on past her, repositioning the brown pack on his back and the sword against his waist. They were passing between a gap in two mountainsides coming together to form a wedge, leading down to a flat surface where dark green shrubbery grew. Looking ahead down the jagged path, Aeric scanned the road for Drakkaidian but couldn't spot the old man anywhere. Raising his brow doubtfully, he was surprised to find the old man appear to his right behind a turn in the road on a boulder. Using his staff to secure a position on its surface and bolster him up as he looked over the road ahead, he jumped down. Landing beside the Grandarian with a grunt, Aeric was again surprised at his agility and endurance and stared at him uncertainly.

"How old are you, if you don't mind me asking?" Aeric asked carefully as he paused and waited for Drakkaidian to rise. The old man merely glanced at him and tucked his black robe tighter around his body as a chilly breeze blew down through the wedge in the mountains.

"I do mind," he returned brusquely, beginning to walk again. Though frowning, Aeric strode up next to him and walked alongside him.

"You know, I appreciate your help us and the sacrifices you're obviously making to lead us to this lake, but since we're trusting you to lead us there maybe you could trust us enough to tell us a little about yourself," Aeric began. "You already know who we are. Are you ever going to tell us who you are?" The old man kept his gaze ahead of him as he continued testing the ground with his staff to make sure his footing was secure before stepping down the slope.

"I don't see how that matters," Drakkaidian replied. "I would have thought you'd be able to surmise from the fact that if a man chooses to live isolated in a place like the Crag Spires beyond the reach of civilization that he doesn't want anyone—the princess of Drakkaidia or not—to know who he is."

"Well since civilization seems to have found you anyway," Aeric pressed on though taking note of the old man's increasingly frustrated tone, "maybe you could at least tell me what you once were to know all that you do. I mean, you're a tracker who knows the Black Peaks, a healer with skills beyond anything I've ever seen, you're knowledgeable about things no one else in Iairia is including the Mystic Sages, and even at your age you're still a skilled combatant against humans and demons alike. If you're going to leave it up to me to piece together who you are, I'd guess you were once someone of great influence in Drakkaidia who must have done or seen something very unfavorable to willingly exile himself to the Crag Spires, of all places."

"Perhaps I just found the Crag Spires an ideal spot to finish out my days," Drakkaidian returned blankly.

"It's hardly a desirable place to retire after an obvious lifetime of service to your country, if what you said yesterday about serving Drakkaidia was true," Aeric said citing the conversation from the previous night.

"It suits me," the recluse said. "A crumbling heap of rocks that have been worn down by the elements over their longs years for a crumbling old man worn down by elements of his own." Drakkaidian turned to stare into the Grandarian's curious eyes then, his face suddenly challenging. "Or perhaps, my naïve Grandarian, I was driven here against my will. Perhaps I was forced to flee here because of my horrible past and the more horrible things I did. Perhaps I am a dangerous criminal once wanted dead or alive for the horrendous atrocities I unleashed on innocent people. What if that were the case, young Tieloc? Would you still want to know about my past then?" Aeric held the old man's admittedly frightening gaze for a long moment as they continued walking, not breaking away.

"If any of that were true," Aeric answered at last, "and you were some long lost killer or whatever you're painting yourself to be, I don't think it matters now anyway. However you ended up out here, you went far out of your way to save Valeri and the rest of us and now you're risking everything to help us save the world. Those are pretty noble intentions if you ask me. You've already revealed the essence of your character, Drakkaidian, so don't waste your time trying to convince me otherwise." Drakkaidian studied the seemingly impervious face of the young man for a long moment after he stopped, his own visage going blank. At last he turned to place his view back in front of him.

"You really are your grandfather's kin," he said, making Aeric narrow his eyes uncertainly. Though about to ask him what that meant or how he knew of his grandfather to make such a statement, he was cut off by Drakkaidian asking a question of his own. "When did he die?" Aeric was silent at this, confused until the old recluse turned to him again. "Your grandfather. When did he die?"

"Several years ago," Aeric answered hesitantly.

"How did he go?" Drakkaidian pressed, his tone emotionless but genuinely curious. Though more curious at why he cared to know, Aeric answered him, thinking back to what he remembered of his grandfather's passing.

"Living out his legacy," the young Tieloc responded as he shifted his gaze into space before him, remembering. "In his last years Grandfather Tavin lived more in Eirinor than in Galantia, wanting to spend most of his time with his family after my grandmother passed away. He was out for a ride one day when he came across a woman being preyed upon by brigands and he drove them away, bringing the woman back to Eirinor. The brigands caught up to them and he fought them off to protect her with his last breath. He died in my father's arms with his sword still in hand. His funeral in Galantia was the most momentous event since the celebration of the Days of Destiny. The whole country was there; everything stopped for that day to honor him. I was only a child but to this day I've never seen so many people. His body was carried in a golden coffin from Eirinor all the way to Galantia and up to the Golden Castle itself with Grandarians lining the road the entire way and following him. It was amazing."

"A death befitting the true warrior," Drakkaidian said more to himself than Aeric, his voice almost lost to the slight wind. "And a hero." After pausing and staring down to the earth with his pace lessening, the old man spoke again.

"What of your grandmother? How did she pass?" Aeric's brow furrowed at this, his curiosity getting the best of him.

"Why would you care what happened to my family?" he asked almost offended. Drakkaidian spun his head to face him with his eyes flaring.

"You expect answers to all your questions but refuse to answer mine?" he questioned heatedly. Aeric frowned but saw his point and decided to answer, not seeing any harm.

"She passed away in her sleep in Galantia almost two years before my grandfather died," Aeric told him. Drakkaidian was quiet again at this, letting a much longer silence hang between them. At last when the two were coming to the base of the sloping wedge and the flat expanse between the mountain basins he raised his head and took a deep breath.

"The details of my life are inconsequential," the old man said, getting Aeric's attention. "I was a warrior who fought many battles on many fronts and learned many facets of life from them all—too many for my own good. I came to the peaks to find rest in the final days of my long life. And yet it seems fate has planned one last venture for me before my time is done. Does that satisfy you, Aeric Tieloc?" Aeric was quiet at this, realizing he should be thankful to have obtained even this much from the reclusive man.

"All right," he confirmed. "Thank you." Drakkaidian didn't say anything but shot another glance at the young Tieloc, coughing and hurrying his pace along the rare flat between slopes. Both he and Aeric stopped as they heard Valeri's voice suddenly soar behind them, yelling out loud. Turning they found her angrily staring down Asthatch at the end of the slope several feet behind them. Looking at the princess to see what had her upset, Aeric could see her face fuming and losing control of her temper.

"I'll say it again, Asthatch—I know what I'm doing!" she shouted. The Drakkaidian captain returned her angered expression, throwing his arms up exasperated.

"We don't know a thing about this man other than Markus recognizing him," he returned struggling to suppress his apparent rage. "He refuses to tell us anything and we have no idea where he may be leading us. How can you trust him?"

"All that is required of you is to trust and obey *me*, captain," Valeri snapped back. "I grow tired of your constant second guessing of my orders."

"Someone has to inform you when you are making a string of irrational decisions, Your Highness," Asthatch returned with his face tightening further. "All I am asking for is the chance to make him tell us our route and who he is so I can ensure your safety. If your father were here he would agree—"

"My father is dead, Asthatch!" she practically screamed, surprising Aeric and all of them as a thin layer of palpable dark energy leapt off her skin into the air around her frame. "I am in charge here! If you want to serve my house, then serve me. If you don't, then I suggest you turn around and head back to Hadecrest. This is our road." Caught up in her storm of emotion, Valeri lost her strength and balance on the sloped ground where she stood. Seeing her about to tip over and fall, both Asthatch and Aeric dashed to her side to grab her before she could. Though Asthatch got to her first and lifted her back up to stand beside him, in her lingering anger and building frustration that she couldn't even stand up on her own, the princess wheeled away from him and pulled her arm out of his grip.

Shooting him an irate glance before spinning around and leaning over with a grimacing face, she met Aeric's gaze with a look that silently told him she needed him. Leaning down to her right side to gently prop her up while she raised her arm behind his back and onto his shoulder, Aeric helped her down from the slope and onto the level ground with Asthatch standing behind them dropping his arms. He stared at the girl with his eyes distraught and wounded at her recoiling from him, having never seen her so upset with him before.

Seeing the Drakkaidian princess wincing as she walked forward with Aeric to help her, the old recluse let out a sharp breath and shook his head.

"You need to rest," he said looking at her. "We'll make camp here tonight. When you build the fire, build it against as much cover as you can and keep it to a few flames. Creatures roam these peaks that see better at night than in broad daylight and would be upon us in moments, if they aren't already thanks to our dramatic little scene." Though Valeri shot the old man an unappreciative glance, she fell further into Aeric, her fatigue from the long day catching up with her. Leading her to a soft spot of soil beside one of the dark bushes growing on the flat, Aeric laid her down and helped the others make a small camp. Darkness descended on them quickly after, making them all nervous at what could be out with them that Drakkaidian warned them of. Asthatch kept his distance from Valeri for the duration of the night, looking to be more distressed than Aeric had ever seen as he watched him eat on the opposite side of the fire and sharpen his massive axe.

Aware the irritable Drakkaidian captain had Valeri's best interests in mind and acted from the heart, Aeric told the princess later in the night that she should try to give him an easier time; that he was probably right to question Drakkaidian for his obstinate nature. Though Valeri responded that her captain needed to obey her without an argument every time they spoke, he made her remember he merely cared for her safety and she was the closest thing to family he had as well. While they ate Aeric quietly told Valeri everything he had learned about Drakkaidian in their conversation before dusk, including his questions about his grandparents. Though Valeri appreciated the clues and sat trying to piece them together for a long time after they finished, she eventually gave up and tried to go to sleep. Once she fell into her dreams Aeric heard Desrum call for him to take over the watch with the other soldier. Though tired, Aeric rose from the princess and wandered to a post on the other side of camp away from the fire beside a bush.

Sitting down with his sword in his lap and his eyes sweeping the darkness of the Black Peaks towering around him, the Grandarian found himself alone with his thoughts again. Though they focused on Mina as they always did when he had a moment to sit and think, the young man found his eyes continually ending up on the silhouette of Valeri's sleeping form across the camp whenever his mind strayed. Having invested so much of himself into her the past few days, he told himself it was only natural he thought about her and the road still laid out before them. In the back of his mind in a place he didn't want to look, though, he knew it wasn't the quest that drew his thoughts to the princess. Shaking off such notions as he sat and tried to imagine life after all this when he was reunited with Mina in Eirinor, an hour slipped by and the rest of his party fell asleep around the embers of the fire.

Just as his shift of watch was coming to a close, Aeric noticed a movement from the right side of their camp and spread his eyes wide to better view it. Though he tensed and prepared to leap up at first, he saw it was only the hobbling form of Drakkaidian wandering into the weak light. Staring at the old recluse as he neared Valeri, Aeric remained still, curious at what he was doing. Looking down at her slumbering form for a long moment, Drakkaidian slowly leaned down to crouch beside her, reaching down for her gray shawl lying next to her. Running his fingers over it, Aeric watched as he lifted up the tip and slowly dragged a finger over the black emblem embroidered on it. Setting it back down, the old man slowly flipped his staff upside down to lift the sharp edge beside the girl's head, lowering it closer to her. Though Aeric tensed at what he saw, his heart nearly leapt out of his chest as he heard a loud shout and witnessed Asthatch leaping over the fire with his cape racing through the embers as he came. Landing beside Drakkaidian with a loud stomp that woke Valeri and the others, he extended the blade of his axe to the recluse's neck and told him to slowly rise.

When Valeri was about to shoot up to see what was going on, she was surprised to see Drakkaidian stab the point of his staff into her shawl with a loud thud. Though Asthatch saw this as a threat and prepared to slice off the old man's head, Valeri lifted up and barked for him to hold. Looking at Drakkaidian still leaning beside her and lifting her shawl with the end of his staff, she narrowed her eyes distrustfully.

"What are you doing with that?" she asked guardedly. The old man merely met her gaze and slowly flipped over her shawl to reveal a large clawed insect impaled through the center by the tip of his staff. Asthatch's expression changed from furious to shocked and he mumbled something.

"A Breok bug," he uttered, staring at the fearsome little creature as it bled liquid from its middle. Drakkaidian rose and pulled off the notoriously poisonous bug with another cloth along his belt and cast it behind a bush. Pulling Valeri's shawl off his staff, he handed it back down to her and wordlessly turned to walk back into the darkness. Realizing he had probably just saved her life, Asthatch loosened his taut frame and slowly placed his axe over his back.

Meeting Valeri's gaze as she looked up to tell him she was fine, he turned to make his way back to his place on the ground, taking care to check for any Breok bugs that might have been around. Though aware Drakkaidian had his excuse for coming to Valeri's side, Aeric sat back down at his place on the edge of camp remembering how he had touched the shawl before saving her. Though he learned a little about the mysterious recluse that day, Aeric couldn't help wondering exactly who he was and what his true motives were for helping them.

Chapter 33

<u>The Trees</u>

After the destruction of Ceruleana and their narrow escape from the Ancients, the Master Sage Revond and his party fled through the night on Alberic's back as far away as they could. Guessing that Dalorosk and Wyrik would converge on the underground city from the north and east, Revond instructed the Ancient of Light to take them southwest into the Grailen Plains. Though the sage asked Lucan if he knew of any rumor of another gathering of people in the south where they could take refuge and hide while the Ancients hunted them, Lucan barely responded, still shaken by the death and devastation he had witnessed that night. The entire party was in dreadfully low spirits as they soared through the clouded skies.

All of them took responsibility for their personal failings that allowed the destruction of perhaps the last free city of humanity in Iairia. Lucan and Maglin were speechless as they traveled, in disbelief they had led the group of refugees that survived the initial attack to their deaths at the molten claws of Moltar, waiting for them at the entrance to the city. Alberic silently cursed himself that he could not better hold off Vorkoise in particular who had heaved up and washed away half of the city in one attack.

Revond was perhaps the most guilt ridden of the group. He couldn't help feeling like he had brought the destruction on them by passing through Ceruleana's door in the first place. Though he didn't believe the Ancients had been tracking them, Golthrout and Moltar arrived too quickly behind Vorkoise for the attack to have been pure chance. His lack of care to keep the group hidden while they traveled had most likely betrayed their position to one of the Ancients in the midlands and resulted in the attack. As they were fleeing the cavern and rising into the sky after their escape, Revond could hear Jax Morrol cursing him and crying out that he had brought this death on them.

The Sarton had been wounded during the escape when Revond seized him and pulled him up to Alberic. His left arm had been broken either by falling rubble from the ceiling or chunks of boulders cast at them by Golthrout. Though Lucan was trying to hold him upright and brace his limb as best he could as they flew, the Blue Maven had been cut down his right leg by a sharp piece of a shell blasted apart by Vorkoise. Steadily bleeding and turning pale as the hours slipped on, Revond knew they were both in bad condition and needed care immediately.

When Lucan and Maglin told Revond they knew of no safe havens or rumored wanderers to the south, the Master Sage was forced to come up with his own idea for their next destination. Though he could think of nothing and no safe place anywhere in the Grailen, when view of the Great Forests appeared on the horizon at dawn, Revond was finally struck with an idea. It was the only place he could think of that might have survived the carnage of the Ascension. If it was still hidden and undamaged it would prove the perfect place to recuperate and reflect.

Directing Alberic toward the woods on the horizon, the party sped toward the Great Forests. Losing hope once more as they reached the boundaries of the western forest, Revond and the others saw the vast trees largely burnt to a crisp. There were sparse pockets of woods here and there that remained only singed and slightly charred, but the vast majority of the forests were blackened and scorched in every direction. Though worried his last hope of a safe haven had been consumed in the fires as well, Revond let Alberic fly on over the forests until all they could see in any direction was burnt trees.

After nearly an hour of watching Revond scan the forests for whatever he was looking for, the others were surprised to find him suddenly shout for Alberic to slow down and take them lower to a small region of woods that were still predominantly green. Dropping their altitude and swinging around to the area Revond pointed to, Alberic slowly passed over the green trees until the sage told him to stop and lower into the forest through the only opening they could see big enough for the winged horse. Dropping down into the tree tops, Lucan and Maglin exchanged curious glances at where Revond could be taking them or what could be out in the middle of the forest. Guessing that they would be as well hidden in the sprawling Great Forests as a needle in a haystack, they trusted Revond and looked out into the trees.

As Alberic descended even farther down, Lucan's eyes widened with surprise to find a series of rope bridges connecting several small wooden huts nestled up against thick tree trunks appearing around him. Spinning his head around to look back, he found an entire village hidden atop the trees with many more of the small huts clumped together around one massive structure resting against the largest tree trunk he had ever seen. Looking down, he observed the village rested several hundred feet above the forest floor, too far below to see. He had never even heard of trees so tall. While he stared down into the endless green of the woods below them, Maglin cast her astonished gaze out to study the strange little huts in the trees, most looking to be hand carved with strange, primitive designs on the walls.

Everything around them was undersized—the huts and bridges looked to be designed for children. There were wooden plank balconies around every tree with a hut, connected by the many bridges swaying back and forth in the open air thanks to a gentle breeze coming down through the trees. Other than the movement of the bridges and the vivid yellow ribbons tied to their edges and some of the houses, the village was devoid of movement. There were no lights in any of the houses; all the torches along the walkways were doused; even the massive structure at the center of the village was tightly boarded up.

As Alberic touched down on the strongest looking balcony he could see in front of the large building and a wide staircase leading up to its doors, Lucan noticed why the village looked deserted. Several of the bridges and huts on the north side had been smashed up and charred as if the fires that consumed the forest had almost reached the village, forcing its habitants, whoever they were, to flee. When the Ancient of Light was finally on the ground with his golden hooves flashing upon impact, he folded in his wings and turned his head back to Revond in silence. While Alberic folded in his feathered wings the Master Sage slowly crawled down from his side and stepped onto the petite balcony. Though Lucan was about to ask where they were the sage heard him

403

preparing to speak and lifted up a hand from his black cloak to motion for silence. Sweeping his eyes through the empty village for several long moments, Revond at last pulled back his hood to reveal his face.

"You can come out, little ones," he called with his voice soaring through the trees into every corner of the village. Lucan and Maglin looked around, wondering if there was someone there they had missed. Seeing no movement of any kind, they looked back at Revond skeptically. "We mean you no harm. I am a friend to the man you once called Graystorm. He was a mentor of mine, and I am a sorcerer like him. My name is Revond. The creature beside me is not one of those that burned the forests—he is an ally of mine, as are the others on his back. We have come to you for help. Some of us are wounded. Please, my friends. Together we can help each other through this dark time. Come out." Baffled at who he thought he was talking to, Lucan and Maglin scanned the trees around them waiting for anything to appear. Though nothing but swaying bridges and ribbons moved for a long moment, at last Maglin caught sight of a little head peeking out from a window of a hut across a bridge from them, followed by a set of hands grasping the side of the hut's doorway.

Rapidly tapping Lucan on the back to get his attention, the Red Maven discreetly pointed out to the hut where the little people were emerging. Noticing them and tilting his head with wonder as he studied them, Lucan felt his jaw slip open as dozens more of the little creatures began appearing from the huts and behind trees, some even dropping down from branches or sliding down trunks. Finding themselves surrounded by over fifty incredibly short and portly people, Lucan and Maglin realized there was no way they could be human, looking more like a strange race of gnomes.

None of them stood more than a few feet tall and they were all dressed in virtually the same primitive green and brown garb. Revond stood motionless as they began to cross bridges and encircle them, staring up with their wide eyes mystified at the white horse standing before them. After several minutes of the creatures gathering around them, they parted to form a path leading to Revond where an older gnome with a long white beard appeared from the crowd to walk toward the sage. Stopping when a few feet away and looking up to his blue eyes so high above his own, the little man spoke.

"Revond," he repeated back to the sage, tilting his head with a sparkle in his eye. Though Lucan wondered if the little humanoid creatures could speak their language or if they were even capable of speech, he doubts were allayed as he saw the man smile and bow. "Any friend of Graystorm's is a friend to the Cronoms. Welcome to Keracon Valley, Revond and friends." The Master Sage let a relieved faint smile appear from the corner of his lips and he bowed his head in response. "I am Yucono, an Elder of Keracon. How can my people assist you?"

"Do you not even wish to hear of who we are in more detail before trusting and helping us, Yucono?" Revond asked. The Cronom merely shook his head and smiled again.

"I knew Graystorm myself when he was still alive," Yucono said. "He saved my life once. If you claim to be his friend we will of course trust you. Come now—which of you is hurt?" Grateful for the Cronom's famed hospitality and kindheartedness that he had read about in writings at the Mystic Tower years before, Revond let out a reassured breath and turned to walk back to Alberic and lift down Jax Morrol, half asleep.

"This man is cut in several places and has fractured his arm," Revond said, looking down at the Sarton he held. "I have another with a deep slash down his leg, and two more in need of rest. I can help you mend this one but—"

"Just carry him into the Grand Hollow behind you, Revond," Yucono replied, turning to motion for several of his kin to come forward. Ordering them to open the hall and prepare the medicine room, a handful of Cronoms rushed forward to climb the stairs to the largest building in the village to open the doors and prepare the way inside. "Take your two wounded inside after my friends. They will see to them. I'm afraid we have lost many of our people to the fires and protecting the valley in recent times, but our home is yours as long as you need it. My people will take the others to a guest hollow at the other side of the village to rest." Kindly thanking the elder for his generosity, Revond rushed up the miniature stairs with Morrol in his arms and disappeared inside the Grand Hollow after the Cronoms, calling for Maglin to help Lucan in after him. Though appreciating her help, Lucan told her he was fine as he dismounted from Alberic's back and limped up the almost comically small stairs behind the sage.

Once his back was free, Alberic transformed back into his human form in a quick flash of light that shocked most of the remaining Cronoms outside and sent a few sprinting back into the village to hide behind huts and tree trunks. When the Ancient of Light finished his transformation he smiled and leaned down on a knee, calling the Cronoms back and telling them not to be afraid. Though hesitant, the small residents of Keracon Valley slowly gathered around him to ask what he was and what he was doing there. Explaining who they all were and what they were doing in their journey across the Southland as best he could to Yucono and the rest of the Cronoms, Alberic told them everything from the truth about the Ascension and the identities of the beasts that had burned the Great Forests to their current plan to stop them.

At the end of his long but summarized story the simple Cronoms were amazed at the tale. When he was finished, Yucono was quick to send for the other elders apparently elsewhere so they could be informed of their guests. Claiming that one of the elders was further hidden on the outskirts of the village tree tops and remaining in place in case the strange visitors they had noticed in the sky in the moments before Alberic appeared were hostile, Yucono ordered for him to be sent for immediately. Asking where the other elder was, Yucono informed the Ancient that she was on the forest floor with a small number of Cronoms checking over the protective fire line they had put in place around Keracon Valley to shield them from the flames that had engulfed much of the forest around them. Again thanking all of them for their help and kindness, Alberic rose and followed them in to the Grand Hollow. While most of the wooden huts around the trees of the village the Cronoms called hollows were very compact, the biggest one he stood in was relatively enormous.

Alberic had seen the valley before millennia ago when it had been much larger and most of it was still on the ground, so he already knew the intricacies of the Cronom's last remaining village after their race fell into decline after the Battle of the Gods and the breaking of the Holy Emerald. The Cronoms were a simple race that lived solely off what they found and crafted from nature. They were a famously good natured race that had become a favorite bedtime story for mothers in the Grailen or the border villages of the Great Forest.

Cronoms lived incredibly long lives, easily tens times that of any human. They did everything together. Several long tables stretched down the central chamber where they all ate as a group once a day. With the exception of the three elders picked from amongst the population, they all took turns fulfilling the daily chores that sustained their small number through their long years. From gathering food and harvesting water from their traps in the leaves that caught rain and dew to lighting torches along the bridges every evening, all of them shared the load of their simple lives.

Since the Ascension Yucono and the other elders had ordered an increased state of cautiousness as they moved about the valley and the forest floor on rare occasion. The flames of Moltar had spread to engulf much of the Great Forest but thanks to their fire breaks and cutting a perimeter around the outskirts of the village they had held the wildfire back and saved most of their homes. Though a great number of Cronoms had died helping to put out the fires around the massive trees of the valley, they endured as they had for eons.

With their guests settling into the Grand Hollow, Yucono ordered his people to disperse back to their own hollows and duties for the day until dinner later that evening. Entering the medicine room adjacent to the entrance of the hollow, Alberic peered in to see Jax Morrol and Lucan lying over two of the three undersized beds in the room with several Cronoms feverishly tending to them. Lucan's leg was already stitched and being covering with a paste they made from crushed white leaves, while Morrol's arm was being set into a splint they had already crafted from scratch. Alberic smiled to see their dedication to the helping others even though they were complete strangers. He didn't have time to enter as Revond appeared from around the corner and exited, asking him to follow him to the steps of the Grand Hollow. Once outside Revond cast his hood back over his head and took a deep breath, looking over the sprawling village of Keracon Valley and silently thanking Granis it was still here. Asking Alberic what if anything he had learned from Yucono, the Ancient of Light informed him how they survived the Ascension and that the other elders were being summoned.

Silently nodding in response, Alberic turned when catching sight of Maglin Byre emerging from the Grand Hollow to walk up to them. She told them the others would be fine and they would be allowed to sleep there under the watch of the Cronoms while the rest of them retired to a guest hollow. Aware she was fatigued after the night in Ceruleana and Alberic was growing tired from the battle and flying them all the way to the Great Forests, Revond told them to go with the Cronoms and rest until evening when they would all meet for the Cronoms' dinner. All too happy to agree, Maglin and Alberic complied and walked down to the little group of Cronoms apparently waiting for them on a balcony leading to a bridge stretching further into the village. Finding himself alone, Revond watched them climb down a short ladder leading to a lower level of the village to be surrounded by bouncing Cronoms with smiles adorning their faces. Turning back to the Grand Hollow, Revond walked back into the medicine room where Morrol and Lucan lay.

Entering to find the Cronoms finishing up the bandages on Lucan and securing the splint on the Sarton's arm, Revond ambled up between their beds. With the Cronoms around him wishing him well and telling him to call if he needed anything, they left Lucan, allowing him to lift both his legs and swing them off the bed to touch the ground again. The Maven smiled up to Revond after feeling his numb leg tingling with some strange sensation brought out by the paste the Cronoms had rubbed over his cuts.

"These little guys are amazing," Lucan said as he watched the last of the Cronoms to have worked on him hopping out of the room. "What is this place, Revond?" The sage shifted in his robes.

"Someplace safe, Lucan," he responded. "The Cronoms are one of the earliest natural races that have existed since the time before the Battle of the Gods. They once occupied every inch of the forests of the world but are now nothing more than a fairy tale, except for this last remaining village, of course. Keracon Valley was built high in the trees so they wouldn't be spotted by humans or Golthrouts that would mean them harm. They are a friendly people who knew Zeroan during his travels so they will trust me. Though they have little dealings with humans, they are expert healers as you will soon be able to attest." Revond turned from the Maven then, looking down to the other man beside him finally sitting up and staring at the sage with a deep frown. "How are you feeling, Sarton?" Morrol's expression remained cold at the sage's question and he sat still and silent for several moments, making Lucan feel uncomfortable as the smile faded from his face. At last he reached down to his side with his undamaged right hand and pulled up the sword fastened into his belt, reaching the tip up to Revond's neck. Though Lucan's eyes widened at what the sage would do, he was surprised to see him remain perfectly calm and still.

"I told you I wanted nothing to do with this," Morrol said, his voice a furious whisper taut with emotion. "I warned you that your actions would only result in ruin for my people. And now thanks to you an entire township was destroyed along with every last person inside." Revond remained calm, speaking sharp and undaunted.

"Except for you," he said, to which the Sarton only pressed his blade closer against the sage's neck. "I am sorry for what happened, Morrol."

"Sorry?" Morrol repeated with his voice shouting. "The last living people I was responsible for were just slaughtered because of you! I knew every last man, woman and child in that cavern! Don't tell me you're sorry, sage. You knowingly brought that destruction with you! You led the Ancients to us!"

"You were the one who opened the doors to your city to me, Sarton," Revond returned.

"You deceived me!" Morrol shouted again, his voice cracking with emotion. "If I had known the Ancients were following you I would have thrown you out of that cavern myself!"

"None of us knew we were being followed, Morrol," Revond replied. "If the Ancients knew our location and were planning a coordinated attack they all would have been there. It is true that the Ancients were looking for us but they stumbled upon your city by unfortunate, random chance. Dalorosk and Wyrik would have been waiting for us in the sky if they knew where we were. Your city would have been discovered if I arrived there or not."

"But they were looking for you!" Morrol barked, a tear falling from his eye down his cheek. Through trying to hold onto his anger to evade his grief and sorrow, the Sarton could not hold out for long and eventually let his sword slowly fall back to his side. Lucan sat silent as he watched Morrol's head fall and his eyes close, weeping. "Now the last of the Southland is destroyed." Though Revond gave him a moment to expel his emotions, he stiffened and stood tall to respond with his voice focused and determined.

"It still has its Sarton," Revond said powerfully. "Which puts you in a unique position, Jax Morrol. I am truly sorry for the tragedy that befell your people. Remember—I have dedicated my life to protecting and serving other lives. I journey to try and save and reclaim as many as I can. And now you have a chance to help me do so. You are perhaps the last Southlander born and raised in the wetlands. You are a warrior and a passionate leader who cares for his people. You are exactly the man I need for the Warrior of Water. As an Elemental Warrior you can aid in saving those who remain and possibly reviving all those who have already fallen. Do not give up on your people now—honor them by taking up this new charge if only until this crisis has abated, Morrol. Help me put an end to the murderous Ancients once and for all." The Sarton was quiet for a moment, his tears subsiding while his face went blank and he stared into the space in front of him. Though speechless for a long moment as he looked back up to Revond, he at last opened his mouth to speak softly.

"It seems as though I have no other choice," he stated with his words still choked with sorrow. "But what use can you get from a warrior with a broken arm, sage?" Revond merely smiled, happy to have his cooperation at last.

"I told you before, Morrol," he replied. "Courage will suffice. Thank you." Morrol merely nodded and laid back on his small bed, resting his head on the pillow and lifting his sword back over his chest. Taking a deep breath, Revond spun around with the tails of his cloak twirling around him and he made his way back to the door to exit the medicine room. As he started for the doors leading out of the Grand Hollow, he heard a voice call for him to wait and he looked back to see Lucan hobbling after him, wincing as he stepped on his cut leg. Waiting for him at the door, the sage observed the concerned and curious expression on the Maven's face.

"Revond," he began stopping before him, "last night in Ceruleana, Alberic told me you two had something to tell me." Revond merely nodded and shifted the weight between his feet as he searched for the words to respond.

"I do indeed," he said. "But it can wait. I need time to think and spread my mind over everything. I am worried our friends in Drakkaidian may not be faring as successfully as us with their venture." Lucan's face locked up with worry.

"Has something happened to Aeric?" he asked quickly with alarm.

"Not that I can sense," Revond returned shaking his head. "But I have sensed Valeri Montrox severely weakened in the past few days and there is... another mysterious power with them. I have sensed it flare up only a few times but it is very potent. And somehow... familiar." Revond trailed off, staring away from Lucan at the end of the Grand Hollow toward a lifted stage where the elders ate every night. "And there is something following them. A terrible demonic power beyond anything I have sensed before."

"Do we need to go help Aeric?" Lucan asked quickly. Shifting his eyes back to Lucan's to see the Maven vexed, Revond raised a hand to place it on his companion's shoulder.

"I'm afraid Aeric and the Drakkaidians are beyond our reach for the moment, my friend," he replied. "We have our own quest to see to, and it may be drawing to its end. For now, just get some rest. We'll meet up this evening for dinner." With that, the Master Sage turned and walked out the door of the Grand Hollow, making his way down the tiny steps into the Cronom village. As Lucan watched him disappear, he looked down at his wounded leg and thought of all the other damage done to their party since they embarked. Lucan could only pray his Grandarian friend was doing better than they.

Chapter 34

<u>The Electric Flat</u>

The recluse called Drakkaidian led the party from Hadecrest deeper north into the Black Peaks for four days after leaving his house on the edge of the Crag Spires, driving them at an arduous pace that surprised them all. Though he led them over some of the most jagged and treacherous mountain roads any of them had ever seen, he pressed on and continually called out for his band to hurry behind him. He usually stood at the front of the group, hiking and climbing with his wooden stick to help him along and his black robe flying back in the wind. Markus Desrum and the other soldier walked behind him, followed by Valeri with Aeric almost always by her side to help her along over the particularly sharp and hazardous obstacles in the road. Though the Drakkaidian princess still needed help on occasion, she had regained much of her former strength in just a few days and her wound looked to be healing at an incredible rate. Though she was still sore and without most of her former mobility, she walked on her own without Aeric's aid most of the time, even jumping and stretching her body to reach rocks she had to lift herself up to as they traveled.

Trailing the two youngest companions in the group was Asthatch at the rear, who had been even more quiet than usual the past few days. Though it wasn't spoken, he and Valeri were still upset with one another and neither of them had any desire to communicate that or try to resolve their conflict, both too proud. The large captain still watched after his charge with constant vigilance and was at her side whenever she needed help, but Valeri brushed him off in favor of Aeric whenever she needed anything. He contained his frustration as they marched but found ways to let it out in between, usually viciously hacking wood for their fire with his oversized axe.

One morning while Valeri ate, he had even sparred with Aeric at the Grandarian's request to try and sharpen his skills with the blade. Obviously the far superior warrior, it was hardly a lesson and more of embarrassment for the Grandarian—constantly parried and batted away to be sent flopping to the ground on his front and back. Though Asthatch insisted he was merely trying to reveal the boy's weaknesses with traditional Drakkaidian discipline, Valeri recognized he was toying with him and purposefully laying him out with each attack. Going to Aeric's side and pulling him back, the princess shot Asthatch a scowl and told Aeric a hardened warrior like the captain could best even her more often than not.

As the group pressed on up a winding incline, Aeric was surprised to see snow falling over the peak of the mountain to their left even in the summer. Remembering how high they traveled as they penetrated deeper into the mountains, he pulled his gauntlets tighter against his forearms and rubbed his chilled shoulders. Drakkaidian had not exaggerated about the terrain on the road to the Lake of the Undead. It was even more dangerous and inhospitable than they had imagined, some regions even rivaling the Crag Spires itself. Large fissures riddled the rock around them dropping into endless darkness.

Though Drakkaidian tried to keep to the straightest and lowest roads possible as he frequently stopped to navigate, most of the ground they traversed was almost too steep, too unsteady, or too jagged to walk. Every hour drained them as if they had walked a day over simple level ground. Watching Drakkaidian every time he halted to scan ahead and around them for the safest path through the dark mountains, Aeric curiously watched as he turned back and looked into the sky with nervous eyes as if something was following them. Aware it was a definite possibility, the young Tieloc continually kept an alert eye on their surroundings for any demonic creature trailing them.

Relief from the constant ups and downs of the mountain roads at last came on the afternoon of the fourth day when Drakkaidian led the party up a wedge in the cliffs to a rocky surface that seemed to level out for what looked to be leagues in every direction. Staring at the unusually flat region ahead with skepticism, Aeric looked around to see blackened soil at their feet with singed roots protruding from the ground and disintegrating as the breeze swept by. Looking around into the rocks around them, Aeric saw faint movements in the darkness and nervously pointed them out to Valeri.

The princess told him they were merely Siarchs sleeping for the day and she was keeping them dormant with her power as they passed. Aeric gulped, remembering his last unfavorable encounter with the little Siarchs. Though they continued on in curious silence for several minutes, Drakkaidian at last came to a slow halt as the rocks around them began to completely fade and they reached the start of the open expanse. Tapping the ground at his feet with the end of his staff and looking back into the sky to scan the clouds, he finally provoked Aeric's curiosity enough to speak.

"Is something out there, Drakkaidian?" he asked softly, catching the attention of the whole group. The old man kept his eyes on the sky for another moment before turning back to look behind them and at last down to the Grandarian who spoke.

"Not that I am aware of," he returned simply.

"Then why do you keep looking around like there's something following us?" Aeric pressed. Drakkaidian frowned at him and leaned down to sit back on one of the last boulders jutting up from the earth around them, holding onto the middle of his staff with both hands and propping it against his shoulder.

"I am merely trying to gauge whether it is safe to cross the ground ahead or not," he answered. Drakkaidian pointed past the empty surface ahead far into the horizon where the peaks reached high again. "The valley holding the Lake of the Undead lies beyond those peaks to the north. The only way in is through a very narrow and razor sharp maze of canyons called the Pass of Jostoc. The fastest way to get there is through the plain you see ahead of us. It has no name other than the one I gave it many years ago: the Electric Flat. This barren plain was once a small forest where trees grew tall. So tall that one day there was a fierce lightning storm that scorched the woods. Perhaps the lightning affected the composition of the ground because ever since this flat has enticed electrical storms. It is very dangerous to cross because if a storm were to break out, we and the steel we carry would be very alluring to the sky. The last time I crossed the Electric Flat most of men I traveled with were killed."

When Drakkaidian paused and looked back into the sky, Aeric and Valeri shot each other nervous glances then looked out onto the scorched flat to watch ash drift by in gusts of wind. Though Markus Desrum was about to comment that he had heard of this place and that Valeri's grandfather had supposedly traveled here once, he was cut off by a crackling of thunder accompanied by a sharp bolt of lightning blasting down from the clouds far ahead in the center of the flat. Jumping in surprise, Asthatch frowned and shook his head.

"This is madness; we're loaded down with steel," he said. "There must be away around this death trap."

"There is," Drakkaidian acknowledged. "To the far east there is another road up the cliffs that leads to the Pass of Jostoc. But those cliffs are near vertical faces and neither myself nor Princess Montrox would be able to scale them in our conditions. That route is also days out of our way, but we can cross the Electric Flat and be at the mouth of the Pass of Jostoc in hours if we cut across straight north. This path is far from safe, but it is the only one available. How many times did I warn you this journey would be perilous?"

"Enough that I don't need to hear it again," Asthatch snapped back, his voice dripping with impatience.

"Do you think it's safe to cross now, Drakkaidian?" Valeri asked, precluding an argument between the two before it could start. The recluse glanced up at the gray billows thick above them and shrugged.

"As safe as it's going to be," he replied. "If we start now we can reach the end by late afternoon. Be swift and watch your footing. There is loose soil that could snare you and we don't want to be stuck out there a moment longer than necessary." Seeing Aeric and the Drakkaidians nodding in compliance with nervous but ready faces, Drakkaidian rose from the rock and told them to hurry behind him. Marching ahead at just short of a jog, the old man quickly led them past the last rocks and into the barren Electric Flat. They moved quietly and carefully in a single file line, careful to watch their footing so as not be snagged by the many burnt roots sticking out of the ground or fall into holes of loose earth.

Lightning usually struck the ground once or twice every few minutes, most of the time either far ahead or to their sides. Though Aeric was the only one who consistently jumped in surprise at each strike, all of them were unnerved and kept an eye on the sky to make sure the clouds wouldn't turn into a storm without them knowing. To their east and west were rising cliffs and craggy inclines on either side of the flat but were leagues away and only barely visible on the horizon. It was as if they had entered a cold, black desert in the middle of the mountains.

The group proceeded on at their rigorous march for nearly two hours before sight of the rocks ahead where the mountains began to lift back up from the flat terrain entered their view. Allowing himself a deep breath of relief to know they were almost clear of the perilous Electric Flat, Aeric looked back to make sure Asthatch was still behind them. The large captain stopped for brief moments whenever he thought he heard something behind them, reaching for his weapon and staring back into the plain before returning to formation. Though Asthatch was still hiking after them, Aeric was surprised to see three bolts of lightning all strike the earth only a hundred feet behind them within a few seconds. The crackling energy from the sky had been coming down with greater frequency over the past few minutes, seemingly growing closer to their position with each strike.

While Drakkaidian kept on moving forward he cast his gaze up into the sky, slowing to a meager walk as he gradually looked back and witnessed another barrage of lightning burn into the earth. Narrowing his eyes distrustfully, he came to a halt. Desrum quickly asked what he was doing, urging him to keep going with the end in sight. Drakkaidian was quiet for a moment as the party gathered around him, shaking his head and whispering something to himself.

"Those clouds behind us are coming fast," he finally said for them to hear. All of them turned around to observe a large bank of thick black clouds on their heals, moving far faster than should have been possible with the wind blowing east and not north. Valeri could guess what that meant and was about to ask if he thought demons were behind them, but before she could another bolt of lightning touched down dangerously close by. Drakkaidian tightened his frame and turned to begin jogging north again. "The storm is building. We must get off the flat with haste!"

The group didn't need to hear any more to be on their way after him. Nearly sprinting toward shelter a few hundred yards ahead, they all looked backed into the sky to see strange red surges of electricity brimming in the churning clouds. Gritting her teeth and drawing her sword, Valeri waited for the first of the Valcanor to appear behind them. Though nothing emerged from the dark mass of clouds, another horrifying image behind them drew her attention and her eyes widened with terror. As the clouds drove on toward them a veritable blanket of lightning was raining down to pound the earth like an ocean wave crashing after them. Rushing forward at top speed, Valeri shouted for the others to look back.

Seeing the coming wave of electricity as well, Drakkaidian told them the storm surrounding the pack of Valcanor was colliding with the clouds already above them and intensifying the lightning. Aware they would be consumed by it if it reached them, he shouted for them to run hard for the end of the flat and not to look back. As bolts of white and red lightning began to drop around them with the roar of thunder filling the mountain air, the ground itself began to seemingly rumble and quake from the assault coming from the sky. Though running as hard as they could, Aeric knew Valeri couldn't keep on like this for long. Her wound had to be causing her a great deal of pain. Trying to keep pace with her as she slowed, the Grandarian wheeled around when he heard the sound of a cry of pain behind them. Turning as well, Valeri saw Markus Desrum sunken into the ground where his leg had punctured the soil and lodged inside.

Though she instantly skid to a halt in preparation to run back for him, she heard both Aeric and Drakkaidian yell for her to keep going. Seeing Asthatch and her soldier rushing back to Desrum, she did as she was told but kept her eyes on them. The soldier reached Desrum first, taking hold of his arm to pull him up. While he worked, Asthatch caught movement from above and jerked his head up to find one of the oval bodied Valcanor plunging out of the clouds. Spotting them instantly, the creature shrieked and narrowed the glowing red eyes in its sunken head, swooping down for them.

Hearing the shriek, Valeri and Aeric looked up and saw the winged demon descending on them as well. It was upon them before the princess could come to a stop and rush back to aid them, flipping upright as it careened toward the earth. Though Desrum saw it coming and furiously tried to pry his stuck limb out of the earth, eventually he shoved the solider out of the way and braced himself for the monster about to drop onto him. Valeri and Aeric watched in horror as the Valcanor slammed into him, crushing the former commander of Hadecrest underneath its clawed feet.

Fragmenting the earth as it landed, the ground under the last soldier's feet crumbled and forced him over while he struggled to draw his sword. Seeing the human fighting to rise back to his feet, the demon swept its hydraulic arm out to snatch him off the ground. Though Asthatch was rushing to the soldier's side with his axe in hand and screaming to get the beast's attention, the lightning began to slam down to the earth in a maelstrom and the Valcanor lifted back into the skies before he could be struck on the ground. Reemerging into the clouds with the screaming Drakkaidian in his arms, Asthatch was left barking furious curses as it disappeared. Though casting his gaze down to the crushed corpse of Markus Desrum, he quickly wheeled around and began sprinting to get to Valeri still frozen in shock ahead.

Reaching back to heave the girl forward, Drakkaidian shouted for them to keep going. Sprinting forward with the lightning coming down faster and denser with each passing second, Aeric felt his heart begin to beat even more wildly as the sight of another Valcanor dropped out of the clouds directly above, obviously coming for them. Seeing it herself, Valeri let her rage course through her and trigger her dark power. Crimson energy swirling to life around her and radiating from her frame, Valeri pointed her blade upward toward the plummeting demon to send a piercing beam of her own electrified energy tearing into its wing while it evaded her as best it could. Crying out and struggling to regain its balance, the Valcanor crash landed in front of them on its belly. Though Drakkaidian tried to lead the others around it as it propped itself up with its arms, Valeri knew it would be back on its feet unless she stopped it and flared her dark aura of power up.

Veering away from Aeric, she flipped her sword around her hand to hold its blade facing away from her and rushed at the Valcanor. Watching her and sensing her considerable power, the demon put all its weight on its left arm and slashed out for her with its right. Seeing the attack coming, the girl ducked and rolled as the clawed hand swept through the air where her upper body had been seconds before. Though cringing in pain from her wound, the powerful princess leapt back to her feet, taking advantage of the Valcanor's position with all its weight on one side.

Slashing out with her sword she released another arching wave of energy that cut into its left arm, forcing it to buckle and send its body down into the ground with a shriek. With its head on the ground, Valeri lifted her sword above her head with both hands and lunged forward. Plunging the pulsating blade down into the demon's sunken head between its eyes, it cut deep inside and blinded the creature in the flurry of crimson energy shining out of the wound.

Jerking up in pain with force that surprised the warrior princess, the Valcanor slammed its head into Valeri to knock her off her feet and send her flying back. Landing on her side, the girl screamed out in pain, her dark power fading to a light red glow around her figure. Feeling the touch of blood on her stomach again, Valeri struggled to rise as the Valcanor lifted back to its feet and began wildly crashing around looking for her in its blinded state. Though it would have caught her in its slashing arms in a few moments, Valeri was surprised to find someone lifting her up and throwing her in his arms.

Being sped away back toward Drakkaidian and Asthatch, Valeri saw Aeric carrying her and running as fast as he could with the burden in his arms. Though Drakkaidian was only a few dozen feet away all of them were shocked to see a bolt of lightning touch down halfway between them. Cursing out loud as he realized the full force of the storm had caught up to them and they would never make it to cover with the demons after them as well, Drakkaidian came to a halt and told Asthatch to stand back.

Lifting up his staff and slamming it back down into the ground, the others watched in awe as a wave of foaming red mist engulfed it. As the old man swung the blur of heavy particles over his head, a silver broadsword appeared from inside, cutting its way free into the air. As the regal weapon completely broke free of the dissipating red mist, Drakkaidian shouted for the others to gather around him and crouch down.

Already on his way, Aeric rushed to the old recluse and ducked down with Valeri in his arms. As he held her and looked her over he could feel her warm blood soaking through her tunic again and shook his head with worry. Asthatch arrived beside them in a crouch, observing her wound as well and beseeching her to hang on. Standing tall amid the falling electricity, Drakkaidian raised his regal sword high into the air and locked his face with determination.

Though sure he was only going to get himself killed, the others were stunned to witness him providing them shelter. Within moments the lightning was attracted to the metal of his sword and began striking it, but Drakkaidian stood tall with his blade beginning to glow with each bolt that hit it. Before long all the lightning coming down around them was crashing into Drakkaidian's sword, charging it white hot with energy bristling off its edges. Dumbfounded at how this could be happening, Aeric stared at the old man struggling to stand tall in the face of the onslaught.

As if they weren't already besieged enough, another Valcanor that had been circling overhead dropped out of the clouds in their direction. Seeing it coming, Drakkaidian took hold of the hilt of his sword with both hands and pulled the weapon into his shoulder. Stabbing upward the next moment, the group was surprised to find an enormous bolt of lighting leaping from the tip of his blade into the sky to slam into the demon before it could even get near them.

Electrocuting its entire body with the force of dozens of concentrated lightning bolts, the creature dropped lifeless onto the ground with its hide smoldering. Though amazed at the old man's powerful display, the lightning kept falling around them and he was forced to throw his sword back above his head to attract it away from their vulnerable bodies. Struggling to hold his ground against the constant bombardment from the sky, Drakkaidian swung his head around to look to the rocks at the end of the flat and saw them teeming with nervous activity of the Siarchs Aeric had noticed on the opposite side. Spinning his head back to face his two younger companions he summoned his voice.

"Valeri!" he bellowed through the sound of the crashing lighting. "I can't keep this up! Use your power to call the Siarchs in the rocks! Do it quickly!" Though Valeri could barely hear him, Aeric repeated the order to her as he watched two more Valcanor descending from the clouds toward the one Valeri had wounded, still blindly thrashing behind them. Though she was confused at his request, when she saw Drakkaidian buckle and kneel down with the lightning slamming into his sword even faster, she did what she was told.

Looking around for the rocks at the end of the flat, she raised her hand to summon the swarming masses of Siarchs out. Though frightened, the Siarchs acquiesced to the Warrior of Darkness' influence and began soaring out of several fissures in the earth in a storm of black wings. Summoning them to her, Valeri watched as they spread out in confusion amid the falling lightning. Though previously baffled at why Drakkaidian would want Siarchs above them, Aeric quickly saw there were so many they created a barrier between them and the sky and the lightning that penetrated through them to the ground was cut in half.

With the constant electric bolts temporarily drawn away, Drakkaidian dropped his sword and fell to his knees, panting in exhaustion. Slowly raising himself back to his feet as he struggled to breath, the sword at his feet shrouded in the red foam again and disappeared. Telling them to rise and hurry before they ran out of Siarchs to shield them, the remaining group continued running for the end of the flat. Though the Valcanor were still airborne and searching for them, the Siarchs proved to be more useful than Drakkaidian had hoped as they created so much confusion the demons lost sight of their human quarry. Just as Aeric thought they had escaped from the demons and the chaos they brought, they all heard another howl from behind them and turned to find a lone Arnosmn charging toward them from back in the flat. Though Drakkaidian told them to keep running, Valeri tightened in Aeric's arms and she saw something else behind them.

"Asthatch, no!" she yelled. Aeric turned his head to see the large Drakkaidian captain taking a stand behind them with his massive axe in his hands. Holding his ground, he did not turn back as Valeri cried for him to hurry after them. Before the weakened princess could even try to worm her way out of Aeric's arms or summon her power, the speeding creature was on top of Asthatch. He stood gripped by his poise and calm even in the face the monstrous foe; he had seen its kind before and learning from it as he had from all his enemies through his long career as a Drakkaidian warrior.

Asthatch raised his axe and swung it out in front of him with all his strength as soon as the agile demon lunged off the ground for him. Sailing through the air toward the lone human, even its great demonic strength and endurance proved to be no match against the brute force behind Asthatch's oversized axe and the perfect timing with which it slammed into its target. Careening into the Arnosmn's side in midair, the blade hammered the demon into the ground with force enough to fragment the earth around its frame.

Staring with incredulous eyes as the fierce Drakkaidian captain turned to wrench his axe out of the demon's flesh while it writhed on the ground, Aeric couldn't believe he had downed a creature with a single blow that others had fought three to one and barely bested. Valeri loosened her tense body seeing her captain safe and the demon dying, yelling for him to start after her again. Though hearing her as she was whisked away in Aeric's arms, Asthatch knew better than to leave a foe as cunning as the Arnosmn alive and he raised up his axe in preparation to slam down and sever its head before he caught up with his party. With the steel axe in the air, the captain forgot the lighting still jetting through the weak spots in the Siarchs and felt a sudden hot surge of pain slam into him, immobilizing him instantly. Seeing Asthatch struck by the lightning, Valeri jerked back and screamed as he limply fell to his side, dropping the axe beside the inert demon.

Fighting to be free of Aeric's arms, she demanded the Grandarian let her go so she could go back for Asthatch. With the remaining Siarchs thinning out and fleeing without Valeri to concentrate on keeping them in the sky, the lighting began to rain back down on the field and Drakkaidian shouted it was too late and their only chance was to make it for cover. Knowing he was right, Aeric gripped Valeri all the tighter and kept running. Hearing Valeri begin to cry he was surprised to feel her slam her fist into his chest to stun him and make him stumble to the ground. Tearing away from him, Valeri tried to stand but fell to her hands and knees, her strength gone.

Feeling tears freely flowing down her cheeks as she looked at her guardian's body lying motionless on the Electric Flat, she tried to crawl back out to him but was stopped by Aeric grabbing her and collecting her into his arms once again. Though desperately crying for him to let her go the Grandarian ran hard, finally arriving amid the rocky terrain at the end of the flat. Running hard after Drakkaidian as they passed into a collection of tall boulders where the lightning began to fade, the trio left the Electric Flat behind them. Despite Drakkaidian telling them not to look back, all three of them did as the fading Siarchs were dispersed by the Valcanor and the bodies of their fallen friends disappeared from view.

Chapter 35

<u>Impulse</u>

Dropping through the air with his massive black wings tucked in against the thick hide on his back, Dalorosk slammed into the barren earth beside the crater leading down into the cavern where Ceruleana had been. Fragmenting the ground and sending crumbling chunks of rock on the edge of the hole falling down into the dark cave from the colossal force of his impact, the Ancient of Darkness raised his horned head with his blood red eyes peering around to spot his brothers standing in their human forms waiting for him with arms folded and impatient looks on their faces. With a light aura of dark energy appearing around his beastly frame, the giant behemoth quickly morphed down to his relatively miniscule human disguise as well. With the dark energy around him fading, Dalorosk marched toward his brothers with his face cringing and ready to explode with rage.

"You let them go!?!" he bellowed in disbelief. "Three of you descended upon him and he escaped?"

"The three of us who cannot fly, Dalorosk," Vorkoise hissed back. The Ancient of Darkness jerked his head toward the one who spoke and raised his arm with a swirling torrent of black energy abruptly surging around it. Though ready to swing his forearm out and blast the Ancient of Water off his feet, Golthrout stepped in front of him with fury in his own eyes.

"Mind yourself, Dalorosk!" he barked. "Lest you betray us and make all of us your enemies. Calm down." Though the rage in his dark eyes only built, Dalorosk halted and wheeled around, slamming his fist into the ground to splinter and break rock again. Pulling his body back up, he spun around and shouted at Golthrout.

423

"Why did you attack before we were ready?" he grilled heatedly. "When you found him why did you not call us all!?! We could all have been here to ensure this didn't happen!"

"It was random chance that I stumbled onto the underground city where he was hiding," Vorkoise told him. "I had no choice but to attack."

"And in the chaos they escaped through this hole in the cave's ceiling," Moltar finished.

"Who else was with him?" Dalorosk pressed.

"His disciple and three other humans," Golthrout said. "He must indeed be gathering new warriors somehow."

"We must return to the Holy Shrine to guard the Sources!" Wyrik stated with authority.

"He would not risk penetrating the shrine again," Moltar said. "He can't know some of us aren't there to stop him if he tried."

"Which way did they go?" Dalorosk asked.

"We were underground, brother," Vorkoise replied annoyed. "How could we know?"

"Well, did you glean any information from the humans about his plans?" Dalorosk asked with his every word escalating his temper.

"We agreed to kill them all on sight, as I recall," Moltar said. Dalorosk turned and threw his fist back down into the ground, punching clear through the rock.

"Not when they have had direct contact with Alberic and might know what he's up to!" the enraged Ancient yelled as he rose and wheeled back around. "Now what do we do?"

"What we should have been doing all along," Wyrik said angrily. "We all go to Drakkaidia and find this resistance he must be using. We break it, interrogate the survivors, and find out where he is. With any luck he'll be there when we arrive."

"What of the demons?" Moltar asked.

"They are of no consequence if we hold our Sources," Golthrout replied. "We should go retrieve them from the shrine before we attack."

"No!" Dalorosk shouted, surprising them all. "We'll need to spread out to find them and may need our mental link if we stray too far. We are strong enough without the Sources."

"Why are you so intent on leaving the Sources as they be?" Vorkoise asked with unguarded suspicion in his voice.

"What took you so long to get here anyway?" Dalorosk glared at the Ancient of Water but slowly pulled a circular stone object out from his back. Pulling it into two halves, he quickly snapped them back together to reveal an empty space in the center.

"Finishing my work," he answered impatiently, tucking the object back behind him. Though all his brothers were about to object, Dalorosk transformed back into his true form and roared for them to follow him. Spreading his bat-like wings he lifted into the air and charged off to the north. Wyrik transformed after him, allowing the others to gather on his back in their human forms. When they were all situated, the Ancient of Wind followed his other winged kin into the sky toward Drakkaidia.

Drakkaidian led Aeric and Valeri on into the rugged terrain leading up to the Pass of Jostoc for almost half of an hour after they escaped the demons. Though the onslaught of lightning over the Electric Flats lessened the further the trio ran into the rugged mountains and night was beginning to fall, all three of them could hear the shrieks of Valcanor still present in the skies behind them. The old recluse insisted they keep moving until they could find better cover at the mouth of the pass to hide. Concerned for Valeri's wound and exhausted after the ordeal on the flat, Aeric protested they needed to rest as quickly as possible.

Drakkaidian completely ignored his dissent and kept dashing through the rocks into the darkness, somehow bolting ahead of them with vitality the Grandarian could hardly comprehend after his display on the Electric Flat. Though they left the electrical storm behind, the thick black clouds remained over their heads and quickly began to cast a soft layer of rain drops falling down over the trio's heads. Tired, wet, cold, and burned with Valeri who was still crying and struggling against him over the loss of Asthatch, it took all the determination and willpower Aeric could muster to keep moving.

The rain fell harder as the minutes slipped by, soaking all three of them to the bone by the time Drakkaidian finally slowed and looked up to a tall cliff wall with an overhang of rock unevenly jutting out. Turning his head to beckon the exhausted young Tieloc toward it, the old man ambled under the rock to a small dry patch where the rain couldn't reach them. Looking around and waiting for a periodic flash of lightning to temporarily illuminate their surroundings, Drakkaidian saw they were enclosed in steep cliffs that led into a narrow cleave in the mountain. Judging it was the safest place they would find in the rain and darkness, he knelt down to catch his breath while Aeric crouched under the rock to work his way inside with Valeri. Taking a look at the princess, the old man saw she had stopped crying and hung limply in the Grandarian's arms, obviously out of energy to resist.

Sweeping his eyes down to her middle, he saw what looked to be blood and silently cursed, reaching out to gently pull up the end of her tunic and inspect her stitched wound. While it held firm, a few stitches had been torn apart and she was indeed bleeding again. Though about to tell Aeric to lay her down so he could mend her as best he could, the three of them heard a howl in the darkness much closer than the Electric Flat. Drakkaidian jerked his head up to stare into the darkness as a rolling thunderclap echoed between the cliffs. Narrowing his eyes, the recluse reached inside a pouch that hung from his belt and pulled out a stiff red cloth, handing it to Aeric.

"Get this wet and press it against her wound," he ordered at once. "I'm going to check our perimeter and make sure we're alone. If I'm not back soon take her further into the mouth of the pass and find the best cover you can." Not liking the sound of that at all, Aeric shook his head and prepared to ask him not to leave. Before he could say a word Drakkaidian slapped the cloth into his hands and was back into the night, disappearing amid the falling rain. Alone with Valeri, Aeric turned back and wiped the dripping wet hair in front of his eyes back over his head. He looked down to find her wincing in pain and reaching down for her right side.

"Don't touch it, Valeri," he told her, grabbing her hands and pushing them back. Holding the red cloth out into the rain and letting the water saturate it, he brought it back under the rock and unfolded it. Lifting up Valeri's tunic to expose her bleeding wound, he spoke to her in a soothing voice. "Just hold on. If this is what I think it is, this is probably going to hurt so brace yourself." The princess looked up to him and started breathing harder as she saw the cloth lowering down to her side, screaming out and tightening her entire frame as it touched her with the burning chemical soaked inside. Every bit as painful as it had been the first time Drakkaidian had applied the substance to her body, Valeri grit her teeth and lifted her upper body to wrench the cloth out of Aeric's hands and throw it back against the cliff wall, tears streaming down from her eyes again. Aeric let out a sharp sigh and saw she was still bleeding from the top of her wound.

Before he could tell her she had to let him help her, the girl pushed away from him shaking her head and crying harder as she had been on most of the way away from the flat.

"Get away from me!" she shouted, summoning her voice. "Who do you think you are, Aeric? Why did you keep me from going back? He needed me! You let him die!" Though empathetic to her pain of losing someone, Aeric couldn't stay calm with her, his own emotions rising high.

"If I had let you go back onto that field you'd be dead too!" he yelled. "Between the lightning and demons none of us could have made it back to Asthatch, especially you. You're hurt, Valeri! Can't you see that?"

"I am a Drakkaidian!" she returned, her voice choking with emotion. "We don't leave our comrades behind no matter what!"

"Well I wasn't leaving you!" Aeric exclaimed. "What do you think Asthatch would have wanted? For you to come back and die alongside him? He would have carried you off that plain with his last breath to protect you!"

"I don't care!" she blasted, struggling to contain her rage. Aware the girl didn't actually mean what she was saying while consumed by her emotions, Aeric bit his tongue and didn't respond, instead moving closer to lean down in front of her. Though she remained hostile and tried to summon the words to scream at him, Valeri was surprised to see him lean in and grab her arms, slowly pulling her into him. Confused and unable to hold onto her anger, the girl fought to keep her plentiful grief from rising out.

"It's alright to cry, Valeri," he told her in a hushed tone. Though wanting to keep her body stiff, she felt it softening against him.

"There's no room for tears in Drakkaidia," she whispered back. "You couldn't understand." Aeric shook his head and wrapped his arms completely around her.

"I understand that beneath all your power and posturing there's a girl inside who needs to feel sorrow right now, not anger," Aeric returned. "Trust me, Valeri. Just cry." Though desperately battling to hold onto her hard exterior and stay strong as she had been taught all her life, in Aeric's arms she felt her armor melting away. She slowly let her body loosen and completely fall into his. Realizing he was right and there was nothing either of them could have done for Asthatch, the princess let her guard down and her true emotions empty out onto the boy holding her. Crying for several long minutes, Valeri felt the young man reach up under the back of her shawl to rub slow circles over her back, not saying anything. After she cried out the full force of her sorrow, Valeri felt a soothing calm begin to fill up the space in her heart previously occupied by the sadness. Realizing Aeric had been right and she felt momentarily tranquil with him there holding and rubbing her, the princess slowly opened her quivering lips to speak.

"He was like my second father," she said with her voice shaking. "He only ever wanted to be there for me—to protect me. And this entire journey all I did was push him away. Take him for granted. I wouldn't listen to him when he tried to warn me about Drakkaidian. What if he was right? There's obviously something more to him than we thought after seeing what he just did..." Though she trailed off for a moment, she sniffled again and turned her head on Aeric's shoulder. "He was the only family I had left and I never even told him I loved him." Aeric stopped rubbing her at this, groping for something to say but failing to think of anything that would alleviate her sorrow. Feeling him stop rubbing her back, Valeri slowly lifted up against him, looking into his eyes as her face passed inches away from his. Though happy to see her guard down and her troubled heart finding some measure of peace, Aeric felt the familiar discomfort of her ardent gaze on him. Dangerously tempted to stare back and keep her in his grasp, he looked away and let his arms down.

Reaching behind her, the Grandarian picked up the red cloth dripping on the rock and brought it back to place in his lap. He kept his gaze down on it away from her eyes as he spoke.

"We need to stop your bleeding," he told her softly as a clap of thunder bounced through the walls of the cliffs around them. Valeri nodded and she wordlessly pulled up her tunic to reveal her slender midsection and the wound on the right side. Observing the last remnant of the open wound, Aeric laid the cloth flat in his open hand and pressed it against her skin. He could feel her muscles tighten as she cringed, struggling not to cry out. Though she stayed tense for a painful moment, he could feel her gradually relax and ease her entire frame.

Keeping his gaze on his hand and the cloth, Aeric watched as she reached up from her lap to put a hand over his. Looking up at her face uncertainly, he saw the princess staring down at their hands with her breathing quickening. Though he spoke her name once to get her attention, the girl remained frozen in place. Closing her eyes and tightening her expression as if struggling with some internal dilemma, the girl suddenly thrust her head up and brought it next to Aeric's. Pressing her nose against his with her eyes closed and her wet red hair sticking to his forehead, she waited. Waited for anything to happen. Feeling the faint touch of the girl's bottom lip against his, Aeric felt his heart beating as fast as it had in the Electric Flat. His every muscle freezing up, all his thoughts and cautions were suddenly overridden by a desperate craving to close the gap between them and kiss her.

Suddenly finding himself staring face to face with the subconscious desires that he had so adamantly refused to even acknowledge in the past few days, Aeric faltered and didn't know what to do. The few seconds of sitting with his face touching the girl's felt like days. He couldn't deny that he wanted to press his lips just a few hair lengths closer into hers—to grab the princess, hold her tightly against him and never let go. But as the seconds ticked by and the urge threatened to act for him if he didn't make a choice soon, Aeric saw the image of Valeri Montrox slowly morph to a flash of Mina Garrinal walking down a grassy hill overlooking Eirinor Village. She ambled barefoot through the bright green grass, turning with her bouncing chestnut hair leaping up from her shoulders to land behind her back. There was a smile on her freckled face that wordlessly called out for him.

A wave of pain washing through him, Aeric dropped his head and pulled his lips away from hers, slowly withdrawing. Feeling a painful breath escape from Valeri's mouth as she was left hanging her head against only the air, Aeric opened his eyes to see her opening hers with more hurt inside than he had ever seen before.

"...I... can't," he managed to whisper with his words almost lost in the sound of the falling rain. "I'm sorry, Valeri." The princess remained motionless for a moment before sealing her eyelids again and letting her head fall as well. As another roll of thunder swept through the air, Valeri pulled back and let Aeric's hand gradually slide out from underneath hers. Holding the red cloth over her side by herself, she looked up at him with a tear falling down her cheek.

"I know," she replied at last, her usually strong and resolved voice shaking with vulnerability she had never felt the likes of before. The silence that occupied the passing moments afterward was deafening. Both of them were held captive by it, unable to move or speak a word. Though Aeric watched in agony as another tear spread down Valeri's cheek, she quickly lowered her head and raised her hand to wipe it away along with the soaked hair on her forehead. He knew full well that was probably the first time she had ever let someone see her naked of the armor she wore to maintain the persona of the warrior princess; it was probably the first time she had ever taken that risk with anyone. And though he knew he had to do it, the hurt and shame of having to push her away was almost unbearable for him.

Though he tried for several long moments to find something he could say to her, he was at last distracted by the sound of something dragging over the rocks behind him. Aware it could be a threat, Aeric forced himself to sharpen and turned around to peer into the darkness. Seeing the silhouette of a hulking mass approaching them, the Grandarian reached down to his belt for his sword and pulled it free, sending the metallic ring into the night. Taking a defensive position in front of Valeri as the silhouette grew closer, a flash of lightning temporarily illuminated the rocky ground before him and Aeric saw what was coming.

A large, hairy beast with a dog-like head and long claws lay limp on the ground. The soaked form of Drakkaidian was in front of it, lugging the creature from behind a rock by its open jaws. Observing Aeric standing with his sword drawn in the momentary flash of light, the old man grunted and dropped the demon's hairy hide. Groaning as he paused and rested his hands on his knees to catch his breath, Drakkaidian stood full length over the apparently dead creature with his silver sword once again in hand.

Lifting it up over his head, he swung down and slashed the hairy corpse down the side deep into its flesh. Flinching in shock as black blood sprayed from the gash, Aeric watched the sword fade from Drakkaidian's hands in a foaming mist. His tired form unhurriedly trudged through the rain up to them. Leaning to pass under the low overhang of rock keeping them dry, the recluse reached up to his face to wipe a streak of blood from his cheek and beard. Though Aeric looked back to the dead demon lying out in the rain, Drakkaidian set his eyes on Valeri, staring up at him.

"May I have that cloth, princess?" he asked through his heavy breathing. Valeri hesitated but slowly pulled the red cloth on her wound free to hand it to him. Hearing his request, Aeric looked back to see Drakkaidian pull apart his slashed tunic by his chest to reveal a light wound where he was bleeding. Without flinching, he pressed the cloth against his skin with an audible sizzling sound escaping into the air. Though the two could see his body tense, he made no sound and took a seat beside them. "That's a Liradd. Slower and more clumsy than the Arnosmn but just as malicious. They relish death but hate the smell of their own. It should keep at least their kind away tonight." Both Aeric and Valeri were quiet at his words, staring at him uncertainly as he dug his fingers and the red cloth into his wound. When Aeric finally glanced back to Valeri, she immediately looked away and slowly rose to make her way to the opposite end of the overhang where she lay down with her back to them.

Though wishing he could say something to her, Drakkaidian told him to rise and follow him for a moment. Replying that they shouldn't leave Valeri, the old man told him it would only be for a moment and he needed his help with something. Doing as he was bid, the young Tieloc followed him back into the rain to the cleave in the cliffs to peer deeper into the narrow passage.

"My eyesight is failing in the darkness these days," Drakkaidian told him. "What do you see down there?" Aeric squinted his eyes and struggled to observe anything out of the ordinary down the opening. When a flash of lightning better illuminated it, he could see rock walls rising on either side but nothing else he considered noteworthy.

"Nothing," he answered at last. "Just the path between the cliffs."

"No fork at the end of the road?" Drakkaidian pressed, water dripping from his beard. Aeric remembered the lightning had indeed revealed several paths at the end of the road and nodded.

"It forks several ways," he confirmed. "Why?" Drakkaidian sniffed in and opened his hand to summon another wave of the foaming red mist stretching out several feet. Lowering it, his wooden staff appeared in his hands and he set it on the ground before him.

"Like I said," he began, "my eyesight is poor in the darkness. I needed to be sure we made it to the right entrance. The Pass of Jostoc is a labyrinth with several entrances that lead to nowhere." Shifting his gaze to Aeric to find him staring at him, Drakkaidian saw the boy panting and keeling over as if his entire body was about to give out on him. Aeric could see his expression half confused and half disgusted as if wondering why a man in his youth couldn't keep up with him.

"I don't know how you do it, Drakkaidian," the Grandarian said shaking his head. "I can barely stay on my feet." The old man sniffed and responded casually.

"It's not whether you get knocked down, it's whether you get up again," he said as he looked back to the overhang on the cliff. "Otherwise there is only trained and untrained. I am the former. What about her? Is she alright?" Aeric turned to glance back as a lightning bolt revealed Valeri's still body lying down behind them.

"She was," he replied softly, hanging his head. Drakkaidian was quiet for a moment but at last put a hand on the young man's shoulder to get his full attention.

"A piece of advice, Tieloc," he said plainly. "For all our sakes, don't get any closer to the princess. Montroxs are as treacherous as these peaks. Trust me." Aeric frowned at this, unsure what the old man meant. Before he could ask, Drakkaidian told him he would be off keeping watch and ordered him to get some sleep. Disappearing back into the darkness, Aeric looked back at Valeri while cursing himself for crushing her and betraying his own heart in more ways than one.

Chapter 36

<u>Earth and Wind</u>

After getting several hours of much needed sleep, Lucan Hauk Erland and Maglin Byre were woken by Alberic in the small guest hollow on the far west side of Keracon Valley. The three of them immediately fell asleep in the miniature beds the Cronoms had prepared for them after Lucan caught up with Maglin and Alberic at the hollow. Much to the trio's surprise, they learned from the Cronom leading them inside that the last people to have stayed there were Tavinious Tieloc and Arilia Embrin themselves over sixty years ago. Unaware the famed Warriors of Light and Fire had spent time in Keracon, they wondered if they too came for refuge during their legendary quest. The interior of the hollow was just as they imagined it would be. Though undersized and furnished only with a bed and table, it was as cozy as everything else in the Cronom village, decorated with simple but beautiful designs of leaves and other works of nature.

The two Mavens were slow to wake when Alberic roused them from their dreams, telling them it was evening and they had to be on their way to the Grand Hollow for dinner. Though doubtful the simplistic race of gnome-like creatures would serve anything familiar or appetizing, Lucan's qualms were easily overridden by his hunger and was quick to spring from his bed and secure his blue scarf around his neck. Maglin was already waiting outside when he emerged from the rickety wooden door of the hollow, staring out at the rope bridges of the village as several merry Cronoms worked to light low torches across the village in preparation for night. Turning to see her old friend emerge from the hollow while tucking his scarf behind his back, Maglin grinned and let out a dry huff.

"So are you ever going to explain this?" she said as he walked up to her and she grabbed the ends of the blue garment around his neck. Lucan rolled his eyes and swatted his scarf out of her grip.

"Does it really matter?" he returned, raising his eyebrows and raising his hands to fold them behind his head. Maglin furrowed her brow and shot him a suspicious look.

"Does it matter?" she repeated almost aghast. "Here you are, once the quintessential boy scout in your little Windrun patrol dedicated to the rule of law, now standing before me wearing a symbol of rebellion and indifference to that law. It's a pretty extreme turnaround, and easily the last thing I would have ever imagined you wanting anything to do with."

"First off," Lucan began right away, "as you might have noticed, the world has had a pretty extreme turnaround since my days as a Windrun Warrior. People had to do pretty extreme things to adapt and survive. And second, what do you mean the last thing I would want anything to do with? As I recall I had quite a bit do with you over the years."

"So because you used to mix with a Maven who worked for you, you felt compelled to become one yourself?" she asked skeptically. "What, is the scarf your way of telling the Ancients and the converts they can shove their new world order?" Though Lucan was prepared to jump back on her and tell her to shut up, he bit his tongue and took a deep breath, lowering his hands back to his sides.

"Maybe it was just a good representation of another life I wished for sometimes," he replied. "Of someone I used to admire who lived that life and did what good she could with all the freedom that came with it." Maglin laughed in spite of herself for a moment but gradually softened as she saw his eyes were sincere.

"I guess I should be flattered," she joked at last, hearing the door to the hollow open a final time to reveal Alberic walking out and stretching in the evening air. "But I guess I missed you too, Erland." Though aware she was half mocking him, Lucan smiled and turned to greet the Ancient of Light. Regrouping and hearing a Cronom calling for them to follow him back to the Grand Hollow, they set off for their dinner.

As they walked, the three companions crossed paths with several of the small inhabitants of the valley, all politely bowing and introducing themselves. Though curious at why virtually every hollow was being emptied of its Cronom occupants as they passed, Lucan remembered that they all ate together in the Grand Hollow at the same time. Making their way up to the large structure tightly built against the largest tree any of them had ever seen, they climbed the ladders and stairs to its open double doors where Cronoms were filtering through to sit along the long tables in the central chamber.

Passing into the primary chamber, Lucan looked around to see plates of green vegetation and steaming soups being catered in by several of the Cronoms, spread evenly over the table tops. While the Blue Maven recanted his earlier doubts of their cooking ability, Alberic spied a figure that dwarfed the others around him at the far side of the chamber where a raised stage stood perpendicular to the tables. Starting toward it through the wide aisle between tables, the two Mavens followed after him, observing Revond taking a seat in a small chair along the table beside the Cronom elder Yucono and a few others. Also beside him was Sarton Jax Morrol, his left arm tightly secured in the sling the Cronoms had made for him, and another figure that puzzled all three of them as they stared at her.

There was another human woman standing behind Yucono happily speaking with the Master Sage. She looked to be fairly young with vibrant blonde hair that stretched down to her shoulder blades and a cheery face harboring a wide smile. She was dressed identically to most of the Cronoms but for the bright yellow lining stitched into her attire. Though Lucan and Maglin exchanged confused glances at who she could be, when they approached the stage Yucono rose form his small seat where his legs had been dangling and beamed at them.

"Greetings again, my friends!" he exclaimed happily. "Please come sit with us tonight! Dinner is being served." Thanking him kindly, the three made their way up a staircase on the left side of the stage and took their seats around the table on the stage. With their entire party, two Cronoms and the other blonde woman taking a seat beside Yucono, they filled every seat along its perimeter. So close together, they struggled to part for servers placing plates of a green salad and bowls for soup in front of them. Standing up on top of his chair and raising his hand with a spoon in it, Yucono cleared his throat and shouted out to project his elderly voice to the end of the Grand Hollow. "Everyone please raise your arms for blessing!" Guessing this was some sort of ritual practiced before eating, Lucan turned to watch the Cronoms all lift their hands into the air and slowly start to faintly hum.

Though quiet at first, the sound grew louder than the Maven had expected until it began to focus from a mess of unharmonious sound to a unified note ringing out as if from a bell. Once they reached the note in astoundingly beautiful harmony, Lucan was surprised to see the Cronoms close their mouths and lower their hands even though the sound lingered in the air. Slowly dissipating, the Cronoms all smiled merrily and began talking once more, digging into their food. Amazed at the simple but beautiful ritual, Lucan turned back to find Yucono sitting back in his chair and chuckling as he swept his gaze over his visitors.

"So please eat, friends," he bid them, motioning toward their bowls. "A good meal is just what you need to recover the last of your strength. Did you all get good rest today?" Alberic was the one to respond for them, bowing his head and nodding as he picked up a wide wooden spoon to dip it into the creamy orange liquid in his bowl.

"I know I did," he replied. "Though my legs hung over the end of my bed it was surprisingly comfortable." He paused to take a sip of his hot soup, smacking his lips and looking around as if to gauge the taste, then smiled again, nodding. "And this is delicious." Yucono cackled to himself, his sense of humor infectious to the others as they all started to laugh with him.

"I'm glad you approve," the Cronom elder said. "But please, I've delayed with introductions long enough!" Yucono turned toward the older Cronom with a white beard that stretched down past the seat of the chair he sat in. "Revond and Jax have already met the other Cronom elder, Jolthop. He is currently the oldest Cronom left among us, having served as an elder for over three centuries, while I myself was only granted the position a few years ago. He was the first one of us to meet Graystorm." The elder named Jolthop turned with a slow smile spreading on his weathered face, looking at Revond.

"Yerbacht and I knew your mentor well, Revond," he said. "The first time I saw him he was being chased by Golthrouts in the woods! We hid him in our tunnels, too small and hidden for the clumsy monsters to find. Yucono here was even the one who led him and his friends out of the

436

caverns of the King of the Golthrouts during the last time we saw him."

"Such acts of hospitality and helpfulness seem to be the norm from your people, Jolthop," the Master Sage said with a smile. Though he didn't need the nutrition of food anymore than Alberic, Revond had lifted a crude stick the Cronoms used as a fork to stab at his salad, not wishing to be rude. Yucono then turned to the woman at his right, patting her forearm with a smile.

"And this is our third elder, also just recently chosen amongst us," he began. Lucan, Maglin and Morrol froze in shock at this revelation, staring at the woman. "Kira Marcell was obviously not born of our people, but she has been our longtime guest turned greatest defender over the years." Revond paused at this, remembering this name from somewhere before.

"Hello everyone," the young woman greeted with a cheery smile. "It's a great pleasure to have guests. Especially fellow humans."

"This is a surprise," Alberic said curiously. "Over my many long years I have never heard of the Cronoms taking in a human before."

"Yes well, as Yucono said, I've been here a long time," Kira replied. "As you all know the Cronoms are a loving and kind hearted race. They found me when I was just a child alone and abandoned in the Great Forest so they rescued me and brought me up to Keracon. I lived with them for many years until I grew old enough to venture out for myself back into the human world. Though I lived in Gaia Village for a time, I ended up spending most of my time in the Cronoms' eastern outpost of the forests. Eventually my duties there brought me back here and I've just been living back and forth ever since until recently. Keracon is my life—I owe the Cronoms everything and living here is so much simpler, so I accepted the honor of becoming the first non-Cronom elder in their history a few years ago."

"I don't mean to sound critical, Miss Marcell," Alberic told her, "but aren't you a little young to be an elder?" The woman smiled as she brushed a lock of her golden hair away from her face.

"Looks are deceiving amid the Cronoms, I'm afraid," she responded with her smile still stretching from ear to ear. "As you know, they live to be centuries old before fading back to nature. I've been among them so long their influence has stretched my life out some. I look fairly young but I'm actually above seventy now." Maglin dropped her spoon into her bowl while Lucan coughed up some of his soup in surprise at this. All of them couldn't help but stare at the woman, in disbelief she had endured so long still looking so young and healthy.

"Well you'd fit right in with some of the people at this table," Lucan finally said, glancing at Revond and Alberic. Ignoring the Maven's remark, Revond kept his gaze on Kira before eventually saying what had been on his mind since first hearing her name.

"Miss Marcell," he said to get her attention, "your father didn't know Zeroan, or rather, Graystorm when he was alive, did he?"

"Both of my parents did," Kira replied with a smile. "Why do you ask?" Revond put down his utensil.

"There is mention of the name Marcell in his writings at the Mystic Tower," the sage told her. "Before and during the Days of Destiny. May I ask what their connection to him was?"

"I'm afraid I can't really tell you," the woman replied with a shrug. "I was just a child when they died and all I ever heard was them talking about their friend named Graystorm. I was later told that my father had inadvertently found a shard of a powerful talisman of magic called the Holy Emerald that was important during the Days of Destiny you're talking about. But I'm afraid it was lost to him by Golthrouts when they attacked our village." Revond stiffened at this news, leaning in closer.

"Who did you learn this from?" he pressed. Kira grinned again as she took a deep breath and looked into the space above her as if remaining times past.

"My childhood hero," she returned merrily. "And though I'm sure he's been gone for several years he still is. Tavin Tieloc the Warrior of Light." The entire group froze at this, gulping down whatever they had in their mouths as they stared at her in disbelief.

"You knew Tavinious Tieloc?" Revond asked. "When did you cross paths with him?"

"Here in Keracon, of course," she answered, taking a sip of water from the cup beside her. "He and Ril were here on their quest for the emerald shards. The Cronoms rescued them from Golthrouts the same as they did for me. After their adventure they came back and told us about it all, including how my father had found a shard in the Great Forests without even knowing what it was." Revond took in her words and made an astounded face.

"The world is always a smaller place than we believe," he responded at last. "Especially during the time of Tavinious Tieloc, the Great Unifier." Revond paused for a moment, collecting his thoughts and finally shifting his gaze back to Yucono chomping away at his green salad. "And now we are in a new time—a darker time. We have all experienced the effects of this darkness. Which is what brings my friends and me here, elders." All of the Cronoms, humans and the Ancient at the table stopped eating, shifting their gazes to the sage as his tone grew serious. "As you know from Alberic's story and your own experience, elders, the fires of destruction have spread across Iairia over the past year. Five of six beasts called the Ancients rose from eons of entrapment and laid waste to the world in search of power. One of these beasts is the King of the Golthrouts you have evaded for millennia."

Yucono and Jolthop exchanged nervous glances at the sage's story, setting down their spoons to give him their full attention and telling him to go on.

"While these Ancients have destroyed much, hope is not lost to stop them and restore life to the world," Revond continued. "I have the power to anoint a group of men and women called Elemental Warriors who can stand up the Ancients and contain them, but first I must gather the necessary warriors to wield this power. As you can see I have found a few but I still need a capable man or woman to assume the role of the Warrior of Earth and the Warrior of Wind. As stewards of the Great Forest you know every inch of it. Do you know of any surviving human villages where I could find such a warrior?" Yucono, Jolthop and Kira all looked back and forth between each other at the sage's question, returning each other's bemused expressions.

"I'm afraid we have not seen or heard much of any humans since these beasts you speak of began the fires in the forest," Yucono replied. "We have been forced to keep mostly to ourselves and watch our own borders."

"Which might mean that we have overlooked some of the forests, however," Kira chimed in with hope in her voice. "The Golthrouts have destroyed much of what the fires did not, but the woods in the south are deep and thick beyond what most can even begin to imagine. It is possible there may be some people lingering further south."

"As always, we appreciate your hopefulness, Kira," Jolthop interjected, "but perhaps we should be slow to build up the hopes of our visitors. After all, even we have not been to the deep forests in many long years. We don't know if any of the old vale villages remain."

"That is true," Kira conceded, "but if anyone would know where to look it is me. You both know my size and the skills you have taught me over the years have allowed me to venture further and faster than Cronoms when exploring to the south. I have found tracks of what must be other humans before—wanderers and foragers most likely. If Revond must have a warrior from the south, that is the only place we can hope to find one. I ask that you allow me to lead them to the deep woods." Yucono let out a huff of air and frowned before turning to face Jolthop who was already scratching his chin through his thick beard.

"There is much risk in the Great Forests of late," he stated to no one in particular. "To be realistic, I doubt anyone could have survived this long outside of our boundaries."

"Yes, and we need you here now more than ever, Kira," Yucono added. "I wish to help our friends as well but I fear we would merely be wasting their time."

"A slim hope is better than none at all, my fellow elders," Kira told them. "And we need hope right now more than anything. My group just returned from the outskirts of our fire blocks. The damage is even worse than we feared. At this rate even we will eventually be routed from this valley and from there we will have nowhere to go. It is my judgment that for the sake of our people as well, I must be of whatever aid I can be to Revond and his friends." Yucono stared at her for a long moment before eventually grinning at her earnestness.

"As usual, Kira, your wisdom shines beyond your years," he told her. "Very well. If Revond will have you we are in agreement that you will help him find anyone that is left within these trees beside us." Revond nodded at this, telling them they would be honored to have her. After deciding on Kira's joining them, the group let the conversation pass to lighter subjects while they finished eating their dinner. They remained in the Grand Hollow for nearly an hour until the sun began to disappear into the western tree tops, ushering in the dark and chill of night. By the time they all rose from the table and made their way off the stage all the other Cronoms had retreated back to their hollows for the evening with the exception of those cleaning up. Over the hour, Lucan and Maglin had quickly come to know Kira better, gravitating toward her genuine friendliness. Despite her age she had held onto a youthful cheerfulness that had long eluded both of the Mavens. It made her all the more interesting to talk to, coupled with the knowledge and experience far beyond theirs.

On their way out of the main chamber of the Grand Hollow, Kira was telling them it would be a week long journey on foot into the heart of the Great Forests where she had seen traces of people years ago. Hearing this, Alberic told her they could make it in hours on his back in the skies. Amazed at the Ancient of Light and curious to see the seemingly normal looking man transform into the creature he apparently truly was, Kira told them they could be off as soon as they wished. Remembering his leg was still sore from the gash he had sustained fleeing Ceruleana, Lucan groaned and lightly ran his hand up his thigh.

"Another trek into dangerous ground. Just what I need," the Maven spoke sarcastically. "I can only hope team Tieloc and Montrox are faring better up north." The Maven was surprised to see Kira come to a halt beside him in the doorway of the hollow, staring at him with wide eyes. Peering back curiously, he spoke again. "What's wrong, Kira?"

"Those names," she said almost in a whisper. "You know a Tieloc and a Montrox?"

"They are our friends, yes," he replied, remembering the woman's affection for Tavin Tieloc. "Tavin Tieloc's grandson and the Princess of Drakkaidia Valeri Montrox are looking for something to help Revond anoint the new Elemental Warriors up in Drakkaidia as we speak." Hearing the conversation unfolding between Lucan and Kira the rest of the group came to a halt on the steps outside the Grand Hollow and looked back at the human elder. Her face was alight with astonishment and she quickly leapt down the stairs to rush to Lucan.

"You never told me the relations of Tavin Tieloc and Verix Montrox were with you!" she exclaimed. She looked over into Revond's hood, drawn down over his face as usual. "This changes things, Master Sage."

"What are you talking about, Kira?" Revond asked confused.

"The last time I saw Tavin was when he had become an old man and was visiting the Southland with Ril. I met them outside of Gaia Village by pure coincidence, but Tavin told me there are no coincidences. We got to talking about what we had done since the last time we met and he told me of all his adventures and duties. I told him I wish I could make a difference in the world like he did but he told me the same thing he did when I was just a little girl—that we all have to make choices that decide our destinies." The girl's eyes were full of energy and passion as she looked around to the faces of everyone around her. "I promised him that if the day came when the world needed me like it needed him I'd stand up for it. Well now is my chance. If Tavin's grandson is a part of this that is a good enough sign for me. It may take weeks to find anyone in these forests if we can find anyone at all. Let me save you the time—I will volunteer for the duty you need fulfilled." The group was quiet after she finished, all staring at her again. Seeing everyone's eyes shifting to him, Revond let out a quiet huff of air and pulled back his hood to better view her.

"Kira," he began softly, "I appreciate your passion and sincerity but I feel that despite your wealth of experience you may not be up to a challenge like this. There is great danger in store for whoever becomes the Warrior of Earth. You would need combat experience and physical strength in addition to your wisdom and character. Besides, you are an elder of the Cronoms. You have responsibilities here."

"The same argument that was true before is true now, Revond," Kira responded without hesitation. "The needs of the many outweigh those of the few, and the many need these Elemental Warriors before it is too late. I may still look young and delicate but I have seen plenty of danger and conflict in my life. I have evaded Golthrouts, fought bandits and survived lost in the woods for months at a time. I am not afraid of danger and I can cope with it as well as any. Let me help you." Revond was silent again but looked down to Yucono and Jolthrop, both staring at Kira. When they eventually looked up to see his gaze on them, they looked at each other.

"She has sworn an oath to defend and serve our people first," Jolthrop said. "There has never been an abdication of her responsibilities."

"But perhaps she serves us best by undertaking this journey," Yucono replied. "It is true that we may not be able to weather this storm forever. If she can stop it she would do far greater good with the sage than here." Jolthrop reached up to his beard again as he swept his eyes around the ground, eventually nodding and looking up to Revond.

"This is true," he stated. "While we worry for her safety above all, we agree that Kira would serve not only the Cronoms but her own kind best by helping you, Revond. Kira has become our greatest champion from many dangers over the years. Most of us can barely remember what we ever did without her. She has a brave heart still as pure as they day we found her."

"I do not doubt her courage or spirit, only her lack of familiarity of the wide world," Revond told them. "There are horrors and evil waiting for us that even one with all of her years and experience in the forests has never seen the likes of. It is a burden she does not have to bear."

"But I want to," Kira answered for herself, almost pleading. "I can help you, Revond. I've been told no before when I asked to embark with heroes leaving our valley. I would be ashamed to have been left behind twice, especially now when I am so desperately needed. Let me become the Warrior of Earth." All of them were quiet again, looking back to Revond. The sage remained still for a moment, at last walking up to her and looking her hard in the eyes. She did not back away or flinch but maintained the confidence and sincerity he had seen her exude since first meeting her.

"Though I'm not sure you fully understand the responsibility this charge will require of you, Kira Marcell," he told her, "I can see your heart is courageous enough to meet that responsibility. So be it. I will anoint you the Warrior of Earth for at least the duration of this crisis. From there we will see." Kira beamed at this, jumping forward to tightly wrap her arms around the sage and his cloak. Though none of them were expecting her to hug the Master Sage himself, Lucan couldn't help but silently worry that despite her many years this woman was still oddly naïve and sheltered. Aware her heart was in the right place and feeling he could trust her completely, however, Lucan shrugged off his doubts and grinned as Revond peered back to him with an uncertain expression on his bearded face. When Kira pulled back and graciously thanked him for the opportunity, the Blue Maven leaned back against the frame in the doorway of the Grand Hollow, folding his arms behind his head.

"Well then," he said smiling, "that was certainly easier than the first two have been. Looks like we're only one Elemental Warrior shy of the full team. Shall we head back east to finish the good fight?" Shifting in his robes and pulling his black gloves tighter against his hands, Revond turned to look at Alberic, standing with his arms folded beside him. Giving the sage a single nod, the Ancient of Light turned back to Lucan and waited for the Master Sage to step forward and speak once more.

"That won't be necessary," he said, catching them all by surprise. Maglin's brow furrowed and she tilted her head in confusion.

"What does that mean?" she grilled. "We still need a Warrior of Wind, don't we?" Revond shook his head.

"I already found one several weeks ago," Revond told her, to which the bedazzlement on her face spread onto the rest of the group. "I just didn't know it until recently." The sage turned his head and placed his focused blue eyes on the Blue Maven standing in the doorway before him. "Alberic and I have been discussing it since Ceruleana, Lucan. We feel you would make for an excellent Elemental Warrior. I offer the position to you." The smile on Lucan's face slowly dissipated and his hands unfolded behind his head to slide to his sides limply. There was a long silence before he eventually narrowed his eyes in disbelief.

"You're joking," he said, trying to read the sage's eyes. The expression on Revond's face did not change in the slightest.

"Have you ever known me to make jokes, Lucan?" the sage asked flatly. Lucan was silent for another long moment but at last thrust himself off the doorway, an incredulous look in his shaking eyes.

"Me?" repeated as if awestruck. "I just signed up to guide you to the people you needed, Master Sage. This was hardly our deal when we set out."

"No it was not, because then I still barely thought you dependable at all," Revond returned, to which Lucan raised an eyebrow unappreciatively. "But you have been true to the right path since I first met you and proved of great worth to us all. Despite your flippancy and the mask of sarcasm you wear to make sense of such a dark and twisted world in which you have lost so much, you remain stouthearted and a good friend. You are a skilled combatant, born of the eastern lands, a leader, and courageous in the face of danger. You fulfilled your task in leading me to the Elemental Warriors I needed—you finished by leading me to yourself." Lucan could barely believe what he was hearing.

"Revond," he began almost exasperated, "you know this isn't what I wanted! This is all on too big a scale for me! I'm just a Maven for Granis' sake!" Maglin Byre stepped forward crossing her arms in front of her and raising an eyebrow.

"What's that supposed to mean?" she snapped. Lucan rolled his eyes at the woman but ignored her.

"Revond, you could barely talk me into leading you to Galantia when we met," he said. "The only reason I even went along with that was because the kid is who he is. What makes you think you're going to be able to talk me into something like this?"

"Because that kid still needs your help to become that man you dreamed he could be when you first learned his name," Revond answered. "You've come this far and survived the Ancients on more instances than anyone alive. Face them a final time. This is the hope your wife saw in you. This is still the opportunity you were looking for. See it through. Let us finish this and take back what is ours." Lucan was still at this, staring at the sage to find a passion and determination he had never seen before in his expression. Though this was the last responsibility he wanted, Lucan couldn't argue with his words. This was his chance. It was what Terrea wanted. And it was his only chance to get her and Lauress back. Looking up to scan the faces of his friends and allies waiting for him, he saw Maglin Byre let a smile spread from the corner of her lips.

"Oh just say yes, you baby," she said, rolling her eyes. Feeling a slight smile appearing on his face as well, Lucan slowly nodded and let out a loud breath.

"You had me at death and destruction, sage," he said for the third time.

Part Four
Elemental Order

Chapter 37

Family Ties

The rain over Drakkaidia stopped sometime in the night while Aeric and Valeri slept. They woke to Drakkaidian sitting next to a fire outside the overhang in the rocks between the cliffs, his hands reached out over the open flames to dry himself. Though it was warm outside both Aeric and Valeri were still damp from the rain the previous night and quickly made their way to the modest fire to dry their clothes as best they could. As soon as the princess opened her eyes she cast them away from Aeric, obviously still perturbed and unsettled from their conversation the previous night. Though she was sore around her midsection again, her wound looked to be fine and the blood that had stained her tunic had been mostly washed away by the rain. After Drakkaidian checked her wound again, he told them to eat breakfast and make themselves ready to start into the Pass of Jostoc.

Aeric in particular was still wary of the demons that had been only a few leagues behind them when they halted for the night. Noting his worry that they would be looking for them and could reappear, Drakkaidian informed the Grandarian the storm that the Valcanor brought when flying in packs had moved on and they had most likely eluded the demons for the moment. Though this put both of the younger companions at rest, the old recluse was quick to remind them their path was still only growing more dangerous. Peering ahead into the narrow road between the cliffs and the fork at the end in the cloudy morning light, Drakkaidian told them the Pass of Jostoc was just as dangerous as the Crag Spires. A series of curving and sharp narrow channels through the lowest part of the mountains that divided them from the valley that lay beyond, he informed them he was one of the few who had ever successfully navigated a way through. Apparently there were a myriad of twisting paths that led to nowhere inside and if they didn't get lost they would certainly have to worry about falling rocks so large and powerful they could cave entire segments of the pass in.

Drakkaidian quickly doused the fire after seeing Aeric and Valeri finishing their breakfasts and rose, gathering his few supplies together. Though both of them had been eager to ask the old man about the previous day and his mysterious sword that appeared from the cloud of red mist, he cut them off by warning them the road ahead demanded as much respect and attention as the Crag Spires and they must remain silent. If they moved fast and didn't get lost he told them it was a two day journey to the valley on the other side. Wanting to get moving again despite his own obvious fatigue, Drakkaidian began walking into the maw of the Pass of Jostoc with his companions behind him. Though forced to stay close together as they traveled in the narrow passage, Aeric and Valeri had little problem following Drakkaidian's order to remain silent. Neither of them even wanted to look at the other, afraid of what they would find in the other's eyes after the scene the previous night.

Though Valeri could walk and climb over the occasional boulder in their path as Drakkaidian took them down forks in the road, the princess was still weak and Aeric knew that despite the discomfort between them he would have to help her keep going forward before long. Finally grabbing her arm to gently help her up to a ledge in a turn in the road, the two made eye contact for a split second but quickly looked away. Though he expected Valeri to pull her arm back and insist on climbing without his help, she let him aid her as she had for the past several days.

Drakkaidian hadn't been embellishing in his warnings of the danger in the Pass of Jostoc. Aeric felt claustrophobic from the moment he set foot inside. The towering but narrow walls of the twisting pathways between the cliffs were never more than several feet wide, sometimes squeezing them so tight they had to squeeze through with their bodies sideways. It was dead quiet inside the pass with only the occasional wisp of wind from far above knocking pebbles down to break the silence. There were open fissures along many of the roads that stretched down into infinite darkness, reminding Aeric of the Crag Spires all over again. Over the hours of the first day weaving into the mazelike mountain pass the trio came to dozens of twists in the road that demanded they choose one of many forks to traverse. Though Drakkaidian occasionally signaled for them to stop and wait as he selected a path, he always came to a decision within a few moments and silently beckoned for them to follow closely.

Aside from a few Siarchs living in a colony high in the cliffs, they didn't see or hear anything alive inside the pass. When night came Drakkaidian continued on until finding the widest gap in the road he could for them to rest, taking care to inspect the ground in the failing light to make sure it was steady for them to sleep on. Though much to his surprise knowing the strength of his two companions, by the time they made a fire and ate some of their remaining rations Aeric found himself with the most energy left in the group. From her wound and the emotional toll of the past few days Valeri was drained and asleep almost as soon as she finished her food and Drakkaidian was not far behind her, his age finally showing through his hard and powerful exterior as Aeric watched him rub his wrinkled hands over his aching muscles.

The next day it was the young Tieloc's turn to wake the others from their slumber, having already packed up their things except for some food, water and the leaves of the fern Lucan had given him to keep their bodies clean and smelling refreshed. Propping himself up with his stick, Drakkaidian rose and pressed on with a gesture of a finger to his lips to signal the need for continued quiet. They kept on moving through the Pass of Jostoc until midday rolled by the next day and they at last came to a series of wider and more spacious passages signaling the end of the pass. Relieved to be able to stretch out his arms without touching rock on either side for the first time, Aeric looked up to see the high cliffs drawing lower with each step they took. Though the uncomfortable silence between all three of them hung on, Drakkaidian at last told them they had made it through the pass.

Weaving out of the last few passages of the mountains and into an open expanse of rock, the trio emerged into the valley Drakkaidian had told them of. Continuing their march for another half of an hour, they made their way over an open basin gingerly sloping down to a large cliff overlooking a sprawling view into the valley. The recluse slowed his pace and diverted from the road he seemed to be sticking to and ambled over to the edge of the cliff top to gaze down onto the scenery far below. Following him to the edge with their eyes going wide, Aeric and Valeri stared in amazement as view of an enormous valley entered their view for leagues in every direction. Aeric felt his heart sink as he scanned the valley, a dark feeling of depression sweeping through him. It was mostly barren and black with no sign of life anywhere, only a wasteland full of rock. Though the valley curved past another cliff and they couldn't see all of it, Drakkaidian slowly nodded to himself before summoning his voice to speak.

"The lake is on the other side," he said slowly. "We will have a better view from further down this cliff as it slopes back into a hillside leading down to the bottom. Be alert. We'll be in the open all the way down." With that he lifted his weight off his staff and started down the cliff, taking care to step farther away from the edge. Aeric and Valeri silently followed, staring down into the sprawling but empty valley as they walked. Several minutes later they came to the turn in the cliffs where Drakkaidian led them to a ledge that stretched down to a hillside gently leveling off into the valley far below. Making their way down, the hidden segment of the valley was revealed with each step they took. By the time they reached the end of the ledge and a rocky series of hills rolling down into the valley, Aeric and Valeri slowed when view of their destination finally caught their mesmerized eyes.

Several leagues in the distance in the center of the previously concealed part of the valley, the trio saw a stagnant body of gray water stretching into the distance. Though a healthy wind blew down from the cliffs into the valley that should have been strong enough to create whitecaps on any body of water, the lake in the distance remained dead calm with only a strange haze hovering over it and the small island they could barely make out in the center. Stricken with the same simultaneous amazement and apprehension as his younger companions, the old recluse gradually slowed until he came to a halt. Leaning his weight back on his staff, he narrowed his eyes at the sight he had not seen in a very long time. Though keeping his gaze fixed on the gray body of water far ahead, he spoke to Aeric and Valeri standing to his right.

"The Lake of the Undead," he breathed as if not wanting to utter the words too loud. "The cursed body of water where the Black Church long sent its enemies after severing their souls from their bodies and binding them to this isolated and forsaken place. We can't make them out from here but the vapors levitating over the surface are the physical manifestations of damned souls reaching out for the sky as if to grasp onto something and pull themselves free." Drakkaidian finally turned and set his precarious, almost fearful gaze on them.

"But there is no escaping the lake once your soul is bound to it—trapped in torturous limbo unto the end of existence. The ground we are about to embark upon teeters on the brink of life and death; sanity and madness; substance and void. Even beyond the waters of the lake the taint that it exudes can ensnare those with wandering senses, and the lake's keeper will not show us welcome. This is our last chance to turn back. I make no guarantees of anything past this point, whether it be the success of our mission or our very survival." When he finished, Aeric could feel a shiver run up his spine from his ominous words. Though he was silent, Valeri let out a dissatisfied huff of breath and turned away from them both.

"When have you ever guaranteed us anything?" she asked rhetorically, more to herself. "We've come far and lost much to get here. We're going down there." Watching her walk away, the two observed the princess unhurriedly making her way to an outcropping of stone jutting out from the hillside to their right. Hiking up it, she stood at its top to better overlook the Lake of the Undead with the wind blowing her hair and shawl back to the south. Aware she was too far away to hear him now, Aeric exhaled a long breath and shifted his gaze back to Drakkaidian.

"She's still very upset about Asthatch," he spoke quietly, accounting for her terseness.

"There is no need to make excuses for the princess," Drakkaidian returned, looking back out into the valley. "Her mood is justified." The old man lifted his staff from the ground and pointed it to the far right of the lake where the rocks began to rise back into a cliff wall. "That is where Sakkdra's hut lies. We should make haste—if I know her, the witch already knows we're here." Aeric swallowed hard and tried to formulate the question on his mind.

"Is she...? I mean, what does she...?" he said, groping for the question.

"Look like?" Drakkaidian finished for him. Though not quite what he was getting at himself, Aeric nodded. "The witch appears as many things—she is not bound to one form.

But while it occasionally behests her to take unconventional or even monstrous shapes, she will appear to us as humanly as she can. Remember, Aeric, Sakkdra is trying to recover her lost humanity. She hates her existence as the thing she has become. She chooses to appear as much like her former self as she can remember."

"What are you going to offer her in trade for the crests?" Aeric asked, his curiosity over this question built up since first hearing about it. Drakkaidian was quiet for a moment but lowered his staff back to the ground to lean on it again.

"If we make it that far, you will see soon enough, boy," he answered cryptically, turning to look at him. Aeric held his gaze for a lingering moment, not sure why he still didn't want to reveal whatever his real plan was even this close to their goal. Letting the matter go and trusting him again, Aeric turned to look back at the outcropping to his right. Gazing up to the young woman standing at its top, he saw Valeri already staring at him instead of the lake. Reading her eyes even from the distance between them, he knew what was on her mind and he forced himself to look away, not having the heart to face her. He knew that even after the night before entering the Pass of Jostoc and the awkward silence to follow in their passing through it, her feelings had not changed and she still wanted something he could not give her. Taking a deep breath he saw Valeri look away from the corner of his eye and begin to slowly make her way down the outcropping.

Seeing the Grandarian discreetly eyeing her as she walked, Drakkaidian shifted the weight between his feet and raised an eyebrow.

"You Tielocs certainly have a way with the Montrox women," he said under his breath, just loud enough for the Grandarian to hear. Aeric spun his head around to face him, watching as the old man shook his head. Seeing the boy's gaze on him, Drakkaidian looked away and lifted his staff in preparation to begin walking down the hills into the valley.

"What?" Aeric asked sharply with an offended look on his face.

"Just the way it was with your grandmother Arilia," Drakkaidian replied to himself as he began walking down the hill. Before he could escape Aeric's reach, the Grandarian shot his arm out to grab Drakkaidian's with frustration finding its way into his expression and body language.

"Just wait, Drakkaidian," Aeric told him harshly, holding the old man where he stood. "What are you talking about? How could you possibly know so much about my family to know my grandmother was originally a Montrox and married a Tieloc?"

"Because they were his family too," another voice answered from behind him. Releasing Drakkaidian, Aeric wheeled his head around to see Valeri coming to a halt behind him, folding her arms in front of her chest. The old recluse shifted his gaze to her, silently staring with his eyes softening. Aeric's face warped with confusion at her statement.

"What did you say?" he asked, his impatience getting the better of him. Valeri kept her gaze on the old man for a long moment, here expression confident but soft.

"He's your family as well, Aeric," the girl replied. "And mine. This old recluse is my grandfather and the former King of Drakkaidia, Verix Montrox." There was a long silence that hung between the three after Valeri finished her sentence. Aeric's eyes widened at first, and he slowly turned to look at Drakkaidian with disbelief. The old man merely held his impassive gaze on the princess, completely still. When he didn't refute her or ask her to explain herself, Aeric slowly shook his head and shifted his gaze back to Valeri.

"Verix Montrox?" he repeated dumbfounded. "How could this man be your grandfather, Valeri? Why would a former King of Drakkaidia be living by himself in the Black Peaks away from Dalastrak and his family?"

"That's what I intend to find out before we go any farther," the princess returned, still staring at the old man. "Think about it. We've seen him do things no ordinary man is capable of, much less one as old as this one is. He killed that Arnosmn in the Crag Spires with a single blow, navigated the most dangerous ground in the world, held back a lightning storm, and killed a Liradd on his own in the dark and rain. He's a warrior that can best demons even in his old age and knows everything about this country, including the exact route through the Black Peaks that my grandfather took in his travels here when he was still a prince. He asked about your grandparents and knows so much about them because they were his sister and brother in law, making you his great-nephew. That is probably why he agreed to help us get here in the first place. And how did he know to come for us when we were in trouble in the Crag Spires? Because he wields dark elemental power of his own and he could sense me using my power against the demons. It's how he knew the exact spire top to find us. This is my grandfather."

Drakkaidian was quiet in the face of the girl's evidence, still just staring at her. Again surrounded by silence, Aeric threw his arms up in the air at the impossibility of what she was saying.

"Valeri, think of how old that would make him!" she exclaimed. "My grandfather was the same age as Verix Montrox and if he were still alive he'd be eighty-two."

"Eighty-one," the old man corrected with what sounded like scorn. Aeric froze at this, slowly grinding his head back to stare at Drakkaidian uncertainly. He couldn't find the words to respond at this, unable to believe the legendary Prince and King of Drakkaidia that he had heard so many tales of from his grandparents could be the wrinkled and impatient old recluse. Eventually Drakkaidian shifted his gaze from Valeri to the young Tieloc, closing his eyes and taking in a long, slow breath. Exhaling, he opened his eyes and nodded. "Valeri is correct. I am Verix Montrox." While Aeric felt his jaw slipping open in astonishment at his words, even Valeri felt her breathing quicken despite already knowing it in her heart. The old man shifted his weight between his legs and staff once again before continuing. "Well done, princess. You are indeed your father's daughter to have pieced together all that you have." Hearing her grandfather acknowledge his identity, Valeri softened and let her arms fall to her sides, her armor slowly falling away as Aeric had seen several times. Opening her mouth as she searched for her next words, the girl shrugged as if not sure what to say at that point.

Shifting his gaze between the two Montroxs, Aeric finally found his voice again.

"How long have you known?" Aeric asked Valeri, to which the girl tried to collect herself and respond.

"I had my suspicions since we first met," she stated plainly. "Besides all the evidence he's given us along the way I could... feel something familiar about him from the first time I saw him. I can almost see my father in him..." She trailed off for a moment, staring with her searching eyes at the man revealed to be her grandfather. "Why didn't you tell us?" Verix Montrox slowly blinked and glanced at Aeric before responding.

"It wasn't necessary for you to know," he told her, earning a frown from the princess. "You never knew me. You have no attachment to me. Creating one in circumstances as dire as ours would only have proven a liability."

"What makes you think I would have grown attached to you?" Valeri batted back, her words cold. Verix merely let an inaudible chuckle escape from his mouth.

"And you are indeed my granddaughter," he said with a dark smile. "I had no reason to assume you would, but nevertheless, there was no reason you needed to know and many reasons not to tell you, so I didn't. But now that you have surmised the truth on your own, I suppose I should tell you why you never knew your grandfather in the first place. Just a year after you were born I decided to pass the throne of Drakkaidia to your father, Valeri. I was telling you the truth earlier when I told you I am simply a warrior who has seen too much for his own good. When I took command of Drakkaidia, I inherited a nation of chaos and despair given to me by my father and the evil he unleashed during the Days of Destiny. Over the years I fought for and accomplished much, from the uniting of our people in the face of civil war to the reform of the throne and Black Church. Peace with Grandaria, only a fool's dream when I was born, had become a distant but possible reality under my rule.

"But my gains did not come without cost to my own person. The stresses of the throne during my turbulent years left me tired, and the battles I had fought through them left scars on my body and mind that needed time to heal before I could pass to the next realm. Drakkaidia is a strong nation that demands a strong king ready to come to her defense from any enemy with power and poise. I had grown old fast. I could no longer provide that strength after the toil my life had wrought on my body. So I passed rule down to your father. He was young and inexperienced, but so was I when my reign began."

"But why did you just disappear?" Valeri pressed, unconvinced. "Why exile yourself to the Black Peaks? Your place was in Dalastrak."

"One of the earliest chapters in my life was still unfinished elsewhere, my granddaughter," Verix returned. "Before even the Days of Destiny I ventured into these mountains on a mission for my father to prove myself to him as a worthy heir to his throne. Much was different then. It was on that journey that I found that house in the Crag Spires once filled with criminals I was sent to rout. I navigated the Electric Flat and Pass of Jostoc, and met Sakkdra the Witch. I... sinned on that journey. A terrible tragedy befell someone that I was responsible for. I have been seeking atonement for that tragedy ever since." Though he softened as he let memories from long ago sweep through his thoughts, Aeric and Valeri watched as his face tightened with anger as he spoke his next sentence. "And there was also justice to be served to others that had a hand in that tragedy. I came to live in the Black Peaks to tie up the loose ends of my life before my old war wounds could claim me. Besides, if I had lingered in central Drakkaidia there would have been protest of my order to pass the throne to Valgard. In the end we both agreed the course of action I took was best. I have been here ever since, dwelling in the peace of my solitude after years of trauma and turmoil."

The former King of Drakkaidia trailed off there, his eyes growing distant and looking into space.

"And yet over the years of my reclusion I found myself with regrets," he said quietly. "I frequently lamented not seeing my son rise to power. Never seeing my beloved sister again, or my old friend and rival Tavin. Or seeing my granddaughter grow up into the woman she has become." He slowly raised his eyes to Valeri who slowly softened at this, staring at him with some masked emotion in her eyes. "I never expected to survive as long as I have, but as the months turned into years my body simply wouldn't fail. Then one day I sensed a familiar power outside my doorstep in the form of my own blood and I found myself with a new task. I meant what I said about you, Aeric. I would not dare deny the destiny of a Tieloc after the things I have seen in my life. Now I think perhaps I was meant to survive all these years so this old man could be of use to Drakkaidia and all Iairia one final time." Verix paused there locking his gaze back on his granddaughter. "I am sorry for keeping the truth from you both. But most of all, my Valeri, I am sorry for leaving you in the first place. It had to be done and I do not expect you to understand, but I am still sorry you never knew your own grandfather."

Valeri remained still and silent when he finished, tears welling in the corners of her eyes. Aeric knew her well enough to know half of her wanted to turn her back on him and leave him the same way he had left her. The other half wanted to rush up to him and embrace him, letting her tears flow. Though aware of her feelings, Aeric also remembered both the Montroxs were Drakkaidians and knew she would not do either. She would stay as calm and controlled as she could and do nothing, containing her emotions as she had been trained. There was no place for a girl's love for her grandfather in Drakkaidia, nor a grandfather's for her. Though he wished it otherwise, the Grandarian wasn't surprised when Valeri stood her ground, held in her tears, and simply spoke three simple words.

"I do now," she said, standing strong. Verix gave her a single nod as a gust of wind blew up the tails of his black robe where he stood.

"I suppose you do," he returned. The three stared back and forth at each other for a long moment before Verix at last broke the silence and lifted his staff up from the ground. "Well, if you still trust me, it's time we make our way to Sakkdra and these crests of yours. I could keel over and die any minute after all. Then what use would I be to you?" Though appreciating his mildly playful words, Aeric didn't smile or laugh. He looked back to Valeri standing behind him with a regretful look in her eyes. When she didn't respond, Aeric told Verix he was still with him and asked him to lead them to the lake. Nodding, the old Drakkaidian king turned and began marching down the hill for the Lake of the Undead in the distance. Turning back for Valeri, Aeric watched as she uncertainly shifted her gaze to him and forced herself to start forward alongside him after her grandfather.

Chapter 38

<u>Bargain</u>

Verix, Aeric and Valeri descended the rocky hills curving down into the basin of the valley over the next hour. All three of their hearts pumped hard as they finally made their way onto the barren plain leading to the Lake of the Undead, arriving in what Verix had warned over and over was the most dangerous place on the continent. It was the most barren place Aeric had ever seen, even having seen nothing but desolation since the Ascension began. The flat and bleak valley surface was nothing but gray rock as far as they could see, only rising into boulders at the valley's edges that were mostly surrounded with vertical cliffs. The trio stayed close together as they entered the unusual depression in the Black Peaks. Aeric and Valeri walked closely at each others' sides with Verix a few steps ahead, the sound of his staff striking the flat ground with each step the only sound they made.

Though all of them were nervous of walking closer to the cursed Lake of the Undead and any hidden dangers in their path, Aeric guessed the silence between them came primarily from the shocking scene that had finally revealed the identity of their reclusive guide. Valeri looked to be the most shaken up despite having exposed him in the first place. As she walked close beside Aeric looking around at the empty valley and the strange haze slowly lofting over the lake, her crimson eyes frequently fell to her grandfather's elderly figure. Aeric could tell there were dozens of questions burning in her mind and things she wanted to say to him, whether favorable or not. She held them all in, her fierce Montrox pride keeping her focused on the task at hand and numb to her emotions the same as her grandfather from whom she inherited the characteristic.

Verix had softened to a point neither of his young relatives had ever seen from him when he first acknowledged

Valeri's accusation. It looked as though a weight had been lifted from his mind and heart, allowing him to look upon his granddaughter and great nephew through his own eyes instead of through those of the ill-tempered recluse trying to keep them at arm's length. They could both see an unidentifiable change in him despite maintaining his usual aloofness. Though it was clear by his words and tone when confirming Valeri's suspicions that he had not wanted them to find out the truth, the revelation was one of the few unexpected rewards their quest had yielded. Aeric still wasn't sure he credited Verix's excuse for withholding his identity from them, but walking behind one of the living legends of Iairia, he found it didn't really matter. He felt a new surge of confidence at his presence no matter how small.

Despite the former king's fabled Drakkaidian coarseness that he had experienced for himself since their first meeting, Aeric also kept in mind the old Montrox's famed heroics and honorable actions over his long years in service of not only his people but of all Iairia as well. He aided Aeric's grandparents in the Days of Destiny by defecting from his own father to stop him from permanently unleashing the Netherworld. It had cost him his life but with the Holy Emerald assembled in the aftermath of Drakkan's defeat, Tavin Tieloc was able to revive him. Twenty years later he backed down from a war he was poised to win when he had the chance to raze Galantia to the ground and possibly conquer Grandaria once and for all at the conclusion of the Third Holy War. Instead he sought truth through a shroud of doubt and lies to realize Drakkaidia and Grandaria had been manipulated into war by the High Priest Zalnaught.

In the wake of the several abuses of power he had witnessed nearly destroy his home in his life, he reformed the Black Church and created a new governing body under the throne in Dalastrak to ensure dictators like his father or Zalnaught never rose to power again. Perhaps his most notable work was striving for peace with his neighbor to the east for the first time in history. Even in the face of his people vehemently opposing such a notion to the point of calling him a traitor to Drakkaidia, the respect he and his beliefs commanded influenced all but the most stubborn of traditionalists over relatively short decades. He made a once treasonous notion of embracing their most bitter enemies an ideal of fellowship. Verix Montrox had arguably accomplished and contributed as much during his lifetime as even Aeric's grandfather Tavin.

Contemplating the actions of the former King of Drakkaidian and feeling himself growing more vested in the idea of his great uncle as more than just their guide but someone he felt responsible for and cared about like the member of his family that he was, Aeric wondered what Verix would do if they succeeded and restored the world now that he and Valeri knew he was still alive. Thinking of the future that might lie in wait for them if they did mange to stop the Ancients and fuse the Sources to create a new version of the Holy Emerald itself, Aeric felt his eyes drawn to the red-haired girl striding beside him. Letting his mind drift, the young Tieloc thought of his usual dream of Eirinor Village bright green and blooming with life in mid spring. As his thoughts passed up the hillside overlooking the vale village to the image of the girl always waiting for him on top of it with a smile, he imagined taking her into his arms and preparing to lean in and gently kiss her soft lips.

Aeric suddenly flinched, his eyes going wide as he realized where his mind had drifted. Though he had not even noticed in his daydreaming, he realized the lips he imagined reaching out to touch weren't those of Mina but the fiery haired princess of Drakkaidia. Noticing him jump with a start as they walked, Valeri shifted her anxious gaze to him and asked if he was alright. Though replying he was fine and just took a bad step, Aeric felt his heart beginning to beat faster in a virtual panic.

Though he could no longer deny his feelings for Valeri despite their fierce difference in personality and their being second cousins, he felt like every step he took beside her without plainly telling her they could never be was nothing short of a betrayal to Mina. The hope of reviving his lost love had been his only reason to live after losing her; it was his only purpose in venturing to find Alberic and then the elemental crests. Not sure what it meant to have found another purpose in protecting Valeri that felt equal to his first charge now consciously driving him, the Grandarian felt a crushing wave of confusion and disgrace crashing into him as if the very notion was a sin against himself and his love.

Though caught up in the storm of emotions and doubts tearing through him at his mess of conflicting feelings, Aeric had little time to dwell on them as he saw Verix quietly turn his head and prepare to speak in a hush.

"It's vital for the two of you to stay as alert as possible as we approach Sakkdra's dwelling," he almost whispered back, shifting his eyes between them. "We draw close now and I don't know what kind of reception we are going to receive. I didn't exactly part with the witch on the best of terms after our last meeting, and she is known for her temperamental nature. Be ready for anything." While Aeric tried to gulp down his worries of what to expect from the keeper of the Lake of the Undead, Valeri merely narrowed her eyes challengingly and swept her gaze around the valley.

"Where is this dwelling of hers?" she asked, looking around the edges of the gray lake. Seeing her peering around the lake, Verix lifted his staff to point over to the south side of the valley where a collection of jagged boulders rose into the cliffs.

"There," he breathed, lowering his staff. "The witch's power is not great but it is enough to ensnare the three of us if we provoke it. Stay silent now—let me do the talking." Aeric and Valeri exchanged apprehensive glances. While Aeric wondered if he would need the Source of Light and Valeri if she would need her sword, they weren't sure if either would do any good. Over the next half an hour the trio drew ever closer toward the cliffs south of the Lake of the Undead. As they neared, Aeric and Valeri were surprised to see most of the boulders beside them not naturally protruding out of the grown but messily cast about as if they had been blown apart and fragmented. When a clutter of wooden logs and boards came into view, Verix slowed his pace, keeping his gaze ahead but motioning with a slow downward gesture of his free hand for his companions to move carefully. Guessing the shambled shack of wood was Sakkdra's lair, Aeric peered into the darkened opening trying to see anything. It seemed as if even the minimal noise of the passing wind and their footsteps on the rock had disappeared as they came within a few yards of the rocks, the dead silence sucking any sound into the shack.

Verix frowned as he noticed the all-pervasive silence, sweeping his narrowed eyes around the rocks for movement. Looking down at a small chunk of a boulder lying beside him with a strange hue compared to most of the rest, the old Montrox reached down with the end of his staff to nudge the end into it. Aeric and Valeri jumped as the rock fell apart with dark purple embers leaping up around it. Watching the stone turn to ash, the two felt their hearts soar into their chests at the resonance of what sounded like a menacing groan echoing from the opening of the makeshift shack. Verix tightened his frame and took hold of his staff with both hands, waiting. Though about to say something, the former King of Drakkaidian tensed further as he saw a mess of several thick tentacles soaring out of the opening in the shack toward them.

Though Valeri was about to draw her sword, Verix shouted for her to remain still and he leapt to his right to swat one of the black appendages to the ground before it could sail into the princess. The moment he touched it the others responded by soaring at him, dripping a smoldering black sludge as they whipped around the air. Seeing the tentacles all converging on him, Verix waited for one of them to grab onto his staff before he released it and jumped back. They all wrapped around it and snapped it into splinters. Fumbling to catch his balance, Verix shouted out a single word into the air.

"Sakkdra!" he bellowed. Though Aeric expected the tentacles to throw the wood down and reach out for them again, they carefully slowed and dropped Verix's staff. Before long, they fell to the rocky ground as if in submission and gradually slid back into the darkness of the shack with the oozing trial of black left behind. As soon as the tentacles were gone, the three heard another faint groan that eventually turned into short laughter. The timbre of the voice was deep and echoing as if coming from several mouths but as it transitioned into an almost giddy laugher, the pitch rose.

"A caller," the voice spoke, still ominously echoing but sounding like it came from a woman. "I have not had a caller in years..." There was a long silence then, with Aeric and the Montroxs merely waiting for the voice to speak again. Though no more words left the shack, the three were surprised to see a dark shadow stretching out of the doorway onto the mess of wood below it, radiating twisting black energy as if embers from a fire. It looked like a puddle of viscous liquid, slowly churning forward onto the rock toward them. When Verix lifted his right leg in preparation to step toward it, the shadow abruptly flew forward and squeezed together to jet under his feet and between the two behind him. Wheeling around to watch the black mass shoot off into the distance toward the lake, Aeric and Valeri exchanged befuddled glances, wondering if what they had seen was the witch.

They got their answer when they turned back around for Verix to see him staring down a darkly dressed woman standing but a few inches from his face. Both Aeric and Valeri jumped in shock but remained otherwise still, remembering Verix's order to let him handle this. The woman was dressed in a long black robe that covered her body from the neck down, fraying into long strands at her feet. She had the blackest hair any of them had ever seen tightly collected into a swirling bun behind her head and dark skin that looked to have been in the sun long enough to tan her to a crisp. Her face was not aged or hideous as Aeric guessed it would be but unblemished and even marginally attractive. Her penetrating eyes staring deep into Verix's were solid brown but for her pupils that shone a strange rotten yellow. There was a curious, even tickled smile on her face as she kept her gaze on the old man before her, looking him up and down.

"I see..." she began slowly, "...a boy I once knew, in the face of this old man." Sakkdra narrowed her eyes, slowly turning to the other two standing beside him. The witch quickly swept to her left like a wraith, sliding in front of the princess with the ends of her robes exuding the same strange radiation they had seen emanate from the shadow moments before. Valeri remained undaunted as the witch peered into her eyes, opening her mouth with her face seeming to soften and grow younger. "I see that boy in this girl, as well. How beautiful you are..." Sakkdra slowly raised a hand up from her robes and reached out for Valeri's face. Though tempted to tear away or slap the witch's limb back to her side, Valeri decided it best not to provoke her unless warranted and remained still as Sakkdra swept the tips of her fingers across her left cheek. They were cold and course as if composed of jagged ice.

Eventually sweeping her piercing gaze to Aeric, the witch suddenly cringed and shrieked out, reeling back and pulling her arm back into her robes. Though all three of them were surprised at her unprovoked recoil, they were more shocked to see her once smooth and striking face warp into that of an old woman's, wrinkled and worn with her eyes turning bloodshot.

"A Tieloc," she stated with disgust as she peered up and down Aeric's frame. "I have crossed one of you before." Where Sakkdra had once revealed her arm, two of the oozing black tentacles they had seen before slowly reached out into the air toward him. "I should snap you in two for insulting me with your presence." Though Aeric watched with his heart racing as the two appendages approached, he saw Verix fire his right hand up to powerfully latch onto one of the tentacles and squeeze it hard, black sludge seeping between his fingers. Sakkdra shrank back as if in pain and spun her head to face him.

"We have come to visit you for a reason, Sakkdra," he spoke ominously quiet. "Don't you wish to know why?" The witches face tightened with her wrinkles compressing but turning red.

"The last time I met you, Verix Montrox, you were here to steal from me what I had rightfully found," she hissed, her voice echoing with power. "I should destroy you!" Sakkdra's eyes suddenly burned with glowing red energy and her skin blackened, strange black embers twisting off her frame as it widened and several more tentacles emerged to shoot around his neck before he could react. Though Valeri grit her teeth and reached for her sword Verix saw her move and shouted for her to stay where she was. Breathing heavily with purple veins broadening under her putrid skin, Sakkdra lifted the old man off the ground and tightened her grip on him. Struggling to breath, Verix looked back into her furious eyes.

"If you keep this up I'll have no choice but to summon my power to hold you back, Sakkdra," the old man managed to utter. "And you know who will be on their way here on claw and wing if they sense power. Would you rather deal with me or face Drakkan's minions?"

"Maybe I'll just snap your neck now before you can!" Sakkdra bellowed with her voice pounding through their bodies.

"Then you'll face my granddaughter and probably be destroyed before her power draws any demons here anyway," he returned, reaching up to try and pry away a tentacle around his neck. Sakkdra was quiet at this, casting a glance down to the girl standing enraged with her hand tightly gripped around the hilt of her sword. Growling and gritting her teeth, Sakkdra grunted and threw Verix away to land on his back several feet beyond on the gray rock.

"What do you want?" she barked as she quickly shrank back down to the size they had first seen her with the tentacles sweeping back into her robes. Valeri and Aeric quickly rushed to Verix's side to help him back up. Slowly lifting back to his feet and wiping away the black sludge around his neck, the former king summoned his voice again.

"You've sensed the beast Dalorosk free and destroying everything in his path, yes?" he asked. The witch spun around with the black radiation leaping off her frame to show him her back.

"The meddling creature has brought Drakkan's underlings out from the pit," she snapped furiously.

"Well, we can stop him for you," Verix told her, standing full height again. Sakkdra slowly rotated her head back to stare at the old man with her eyes narrowing and her pale yellow pupils widening. Though still and silent for a moment, the witch eventually turned her entire body around and began sliding toward them again with a knowing smile lifting the corners of her mouth. When in front of Verix she began circling them with her face returning to its attractive state and her voice serene again.

"You still command your dark power, old Montrox," she said almost seductively, "but your frail body awaits death's swinging scythe. You cannot stand up to one as powerful as the behemoth, even with these two. And why would you want to help me?"

"We occupy the same world, Sakkdra," Verix told her as she swept in front of his eyes to circle him again. "If we work together we can end this threat to us all." Sakkdra's smile widened as she glanced at Valeri and Aeric, aware she was growing closer to the real reason they were there.

"You still have not told me what you want," the witch said, pressing her lips closer to Verix's ear as she slipped behind him. "What would you need from me?"

"Many years ago you gathered six talismans that can repel the beasts," Verix told her slowly. "We need you to give them to us." Sakkdra slowed to a stop as she neared Verix's front again, staring into his eyes.

"Six talismans?" she repeated confused, obviously unsure of what he could have been referring to. "What makes you think I have these talismans?" Sakkdra's face darkened again as she frowned. "Do you accuse me of stealing them? Are you calling me a thief?"

"I didn't say that," Verix replied quickly. "I just remember your collection of rare items is far more expansive than any other. We are looking for six coffins that were once buried in the east." Sakkdra slowly smiled again and let her tense face relax.

"Ahh..." she murmured, sliding a few feet back and nodding. "Perhaps I do have what you seek." She set her disturbing eyes back on the three, looking over their faces. "But why, Verix Montrox, would I give this power to you?"

"Eventually Dalorosk and his brethren will find even you here in their rampage," Verix responded. "Together they could defeat even you. It's in your interest to help us."

"Is it?" she asked. "It seems I already possess whatever power is hidden inside these coffins for myself. Why don't I just hold onto it in case Dalorosk ever does find me? What do I care about any of you?"

"The talismans we need are worthless to any but the Elemental Warriors appointed by the sages," Verix told her. "They will do you no good unless you give them to us." Sakkdra raised an eyebrow and leaned forward.

"And yet you are no more an Elemental Warrior than I," she returned. "I gain nothing by this. You have nothing I want. So you will get nothing." With that, the witch turned her wraith-like form and started to glide back toward her shack with the dark embers twisting off her body as she went. Before she could get far, Verix shouted out to her.

"I have something you've wanted for years," he said, catching her attention. She halted again and looked back.

"I think not," she replied, though unable to hide the obvious curiosity in her voice. "What could you possibly have for me?" Verix narrowed his eyes and took a slow step forward.

"My power," he told her. "Have you forgotten our last meeting? You tried to barter my soul to harvest its power. I am old, but you admit yourself it remains." Aeric and Valeri shot each other astounded glances, unable to believe what he was saying. "Well, now is your chance to take it. Let us barter. Grant us the talismans we seek and I am yours." Sakkdra had slowly turned around to face him by the time he was finished, staring at him distrustfully. Aeric was awestruck at the reclusive king's offer. He could never have imagined that his secret leverage over the witch would be his very soul. Though compelled to say something to Valeri that they couldn't let this happen, after a long pause, Sakkdra shot over to Verix in a black streak until abruptly inches from his face again.

"You offer your soul to me," she said as if to confirm it to herself. "I do not deny that I have hungered for your great power since I first felt it—witnessed it tear through your enemies and explode with energy I had rarely seen over the years." The witch reached out with her arm to slide her fingers up and down the old man's hard body. "And through your life I sensed and saw it grow with each of your many battles, ever expanding. You are truly a titan of this world, Drakkaidian King." The witch pulled her other hand free from her robes, holding what looked to be a flask with a wide wooden lid at its top. Both Aeric and Valeri could see a strange glowing haze around it similar to the haze above the Lake of the Undead behind them. "You remember this, don't you?" Verix stared down at the flask with his face tightening with quiet rage.

"You swindled my friend's soul with that cursed bag," he told her with ice hanging from his words. Sakkdra's face morphed into the old woman's, twisting with rage.

"Watch your tongue, old man," the witch barked. "I swindle nothing. I take only what is promised to me, though my flask can take anything I want. If he crossed me I could steal the soul of Dalorosk himself with this, so I could most certainly take yours now. Such an addition to my collection would be a mighty one indeed." Sakkdra lifted the flask up to his chest and set her fingers over the lid, preparing to lift it free.

Though holding steady for a long moment, her once wanting eyes narrowed. A look of disgust came over her face and she withdrew her flask back into the folds of her dark robes.

"But while your power remains it is dwindled and a shell of its former potency. Your soul is hardly worth offering to Drakkan in such decay." Sakkdra looked past Verix's head to the younger pair behind him, her smile returning. "But luckily for me, that same power exists again in its youthful state." Sakkdra slid around Verix and slowly raised herself as she approached Valeri to cast her glare down on her. "This one is still ripe and with power that will one day rival your own. I will take her soul." Valeri's eyes widened in shock at this, the breath in her lungs escaping her. Aeric responded to her offer first, shoving his body between the witch and the princess and glaring up at her. Before either of them could say anything Verix was turning around and shaking his head.

"No," he answered. "It is my soul that is offered. The girl is young and her power still undeveloped. I am—"

"Not what I want," Sakkdra interrupted him, looking back with a glare. "She is young but I will take such... beautiful innocence primed to ascend into maturity, long before I take a shriveled old man virtually ready to collapse before me. This is the only way you will get anything from me. If I get what I want the coffins are yours. I will take your young relative."

"Then take me instead," Aeric interjected desperately, catching them all of guard. Valeri instantly spun to face him with anger in her eyes.

"Aeric shut up," she told him threateningly. "You're not—"

"I am also related to Verix Montrox but my blood carries potential for dark and light power," Aeric told Sakkdra, ignoring Valeri. "I would be of far greater use to you." Sakkdra shifted her gaze to the young man but violently grimaced.

"The only use I would have for you is to watch you die, maggot," the witch bit at him. "I have tried to absorb one of you Tielocs before but my efforts ended in catastrophe. For all I know you have a vessel of Drakkan inside you as well. The trade will be the talismans for the young Montrox." Growing frustrated, Verix stepped forward and told her to listen to him. Before he could reach her, Sakkdra tightened and threw one of her black tentacles out from her robes to slam into the old man and throw him off his feet to send him falling to his back once again, temporarily stunned. With Valeri's grandfather incapacitated for the moment, Sakkdra loosened her face back into its soft appearance and set her yellow eyes back on the princess.

"What of it, girl?" she asked soothingly, pulling her strange glowing flask from her robes. "Do we have a deal?" Though Aeric waited for Valeri to tell her to go to hell like he expected, she was silent. Shifting his view to the princess, Aeric saw her strong gaze replaced by a strange passivity he had not seen before.

"What assurance can you give us that you'll honor your word if I agree?" she asked. Aeric's mouth fell open and his heart leapt into his chest at this, shocked at her reply.

"Valeri, you can't!" he shouted with his emotions seizing control of his words. The princess spun to face him with an indomitable expression.

"Don't even try to tell me what I can or can't do with myself after offering yourself to her too, Tieloc," she snapped, struggling to hold onto her anger. Aeric was shaking his head, grabbing her by the shoulders and pulling her around to face him.

"Valeri, no," he pleaded, desperation in his voice. "The world needs you. You're our Warrior of Darkness. We need you..." Valeri was quiet at this, unable to hold onto her strength. She met his gaze, her eyes almost trembling.

"I'll do whatever I have to for Drakkaidia," she told him. "And for you. You still have to face the Ancients with the others. This is our only chance."

"I don't care," Aeric told her, tears welling in his eyes as he saw one roll down Valeri's cheek. "We'll find another way. We'll get Revond and Alberic and come back here and make her give us the crests. I can't lose you."

"He's right, Valeri," Verix said as he tried to rise from the ground where Sakkdra had laid him flat. "I won't let you do this. Your father didn't raise you to die like this."

"Well you didn't raise my father to die like he did either, but he gave his life to stop the Ancients the same as you would have," Valeri told him passionately. As another tear rolled down her cheek, she looked back at Aeric. "The same as I have to do now. You know there's no other way." Aeric didn't know what to say to her, aware there was no way to deter the willful Drakkaidian princess. She leaned closer to him, desperately wanting to say something but held firm and kept it in. Aware the Grandarian would do anything he could to stop her, the princess quickly kissed him on his cheek then raised her arms to forcefully shove him falling onto his back. Spinning around to the witch still towering in front of her, Valeri nodded in defiance of her fear. "You have a deal. Do it." Sakkdra let a dark grin spread across her face as she reached into her robes with her free hand. Hearing his granddaughter's words, Verix forced himself back to his feet.

"No Sakkdra!" he bellowed. "I forbid this!" The witch did not look back at him as she responded.

"I do not need your consent, old man," she replied as she raised the flask up to Valeri's chest and put her hand on the lid. "We have a deal." As soon as she finished her sentence, Sakkdra pulled the lid off her flask and Valeri went stiff, her eyes wide. Though Aeric screamed for the witch to wait as he scrambled back to his feet, it was already too late. The soft haze emanating around the flask shot upward and raced out to spread around Valeri's immobile body while an ominous blue light from inside the opening began pulling in the air around it. Once the haze had completely surrounded the Drakkaidian princess, she began to levitate off the ground with her eyes slowly closing. Watching in horror, Aeric witnessed a transparent blue copy of Valeri's frame rush out of her body into the air to be compressed and sucked into the witch's flask.

Once all traces of the blue light from Valeri's essence had been pulled into the opening, Sakkdra sealed it with the lid once more. The young woman's lifeless body dropped from where it hung the next moment, falling in a limp heap over the gray rock. Though previously frozen in his shock, when he saw the princess' body fall Aeric rushed toward her and slid to her side to collect it in his arms. Though he spoke her name in anguish as he lifted her limp upper body, he could feel her suddenly cold and noticed her entire body had turned a pale shade of gray. Unable to contain his tears that had been welling in the corners of his eyes as he watched the girl's soul being sucked out of her, the Grandarian lifted Valeri's head to press it against his forehead in the silence. He tightly closed his eyes and cried, unable to believe the fate that had just befallen the stubborn princess.

Verix Montrox stood behind Sakkdra, slowly walking around her to look down at his lifeless granddaughter with pain in his eyes he hadn't felt in many long years. Lowering his head in shame of what he had allowed to happen, the former King of Drakkaidia stood in the torturous silence only broken by Aeric's anguished weeping. This was his fault. He knew the risks of bringing the two before Sakkdra—he knew his gambit would probably be the death of them both. He never would have brought them here had he known this was the fate that would await his own granddaughter. Aeric grasped Valeri's body tighter with both arms but lifted his head off hers, sniffling as he stared down at her gray face.

"I will bring you back, Valeri," he whispered to her through his tears. "I swear I'll put this right. Whatever it takes..." Though staring at Aeric while he embraced the empty body of the princess, Verix shifted his gaze to Sakkdra as she tucked her flask into her robes and pulled free a forbidding looking amulet hanging around a black necklace of twine. There was a miniature skull at the center of the triangular amulet, dripping red with what looked like blood. She threw it down at Valeri's feet, the sound catching Aeric's attention. Sniffing back his emotion, he turned his head to look at it.

"This necklace is called the Immortal Pendant," Sakkdra told him plainly. "Wearing it, one of you will be able to cross the Lake of the Undead to the island where I keep my spoils. I will be waiting for you to return it to me and to make sure you don't take anything more than your coffins. Make haste—I haven't got all day." Though Aeric shot the soulless witch a look of deathly revulsion, he slowly reached out to take the necklace into his grasp. Feeling the viscous blood drip off the amulet, he looked back at Verix Montrox staring at him. Knowing what he had to do, Aeric's expression grew grave. After putting the necklace around his neck, he knelt over Valeri to gather her in his arms and lift her. Standing tall with resolve pumping through his heart as he had never felt before, the young Tieloc locked onto the witch smiling at him with eyes so hateful he stole her grin away.

"This isn't over, witch," he spoke powerfully. With that, he turned and began walking toward the Lake of the Undead in the distance carrying Valeri in his arms. Taking a deep breath and focusing on the task at hand, Verix Montrox started after him, shooting a glare toward Sakkdra as he passed. The witch merely narrowed her eyes with her rotten pupils watching them walk toward the evil lake in the distance.

Chapter 39

<u>Found</u>

After taking the night to rest in Keracon Valley and allow Morrol and Lucan time to recuperate, Revond, Alberic and the four soon to be anointed Elemental Warriors departed the Cronom village high in the trees. When they awoke, the cut in the Blue Maven's leg had completely healed without so much as a scar present and the Sarton's arm was fully mobile again as if it had never been broken. Though Revond and Alberic had heard of the amazing healing abilities of the Cronoms, neither of them had anticipated so quick a recovery and were surprised to find the once ailing men walking to the Grand Hollow as fit as ever with Maglin and Kira that morning. The Master Sage and Ancient of Light had been waiting above the Grand Hollow since dawn, talking on its highest level beside the fabled Sapphire Pool Tavin Tieloc had used to speak with Zeroan during the Days of Destiny.

The two could both feel Dalorosk and the other Ancients rampaging through Drakkaidia, obviously on the hunt for the resistance base. Aware they had to get back and prepare the fortifications of Hadecrest before they found it, they decided to leave as soon as the others were up. After eating a healthy green breakfast laid out by the Cronoms, the party bid them goodbye outside the Grand Hollow, all of them expressing their gratefulness for the incredible hospitality they had been shown. Yucono and Josthop told them they were happy to help and it was they who were indebted to the sage and his warriors for fighting for the survival of the entire world. The mob of Cronoms that had assembled around them to see them away were in tears at the sight of Kira climbing up on Alberic's back. She had hugged each and every one of them over the course of a half an hour, promising them she would be back.

When they were all situated onto Alberic's back, the Ancient of Light spread his magnificent white wings and lifted off into the trees with the Cronoms below waving goodbye to them. Though Kira in particular was nervous to be squeezed so tightly onto the winged horse's back with four others, Alberic knew he could not afford to take his time in transporting the Elemental Warriors back to Hadecrest. He could feel the Ancients drawing close and there was no sign that Aeric had retrieved the crests. Revond and Alberic had decided that morning that while the sage prepared Hadecrest's defenses and the recruits for their anointment, Alberic would take off for the north to try and find Aeric and give him what assistance he could on his quest. Though confident he and Valeri Montrox had found the recluse living in the Black Peaks by now, neither of them was sure their party had any clue as to the whereabouts of the crests.

Traveling on over the clouds of the Iairian skies for three days as fast as he could fly while taking as few breaks as possible, Alberic and the humans on his back at last arrived in Drakkaidian airspace. Having never been to the dark nation to the northwest, Maglin, Morrol and Kira were shocked at the desolate black wasteland they saw, wondering out loud how people could have lived there even before the Ascension. By the time they reached the easternmost mountains of the Black Peaks, Revond could not only sense the Ancients nearby but see explosions of flame and dark power on the horizon to the east. Watching as enormous plumes of smoke rose in the distance, the others all gulped, realizing it wouldn't be long before they would have to face the beasts responsible for the disturbance.

By noon Alberic dropped out of the clouds for good to descend toward the wedge in the mountains that revealed the stronghold of Hadecrest. Soaring down through the rolling black vapors with his golden hooves leaving the usual contrails of light shimmering behind, the group looked down to find the small castle atop the wedge. Banking to his left, the Ancient of Light sped inside the wedge with his wings spread wide to gradually slow his dropping form as it neared the wall built into the cliff. As they approached all of them could see a handful of Drakkaidian soldiers mobilizing along the wall and shouting out to each other upon sighting the winged horse. Though he guessed the Drakkaidians of the resistance had merely been excited by Alberic drawing near, as Revond heard another distant explosion reach his ear from far behind them he couldn't help but worry that they were already out of time.

When Alberic reached the fortified wall in the cliff he beat his expansive wings against the wind to decrease his momentum until he hovered over the wall. Waiting for the excited Drakkaidians below them to make way for his landing, the white Ancient carefully touched down with his hooves of majestic light shimmering at the touching of the ground. Revond was the first to leap off Alberic's back, looking around for any sign for Aeric Tieloc or Valeri Montrox. Seeing only a mass of Drakkaidian soldiers rushing toward him with amazed faces, the sage scanned their uniforms to determine which of them was a ranking officer. Finding a man in full black armor with a tattered red cape on his back, Revond took a few steps toward him with the wind whipping up the ends of his black cloak.

"Are you in charge here?" Revond asked quickly, to which the Drakkaidian nervously glanced around to be sure the sage was speaking to him. Eventually nodding, the man replied yes.

"It would seem so," he imparted sheepishly. "In the princess' absence along with Commander Fauldrov and his patrols not returning, we're in a bit of chaos at the moment."

"The princess has still not returned, then," Revond stated more than he asked. "What's all this about patrols not returning?"

"Mid-Commander Fauldrov embarked with three patrols two days ago to investigate the columns of smoke on the horizon and the earthquakes we've been feeling," the Drakkaidian officer replied as he was jostled by a soldier frantically running by. "None of them returned but for one man who made his way back this morning half blown to the Netherworld. He said they were attacked and destroyed by one of the Ancients rummaging around the plains just several leagues beyond the Black Peaks. We've been mobilizing for battle ever since but with the council members arguing with our few military commanders over what should be done, we're in disarray." Taking in the Drakkaidian's report, Revond turned back to his companions. The others had all dismounted from Alberic's back and were nervously looking around at the chaos along the wall while the Ancient of Light stared at Revond, having heard the report for himself.

"Aeric and the crests are still missing?" Alberic asked, confirming the most pressing issue before them. Revond slowly nodded, trying to collect his thoughts as he swept his eyes across his environment.

"They are," the Master Sage confirmed. "We'll need to try and find him as quickly as possible. If it was indeed an Ancient that destroyed these Drakkaidian patrols and not some demon we may have little time. I will stay here and prepare the defenses of Hadecrest as best I can while I make our recruits ready for their anointing. You take to the skies and try to find Aeric. I couldn't feel the exact location because of the distance between us but I'm sure you felt Valeri's energy signature disappear this morning as well. If she has fallen, Aeric's last defense will be the Source of Light and we'll need a new Warrior of Darkness."

"Something did indeed happen to her life-force but I don't believe the princess is dead," Alberic returned, shifting his gilded eyes into the sky to the north. "And while I don't wish any harm to befall them, I fear the only way I'll be able to discover their exact location is if Aeric has need to use the Source of Light. Otherwise the best I can do is to find these Crag Spires and pick up their trail as best I can." Revond frowned at this, aware he was right but that it would take precious time for even Alberic to scour regions as vast as the Black Peaks with no indication of where they could be.

"I suppose you'd better get moving, then," Revond returned. "Fly hard, my friend." Nodding his majestic white head, Alberic spread his wings wide again and lifted off the wall back into the air. With his cloak flying up in the wind from his wing beats, the Master Sage turned back to face Lucan and the others waiting behind him. It was the Blue Maven that spoke first.

"What if he doesn't find Aeric before the Ancients find us?" he asked worriedly. "Your new batch of Elemental Warriors won't do anyone much good without those crests."

"In truth, there is no indication Aeric has even found the crests, much less that he is on his way back here with them, Lucan," the sage responded plainly, surprising the four recruits with his bleak hopes. "But if this stronghold is compromised before the crests are recovered, we cannot flee. There are hundreds of refugees and Drakkaidians above us who will fall to slaughter without a fight, and too many innocent people have already perished at the claws of the Ancients for us to run again. We must at least try to make a stand. In the meantime I will prepare you all as best I can for the power you have been chosen to receive. If the crests are anything like the Sources themselves, your master over the element they wield should be a natural and simple ability to learn. But I fear—"

A painful yell from far above them cut Revond short, loud enough to catch the attention of the entire stronghold. With hundreds of heads spinning up to the sky to see where the bizarre sound had come from, Revond and his recruits were shocked to see the white body of Alberic plummeting over the top of the mountain wedge upside down in freefall. Though the Ancient of Light struggled to regain his balance and spread his wings to flip upright again, he slammed down the side of the cliff and onto the wall before he could point his feet back to the ground. With the Drakkaidians leaping clear as he crashed into the wall top with fragmenting force, Lucan and Maglin immediately rushed over to him while Morrol and Kira stood awestruck with most of the resistance soldiers.

Knowing something was terribly wrong, Revond jerked his gaze back up to the top of the wedge on the cliff to see an orange glow soon followed by passionate flames slowly emerging. Within a moment, the fiery coated form of Moltar was standing above them looking down on the wall in the cliff, his burning red eyes quaking. Seeing the downed form of Alberic flipping himself upright and the throng of humans working themselves into a panic, the Ancient of Fire turned his head and looked out into the horizon toward the rising columns of smoke. Aware of what the blazing cat was doing, Revond cast his hood back and quickly acted before the Ancient could telepathically summon his brethren. Throwing his gloved hands up to reach out for the ground Moltar stood on, Revond tightened his mystic grip and violently cleaved the stone around his feet free. Lifting the thick and wide square of rock with his power, Revond violently cast it away from them to plummet down the long cliffs to the bottom of the field far below.

Though nervously tensing as he began to freefall on top of the rock he had clawed his molten feet into, the Ancient of Fire would not be so easily bested and spun his head to the wall he was about to pass. Leaping off the falling rock his stood on, the Ancient of Fire dove through the air straight at the north end of the wall at two humans he had seen before in Ceruleana. Though Lucan and Maglin froze in terror as they saw the image of the beast lunging at them with claws stretched out, they were surprised to see Alberic back on his feet racing in front of them with his head tucked low. Rearing as Moltar sailed into him, the Ancient of Light thrust his large head up to slam into the cat and blast him back over the side of the wall. Though Moltar desperately reached out to claw onto the cliff as he dropped past the bulwark shields, Alberic made sure to hit him hard enough so he would not be able to claw his way back up.

Clutching their hearts at their narrow rescue, Lucan and Maglin realized they were safe for the moment and raced past the Ancient of Light to look over the side of the wall top and watch their fiery foe drop to the bottom of the cliffs far below, shrieking out. Lucan grinned darkly and pumped his fist as he saw Moltar slam into the ground with his flame extinguished.

"Good riddance," he breathed with acid dripping from his words. "Do you see what happens when you mess with the best, kitty!?!" Revond rushed to their side with Morrol and Kira behind him, all checking Alberic to make sure he was alright. Seeing no wounds or significant damage to his shining frame, Revond swept his view down to the bottom of the cliffs and shook his head.

"He'll be back," he said gravely. "With bigger help." Revond turned back to Alberic to look him in his gilded eyes. "He surely had time to alert the other Ancients of our position. You'll have to remain here now to try and hold off whichever of them arrives and to ferry the Elemental Warriors out if we are overwhelmed."

"There is no point in trying to hold the stronghold, Revond," Alberic returned. "If they are coming it is already lost. Without the anointed Elemental Warriors we cannot stop them."

"Maybe, but if you go off in search for Aeric while the recruits and I are destroyed we will still be missing half of what we need to stop your brethren. You must stay." Though Alberic was about to respond, they heard another loud explosion much closer to the Black Peaks with smoke and dust rushing into the air. Not far behind it they heard a furious roar, ripping through the air in all directions. Before any of them could guess which of the beasts it belonged to, they were terrified to see the black body of Dalorosk tearing out of the smoke with his massive wings furiously beating to rush him toward the wedge in the mountains in the distance. Revond locked his body with resolve and shouted as loud as he could for the resistance soldiers to make ready for combat. Though the battle hardened and disciplined Drakkaidians lined up and ran to their positions on the wall, all of them glanced back and forth at each other, nervously wondering what chance they had to hold such a formidable creature when even Valgard Montrox himself had fallen fighting it.

Looking down to Revond as he spread his wings, Alberic gave him a single nod and thrust himself back into the air with his golden hooves glowing bright. Revond quickly ordered Lucan, Maglin, Morrol and Kira to stay together and watch each other's backs because all of them had to survive no matter what happened to Hadecrest. Determined not to let another city fall to the wanton beasts, Morrol was the first to draw his sword and direct the others to a defensive position in the cliff where archers were lining up. Aware they would be safest with the Sarton leading them, Revond turned his attention back to the fields outside the mountain wedge. Pulling his hood back up over his head and clenching his fists in preparation to unleash the height of his power to hold the creatures as bay, he watched as Golthrout lifted free from the rocky earth far in the distance and Wyrik dropped down out of the sky just behind Dalorosk. Only a miracle would be able to save the stronghold. The battle for Hadecrest had begun.

Chapter 40

Barrier of Seven

With Valeri's lifeless body in his arms, Aeric Tieloc silently marched his way away from the corrupted witch named Sakkdra who had taken the princess' soul. Though half wanting to charge back and wrestle the witch's flask away from her to retrieve Valeri's essence, he knew Valeri would want him to keep going and finish what she sacrificed everything for. It was up to him to find the crests across the Lake of the Undead and then after all this was over somehow restore her lost spirit to her body. Even after first setting out with Revond and Lucan in hopes of finding Alberic and in turn find a way to save his beloved Mina, the Grandarian had never been gripped by such resolve or desperation to succeed at any cost. He had already failed one girl he cared about. There was no way he would allow Valeri to be lost because of failure on his part.

Caught up in his renewed purpose as he walked, Aeric didn't pay attention to the footsteps of Verix Montrox ambling behind him until they finally caught up with him and he found the former Drakkaidian king at his side, staring down at him. When Aeric looked up to meet his gaze neither of them said anything. There was nothing that needed to be spoken aloud; both of them knew what had to be done. Verix could see the strength and resolve in Aeric's eyes the same as another Tieloc before him. He knew full well that nothing would be able to stop this young man from reclaiming what he set out to find.

Glancing down at the body of his granddaughter, the old Drakkaidian's eyes softened. He knew that if there was a way to save her Aeric, would find it before this was over. He remembered how treacherous and crafty Sakkdra was when it came to her collection of harvested souls and power. Even if they succeeded, it would take power and leverage beyond what he knew to convince her to relinquish Valeri's spirit. Aware that the only way they would ever be able to help the princess was for him to help Aeric get the crests and safely return to Hadecrest, the senior Montrox strapped an expression of his own renewed determination on his haggard face and cast his gaze ahead toward the gray body of water.

Aeric and Verix marched across the barren valley for a half of an hour before they arrived at the banks of the Lake of the Undead. A short basin of strange gray soil surrounded the lake on all sides, almost sinking as they began to slowly walk through it. Though his unflagging determination remained, the expression of Aeric's face began to gradually shift from focused to awestruck as he neared the cursed body of water. By the time they neared the banks of the massive lake he could make out the true form of the haze blurred into a simple gray fog from further away. Slowly churning spirits of decayed and skeletal bodies drifted over the waters of the lake, some dipping up and down from the stagnant surface with their transparent bodies disappearing under the thick and cloudy water.

As they drew near the lake Aeric was perturbed to see several of the translucent faces of the corrupted souls turning to ogle at him and Verix. The Grandarian gulped as he looked over the hundreds of floating apparitions silently drifting over the enormous lake. Though shooting a quick glance down to the bloody Immortal Pendant around his neck that Sakkdra had given him to cross the cursed water, he suddenly wondered how he would get out to the tiny island in the center of the lake hundreds of yards away.

"Verix," the young man whispered through the still air, "how do I get out there? Am I supposed to... swim?" The old Drakkaidian looked down to Aeric with his gray brow furrowing.

"Even with the witch's talisman," he began equally hushed, "you would never survive beneath these evil waters. There must be a way Sakkdra ferried objects as large as the coffins through the lake to the island..." Verix came to a halt then, slowly scanning the edges of the Lake of the Undead for a way across. He found it far to their left in the form of a makeshift boat pieced together with black wooden planks. Though in distressed condition, it appeared large enough to fit several occupants or even heavy cargo if it was indeed the means for the witch to cross the lake with her pillaged treasures. Pointing out the black boat lying over the shore of the lake several hundred steps to their left, the two set out for it as a chilled wind blew down from the thick clouds high above them.

As they walked with the wind assailing their faces, Aeric looked up to Verix to see the old man clutching his black robe tighter against him and grunting with each step, obviously growing tired from the long trek even with his great power. Before he could ask if he was alright and could keep going, the former king spoke first with his eyes shifting between Aeric and the lake.

"The boat doesn't look like much but if Sakkdra uses it through such treacherous waters as these it must be worthy," he said. "Once you start across the lake you cannot turn back. Even with that pennant there is grave risk. If you disturb the water too much or agitate the evil spirits they will try to ensnare you no matter what protection you carry. Row forward slowly but steadily and keep your eyes ahead or in the boat; don't look at the phantoms."

"Sakkdra's pennant won't protect us both?" Aeric asked.

"I cannot go with you," Verix answered, aware of where his question was leading. "I will remain on the shore with Valeri and to make sure the witch doesn't try anything." Verix paused there, narrowing his eyes and looking around as if feeling something out of place. "There is something... not right. Since we stepped into the valley I have sensed something very dark hovering around us, as if it is waiting."

"Is Sakkdra trying to set us up?" Aeric worried out loud. Verix gradually shook his head no as he continued sweeping his gaze around the valley.

"This presence is beyond the witch," he returned in a whisper. "Far beyond her. There is great energy hiding behind whatever is out here. But what troubles me most is..."

"What?" Aeric pressed.

"...It feels familiar," the old recluse answered, slipping his eyes onto the lake to scan its surface. Looking past the hundreds of damned souls slowly slipping in and out of the water with their decayed faces and attire, Verix spotted something with solid mass floating over the surface halfway between them and the island. Freezing as he locked onto the image, the former king observed it was similar to many of the wraith-like specters hovering above the waves but for its tangible black robes tightly wrapped around its body. Staring at the dark figure for several long moments while Aeric came to a halt beside him wondering what had earned his attention, Verix at last caught sight of something that froze his heart in his chest and drew the air from his lungs. As the black figure slowly turned its hooded head toward them, the old Drakkaidian could barely make out a bloodied and decayed face inside with its eyes missing from its sockets.

Tightening in alarm, Verix violently grabbed Aeric and dropped him to his knees where he stood, leaning in close beside him. Aeric was instantly distraught as well, wondering what the old man had seen to frighten him when before seemingly nothing could cause him distress. Verix quickly pointed out with his forearm to the black wraith levitating over the water ahead of them until the Grandarian caught sight of it for himself.

"What is that?" he asked curiously. Verix swallowed hard before letting his hand drop and summoning the words to respond.

"Something I never thought I'd have to face again," he replied with his words half petrified and half furious. "I should have sensed it before, and the others are probably close by." Confusion threatening to suffocate him, Aeric rested Valeri's legs on the ground and reached up with his free hand to grab Verix's cloak and gently tug it toward him.

"Verix, you didn't answer me," he said apprehensively. "What is that?" The old man quickly shot his eyes down to the boy's, frightened for the first time Aeric had ever seen.

"Your grandfather told you stories of the Black Seven, did he not?" Verix asked ominously. Running the familiar term through his head, Aeric thought back to his grandfather's stories from the Days of Destiny and remembered a group of demons that had almost destroyed him, his grandmother, and Verix on more than one occasion.

"The Dégamar?" Aeric asked, not even sure if that was the correct name. Verix slowly nodded, peering back out onto the lake to make sure the creature hadn't spotted them.

"They are here," he replied with a single nod. "I should have guessed that if demons were breaking free into this realm the most powerful of their kind would be among them."

"I only see one," Aeric said, staring at the lone black wraith.

"Where there is one, the others are surely nearby," Verix responded, sweeping the lake again. Pointing up, he revealed the location of another two of the Black Seven also hovering above the waters of the Lake of the Undead. Spotting them as well, Aeric's breath began to escalate to a faster pace.

"Why are they here?" he asked anxiously. "What are they doing out there? They look like ghosts."

"They are," Verix affirmed, shifting his gaze to the Grandarian. "The Dégamar are the shells of seven Dark Mages who lived during the First Holy War and traded their souls to Drakkan to gain greater power."

"So they're like Sakkdra?" Aeric asked bemused.

"Only insofar that they are soulless," Verix answered quickly. "That is how they can hover above this cursed lake—they have no souls to be stolen from their bodies. They are far more powerful than the witch, though. The Dégamar got what they wanted in their deal with the dark god—power unrivaled among their demonic brethren. They are Drakkan's personal vanguard. After the Warrior of Darkness' defeat in the First Holy War they were trapped in the Netherworld until the Days of Destiny when my father summoned them out with a shard of the Holy Emerald."

"But I thought they were destroyed by my Grandfather Tavin," Aeric said.

"As long as Drakkan's soul remains intact in this world or the void he is currently trapped in, the Dégamar will endure," Verix said with hatred dripping from his words. "Though I recognized their presence on the way here, I couldn't tell they were among us until seeing them. They feel... different. Perhaps it is because their evil master is gone from the world and they find themselves purposeless, but they are changed from the last time I met them in battle. I would bet even Sakkdra doesn't know they are here—she would never have left her shack if she knew the Black Seven were nearby." Verix paused for a moment, studying the way the three undead mages he could make out moved, occasionally reaching out for the shades of corrupted souls floating amidst them. "Yes, they are complete wraiths now—all traces of their former humanity gone. Such is the price paid for living in the Netherworld. They were probably drawn here by the concentrated souls moaning out into eternity. Perhaps they are here looking for their own souls. Can you see them reaching out as if to grasp them?" Aeric watched the closest of the black wraiths slowly dipping a skeletal hand into the water as if to take hold of a passing spirit.

"So what do we do?" Aeric asked, attempting to focus the obviously frightened Drakkaidian. "Do we have anything to fear from them now that they are cut off from Drakkan? Maybe we can just slip by them—" Verix cut the Grandarian short by spinning his head back to face him and shaking it no.

"There is no slipping by the Dégamar," Verix said gravely. "Even without a master the Black Seven are still demons—they will instinctively attack anything they see, and there is no way they won't see you crossing the lake. They would kill you for certain." The Drakkaidian king stopped again, controlling himself and peering back out to the lake. His hard expression slowly morphed back onto his face, letting a long silence hang as he stared at the demonic mages. "Unless we can distract them." Aeric raised an eyebrow at this.

"How do we do that?" he asked uncertainly. Verix looked down to his great-nephew then at his granddaughter, still limp and gray in his arms.

"I will do it," he responded at last. "I will summon my power and draw them away form the lake while you cross it." Aeric tightened upon hearing this, immediately shaking his head.

"But you'd be killed," he said. "My grandfather told me the two of you together couldn't hold back all seven. There's no way you could do it now, especially at your age."

"No, I couldn't," Verix affirmed. "But I can at least buy you a little time to make it out to the island to retrieve the crests." Aeric couldn't believe what the old man was proposing and was quick to deny him by reaching for the white medallion still under his blue tunic.

"There is no way I'm letting you do that, Verix," the young Tieloc told him. "I still have the Source of Light. We can use it to drive them away the same as any demon." Verix shook his head.

"If you use the Source you will attract Dalorosk and the other Ancients," he stated. "If they find us we will be destroyed anyway. Not even your Master Sage or Alberic with the Source can stand up to all five. It is too great a risk. You cannot use the Source. I must do this."

"Verix, no," Aeric denied passionately. "If these things are as strong as you say, you wouldn't last a minute. We need you to get us back to Hadecrest. You can't die. And what if they come after me the same as you?"

"The Dégamar and I have tasted each other's power and blood before," Verix stated with his voice growling. "They will not have forgotten—I guarantee they'll all come to me." The former King of Drakkaidia turned his entire body then and looked Aeric hard in his blue eyes. "If I don't draw them away you will never make it to the crests alive. This must be done, Aeric. If you have to you can find your own way back. You are a Tieloc. And though you are not the same man as the one I knew, I see his strength alight in your heart. You can make my granddaughter's sacrifice worthwhile. Get the crests to your sage, destroy the Ancients and revive her with this master Source you plan to create. Her life is just beginning—mine is at its end." Aeric didn't know what to say to his great-uncle, emotion rising from his chest to make his eyes water.

"You don't deserve this, Verix," he said with his voice shaking.

"I am a warrior, young Tieloc," the old Montrox told him proudly. "This is the fate my life has always been aimed for. It is an honorable death—a death befitting a Drakkaidian king. I stood against these creatures for your grandfather once before, Aeric. I am honored to stand against them again for you." Though he didn't want to admit it, Aeric knew what the old Drakkaidian said was true. This was the only way and he was not about to deny the legendary warrior Verix Montrox his final battle. Humbled and privileged by his great-uncle's words, Aeric slowly reached up with his free arm to reach behind his back and embrace him.

"I will bring you back, Verix," Aeric avowed as he struggled to choke down tears. He felt the old man gently return his embrace and shake his head above his.

"There is no need," Verix told him quietly. "I have lived too long as it is. It is time for me to shuffle off this world for the next. All my affairs are done and I have grown to see my family become better men and women than I. Now I know why my destiny stretched on as long as it did." The two held firm for a long moment before Verix released the young Tieloc and let him pick up Valeri in his arms again. "Hurry now. Make for that boat with Valeri and start across the lake once you see the Dégamar coming for me. You won't have much time but I have one last trick up my sleeve called a Final Rush. If

I can unleash it on them while they're all together, even this tired old man will be able to send the cursed mages flying to the other side of this valley. If not, you'll have to evade them as best you can and risk using the Source of Light if they catch you. Do you understand?" Aeric quickly nodded and tried his best to suppress his emotion. "Then get moving and stay low. I'll draw them to me once you're inside the boat."

Aeric was motionless for a moment, not sure if there were any words to relay his gratitude for the sacrifice Verix was about to make for them. Seeing the young Tieloc speechless but desperately wanting to say something, Verix merely nodded.

"Godspeed, Aeric Tieloc," he said with a faint smile before turning and rising to quickly stride back toward the end of the banks and into the valley. Watching him running away, Aeric forced himself to turn as well and swiftly make his way to the boat on the shore. Though struggling to stay low with Valeri in his arms, the Grandarian kept a watchful eye on the slowly moving Dégamar that he could see out on the Lake of the Undead. He could barely believe he was about to lose another Montrox in his quest to retrieve the crests. Though he had retained his doubts about the old recluse revealed to be his great uncle until the very end, he now saw he was every ounce the hero and warrior his grandparents had always told him he was. It was all he could do to pray the old Drakkaidian could muster enough strength to buy him the time he needed to get on and off the island without being noticed.

Though remembering the term Final Rush from something his grandfather had once told him and wondering what it could be to allow one as old as Verix the power to fend off the most powerful demons in the Netherworld, Aeric had little time to dwell on it as he quickly reached the black boat sitting on the edge of the lake. It was bigger than he had noticed before, easily with the space to ferry several large objects as big as coffins across the surface of the waters. Rushing up to it and gazing up to the floating Dégamar to ensure they hadn't caught sight of him, Aeric gently slipped Valeri's body inside and crawled into the boat after her. Inside he saw two oars lying next to the princess' body. Reaching down for one, he picked it up and shoved it against the ground behind him ready to shove them off as soon as it was safe. All he could do was wait for Verix.

Looking back into the southern valley he could see Verix Montrox standing still on the edges of the basin leading down to the lake several hundred feet back. Though staring at the boat, the old man slowly pivoted his head back to the middle of the lake as the wind whipped his gray hair and black robe back behind him. Standing tall with his muscular body taut and his expression as hard and resolute as ever, the Drakkaidian slowly raised his right hand from his side into the air. As soon as it was perpendicular to his body a familiar wave of red, foaming mist spread from his open hand up to cover the coming weapon to be revealed. Letting the red foam expand beside him for a long moment, the Drakkaidian king abruptly clenched his fist around the hilt of his weapon inside and thrust it down out of the mist. Though there was no sunlight to reflect off the edge of the sharp blade, his old silver sword shone brightly as it broke free of the dissipating mist as clean and ready for battle as ever.

Holding his weapon, Verix took a deep breath and began flexing his once titanic power from deep in the confines of his soul. Awakening as much of the long dormant energy within as he could find, a faint layer of crimson energy began to pulsate around his frame, widening and expanding by the second. Within a few moments of seizing the bulk of his dark power, the soft aura began swirling and churning into an explosive field of flashing black and crimson energy encircling and rising from his body. Letting it charge and build to the highest peak he could reach, Verix at last reached through his rising field of energy and thrust his other hand around the hilt of his sword, setting it in front of him. Though Aeric would have guessed his great-uncle's power completely brought to bear, he was surprised to see the continually rising and expanding power suddenly flare up further and explode into a final maelstrom of energy that pushed loose rocks away from him and split the earth at his feet.

Finally reacting to the monstrous power detonating to life beside the lake, the black wraiths that Verix had spotted at last jerked their heads up and cast their eyeless gazes his way to observe the swirling field of crimson energy they had seen many years before. Though Aeric had been captivated by the amazing display of Verix's power, he quickly remembered the Dégamar when he heard several shrieks tearing into the air from around the Lake of the Undead and shot his head back to see several black figures rising up into the sky to come soaring forward toward the power flaring to life ahead of them. Though Aeric counted only five at first, he quickly saw the other two demonic mages rising from behind the island and soaring out to meet Verix. Seeing them depart from the lake, Aeric shoved off from the shore and began his trek across to the island. Sitting in the middle of the boat and dropping both oars into the water to slowly paddle him forward, the Grandarian silently prayed for Verix's battle to be long and that his death be painless.

Observing all of the Black Seven racing toward him, Verix grit his teeth and flexed his power around him challengingly while stepping into his long perfected battle stance. Not surprised that the Dégamar rocketed toward him quicker than he had ever seen them before, Verix was left with little time to plan his defense and merely let instinct take over. Though not bunched together, they would strike him rapidly once they reached him and he would soon be overwhelmed by all seven. Charging his blade with power and black electricity dancing along its edges, Verix slashed it forward to send his first attack slicing forward in the form of an arching wave of power headed for the first of the wraiths. The Dégamar saw it coming as it reached the shore of the lake and nimbly ducked underneath it as it sliced past it. Though an edge of the attack caught another of the seven and veered it off course, it did little damage and Verix was forced to prepare for melee combat.

The first of the undead mages descended on him from above, hammering down with a hand of decaying flesh reaching down as if to stab him with its protruding bones alone. Fully empowered, Verix sidestepped the attack and drove his already swinging blade down to parry it away, immediately raising the sword again to deflect another blow from the assailant behind him. Though Verix could handle the intense speed at which his attackers dove on him, Aeric felt his heart racing to see his great-uncle dexterously swatting them away and blocking their initial attacks with both hands heaving his blade back and forth.

The Dégamar were relentless in their assault, quickly recoiling from being parried away and reaching out for him again in seconds. When one of them slashed out for the former king's feet, Verix leapt off the ground and flipped his blade downward, stabbing its tip through the creature's hood and into the rock below. Temporarily pinning it down, he saw another of its kin slash its bony hand toward his head. Ducking and rolling into a crouch past his sword, he flipped upside down on his hands and to land and start running. Charging ahead with his crimson energy burning around him, Verix leaped out while reaching with both hands to grip one of the Dégamar's necks, heaving it down with his momentum.

On the ground again, Verix summoned an intense charge of dark power into the palms of his hands to blast free into the demon's hooded face. The swirling crimson energy exploded into the ground and sent a wave of dust and debris flying up. Seemingly stunned by the haze, the other Dégamar failed to notice Verix rise and charge back to his sword. Wrenching it out of the ground, he tore loose the hood of the mage it was still planted in struggling to be free. Screaming with some of its flesh and black blood staining the rock as the sword pulled through its head, the wounded Dégamar furiously slashed out for the crimson warrior with an enormous lance of dark matter materializing out of its robes. With his sword back and in hand, Verix blocked the attack but was gripped by another of the mages around his ankle.

Before he could be lifted off the ground Verix quickly flexed his power around him and slashed his sword into his own foot to nearly cleave through both the demon's hand and his boot. Deflecting a passing wraith with the flat of his sword swiping backwards, the Drakkaidian opened his other clenched fist and grabbed onto a fistful of another demon's robes as it dove on him. Though slicing its bony hand into his chest, Verix only grit his teeth and heaved the demon over his head by his attire to slam it into the returning Dégamar he had deflected with his sword.

Jerking them into the ground with fragmenting force, Verix wheeled around to impale the creature with the wounded hand and lift it off the ground. Screaming with power and untold rage, the energy around his blade pulsated and detonated with life in the Dégamar's center. Burning and smoldering, it squirmed free to lift high into the air. With his rage building and his focus dwindling again, Verix was slashed across his back by a passing wraith and gripped by his robe by another. Thrown off his feet, Verix was heaved high into the air far above the valley's surface.

With his view of the battle previously obscured by the cloud of dust and debris, Aeric felt his heart fly high into his chest as he caught sight of Verix soaring into the sky. Five of the Black Seven were immediately after him, shooting into the sky. Seeing them coming, Verix cast his sword over his back only to throw it back down as hard as he could with crimson contrails bleeding off its gleaming hilt. Speeding like a lightning bolt, it soared into one of the demons and pinned it back to the ground. The others rushed past their kin to be greeted with a colossal beam of electrified energy bursting from the king's open palm of his right hand. Though three of the Dégamar were caught in the beastly attack, the others raced around his beam and hammered into his exposed back to beat him back to the ground. Verix slammed into the rock with his power fragmenting it. Immediately rolling to his right to avoid the attack he knew would come, the Dégamar furiously stabbed into the ground where he had been with dark lances of energy.

Flipping back to his feet, Verix had little time to brace himself as the other two Dégamar still in the original cloud of dust came sailing at him with their own spears of sharpened dark power. Standing his ground, the Drakkaidian warrior sidestepped one to catch the lance under his arm and then leapt to his right to evade the other and catch it the same way. With both dark weapons caught under his flexed arms, Verix screamed and spun his body to the right to heave them away with monstrous strength.

As soon as they were gone he opened his right hand to summon the crimson mist and in turn his sword from the point in the ground it had been lodged a moment before. Hearing a coming demon mage screaming for him as it charged, Verix took his weapon in both hands and swung it out for the creature like a bat. Though cleaving into the Dégamar's hood and head, Verix was surprised to find another of them charging behind it to fly into him and knock off his balance. Seeing their quarry stunned, all of the Black Seven were back on the attack, sailing into him with ripping hands and stabbing lances tearing chucks of flesh from his body.

Seeing his great-uncle's power dwindling and his defense waning with each blow, Aeric nearly dropped the oars in his hands as he continued making his way across the Lake of the Undead. Rushing to the back end of the boat with tears welling in his eyes, he watched the Dégamar slam a lance through Verix's left leg from behind. With his balance completely lost, the former King of Drakkaidia was caught in one of the mage's telekinetic grip and heaved off his feet only to be slammed back down into the ground the next second. Verix could feel the life draining from his several wounds as the Black Seven gathered around him, aware he would no longer be a threat. Remaining still as one of them picked up his sword and prepared to slam it down into him, the old warrior grit his teeth and flexed his power again. Reaching up just as the demonic mage thrust his own sword at his head, Verix clenched his fingers around the blade to hold it back.

Amazed the old man could match their prodigious strength even as he lay dying, the Dégamar were further shocked to see his field of crimson power charge around him a final time. Yelling out in fury, Verix threw his sword back knocking the mage holding it off his feet and into several of the others. Aware this would be his last chance to use his trump card, Verix flipped back to his feet with his energy suddenly spiking to its peak once again. With the Dégamar all assembled before him charging forward with their blades of dark energy stabbing out for him to end the battle once and for all, Verix threw both of his suddenly fiercely glowing hands together in front of him just as the tips of the Dégamar's blades came slicing into them.

In an explosion of power Aeric had only ever heard stories about from his grandfather during the Days of Destiny, Verix let out a colossal scream louder than anything he had ever heard and released a blinding wave of electrified crimson energy blasting to life from his open palms. Careening forward in a massive beam that doubled his height and arm span, the swirling crimson power slammed into the seven Dégamar that forced them off their feet and flying away into the valley. Verix held the attack of rushing energy somehow charged out of nowhere for several long moments, breaking the ground at his feet and quaking the entire valley to the tops of its cliffs.

Then, as quickly as it had started, it was over. Fading as if having been sucked into the void world like Drakkan at the end of the Days of Destiny, the crimson energy around Verix Montrox faded and his mammoth beam of power died. Though his powerful war cry continued to echo across the valley for several moments, the old king was silent as his energy disappeared. When the last remnant of blinding light was gone and Aeric could look back out on the field, he saw the Dégamar had vanished from view, obviously blown to the opposite side of the valley as Verix had hoped. Locking his view onto his great-uncle, however, Aeric saw he was motionless with his arms still outstretched ahead as if locked into position from the massive attack. Watching in horror, Aeric saw the old man's limbs slowly drop to his sides followed by his entire body falling to its knees. Though standing erect for a long moment, the senior Montrox at last dropped onto his front to lay over the fragmented rock, completely inert.

Watching the former king's body for almost a minute praying for him to get back up or even twitch, Aeric felt tears stream down his cheeks in realization the old Drakkaidian was gone. He had given the Dégamar every last ounce of his strength in his final attack. Running these words through his head, Aeric's brow furrowed in remembrance of the Final Rush Verix had told him about. The technique was something his own grandfather had explained to him when he was just a child. Though it could only be used once, it immediately called upon every pocket of strength and power in a warrior's body and let it go in one last flurry of energy. It could be summoned all at once since it called upon the very life-force of the warrior but therefore left the user with no energy left to breathe or sustain a heartbeat. It was a Warrior of Light or Darkness' last defense and Verix had used it at the cost of his life.

Staring at the lifeless body of his great-uncle lying out in the empty field with dust settling around him, Aeric remained still and silent for a long moment, reflecting on his sorrow over both the loss of a member of his family as well as legend of Iairia. Though desperately wishing the old Drakkaidian was still with him, Aeric knew it was a death he had probably always craved. It would be up to him to make sure that death wouldn't be wasted. Taking a long last look at his great-uncle, Aeric slowly turned back to sit down in the center of the black boat and wiped the tears off his face with his dirtied blue sleeves. Reaching down to grab the oars as his side, he again dipped them into the water of the Lake of the Undead and began rowing forward to the island before him.

Chapter 41

The Mae Fountain

Alberic beat his feathered wings as hard as he could as he rocketed over the sky in the mountain wedge to meet Dalorosk head on, his golden hooves leaving their contrails behind him. His gilded eyes were narrowed with resolve as they watched his dark brother charging at him with indescribable rage. The two had not battled headlong in their true forms since halfway through their elemental war eons ago, before Alberic left to find the Staff of the Ancients that would eventually bring about the black Ancient's downfall. Roaring with deafening fury while foam frothed around his jaws, the enormous behemoth raised his fists to prepare to crush his small brother as they sailed into each other.

Before Dalorosk could slam his fists down on the white horse, Alberic beat his wings hard to lift him high above the large beast's head and soar down to pummel his black hide with his shining hooves. Dalorosk screamed in a furious pain as the hooves seared into his back, reaching around to try and grab the nimble horse with his clawed hands. Once again evading the Ancient of Darkness with his superior speed and maneuverability, Alberic lifted free and pulled higher in the skies. Roaring out again, Dalorosk pulled one of the black swords out of his thighs and beat his right wing to spin his body around. Heaving the blade at his brother, Alberic was forced to lunge to his left to avoid the speeding missile. Taking advantage of the winged horse's forced trajectory, Dalorosk reached out with his other massive sword and swatted the flat of his blade into Alberic to send him plummeting down to the earth yelping in pain.

While Alberic regained his balance in the air and prepared to face his brother descending on him, the Master Sage Revond stood in the center of the wall of Hadecrest summoning the glowing white energy of his trained Hallador

Might around his fists in preparation for Wyrik swooping down from the dark sky. Shrieking out with its two heads, the enormous wyvern shot down for the soldiers along the left side of the wall with open jaws. Before he could reach the wall Revond threw up an arm to send a flaming ball of white flame racing from his open hand to meet the creature when it slowed to prepare for landing. Burning into its side to char its unique scaly feathers, Wyrik held his position in the sky and looked to the center of the wall to find Alberic's disciple shouting for the other men to take aim at his heads. The Drakkaidians did what they were told, showering the beast with arrows from all corners of the wall. Though screaming out as they began lodging themselves into the front of his body, Wyrik slammed down onto the wall and raced for the Master Sage.

Seeing the beast coming, Revond summoned a long shaft of white energy in his hand to grab like a sleek sword. Waiting for Wyrik to snap one of its heads out for him as he had seen it do before in his first encounter with the beast as a young man, the sage strafed to his right just as the creature's jaws clamped shut where he had been. Taking hold of his white saber with both hands, he drove it down into Wyrik's neck to slice almost halfway through. Jerking up in pain and feeling the cut of steel from arrows and swords all over its body, Wyrik spread its wings and lifted back into the sky to retreat for the moment. Though the resistance soldiers cheered as it fled, Revond had felt the tremors in the ground over the past few minutes and spun his head to the edge of the wall to see a massive rocky hand reaching over the edge. Though the Drakkaidians fired arrows at the bull-like head of Golthrout as it lifted above the edge of the wall with its eyes burning scarlet energy, they could not penetrate the rock and the beast threw its other hand down into the right wall to cleave it in two and send several soldiers flying into the air.

Not waiting for it to attack again, Revond charged forward to raise his white sword above his head and slam it down into the minotaur's hand on the wall. Thrusting it down with all his strength, the scarlet light flowing under Golthrout's rocky skin shone and it recoiled in pain. Lifting his white blade free, Revond cast it like a spear into the beast's face between its eyes. Before it could grab on to another hold on the wall, Revond lifted an entire segment of the smashed wall top free with his mystic grip and heaved it up into the Ancient of Earth's face. Roaring out in shock and rage, the beast fell back down the cliff desperately clawing out for the rock again.

Just as Revond was about to rush to the side to make sure the beast had fallen, he was surprised to see Moltar leaping back over the edge right where he had fallen with his molten claws reaching out for the sage. Striking so quickly, Revond never had a chance to swat him away and he was pinned down. Screaming in pain as the flaming cat's claws seared into his shoulders, he desperately tried to summon his power before the Ancient of Fire could finish him once and for all.

Aeric rowed the black boat on through the surface of the Lake of the Undead for several long minutes, keeping his determined eyes toward the small island off his bow and not at the tainted apparitions in the water that the small vessel divided with each paddle stroke. Though caught in a sweat from watching Verix's final battle, the air was freezing over the cursed water. Aeric could feel chills run up and down his spine with every movement of his arms rowing them forward as if death itself tingled along his back, tickling him and begging him to cast his gaze down to the tormented souls reaching out for him. Though worried that the Dégamar would return and not sure how much time he had, the Grandarian kept on at his steady pace Verix had warned him to stay at so as not to provoke the evil souls any more than necessary. It was dead quiet over the lake; he couldn't even hear the sound of his paddles churning water.

After another few minutes Aeric was surprised to feel the hull of his boat striking something solid and he looked up from his boots to see the boat sliding onto the rocky shore of the island. Rising from his seat with his heart pounding in anticipation of finally reaching the coffins he had set out to find, he pulled the boat further up the shore so he could step out without touching the evil water. Though at first choosing to leave Valeri in the boat where she would be safe, he quickly negated his decision, not wanting to let her out of his immediate care for more than a moment. Picking her up in his arms and lifting his legs out over the boat to stand on the island shore, he looked around to find an amazing view before him.

The island wasn't as big as he had imagined it would be from the shore of the lake. Stretching only a few hundred feet ahead and across at its widest point, its gray rocks and soil were almost completely obscured by the gluttony of messily arranged objects scattered over its surface. Aeric's eyes were wide as he started slowly ambling forward. There were all kinds of strange objects Sakkdra had scavenged, some looking to be powerful treasures while others were mere garbage. As he began wading into the muddle of pilfered relics and goods, Aeric saw boxes full of crowns and armor; an assortment of weapons of both Grandarian and Drakkaidian origin loosely tossed in piles; dead and shriveled plants as big as trees that had been uprooted; even the skeletal remains of warriors with weapons still cleaved into their bones.

While Aeric recognized some of the weapons and objects around him, the majority of what he saw he had never seen anything like before. There were smashed statues rising from the far side of the island beside entire archways of white stone with bizarre designs carved into them. Around his feet were countless medallions and jewelry, some plain and dirtied but some gilded and still shining. Though carefully checking the smaller objects to make sure none of them even faintly resembled the crests he was there to find, he knew he would have to find the six coffins of the original Elemental Warriors first and forced himself to press on.

Captivated by the seemingly myriad supplies and talismans Sakkdra had gathered, Aeric couldn't help but gaze intrigued at everything that entered his vision as he ambled on. Though there were many large objects, he didn't see any sign of the coffins. Beginning to feel a stressful pang tearing at his heart, the young Tieloc was surprised to hear the breaking of glass under his feet and he quickly looked down past Valeri to observe several darkened little crystals on the ground. Immediately recognizing them from somewhere before, the Grandarian bent down and picked one up to lift it to peer into. It was a golden gem big enough that he couldn't quite close his entire hand around it, angled like a kite. Trying to remember where he had seen such a crystal before, Aeric's eyes suddenly widened and he recalled a picture of the Sword of Granis his grandfather had shown him years ago. It was a Granis Crystal, the sentient miracle gem that empowered the Sword of Granis.

Staring at the crystal in amazement, he wondered why it was so dark and lifeless when his grandparents had told him stories of the little talisman shining with life every time Tavin held it. Guessing its power was still somehow dormant, he looked down to all the other crystals at his feet in awe at the potential power at his fingertips. Though he had no idea where Sakkdra had found so many when the last Granic Crystal was supposedly fixed to the Sword of Granis, he remembered her warning to take only what they agreed and let go of his temptations to tuck one into his pocket. Rising to continue his search for the coffins, the young man kept walking through the scattered junk to the high center of the island where he could see everything else. Standing on top of a broken steel crate, Aeric spun around to search the entire island's contents for anything that resembled a coffin.

Desperately wheeling around sweeping his eyes through the junk, Aeric at last spotted six long boxes covered with dirt on the opposite side of the island from where he had come. With his heart leaping into his chest, he jumped down from the crate and began dashing around piles of weapons and empty boxes to rush down to the coffins. As he passed the large white archway he had seen earlier, he noticed another large edifice sitting behind it previously hidden from view. Gazing up at it, he identified it as a large blue and white fountain, beautifully curving and carved from a metallic material he had never seen before. Sweeping his gaze up and down its surface, Aeric jumped with alarm and slid to a halt when he saw what looked to be the body of a small girl sitting against the base of the fountain between he and the coffins. Though amazed at her appearance with her entire body made up of a thick liquid substance, he was most shocked by the sight of her chest moving up and down as if breathing.

Feeling his jaw dropping in astonishment, Aeric slowly leaned down to her level to better look at her. She was more the outline of a person that an actual human body, with the curves and figure of a girl but no distinguishing features or clothes. She had hands and feet but no fingers or toes. The girl was small, only half of his or Valeri's size, with flowing blue hair that stretched down to her waist. Her entire form was made up of the strange blue liquid that slowly churned under her surface in tiny circles. Her head was leaning down over her chest and her legs were spread with her arms limply hung between them. With no idea what she could be or if she was even really alive, Aeric leaned his head down past hers to look up and see if she had a distinguishable face.

Just as he caught sight of the face underneath her hair, Aeric was shocked to find her head suddenly lift up and her once darkened and pale blue body begin to glow. So startled by her movement that he lost his balance, the Grandarian fell onto his backside over the ground next to her with Valeri still in his arms. Staring in awe, Aeric sat frozen still and watched as the girl lifted her head to reveal her face. It was like the rest of her body: human-like but lacking any distinguishing features. She had a small nose and open eyes, but they were bland and devoid of irises or pupils—just glowing blue like the rest of her. Though he couldn't tell for certain, Aeric could feel like her eyes were on him as she slowly levitated off the ground with the blue light from within her glowing brighter. The little circles moved faster as if to illustrate her heart beats increasing. Slightly tilting her head as their eyes met, the girl looked the boy up and down before blinking.

In a bright flash of blue, a wave of color began expanding from the miniature lines circling inside her to wash out over the girl's bland outline. Spreading onto her skin, it began drawing on human detail to her frame ranging from shining blue eyes to exotic flowing attire around her upper body and waist. Her skin remained a strange blue hue but instead of leaving the glowing liquid within visible, the beautiful lines of flowing light took shape over her. Keeping her penetrating blue eyes on the Grandarian, she slowly swept in closer and opened her mouth.

"Who are you?" she asked with a gentle but otherworldly voice. Aeric was shocked to hear her speak but realized that whatever she was, it would be prudent to answer.

"My name is Aeric," he replied timidly.

"What brings you to a place such as this, Aeric?" she pressed, looking down at the lifeless girl in his arms.

"I've come for something on his island," he answered. "What... who are you?" The creature looked up from Valeri and set her gaze back on him, swiftly pulling back to levitate over the ground where he had found her.

"Celestrians have no names," the girl told him. "We do not need to be identified that way. We all know who we are." Aeric narrowed his eyes and took in what the girl told him.

"You're... an angel?" he asked mystified.

"No," she replied simply. "I am not of Granis' creation. Celestrians predate even Granis and his brother Drakkan. I am one of the last surviving members of the race that once spread the world as yours does today. We do not have gender like your people, but if you must call me something, you may call me Female." Aeric stared at the strange creature for a long moment, remembering how Alberic once said something about one of the old natural races from before the Battle of the Gods simply known as Celestrians. With dozens of questions buzzing through his head, he asked the first one he could formulate into words.

"How did you get here?" he questioned. "Did Sakkdra..."

"I have been here for several hundred years now," the Celestrian began, aware of what he was trying to ask. "In the wake of the Battle of the Gods, most of my kind were destroyed, but I remained, as I am bound to this fountain." Female turned sideways so she could extend one of her slender arms up to the beautiful curving fountain behind her. "It is called the Mae Fountain. The dark woman stole it long ago, and me with it. I am bound to it—charged with protecting it. And while I lacked the power to stop her from stealing it from its rightful place, she was unable to purge me from it. So I have been here in the middle of this lake ever since. Celestrians are immortal unless killed by forces greater than ourselves and our souls cannot be so easily ensnared as a human's, especially by the corrupted spirits over this lake, so I have remained alone here for a long time."

"What is so unique about that fountain that you are eternally bound to it, Female?" Aeric asked, looking behind her to the large fountain. Though there had never been a smile on the Celestrian's face, Aeric could see her expression darken and she swept in toward his face again.

"That is not your concern," she said in her soft tone but with an added layer of hostility. "You have still not answered my question. Why are you here? You were not brought here by the witch." Aeric wasn't sure how detailed his response should be.

"I don't know if you know this," he began, "but several evil creatures have destroyed the world. I'm looking for six talismans called elemental crests that can control the creatures and help restore Iairia. They are hidden inside those coffins." Female glanced at the coffins to her right before looking back to Aeric and responding.

"I have come to watch over all of the treasures and powers the witch has brought to this island," the Celestrian told him, catching him off guard. "Why should I let you take something from here? How can I trust what you say is the truth and not some deception as the witch once told me? You come here with no proof of your character but a dead woman in your arms. You hardly seem trustworthy." Aeric was speechless for a moment as Female stared at him with skeptical eyes.

"You must believe me," Aeric pled. "I carry this girl because she sacrificed her life to help me get here, as others have sacrificed. I need those crests to bring her back; to bring them all back." The Celestrian tilted her head as she ran Aeric's words through her head, probing him with her glowing blue eyes. Eventually she leaned back to hover beside the structure she called the Mae Fountain once again.

"Time will tell where you heart truly lies," she said passively, raising an arm toward the coffins lying to her right. Guessing she was letting him proceed, Aeric gave her a single nod and rose back to his feet. Turning and walking up to them, the Grandarian gently set Valeri down to lean against another crate beside him and set to work opening the coffins. He approached them slowly, looking up and down their long structures in disbelief he had finally reached the ancient bodies of the first Elemental Warriors. They were simple rectangles of sturdy wood with emblems of what he guessed to be the crests themselves on the lids. Brushing off several large chunks of old dirt from the top of the first one he came to, he saw a circle with a design of a dancing flame inside. Guessing it was the coffin containing the crest of fire, he looked to the side to find an opening.

Though expecting he would have to pry the lids off with one of the swords he had seen behind him, he was relieved to find four large locks holding the lids down on each corner of the coffin. Reaching out for one of them and what looked to be a handle along the side, Aeric was surprised to find it lift the lock free with little leverage. Doing the same to the other three handles, Aeric prepared to shove the heavy lid off and reveal the coffin's contents. With his heart racing, he heaved the lid free and dropped it to the ground with a loud thud. Gazing down into the wooden coffin, Aeric saw something that made his heart skip a beat.

Nothing.

The coffin was completely empty. All that was inside was a few clods of dirt and the remains of a single bone in one of the corners. Aeric was motionless for a long moment, trying to comprehend what his eyes were telling him and what it meant. He slowly shook his head, not able to believe what he saw. His worry growing, he jerked around to another coffin beside him bearing the crest of earth with a leaf in the circle and unfastened the four locks. Throwing off the lid, he felt his heart sink further into his stomach to find it empty as well. Feeling desperation and madness taking hold of him, he rushed to the other coffins and opened them one by one, each time finding them empty until he had thrown off each lid.

Spinning around and feeling short of breath, Aeric looked around for any sign of the bodies or crests on the island. They had to be there. These had to have been the coffins of the Elemental Warriors and Sakkdra wouldn't have discarded their contents. Seeing Female's eyes on him as he looked around the island, he quickly stepped closer to her and summoned his shaking voice.

"Do you know where they are?" he asked her quickly, his words slurring together. Female slowly looked out to the waters of the Lake of the Undead.

"Often times Sakkdra throws her stolen objects into the waters if she does not believe them to be of use to her," she answered impassively. "As I recall, she opened the coffins and threw everything inside them into the lake many years ago." Aeric felt the air in his lungs rushing out of his gaping mouth. The strength in his legs gave way and he fell to his knees, a numb sensation sweeping over him. He couldn't believe it. After all he had gone through to get this far and all the sacrifices his allies had made along the way, it had all been for nothing. The crests were gone—cast to the bottom of the Lake of the Undead. If they had ever been there at all. If Sakkdra had thrown the contents of the coffins away, maybe they didn't belong to the Elemental Warriors. Perhaps she had never even taken them in the first place and something else had stolen the crests.

Aeric felt tears welling in his eyes as he looked back at Valeri's gray body. One thing was for certain: wherever the crests were, they were beyond his reach. Hope was lost again. Without the crests, there could be no Elemental Warriors and the Ancients would be free to continue destroying the world until they eventually found him and the Source of Light to complete their conquest. Valeri and Verix's actions had been in vain, as well as Revond's and the others depending on him. He would never get to see Mina again. Everything was gone. With the finality of all the death settling in around him, the hope of him one day restoring everything dissipated and the reality of all he had lost sank back in as it had when he first failed Mina.

The tears in the corners of his eyes streamed down his cheeks and the young Tieloc leaned his head down to cry over the dark earth in the center of the cursed lake. He felt sick to his stomach. He had never felt so forsaken and alone. All that was left was death. As he sat crying and losing himself to his grief, Aeric saw the grays and blacks of the lake and valley begin to slowly be colored by a strange mist.

"You are in pain," a familiar voice told him. Aeric looked up and opened his eyes wider to see Female floating in front of him with a mist of soft watercolors filling the air around her. Looking to his left to the source of the strange mist, he saw the fountain softly spewing spray from its many openings. Female slowly swung in and drew her face close to the Grandarian's. "I can ease your pain." Aeric didn't respond with words, unable to summon his voice, but curiously looked her in her radiating eyes. "The Mae Fountain is one of the oldest treasures of the city I once lived in. When Celestrians would sleep there, this fountain would spray its vapors into the air to make our best and brightest dreams come alive. It was as if we could live out our fantasies as we slept. With the Mae Fountain, most found it impossible to distinguish between dreams and reality."

The Celestrian paused there, turning to allow Aeric to see past her to what the vapors of the Mae Fountain were creating while she talked. Though blurred by the tears in his eyes, Aeric was surprised to see the once gray world around him slowly swirling into a field of green. Taken aback by what he was witnessing, the Grandarian wiped away the water in his eyes and focused them to see the green shaping into fields of grass in front of him, stretching on into the horizon where rolling hills met a cloudless blue sky. Staring around him at the grassy environment he suddenly found himself kneeling in, he was surprised to feel a sensation of warmth shining down on him that wore away the biting cold of the Lake of the Undead. Peering up, he saw the sun shining above him for the first time in as long as he could remember. Raising a hand to shield his eyes from the light and placing another on the ground to balance him, he felt the touch of the long grass with morning dew still clutching to the blades.

"No matter what you have lost in your world, I can restore it for you with or without these crests," Female told him as she slowly drifted down out of the blue sky where Aeric had been staring at the sun. "All you need do is fall asleep, and I can return all that you lost. You would be reunited with your loved ones, given back your possessions and the life you always dreamed of. You would forget the cruelty and sadness of this world forever. Affected on a human, the vapors of the Mae Fountain could keep you alive in your dream for a full human life. You would never even remember this reality."

Unable to believe what he was seeing and feeling, Aeric was further amazed to hear the sound of his name being called from behind him from another familiar voice. Turning his head, he found a sight he had all but forgotten except for in his dreams. His home village of Eirinor sat nestled in its green vale behind him, with a figure materializing out of the mist of colors on the hill he sat on. Slowly rising to his feet and turning to face it, the Grandarian felt his sorrow slowly drifting as he saw Mina standing on the hill waving at him and coyly smiling, waiting for him as she had when she was just a child. Aeric slowly blinked as another tear fell down his cheek and he slowly took a step toward her. Seeing her giggle and grin wider, Aeric began hurriedly walking toward her through the long summer grass until she was only a foot away.

"I've missed you, Aeric," she whispered as he stopped in front of her. Her voice was exactly as beautiful as he remembered. She looked exactly like his lost love—her curly chestnut hair even had the same bounce when she moved. Mina reached up with her right hand and set it on the boy's wet cheek, slowly drawing closer to press her lips into his. Feeling the moist touch of her soft lips against him,

Aeric began losing himself to the sensations of the dream world. Though he tried to remember this was all false and the real Mina was still gone, her touch now felt more real than he could have ever remembered. He couldn't believe what he was seeing, but as the seconds ticked by he found himself caring less and less. He desperately wanted to give in and pretend this was all real. In time he could tell with an absolute certainty he would forget it wasn't. The touch of Mina's lips was intoxicating like nothing else. He had been without softness, color, or life for so long he would take it any way he could. Aeric had told himself he would do anything to feel this again, if only just once more.

As he stood with Mina pressing her body against him and reaching in to kiss him again, he felt himself drifting into the dream as if to accept it and replace his reality with it. Female was right—he couldn't even tell the difference. All traces of the bleak world he had left behind had faded from view. He was free from the burden of responsibility; free from the demanding legacy of his name that the world expected of him. It was his chance to just be another man the same as any. As the thought of his family echoed through his mind just before he completely gave into Mina and let his senses believe in the dream world without hesitation, the image of the other girl he had left lying next to a crate in the darkness of the forsaken lake flashed to life in his mind. He saw Valeri, soulless and gray because of the sacrifice he knew she had made for him.

With Valeri came the thought of Verix falling to ensure he could collect the crests and bring his granddaughter back. The legendary Drakkaidian king who trusted him the same as he trusted his Grandfather Tavin. After Verix came Revond and Lucan who both entrusted him on his own to recover the crests. After everything they had all done for him to bring him this far and fight to preserve the world they all inhabited, Aeric knew he couldn't dishonor them by selfishly seizing his own personal paradise and leaving them in darkness. Even if the crests and all hope was lost, he wouldn't abandon them this way. Though painful to push away from the arms of his greatest love, Aeric took a step back, shaking his head and closing his eyes to block her out.

"No," he said out loud, trying to concentrate on Valeri and the real world somewhere past the illusion the vapors the Mae Fountain had pulled around him. Swinging his arm up as if to bat the false world away, he cast his forearm clear through Mina and sent a mist of colored particles flying through the air. Opening his eyes to see her dissipating, the rest of the green world followed in suit. Feeling the warmth of the sun and the softness of the grass disappear, Aeric felt a sharp pain strike his body as the chill of reality set back in and he found himself standing back on the island of the lake. Feeling dizzy and losing his balance as the vapors of the Mae Fountain faded in the air, Aeric fell back to his knees. Turning to see Valeri's lifeless body still sitting behind him, the Grandarian crawled back to her to gather her in his arms and lean her against him, setting his own back against the crate.

Breathing heavily from the physical and emotional shock of refuting the paradise given to him for the dark valley high in the Black Peaks, Aeric held onto Valeri and just sat in the silence. If this was the end, it was the one he owed his friends. As he sat just breathing and thinking of nothing, he saw the levitating form of Female drop back in front of him with the continual impassive look on her face. She stared at him for a long moment before opening her mouth to speak.

"You choose not to embrace this paradise," she stated more than she asked. "To hold this lifeless girl instead of your love." Aeric was silent for a long moment but eventually looked at Female with exhausted, languid eyes.

"I'd rather be worthy of her memory," the young man replied at last. The Celestrian tilted her head at this. Though remaining still, she faintly smiled for the first time and lowered her body closer to Aeric's.

"And so your character is revealed, Aeric," she said. "Any man who would reject his own personal paradise for the sake of another has a true heart, as is yours. I had to be sure." Aeric shot her a confused glance but watched in wonder as she reached behind her back with both hands. Bringing them forward again, she revealed six flat objects in her hands that stole the breath out of Aeric's lungs. They were circular stone emblems with six different elemental designs in each.

"...What?" he asked in a whisper.

"I already told you," Female began again, "since being here I have taken it upon myself to look after all of the witch's stolen spoils. I took these crests from the coffins shortly after she brought them here. I could not trust you at first but now

I see you will only do good with them, so I relinquish them to you. Take these crests and restore your life as it should be restored." Aeric was speechless again, but slowly reached up with both his hands to grab onto the six crests and take them. As soon as his fingers touched them he could feel incredible power flushing through him, warming him and energizing his fatigued body just by holding onto them. Looking back up at Female, he saw her smiling at him. Though lost in thought over all that had just befallen him, now that he held the crests it was all he could do to return her smile.

Finding his energy again, Aeric set Valeri down and rose to place the crests in his back pack. Tightly securing it, he reached down and grabbed the princess again. Before he could say anything to Female, he was surprised to find the Celestrian reaching out for Valeri's chest with one of her hands. Though unsure of what she was doing, Aeric remained still and let her press her fingertips against Valeri. The blue glow that radiated from the circular veins of light within Female when she first awakened sprang to life around her hand and onto Valeri's chest.

"What are you doing?" Aeric asked in a whisper.

"We Celestrians endure with great longevity because of our ability to heal in ways you can't quite comprehend," she said quietly. "As long as a body is intact, my power can revive its spirit, even if that spirit dwells somewhere else." Having said this, Female's body flashed again and her liquid blue form returned. Though her fingers morphed back into a single limb over Valeri, a wave of bright blue energy spread from her hand over the princess like a calming ocean wave sliding up a sandy beach. When the humming blue light had engulfed her entire body, it seeped through her clothes into every cell and restored her color. Watching as Female turned her head south, Aeric saw a flash of speeding light flying across the Lake of the Undead onto the island to shoot into Valeri. The moment it merged with her frame, the princess' body jolted with life and her eyes spread wide, vibrant and colorful as ever.

Feeling her move, Aeric felt his jaw dropping and his heart racing with joy. Holding her as she came awake, he watched as the energized princess looked up to stare at him in surprise.

"Aeric?" she said vivaciously. Hearing the young Montrox speak, Aeric felt his mouth beaming with a smile and he set her down. The moment her boots touched the ground Valeri shot forward with her arms tightly pressing her body into him, tears welling in her eyes. Aeric was quick to match her emotion, returning her forceful embrace and feeling new tears trickling down his cheeks.

"I told you I'd bring you back," he said with a hand pressed against the back of her head. "I told you." Valeri didn't say anything but he could feel her nodding and crying with her head buried between his neck and shoulder. The two stood there in each others arms for over a minute, releasing their emotions before finally separating and opening their tear stricken eyes to look at each other.

"How?" was all Valeri could ask as she smiled broadly.

"It's a long story," he told her, not sure if he even had time to begin. "But we have the crests."

"And now you must deliver them," Female said, catching both of their attentions. Though Valeri was shocked to see the strange levitating girl, Aeric looked at her confused. "Among the witch's spoils there is another relic of my people's civilization: a portal that can transport you wherever you concentrate the hardest. It lies on the other side of the island beside your vessel. Use it while you still have time." Aeric nodded and smiled, not sure how to express his gratitude for all the Celestrian had done for them.

"How do I thank you?" he asked flabbergasted. Female merely smiled back.

"Perhaps when you restore your world you can send me back home," she said softly. "Now go." Though feeling there was something more he should say to the Celestrian, Aeric merely bowed and took Valeri by the hand, running back through the mess of stolen items littering the island with the princess close behind. Though she asked him who the mysterious girl was on the way and what had happened to Verix, the Grandarian told her he would tell her as soon as they had time but he had the feeling they had to get back to Hadecrest as quickly as they could. Finding his way back to the boat, Aeric scanned the ground for anything that looked like a portal. Valeri pointed out a circular dais lying at her feet with similar curving edges as the Mae Fountain. Guessing that was what they were looking for, Aeric stepped on with Valeri behind him and told her to close her eyes and concentrate on Hadecrest.

Doubtful but doing as she was bid, Valeri remembered the mountain stronghold and focused on it as hard as she could. As the two thought of their destination, they felt the rush of a strange sensation rippling up their legs and into the rest of their bodies. Looking down, they saw a swirling white light engulfing them until it reached their heads. Concentrating on Hadecrest again, the two disappeared from the island in the Lake of the Undead in a brilliant flash of blue light that illuminated the entire dark valley. As soon as it vanished, so did Aeric and Valeri, leaving the lake in silence again.

Chapter 42

<u>Anointment</u>

Though Revond had freed himself from under Moltar's claws by blasting a wave of white mystical liquid into his sensitive belly, the fiery cat was quick to pounce on him again. Knocked to the edge of the wall with his black robe on fire from the attack, Revond lost his balance amid the rubble and fell onto his back again. He barely had time to grab a slab of a bulwark shield with his mystic power to hold in front of him and shield his body from Moltar leaping into it. Struggling to hold the slab of rock in place with the mighty weight of the Ancient of Fire pressing down on it with all his strength, desperate for the sage's blood, Revond knew hope was slim. Wyrik was already descending to the right side of the wall killing most of the soldiers and he could hear Golthrout climbing back up the side of the cliff. Even with he and Alberic to bolster the resistance he knew they were ultimately doomed.

Though about to try and break the slab of rock and fire a flurry of white spikes into Moltar before he could break through on his own, Revond was surprised to see a brilliant flash of blue explode into view from beside him on his left. Forced to close his eyes for a moment, he opened them to find something he never could have dreamed standing before him. Tightly wrapped in each others arms were Aeric and Valeri, slowly opening their eyes and looking around as if confused at the chaos erupting around them. Though Aeric was the first to see Revond pinned down by the Ancient of Fire, Valeri caught sight of the Ancient as well and told him to stand back as she drew her sword. Charging forward with an electrified wave of darkness rushing up her blade, she slashed down as she raced up to the fiery beast and cut deep into its side with crimson energy leaping off from the wound. Moltar quickly flung off the slab of the shield back to the other side of the wall, spinning around to roar out at his attacker.

Lowering his body to pounce, Moltar leapt into the air toward the princess with his claws reaching out for her glowing body. Seeing him coming, Valeri rolled onto the ground in front of her while clenching her free hand into a fist and charging a surge of dark power around it. As she felt the heat of the flaming cat above her, she opened her fist and released a blast of electrified energy out of her palm to smash into her foe. Coupled with his incredible momentum, Moltar was blasted high into the air to sail over Aeric, still several feet back, and land painfully on his head. Jumping back to her feet Valeri dexterously swung her blade around her hand and charged after the Ancient of Fire.

"Get to Revond!" she ordered as she ran past Aeric. "I'll handle him." Though not wanting to leave her, Aeric did what he was told. Judging from her returned strength and agility, he guessed Female had also healed the once grievous wound in her side. Spinning around, Aeric ran past a group of Drakkaidians struggling to get to the right side of the wall toward the downed form of the Master Sage. Still amazed at the Tieloc's presence but acting fast in the dire situation he found himself in, Revond heaved away the slab of rock levitating above him and rolled back to stand full length before his young friend.

"Aeric?" he asked, the most dumbfounded Aeric had ever heard him. "How is this possible?"

"It's a long story, Revond," he answered as a tremor in the ground nearly knocked him off his feet. "The important part is we found the crests." Reaching to his back to pull off the tattered leather pack, he opened it to reveal the six stone talismans resting inside. His eyes going wide, Revond found himself speechless for a moment. He had no idea how Aeric had so suddenly arrived but knew their hope was restored. Reaching in to grab hold of all six, the sage flipped his head up to one of the archery holes in the cliff and shouted out as loudly as he could.

"Lucan!" he bellowed. "Bring them all down!" Looking up as well, Aeric saw the Blue Maven Lucan Hauk Erland standing in an archer's hole with three others. When Lucan looked down to find Aeric standing beside the sage, his eyes lit up and he hurriedly dropped his bow to push the others down the stairs leading to the wall top. Seeing them moving,

Revond placed his gaze back on the stone crests and released them. Spreading them out in an arch before him with his mystic power, he placed his hands on each other in front of his chest. Slowly spreading them out to pass over the crests, Aeric was amazed to see each one glow with unique life and color. The fire crest burned with small flames from its red emblem while the water crest dripped with clear liquid from the blue water drop design in the middle.

Casting his gaze to the crest closest to him, he saw it shining white with a star-like emblem inside. Having awoken the crests, Revond reached down to pluck the white one from the air and hand it to Aeric. The Grandarian was confused but looked up to peer into the sage's hood to find a tired but true smile behind his bearded face.

"I'm not sure how you managed this, Aeric," Revond told him, "but well done. Here—this is yours now." Looking back down at the shining crest in the sage's gloved hand, Aeric reached and took it into his hand. The moment his fingers fell upon it he could feel a familiar sensation of warmth and power emanating into his entire body that shone brighter with the crest in hand. Before he could ask what to do, Aeric saw Lucan dashing out of a hole in the cliff leading onto the cliff with the three others he had never seen behind him. Assuming they were the Elemental Warriors Revond had recruited, his guess was confirmed when the Master Sage spun around and pushed the crests out to them.

"Aeric has succeeded in his quest and brought the crests to us," he said quickly as he heard Wyrik scream behind him. Catching each other's eyes, Lucan and Aeric beamed at each other but didn't have time to say anything as Revond was quick to continue. "Take the crest of your element, quickly!" The four did what they were told, each of them reaching out for the floating crest that looked to hold an emblem resembling their element. When Lucan, Maglin, Morrol and Kira all had their crests in hand beside Aeric, Revond swept his open hands out over the crests again. As his arms flew by them, the group could feel the power in their hands radiating into them deep into every cell in their bodies. "The crests are now activated and can be used through your will. I will anoint you formally later but for now spread out and engage the Ancient that corresponds with your power. They are comprised of your elements—use that against them!"

The sage was interrupted by another large tremor rumbling around their feet and the sight of Golthrout's hand clutching onto the wall once again. Opening the palm of his own hand Revond summoned the white energy of his Hallador Might and formed another long shaft of light. Piercing it into the ground, the newly christened Elemental Warriors watched in awe as a trail of white spears blasted out of the ground in a line all the way to the massive rocky hand to stab it repeatedly. Though roaring out in pain, the Ancient of Earth still swung his massive head up to the wall with his mouth opening to charge a blast of swirling scarlet energy in his jaws. Sensing the energy building, Revond rushed past Lucan and Maglin to grab Kira Marcell's shaking form and lean down. Yelling into her ear to make sure she heard him over the chaos of battle, he told her to concentrate on the beast's rocky skin and pull it apart. Though not sure what to do, Kira held the circular crest in her hand out toward the minotaur and focused on what the sage told her.

Bracing herself with courage she had long prepared for the day she could finally avenge her parents' deaths to the Golthrouts, she took another step toward the rock monster and tightened her body with resolve amid the quaking ground. Concentrating on the beast's rocky hide, she saw the crest of earth in her hand glow green and fragments of stone began chipping off the beast's face. Seeing her elemental power working, Kira continued stepping toward the beast as chunks and slabs of rock began breaking free from the Ancient's bull head. Though only mildly agitated at first, Golthrout clamped its jaws shut and sealed off his power as it felt an entire side of its face lift free to reveal the scarlet energy within. Roaring out in obvious pain, it felt one of his long horns atop its head crumble and break off, falling behind it down the cliff. Aware it would be left defenseless if stayed standing before the girl holding the green talisman, Golthrout released the wall and dropped down to take refuge lower on the cliff.

Hearing the resistance soldiers and her fellow Elemental Warriors cheer as the Ancient of Earth retreated, Kira spun around with an uncertain smile to see Revond approaching.

"Good work, Kira!" he yelled. "Stay on the edge of the wall by those archers and keep tearing away at him!" The sage was interrupted by Moltar's roar as he batted Valeri back against a patrol of Drakkaidians rushing to their princess' aid. Hearing Wyrik descending on the right side of the wall simultaneously, Revond stiffened with resolve and pulled back his hood to reveal his face. He looked over to Maglin and pointed over to the Ancient of Fire. "Maglin! Go help Valeri! Lucan! With me! Aeric, stay with Kira!" With that, Revond bolted around and grabbed Lucan's scarf, tugging the Maven after him as he ran to the right side of the wall. The Ancient of Wind had dropped to the edge of the wall and was hovering over it while snapping its jaws down at the soldiers still bombarding it with arrows. Reaching forward to grab a loose slab of rock and heave it up at the wyvern to get its attention, Revond spun his head back to shout at Lucan.

"Blow this beast into the ground, Lucan!" he ordered, to which Lucan doubtfully glanced between him and the glowing purple crest in his hand.

"How do I do that?" he returned frustrated as Wyrik lifted higher to whip around and slam his spiked tail into the ground just in front of them.

"Visualize the wind in your mind," the sage commanded while he stopped the rubble of the wall from landing on them with his power. "Focus on the air as it rushes by you! Unleash it onto Wyrik!" Though again not sure he was the right man to pull off such a feat, he lifted the blustery crest of wind in his hand up to Wyrik and focused the air rushing around it up. Though nothing happened at first, he could gradually feel the light headwind shifting and blowing at his back as he concentrated. Within a few moments a gale of wind was rushing past him nearly knocking the Drakkaidians around him off their feet and over the side of the demolished wall top. Wyrik was affected little at first, merely beating its wings harder to compensate, but as Lucan pressed the wind harder against it into a howling storm the wyvern was blown back from the wall screaming from both heads.

"I don't think I can hold him!" Lucan shouted to Revond as the sage held onto a heavy weapons container bolted to the ground.

"You are creating wind from the crest itself!" the sage responded. "Use the air already present around him! Trap him in it! Use the clouds!" Realizing his gale was coming from the crest as Revond told him, Lucan shifted his concentration onto the rolling billows above the Ancient of Wind. Narrowing his eyes as he lifted the crest up to them, he saw a swirling whirlwind taking shape amid one of the clouds that reached down to circle over the winged beast as he began to regain his balance in the sky. Focusing harder, the whirlwind quickly strengthened into a violent tornado ripping down from the clouds to sweep even the enormous Ancient up. Unable to lift free or escape the wind's power, Wyrik spun around inside like a leaf caught in a storm.

Seeing the Ancient of Wind trapped, Revond stood full length on the calm right side of the wall and lifted his hands perpendicular to his body on either side. Summoning a charge of white electricity around either limb, he threw his hands together to release a flying charge of lighting. A thunderclap cracked through the air the moment his hands came together, catching the attention of everyone on the wall. While the electrical surge slammed into the tornado to shock Wyrik's entire form, Valeri glanced to her side on the opposite end of the wall to see what the commotion was. Seizing on the girl's hesitation, the Ancient of Fire still locked in battle with the Drakkaidian princess shot his head forward to bite at the sword lodged in her hands.

Tearing her weapon away and batting Valeri against a column of rock behind her, it left the princess momentarily stunned and lowered its head to pounce on her again. Stretching its molten claws as it prepared to leap at her, Moltar was surprised to feel a painful sensation tear over its entire form as if the air was being pulled out of its lungs. Wondering why the creature hesitated to attack, Valeri finally recovered from the stun and focused her eyes to see the bright coat of fire over its body dimming and puffing out until it was left with only charred smoldering skin and its burning eyes. Wondering how it was possible, both Moltar and Valeri looked to the left side of the wall to see Maglin Byre standing there with the burning crest of fire in her hands.

"You've been playing with fire for too long, kitty," Maglin breathed with acid dripping from her words. Though weakened and in pain without the fire burning around its body, Moltar turned to face her and prepare to leap at her instead. Seeing it change targets, Valeri Montrox rose full length and clenched her fists, charging her field of dark power alive around her frame. Gritting her teeth and running at the cat before it could jump, she planted one leg on the ground and threw the other up to send her boot slamming into the beast's side. Her kick was so powerful she sent the Ancient of Fire flying over the wall and toppling off the edge to plummet down the cliff a final time. Dropping her right leg down to the ground, the princess let her swirling aura of power wane to a crimson layer of light around her body and she turned to look at the auburn haired Warrior of Fire standing beside her.

"I like your style," Maglin said, giving the princess a nod.

"Likewise," Valeri returned with a dark smile. Though about to ask the Warrior of Fire's name, Valeri caught sight of something rushing toward the wall all the way from the bottom of the mountain wedge. Her eyes going wide with panic, she spun around and shouted out Revond's name as loud as she could. Though the Master Sage was nearly a hundred feet away and still electrocuting Wyrik in Lucan's tornado, his acute senses picked up her voice amid the chaotic activity around him and he spun his head to her. Before he could even set his gaze on her, he caught sight of the blue torrent of water beaming toward the wall top from the mouth of Vorkoise far below them. Aware the high powered stream of water could blast the wall apart even from such a distance, Revond immediately cut off his attack and rushed to the center of the wall before the watery beam could reach them.

Holding out his hands with his fingers spread, he caught the blasting water just before it slammed into the ground at his feet, holding it back with his mystic energy and sending liquid spraying off in all directions. Throwing his shoulder down as if helping him to hold back the invisible wall of his power, he turned to yell at Lucan.

"Lucan!" he shouted as loud as he could as he struggled to hold back the water. "Get Morrol closer to Vorkoise! Now!"

"What are you talking about?" he asked as he let go of the tornado around Wyrik and dashed over to the sage.

"You are the Warrior of *Wind*!" Revond snapped angrily. "Use it!" Though still not sure what that meant, Lucan stopped when he reached Jax Morrol and shrugged. Lifting the crest of wind to the Sarton of the Legion's feet, he gulped and summoned a gust to lift him up and gently balance him in the air. Raised off his feet by the fiercely blowing wind, Morrol shot the Maven a nervous glance.

"Do you know what you're doing?" he asked nervously.

"Of course," Lucan lied, moving him to the edge of the wall. "Just hold on to... well, don't hold onto anything, just trust me." With that, the Warrior of Wind created a gust of wind to shove Morrol down from the wall and gently but quickly slide him down along the stream of water to its source far below. Racing along the water so close he could feel drops of it spraying onto his face, Morrol caught sight of the serpent that had destroyed Ceruleana waiting at the floor of the mountain wedge and narrowed his eyes with fury. Though not sure how he could attack the Ancient of Water when he had no water to manipulate, he knew all the liquid spraying from the beast's jaws had to come from somewhere and raised the crest of water. Concentrating on the water he knew flowed through the serpent, Morrol yelled out loud and pulled it out wherever it was to spray through his scaled body.

Feeling his long body tearing as water ruptured his thick hide, Vorkoise ended his attack and painfully looked up to the levitating Warrior of Water beside him. Though about to snap its jaws out for him, jets of water exploded out from his head and the serpent was left inert, dropping to the rocky ground crippled. Watching the blue beast fall from high on the wall the other Elemental Warriors cheered and looked around to find the four Ancients of the neutral elements contained. Golthrout, Moltar, and Vorkoise lay sprawled out next to each other at the bottom of the cliff while Wyrik had crashed into the wall top, stunned and unable to move from the dizzying storm of electricity he had been caught in. As the Drakkaidians began to cheer, Aeric and Kira moved from the edge of the wall to converge on the center where the others were gathering.

Looking up into the sky above them at the sound of roaring, Aeric saw the Ancient of Darkness swinging his clawed hands out for the white horse spinning contrails of light around him. Though watching Alberic continually pummel the behemoth with his golden hooves for several moments, the Grandarian was shocked to see Dalorosk at last snatch him out of the air and slam a fist down into him. Tucking in his bat-like wings to soar down after him, the black Ancient tore free the sword in his thigh to cast it out for his brother to release an arching wave of black energy slicing into him. With his golden hooves dimming and a flurry of white feathers exploding into the air, Aeric and others watched as Alberic plummeted out of control down into the top of the cliff to tumble down it until landing on the right side where Valeri had battled Moltar.

Splitting the ground from the bone breaking force of impact, the Ancient of Light did not move except to blink his golden eyes. Aware he was weakened and unable to continue fighting, Aeric tightly clutched the crest of light from under his tunic and raced toward him in spite of Revond shouting for him to remain at his side.

"Aeric no!" Revond bellowed. "Do not put the Source of Light at risk!" Pushing past the Drakkaidians and even Valeri to get to the downed Ancient, Aeric ignored the sage, aware that if he didn't reenergize Alberic he would be killed. Running as hard as he could, Aeric was surprised to see a large shadow spreading over the ground in front of him and looked up to see Dalorosk dropping down from the sky to rip into the cliff and slide down it until crashing into the ground beside Alberic. Roaring in fury, the behemoth gripped the hilt of his black sword and swung it above his head with a roar so loud most of the resistance members were forced to drop their weapons and cover their ears.

Aware he had to act fast, Aeric raised up the crest of light to try and fend him off. Seeing the white light in the boy's hands, Dalorosk quickly swept forward to slam his fist down and try to destroy him before he could use the talisman. While he might have been crushed, Valeri was there to pull him back as the bulging fist came down where he had been.

"Valeri!" Revond yelled, still holding the crest of darkness. Throwing it out to her, the girl looked back just in time to catch the crest in her left hand and stand to ward the beast off with her own power. While she charged the talisman in her hands, Dalorosk looked down at the boy and recognized him as the one who had freed Alberic from the Holy Shrine and used the Source of Light against him. With his black heart suddenly pumping, Dalorosk acted faster than ever before. Lunging ahead and surprising them all by transforming into his human disguise, the Ancient of Darkness rolled up to his feet on the devastated wall and rushed toward Aeric and Valeri. His arm quickly mutated with bulging and twisted muscles shrouded in black energy. Screaming and spreading his jagged fingers wide to release and blast of dark power into Valeri before she could use the crest against him, he blew her away with the sheer force and slammed his free fist into Aeric, dropping the Grandarian to the ground.

Kneeling over him with his foot pressing hard on the boy's chest, Dalorosk pulled free a black stone circle tucked into the back of his belt. Reaching down to swat away the crest of light in Aeric's hands, he ripped the boy's tunic open to reveal the white medallion Aeric was desperately fumbling to open on his chest. Again slapping his hand away with his powerful brute force, the Ancient clasped his black stone around its edges and closed it inside. It snapped tight in a perfect fit, just as he had designed it. Once in his reach the black Ancient let a grin of disbelief spread across his face and he rose from Aeric's chest to raise the contained Source of Light above his head. As he stood laughing, Revond rushed forward telling the other Elemental Warriors to attack him as quickly as possible. Seeing Alberic's disciple rushing him with white power alight in his hands, Dalorosk growled and transformed back into his enormous true form with the Source of Light and the strange container he held it in disappearing from view.

"All six Sources are mine!" he bellowed as Revond fired a flurry of white spears into his front. Ignoring the pain, Dalorosk leapt off the wall top and spread his wings to keep him hovering above them. Seeing him free and laughing maniacally, Wyrik summoned what strength he had left to speak from his twin heads.

"Help us, brother," he said just loud enough for Dalorosk to hear. The Ancient of Darkness spun his head to the felled wyvern and shook it with a disgusted frown appearing on his face.

"Did you really think I would share rule of this world with the likes of you, you pathetic fool?" he asked mockingly. "You were always my enemy the same as Alberic. And once I create the Source of All you will taste the same death as him!" Pulling one of his swords free, Dalorosk roared with fury and slashed down to cleave through both of Wyrik's heads and deep into the rock wall. "Mine is the face of the future!" Wrenching his weapon free, the behemoth started laughing again and turned to shoot off into the sky toward the east and the other Sources waiting for him at the Holy Shrine. As he slipped out of their range, Revond and the other Elemental Warriors watched in horror as all their efforts to stop the Ancients vanished. Dalorosk flew away to unleash the ultimate power in the universe.

Chapter 43

<u>The Warrior of All</u>

As Dalorosk disappeared into the dark horizon, the wall top of Hadecrest fell silent. The chaotic clamor of battle dissipated into the suddenly quiet Drakkaidian air, replaced by the sounds of the resistance soldiers slowly looking back and forth at each other wondering what had just happened. Though some of the Drakkaidians cheered in seeing the Ancient of Darkness flee from Hadecrest and the other Ancients all defeated by the newly christen Elemental Warriors, most of them knew something was wrong from the way Dalorosk had departed with maniacal laughter and the way the warriors who had saved them hung their heads in defeat.

Still watching the behemoth disappear into the distance with the Source of Light he had been charged to protect, Aeric felt his heart sinking to mesh with his guts and the strength in his legs giving out the same as when he opened the coffins of the original Elemental Warriors to find them empty. The distraught Grandarian slowly leaned down and set a knee on the ground to brace himself, once again feeling a wave of hopelessness overcome him. He couldn't believe what he had just let happen. After all he had gone through to retrieve the crests and defeating four of the five Ancients, he had practically handed the final Source to the black Ancient in his foolish charge to help Alberic. Now all hope was lost.

Valeri stood beside him after being blown off her feet and rising back to his defense, staring at the horizon where Dalorosk vanished with a befuddled expression on her sweating face. She couldn't believe what had just transpired any more than Aeric. Though turning to look back at the Master Sage Revond and the other Elemental Warriors grouped around him, she couldn't find the words to address him. The sage had a mortified expression on his face, cast down to his feet after witnessing Dalorosk make his escape. Though desperately reeling for an idea of what could be done to stop him, the sage gradually let his despair and anguish take hold. He had been so close—so close to putting everything right. In the pandemonium from the heat of battle he had let the Ancient of Darkness' final key to the Source of All slip away.

As Revond stood silent with his ripped cloak still smoldering from being seared by Moltar's claws, Lucan Hauk Erland stared at him waiting for the wise sage to snap back to his senses and tell them what to do. When the silence only hung on and no confident orders came, he took a step toward Revond with his expression dire.

"What do we do now?" he asked for all of them. His question reaching the ears of all the others around them, they all slowly turned their heads to stare at the Master Sage and wait for him to respond. Revond slowly raised his weary blue eyes to the Warrior of Wind, staring back for a long moment.

"Nothing," the sage whispered back at last, lowering his eyes back to the ground. "We tried our best but Dalorosk is gone with the last Source. It is over." Another long silence lingered over the wall top. Though Lucan was stunned by the sage's reply, he shook his head and narrowed his eyes.

"No," he returned. "No, no, no! It can't end like this—there has to be something we can do! Let's go after him! I just flew Morrol down the cliff; maybe I could—"

"Even if you and your crest had the energy to fly someone across the continent to the ruins of Galantia," Revond interrupted, "which you don't, you could never beat Dalorosk there. He will have reached the Holy Shrine before you even get out of Drakkaidia." Lucan frowned but ignored the sage's dismissal, still groping for an idea. Spinning around, he looked for Alberic and started speaking before even knowing what he was saying.

"We could ride Alberic," the Maven said frantically.

"Look at him, Lucan," Revond responded gravely. "He isn't even conscious, and without the Source of Light—"

"Aeric has the crest of light," Lucan cut him short. "You said it's a copy of the Source! That could energize him!"

"The crests are copies of the Sources, not the Sources themselves," Revond told him. "Only an actual Source can empower an Ancient. He cannot help us anymore. Dalorosk will return to the Holy Shrine, fuse the Sources together as he has planned all along and achieve power rivaling that of the Holy Emerald itself. There is nothing more we can do." Having never heard the wise and confident sage so negative and depressed, Lucan didn't know what to do. Though wanting to throw his arms in the air and scream that they had to try something, he was surprised to hear a small voice speak out from behind him.

"What if we did what he's going to do?" the feminine voice spoke in a nervous quiver. Lucan slowly turned to see Kira Marcell standing behind him with her long blonde hair falling across the glowing green crest in her hands. Revond looked up and tilted his head at her uncertainly.

"What did you say, Kira?" he asked confused. Kira looked around to see all eyes falling to her but she cleared her throat and took a step forward to stand beside Lucan.

"Well, if Dalorosk is going to combine the elemental Sources and make a master power," she began, "maybe we could combine our crests and make a master power of our own." Lucan raised an eyebrow and cast his gaze up to Maglin and Jax standing across from him, both staring at her with uncertain but captivated faces. Aeric and Valeri shot each other curious glances standing on the right side of the wall before the princess helped the Warrior of Light back to his feet and they began slowly walking over to the others. Revond merely let out a long breath at the girl's idea and slowly blinked.

"I appreciate your creativity, Kira," he told her, "but as I told Lucan, the crests are not the same as the Sources. They are physical talismans and not mere energy—they cannot be fused."

"Well what if we fused their energy together into a something else?" she pressed.

"With the exception of the Sources that were formed over a very long time by creatures of pure elemental energy, all power in this world needs a conduit in which to flow, Kira," Revond told her. "Magic and energy need a medium to emerge, whether through life or an inanimate talisman like the crests."

"But you said the energy of the crests flows inside us when we use them, Revond," Lucan exclaimed hopefully. "We are the conduits the power needs!"

"Are you saying we should fuse ourselves together, Lucan?" Maglin asked mockingly with her eyebrow raised.

"What if we combined the power of the crests into one person?" he said, ignoring her. "We could create a... well, Elemental Warrior of All!" Revond let out a sharp huff and shook his head.

"This is ridiculous," he said growing frustrated. "There are six Elemental Warriors, one for each element, for a reason, Lucan. The crests were not designed to empower one person alone. One body could not sustain the presence of all six elements within."

"Why not?" Lucan pressed. "Do you really know that? If the very Sources of all elemental energy in the world can be fused together, why can't the energy of these crests combine too? We should at least try!"

"And which of you will volunteer to throw yourself in the middle of this maelstrom of power?" Revond asked heatedly. "Even if what you're proposing is physically possible and one of you could act as a means to control such power, there is no assurance the energies of the crests would do anything more than resist each other and tear you apart. Will you assume this risk Lucan?"

"I will," came another voice from outside the circle around Revond. The group spun their heads to the right side of the wall to see Aeric standing there, a determined expression on his face. "This is my fault. I let the Source of Light go. I'll get it back. Let's do it." Valeri was the first to step up to him with incredulous eyes.

"You?" Valeri said shocked. "Aeric, you can barely handle a sword. If anyone is going to try this and stand up to Dalorosk it's going to be the warrior of the group, and that's me." She spun around and looked at Revond. "I'll do it."

"No one is doing anything," Revond said throwing his hands up, exasperated. "You don't know what you're proposing. For this to work you would all have to concentrate the exact same level of power together with every ounce of energy in the crests. You all just received them—it would take weeks for you all to master your new powers and feel out the limits of their strength."

"We don't have weeks, Revond," Aeric said. "We probably only have a few minutes. I haven't—we haven't come this far to just give up now and wait for the end of the world. If there's any hope of stopping Dalorosk, we're going to do it." Empowered by the young Tieloc's resolved avowal, Lucan nodded and walked over to stand beside him. He was quickly followed by Valeri and Kira, then Morrol and Maglin. Facing the line of Elemental Warriors all staring him down, Revond let out another deep breath and raised one of his gloved hands to sweep his fingers through his black hair.

"Very well," the sage caved in at last. "I respect your courage, all of you, but I fear we will do nothing more than kill whoever we try to empower. Nothing like this has ever been attempted before." Dropping his hand back into his robes, the sage ran his jumble of thoughts through his head and tried to think of what he should have them do. "All of you form a circle then, I suppose." The Elemental Warriors exchanged anxious glances but did what they were told and stepped into a circle with equal distance apart from each other.

Revond quickly positioned them into a more exact formation, walking around their perimeter to look over their crests all glowing in their hands.

"Listen closely, my friends. For this to have any chance of success you will all have to summon the complete power within your crests and extend them out to our Warrior of All. Their full power must be brought to bear for there to be an equilibrium and a successful fusion of energy. This will take your complete concentration and willpower to maintain it. If one of your crests is out of sync or too weak, the energy will collide instead of fuse and destroy you."

After Revond had trailed off, Valeri prepared to ask him if she should stand in the center or stay in the circle. Before she could, she felt Aeric grab her arm and hold her in place.

"Valeri, I have to do this," he told her, earning an instant frown. Before she could rebut him, he spoke again to cut her off. "I'm the Warrior of Light. I'll have a better chance to contain him and take back the Source of Light that he stole. I know as well as you I'm not the warrior you are but with this power hopefully I won't need to be. Please. You have to trust me. I haven't let you down yet. I won't. I promise." Valeri's harsh expression faded at this and she didn't know what to say.

"Aeric is right, princess," Revond said from behind them. "He has the potential for both light and dark power in him already from his Tieloc and Montrox blood. He has the better chance to survive the transformation." Valeri glanced back at the sage before looking down, tears forming around her crimson eyes. Choking them back, she raised her head to face Aeric and grabbed onto him as well.

"This is a horrible idea," she said, tightly embracing him. "But I trust you." She placed her head between his shoulder and neck, holding him for a long moment while she suppressed her tears. "Just don't make me say I told you so." With that she released him and blinked away the water in her eyes. Nodding and giving her a faint smile, Aeric looked back at Revond who motioned for him to stand in the center of the circle. Slowly ambling inside the Elemental Warriors, Revond told them all to raise their crests toward Aeric and reach deep inside their minds to summon as much raw energy from the talismans as they could. Clutching the crest of light against his chest and doing the same, Aeric closed his eyes and prepared for whatever fate had in store for him. Curious at what was about to happen, the Drakkaidians slowly gathered around the circle of Elemental Warriors with eyes agape.

With their crests all glowing bright colors pointed out to Aeric, Revond told them to begin casting as much power as they could toward him. Following his orders, the crests burst alive with radiating power and flowed out into the circle to spread around Aeric and swirl into each other. Though Aeric felt an uncomfortable pain fermenting around his middle as the energy slid over him, before long a strange numbing feeling spread up and down his body making it difficult to grasp onto the energy of his own source. Seeing the Grandarian falter, Revond yelled out for him to stay strong and keep focusing his power. Tightly closing his eyes and concentrating as hard as he could, Aeric squeezed the shining crest of light in his hand and felt its brilliant warming power surging to life amidst the others.

While Lucan, Kira, Maglin, Jax and Valeri found it difficult enough to keep their crests' full strength blaring forward into each other, Aeric was quickly overwhelmed by the full force of accepting not only his own element but theirs as well. Screaming out in apparent pain as the colors rapidly pulsating with life around him began to flare up with white light searing into his flesh, Aeric heard Revond shouting for him to keep holding strong. Though the sage would have ordered them to stop under any other circumstances, he knew this was the world's only chance and Aeric understood the risk. Biting his tongue and raising his arm to shield his eyes from the intense light shining out in the swirling storm of power in the circle of Elemental Warriors, the Master Sage could only pray to Granis that Aeric would survive. Though Valeri and the others cringed at the thought of Aeric in pain with them only concentrating on it harder, they thought of all they had lost during the Ascension and remained focused on unleashing the power the young Tieloc would need to set it right.

With the entire mountain wedge that held Hadecrest caught in the white glow exponentially brightening over the next few moments, all the occupants on the wall top were shocked to see the crests simultaneously burst in the hands of the Elemental Warriors, shattering as if mere dirt clods in their grip. Terrified and astonished to feel the circular talismans break, the five warriors surrounding Aeric felt a massive surge of power rush out from the center of the circle that blasted them off their feet as a column of white energy exploded into the sky. Landing on his back beside the other felled Elemental Warriors, Revond stared up into the sky to watch the clouds part around the beam of white light piercing them. As the vapors withdrew, a faint rim of blue sky appeared beyond. Struggling to remain where he lay while the force from the power of the beam pushed everything around it away, the group watched in amazement as it suddenly widened and expanded over the entire mountain wedge in mere seconds then faded as silence gripped the Black Peaks.

There was no sound for a long moment even as loose rubble and weapons from the wall fell down around them from being lifted up by the surge of power. The beam was gone but a brilliantly shining figure covered in radiating white light hovered above the ground where Aeric had been. Revond and the warriors slowly lifted their backs off the ground and stared at it as the light gradually dissipated, revealing the body underneath. Feeling a tear roll down her cheek, Valeri found herself staring at Aeric limply levitating off the ground. He was caught in a field of the most intense power she had ever felt—beyond her ability to categorize or identify. The Grandarian was inert but his entire frame was restored; all his wounds and the rips in his clothing were gone. He looked fully recuperated but remained motionlessly floating in the grip of the amazing power.

Though Valeri attempted to stand and run to him, Revond was quick to reach out for her leg to keep her standing beside him.

"That power is strong enough to incinerate anything it touches, Valeri," Revond told her though his voice was almost lost in the strange silence hanging around them. The princess turned her head to look back at him, gradually rising himself as he stared at Aeric.

"What happened to him?" she asked quickly. "Is he...?" Revond kept his eyes on Aeric, squinting them as if to sense if the boy was even alive.

"I'm not sure," he replied, dumbfounded. "I believe we succeeded in forming a combined energy of the six elements, but it is radiating raw, unrestrained energy of impossible strength. Aeric isn't in control, he's just..." The sage wasn't sure what to say, unable to judge what state the boy was in. He couldn't feel or sense anything but the incredible power before him. While the other Elemental Warriors rose around Aeric, they all stared at him nervously, waiting and praying for something to happen. As the seconds slipped into minutes with Aeric still unmoving, Lucan let out a deep breath of lament, guessing his gambit had done nothing more than take his young friend's life. Standing horrified with her hands over her mouth, Kira Marcell let tears fall from her cheeks, turning to look at Jax Morrol standing beside her, slumped over in defeat.

Revond let out a final huff and slipped his eyes to the ground again. Seeing the sage and the other Elemental Warriors casting their gazes down and slouching in mourning, Valeri shook her head, unable to accept he was dead. Balling her fists, she took a step toward him and the field of shining white energy. Though it pushed against her and burned into her as she neared, the princess shot her head forward and yelled out with emotion choking her voice.

"Wake up, Aeric!" she commanded as a tear fell from her eye. "You promised me! You can't die! You've never given up before—you can't now! Wake up!" Though nothing happened other than the incredible power singeing Valeri's shawl and burning her skin as she remained where she stood without backing down, all of them were surprised to see the potent energy suddenly shrink back and shift into an easier, slowly radiating aura around the boy. Feeling the painful field disappear, Valeri's eyes widened when she saw Aeric's eyes slowly twitch and lift open, revealing his shining blue irises. He remained inert for a long moment but eventually turned his head up to fix his gaze on the Drakkaidian princess. Staring at her for a long moment while Valeri's face beamed, he flexed his muscles and made his body erect, slowly dropping to touch down on the ground. Looking away from Valeri to raise his own hands and stare at them as if in awe, the empowered Grandarian reached out as if to touch the field of rising energy around him. Seeing it follow his hand, he felt the power was indeed radiating from him and looked up in amazement to Revond, already staring at the young Tieloc in awe.

"I don't believe it," the sage whispered to himself.

"We did it!" Lucan shouted from behind Aeric, throwing his arms into the air and leaning back to shout out in glee. Hearing the Warrior of Wind's cheer, Valeri jumped forward to ran at Aeric and drape her arms around his neck, tightly hugging him and letting her tears flow freely. Returning her embrace, Aeric looked up past her red hair to see Revond slowly approaching.

"I feel..." Aeric began, trying to say something to both Valeri and Revond. "Strong." Revond slowly nodded, looking him up and down and spying the broken crests lying at his feet.

"I believe you are, my young Tieloc," Revond said. "I think you have absorbed the power of the crests. Our risky ploy seems to have worked. You are radiating power I have never dreamed possible. You are a Warrior of All." Aeric gently pushed Valeri back and gave her a comforting nod that communicated he was alright.

"Then I need to move," he said with his every word exuding fortitude.

"I agree, but listen well, Aeric," Revond told him, raising a hand in caution. "You possess power unrevealed right now, perhaps even greater than your grandfather did as the Warrior of Granis in the Days of Destiny, but it will not avail us if Dalorosk is allowed to fuse the Sources. The crests were powerful but only copies of the true energy created from the energies of the Holy Emerald. Even with your new strength you will not be able to stop him if he assembles the Source of All. You must stop him before he gets back to the ruins of Galantia and his shrine. Use the element of light—burn him to a crisp."

"How is he going to get there?" Lucan asked from behind them. Though Revond was about to remind him that Aeric possessed a weak version of the Holy Emerald itself within his body and therefore the power to do nearly anything he could imagine, Aeric turned back to face his Maven friend. Balling a fist with a charge of shining white power emanating from his knuckles, Aeric stared him in the eyes.

"I can get there," he said simply, leaving Lucan confused. "I can feel the Sources. And Dalorosk. I... I don't know how, but I know what to do." Turning back to face Valeri, he stared into her watery red eyes and grabbed her by the shoulders. "I'll be back," he told her softly, to which she nodded and wiped tears away from both cheeks.

"I believe you," she returned. Aeric nodded, releasing her. Before he could back away and prepare to depart, Valeri leaned in and kissed him on the cheek. "Pummel him for me, Aeric." He faintly smiled but didn't say anything, backing away from her and lifting off the ground with his field of power intensifying again.

"Is he going to fly?" Maglin asked, leaning in to ask Lucan. Though about to reply he wasn't sure, he was astonished to see Aeric merely strap a determined look on his face and ball his fists. With a white flash exploding around him, his body was covered in the bright energy and suddenly disappeared out of the air. As the white energy completely dissipated within a few seconds and all traces of Aeric were gone, the warriors on the wall of Hadecrest could only wait and hope he would return soon with good news.

"Revond," Lucan said, catching the sage's attention. "Honestly—is he strong enough to do this? He's not a warrior. Even with all that power Dalorosk is still the veteran." Revond turned to look into the distance toward the east, answering slowly and softly.

"Where Dalorosk has experience, Aeric has courage," he replied. "Where Dalorosk has desperation, Aeric has determination. Where Dalorosk has hatred, Aeric has love." He paused again and blinked slowly, relaxing his frame as he found his own words convincing him to accept the hope he was trying to impart to the others. "Yes. Aeric will do this."

Chapter 44

Indemnity

The dark and desolate ruins of Galantia were illuminated by a massive flash of brilliant white light appearing out of the air directly over the top of the false Holy Shrine. When the momentary column of light disappeared, Aeric Tieloc was left floating in the air with his balled fists in the same position they had been when disappearing form Hadecrest. Guessing he had teleported himself to the Sources he could now feel directly below him, the Grandarian cast his gaze down to see five of the six spheres of elemental energy lying at his feet. Aeric gulped and looked into the tempestuous westward skies for any sign of his enemy. He had made it, but now that he was here he wasn't sure what he should do. Dalorosk was still obviously on his way back, giving him at least a few minutes. Looking back down to the Sources, he wondered if he should try to move them. He could feel the power of all six elements inside him; he might have been able to at least gather them and hide them in case the worst should happen.

Aeric shook his head at the idea, realizing that if he failed to stop Dalorosk this time there would not be another chance for anyone else to do so. He was the last line of defense. Locking his eyes back on the overcast horizon, Aeric knew the future of Iairia rested on his shoulders alone. He had to destroy Dalorosk at any cost before he could reach that shrine. Clutching his fists with determination and summoning a wave of bright white energy around his body, the young Tieloc flexed his power and began to slowly fly west away from the shrine and over the destroyed city. He could feel Dalorosk charging toward him in the distance faster than the behemoth had ever moved before, desperate to reach the Sources and achieve his ultimate power.

Aeric's face was hard as the wind blew through his field of radiating energy and cast his black hair back against his forehead while he flew. Though trying to stay focused, now that he was at the end he couldn't help but think of everything that had transpired since the day he and Mina witnessed Galantia fall and all the destruction that had ensued. Though he had vehemently resisted this destiny for years, as he felt the power of the six crests emanate from his every cell, he knew that the fate of the world had fallen to him the same as it had his grandfather. Though he was no warrior or champion he knew what he had to do now. Dalorosk could not be allowed to get past him.

As the Grandarian gently accelerated over the ruins of the former Grandarian capital, his thoughts were interrupted by a distant roar blasting through the sky to his ears. Peering ahead as he noticed the horizon growing darker, Aeric saw the muscular behemoth he was waiting for drop out of a rolling thundercloud with the dark vapors trailing off his sharp wingtips. With his enemy in sight, Aeric tightened his frame and leaned forward to continue accelerating until his power began to leave a white trail of streaking energy behind him. He could tell Dalorosk had spotted him by the way he roared challengingly again and reached to his thighs to wrench free his duel swords, black surges of electrified energy racing up and down the blades. Hastening to his top speed and bolting through the air like a raging comet, Aeric grit his teeth and let his emotion seize control. He hated this evil creature that had taken so much from him. He was going to unleash everything on him until all that remained was his blackened ashes.

Aeric reached into the layers of elemental power within and began to take hold of the full power of light, remembering the Ancient of Darkness' vulnerability to it. Plowing through the skies at Dalorosk, Aeric saw him heave his blades up with dark power shrouding them. He knew that even with his new power he was still no match for an ancient warrior like his opponent and he would have to completely cripple him in one attack before they collided. Feeling the light energy pulsating around his fists and almost blinded by the intense rays shining out, Aeric raised his arms above his head and shot upward into the sky just he and Dalorosk were about to slam into each other. Though he had never imagined being able to command and unleash elemental energy like his grandfather had throughout his life, somehow Aeric knew exactly how to use it as if it had been with him all along. At his elevated position, Aeric screamed with all his might and threw his arms down with open hands to unleash a barrage of light power blasting down into the behemoth.

The entire Grandarian sky was suddenly engulfed in piercing white light beyond even the borders of the Valley of Galantia to the point where Aeric couldn't even see his hands in front of him releasing a mammoth discharge of righteous energy slamming down into Dalorosk. His emotions fueling the rush of energy beaming away from his palms, Aeric's passionate scream blasted louder than Dalorosk's howls of loathing until he was sure it was shaking mountaintops in the distance. Listening through his scream as the beast grunted and the sound of his wingtips fell away, he guessed his colossal attack had served its purpose and the Ancient had been sent plummeting to the ground. Releasing his hold over the massive light energy detonating from his open hands, Aeric relaxed his spread fingers and his entire body. The beam of energy faded and the light gleaming over the entire countryside with it. Hovering in the air over the outskirts of the ruins of Galantia, Aeric found himself breathing hard from the expenditure of so much energy for the first time and looked to his hands to see them quaking uncontrollably.

Peering past them to see what his attack had done, he observed the sprawled out body of Dalorosk lying on the barren earth hundreds of feet below. Though he hadn't heard or felt it while concentrating so hard on unleashing the barrage of light energy, his attack had drove into the ground along with the black Ancient, leaving an expansive crater around his enormous body. Aeric remained frozen in place for a moment, wondering if he had done it. The Ancient of Darkness wasn't moving; he looked dead. Letting his guard ease, the Warrior of All slowly began to descend through the dark atmosphere toward the crater he had made. With his brown boots gingerly touching down to the smoldering earth, he nervously dropped beside Dalorosk's fearsome head, lying inert with eyes closed. Letting the passionate field of united elemental energy swirling around him dwindle to a faint aura around his body, he took a deep breath, guessing his colossal attack had finally done justice upon the dark hearted fiend.

Not sure what he should do in the wake of his victory other than thank Granis his long struggle was over, Aeric remembered the behemoth had stolen the Source of Light from him at Hadecrest and decided he would have to somehow retrieve it. As he was about to use his elemental sway over the earth to lift Dalorosk's body and turn it over, he was shocked to see the beast's massive eyelids shoot open to cast Aeric's entire body in their ominous crimson glow. Though tensing in shock, Aeric couldn't react quick enough to avoid being snatched up by Dalorosk's fist suddenly heaving free from his side and hammering down to clutch the empowered boy. Squeezing the Warrior of All with strength that would have instantly crushed anyone without such incredible power surging around him, Dalorosk growled and quickly flipped back up to his feet with tremors shaking the earth as he did.

"You again!" the beast roared, squeezing Aeric so hard the Grandarian could feel his bones threatening to snap even with his power to protect him. "Your power over light will not stop me now, boy! Did you think I would have remained captive under your pathetic race for this long without having devised the means to turn my only weakness into a strength? The power of the Source of Light flows alongside mine now! And while you may possess the other elements you will not get the chance to use them!" With that, Dalorosk raised Aeric high into the air and heaved him back out of his grip into the rocks behind him as hard as he could.

The Warrior of All slammed into the earth with slabs of rock and boulders flying up around him while Dalorosk spread his massive wings and shot back into the sky toward the Holy Shrine at the top of the ruins. Though Aeric was stunned from slamming into the rocks, his elemental powers continued to protect him and he was quick to rebound, flexing the white energy around him with force that blew away the slabs that had settled on top of him. Though not sure how, Aeric guessed that the black stone case that Dalorosk had used to steal the Source of Light from him must have somehow nullified its power and converted it to flow in sync with his own. Standing full length in the crater furious that he had been tricked by the black monster, Aeric forced himself to sharpen his hazy senses and act.

Looking up to see his enemy driving toward the Sources on the shrine, the Warrior of All threw up his hand to summon a fierce gale of wind down out of the clouds rushing against Dalorosk. Though it slowed the creature down, he was not blown away and kept beating his wings to propel forward. Aware it would take raw power to bring the Ancient of Darkness down, Aeric grit his teeth and kicked off the ground to soar into the air after him. Hearing the explosion of power behind him as the Warrior of All charged off, Dalorosk turned his head back to see him coming. Growling in fury, the behemoth spun around to look down at the base of his Holy Shrine and bark out loud through the windstorm. Though nothing happened at first, eventually a swirling jet of hundreds of Siarchs emerged from an opening in the fortress, slicing upward into the turbulent air in a frenzy.

Aeric noticed the storm of Siarchs and remembered they answered to Dalorosk but dismissed them as an act of desperation—with his new power he could control them as easily as the Ancient of Darkness himself. Plowing through the air in a bolt of white light, Aeric quickly caught up to Dalorosk with his fists clenched and surging with dark energy. If he couldn't use light against the behemoth, Aeric thought, maybe he could overpower him with his own element like he had seen Valeri and Verix do to demons. Firing underneath Dalorosk faster than the monster could keep up with him, Aeric shot up directly into his flight path and slammed a fist into the creature's skull with waves of black and purple electricity surging around his arm and over Dalorosk's forehead. Blasted back by the raw force of the powerful Warrior of All's attack, Dalorosk roared in fury and struggled to regain his balance in the air. Not letting him have a moment to breath, Aeric charged forward with both fists slamming into the behemoth's middle. Racing up his body he shot up into the Ancient's chin to uppercut him with force that snapped even Dalorosk's black bone in two.

Quaking with rage at the insect buzzing around him holding him back from the power lying just up the hill that he had awaited for eons, Dalorosk's mouth began frothing with brown foam and he reached up with one of his clawed hands to snatch the Warrior of All again. This time prepared with his power charged, Aeric merely flexed and began burning his field of power into the Ancient's flesh. Feeling his own blood slipping out of his fist, Dalorosk was forced to release him before his entire hand was burned away. Free once more, Aeric threw back a hand and charged it with a fiery wave of dark power. With two elements twisting around each other, Aeric screamed and shot his open hand forward to release a flaming beam of black energy pounding into Dalorosk's chest and forcing him back to just a few dozen feet above the ground.

Observing the wave of Siarchs beginning to swarm around Aeric, Dalorosk fought his way free of the beam with his chest seared and charred. Fiercely beating his wings to regain his altitude as Aeric fired a series of dark blasts after him, Dalorosk tightly grasped the sword in his left hand and drove up, narrowly evading one of Aeric's fireballs. Banking to his left, Dalorosk swung his sword into the boy with all his might to strike him with the flat of his blade and send him tumbling through the sky. With Aeric momentarily stunned again, Dalorosk turned into the storm of Siarchs and reached inside their large column rising from the shrine for something they carried atop of their masses. Flipping upright in the sky, Aeric prepared to fire back at the Ancient and finish him off. Observing the beast reaching into the storm of Siarchs, Aeric suddenly froze when he saw the Ancient of Darkness grab something from their teaming masses. A dark grin appearing on his beaten face, Dalorosk slowly grinded around to face Aeric and hold out his fist and present what he held.

Aeric squinted his eyes to make out what it was, obscured by the Siarchs dispersing and fading back into the Holy Shrine or the rocks around its rear side. It was a body of someone covered in the same Siarch slime he had found around Revond and Alberic in central Drakkaidia. Though he couldn't make out who it was, he was further surprised to see Dalorosk slowly open his fingers and lay his hand flat to fully reveal the human he held. His eyes widening as they fell onto the fragile body, Aeric felt his own body going limp and his heart miss a beat before racing out of control.

It was Mina.

She lay sprawled out over Dalorosk's palm, motionless but for her chest slowly rising and falling. Even from the distance between them, Aeric could see she was somehow alive. The Grandarian was frozen in disbelief. Though he had never seen Mina die the night he lost her over a year ago, Revond assured him she had been killed. Yet now she lay before him after so much time still drawing breath. The Ancient of Darkness' grin spread as he saw the boy's field of power diminish in his shock, having counted on such a reaction.

"Humans and your emotions," Dalorosk said shaking his head. "You're as predicable as the sun and moon rising and falling. That's why I kept these two with me all this time, just in case this moment came." Hearing the Ancient mention two, Aeric scanned his palm again to notice the small purple body of Revond's sky sprite friend also laying beside Mina. "You will not stop me! *Mine is the face of the future!*" Before he could do anything, Aeric watched in horror as the black Ancient clamped his fingers over the two and reached back over his head to throw them westward as hard as he could away from both Aeric and the Holy Shrine. Caught by his instincts and so shaken by his love revealed to be still alive, Aeric completely forgot the behemoth and fired off in an explosion of white light after the two bodies sailing through the air away from him.

As Aeric sped to catch his love and the Sky Sprite, Dalorosk instantly spun around and thrust in the direction of the Holy Shrine. Beating his wings harder than he had ever flown in his life, the Ancient drove forward and reached ahead toward the top of the shrine as if to seize it so he could not be ripped away again. Letting him slip by unchallenged, Aeric soared in front of Mina's limp body to catch her and Zephyr in his arms before they could fall to the ground. Landing in a crouch on the earth the next moment, Aeric felt tears welling in his eyes as he reached up to wipe away a lock of his love's chestnut hair dripping with the clear ooze from a Siarch's coagulation net. Unable to believe she was still alive, Aeric completely forgot Dalorosk until he heard the crash of the beast slamming into the top of the Holy Shrine. His heart flying into his chest as he realized he still had to stop the Ancient of Darkness, Aeric set Mina and Zephyr down on the ground and prepared to shoot back into the sky with all his energy.

By the time Aeric could crouch down and prepare to lift off the earth, however, it was already too late. Having seized on Aeric's oversight, Dalorosk dropped onto the top of the Holy Shrine and immediately transformed into his small human form. Landing in a roll, he shot up to race for the empty pedestal where he had long imprisoned Alberic. Reaching behind his back to pull free the Source of Light encased in his dark stone amulet, he lifted a fist to smash the glass door of the white medallion and threw it onto the pedestal. The moment it touched down the shining Source of Light emerged

537

from the talisman to expand into the full sphere of white light hovering over the pedestal. Though temporarily blinded and seared by its righteous power falling onto his flesh, as soon as the white orb regained its full appearance, it and all the other five Sources around the perimeter of the shrine flashed with light. The next moment a wave of invisible force leapt from the center of the roof and spread out to pass through all matter around it. Though they couldn't see it, both Dalorosk and Aeric could feel it sweep through their entire bodies negating their power for a fraction of a second.

Identifying it as the same sensation his grandfather had told him of when Valif Montrox assembled the Holy Emerald, Aeric flared his power back around him and jerked his head up with dread in his eyes. He could see the six Sources all moving together on their own with Dalorosk rushing to the center where they were converging. Not expecting the Sources to merge on their own, Aeric desperately shot skyward toward the Ancient of Darkness and charged a fist of shining energy around him to try and blast him off the roof of the shrine before the converging Sources could reach him. Though shoving his open hand forward to fire his blast of energy to the shrine, the moment the six spheres of light touched, a blinding wave of energy exploded out throwing both Aeric and everything else around the shrine back.

Driven away and tumbling through the air out of control, Aeric painfully landed on the rocky ground. Looking up through the light, he saw the six colors of the Sources slowly painting the sky before merging into a white light beaming off the top of the shrine. As the seconds ticked by with a strange power Aeric could sense but barely comprehend appearing in front of him, he lifted his upper body off the ground and watched as the entire fortress gave way under the force of the power emerging and caving it in. Shortly after the cloud of dust and debris rushed over the ground to swallow Aeric, the light abruptly faded and the massive energy signature slipped away from his senses. The Warrior of All slowly stood in the quiet, looking back to find Mina and Zephyr. Running through the dust he came upon them blown back against a wall of an old building but otherwise alright. As Aeric rushed to his love's side to make sure she was unharmed, he was surprised to see the dust shrouding them suddenly rush away faster than wind could blow.

Turning back toward the clear air where the Holy Shrine had been, Aeric felt his heart sink to mesh with his guts as view of a figure in black slowly descending through the air entered his sight. Dalorosk hung over the pile of rubble with white light shining from his chest and over his entire body until it radiated off and leapt into a strange black flame. Over his chest where he once held the Source of Darkness, the Ancient of Darkness reached up to tighten a new medallion containing a white light shining like a captive star. Looking down over the ruins of Galantia, Dalorosk spied Aeric staring up at him with dread and let a dark grin spread across his face. Looking down at his body as if to inspect the medallion now that it held the power of the universe, the black Ancient began laughing. Though a slow chuckle at first, as the seconds ticked by he threw his hands into the air and bellowed his laughter into the air so loud it could be heard across the entire continent. Aeric shook his head in shame and disbelief.

He had let Dalorosk assemble the Source of All.

Chapter 45

<u>Tieloc Ingenuity</u>

Aeric leaned over Mina's body to wrap her in his arms, watching in trepidation as Dalorosk slowly drifted down for him. The fear and dismay in the Warrior of All's eyes was palpable and he knew Dalorosk could see it as his dark grin only spread. The power radiating from the Ancient of Darkness and the medallion shimmering with white light on his chest was beyond Aeric's ability to grasp. He couldn't believe he had let this happen. The universal power equal to the Holy Emerald itself was in Dalorosk's grip; there was no way to stop him anymore. As the empowered Ancient continued lowering toward the two Grandarians, Aeric violently rejected the idea there was nothing he could do. The God of Darkness had assembled the Holy Emerald itself and possessed its all prevailing power before but Aeric's grandfather had still found a way to best him. He had to be creative and think of something—anything. His mind reeled for any semblance of an idea but nothing came to him. Revond himself had told him his last chance was to stop the black Ancient before he could assemble the Source of All. There was no power left to stand up to him.

Though unable to think of anything he could do to stop his imminent death and save Mina, Aeric narrowed his eyes with trembling fortitude. Even if all hope was lost and this was the end, after all he had come through since the Ascension there was no way he would remain on his knees now. Taking in a deep breath as Dalorosk dropped in front of him, Aeric gently set Mina down beside Zephyr and rose full length before the levitating Ancient radiating with power. Observing the boy stand to meet him with a challenging expression and his fists clenched, the broad smile on Dalorosk's face gradually faded and a disgusted look raced across his face.

"You are either misguidedly brave or foolish beyond measure," he stated with a huff of revulsion, his voice spacious and all-encompassing. "Why would you do anything but grovel for your life now? I have but to wish and my thoughts become reality." Dalorosk raised both of his hands down to the ground at Aeric's feet, spreading them over the barren earth around them. As they swept, the earth crumbled and caved in everywhere but around Aeric and the unconscious pair behind him, revealing gaping chasms with jets of ferocious flame leaping out as far as the eye could see. The Ancient's smile renewed, he glanced down into the fires and raised his hands to bring several towering pillars of bizarre twisting steel out from the hellish chasms. Rotating as they soared into the suddenly electrified sky, enormous plates and bridges dropped down from their distorted surfaces to reveal living swords firing out to spread their blades like wings and circle the air above them. "My every whim is law, boy."

Aeric remained trembling at the fearsome display but held firm, flexing his body and summoning his field of white power of the combined elements around him. Seeing the boy still defiant in the face of his universal power engulfing the world around them, Dalorosk sneered and reached forward with impossible speed to seize Aeric by his throat. Effortlessly plucking him off the ground and extinguishing the Warrior of All's power, the Ancient of Darkness heaved him into the air to send him flying across hundreds of feet up into the side of one of the rising towers of metal. Hurtling through a swarm of the living weapons slicing through the air, Aeric painfully careened into a wall of twisted steel and dropped onto a lowered bridge. Hanging over the edge looking down on the hell below him, Aeric struggled to restore his breath and slowly propped his upper body up with his forearms. Hearing Dalorosk's laugh pounding through the air again, the young Tieloc knew he was only still alive because he was being toying with. He would only last as long as the Ancient felt like playing his games.

While considering just lying back down and waiting for the end, Aeric felt a warm sensation slowly spreading across his chest and looked down to see blood dripping from his tunic down onto the metal ground where he laid. Not feeling the pain of a wound, Aeric wondered where it had come from and looked under the cloth to observe something hanging inside his tunic. Reaching inside to pull out the necklace hidden within, he saw he the Immortal Pennant Sakkdra had given him still draped around his neck and dripping blood from the skull amulet at its center. He stared at it for a long moment, remembering its function and the place from where it had come. A thought racing through his mind, all of Aeric's other deliberations and reflections came to a sudden halt, recalling something the witch who had given him the amulet had said. His blue eyes slowly widening and brightening with color as a sparkle of hope flashed across them, Aeric slowly peered away to the northwest sky with a final idea racing through his mind.

As he was about to rise and summon his power, Dalorosk smashed up through the steel behind him in the tower with the metal melting around him. Praying to Granis the Ancient of Darkness would keep playing with him before simply wishing him dead, Aeric rolled up to his feet with his white field of power flaring to life again. Seeing the Warrior of All spread his legs and ball his fists in preparation to fight once more, Dalorosk raised his eyebrows as if aghast. Firing forward to grip his neck again before Aeric could even see him move, the Ancient shook his head in confusion.

"You learn slowly, don't you?" he asked hatefully. "Well I don't have the patience to educate you so it's time I sent you back to your feeble creator." Hearing this, Aeric knew he had to act as quick as possible to hold onto any chance of his idea working.

"You'll have to find me first," he managed to utter. Closing his eyes and raising his fist to his chest, a white surge of energy swirled to life around it and spread over Aeric's entire body, teleporting him out of the Ancient's grip and the former Grandaria altogether. Surprised to see the determined boy disappear, Dalorosk guessed he had fled elsewhere in a vain attempt to escape. Levitating off his black boots and away from the tower of steel, the Ancient narrowed his eyes to feel out the boy's position. Sensing him far north in Drakkaidia, Dalorosk blinked and vanished from the air to reappear in an enormous explosion of white and black energy in a barren, gray valley surrounded by mountains. Looking around to see where Aeric had led him, Dalorosk spied a placid body of water just before him with ghostlike apparitions slowly levitating above the water. Raising his eyes curiously, the black Ancient spied Aeric hovering a few feet above the lake and staring at him challengingly.

"Well what are you waiting for, you murdering sack of garbage?" Aeric shouted furiously. "Here I am! You want my life—come get it! Come get me! Come on!" Dalorosk remained levitating beyond the shore of the gray waters, peering at the boy suspiciously as if trying to decipher what he was up to. Seeing him hesitate, Aeric continued desperately shouting with his heart pumping. "I said get over here, you damned abomination! Come get me! *Come on!*" Shifting his gaze down at the decaying spirits floating just below Aeric's feet, Dalorosk let a faint smile spread across his face and his black eyes shifted back up to the Warrior of All.

Raising one of his hands with binding electricity dancing over his fingers, Dalorosk seized Aeric with his powerful grip and began slowly pulling him back over the water toward him. Caught in the Ancient's pull with similar electricity keeping him bound, Aeric violently shook his head and tried to resist but with no avail. Still screaming for Dalorosk to finish him now and come out to meet him, the Ancient of Darkness merely remained silent with the knowing smile on his face growing until he gradually pulled Aeric back to the shore. Raising his other hand to grab onto Aeric's tunic, he looked down to see the bloody amulet on his chest.

"Very clever, boy," Dalorosk complimented. "I may have never seen this place before but I can sense what would happen to me if I passed over those cursed waters. You must have some immunity to these ruined spirits and planned for them to rob me of my soul." Still caught in Dalorosk's power, Aeric shook his head.

"Not quite," he returned. "You weren't the one I was talking to." Aeric shifted his gaze to something behind the black clothed Ancient. "I swindled you out of one soul, Sakkdra. I brought you another." Hearing this, Dalorosk's smiled dissipated and he turned his head back to observe whatever the boy was talking to. Looking back, he saw an unfriendly woman standing behind him curiously peering into his eyes with rotten yellow pupils of her own. Seeing the Ancient of Darkness about to react, Sakkdra defensively raised a tattered flask from her black robes and opened its lid up toward the black Ancient. The moment it slipped free the blue haze hovering around it shot up to cover Dalorosk's skin and freeze him in place. A horrified look encompassing his face, the Ancient of Darkness watched helplessly as Sakkdra raised her flask higher up to his body and began pulling all matter around it.

Released from Dalorosk's grip the moment Sakkdra opened her flask of souls, Aeric shot his arm forward to latch his hand onto the shimmering medallion fixed to the Ancient's chest and twist it free. Heaving it back just as Dalorosk's essence lifted free, he watched as the spiritual copy of his body screamed as it was slowly sucked into Sakkdra's flask. Though the image of his soul transformed into his true form and desperately clawed at his levitating body, it was too late and his entire soul was pulled into the flask. When the last trace of blue light was gone, Sakkdra slipped the lid of her flask back down and the haze around it fell passive once more. Watching his body turn gray and fall to the barren shore of the Lake of the Undead, Aeric fell to his knees in shock that his gambit had worked. Struggling to regain his breath, the Warrior of All looked down to the simmering white medallion in his hand, realizing he had out thought Dalorosk even with the universal power of the Source of All.

Staring at the shimmering talisman in his hands, Aeric felt its incredible power surging through him even though the Source was closed off inside the medallion. His strength returned with a mere thought, Aeric looked over the lifeless body of Dalorosk lying on the ground before him and the black embers leaping off of the witch standing beyond it. Peering to meet Sakkdra's gaze, he saw her eyeing the Source of All in his hands. Pulling it back and standing with his field of incinerating white power surging to life around him to ward her off from any thoughts of taking it for herself, Sakkdra frowned and hissed in disgust.

"Be gone with you, cursed Tieloc," she snapped, reaching out with her oozing black tentacles to grab onto Dalorosk's body. Giving her a single nod as if to thank her for playing her part, Aeric slowly lifted off the ground back into the air. Watching the witch toss Dalorosk's corpse into the water of the lake and then slip into her puddle of shadow to retreat back to her shack in the distance, Aeric found himself alone in the valley with the Source of All in hand. He couldn't help but smile to himself, knowing he had saved the world the same as his grandfather had before him. Even though he had let Dalorosk assemble the Source of All as Drakkan had assembled the Holy Emerald, his quick thinking and luck had still triumphed over the incredible odds set against him. It was finally over.

As he turned to fly off and teleport back to Grandaria to retrieve Mina and Zephyr, he spied the island in the center of the Lake of the Undead and remembered he wasn't alone. Shooting across the waters of the lake to the island and lowering to its surface, he saw a familiar creature comprised of blue light staring up at him as he descended. Though neither of them said anything for a moment, Aeric watched as Female the Celestrian took on her familiar human appearance again and smiled up at him.

"I told you I was a good judge of character," she said almost playfully. Aeric returned her smile and gave her a single nod.

"I haven't restored the world yet, Female," Aeric told her looking down at the medallion in his hand again, "but with this I can send you home as you wished." Female's smile faded a little at this but a look of deep contentment spread over her face. She closed her eyes, exhaling a deep breath.

"Thank you, Aeric," she returned, slipping back into her blue liquid appearance. Levitating up to the top of the Mae Fountain, Female stood on its tip and smiled up at him. "I wish you grace and compassion until the end of your days, my friend." Bidding her goodbye as well, Aeric watched in amazement as her blue body turned to what looked like glass and she froze solid atop the fountain. Though not understanding what she was doing or where he was sending her, Aeric reached out the Source of All and wished her and the Mae Fountain to wherever she called home. Sparkling white energy surrounding the fountain, it gradually faded and disappeared along with the brilliant light. With Female gone, Aeric smiled again and looked back into the cloudy sky. Lifting up the Source of All, he made a sweeping gesture that cast away the overcast clouds if only for a moment to let a ray of sunlight fall down on his skin. Closing his eyes in the warmth and letting himself relax for the first time in what seemed like forever, the boy brought the Source to his chest and summoned the white energy over him to teleport him out of the valley for the final time.

Chapter 46

<u>Recovery</u>

The Elemental Warriors had nervously gathered around Revond who nearly dropped to his knees with distress upon feeling the negating surge of power from the formation of the Source of All. He had read of the phenomenon caused by the forming of the Holy Emerald from writings of the Days of Destiny and knew what it meant. Though he couldn't know for sure that it was Dalorosk who had assembled the master Source and harnessed its power because he could still feel Aeric's energy signature present and alive, its formation with no apparent change on the face of the world had him worried. Remaining on his feet and trying to quiet his mind to sense what was occurring between Aeric and Dalorosk, he ignored the desperate calls from the warriors around him, most of all Lucan, asking him what was happening and if Aeric was alright.

Hearing nothing from the Master Sage as the seconds dragged on into minutes with no clue of what had Revond so vexed, the five Elemental Warriors periodically exchanged apprehensive glances through the silence and swept their gazes over the horizon to the east. Though Lucan was the most restless as he impatiently waited for Revond to say anything, he caught Valeri Montrox slowly making her way to the edge of the blasted wall top with her hands over her heart and tears welling in her eyes as she stared out into the cloudy sky. Though not expecting the emotional display from the fierce Drakkaidian princess, Lucan felt his impatience being drowned away by empathy as he watched her dip her head and close her eyes to try and suppress her tears, quietly whispering Aeric's name to herself. Wondering if she could sense something Revond couldn't that might have indicated the fate of the Warrior of All, Lucan felt his heart slowly sink and his body loosen in depression.

As the Warrior of Wind was about to ask Revond if his young friend was dead, he was cut short by a brilliant flash of white light flaring to life and disappearing before he could even blink in surprise. Spinning his head to the left side of the wall top beside a toppled rack of swords and several startled Drakkaidian soldiers, Lucan's eyes went wide to see Aeric hovering inches from the ground engulfed in sparkling white light gradually evaporating off of his frame. Though confused at the sight of the girl limply hanging in his arms, he was far more shocked by the shimmering talisman in his left hand that the amazing energy originated from.

Having spun around to observe Aeric hovering before them as well, Revond and the other Elemental Warriors watched in awe as he touched down over the wall with the last remnants of the mystical light fading around him. Though all of them were in shock and not sure what to make of his dramatic return, the sage slowly stepped forward staring at the young man while their eyes met. Recognizing both the girl and medallion in his grasp, Revond slowly lowered his hood again and shook his head with an incredulous expression on his face.

Unable to find the words to speak, he waited for Aeric to slowly take a deep breath and let a faint smile appear on the corner of his mouth. Watching as the Grandarian gave him a single nod to communicate the outcome of his final confrontation with the Ancient of Darkness, Revond found a smile of his own slowly building and his mouth hanging open while he groped for his voice.

"You did it, then," he said at last. Aeric nodded again and looked over to Valeri staring at him with tears flowing down her cheeks.

"We all did," he returned, confirming all of their hopes. Hearing this, Lucan beamed and threw his arms into the air to shout as loud as he could in unbridled joy.

"Aeric Tieloc defeated Dalorosk!" he boomed so the entire wall could hear. Though the silence hung for a second while the resistance soldiers looked back and forth at each other, seconds later the wall exploded with cheers. The Drakkaidians raised their weapons high and threw off their helmets in celebration. The five Elemental Warriors including the three who had never even formally met Aeric were quick to gather around him as they cheered and raised their hands in victory, patting the Warrior of All on the shoulders and congratulating him. Though Lucan wanted to pick him up and hoist him into the air, he looked down to the girl in the Grandarian's arms and held back, asking Aeric who she was. Aeric was about to reply but he saw Revond part through Lucan and Maglin, staring down at the talisman in his hands.

"How is this possible, Aeric?" he asked exasperated. "How did you do this?" Aeric cleared his throat and looked down to Mina.

"There's much I need to tell you," he began, "but right now these two need healers. I'd use the Source to revive them but in all honesty I'm scared to death of it. I don't want to hurt them by accident." Hearing the Warrior of All speak of two, Revond looked more carefully at the girl to observe the small form of a purple feathered Sky Sprite lying over her against the folds of Aeric's body. Feeling his heart jump into his chest, the Master Sage slowly reached down to gather his oldest friend in his hands and look down to him with a smile. While Revond grabbed hold of Zephyr, the others looked down to the shimmering Source of All in Aeric's hand with their eyes going wide.

"Is that what I think it is?" Lucan asked softly as if afraid to even speak in its presence. Aeric nodded with a smile.

"The Source of All," he confirmed. Before saying anything more he turned to Valeri wiping the tears from her eyes and silently laughing with joy. "Mina needs a healer, Valeri. Are there any still around here?" Valeri's eyes widened in surprise upon hearing the name of the girl in his arms and looked down to her slime covered body as if she had just come from a Siarch coagulation net. Her smile somewhat fading as she glanced back up to Aeric, she swallowed hard and spun her head for two Drakkaidians standing nearby. Shouting out for them, she quickly ordered them to take the girl into the castle and have whatever healers weren't on the wall seeing to wounded soldiers set to work on her immediately. Racing up to Aeric and holding out their arms, the Drakkaidians gently accepted her limp body from him and rushed her off the wall toward the castle. Though wanting to follow after her, Aeric found himself preoccupied by Lucan rushing forward and lift him into the air in a massive embrace.

Laughing as the Blue Maven swung him around while cheering out his name, Aeric was surprised to hear the resistance soldiers chanting "Tieloc" after him within moments. When Lucan at last set him down amid a mob of soldiers clamoring around them, Aeric found Valeri standing beside Revond staring at him with happy but uncertain eyes. Ignoring the other Elemental Warriors and Drakkaidians congratulating him, the Grandarian walked up to her and opened his arms. Valeri instantly dropped her pride and leapt into him, telling him she was so proud of him. Holding her while she cried tears of happiness, Aeric eventually released her to face the others and receive the massive plaudits from the entire wall top. Though celebrating for several long minutes, Revond quickly gained control of them all afterward. Giving Zephyr to another of the Drakkaidians to ferry up to the infirmary of the castle, he told Aeric to follow him to Alberic and the others to head to the castle to rest and see to their wounds. Though wanting to stay beside Aeric's side, Valeri was quick to resume her royal demeanor as the situation demanded and she began coordinating her wounded men back up to Hadecrest. She ordered the wall to be refortified as best as possible until she knew for certain what had happened and that the threat of the Ancients was no more.

While Valeri and the other Elemental Warriors began helping wounded resistance soldiers off the wall, Revond led Aeric to the downed form of the winged horse lying unconscious to the right side of the wall. Heaving several large chunks of rubble and rock off of him, the Master Sage bid Aeric to use the power of the Source of All to restore him. Though Aeric was nervous to use the all-pervasive power of the Source, Revond merely told him to summon the Source of Light somewhere within and cast its energy down on him. Trying his best, Aeric shone down the shining golden rays of the element of light onto Alberic, instantly waking him and brightening his white coat once more. Witnessing his gilded eyes slip open, Aeric and Revond watched the Ancient of Light stand once again. Alberic looked down to Aeric with the fully assembled Source of All in his hands, his eyes widening. Quickly transforming into his human form, Alberic beamed at the Grandarian and bowed his head to him, aware of what he had obviously done.

With Alberic back, he and Revond asked Aeric to see to the others in the castle. Though Aeric offered to give the Source of All to either of them, Revond declined and asked him to hold onto it and safeguard its power until later when they were organized and prepared to use it on a broader scale. When Aeric agreed and set off after Valeri and the others, Revond and Alberic quickly set to work dealing with lifeless or damaged bodies of the other Ancients strewn around Hadecrest. All of them had been weakened by the crests and were powerless to escape without the Sources to rejuvenate their battered bodies. Piling them near the base of the cliffs in the wedge and making sure they were powerless to escape or pose any further threat, the two Master Sages made their way up to the castle as well to find the Grandarian who had saved the world.

Throughout the afternoon while they cleaned up the mess of Alberic's kin, Aeric remained at Mina's side while Valeri dealt with her soldiers and her council, eager to hear of what had transpired. Though the princess told them not to worry and that they had defeated the Ancients, she went to Aeric several hours into the afternoon to ask him when he would be ready to speak. Turning his attention away from Mina as healers slowly scrubbed her body to purge the numbing poison of the Siarchs from her, he told her he just wanted to sit and relax for a while but he would tell them all what happened that evening if it was all right with her. Replying he could take all the time he needed, Valeri relayed the message to her council and the others, including Revond and Alberic who returned from the wall before dusk.

Stepping out of the infirmary to speak with the princess quietly in the halls, Aeric and Valeri embraced again for a long moment. Though aware she wouldn't have enough time to truly talk to him there, she asked if Aeric could use the Source to bring back Asthatch and the others they had lost on their journey sooner rather than later. Though not sure he knew how without Revond to help him or if it was safe, when he looked into her eyes to see the longing he couldn't deny her and pulled free the shimmering medallion hanging around his neck as the Source of Light had for so long. Focusing on what he wanted and closing his eyes, Aeric opened them moments later to see Asthatch, Markus Desrum, and the Drakkaidian soldiers lost to the Black Peaks assembled behind Valeri. A gentle mist of gleaming white particles hung around their bodies for a moment while their eyes slowly opened, gradually looking around as if confused.

Seeing Aeric's eyes on something behind her, Valeri spun around to see them as well and leapt into her captain to squeeze him tightly with fresh tears on her face. Though dumbfounded at how he was back in the castle, Asthatch gently took hold of his princess and returned her embrace, glancing up to see Aeric standing before him with a smile. Bowing their heads at each other, Aeric took a deep breath and looked behind Desrum to see another Drakkaidian he had wished back not among them. Frowning but remembering what his great-uncle had told him about it being his time to pass, Aeric guessed Verix had chosen not to come back. His grandfather had told him that even the power of the Holy Emerald lacked the power to revive a soul at eternal peace.

After explaining to Asthatch and the others what had befallen them since their deaths in the mountains and finishing coordinating her forces back and forth between the wall and castle, Valeri turned her attention to other matters. Ordering a massive meal served from what rations they had left for all of Hadecrest's occupants, she declared to the hundreds of refugees before dinner was served that the Ancients had been destroyed and their world was about to be returned to them. Met with roaring applause and celebration in the mountain base around the castle, dinner began both outside and in the fortress. Valeri's council and the Elemental Warriors gathered in the primary food hall of the castle, joined by the revived members of the party that set out with Aeric and Valeri for the crests as well as Revond and Alberic. With food everywhere and in the best spirits he had been perhaps since his youth, Revond set aside his inhibitions and joined Alberic in the feast.

Though the group ate for nearly an hour on their own, eventually Valeri entered the room refreshed. She was dressed in regal, dark crimson clothing with a thin crown around her short red hair that shone like silk for the first time since she set out from Hadecrest. She was announced by two sentries prompting the entire room to rise and fall silent at her coming. As she entered with an uncharacteristic smile on her face, she bade them to remain on their feet.

"It is now my honor to introduce the man to whom we all owe our lives," she said turning back and sweeping a hand up to the arching door. "I give you Aeric Tieloc." Aeric came around the side of the door after her, nervously scanning the room's occupants before quirkily smiling at Valeri. Upon seeing him the entire room burst with plaudits. The Warrior of All was dressed in a silver tunic with his cleaned brown pants and boots on, though his usual leather gauntlets and belt were gone. With his hair recently cut and washed, he ran one hand through the damp locks as he walked up to the Drakkaidian princess and bowed to her. Taking a seat beside Revond, he and the princess joined the others in the meal. All eyes were on the two as they ate, waiting for them to elaborate on their quest to recover the crests and Aeric's last clash with Dalorosk.

Observing his various allies watching him and patiently awaiting his story, Aeric eventually looked to Valeri to ask her if she wanted to help him narrate the tale of their quest to the group. Agreeing, the princess called for the chamber's attention and told them she and Aeric were ready to recount their story. Beginning with their trek through the Crag Spires and ending with finding the Lake of the Undead, Aeric and Valeri told their listeners everything about fleeing from demons, finding the recluse called Drakkaidian, the tale of Sakkdra, and their travels north to her hideaway near the Lake of the Undead. When they came to the Electric Flats, Asthatch and Markus Desrum winced in remembrance of their deaths at the hands of the demons and the lightning storm they brought with them. Recalling the next stage of their journey the night after the Electric Flats, both Aeric and Valeri omitted certain details while uncomfortably glancing at each other and moved ahead to their trek through the Pass of Jostoc.

The revelation of the recluse named Drakkaidian came as the largest surprise in their narrative, particularly shocking the Drakkaidians in the chamber. Not sure if it was necessary to reveal the truth about Verix Montrox, Aeric waited for Valeri to make the decision to include it in their story. She saw no reason to hold it back and told them all the truth of why he departed from Dalastrak from the little he had told them. Though barely able to believe their former king had exiled himself in his final days, the group was distraught to learn of his death after the meeting with Sakkdra and Valeri's sacrifice to allow them a way to retrieve the crests. From here Valeri turned from speaker to listener to hear of Aeric's encounter with the mystical Celestrian that had bestowed him with the crests and revived her. Even Alberic had never spoken with a Celestrian and was mesmerized by the account of her aiding the Grandarian.

After telling them of their return using the strange portal on Sakkdra's island, Aeric told them all of his final confrontation with Dalorosk. The group listened intently of their initial clash but was horror stricken to learn how the black Ancient exploited Aeric's love for Mina to get to the Sources unchecked. While Revond couldn't believe the bloodthirsty behemoth had possessed the foresight and patience to plan for such a contingency, Alberic was not surprised and reminded them that he had even planned to betray his brothers by constructing a talisman to contain the Source of Light and somehow use its power as his own. All of them were surprised to learn of Aeric's gambit to lure Dalorosk to the Lake of the Undead but were even more shocked that Sakkdra had been the key to finishing the Ancient of Darkness and saving them all.

Aeric concluded his story by telling them how he went back to collect Mina and Zephyr then returning to Hadecrest, not sure he should attempt to use the Source of All to revive the world without consulting Revond first. The Master Sage agreed with his decision, telling Aeric to continue to hold onto the Source until the next morning when they could muster all their energy into using it to restore Iairia. Applauding Aeric's courage, creativity and foresight in defeating Dalorosk and recovering the Source of All, Alberic rose and called for another ovation for Aeric as well as Valeri, Revond and the Elemental Warriors he had recruited. Standing with the others to receive his praise, Aeric smiled at Lucan already laughing and victoriously shaking his fists together above his head. Glancing down the ranks along the tables to the redheaded girl beside him, he found her already staring at him with a distant smile. Aware there was something on her mind despite her holding it back in front of the crowds, Aeric knew he had to speak with her before he left to return to Mina's side after dinner. The two did not converse during the rest of the meal, instead talking to those around them and exchanging restless glances between sentences.

When the end of the meal came and the groups present began to depart back into the castle and fortress below, Aeric rose and prepared to make his way to Valeri who had already risen to speak with Markus Desrum, Alam Tielance and Condom Broll at the rear of the room. Seeing Asthatch and another two Drakkaidians descend on her bringing progress reports of the fortification of the wall and other matters for her to see to, Aeric paused and halted, guessing it wasn't the best time to talk. Catching Aeric standing beside her near the end of the longest table in the chamber, Valeri fixed her gaze on him apologetically. Aware she had been bogged down by more pressing matters for the moment, Aeric merely smiled in her direction and gave her a slight bow. Returning it, Valeri watched as the Warrior of All turned to make his way for the doorway of the chamber. Hearing him tell Revond he was going back to the infirmary to stay at Mina's side, she let out a deep breath as Aeric disappeared from the chamber.

Chapter 47

<u>Restoration</u>

Aeric woke to the faint breeze from outside the walls of Hadecrest blowing in through a window of the infirmary, rustling his black hair against his forehead. Slowly opening his eyelids, he glanced around the room to remember he had fallen asleep beside Mina's bed the previous night. Gazing down to the bed at his left, the Grandarian saw Mina Garrinal lying fast asleep beneath the white sheets he had gently tucked under her figure. Though she had been in a sweat most of the night and remained pale by the time he finally fell asleep beside her in the wooden chair, she looked to be on the mend with the rosy color on her freckled cheeks returning. Wiping a hand over his face to push his eyelids and force them open, Aeric leaned in close to set his face above hers. Tenderly kissing the tip of her nose and looking around to make sure one of Hadecrest's healers was still in the room to see to her, he rose from his seat and stretched his body.

As his hands passed above his chest, he noticed the familiar warmth radiating to life and looked down to see the shimmering light from the Source of All shining through his tunic. Somehow instantly refreshed and energized as he peered down ay the brilliant luminosity, Aeric smiled and turned around to shift his gaze to Mina. Silently promising her that one way or another he would see her revived by the end of the day, he turned to slowly amble away from her bed around a corner where he found a large tub of water beside a collection of supplies and bottles in the infirmary. Splashing some on his face and rinsing his mouth, Aeric took a deep breath and exited the room to search for Revond and the others. Though still unsure how he would do it, he knew today was the day he had to restore the world. He was nervous of the responsibility and power he would have to wield to accomplish such a feat, but remembering all he had overcome to reach this point he knew he could do it. Against all odds he had already won. All that was left was restoring the life that had been ripped from him.

Though heading down a hallway of the castle toward his bedroom where he had left his few belongings, he was pleasantly surprised to observe Lucan Hauk Erland opening the door to his room as he walked by it, stepping out with a broad grin and latching onto him almost before Aeric knew who it was. Laughing and returning his friend's embrace, Aeric greeted him and asked if he knew where the others were. Responding that he was just on his way to breakfast and their comrades were likely in the kitchen, Lucan bid him to follow him for some food while joking that even the Warrior of All still had to eat.

The two arrived in the central castle foyer and the kitchen branching off from its right side a few minutes later to find several smiling faces looking up to them as they entered including Maglin Byre, Jax Morrol, Kira Marcell, Asthatch and Alberic. Greeting them all warmly, Aeric took a seat beside Asthatch who gave him a begrudging smile and a sturdy handshake. Though guessing the last Princess of Drakkaidia was busy with business of her council elsewhere, when he asked Asthatch as to her whereabouts he replied he didn't know but that she was probably still resting in her chambers from their previous trying day. Remembering how much they had been through in the last few days before the culmination of their quest, Aeric guessed even the powerful princess would be exhausted. Turning his attention to Alberic to ask about the Master Sage, the Ancient of Light set down the goblet he was drinking from and smiled.

"Revond just left actually," he replied. "I believe he and the princess' council members are preparing for us on the wall of the fortress."

"Preparing?" Aeric asked confused.

"Revond wants a contained and controlled environment for you to use the Source of All," Alberic answered. "The Elemental Warriors and I were just about to head down there ourselves. We are in no rush but whenever you're ready, Revond will be ready to help you wield the Source and finsh what we set out to do." Returning the Ancient of Light's smile, Aeric nodded and replied that they had waited long enough and he was ready. Telling them he just needed to go back to his room to fetch his belongings, the others rose and told him they would be waiting on the wall with Revond. Making for the door the group split up, leaving only Aeric and Asthatch remaining in the foyer. Informing Aeric he would send one of his men to find Valeri wherever she was, Asthatch stood patiently by the hallway in wait for Aeric to go to his room and return. Promising to be quick, the Grandarian made his way back into the torch lit halls of the old Drakkaidian fortress past Lucan's door and to his own.

Slowly pushing it open, he sauntered in to feel a chilled breeze sweep around him. Observing the solitary window along the outer wall of the castle open, Aeric remembered the last time Valeri had climbed through it his first night there. Peering around the room with his eyes wide, he found himself disappointed that the redheaded intruder was nowhere to be found. Slowly exhaling, he drifted toward the window shutters to close them. Wandering back to his bed, he picked up his leather gauntlets that he set there the night before and pulled them over his tunic sleeves. Strapping them tight along with his thick carpenter's belt, he looked around the room to make sure there was nothing else of his he was forgetting.

Aware it didn't really matter if he left anything because everything he ever needed was about to be returned to him, he nodded to himself and turned around. As his eyes shifted to the doorway, they opened wide in shock to see Valeri standing in it, waiting for him. Seeing his surprise she faintly smiled and entered the room. She was dressed in her usual attire but had swapped her chinked crimson armor for regal but jagged Drakkaidian grieves and gauntlets as black as night. She even wore ceremonial black shoulder plates and a thin crown around her hair with a pointed scarlet jewel in the front.

"I hope I didn't startle you again," she said softly from behind her smile. Aeric was quiet for a minute as his eyes drifted back up her frame to her face. Eventually he forced himself to loosen and shift his weight between his feet.

"Not at all," he returned offhandedly. "You used the door this time." Valeri's smile widened and she looked down at the floor with a coy grin. Stepping to within a few feet of him, the princess looked back up with her expression growing serious.

"How is Mina?" she asked, to which Aeric stared at her uneasily but forced himself to find his voice.

"Still can't wake up," Aeric replied, "but in a little while I guess it won't matter anymore. Everyone will be fine." Valeri was silent to this but looked down to see the glowing white light from underneath his tunic. Taking a step closer to him and raising her right hand she slowly reached up to it and slid her fingers along its circular outline. Feeling its warmth seep into her very core, Valeri looked back up to Aeric.

"Not everyone," she returned in a whisper. "I almost wish we hadn't found this yet. So our time wasn't over. I don't want you to go." Aeric wasn't sure what to say to this, unable to look away from her intense eyes fixed on him like never before.

"It's not like we can't ever see each other again, Valeri," he told her. "Our lives are still just beginning. This isn't the end."

"Then why does it feel like the end?" Valeri asked, closing her eyes to keep the tears welling inside them from dropping out. Sighing, Aeric slowly reached up and pulled her close to him to hug her and gently sway her back and forth. Valeri slowly raised her arms to return his embrace while her tears trickled down her face. Feeling the salty water on his skin as their faces touched, Aeric pulled his head back and lifted a hand to her chin to prop her head up.

"Valeri, look at me," he told her gently. The princess slowly opened her watery eyes and set them on his, searching like they had many times before. "You're the strongest person I've ever known. Even now your eyes are always full of courage." Valeri blinked and silently let a huff of shame escape from her mouth.

"Only because they're usually looking at you," she replied softly. "If I had an ounce of courage for every time I've thought of you since I met you I'd be brave enough to say that..." She trailed off there, stopping herself short before her feelings could escape. Though she left her sentence hanging Aeric knew what would have come. Feeling her hands slipping down his chest about to fall back to her sides, he reached up to catch one of them in his and hold it by his heart.

"We may have completely different lives in completely different places, Valeri," he began, "but we'll always be family, and you'll always have my love. I owe you everything. Without you I wouldn't still be here. I can't forget that; I won't forget you. How could I?" The princess looked into his eyes as vulnerable as Aeric had ever seen her. Though just staring at him for a long moment, she eventually gave him a single nod and felt a smile materializing on the corners of her lips. Beaming back,

Aeric leaned in to hug her again and gently kiss her on her cheek after wiping her tear away. Taking a deep breath, Valeri nodded to herself and stepped back from him while wiping the residue of her tears away.

"I guess I should let you leave then," she said lifting her head back up to his. "I had been planning on just locking you up in Dalastrak so you couldn't, but I suppose it would be selfish of me to deny Grandaria a carpenter of your skill." Silently chuckling at the girl's attempt at humor, Aeric nodded and followed her out of the bedroom into the halls. Walking beside each other, the two emerged back into the central foyer of the castle to find Asthatch patiently waiting for them with his long red cape gently wafting in the breeze from outside. Bowing to them both, he informed Valeri everything had been assembled and the Master Sage Revond awaited them on the wall top. Following the captain down out of the castle into the mountain stronghold, the trio appeared on the left entrance to the nearly decimated wall several minutes later. Emerging into the open air in the cloudy Drakkaidian atmosphere, Aeric was surprised to find the wall lined with Drakkaidian soldiers from one end to the other all slamming lances down at Valeri's presence.

Slowly walking through the soldiers behind Asthatch, the trio observed the other four Elemental Warriors, Alberic and the council members of Hadecrest including Alam Tielance, Markus Desrum and Condom Broll waiting for them behind one man in black robes ahead of them. Lowering his hood as the three approached, the Master Sage Revond revealed his clean bearded face and deep blue eyes. Smiling, he waited for Asthatch to step aside in front of the row of soldiers and Valeri to walk behind him beside the other Elemental Warriors. Standing alone before the tall sage, Aeric waited for him to speak.

"Good morning, my young friend," Revond said warmly. "Are you ready to repair Iairia and restore the world we lost?" Though nervous Aeric nodded confidently.

"I am," he returned boldly to which Revond smiled wider.

"I am very proud of you, Aeric," he said. Revond turned to the others standing behind him, looking over the faces of his Elemental Warriors. "I am proud of all of you. Thanks to all of your bravery and determination we have overcome one of the greatest evil powers in existence and triumphed over apocalypse." While Revond turned back to Aeric, Alberic stepped forward and smiled at the Grandarian.

"And now, Aeric Tieloc, comes the spoils of your courage and sacrifices," the Ancient said. "You now have the power to decide the fate of the world the same as your grandfather did in the Days of Destiny. In that medallion lies power equal to the Holy Emerald itself. With it you can carve the destiny of Iairia any way you choose. And while you are right to be humbled by such power, it is nothing for you to fear. You have but to open the medallion, touch the Source of All, concentrate on your wish, and it will be so." Aeric reached inside his tunic to pull free the shimmering white talisman. All eyes shifted to it as he held it in his palm, once again at a loss for what to do.

"Well I can envision my own life, Alberic," Aeric began, "but what about the rest of Iairia? How can I restore the lives of all those people who died when I don't know the first thing about them?"

"I suggest you merely wish the world back to the state it was in before the Ascension," Alberic answered with a smile. "Though it is difficult to comprehend how, the Source of All can take care of the details from there."

"Well what about all of us?" Aeric pressed, looking around the faces of the men and women who had battled alongside him to reach this moment. "If I wish everything back to the way it was before the Ascension will we even remember any of this? Will it even have happened at all?"

"You forget that even the universal might of the Holy Emerald in that Source cannot interfere with the free will of a soul in any plane of existence," Revond answered. "The Source will restore the life that was lost and reverse the damage done to the world, but none who remember these events will forget them if they do not choose to do so. Just because you are reverting the physical shape of the world to a former state does not mean all that transpired between then and now did not occur. We who lived through it will endure as we are, and I highly doubt any of us would choose to forget such an experience."

"Well what will become of the Source of All?" Aeric asked.

"That is also a choice you must make, Aeric," Revond said. "But if you wish to return the world to its former state it will mean the Source will once more separate into the six for each element to reside in their respective Elemental Temples.

From there I will be paying the four Elemental Warriors of the Southland a visit to be properly anoint them in the Sources. Though the Ancients will be gone, it is still imperative that they remain. As for your own power of all the elements, Aeric, that will be yours to do with as you wish." The wall fell silent at this, all eyes back on Aeric and the medallion in his hands. Still looking over the faces of his comrades, Aeric felt emotion tugging at him.

"Will I see you all again?" he asked suddenly. Revond silently laughed and nodded his head.

"I have no doubt of that, young Tieloc," he responded, looking back to the founder of his order. "I'm sure even Alberic will be by on occasion to visit you."

"I wouldn't miss it," the Ancient of Light said merrily. "I've tasted your mother's cooking wares at past Festivals of Radia. Perhaps I can get a full meal now that I'm a family friend." It was Aeric's turn to laugh then, telling him that it would be his pleasure to arrange. Turning his attention to the others, Aeric bid them goodbye one by one starting with Asthatch and working his way through the council members and the Elemental Warriors. Shaking most of their hands, when he came to Lucan, the Blue Maven lifted him off his feet with a hug.

"Looks like my instincts on you were right after all, Tieloc," he said. "I owe you the life of my wife and daughter, not to mention my own. Anytime you need anything, I'm yours."

"I'll see you soon then, Lucan Hauk Erland," Aeric replied. "Tell Terra and Lauress I look forward to meeting them someday." After shaking Lucan's hand again, Aeric turned to the last person he had to say goodbye to standing beside him with her gray cloak that once belonged to her grandfather flapping in the breeze. Trying to hold her Drakkaidian strength in front of all her men, Valeri kept back her tears as best she could and waited for him to walk in front of her. Though not sure what formal goodbye would be appropriate for the Princess of Drakkaidia in front of her subjects and prepared an awkward bow, when she saw him bend forward she instantly reached down and pulled him back up.

"We'll do the bowing, Aeric Tieloc," she said quietly, taking a step back to bow her upper body. Following the princess' lead, all the Drakkaidians bowed to him followed by the other Elemental Warriors, Revond and Alberic. Though feeling uncomfortable as he swept his eyes across the many

Drakkaidians, he was surprised to see Valeri break her formal manners and rise to walk forward and hug him tightly. Wrapping his arms around her waist as hers came around his neck, the two held together for several moments longer than they probably should have though not even Asthatch showed a sign of frustration. When they at last came apart, Valeri backed away beside the other Elemental Warriors with a sad smile. Looking back to Revond who gave the young Grandarian a nod, Aeric brought the Source of All back up in front of his chest and raised a hand to open the glass case covering it. As soon as it lifted free a brilliant flash of white light engulfed them all and when they opened their eyes a large orb of shimmering energy hovered between Aeric and the others. Doing what Revond had bid him, Aeric nervously reached up to the side of the large sphere through the sparkling energy to rest his fingers along its surface.

Closing his eyes and concentrating hard, he silently prayed to Granis for his wish to work and began focusing on what he wanted. Seeing visions of Grandaria, Eirinor and Mina flashing before him, Aeric felt a sudden weightlessness beneath his feet and opened his eyes to see the Source expanding and exploding to create a sparkling white world around him with images of Iairia speeding by in streams of bright light that looked like shooting stars. Marveling as they passed by, Aeric could see the devastation of countless locations he had never seen brightening with color and life. From barren fields blossoming with grass and flowers to the Great Forests and their singed trees stretching with green leaves again, Aeric found himself witnessing the Source of All repairing the world. All the destruction from the piles of rubble of the former Elemental Temples, the underground city of Ceruleana, the golden capital city of Grandaria and even his own home village of Eirinor, everything was rebuilt and healed before his eyes.

Before long the speeding images of the world along trails of starlight began to expand and he found the swirling world of white slowly transforming into a familiar sight. With overcast skies above him parting to reveal blue and sunny skies with long grass rising around his feet, Aeric watched in amazement as it spread around him to cover the world in rolling green hills as far as the mountains in the horizon. Feeling the touch of the long grass against his fingers and gravity returning as he stood on the earth, the jets of sparkling white energy began to dissipate and the green world before him was left exactly as he remembered it. When the last remnant of the Source of All had vanished, Aeric realized he was standing in silence on a hilltop overlooking the Hills of Eirinor. He could feel the warmth of the summer sun and the breeze swaying against him. The grass he stood in gently swayed as the sound of birds chirping appeared behind him. Aeric smiled as his mouth slipped open. He was home.

Letting a slow but beaming smile overtake his face, the Grandarian raised his arms high above him to bask in the sunlight for what seemed like the first time in as long as he could remember. As he was about to start laughing or crying, Aeric heard his name being called from behind him and wheeled around. His heart racing and his eyes moistening, he saw Mina standing behind him with a bemused expression but a smile appearing the moment she saw his face. Unable to move at first, Aeric forced himself to take a step toward her and look down past the ridge she stood on. It was just like the dream Female had given him with the vapors of the Mae Fountain. Eirinor Village lay behind Mina nestled tightly in its little hamlet valley, smoke rising from a few chimneys and townspeople coming out of houses into the streets to look around as if they had all just come out of a dream. He could see his mother and father as well as Mina's family emerging down the streets with confused and curious faces, looking up to notice Aeric and Mina on the ridge above the village.

Tears streaming down his cheeks at the sight, Aeric set his eyes back on his love and strode toward her as if intoxicated with joy. Seeing him coming, Mina raced up to him with tears of her own appearing and leapt at him to wrap her arms around his neck. Holding her tighter than he ever had before, Aeric started crying hard and lifted his hand up into her chestnut hair, desperately wanting to remember the touch. Struggling to speak through her tears, Mina began repeating over and over that he saved her. Just holding onto her as if she was his very life, Aeric opened his eyes and looked past her to see their families rushing up the hillside toward them. Staring into the blue sky, Aeric Tieloc leaned in to kiss his love.

Chapter 48

<u>Beginnings</u>

Two weeks after restoring Iairia and returning to Eirinor, Aeric Tieloc found himself leading one of the Garrinals' horses to the outskirts of the hamlet village in central Grandaria where he and Mina had embraced upon their return. It was a sunny summer morning with a breeze rustling the long grass of the hills and the leaves of the trees around the village. There wasn't a cloud to be seen in the endless blue sky. Mina stood waiting ahead of him beside her uncle's house where they kept the horses, tightening the straps of the saddle on her steed and casting her gaze at Aeric with a beaming smile as she heard his horse's hoof beats approaching. Like him, she was dressed in a blue tunic with shortened sleeves to keep her cooler in the summer heat. Her curled chestnut hair was collected behind her in a ponytail, bouncing to life as her head turned to see her love walking toward her. Finishing tying down all her supplies onto her favorite brown horse, Mina turned back to the stable behind her adjacent to her Uncle Jac's house where he and her father were working.

Bringing his horse up beside Mina's, Aeric momentarily released its reins so he could walk over to the three Garrinals hugging each other. Seeing him draw near as he released his daughter, Roan Garrinal tightly embraced the young Tieloc as well. Wishing both Aeric and Mina well on their journey, the two brothers watched as the pair took their horses and each others' hands, beginning their walk down the village's primary grassy road to the outskirts. Casually strolling hand in hand, the two Grandarians glanced at each other then back to the Garrinals' stable to see Mina's father and uncle disappear inside. Smiling, Mina turned back to kiss Aeric and giggle.

"Now don't you feel bad that you tried to leave without saying goodbye first?" Mina asked jokingly scolding. Aeric rolled his eyes and returned her grin.

"If your father thanks me one more time I'm going to lose my mind," he replied. "It's only been a couple of weeks since we've been back and I've already been smothered with more attention and gratitude than I'm going to get at this ceremony in Galantia. I still have no idea how this happened but this was supposed to stay our little story. Now all of Grandaria knows."

"Oh come on, Aeric," Mina told him, grabbing onto his arm and leaning against him as she walked. "At least this will be good for business once you open shop next month. You'll be the most famous carpenter in the history of the trade."

"That wasn't exactly what I had in mind when I got into this business," Aeric reminded her with a coy smile, "but I think I'm learning to take these things in stride." Mina laughed and lifted free of him to hold his hand tighter and stare up into the clear morning sky while they walked. Though neither of them were sure how, somehow after their return the entire world knew of their ordeal with the Ancients and Aeric's adventure to stop them. Supreme Granisian Gilentium had even seen fit to order a grand ceremony be held to honor Aeric much like his grandfather had been after the Days of Destiny. He and all his comrades who had played a part in the quest had been summoned to Galantia for a celebration of epic proportions. While Darien Tieloc had been summoned right away to meet with the Senior Galantia Council under Gilentium, Aeric's father had sent for him and Mina shortly after the celebration was announced. Apparently the Elemental Warriors, the Drakkaidians under Valgard and Valeri's resistance, and the Master Sage Revond had all been sent summons as well. Though the event wasn't to be held until another few weeks to give those it was intended to honor time to arrive, Aeric and Mina decided to take their leave at once, seeing as the sovereign of Grandaria had asked for them right away.

Though he had been looking forward to relaxing in his home village with Mina and such recognition wasn't what he had desired after his ordeal, Aeric found himself with little choice but to accept it. He knew that even once the commemoration of the Ascension was over in Galantia and he was free to pick up the pieces of his simple life, he would never be the same afterward. Though the power of the six elements had faded from him as he wished and people would slowly forget his name over the years as he fell out of sight in a village as small as Eirinor, his adventure had changed his life forever. He had finally come to accept and recognize the legacy of his grandfather's courage and determination alight in his heart and soul. Though the two Tielocs were their own distinct men, they were the same in every respect that mattered.

As Aeric reflected over his new attitude for life and the way he knew he had to lead it from then on, he was brought back to his senses by Mina suddenly pulling on his sleeve while they walked up a hill out of the village. Turning to face her, he saw his girlfriend looking down a hill to the south where a lone rider on a black horse was unhurriedly trotting along toward them. Though paying him no mind at first and wondering why Mina was so taken with him, Aeric found himself slowing his pace and his heart beat picking up as he noticed a familiar gray hood and cloak on a large man otherwise encased in dark blue garb underneath. As the horse and rider grew closer to them, Aeric and Mina came to a complete halt on the hillside, watching with amazed smiles as the figure trotted up to them and pulled back his concealing hood to reveal his bearded face.

"Hello, my young Grandarians," Revond said in a contented tone, smiling down at them with amiable eyes. Though shocked to see the Master Sage, both Aeric and Mina smiled as he dismounted from his midnight black steed, tucking his robes around him as if unaffected by the sun's hot rays.

"Revond," Aeric said as if awestruck. Though fumbling for something else to say, the sage merely let out a silent chuckle from deep in his throat.

"Indeed," he affirmed. "It is good to see you, Aeric. And you, Mina Garrinal. I am glad to see you back in full health." Mina bowed and politely greeted the Master Sage in a similar fashion.

"Are you on your way to Galantia, Revond?" Aeric asked hopefully. The sage smiled but shook his head.

"Not quite yet, Aeric," he replied. "I did receive the summons from the Supreme Granisian, but I have errands elsewhere to see to first. I wanted to see if you were here before you made your way to the capital. Fortune seems to have smiled upon us at last." Aeric laughed at that and looked over the black steed beside the sage.

"Errands?" Aeric repeated almost worriedly. "Don't tell me there's something else out there still threatening the world." Revond chuckled again.

"No, I'm afraid not," he said lightheartedly. "I merely have loose ends from my own life to tie before I can officially begin my work as the Master Sage. Thanks to you and the efforts of generations of your family, the last of the great powers in Iairia have been contained or cast away. Life in Iairia is all as it should be once and for all. Drakkan is sealed forever with a new strong Granic Crystal to hold him at bay; the Elemental Warriors are soon to be restored to the lands; the Ancients are permanently banished and their troublesome offspring with them; the unique and powerful bloodlines of your family and the Montroxs endure; the Order of Alberic is restored with myself primed to fill its ranks once more; and the last of the prophesies of old left by Granis are all fulfilled. The last of the great evils have been purged from the world, and Iairia can go forward in what I hope to be undying peace."

"Do you think it will last?" Aeric asked, sincerely curious. "You really believe the last dark powers have been dealt with?"

"Don't get me wrong, my friend," Revond said. "There is still much in our world that lies unknown and other powers exist I'm sure we will one day encounter. But while I believe we are merely on the cusp of what our civilization will one day become, for now, this age of our existence is safe. In no small part thanks to you, Aeric. All of Iairia is restored exactly as it was before Dalorosk and the others emerged. You did very well."

"Everything is as it was except that for some reason everyone in Iairia knows of our quests," Aeric immediately filled in. "You wouldn't know anything about that, would you?" Revond smiled and shrugged knowingly.

"I may have had a hand in that," he confessed, to which Aeric raised an eyebrow. "Quite literally, in fact. From behind the other side of the Source of All I touched the orb as well and made a slight alteration to your wish so your efforts would be known."

"And why would you go and do a thing like that?" Aeric asked skeptically. "You above everyone but Mina know I like to stay out of the limelight. Now every light in the world is on me."

"Yes, well, I apologize for inconveniencing you," the sage answered sarcastically, "but the events of your tribulation during the Ascension needed to be known for more reasons than one. We three and many others have been the victim of past history falling out of memory. The consequences of such a lapse nearly destroyed us. As the Master Sage I cannot allow such a significant period of history to be forgotten or ignored. In addition, the confusion of being brought back to life after the populace of the world remembered dying could have created a great deal of unrest if not dealt with. The truth is more appropriate than a lie." Revond's serious expression softened then, as he looked off into the horizon past the two Grandarians. "On a more personal note, there had already been a tale of a Tieloc saving the world that no one knows of but me. I could not sit back and let another generation of your family's heroism slip by unnoticed. You deserve recognition and reward for your bravery and selflessness, my young friend. As do the others who fought alongside you." Aeric tilted his head and furrowed his brow in confusion at something the sage had said.

"What do you mean there was a generation of my family that slipped by unnoticed?" Aeric asked puzzled, thinking back to an earlier conversation in the Mystic Tower. "Is this why you asked me whose son I was when we first met?" Revond faintly smiled again before giving him a single nod.

"That is another story for another day, my friend," Revond answered mysteriously. "After the ceremony, I will tell you a tale of your family that has long needed to be told."

"Why not tell us on the way?" Aeric asked. "Come with us to Galantia." Revond took a deep breath but shook his head and turned to mount Nighcress again.

"I'm afraid it will have to wait, Aeric," he replied with a smile. "I have unfinished business to attend to in the Border Mountains that was interrupted by the beginning of the Ascension. But I will look forward to seeing you both at the ceremony. I just saw Lucan a few days ago. I believe he and the others will be on their way within the week."

"I know things are still rocky between Grandaria and Drakkaidia," Aeric began, "but do you think Valeri and her council from Hadecrest will come?"

"You can answer that question better than I, Aeric," Revond stated. "I'm sure even the King and Princess of Drakkaidia can find the time and tolerance to enter Grandaria for a celebration of such magnitude." The Master Sage paused then, staring down at the Grandarian hero. "I hope you appreciate the amazing feat you have accomplished in your venture, my friend. Though your grandfather may be lauded as the greatest champion in the history of your nation, your role in saving the world matches his in every way, if not surpasses it. Like him you battled through darkness and despair and defeated an enemy of unthinkable evil who possessed the definitive power in the universe, ultimately with nothing more than your quick thinking and determination. Though you were broken by loss when we started out, we witnessed you become the man your family is known for. It may be modest, but your courage is equal with any Tieloc who has come before you. It is my honor to count you as my friend." Aeric was at a loss for words when the sage was finished, opening his mouth and blushing red as he glanced at Mina beaming at him.

"I never even would have made it out of Grandaria without you, Revond," the Grandarian confessed. "You were the one who believed in me even when I didn't. I just did what I had to."

"That is what makes you the man you are, Aeric," he replied. The sage looked down at them for a long moment as the silence hang comfortably between the three. At last he widened his smile and reached up to his chest to tighten the silver emblem of the Mystic Sages holding his cloak together. "I will see you soon then, my dear friends. Safe journey."

"And you, Master Sage," Aeric returned as Revond nudged Nighcress forward. As the Morlan began walking past Aeric and Mina into the green Hills of Eirinor, the Master Sage flipped up his gray hood without looking back. Watching as Nighcress began to pick up speed into a gallop, Aeric and Mina stood on the hillside hand in hand as they disappeared over another hill. Turning to look at each other with broad smiles, they kissed and mounted their horses to begin their journey to Galantia.

Finding himself once again traveling to the portal of the void at an unhurried pace, the Master Sage let Nighcress proceed at a casual trot after departing from Eirinor Village. Since appearing back at the restored Mystic Tower, Revond had taken a well deserved rest. Though eager to inspect the six Elemental Temples across Iairia to ensure the Sources had been restored and to formally anoint the Elemental Warriors he had recruited within, he could sense the five Ancients responsible for the Ascension gone into oblivion along with their troublesome races. With the threat finally gone there was no hurry to gather the warriors too fast. They would all need time to rest and rejoin their lost loved ones the same as he did. Finding Zephyr sweeping down from the skies to merrily land on his shoulder and hug him within moments of returning to the Sage's Valley, Revond decided to take a week to simply relax for perhaps the first time since stepping out of the tower doors as the Master Sage.

After relating his entire tale to his Sky Sprite partner about the year that had passed since their last parting and resting for the week he set aside for himself, Revond called for Nighcress to take him north. Though he had been summoned to Galantia by the Supreme Granisian for a ceremony to honor Aeric and all those who battled to revive the world during the Ascension, he decided to leave early to pay the Sword of Granis and its Granic Crystal another visit before resuming his duties as the Master Sage. Having been cut short by business the last time he went to visit the Border Mountains, he proceeded up to Grandaria at a brisk pace. Along the way he visited both Lucan Hauk Erland and his family in Aggiest Village, followed by seeing Aeric and Mina on his way through the Hills of Eirinor.

Riding out of the hills with only the silent Morlan and his thoughts, he smiled while thinking over the memories of new friends he had made during his first experience as the head of his order. Though Zephyr had returned to Haven to see his kin for a while, he found himself excited to see the others he befriended at the coming ceremony. Remembering his first encounters with the Elemental Warriors and others from his journey, his thoughts frequently ended up with the legendary Ancient of Light. Unable to sense his presence or guess what had become of Alberic after their departure from

Hadecrest, the Master Sage was left to wonder if he would ever see the original head of his order again. He knew Alberic saw himself as an outcast from the world of humanity even though he lived amongst them in disguise. He wouldn't have been surprised to never hear from him again.

No sooner than his thoughts ended up on questions about the fate of the Ancient of Light, Revond heard a faint sound of another set of hoof beats coming from over the grassy Grandarian hillside to his right. Peering over it curiously, he was surprised to find a brown horse trotting into view with a white rider on its back. His eyes widening in disbelief, Revond identified the familiar face of the rider, smiling as he directed his steed beside Nighcress. Pulling back his gray hood to reveal his bearded face, Revond gazed at the deceptively youthful one staring back at him and faintly smiled in confusion.

"And here I was just wondering if I would ever see you again," Revond said casually. The man in white shrugged with his grin widening. "I had forgotten you can probably sense where I am at any given time."

"More or less," Alberic returned. "And I couldn't try to depart without saying a final goodbye." The sage's brow furrowed at this.

"Depart?" he repeated. "You won't be in Galantia for the ceremony then?" Alberic shook his head, reaching down to stroke Nighcress' side as they rode.

"There are plenty of heroes from the fight against my brothers to be honored without me there to complicate things," he said. "The last of my race of Fethiotts roost out in the Filriss Islands. I thought I would venture out to spend some time with them for a while."

"A while," Revond repeated with a knowing smile. "I imagine that will be a long time by my standards."

"Well I can't be gone too long," he returned. "I promised Aeric I would pay him a visit to enjoy his mother's cooking, didn't I?" Revond silently chuckled.

"I suppose so," he agreed. "Just be sure you don't needlessly exile yourself, Alberic. This world is as much your home as anyone's. You have earned that right whether you are of Granis' creation or not. I know you think of yourself and your dealings on behalf of my race as a mere complication to the natural order of the world, but without your aid this world would have perished long ago. Now that everything about your origin is exposed I hope you will feel free to call the Mystic Tower your home again. You will always be welcome there as long as I sit at the head of our order."

"Well thank you for the hospitality, my friend," Alberic returned with soft laughter, "but I think you know I will have to decline the latter part of your offer. While I certainly don't see myself as heading into exile and I will most definitely continue to live among humanity unto the eventual end of my days. I have finally played my last part in the forging of mankind's destiny. With my brothers gone and the sages returned, my work is done. I leave the order and its tasks to men far wiser than I." Alberic paused for a moment and stared deep into Revond's eyes. "But I do appreciate your words, Master Sage. All these long years I ultimately saw myself as a meddler in history, forged from pure accidental chance, but thanks to you and Aeric I think I finally feel purpose in my presence as well. I now see for myself why you had so much faith in the boy. Thanks to him and his family over the years, all of the great powers have been contained so the world may continue to grow free from the burden of outside influence."

"Almost," Revond replied, raising an eyebrow knowingly. Alberic turned to glance at him with a curious smile. "While I recuperated at the tower I read the remaining pages of your Cebrach book, Alberic. It seems there is still much beyond the shores of Iairia we have left to discover and come to grips with."

"Indeed there is," Alberic returned with his smile growing. With that he stopped his horse and slipped off its bare back, gently patting its backside to prompt it away into the hills to run free. Stopping Nighcress beside him, Revond watched the Ancient of Light stretch and smile contented as the sunlight shone down on his skin.

"Is that all you'll say about it?" Revond asked curiously. "Have you no advice for me? I will obviously have choices to make regarding the contents of that book before my time is done." Alberic took a deep breath before smiling up to the sage with his hands on his sides.

"Advice?" Alberic repeated. "Well, a hardnosed realist once told me the role of wisdom is to see the difference between right and wrong and to decide what to do with such choices as those that face you now. I suggest you do what you judge best, Revond." Revond smiled and silently laughed again, remembering the Ancient was quoting back his own words.

"I suppose Zeroan was right, then," he said. "Will I see you again, Master Alberic?"

"Not if you're looking for an old Master Sage or the Ancient of Light," Alberic returned. "But if you're looking for a friend to talk to here and again, I'd say it's almost a certainty." Smiling up to Revond a final time, Alberic unhurriedly turned to begin walking away on the hillside. As he ambled through the long grass a gleaming aura of white energy spread over his figure and his human frame quickly morphed into his true form. His majestic feathered wings spreading wide, the Ancient of Light began to run with his golden hooves shining in the grass. Beating his wings hard, he jumped to soar into the air for the east and the sea that lay beyond. Watching with a smile as the white horse disappeared into the blue sky with his golden contrails streaming behind him, the Master Sage took a deep breath and looked ahead to the north. Reaching down to pat the side of Nighcress' neck, the two continued on for the Border Mountains.

Tales of Iairia
Ashes of Ascension
The End

About the Author

Tyler Tullis is a young author from Washington State. He began writing his *Tales of Iairia* trilogy in high school and published the first installment, *Shards of Destiny,* before graduating. While attending college at Gonzaga University, he published two sequels—*Trial of a Maven* and *Ashes of Ascension.* He is currently working on a science fiction/mystery series called *Sophie.* Upon finishing his third novel Tyler was 21 years old.

Printed in the United States
222303BV00001B/1/P

9 781449 011826